T K
Po6

MISSOURI GATEWAYS

*Four Romances Packed
with Culture and Grace*

AISHA FORD

BARBOUR
PUBLISHING

Stacy's Wedding ©1999 by Barbour Publishing, Inc.
The Wife Degree ©2000 by Barbour Publishing, Inc.
Pride and Pumpernickel ©2001 by Aisha Ford
Whole in One ©2002 by Aisha Ford

Cover image © GettyOne

ISBN 1-58660-965-3

All Scripture quotations, unless otherwise noted, are taken from the King James Version of the Bible.

Scripture quotations marked NIV are taken from the HOLY BIBLE, NEW INTERNATIONAL VERSION®. NIV®. Copyright © 1973, 1978, 1984 by International Bible Society. Used by permission of Zondervan Publishing House. All rights reserved.

All rights reserved. No part of this publication may be reproduced or transmitted in any form or by any means without written permission of the publisher.

Published by Barbour Books, an imprint of Barbour Publishing, Inc., P.O. Box 719, Uhrichsville, Ohio 44683, www.barbourbooks.com.

ecpa Member of the
Evangelical Christian
Publishers Association

Printed in the United States of America.
5 4 3 2

MISSOURI GATEWAYS

AISHA FORD is a writer who resides in Missouri with her parents and younger sister. She was home schooled during the course of her entire academic career and received her B.A. through an independent study program.

Her goals for writing are to "Write stories that appeal to a wide audience and present an example of how we are supposed to live and grow and change as Christians, in addition to writing material that will positively represent African Americans in the growing field of inspirational fiction."

The main message she hopes to present in her writing would be: "The best guide for living is to follow the biblical example of Jesus Christ. No matter how hard it seems or no matter how much it may hurt to do things His way, God's way of living life will always be the best way—the route by which we will reap the most lasting rewards. But I also want to show that none of us is perfect, and even though we make mistakes, God is the inventor of grace, and He is patient above and beyond what we can ask or imagine."

E-mail is welcome at aishaford@yahoo.com

Visit www.aishaford.com for more!

STACY'S WEDDING

Dedicated to my Lord and Savior, Jesus Christ,
who gave me the ability to write.
And to Tracie Peterson and Rebecca Germany
for their encouragement, patience, and writing advice.

Chapter 1

Y ou may kiss the bride." The former Lisa Abrams, now Mrs. Brad Winters, beamed at her new husband as he lifted her veil and prepared to kiss her. On the third row of the congregation, Mrs. Abrams dabbed at her eyes. Mr. Abrams put his arm around his wife's shoulder and blinked to hold back a threatening tear. On the groom's side of the congregation, Brad's parents were the mirror image of Lisa's. Out in the foyer, Stacy Thompson paced as she held her cellular phone to her ear and prayed someone at the reception hall would pick up the phone. Why did the ceremony have to be so short? she wondered. It felt as though this were the quickest wedding ceremony she had ever attended. Time was running out, and she couldn't afford to have this mistake hanging over her head. Lisa Winters was the daughter of one of Kansas City's well-known businessmen. The wedding and the following reception had to be perfect because Stacy was the wedding coordinator and her name and business were on the line.

"Hello?" Her assistant's voice answered the phone.

"Courtney, how are things going?" Stacy asked nervously.

"Well. . .not too good. We're working on Plan B, but something tells me Lisa and her family might not be thrilled with it. Stacy, you'd better get over here. And you'd better try to keep them from coming too soon."

"That bad, huh?" Stacy's heart plummeted to her stomach and sat there like a heavy rock.

"Worse," said Courtney as she hung up the phone.

Two ushers opened the door, and the sound of "The Wedding March" echoed loudly throughout the church. Moving aside for the bride and groom to come down the aisle, Stacy hesitated. She felt bad about heading over to the reception before speaking with the bride's parents, but she knew if she didn't, she would have a very slim chance of salvaging the reception. In fact, she hadn't wanted to come to the ceremony, but it was part of her job that she couldn't shrug off. Lisa and Brad were heading out to the limousine, and if she didn't leave now, she would get stuck in the crowd of more than three hundred guests.

She hurried to the side door and ran out to her car. As she ran, she moved her hand around in her purse to locate her keys and felt sick when she didn't feel them. She was notorious for locking her keys in the car. She closed her eyes when she got to her car, afraid of what she might see. "Please, Lord," she breathed. "Not today. If my keys are in there, could You please unlock the door? And if possible, could You do me a wedding miracle over at the reception hall?" She opened her eyes and gasped. Sure enough, the door was locked, but the keys

9

weren't in the ignition. She moved around the car, looking in all the windows, but the keys were definitely not in the car. She looked back at the church. Where could they be?

People were beginning to file outside and were moving toward their cars. She wouldn't be able to get to the reception hall in time to help Courtney and the others, let alone in time to personally apologize to Mr. and Mrs. Abrams. Maybe she should go break the news now. She looked down at her shoes and tried to find the inner strength she would need to face the bride's parents. "Why does stuff like this happen to me?" she said quietly. A tiny tear escaped the corner of her eye and dropped to the ground. *Oh, no. I'm not going to start crying. I'm just going to explain the situation and hope they forgive me.*

She wiped her cheek and stared at the pair of masculine black shoes that were directly in front of her dainty lavender pumps. She looked up into the face of a very handsome man.

"Did you drop these?" he asked, holding up her key chain.

"Yes, I did!" Stacy said, grabbing the keys. "Thank you so much. I wish I could say more, but I'm in a really big hurry," she explained as she unlocked her car door and got in. She fastened her seat belt and started the car. "Thanks again," she called as she pulled out of the parking lot and left the man standing there, looking puzzled.

❧

Two minutes earlier, Max Edwards had escaped his back row seat at the wedding and hurried to the nearest exit. Another wedding! And still the reception at which to make an appearance. Loosening his tie, he noticed the woman in the lavender suit hurrying out the side doorway. He also noticed her keys fall out of her purse and land on the thick carpet in the foyer. He picked them up and followed her to her car. As he moved closer, he took note of her appearance. Tall and graceful, she had cocoa brown skin and shiny black hair cut close to her head, brushed down and curling at her ears. Her oval face was accentuated by a long neck and wide, round eyes. When he handed her the keys, he noticed her long, slender fingers and her light brown eyes, shiny from tears. He wondered why she was crying, but before he could ask if she was okay, she jumped in her car and left. He shrugged his shoulders. *She might be at the reception,* he thought. *Maybe this won't be such a dull event after all.* He smiled and headed to his car.

❧

A cakeless wedding. *It seems unreal,* thought Stacy. "But it's true," she said aloud. "How can this be happening to me?"

"What do you think we should do?" asked Courtney. She had been Stacy's best friend since the fourth grade. They were both the same height, but that was where their physical similarities ended. Courtney had long, straight, honey brown hair that wouldn't curl even if she fell on her knees and begged it to. Her eyes were jade green, framed by long, thick lashes. She looked much younger than her twenty-five years, which was the reason she was convinced she didn't have a steady boyfriend. "Men are just too afraid to ask me out," she would wail to Stacy. "If you were a man who was twenty-five or older, would you ask a woman on a date if she looked like she was seventeen?"

Stacy would always laugh and reply, "Any man could ask you how old you are. And besides, if you really wanted to look older, you could just get a makeover, or start wearing more makeup or something." Courtney was an invaluable assistant to Stacy. Their firm friendship helped the business run more efficiently. They were the two most dedicated employees, because they both loved creating fantastic, memorable weddings for their customers. When something went wrong, they both attacked the problem and wouldn't give up until it had been resolved.

"What should we do?" asked Stacy. "Like we have a choice! The question is, what can we do?"

"There's no way we can get a new cake now. The baker has several sheet cakes ready, but the tiered one is definitely ruined," said Courtney, shaking her head.

"I guess I'll just have to tell the Abramses what happened. Maybe they won't blame me personally. . . . I mean, it was the baker who tripped and landed in the cake, not me."

"Yeah, poor guy, he feels so bad about it. He's back in the kitchen feverishly decorating all those small cakes. In fact, they almost look fancier than the original cake." Courtney's laugh was nervous.

"There's nothing we can do about it now. But I had really hoped this was some sort of joke. The wedding was just about to start, and then you call telling me the cake is smashed. . . ." Stacy sighed. "Let's start putting those cakes on display."

Not quite ten minutes later, the wedding party began to arrive. Stacy waited a few moments, then quietly pulled Mrs. Abrams off to the side of the room. "Mrs. Abrams," she began, then cleared her throat. "We have a, um. . .a little problem with the cake. Could you come in the kitchen with me for a moment?"

"Okay," said Mrs. Abrams cautiously as they moved toward the kitchen. "I take it this is one of the problems you have to show someone, rather than try to explain—Oh!" Mrs. Abrams's eyebrows shot up almost to her hairline as she stared at the smashed cake. Formerly a towering masterpiece, it was now nothing more than a huge mound of hunks of broken cake and smushed icing. "What are we going to do?" Her face registered panicked. "I have over three hundred people out there and no cake."

"Well, not exactly no cake. The baker has prepared some smaller cakes that we can serve to the guests. I think they're just as pretty and I'll deduct the cost of the other cake and pay for these myself." Stacy inwardly winced. That cake was the most expensive cake any of her customers had ever ordered, and now she had to pay for it. Hopefully, the baker would not charge full price. She waited for Mrs.

Abrams to answer in agreement. The woman still looked to be in a state of shock.

Stacy decided it was not helping matters to let her stare at the ruined cake. "Why don't we go and look at the new cakes?" she suggested. She gently took Mrs. Abrams's arm and led her to the cake table.

Mrs. Abrams brightened a little at the sight of the replacement cakes. "Well, of course, I liked the other cake better, but there's nothing we can do about that. These are fine. I suppose it would be really terrible if we had no cake at all. By the way, what exactly happened to the other cake?"

"The baker accidentally tripped and fell on top of it," explained Stacy.

Mrs. Abrams's face softened even more. "Well. . .accidents happen." She patted Stacy on the arm. "Don't look so upset. You look like you're at a funeral. Try to look happy, Girl. At least for his sake. He's been watching you for a few minutes now." She angled her head in the direction of the man who had found Stacy's keys. "He's an executive at Baker, Shepard, and Morris. I must say, I am surprised. That man is the epitome of the bachelor." She paused for a moment. "Well, I'm off to find my husband. See you later." Mrs. Abrams moved away.

"Oh, Mrs. Abrams? What is his name?"

The woman turned around. "Max Edwards," she said. With a mischievous glint in her eye, she added, "But I'm sure he'll tell you that."

Stacy shot a glance at him. She knew she should go and thank him about her keys and apologize for being so abrupt in the parking lot, but she was not very good at striking up conversations with men she didn't know, even if it was concerning business. She just guessed that after many unproductive relationships with former boyfriends, she had grown to be shy. *And you can't get burned if you don't play with fire,* said a familiar voice in the back of her mind.

Max was staring at her now, and she started to feel flustered. *I need to find something to do so I don't do something silly, like trip over my feet, or even worse, somebody else's feet.* She hurried into the kitchen and shut the door, sighing with relief. She was safe for now. Later she would work up the nerve to thank him, but right now she had work to do. *After all, I'm not here to have fun. This is my job. I'm at work, and he's at a party. It's silly to think he could be interested in me. . . .*

"Stacy, the DJ needs to speak with you right away," said Courtney, briefly coming into the kitchen and then quickly disappearing out the door. *Why was I even worrying? I'm going to be so busy, he won't get a chance to talk to me,* thought Stacy as she went off to see what the DJ needed.

❧

That evening, Max sat at his desk and tried to concentrate on the reports he was supposed to be reviewing. But he couldn't stop thinking about that woman at the wedding. Mrs. Abrams had told him her name was Stacy Thompson and that she was the wedding coordinator, but that was all he knew. He had been ready to speak to her, but she had seemed frightened and had pretty much run away.

He didn't think he looked bad enough to scare her, but he knew he couldn't force her to talk to him. After all, she had thanked him for finding her keys, and she wasn't really obligated to say much more beyond that. He would have liked to have gotten to know her a little better, but he wasn't going to rush her.

He flipped a few pages of the reports and halfheartedly glanced at some numbers, but he knew he wouldn't get any work done. He went to the kitchen and searched for something to eat. All he could find was a box of graham crackers, so he took those and headed off to his computer to see what was new on his favorite Internet book discussion group.

❧

Stacy sat watching the late news while munching on graham crackers and whipped cream. She loved this snack and had convinced herself it was healthier than plain old ice cream and cookies. Her feet ached from standing so long, and she was glad the Abrams-Winters wedding was over.

Her south Kansas City townhouse was decorated simply but comfortably. The walls were either eggshell or bright white. An abundance of windows flooded the interior with natural light, which also reflected off the pine woodwork, flooring, and cabinetry.

To further complement the look, she had decorated with easy and spacious furniture upholstered with dainty patterns in periwinkle, rose, and buttercup. Her extensive collection of crystal vases and mirrors in varying shapes and sizes added an elegant finishing touch. The housing complex was quiet and well kept, fenced with intricate wrought iron and lit with lights that were made to resemble old-fashioned coach lights. Outdoors, the landscaping was simple, with small shrubs and young trees decorating the homes, and in season, begonias and impatiens dotted the landscape, painting the outdoors with cheery splotches of vibrant color.

Stacy sighed and stretched out on the oversized chaise in her living room. It had been a long and trying day, starting with the cake, and she hoped nothing like that ever happened again. She would have to check into a cake insurance policy or something. Then she remembered Max Edwards. He was certainly interesting. He was probably about six feet tall, give or take an inch. He had smooth skin the color of the finest dark chocolate. His eyes were dark brown pools that seemed to dance as if he were always laughing to himself. The memory of his compassionate smile warmed Stacy's heart as she thought about the way he had smiled at her when he handed her the keys. She probably should have talked to him, but she knew she would not have been able to think of anything to say. As she walked to the kitchen to put away the crackers, the phone rang.

"Hello?" asked Stacy.

"Stace, it's me."

"Hi, Maddy. What's up?"

"I was just calling to let you know when to pick me up at the airport. School is out, and I can't believe the fun I'm going to have this summer. I've been telling everyone that I've landed a dream job for the summer. Nothing but weddings, weddings, and more weddings!"

Stacy listened as her younger sister chattered on and on. Madison was a junior in college, and her bubbly personality sometimes made her seem younger than her twenty-one years. Stacy was only four years older, and she was beginning to wonder if she had bitten off more than she could chew by offering Maddy a job this summer.

"You know, Maddy, I'm beginning to wonder if you would really enjoy working for me. I'm your sister, but I'll still be your boss. And it would be almost impossible for you to get weekends off because my busiest days are Thursday through Sunday. Weddings are usually held on weekends, you know."

Maddy was quiet for a few moments. "I don't really mind. And really, it'll just be fun to be home. I'm so excited about staying at your apartment! This is going to be so great!"

Again Stacy wondered what she had been thinking when she told Maddy she could live with her. She had mentioned the possibility when Maddy was home for Christmas, but she hadn't thought Maddy would want to live with her. Their parents lived in Kansas City also, not even twenty minutes away. She figured Maddy would want to go home to her old room and remain close to her old neighbors and friends.

She sighed and shook her head. It was going to be some summer. Maddy would soon be here in her apartment with all of her chattering, her beauty recipes, her squeals of excitement over little things, and her habit of staying up until three or four in the morning, then sleeping in until noon or so. At least they both loved graham crackers and whipped cream. Stacy smiled and closed her eyes as she listened to Maddy. *I have to admit, I'm getting excited too.*

Chapter 2

Max sat at his desk at work and watched specks of dust, highlighted by the sun, float through his office. He really wished he had spoken to the woman at the wedding. He at least wished he had her phone number. He inhaled deeply and then exhaled. There wasn't a big chance that he would happen to run into her again anytime soon. He leaned back in his chair, deep in thought. Suddenly, he sat up and called his secretary. "Celia! I need you to find a couple of phone numbers for me."

Celia peeked in the door of his office with a pen and paper in her hand. She was a short, thin woman in her late fifties. Her short, salt-and-pepper hair was styled elegantly. She always dressed sharply and favored wearing jewel tones like ruby, emerald, and royal blue because these colors complemented her dark brown skin. She was a loyal employee who had three children who were all married, and between the three of them, she had seven grandchildren.

She treated Max like one of her own children and was always trying to set him up with some neighbor's or friend's daughter or some young woman from her church. Hardly any of these many women had gone out a second time with Max. She couldn't figure out what kind of a woman he liked, so she had stopped trying recently. If Max ever got married, she would probably be just as happy as his mother.

"What numbers do you need, Sir?" she asked.

"I need you to find a residential listing for Stacy Thompson, and a business listing for a wedding coordinator by the same name."

Celia quirked one eyebrow up in response but said nothing as she went to look for the numbers.

A short time later, Celia returned to Max's office. "There was no residential listing, but I did find a number for Stacy Thompson adjacent to a listing for Creative Wedding Services." She handed him the number and stood there for a moment.

Max looked up from the number and said, "Thanks, Celia. Did you need something?"

Celia looked at him curiously for a moment, then shook her head. "No, Sir. I'm going to lunch, but I'll be back in thirty minutes or so."

Max smiled as Celia turned and left. She was probably itching to know what he was up to. She never liked to come out and ask him details of his personal life, but her ears certainly perked up when he volunteered to share any information with her. And since he was asking about a wedding coordinator, he couldn't blame her for being curious. But judging by the way Stacy Thompson had dodged him yesterday, there was no use getting Celia's hopes up. . .or his. He looked at the number again. It wasn't like he could call her up and pretend he had business to discuss. He could imagine the conversation now.

"Um. . .how much does a wedding cost?" *Nope, scratch that,* he thought. *Why would she be interested in me if she thought I was getting married? I'd have to say the wedding was for a friend of mine. But she'd probably want to know why my friend wasn't calling to plan his own wedding. . . . And I doubt many men ever call a wedding coordinator. Their fiancées probably do that. She would just think I was stupid. Or worse, she might think I'm stalking her, and then she'd be even more frightened of me.*

"No, this is not going to work," he said aloud. *Why couldn't she sell insurance or be a stockbroker or something so I could have an excuse to call her?* There had to be a way he could get to see her again.

"Yes, I understand. But the problem is, I'm already working that day." Stacy leaned back in her chair and rested her head in her hand. She had a terrible headache, and it was only 1:30. She had dealt with what seemed like hundreds of little problems this morning. She was also battling the sneaking suspicion that she was forgetting to do something, and now this. *I need more employees,* she thought as she listened to the woman try to persuade her to help with her wedding. *I can't keep turning down jobs like this. But where can I get somebody on short notice who already knows what she's doing?*

"So you see, it would be just wonderful if you could find space to squeeze me in." The woman paused expectantly.

"Well, Miss, I really wish I could help you, but the truth is, unless someone breaks their engagement, I'm all booked up for the summer. I've got at least two, sometimes three, weddings every week. All of my employees are working overtime, and there is no way we can add another wedding. In fact, we actually like to start planning six to eight months in advance. I've never done a wedding in under three months. But best wishes to you and your fiancé. I hope everything works out well."

"I see. But in case someone cancels on you, could I leave my number so you could let me know?" the woman asked.

"Sure. Let me get a pen." Stacy listened as the woman recited her number, reminding Stacy to call her the minute someone canceled because she was willing to hold her wedding off for a few more weeks if Stacy's company could coordinate it.

"Who was that?" asked Courtney as Stacy left the office and entered the showroom.

"A lady begging to get her wedding coordinated. She wants us to call her the very second someone cancels so we can get to work on her wedding. I really think she's hoping some unlucky couple breaks up."

"How morbid," said Courtney, making a face. "But that's the third wedding we've turned down this month. We can't keep telling people we're booked for the summer."

"But we are!" Stacy threw her hands up in the air. "I had no idea so many people would hire us when I started this business. I thought we'd do well to get a couple of weddings a month. But this is amazing. We had to double the employees after six months, and now we need more." Stacy sat down behind her desk and frowned.

Courtney giggled. "Stacy, you're so dramatic. You make it seem like you went from having forty employees to eighty. But we only went from two to four!"

Stacy ignored Courtney's joke and continued. "What really scares me is that I'm so busy working on other people's weddings I'll probably never have time to meet anyone myself and fall in love."

"What about the guys from your church?"

"Uhmmm. . .not too much success there. I'm not really attracted to any of them. I tried, but I didn't think the Lord was leading me in their direction."

"Yeah, and the fact that you're too shy." Courtney started dusting one of the floral displays in the showroom.

"What do you mean, I'm too shy?" Stacy countered.

"You know exactly what I mean. Like that guy at Lisa Abrams's wedding. You ran from him during the entire reception. The look on your face was pure fright." She laughed softly as she moved on to another arrangement.

"I was not scared. I just had work to do."

"Oh really?"

"Yes, really." Stacy lifted her eyebrows and sighed, waiting for Courtney to add another argument to her case.

"So you're saying that if you hadn't been working, you would have paid more attention to the guy?" said Courtney, chuckling again.

"Of course. If I was attracted to him."

"Are you?"

"Am I what?"

"Attracted to him. And don't bother answering. I know you are. I just want you to prove to me that you're not scared of him."

"Well, I would love to, only I'll probably never see him again. So you'll just have to take my word for it."

"Oh, no, I don't," said Courtney.

"Now what are you talking about?"

Courtney laughed again, this time really enjoying herself. "Because that same guy from the wedding has been pacing back and forth outside the shop for the last ten minutes, and now I think he's about to come in!"

"Oh, no! Tell him I'm not here," Stacy said, heading for the office in the back.

"Too late for that. I'm sure he's already seen you. Besides, you said you'd

17

prove to me you weren't scared of him. But you won't have to feel like you have an audience. I'll make myself scarce," she singsonged as the door opened and Max Edwards entered the shop.

"Hello," he said, looking at Stacy.

"Hello," she said, trying to sound businesslike. "What can I help you with?" she asked, hoping her voice wasn't affected by the way her heart was pounding.

"I'm going to be in the back, proofing the engraving on the invitations we got in today," said Courtney as she headed for the office. "Call me if you need me," she said as she winked at Stacy.

Max softly cleared his throat, and Stacy looked at him expectantly. "I want you to know that I don't usually do things like this, and I feel kind of funny about this now, but I was wondering if you'd want to go out to lunch with me," he said, his words spilling out in a rush.

"You want me to have lunch with you?" asked Stacy, her voice cracking a tiny bit.

"Yeah, if you don't have anything else on your schedule. I know a great little café. . . . Actually, I kind of already made reservations."

"Oh, I see. I hate to tell you this, but. . .if you're planning to get married this summer, I can't do your wedding. The earliest opening I have is the end of September." There, she'd said it. Stacy held her breath awaiting his answer. She'd taken an extremely roundabout way of inquiring if he was in a relationship with someone. Why else would he want to go to lunch, except to discuss a wedding?

Max laughed. "No, I'm not getting married. . .at least not this summer. Unless you and I decide we're extremely in love with each other over lunch. Then how soon could you fit our wedding in?" A little smile touched his face. He was not going to let her run away from him now.

Stacy, feeling a little frazzled by his direct comment, reflexively reached for her schedule book. "I, um. . .well," she said, flipping pages. Then, understanding his little joke, she shut the book and looked at the floor. She couldn't believe she had fallen for that. "I'm sorry, Sir, but I don't have any free time today."

"Call me Max," he said, taking a seat on a small sofa near Stacy's desk. "And may I call you Stacy, Miss Thompson? It is Miss, isn't it?"

"Yes," she said, meeting his eyes briefly, then looking away. *If I find a reason not to go out with him, Courtney will tease me forever about this, and besides, I would like to have lunch with him.*

"Stacy, I'm sure there's a spot somewhere in that book that says you can have lunch with me this afternoon."

"Sure, why not?" Stacy said brightly, not quite believing her own courage.

Max stood up and said, "Then let's—"

The door suddenly opened. Madison Thompson stood in the doorway, looking upset. She was just under five feet tall, and most people described her as cute. She had cute eyes, a cute nose, a cute round face, and cute figure. Her skin was honey colored, and her eyes were hazel and seemed to sparkle constantly. She wore her hair in a smooth, simple, ear-length bob. At this moment, however, she did not seem very cute.

"Well, I am shocked! My own sister left me stranded at the airport for over an hour. I paged you hundreds of times because I didn't have the number here, but you didn't call me back, so I had to take a cab." Maddy dumped her bags on the floor and went out to the cab to retrieve the rest of her luggage.

Stacy couldn't speak. *Now I remember what I was forgetting*, she thought as she pressed her palm to her forehead.

"If you didn't want me to come, why didn't you just say so the other night?" Maddy asked plaintively.

"Why didn't you call Mom and Dad, Maddy? They would have picked you up."

"I did, but no one answered the phone. Anyway, I'm sorry to interrupt things with you and your boyfriend here, whom, I might add, you've never once mentioned to me, but I need you to pay the cab driver."

"Here." Stacy reached into her purse and handed her credit card to Maddy, who, still frowning, turned in a huff to pay the driver. Then Stacy addressed Max. "I'm sorry, Mr. Edwards, but I need to cancel our lunch before my melodramatic sister delivers an Oscar-winning performance."

"Why don't we take her with us?" Max couldn't believe his own ears, but he figured if he gave up now, he might never get her to agree to go out with him again.

"I don't think. . ."

Max turned to Maddy, who had reentered the shop. "I'm sorry about the mix-up, but I'm sure Stacy didn't mean it. Why don't you join us for lunch?"

Maddy stood silent for a moment, as she directed a questioning look toward Stacy. Before she could reply, Courtney hurried out of the office and said, "Maddy, I'm so glad you're here. I need you to run some errands with me. I've got a ton of stops to make, but we'll stop and get something to eat before we get started." She fished in her purse for her keys and added, "Why don't we put all your luggage in Stacy's car? After we're done, I'll drop you off at her apartment, and she can bring your stuff home." Courtney lifted a suitcase and held open the door for Maddy to follow.

Maddy obediently picked up some luggage, then asked, "If we're going to be gone, and Stacy's going to lunch, who's going to watch the store?"

"We usually close the store early on Mondays and Tuesdays so we have time to run errands. Sometimes Julia or Ben will come in to catch up on work and they'll open the store, but probably not before two or so," explained Courtney.

Max glanced at Stacy, who was very quiet. "Well, I guess that we can return to our original plans for lunch now. You haven't changed your mind, have you?"

"Um. . .no. I'm ready when you are." Stacy offered a small smile.

"Then let's go," said Max, holding the door open for Stacy. Waving good-bye to Courtney and Maddy, he said, "It was nice meeting the two of you. See you again soon." During the short ride to the small café, Max and Stacy made small talk, mostly about the weather. Once they were inside and seated at a small table, they both began to relax and the conversation picked up. Max ordered a turkey club sandwich and potato salad, and Stacy ordered the Greek salad with a rye bagel.

"So how long have you lived in Kansas City?" asked Max.

"All of my life," Stacy answered. "How about you?"

"I've lived in Missouri all my life, but I'm originally from St. Louis. I've only been in Kansas City for the past fifteen years. I came here when I was eighteen for my freshman year at UMKC. And I liked it here, so I stayed."

"So all of your family is still in St. Louis?"

"Yes. My parents, three sisters, four brothers, and several aunts and uncles."

"That's a big family," said Stacy. "I only have one very dramatic sister, whom you met today. But she also does pretty good comedy." They both laughed. "I just can't imagine moving to a city where I didn't know anyone. I went to college in Texas, but my mom's originally from there, and I stayed with her sister and her family my freshman year. And my friend Courtney, who's now my business partner, went to the same school. In fact, my aunt and uncle have a daughter who's my age, and we went to school together. So our sophomore year, my cousin Sabrina, Courtney, and I got our own apartment near campus. I wouldn't have considered going to college alone. And of course, I came back after graduation."

"I didn't mind," said Max. "For me, it was kind of like an adventure, a way to strike out on my own. I was always surrounded by friends and family, and I wanted to get away for awhile."

"Do you think you'll ever go back?"

He rubbed his chin and sat quietly for a few moments. "I don't know. I visit whenever I can. It's not a long drive. But I've kind of gotten comfortable here. I've got a good job, a church I love, and I bought a house about five years ago. I guess I've put down more roots than I realized." He stopped and took a bite of his sandwich.

Stacy cleared her throat nervously and said, "I forgot to really thank you for finding my keys, but. . .thank you. You really did me a big favor."

"No problem. It wasn't a big deal."

Stacy nervously fingered the edge of the tablecloth. "I hope you don't mind my asking this, but. . ." He looked up and waited for her to continue.

Go ahead and ask, she told herself. *But it seems like such a stupid question. How can I politely ask, "Why did you ask me out?" On the other hand, I want to know for the sake of my own feelings. He's a nice guy, very attractive, and a Christian, but what if he's the type who has fifteen different girlfriends at his church or something? Why should I throw my emotions into a mess like that? But what if he's really interested in me, and he's not seeing anyone else? But what if he's seeing someone else and he wouldn't tell me even if I asked? Oh, no, this is pathetic! I shouldn't ask him now. Everything seems to be going smoothly, and if he really likes me, he'll ask me out again. I hope he does, but if he doesn't. . . I don't need to make a fool of myself by asking him what his intentions are halfway into our first date.*

He was still looking at her, waiting for the question.

She exhaled, then said, "Never mind, it wasn't important."

"No, go ahead. Ask me. I'll do my best to answer. I don't mind. . .really."

"Okay," she said, trying to come up with a replacement question. "I was just wondering, what's your favorite Bible verse?" *It's not the most clever sounding question, but it's not so embarrassing as the one I almost asked.*

His eyes widened a little. "Well, that's a question people hardly ever ask me, but I like it. To tell you the truth, my favorite Bible verse changes a lot, depending on what I'm going through or what type of Bible study I'm doing at the moment. So I guess I have several favorites. But one that I've always liked quite a bit is Matthew 10:28: 'And fear not them which kill the body, but are not able to kill the soul: but rather fear him which is able destroy both soul and body in hell.' "

"Why that one?" she asked curiously.

"Well, when I was younger, I spent a lot of time trying to please people and wondering what would happen and how I would be treated if I didn't do what other people expected me to do. That verse just helps me to keep in perspective that I'm truly accountable to my heavenly Father. I still struggle at times, especially when I feel like people are taking advantage of my kindness, but that verse saw me through a lot of unhealthy peer pressure in college."

"So what's your favorite verse?" he asked in turn.

"Proverbs 4:23," she answered without hesitation. " 'Keep thy heart with all diligence, for out of it are the issues of life.' " Without waiting for Max to comment, she continued. "I like that one because it's helped me to learn the importance of guarding my heart against. . ." She stopped. Shrugging, she said, "Well, I've learned that I should be careful where my heart is concerned." She quickly changed the subject. "So what type of work do you do?"

They talked for another two hours and then decided they should be getting back. Max dropped Stacy off at her office and waited for her to get in her car. "Would you be interested in going out again sometime soon?" he wanted to know.

"Yes, that would be fun," was Stacy's reply.

"I'll give you a call then. Talk to you later," he said before driving away.

"Max Edwards, I hope you're as sincere as you seem to be," said Stacy softly as she buckled her seat belt.

Chapter 3

Courtney and Maddy arrived at the apartment at six o'clock, carrying bags full of takeout cartons. "We want to hear everything. We went ahead and brought dinner so we wouldn't have to waste time cooking," said Courtney as she entered the front door.

Maddy was excited, as usual. "Courtney filled me in on how the two of you met. That's so romantic. Imagine, meeting the perfect guy at a wedding. So what happened at lunch?" she wanted to know.

Stacy sighed. "To tell you the truth, I'm more interested in what's in those bags than giving you a minute by minute description of my lunch with Max. I suggest you all dig up plates and forks. I'll get the sodas and meet you in the living room for the big discussion," she said with a mischievous smile on her face.

A few minutes later, they were all seated on the floor of Stacy's living room, Maddy and Courtney listening attentively as Stacy told them details of her date.

After Stacy had finished, Maddy said, "You are so lucky! He was probably in love with you from the second he handed you your keys. In fact, he might have fallen in love with you before he even gave you the keys."

"You're saying that he fell in love with me by looking at my keys?" Stacy asked, giggling. "Maybe he just fell in love with my keys!"

"So when are you going to see him again?" Courtney wanted to know.

"He said he'll call me, but I'm pretty sure it'll be soon. He mentioned going to church together, so we'll have to decide if we want to go to my church or his church. I really would feel more comfortable if he came to our church. I'd be around people I already know, and he doesn't seem like he'd have any trouble making new friends."

"Yeah, and if he came to our church, you could show him off to everyone," Courtney said as she jokingly wiggled her eyebrows. Standing up, she yawned. "I'd better be going. But I'll see you two in the morning."

"I'll walk you to the door," said Stacy.

"No, that's okay. I can let myself out. You two need some time to catch up on everything. If you need to come in late tomorrow, just give me a call. Julia's scheduled to be working in the shop anyway, so if you and Maddy want to spend the day together. . .things at work will be okay."

"Thanks, Courtney, but I don't think that's necessary. Remember, I have the Allman-Kamrick rehearsal dinner tomorrow night. I'll need to come in to get some of their paperwork done. See you in the morning."

As she returned to the living room where Maddy was watching television, she snapped her fingers. "I almost forgot! Maddy, a huge box came for you this afternoon right after I got home. I just had the delivery guy set it outside the door, then I dragged it inside to the hall closet. Whatever it is, it's really heavy."

Maddy bounded to the hall closet and flung open the door. "My computer!" she squealed. "I have to get it hooked up tonight. You'll have to let me introduce you to the Internet."

A few hours later, Stacy sat in front of the computer as Maddy tried to interest her in some of her favorite Web sites. However, after an hour of looking at screen after screen of makeup tips and fashion advice, Stacy was growing lethargic and Maddy was getting frustrated.

"Honestly, Stacy. How can the Internet not be interesting to you? If you don't like my favorite sites, there's got to be something you'd be interested in. What do you want to look for?"

"Maddy, I work with computers when I'm at work. I don't have a computer here because it would remind me of work," said Stacy.

"Well, you need to know more about the Internet, anyway," Maddy retorted.

"I know about the Internet. The computer at work has an Internet connection. I just don't want to use it for recreational purposes."

"Lighten up a little. Come on, what interests you just a little?"

"Okay. . .are there any wedding planning sites?"

"Stacy," Maddy groaned. "How about staying away from sites that are work related? Isn't there anything you like to do besides work? Do you want to chat with some people?"

"No," said Stacy emphatically. "I've heard way more bad news than good about Internet chat rooms."

Maddy sighed. "Not all chat rooms are inherently bad. You just have to pick them carefully and be careful of whom you talk to and what you say. C'mon, think. What are your hobbies?"

"I don't know. . . ," Stacy began, shrugging her shoulders.

Maddy snapped her fingers. "Don't you like to read? What was the last book you read?"

"Well, I started a book last week, but I haven't had time to finish it."

"Doesn't matter. You can probably discuss it with some other people in a discussion group somewhere. What's the name of the book?"

The last thing Stacy wanted to do was discuss a book with some people on the Internet, but she didn't want to hurt Maddy's feelings either, so she told her the name of the book and waited patiently while Maddy spent a few moments typing and clicking away on her mouse. "Here we are. It's a book discussion website. Look, here's a discussion group for that book, *Famine* by Archer Mason. It looks like it's been on the bestseller list for a few weeks. Must be some mystery."

"Well, from what I've read so far, it's pretty good. But I like all of Mason's books. I haven't read the whole thing, so I don't think I would sound very intelligent trying to discuss it with people who have. . ."

Stacy trailed off. Even though she hated to admit it, she was getting excited about this book discussion. Reading was her favorite hobby, and the only downside of her hobby was that she rarely got the opportunity to discuss books she'd read with others. Most of her friends were into Christian romance novels, while she was a big fan of mysteries and adventure, especially those written by Archer Mason.

It wasn't that she didn't like Christian romances—in fact, she loved them. However, after planning weddings for happy, excited couples day in and day out, sometimes Stacy found it to be more discouraging than encouraging to pick up a novel about another woman who meets the perfect man. She supposed she was more sensitive to this than most of her friends due to the nature of her job and the fact that she rarely dated. At any rate, she decided that if she could finish the book quickly, maybe this discussion group was worth a try.

"Look, Stacy, you don't have to read the whole book," Maddy was saying. "They're on a time schedule. You only have to read two chapters every Saturday and discuss those chapters for a week."

"Oh, I think I've covered at least two or three chapters. What time do they have the discussion?"

"No particular time," said Maddy, who was staring at the screen. "It's a threaded discussion group. You just write a message about what you think, and people will reply to it when they get a chance. Meanwhile, you can read the messages that everyone else is posting and respond to what they've said."

"You mean I can start now?"

"Sure. Go ahead. You need any more help?"

Stacy shook her head. "I think I can figure it out. I do know how to use a computer. But I'll call you if I need you."

Maddy giggled. "I guess that's my cue to leave. I'll be in my room, getting unpacked."

Stacy spent the next hour reading the comments already posted on the message board before adding her thoughts, because she didn't want to write something redundant. There were probably nine or ten people who seemed to be actively posting, but two or three seemed to be the more dominant posters on the board. The people really seemed to be having a good time with this discussion. One poster, named Flyer 87, had started a thread entitled: "Watch out for Debra Foster!!!"

> *Flyer 87: I think Kent Lennox has his work cut out for him. I seriously doubt this Foster woman's cousin has really disappeared. It's probably some type of setup.*
>
> *Booknut: No way!!! Besides, he's a private eye. It's his job to take risks. And I think Debra's cousin IS missing.*
>
> *Sherlock: I agree with Booknut. Jill Austin is really missing, and I*

think it has something to do with her line of work.

Flyer 87: *Her line of work!? She's a nutritionist!! Why would she be missing?*

Grandma: *Jill is missing and it does have something to do with her job. . . .*

Leslie: *C'mon, Grandma. I know you're a fast reader, but this week is chapters 1 and 2, remember. I barely finished reading that much! My twins and my husband have the flu and my other two kids are due to catch it any second.*

Grandma: *Sorry, Leslie. I won't divulge any more, but it's so tempting!!! How are the dogs?*

Leslie: *They're fine. . .all 4 of 'em. And Fred and Ethel (our cats) haven't been aggravating the dogs as much lately.*

George: *We're having a sale at our bookstore and I need to do inventory. . . . I really need to hire another employee. But that's the fun part of owning a small business. So. . .I don't have much time, but my vote is with Flyer. Debra's a decoy. I think she might be working for Patrick Edger.*

Sherlock: *Edger!!! That was three books ago. Edger is history. No way he would even try to tangle with Lennox again.*

Stacy paused. *I remember the book with Edger. It was never really clear what happened to him in the end.* Stacy decided to post a message in reply to Sherlock. *I need a handle,* she thought. *Since this Sherlock character thinks he knows it all. . .*

She thought for a few moments. Back when she was younger, she loved to read Nancy Drew novels. She was pretty good at figuring out mysteries in movies and books, and sometimes her friends used to jokingly call her Nancy Drew.

Feeling a little mischievous, she began typing: "All right, Sherlock, what do you say to Nancy Drew? And that's Ms. Drew to you."

It had been a long night, and Max was tired. When he'd dropped Stacy off at her shop, he'd gone back to the office and taken a pile of work home with him. He lived in the older neighborhood of Brookside, which had the feel of a small village nestled in the center of a big city. The people there shared a strong sense of community. Most of the homes were at least half a century old and were situated on quiet, tree-lined streets that twisted and curved in many different directions. The architecture of the homes ranged from bungalows to medium- and large-sized colonials and Dible and Tudor styles. Almost every home had a screened-in porch, located on either the front of the home or the side. Many of the colonials were three-storied and featured attic dormers and columns on the front porches.

Located along the outskirts of the community were many small shops and businesses that were housed in old buildings and added to the feel of being in a small town. The shops included a newer grocery store, a children's clothing boutique, an ice cream shop, a dime store, a bakery, a barber shop, a pharmacy, a bank, a tailor's, and a few restaurants. One could live quite comfortably and never travel outside of the general vicinity, and many of the older residents did so.

Max's home was a small brick Dible with an old-fashioned cobblestoned walkway that led to the arched front entry. The backyard was small and well shaded with mature trees. One corner of the yard housed a small shrub and herb garden which the previous owners had planted and cultivated. The interior featured a harmonious blend of history and the present. Area rugs accented deep cherry hardwood flooring. Much of the oversized and heavy furniture was made of wood or comfortable leather with bulky wooden and cast-iron framework along with clunky feet and legs. Traditional golds and maroons mixed with contemporary additions of eggplant and blue completed the color scheme. The blend of colors from room to room, along with lighting from sturdy lamps, saturated the home with warmth.

Max frowned as he tried once again to finish reading the report he was staring at. Normally, he'd have finished these reports in no time, but tonight, he kept thinking about Stacy. He was very attracted to her, but he couldn't quite tell if she felt the same way. On the outside, she seemed friendly, if sometimes a little distant, but something in her eyes made him feel as though she was longing for something. He couldn't quite figure what he saw in her eyes.

Whatever it was, it made him wish that he was what she was longing for. He wanted to protect her, to hold her in his arms and comfort her when she needed comforting. She seemed the type of woman who would be an ideal wife.

Max shook his head as if he were waking up from a dream. "Whoa. Where did that come from?" he asked himself. He wasn't against marriage, but he barely knew the woman. He'd never considered marrying anyone after one date, but maybe God was trying to tell him something. After all, he prayed every day for the woman who would eventually be his wife. *Maybe it is God, but probably not,* he decided. *More likely, it's lack of food and trying to do too much work late at night. My mind always wanders when I'm hungry. I'll get some graham crackers and check my E-mail. No more daydreaming tonight,* he thought as he headed for the kitchen. He checked his E-mail but found that his mailbox was empty. *Guess I'll see what's going on at the discussion group.* Skimming through the posts, he saw some of the usual posts and reactions to posts. *Flyer 87, as usual, disagrees with me,* thought Max, shaking his head and smiling. *Grandma has already read the whole book, and she's practically bursting trying not to tell everyone how it ends. George doesn't have a lot of free time, so he posted his usual compact, to-the-point opinion. The Butler's visiting his grandkids in Portland this week, but he'll join in when he gets back. Booknut agrees with me, and so does Lizzy. Leslie's trying to keep an eye on her four kids and six pets while sneaking in a page or two now and then. And Ms. Drew. . .* Max narrowed his eyebrows as he noticed a post entitled "Sherlock, I think you're mistaken."

"Who is Ms. Drew?" said Max, clicking to read the post.

> *Ms. Drew: I really think George might be on to something here. In* Fire on the Horizon, *Patrick Edger disappeared after the trial, when his buddies helped him escape. It was implied that he was hiding somewhere in Europe. If anybody would tangle with Kent Lennox, Edger would be the most probable suspect. Besides, if my memory serves me correctly, his sister's name was Debbie. This could quite possibly be a trick.*

Max exhaled and realized he had been holding his breath. How could he have forgotten about Edger's sister? Oh, man! Max slapped his palm to his forehead. This Ms. Drew was making him look bad. As Sherlock, Max had a reputation in the discussion group for solving the mystery before most of the others. His goal was to solve the mystery at least halfway through the book. He was good at it. But now he'd slipped up, and Ms. Drew had caught it. He'd have to post a reply soon so it wouldn't look like he was embarrassed.

~

Stacy's alarm went off at six the next morning, but she turned it off, called Courtney, and took her up on the offer to take the day off. She turned off the ringer on her phone and turned on the answering machine so she wouldn't be awakened by the phone. Stacy didn't wake up again until 1:30, and since Maddy was still asleep, she decided to see if anyone had responded to her post. Upon her arrival at the Web site, she found three responses to her post.

> *George: Way to go, Ms. Drew!!! You sure are one for details. . . . I had totally forgotten about Edger's sister, Debbie. Gotta get some sleep before I head to the shop, but I'm sure everyone in this discussion group agrees with me when I say "Glad to have you aboard!"*
> *Lizzy: Hey, Ms. Drew, good to see another detective type around here. Sherlock may get a little miffed since you've shot a hole in his theory. But I've got to warn you—he's usually right in the end. :) Bye!!! P.S. To Everyone: Happy 26th Birthday to ME!!!! Just thought I'd let you all know.*
> *Sherlock: All right, Ms. Drew. You've got me there. This could be Edger's sister. But, aside from revenge, do you have any brilliant ideas about why she's here? I am inclined to believe that her cousin Jill is really missing. You know, I've read all of Archer Mason's books, and it's not like him to deliberately mislead the reader. I believe this plot is supposed to center on finding a missing woman. Do you want to challenge that?*

Stacy laughed out loud, shaking her head in disbelief. This was why she'd been so wary of the Internet. These people were serious. It was as if this discussion group was their private little neighborhood. They knew each other's lives, their personalities, even the way they analyzed books, but they'd probably never even seen each other! And this Sherlock guy seemed to think he was the king of the block and he was offended that she was trying to usurp his book-solving ability or something. *Who would want to live to spend so much time on a computer talking with people you don't even know?* Stacy began typing a rebuttal message to Sherlock.

Obviously he is very narrow minded and completely against a new twist in the story every now and then. I know his type, because I've dated too many guys like him.

Afterward, she felt a little guilty. *What in the world came over me? This discussion group could get me into trouble. I'll have be more careful about what I say and make sure I watch the amount of time I spend on the Internet. The last thing I want to do is end up being addicted to a computer.*

She checked on Maddy to see if her sister wanted to do anything special, but Maddy was still asleep, so Stacy went into the kitchen to make tea and have her daily devotions while she waited for Maddy to wake up.

Chapter 4

Max was sitting at his desk wondering when Stacy would check her answering machine and return the call he'd placed early that morning. Would she have gone to work before 7:15 this morning? It was almost time for lunch, but at the rate he was going, he'd have to skip lunch to make up for the work he was falling behind on.

Celia peeked her head around the door. Max sat up straighter and tried to look as though he'd been busy working. He knew she was checking on him whenever she came into his office to deliver a message instead of using the intercom. Her eyebrows lifted slightly as she said, "Mr. Edwards, there is a Miss Thompson on line one for you."

Max quickly reached for the phone and hesitated before picking up the receiver. He cleared his throat. "Celia, is there anything else?"

She smiled and said, "Not at the moment. Everything is fine right now," and she disappeared back behind the door.

"Hello?" said Max.

"Hi, it's Stacy. I was returning your call."

"Yeah, I was wondering if you had gotten it."

"Well, I took off today and slept in. I stayed up late last night with my sister," she explained.

"I wish I could do the same. I'm up pretty late every night."

"Your work keeps you up late every night?" she asked.

"Well, my work. . .and hobbies," he added.

"What hobbies keep you up late at night?"

"Oh, you know, the usual. . .the news, stuff like that. I just like to find stuff to do that takes my mind off work. I just try to unwind." He didn't exactly want to tell Stacy about his book discussion group. For some reason, he always felt it was like telling people he belonged to a quilting club or something.

Stacy felt a little pang of guilt. He tried to unwind, while she'd gotten all wound up over some character on the Internet. Her mother would say it was her competitive spirit coming to the surface. From the time she was a little kid, she couldn't bear losing. She tried to stay away from highly competitive situations, but sometimes, something inside her just exploded. Like that little message she'd left for Sherlock a few minutes ago. She was going to really have to spend more time in prayer about those competitive urges. Max was waiting for her to answer a question, only she hadn't heard what he'd asked. *Pay attention*, she told herself.

"I'm sorry, I wasn't paying attention. Would you repeat the question please?"

Max laughed. "I know how it feels when your mind wanders. I was wondering if you wanted to get together before Sunday. Maybe Friday night?"

"That would be good. . .except I need to work."

"On a Friday night?" asked Max.

"I work practically every Friday night. A lot of people have their wedding rehearsals then." Stacy was disappointed, but what could she do about it? This was her job. *I could invite him to come with me, but that wouldn't be much of a date, and plus he might think I was sending him hints about marriage and I don't want to scare him off.*

They were silent for a moment and then Max spoke. "Well, what if I came with you? I know the rehearsal wouldn't be much of a date, but maybe afterwards we could go for dessert or something."

Stacy's heart flipped. "You wouldn't mind?"

"Nah. I might as well sit in on one of these rehearsals. Then I'll be that much ahead at my own wedding," he joked.

At his own wedding. Stacy felt a knot form in her stomach. "Well, the rehearsal's at five. We'll probably be done around seven."

"If I pick you up at four-thirty, will you get there in time?"

"Actually, I could ride over with my sister. She works for me, but she's going to meet some of her friends when we're done and I'm letting her borrow my car. So I would need you to drop me off at my house afterwards."

"Well then, I'll meet you at the church at five."

"Sounds good. Let me give you the address," said Stacy.

Friday afternoon, Stacy left work a little early to get ready for the rehearsal and her date. She did a quick check to see if Sherlock had replied to the little note she'd written him Tuesday, but there was still no reply. Now she was beginning to feel really awful. She must have bruised his ego so badly that he had left the discussion.

Maybe I should write an apology. But on second thought, he had it coming, she decided. *He needs to learn how to maturely handle a conversation with people who don't always agree with him. If I'm the one who had to teach him, so be it. Oh, well. Enough time wasted. I need to get ready so I'll be at the church on time.* She stood looking in her closet, wondering what she should wear.

Maddy passed the door and noticed Stacy just standing there. "Are you nervous?" she asked, taking a seat on Stacy's bed.

"A little. I just don't know what to wear. I don't want to look overdressed for the rehearsal, but I don't want to look too casual for my date with Max."

"What about a pair of jeans and a nice shirt? Maybe a blouse, kind of lacy or something," suggested Maddy.

"Well, I was thinking a little dressier, just not too much. Maybe a dress, kind of a casual one?" Stacy pulled a long white linen dress from the closet.

"Okay, a dress is good, but not that one." Maddy shook her head. "He might think you're trying to go bridal on him. Not to be nosy or anything, but do you really like him?"

Stacy sighed and sat next to Maddy. "It's a little strange. I really do think he's a nice guy. He's a Christian, he seems honest and sincere, and of course he's good looking. To be honest, he seems to be the type I could picture being married to and having kids with and spending the rest of our lives together. But I don't know if I'm his type. Besides, we only had the one date. Hardly enough time to get to know one another. I do know that I pray for my future husband every day, and I ask God to protect him and lead him to me. . . ."

She paused, her eyes excited. "He could be the one, but I'll just keep praying for right now. I get the feeling he is the marrying type. Why waste time with someone who's not?" She laughed as she put the dress back in the closet and began searching again. "Maybe he just wants to be good friends with me so I can coordinate his wedding and give him a discount."

"I. . .don't know." Maddy shrugged.

"It would be different if I wasn't a wedding coordinator," she shrugged. "If I were a lawyer or a doctor, he would just date me because he was interested in me."

"Or he might go out with you to get free legal advice or a discount on surgery." Maddy playfully rolled her eyes. "Honestly, Stacy, you spend too much time worrying about 'what ifs,' and then you chicken out on even developing a relationship."

"I don't chicken out."

"Yes, you do. You never stick around in a relationship to find out why the guy likes you. You second guess him, and then you back out and blame it on work or school or time or. . .or something. It never fails."

Exasperated, Stacy ignored Maddy and went to the bathroom to brush her teeth. Maddy followed her and began naming guys Stacy had previously dated. "Why is it that you can't let a guy like you for who you are? Remember Robert? You broke up with him because you thought he only liked you because you were good at English and he needed a tutor."

"That was high school," Stacy said around a mouthful of toothpaste.

"Well, then, moving on to the college years. You broke up with Greg because you thought the reason he really liked you was because you were a good cook. Andre asked you to marry him, but you had a year of school left and you didn't think he wanted you to be a wedding coordinator but he wanted you to help him start his computer business."

"Can you blame me for wanting to finish college?" asked Stacy, focusing on applying mascara.

"No, but what about Martin? Weren't you worried that he only pretended to like you because he asked for advice about starting his own business?"

"Yes." Stacy stared at Maddy. "You're my own sister, and you're siding against me?"

"No, I'm just asking why you didn't ever confront any of these guys? You never bothered to tell them how you felt. You just assumed you knew where they were coming from and then you fled the relationship. Why don't you at least give Max a chance? Not every guy has a hidden agenda or wants something from you. Maybe God sent him to you, not necessarily to be your husband, but maybe just to be a good friend to you. Maybe he needs a good friend. Maybe you both need to help each other learn how to be good friends."

Stacy sighed wistfully. "I guess you're right. I'll just relax a little and try not to be suspicious. I'll keep praying about it." She smiled and continued. "I know it's strange, but whenever I imagine Max's dating someone else, I get a knot in my stomach. It's like I'm jealous of someone, but I don't even know her. . .and I don't know why."

"Just keep on praying," Maddy singsonged as she walked down the hallway to her room. "Now get dressed because we have to leave in ten minutes."

A few minutes later, Stacy joined Maddy in the car. She was wearing a cap-sleeved, scoop-necked, flowing violet linen dress that reached to her ankles.

"Wow, that dress is awesome. It's perfect. . .very, very feminine, but not too dressy. He'll love it," said Maddy.

"I hope so," said Stacy.

$\sim$

Max was standing outside the church when they arrived. "I got here early but you weren't here. I felt a little funny about sitting in there with people I didn't know."

He held the door open for the sisters as they entered the church.

Throughout the rehearsal, Stacy tried her best to focus on her job. She walked through the whole ceremony with the soon-to-be husband and wife, along with those who would be a part of the ceremony. Max watched intently the entire time, his gaze so steady that Stacy began to feel self-conscious. This old church building had been restored to its original condition and was now a museum, but people often rented it for weddings and social gatherings. The large cathedral felt hollow unless there were many people inside of it. Still, even when it was full, a slight echo could be heard when people spoke. She could picture herself getting married in the building someday, but not anytime soon at the rate her life was going.

Catching a glimpse of Max from the corner of her eye, she reflected for a moment on what it would be like to be his wife. At that moment, Max felt her eyes on him and smiled, almost as if he could tell what she had been thinking. Stacy's face grew warm and she turned away, embarrassed. She spent the rest of the time focused completely on her job, allowing herself no more time for daydreaming.

After it was over, Stacy gave last-minute instructions to the members of the wedding party, then happily settled into Max's car, excited to be going out with him again.

"I thought we could go to the Cheesecake Factory," said Max as they were driving away from the church. "Is that okay with you?"

"Sounds like fun," said Stacy.

The drive to the Cheesecake Factory was short, and the conversation was focused on the rehearsal they'd just left.

After they were seated, Max said, "I never really thought about how much work you put into weddings. I mean, now that I think about it, you must work every weekend, don't you?"

"Pretty much," said Stacy. "But I don't really mind it."

"So why'd you decide to get into the wedding business?" Max wanted to know.

"Well. . .I guess I've always loved helping plan parties and things like that. Back when I was in high school, other people would ask me to be in charge of planning their parties for them on a regular basis. And I've always loved weddings—they're some of the most exciting parties you ever go to." She shrugged her shoulders. "I guess that sounds pretty silly to you."

"No, it doesn't sound silly at all. I just wonder if you ever feel—" The waitress had come with their cheesecake, and the interruption halted the conversation. "Looks delicious," said Max, while Stacy nodded in agreement.

A few minutes later, Stacy said, "What was it you wanted to ask me back when the food came?"

"Oh." Max looked at Stacy. "I was just wondering, since you have to be at the rehearsal and all, I guess you can only do one wedding every week?"

"Actually, we used to only be able to handle one, but since we've hired Ben and Julia, we can do at least two. A couple of times, we've done three. Some weeks we only have one, like last Saturday. But two is pretty much our comfortable number."

"Anything ever go majorly wrong?"

Stacy laughed. "Yes. In fact, last week the baker fell on the cake. It was like something in a movie." She stopped smiling. "Only it was not funny at the time." She explained to him the circumstances surrounding the loss of her keys and telling the Abramses about the cake.

"Do you ever feel funny always being at someone else's wedding and never your own?" asked Max.

Surprised at the frankness of his questions, Stacy was speechless. She struggled to come up with an answer. "Well, I–I, uh. . ."

Uh–oh, why'd I say it like that? Max asked himself. "I'm sorry. I know that sounded terrible. It didn't come out the way I meant it to. Just forget I asked it. I'm really sorry," Max said, reaching across the table to softly rest his hand on Stacy's.

At the touch of his hand, something in her heart melted, sending rays of warmth throughout her body. "No, I'm not offended. It's just no one's ever really asked me that question before." She paused. "I do love planning weddings and I enjoy seeing the happiness of the bride and groom, but it does kind of. . .tug at my heart, the more weddings I do. I find myself wondering more and more, 'When will it be my turn?' I have everything I need to put together my own wedding," she laughed. "All I'm missing is the groom."

They both laughed, then fell into nervous silence momentarily. The waitress came and refilled the coffee cups, and Stacy struck up a conversation on the subject of favorites to get things going again. This topic of favorite books, movies, sports, etc., began a lively conversation that lasted for almost two hours, during which time the two of them discovered they had much in common, ranging from golfing to snacking on graham crackers. They slowly savored their cheesecake and numerous coffee refills.

As the crowd inside the restaurant began to dwindle, the ebb of the noise reminded Stacy of the rest she was looking forward to at home, after a long day at work. She stifled a small yawn.

"Am I that boring?" Max asked, his eyebrows wrinkling in mock concern.

She laughed. "No, it's nothing like that at all. I've just put in a really long day. My Friday nights aren't normally this long. My Saturdays are much more tiring, and so I usually rest up for Saturday on Friday night."

Max stood and held out his hand for Stacy to hold. "Then I guess I should stop talking and get you home. But only if you agree to go out with me again. . .soon."

Stacy smiled as she stood and took his hand. "I think I can manage to fit you in," she laughed.

"Then it's a deal," said Max.

On the way to Stacy's home, the conversation flowed much more easily than it had on the way to the restaurant. Stacy found herself relaxing in Max's company and was glad she'd accepted his invitation to go out again.

When they reached her home, Max walked her to the door and held her hand. "What are you doing tomorrow night?" he asked.

"Working," she said.

"That's right, I forgot," said Max. "How about Monday? If you're free, I have tickets to the State Ballet performance."

"I haven't seen a ballet in ages," said Stacy. "In fact, I haven't really thought about ballet since I stopped taking lessons in the eighth grade. But yes, I'd love to go. It sounds like fun."

"Then I'll pick you up Monday around six."

"See you then," she said, as she opened the door.

Max waited until she was inside before turning to leave. Once she was inside, Stacy watched at the front door until Max got in his car and drove away.

Chapter 5

After getting home that evening, Max spent some time praying about Stacy. He felt relieved that she'd agreed to go out with him again. The next morning he got up early to mow the lawn. After that, he checked his answering machine, hoping in the back of his mind that Stacy might have called. However, there was only a message from his buddy Frank, inviting him to go out to dinner with some of the other guys from church.

Max hesitated, but then he remembered that he couldn't see Stacy because she was working all day. He didn't exactly want to sit at home all night, so he told Frank he would meet them at the restaurant at seven. He looked at his watch and saw that it was only twelve-thirty. He was glad he had something to do tonight, otherwise he would be too fidgety at home. He took a shower, then decided to check the new posts on the discussion group, since he hadn't checked since his encounter with Ms. Drew Monday night. *She probably thinks she ran me off,* he thought, shaking his head.

Sure enough, there was a message to Sherlock from Ms. Drew, written Tuesday morning:

> **Ms. Drew:** *Well, Sherlock, I see you're acknowledging the fact that Edger's sister's name is Debbie. But you didn't have to be such a crybaby about it. So you overlooked something. I don't think you're required to know everything about the book. It is a MYSTERY, you know. And sometimes other people might happen to pick up on something that you've overlooked. Big deal, it's not the end of the world—although one might think so judging from the reply you wrote me. That's all I have to say for now, but I hope you'll read this and take it into consideration in your future posts.*

"Take it into consideration? Who does she think she is?" Max asked himself as he began typing a response. *Why did she pick me to be her enemy? Well, if that's the way she's going to act, that's the way it's going to be. It's too bad she's not more like Stacy—quiet and sweet. There's no way I could ever spend more than twenty minutes with a woman like Ms. Drew,* he thought.

❧

The next week passed quickly, and on Saturday, at the wedding, Stacy's co-workers kept teasing her about her unusual cheeriness.

"I think it has something to do with the ballet on Monday and the movies last night," said Courtney.

"And, of course, a certain man whose name begins with the letter M," added Julia.

"I think he would be the same man who calls almost every day, just to see how Stacy is doing." Maddy smiled.

Stacy laughed and tried not to look flustered. She really did enjoy spending time with Max, and she found herself hoping it was Max whenever the phone rang.

Late that night, Stacy and Maddy arrived home from the wedding. Maddy was still getting used to the overwhelming job of a wedding coordinator. The work was more demanding than she had expected it to be, and she was drained. She changed into her pajamas and began watching a movie but promptly fell asleep. Stacy took a shower and sat at the computer, hoping to get in a little book discussion time before she went to bed.

It appeared that Sherlock had finally answered her post, and he seemed to be pretty upset. But she didn't care. "There's no way some person I've never even met is going to keep me from voicing my opinion," she said. "It's a free country." She browsed some of the other posts. Everyone seemed to be responding to a post by Leslie.

> **Leslie:** While my kids were napping today (rarely do they ever take a nap at the same time, but they did today), I got a chance to read the chapters for the next round of discussion. Now I know we're officially supposed to start the discussion on Sunday, but since I don't know when I'll get a chance to post again, I'll go ahead and give my two cents' worth. If you haven't read the chapters yet, read no farther; there are major spoilers in this post. . . .

Leslie's post went on to detail some key parts of the next chapter, and the replies were abundant.

> **George:** I don't know, Leslie. I haven't read the chapter yet, so I'm a little confused. Could somebody explain this whole "Nutrilack" thing to me a little more clearly?

> **Flyer 87:** Hi George! As you know, the book takes place in the year 2087, and it seems that for the past three years, some type of virus attacked the soil on earth and has been altering plant life. It mutates the cells so that seeds are producing less food over a period of time. For example, if an apple tree normally grows 100 apples every year, next year the crop would decrease by 20% and would keep decreasing until the tree wouldn't produce any apples at all. (I know my numbers aren't exactly accurate, but I was just trying to come up with an illustration.)

> **Booknut:** To add to Flyer 87's post, scientists have determined that it

would be impossible to kill the virus, but instead, they decided to let it run its course. It will take five years for the virus to die off, and after that, they've estimated that the world food supply would be depleted in 7 or 8 months. Then there would be a two-year period of worldwide famine or absolute "Nutrilack."

Lizzy: Well I think the answer is simple. Each country's government should start holding back some food every year, then they can ration it during the famine.

Sherlock: But Lizzy, you're forgetting that crops are getting smaller each year. By the time the virus is starting to die, the crops produced that year will barely be enough to feed everyone.

Leslie: What about a synthetic soil?

Sherlock: That's a lot of synthetic soil—I'm guessing the scientists didn't have enough time to take action with a plan of that magnitude or expense. Plus, virtually every seed on earth has been infected with the virus. I'm not sure they would produce well even in a synthetic soil.

The Butler: Hello, everyone! I got back a little early. I think I'm following everything so far, but doesn't it seem like we're getting off the subject? Isn't this story about finding Jill Austin, the missing cousin?

Grandma: I don't think so. Jill was a nutritionist, and Debra said she was working on a project that seemed to be really stressful. On page 37, Debra said to Kent, "Sometimes she acted like the world depended on the outcome of her research." I'll bet Jill was working on some type of antidote for the soil.

Sherlock: You've got a point there, Grandma. Plus, it looks like the world leaders are having a little trouble negotiating the rationing of food for those 7 or 8 months. If Jill was working for the U.S. government, some other country could have sent someone to kidnap her, out of fear that the U.S. was on the verge of a solution to the problem.

Leslie: Why would they do that? I'm sure other countries are working on the problem. Wouldn't the first country to find the solution tell the other nations?

The Butler: If the solution got passed around, it wouldn't be without a hefty price tag. . . .

Lizzy: C'mon, we're talking about worldwide famine, here. I think it would be most humane to work together and share the solution free of cost.

Booknut: Maybe it would be humane in real life, but in these books, Kent Lennox is always fighting against some greedy person. This kidnapping has something to do with the money that Jill's solution would make.

The Butler: Got to head out for now. I've got to say hello to my friends in the baseball chat room. I'll be back later.

Booknut: Not to get off the subject or anything, but it's kind of eerie, isn't it? I mean, all of the people have just learned about the whole Nutrilack thing and people are really starting to get scared.

Leslie: Yeah, I know what you mean—the "no hoarding" policy at the stores, restaurants closing all over the place, and remember when the president came on TV and asked everyone to cut down on snacks? It is pretty strange.

Sherlock: I've got somewhere to go tonight, but this discussion is really starting to pick up. Anybody in favor of reading two more chapters and discussing them Monday?

Grandma: That sounds like a good idea (especially since I've already read the next 6 chapters). It would also be fun if we could all be on-line at the same time Monday night. Believe me, the way the story starts moving, we'll need to be able to post at the same time!

George: Sounds like a great idea, but I can't Monday night. My fiancée and I are going to her aunt's birthday party. If I cancel, I'm in big trouble. But Wednesday is good for me.

Flyer 87: Tuesday and Friday are good for me. I'm flying the rest of the week.

Lizzy: I'm fine with Monday or Tuesday. But I think we should see what times are good for The Butler and Ms. Drew before we decide.

Sherlock: I've got church Wednesday, and Friday is definitely out.

Church?! He goes to church? With an attitude like that! Then her conscience pricked her. *Uh–oh! That wasn't too nice! I'm just as bad as he is.* Stacy prayed and repented for judging him so quickly. *I don't have any right to judge him. Maybe he was just having a bad day. But I still don't think I can get along with him. He's certainly nothing like Max. Max would never be so rude to someone over a book discussion.* While she was thinking about Max, she said a quick prayer for him, then went on to read the next post.

George: Tuesday's best for me.

After that there were no more messages, and Stacy had already read the chapters they were currently discussing, so she decided to post a response. *And be nice,* she told herself.

Ms. Drew: Hi guys! Sorry I haven't posted in a while. My weekends are usually pretty busy. Anyway, I think that Jill is working on a solution for this Nutrilack. But I don't think she's working on something to fix the soil. If everyone has accepted the fact that the soil won't grow anything for two years, Jill might be trying to come up with something that everyone can eat to survive those two years. Remember, she's a nutritionist, not a biologist.

Stacy posted her message, then went to find her calendar to find out what day would be good for her to discuss the next couple of chapters. When she came back, there were two responses to her post.

> **Leslie:** *Nancy (do you mind if I call you Nancy?), I think you've hit the nail on the head! If Jill is working for the government, she would be working on something concerning nutrition or food to save everyone.*
>
> **Grandma:** *I like Nancy better too. It's less formal than Ms. Drew. I can tell you, you're on the right track, Nance!*

Stacy laughed. "Nancy it is then," she said as she began typing her response. The three of them traded ideas for the next hour and a half, and when they were done, Stacy read the next couple of chapters for the big discussion that would occur later in the week. She'd put in her vote for Tuesday or Thursday, and she'd made it clear that she was absolutely unavailable Friday evening. In the back of her mind, she was leaving the time slot after Friday's rehearsal open in case Max wanted to do something. She would have to check back Monday to see how everyone else had voted.

Stacy went into the living room to find Maddy watching television and eating graham crackers and whipped cream.

"I thought I would have to come and unplug that thing," Maddy joked as Stacy sat down on the couch with her.

"Very funny," said Stacy, nibbling on a cracker. "I wasn't on-line that long."

"Long enough. Too long for someone who refused to even consider the discussion group at first," said Maddy, laughing.

❧

Sunday morning, Max attended church with Stacy and then went to lunch with her and Maddy at their parents' home. Stacy's parents were impressed with Max and made him feel welcome immediately. As they left the house, Stacy's mom took her aside and whispered, "He's a keeper!"

Stacy nodded and answered, "I know."

"Come back and visit us soon," said her father as he shook Max's hand.

❧

Late Thursday night, Max shook his head as he turned off his computer. Tonight's book discussion had been an absolute circus. Ms. Drew had spent much of the discussion trying to make him look silly. The only way he could defend himself was to do the same thing to her. Max fell into his bed, exhausted. Trying to look at the bright side of things, he thought, *At least I have a date with Stacy tomorrow night.* She could teach Ms. Drew a thing or two about making friends.

That Friday, Max took Stacy and Maddy to Shakespeare in the Park after they got off from work. The park was full of spectators mingling with the actors and performers clad in Shakespearean costume. There were jugglers, sword fighters, and dancers, along with food vendors who claimed to sell food that was similar to what those who went to the theater in Shakespeare's day might have eaten.

After the play was over, Max went to their house and sat and talked with Stacy for awhile. Although they had spent several hours on the phone getting to know each other better, it seemed that they never ran out of things to discuss.

The two were discussing their love of kids and happily sharing how many children they wanted to have someday, when Maddy came in.

"It's really a lovely coincidence that you both want to have four kids, but it's almost one in the morning. Stacy, you know we have to get up early for that wedding in the morning," said Maddy.

"Oh. . .is it that late?" said Max, glancing at his watch.

"I didn't even notice," said Stacy. "Before I forget to ask, my parents are having a barbecue tomorrow evening. Would you be free to go?"

Max thought for a moment. "I don't think I have anything planned. . . . Sure, that'll be fun. What time should I pick you up?"

"Why don't you just meet me there around eight? Maddy and I will come straight from work."

"Sounds like a plan." Max stood up. "I'd better be going. But before I leave, what are you doing Tuesday?"

"Tuesday?" asked Stacy.

"Yes. In the late afternoon, maybe around three or four?"

"It depends on what you have in mind," said Stacy, playfully.

"I was thinking we could play a friendly round of golf, which I would win, of course."

"Of course," said Stacy, in mock seriousness. "I'd love to play golf, but the winner won't be decided until it's over." She smiled.

"All right, then, I'll call you and let you know what time it'll be for sure," he said before turning to leave.

Chapter 6

"**M**ax! It's good to see you this morning. We missed you at the singles' picnic Friday. You were supposed to bring a salad, remember?" said Vivianne Hughes as the congregation milled around before the service Sunday morning.

Max slapped his hand to his forehead. *So that's what I forgot about!* The night before at Stacy's parents, he'd had the feeling that he was supposed to be somewhere else. "I'm sorry about that, Vivianne. I know you put a lot of work into planning that. I must've forgotten to put it on my calendar and then I made other plans."

Vivianne laughed as she lightly squeezed Max's arm. "I'm not upset, Max. But I was worried. We thought something might have happened to you."

"No, nothing happened. I just had another. . .thing come up." He didn't exactly want to say anything about Stacy right now. For one thing, he wasn't sure if he should, considering they weren't really a couple yet. Second, Vivianne had, as of late, convinced herself and many of the other members of the church that she and Max were meant for each other. Although some women still seemed to be interested in him, Vivianne was viewed as the favorite for the position of Max's wife. She glued herself to him at every church function, and Max, not wanting to be rude, had probably let it go too far. He held doors for her, gave her rides when she needed one, and had been on a couple of dates with her. He sometimes even called her by her nickname, Viv. He knew she had a temper, and if things worked out with Stacy, she and several members of the church would be upset, and it would partially be his fault.

After all, he reasoned, *I haven't done the greatest job of actively discouraging her.* Vivianne was a little intimidating. She was extremely attractive. Tall and slender, but curvy, she dressed immaculately and her beauty caught the attention of many single men in the church. She always seemed to know what to say and had a gift for organizing things and events and getting a job done well and fast. She would make a good wife, but. . .she just wasn't Stacy. *But until I know more from Stacy, there's no need to upset everyone here.*

Even the pastor would be disappointed. He and his wife had befriended Max when he'd first come to the church and had treated him like a son. Last fall, when Viv had moved to the city and joined the church, they took her under their wing also. Max had gone along with the dinner parties and assorted get-togethers they hosted to introduce Viv to other singles, but after awhile it became clear that they thought he and Viv would be a good couple. He hadn't totally pulled away simply because he didn't want to lose the respect of the people who had been so kind to him.

Max made his way to a seat where he and Viv could sit, since she had her arm looped through his and didn't appear to have any intention of letting go.

Pastor Winslow preached from Proverbs 31, while casting knowing glances toward Max and Viv. Max tried his best to keep from squirming excessively. Soon, he knew, he needed to either make a move toward Viv or put more distance between them. The latter would be hard.

Once again, Vivianne had left her Bible in the room where she taught Sunday school, and Max, being courteous, offered to share his with her. He tried to concentrate on the message, but he was having a hard time concentrating on anything other than the scent of Vivianne's hair right beneath his nose. Her hair hung a few inches past her shoulders and was always perfectly curled. Whenever she moved, her hair smelled like a fresh, cool breeze. He also knew that her hair was soft, from the many times it had accidentally brushed his arm or his cheek on the occasions when she had impulsively hugged him.

"She seeketh wool, and flax, and worketh willingly with her hands," read Pastor William Winslow.

Viv looked up at Max and smiled. If something needed to be found, there was no question Vivianne could find it, he thought. She would leave no stone unturned—and she was good at hands-on, craft-type things. The church was buzzing about how she had already made the angel costumes for the Christmas pageant, and it was only June. But Stacy worked with her hands too. It took a lot of expertise to organize weddings, especially the one he'd attended for the Abramses' daughter.

"She girdeth her loins with strength and strengtheneth her arms."

Neither Viv nor Stacy seemed to be incredibly weak. They were both capable women. . . .

"She is not afraid of the snow for her household."

Max had never seen Viv appear to be afraid of anything. Stacy, on the other hand, didn't seem like she was fearful, just careful. But he didn't mind. It just made him feel like he should protect her, and he liked that.

"She maketh herself coverings of tapestry; her clothing is silk and purple."

He didn't know if either of them made their clothes. When he'd first seen Stacy, she had been wearing a pale violet suit, and Friday night she'd worn the same shade. Viv's favorite color was red, but she wore a lot of brightly colored clothing, sometimes purple. Today she was wearing a yellow suit.

"She looketh well to the ways of her household and eateth not the bread of idleness. Her children arise up and call her blessed; her husband also, and he praiseth her."

Max shook his head. Why was he even thinking about marriage, anyway? Why did Stacy's image keep popping into his mind? For all he knew, Viv could be the one he should marry and he hadn't really given her a chance.

"Give her of the fruit of her hands; and let her own works praise her in the gates."

Max had now had some time to think through his relationship with Stacy. He really knew very little about her. In fact, he knew more about Viv than Stacy. But he knew he wanted to get to know Stacy better, and he planned to be honest with her about that.

After the service was over, he accepted the Reverend and Mrs. Winslow's invitation to dinner that afternoon. He was even looking forward to some of Vivianne's peach cobbler that she told him she'd baked for the occasion.

❧

Monday morning, Max called Stacy at work to set the time for their golfing date. They agreed to meet at Swope Park Golf Course at 3:00 P.M. Tuesday.

Stacy hadn't played in several weeks due to her busy schedule, so Max, who usually managed to play at least once a week, won, shooting a 79 compared to Stacy's 81.

Afterward, Max suggested they stop at a nearby bagel shop for a bite to eat. Since it wasn't quite dinnertime yet, Stacy ordered a chocolate chip bagel with chocolate cream cheese, and Max had a double chocolate muffin. After a few minutes of small talk, Max put the last bite of his muffin in his mouth and cleared his throat.

Stacy could sense the mood had changed somewhat. Although it was not a bad change, she felt a little uneasy and tried to fight the urge to make a joke and change the subject before Max could start talking. Sensing that he needed to say whatever it was, she kept her mouth shut and waited intently for him to begin.

Max began in a rush. "I feel like I need to tell you something—or ask you."

Stacy nodded in response and waited quietly for him to continue, but her heart was pounding so fiercely, she felt it might jump out of her chest any second and go flying across the room. She took a deep breath and thought, *Why is he being so serious? What on earth is he about to say. . .and why am I so nervous?*

He cleared his throat. "I really like you, Stacy. That's why I didn't give up trying to meet you even when you ignored me at the wedding. I've never really dated much, and I. . .I know we haven't known each other for a long time. But I want to get to know you better. I would like for us to really spend time together. . .learn what we have in common, and your likes and dislikes. I want to find out what's important to you and share our views of life in general. I know it sounds silly, but I've never met anyone like you. And I want you to know that I feel this way." He paused and looked her in the eye. "Am I scaring you, or do you agree with me even a little bit?"

For some reason, Stacy felt a sense of relief at his statement. As she opened her mouth to reply, she realized she had been holding her breath. What had she been afraid of anyway?

"I agree that relationships should not be taken lightly." She swallowed. "As for everything else, I feel very flattered that you had such respect for me to be so honest. I really do want to get to know you better, but before we do, I'd like to have a little time to pray about it, if that's okay with you. I just feel a little unsure of what to say right now. My emotions are doing all of the talking, and my brain will probably spend the next several hours trying to process everything. . . . I just don't want to say yes because it feels so romantic. I want to say yes because God told me to."

Max exhaled, feeling relieved. At least she hadn't jumped up and run away. If she wanted to pray about it, that was fine. "Well, you responded better than I thought you would. I was so nervous that I could barely think all day. Why don't we both take a few days and pray? I'll get back in touch with you in a few days. Maybe we could meet this Friday."

"That sounds like a good plan," said Stacy. "Why don't we plan for Friday after I get done with my rehearsal? I'll give you my cell phone number so I can let you know about what time I'll be done."

"That's fine with me. Why don't we go back to the Cheesecake Factory, since they stay open pretty late?"

"Sounds good," said Stacy. Then she stood. "But I really need to get moving. I've got some last-minute stuff to do for this week's wedding and I've had a headache all day long. I should get home and get some rest before tomorrow. Things always pick up on Wednesdays and Thursdays at my job."

He stood and walked with her to her car. "I'll see you Friday," he said.

"Okay," said Stacy as she began searching her purse for her keys. She felt a familiar sinking feeling in her heart that turned to panic when she couldn't find them.

"What's wrong?" Max asked.

"I can't find my keys," said Stacy.

"They're not in the car," Max said, glancing through the window.

As Stacy searched her purse again, Max looked on the ground in case she'd dropped her keys. Their search was interrupted by the voice of a girl coming out of the café.

"Excuse me, Miss, did you lose these keys?" asked the girl. "They were sitting at your table when you left, and I figured you wouldn't get far without them."

"Thank you so much," said Stacy, reaching for the keys.

After the girl went back inside, Max jokingly asked, "Do you do this often. . . lose your keys?"

"I hate to admit it, but it happens quite a lot. I need to come up with a plan to stop losing them before it really gets me in a jam."

"Maybe you should keep me around. You always seem to get your keys when I'm around," Max pointed out.

"I'll keep that in mind," said Stacy as she got in her car.
"Be careful," said Max before she drove away.

≈

The Butler: What do you all make of this turn of events?

Grandma: Took you long enough to read this far! But Nancy Drew did a good job of guessing—at least part of it!

Sherlock: I think you're giving too much credit where not that much is due. So Ms. Drew figured out that Debra is Edger's sister. Is anyone wondering why Debra volunteered this information to Kent in only the sixth chapter? This woman also claims that her brother (Edger) is dead, but she is living on the money he left her in his will.

Ms. Drew: Sherlock, I think you're a little paranoid. Debra is Edger's sister. Let's try to get past that point. I think the main issue of the last few chapters is where Jill might be. After Kent and Debra searched Jill's house and found those notes, I have to agree with something Grandma and Sherlock said a few days ago. If my memory serves me correctly, the notes they found in Jill's cabinet had a lot to do with vitamins. Also, the cages of mice in her office— Kent and Debra were surprised the mice were still alive and even didn't seem to be lethargic even though Jill has been missing for over two weeks.

Lizzy: Yeah, I wondered about that. But I think Debra is working for the people who kidnapped Jill or someone who wants to kidnap her from the kidnappers.

Booknut: She would do this to her own cousin?

Sherlock: I wondered about that too, George. But I checked back a few chapters, and there was really nothing Debra said that PROVED Jill is her cousin. I could TELL you that Grandma and I are cousins, but my just telling you doesn't really prove it.

Leslie: But if she's not really Jill's cousin, how would she know where to find Jill's secret house key?

Booknut: If Jill's research is this valuable, then Debra could very well be working for some kidnappers. Remember when Kent talked to Jill's co-workers? They said she was extremely smart and an excellent researcher, but she was also clumsy and forgetful. Someone planning to kidnap her would watch her for a while to get a feel for her routine. Maybe one day, she lost her keys and had to use her spare to get in the house and, bingo! The kidnappers know where her spare key is.

Flyer 87: Which would explain why, although her house was ransacked, no doors and windows seemed to be damaged. The kidnappers just let themselves in.

Ms. Drew: But why would the kidnappers enlist the services of Kent Lennox if they've already got Jill?

Sherlock: *Maybe she won't talk, and they want Kent to figure out what she was up to—he might be able to find a piece of information that she's hidden. . .or lost. Maybe this is a second set of kidnappers, like Lizzy said. The other kidnappers beat them to the punch, and they want to kidnap her from the other criminals.*

Ms. Drew: *Or maybe Jill suspected she was about to be kidnapped, and she went into hiding. Maybe those mice aren't dead because she's been sneaking back to feed them.*

Sherlock: *I don't care how clumsy or forgetful you are, no one would do something that risky. If she thought she was in danger, she would also realize her house was being watched. She would have either taken the mice with her or left them for good. No way would she risk her life to feed some mice every day.*

Ms. Drew: *Well, she doesn't seem like the type of person to be deliberately cruel to animals.*

Sherlock: *Isn't that just like a woman? Ms. Drew, why is it that you can't even read a fictional mystery without getting all weepy-eyed over a furry little animal? Pathetic!*

Ms. Drew: *You didn't have to get all hot under the collar. So what if I care about the welfare of the mice, while you're just a cold, unfeeling person? I have tried to be civil to you, and now I've had enough! No more will I try to spare your feelings. I will post my ideas whether you like them or not. Get ready to have your precious little toes stepped on!*

Sherlock: *Go right ahead, Ms. Drew, since you think you're so smart. But when we all get to the last page, you will see that I am right, and I will not let you forget it, either. You can't be a good detective if you let your emotions get in the way of logic!*

Ms. Drew: *I think that by the end of this book, you will realize that my intuition will have helped me solve the mystery far better than your "logic" ever could.*

George: *Sorry to interrupt such a heated argument, but getting back to the subject. . . If Jill was working on something to feed everyone during Nutrilack and the mice are her subjects, they might be alive because she's succeeded. Remember all of the tubes outside of the cages? Maybe that was the formula she was working on.*

Lizzy: *The only thing in those tubes were liquid vitamins. It said so right on the tubes. And I don't think liquid vitamins would sustain the whole world for two years.*

Flyer 87: *I agree with you, Lizzy. But maybe she was working on a supplement that was vitamin based. . .like a super vitamin or something.*

The Butler: *Sorry to throw a wrench in things, but what about that theory about Jill working for the U.S. government? If she needed to hide, she* might be under government protection. And here's an even bigger question: Regardless of whether someone took Jill or if she went into hiding, if her secret formula is in those tubes, why would she or the kidnappers leave the tubes? Anyone could walk in, steal a tube, and have the formula analyzed. Anybody got anything to offer here?

Ms. Drew: You've got a point, Butler. But my "emotions" tell me that that's not the whole formula in those tubes. If it was the formula, I don't think she'd list the ingredients right on the tubes. I've got a feeling that those mice have not been neglected since Jill has been missing.

Sherlock: It's unfortunate that we disagree again, Ms. Drew, but "logic" tells me that the mice have not been fed since Jill's been missing and the formula IS what's in those tubes.

Booknut: Does anyone here know how long a mouse can live without eating?

Grandma: I'm not exactly sure how long a mouse can go without eating, but you two sure add an interesting element to the discussion group. The tension is so thick you can cut through it with a knife. . . .

Chapter 7

I understand how you feel, Mrs. Harris. I can't stop you from hiring your nephew's fiancée as the florist for the wedding, but I can't guarantee her work, simply because I normally use a different florist."

Stacy tried to listen as Mrs. Harris continued her story. Meanwhile, she felt as though she might faint. Maddy had come down with a bug Tuesday night, and Stacy felt like she might have it now. She'd been suffering from chills all morning long, and her slight headache from Tuesday had evolved into a pounding headache. She hadn't eaten anything because if she had what Maddy had, she knew she wouldn't be able to keep anything down. On top of that, she was nervous about the evening's date with Max. She knew that she wanted to have a more serious relationship with him, but she was scared of being hurt again. The thought of a serious relationship sounded good, but her heart was telling her to slow down and get to know him as a friend first. But if she kept feeling like this, she'd have to cancel their date, and she wouldn't even get to see him tonight.

"Okay, Mrs. Harris," she said wearily, "I'll give her a call and see what type of an arrangement we can work out. . . . Okay. . .I'll call you Monday then." Stacy hung up the phone and laid her head on her desk.

"Is it okay if I take my lunch break now, Stacy?" said Julia as she entered the office. Looking at Stacy, she said, "Or I could stay here and you could go home. You don't look too good. Do you feel okay?"

Stacy sat up and tried to focus on Julia. "No, I don't. The room is spinning, and I'm seeing double—no, make that quadruple. I can see four of you. I think I need to go home and take some medicine, maybe take a nap. Is Ben coming in this afternoon?"

"No, he isn't." Julia launched into a lengthy explanation. "Remember how the rental service forgot the candelabras for Laura Fields's wedding? Well, this morning I called and asked them if they would deliver the candelabras to the hall for the rehearsal, but they said their delivery trucks would be gone all day, making deliveries on the other end of town. Since Ben doesn't live too far from there, I called and asked if he would mind picking them up. And after that he's going with Courtney to Rachael Dobb's rehearsal. . . . So you and I are the only ones in the office today."

Stacy rested her head on the desk again and sighed. She had a feeling that if she went home now, there was no way she'd be able to drag herself out of bed for the Fields-Porter rehearsal. But she couldn't send Julia by herself.

"Julia, what time does the Dobb rehearsal start?"

"I'm not sure what time it starts, but I remember Courtney telling me that she would be finished there by four-thirty or five at the latest."

"Good," said Stacy, sitting up carefully to ease the dizziness. "I need you to call her and see if she can cover my rehearsal tonight." Stacy closed her eyes and shivered as she waited for Julia to get off the phone.

"Okay," said Julia. "She said she can handle the rehearsal tonight, but if you're sick tomorrow she doesn't know what she can do. You and I were supposed to do the Fields-Porter wedding while she and Ben worked at the Dobb-Benson wedding. Do you think you'll feel better in the morning?" Julia sounded and looked worried.

Stacy stood slowly and reached in her purse to find her keys. "I hope so, but I can't count on it. Maddy had this for three days. I wonder if you and Ben could do the Dobb wedding while Courtney and Maddy do the Fields wedding? I'll call Courtney tonight and see if we can come up with a plan in case I'm sick tomorrow."

Stacy was glad when she made it home and was able to sink into her bed. Maddy, who was feeling pretty normal again, gave her medicine and tried to feed her, but all Stacy wanted to do was sleep. At five o'clock, she awoke suddenly. She had to call Max and explain that she couldn't make it tonight. First she tried his office, but no one answered, so she called him at home. As the phone rang, she cleared her throat and hoped she didn't sound as bad as she felt.

"Hello?" The sound of his clear, strong voice made Stacy's stomach flip-flop. *Or, it could be this bug.*

"Hi, Max, it's me, Stacy." She hurried to continue. "I'm not going to make it tonight." She paused to catch her breath.

"Is something wrong? Did I do something to upset you?" Max wanted to know.

"Oh, no, I think I caught the flu from my sister," Stacy said quickly as she explained the whole situation.

"Oh, no," said Max, sounding disappointed. "Is there anything I can do? Bring you some medicine or something? I could buy some soup. Actually, I'd make some, but I don't want to make you sicker," he joked.

"Thanks, but I'll be okay," giggled Stacy. "I'm trying this flu medicine my sister took. She says you feel better pretty quickly, but it's been making me really sleepy. I'm hoping I can just sleep this thing off."

"Okay," said Max gently. "I hope you feel better. I'll call back tomorrow and check on you."

"Thanks," said Stacy wearily.

"And when you're feeling up to it, we'll reschedule for tonight," said Max.

"Of course," said Stacy.

"I'll let you get some rest. In the meantime, take care," Max said before he hung up the phone.

As soon as she hung up, she quickly fell into a deep and restful sleep.

At 1:15 A.M., Stacy awoke to the sound of the ringing phone. "Hello?" she said groggily as she reached for the receiver.

"Stacy, it's me, Maddy. I know you don't feel good, but I need you to do me a huge favor."

"Right now?" asked Stacy, feeling confused. "What's going on?"

"After the rehearsal, I went to the movies with some of my friends and then we went to this all-night café. But now I'm stuck here, because Mom's car won't start. So could you come and get me?"

Stacy shook her head and groaned. Their mother's car was forever breaking down. Considering all of the times she had taken it to the shop, she probably could have bought two new cars, but she refused to get rid of the old thing. "Where are your friends?" asked Stacy.

"They left. I was the last one to get in my car, and my car always takes a long time to start."

Stacy sat up suddenly and held her aching head. Although she didn't feel spectacular, she didn't feel nearly as bad as she had earlier. The flu medicine she had taken seemed to be working, and her stomach growled from hunger instead of nausea. "Give me the address," she told Maddy. "I'll be there as soon as I can. Don't talk to anyone, and wait inside until I get there."

Stacy hurriedly pulled on a pair of jeans and a knit lavender tank top that was a little dressy, she admitted to herself, but the color seemed to help her feel a bit better. Along with that, she slid on her high-heeled sandals that she'd kicked off near the door and a pair of sunglasses to keep the glare of oncoming cars from making her headache worse. On the way to the diner, her hunger pangs intensified. She hadn't eaten anything all day, and now she had a craving for an ice cream sundae. By the time she made it to the diner, she'd decided to risk having some ice cream even if it made her sicker. At least she would feel better for the moment.

"Hopefully Maddy won't mind staying for a little while longer," she said as she got out of her car and walked through the front door of the brightly lit diner.

Inside, Maddy waved to Stacy from the table she and two men sat at in front of a big window. Once she reached the table, Stacy sat down, a questioning look on her face. Maddy introduced the men as Paul and Marcus, two friends she'd gone to high school with. "They offered to bring me home, but when I called you back, you'd already left. I feel so bad about making you come out when you're sick," said Maddy.

"Actually, I don't mind," said Stacy. "All of a sudden I want some ice cream. I think it might help me feel better. So if you don't mind, I'd like to order a sundae or something like that."

"I don't mind," said Maddy. "In fact, ice cream sounds pretty good to me. Why don't we all have some?"

Her two friends agreed, and they all ordered ice cream and sat around for the next hour eating ice cream and laughing and talking. Stacy still felt ill, even though eating did seem to ease her headache a little. After they were finished, Maddy's friends walked the sisters to their car to make sure the car started and then got in their car and followed them to the highway to make sure they got on safely.

⟋⟍

Early Saturday morning, Max sat with a newspaper and coffee, mulling over the events of the night before. When Stacy canceled their date, he'd gone to his church for the men's all-night basketball tournament that was held once every three months. He'd actually wanted to stay home, but Frank had urged him to come along. He missed Stacy, but he'd had a good time up until around 2:00 A.M.

He'd gone out to his car to bring in a new CD he wanted to play for some of the guys, and as he got in his car, a familiar car pulled around the corner and into the parking lot of the diner across the street. Something made him keep watching the car, and to his surprise Stacy stepped out of the car a few moments later, to walk inside and meet Maddy, along with two guys. They sat there for a long time, eating and talking. Max went back inside and almost an hour later, he peeked back outside to find the two guys walking to the car with Stacy and her sister. Then he watched the two cars pull out of the lot at the same time.

The memory still smarted. *Sick, my foot!* Max thought as he headed outside to wash his car. *If she had another date lined up, why didn't she say so instead of concocting some elaborate lie?* As he soaped the shiny exterior of the car, he wondered, *How on earth did I fall for that, anyway? The flu in the middle of July? She must think I'm really naive.* He guessed that he wouldn't be hearing from her anytime soon. And if she did have the nerve to call him, he'd find some excuse to brush her off. *The last thing I want is to be in a relationship with someone I can't trust.*

Chapter 8

A little over a week later, Stacy was just starting to feel like her old self again. Three days after she got sick, she couldn't seem to shake the bug. It seemed like she would feel fine for a few hours and then she would start feeling awful all over again, so she went to the doctor, who prescribed antibiotics and lots of rest. The doctor said her immune system was weakened due to stress, probably from work.

During her time off, she tried to call Max several times, both at home and at work, but she seemed to always get his answering machine or his secretary. For some reason, she sensed he was giving her the brush-off, but she didn't understand why. After a few days of trying unsuccessfully to reach him, she gave up. If he was still interested, he'd have to call her, because she didn't want to play games.

Stacy's mother, Berniece, came over daily and nursed Stacy while she was sick, and after she learned how Stacy couldn't seem to reach Max, she determined that if he didn't have time to return her call, he wasn't good enough for Stacy.

At any rate, Stacy was determined to put all thoughts of Max out of her head and start healing emotionally. Work was a good place to start; because she was so busy, she didn't have much time to think about Max. . .except whenever her thoughts strayed to daydreams of her own wedding day, which happened nearly every day. The Wilson-Becker wedding was fast approaching, and it was such a big job, both Stacy and Courtney had to attend, along with Julia, Ben, and Maddy.

Late one night, a couple of days before the wedding, Stacy sat down at the computer to see how the book discussion was going. She had spent quite a lot of time there over the past two weeks, since during the time she was sick, the only thing she could do besides read her Bible and watch TV was surf the Internet. She had gotten an E-mail account and exchanged E-mail addresses with Grandma and Leslie, and they wrote each other often. However, as the days passed, things between Ms. Drew and Sherlock grew more strained. They had a severe dislike for each other that revealed itself through their curt posts to one another.

Today was no exception. Sherlock had managed to prove her wrong on an assumption she'd made a couple of weeks ago. *What does this guy do, keep a record of everything I say, so in case I mess up, he can gloat?* she wondered. It was time to set him straight.

Ms. Drew: *Okay, Sherlock, you win. Jill hasn't been feeding the mice. But since you claim they were fed her Super Vitamin formula before* *she was kidnapped (or went into hiding), why are the mice dead now? And I would appreciate it if you didn't feel compelled to remind me of every mistake I make. If I did the same to you, I could fill pages and pages with your blunders. Let's try to remember that this is supposed to be a "friendly" discussion group. I'm not the type to ask people to leave— especially if they were here before me—but I really think it's coming down to me or you around here. A few days ago, I was sorry your girlfriend broke up with you, but now, I don't really care. Boo hoo! I considered letting your nasty mood slide, due to your emotional distress, but has it ever occurred to you that other people in this world have bad days, weeks, and even years? What makes your problems so big?*

After she posted the note, Stacy went on to read a few posts from the other members. A few minutes later, she saw that a new message had been posted. It was pretty late, and she was surprised to see someone else posting at this hour. Her excitement faded as she read the topic of the post: "Then by all means, Ms. Drew, GO AWAY!"

"Of course, it would have to be from Sherlock," she said, clicking to read the message.

> **Sherlock:** *You said it, not me. I was here first, and if you can't bear to be wrong every once in a while, then it would probably be best for you to leave. I am not in the mood to continue these immature, childish arguments with you. And as far as the woman is concerned, she wasn't my girlfriend, we were just dating. And I might add, I wrote that post specifically to The Butler for his advice, and although I didn't mind if anyone else read it, it was not your place to reply to a message that wasn't posted to you. Since your name is not The Butler, there was no need for you to comment. I wasn't talking to you, so mind your own business!*

Stacy leaned backed in her chair. *Well, I can see why that woman wouldn't have anything to do with him. Since he's awake, I might as well reply so he'll be sure to get the message.*

❦

That Saturday morning, Max awoke with a headache. Two hours later, headache still pounding away inside his head, he was in his car on his way to Viv's house. It was actually the last place he wanted to be, but in a moment of weakness he'd agreed when Viv had asked him to be her date at her friend Stella Wilson's wedding. He was still troubled about the way he'd let things dissolve between Stacy and him without really making himself sit down and try to talk things out with her. Being at a wedding would only make him think more about Stacy, making it even harder for him to forget her.

When Viv answered her door, Max inhaled and tried to slow his heart from beating too fast. She wore a royal blue dress with a fitted blazer of the same color. He didn't think he'd ever seen her in this outfit before. The blue perfectly accentuated her deep skin tone and made her look stunning. Her eyes seemed to sparkle more than usual, and when she looked at him from beneath her long eyelashes, Max promised himself again that he would give Viv a fair chance.

He wouldn't let his feelings toward Stacy dictate the way he viewed Viv. He was going to the wedding with Viv, and he would focus his attention on Viv. She was a human being, and he wouldn't hurt her by dating her and constantly thinking of Stacy.

❧

A few more hours and I'll be at home checking out the book discussion, soaking my feet, and enjoying a snack, thought Stacy as she looked over her to do list. She, Julia, Courtney, and Maddy had been at the reception site all morning, while Ben had been at the actual wedding ceremony.

"Stacy, the guests should start arriving any minute now. Are we ready?" Ben's voice came over the headphones they used to communicate with each other.

"Everything's okay. Where are you, by the way?" she replied.

"I'm right outside the front door. I just got here."

"Any idea when the wedding party will arrive?" was Courtney's question.

"I'd give 'em about five more minutes," said Ben. He was now in the main room of the reception area, and he made his way over to his boss. "I love these headphones. Whenever we wear them, I feel like I'm on a secret spy mission or something."

"You might love them, but not us women. They don't do anything flattering for the hair," said Courtney.

"No kidding," was Julia's reply. "I'm glad we only use these for big weddings—Oh! The bride and groom are here. I'm going to go in the foyer and get the receiving line started."

"Stace, can you come in the kitchen and give me a hand?" Courtney wanted to know. "The caterer and I are having a little difference of opinion about the correct serving temperature of the paté."

"I'm on my way. And Maddy, you stick with Ben and do whatever he asks you to do," said Stacy.

"Gotcha," was Maddy's enthusiastic reply.

A few minutes later, Julia spoke. "I'm out here with the receiving line. How are things in there?"

"Fine in here," said Ben.

"Stacy and I are setting things in order in the kitchen," Courtney reported.

Julia went on. "Don't you think today would be a beautiful day for a picnic?"

Ben answered again. "I think it gets really confusing to have business and personal conversations on this intercom system, so let's try to save all of the non-work-related conversation till the reception's over, okay?"

"I agree with you, Ben. It can be a little confusing, since all of us are on head-phones today," agreed Stacy.

For the next ten minutes there was silence on the headsets until suddenly Maddy gasped. "Uh-ohhhh. . .this is not good."

"What's not good, Maddy?" Ben sounded anxious. "Please don't tell me you dropped something or broke anything."

"No, it's not that kind of bad. . ."

"Then what is it, Maddy?" Stacy sounded slightly irritated. "Courtney and I are busy with the caterer, and we can't come out right now."

"It's not catastrophic or anything, but. . ."

"Maddy, will you just tell us?" begged Julia.

"Okay. Stacy, that rat is here!"

"Rat!?" exclaimed the other four in unison.

In a low tone, Ben said, "This place does not have rats. And don't talk so loud. The point is for us to quietly communicate with each other, so the guests don't hear what we're saying. It creates a more pleasant environment."

"Okay, okay. But he's here with another woman, Stacy," Maddy whispered.

"Who?"

"You know who. And I'm coming in the kitchen."

"Ohhh. Max is the rat," was Julia's quiet reply.

"Who in the world is Max?" Ben wanted to know.

"Now you need to lower your voice," said Julia. "Tsk, tsk. The guests can hear you. Let's try to create a pleasant environment, remember?"

Stacy stood in the kitchen, at a loss for words. Maddy burst in and hugged her.

"You can't let him get you upset. Just ignore him."

"I can't ignore him. I have to do my job."

Courtney spoke. "And I don't think you should try to hide from him. Don't let him have the satisfaction of throwing you off balance."

"She's right," said Maddy. "Go out there and be strong. Hold your head up, because you didn't do anything wrong."

Stacy took a deep breath and a step forward. She lifted her chin and said, "I won't let him get the better of me. I don't even know why I let myself trust him in the first place. If he wants to play games, fine. I will not suffer because he didn't have the decency to honestly let me know he didn't want to date again, instead of dodging my phone calls. As a matter of fact, I feel sorry for the woman that he's here with."

"Don't feel too sorry for the competition. She's gorgeous," said Maddy.

Suddenly at ease, Stacy laughed. "Well, thanks a lot, sister dear! Are you on my side or hers?"

"Yours, of course, but I wanted to give you a warning before you saw her."

"Thanks, but it's not necessary. It's over between Max and me, so she isn't competition."

Suddenly Ben's voice came over the headsets. "That was almost as moving as a Hallmark commercial, but could some of you people get out here? Three of you are in the kitchen, Julia's trying to figure out which one is Max, and I'm the only one getting any work done."

"Okay, okay," said Stacy. "Folks, let's get going. We've got a reception to coordinate."

❧

Max blinked when he saw Stacy. *Oh, nooo. This isn't fair, Lord. As soon as I decide to not think about Stacy, she shows up at this wedding.*

"Max?" Viv was shaking his arm. "I said, would you mind getting me some water, please?"

"Oh, sure." He headed to the refreshment table, but Stacy was standing there, talking to a man. Actually, she was laughing with this guy. It looked like they were sharing an inside joke. Max's headache, which had subsided during the wedding, came back with a vengeance. He turned abruptly and returned to Viv's side.

"Max, this is Karen Wilson, Stella's sister," she said, looping her arm through his.

"Nice to meet you," he said, glancing over his shoulder, trying to get a good look at the guy Stacy was laughing with. Now they weren't laughing but seemed to be looking at a sheet of paper, their heads close together. He must be Ben, the guy she works with. Max felt relieved for the moment. He tried to listen to the conversation Viv was having, but his mind kept wandering.

"Max, what in the world is wrong with you? Why do you keep looking over your shoulder? And where is my water?" Viv wanted to know.

He'd forgotten all about the water! "Umm, the water. They wouldn't give me any!" he joked.

Viv's eyes narrowed. "They wouldn't serve you any water? That's strange."

"Extremely strange, considering what she charges," said Karen. "I think I'll have to go and have a talk with Ms. Thompson. You would think she could at least offer water to our guests."

"No, no, don't do that!" said Max.

The two women stared at him.

"I was just joking. But are you really thirsty now? You know, I think I read somewhere that you shouldn't drink ice water before you eat a meal. It's bad for the metabolism." He hoped Viv would forget about the water, because the last thing he wanted to do was face Stacy right now.

"I can assure you, there is nothing wrong with my metabolism. Are you implying that my metabolism is messed up?" Viv demanded.

Max sighed. It was going to be a long reception. "No, that's not what I meant at all."

Stacy took a deep breath. Max and the woman were moving closer to where she stood. Abruptly she turned and spoke into her headset, "Courtney, I think we need to start the meal. Is the caterer ready?"

"Already getting started on that," said Courtney.

"I thought you weren't going to run away from him," Maddy's voice broke in.

"I'm not running. I'm making sure the guests are fed," said Stacy impatiently.

"Ladies, let's not start this conversation again," said Ben. "Remember, we're working. Talk about this later."

During the meal, Stacy and Courtney got the cake table ready for the cutting of the cake.

"He keeps looking at you," said Courtney.

"Really?" asked Stacy.

"Maybe you should talk to him," whispered Courtney.

"No, I can't," Stacy whispered back. "It wouldn't look right. He's here with another woman, and I'm here to do a job."

"You're right, but maybe you could call him later?"

"I don't think so. I'm pretty sure it's over."

"Then why does he look so upset whenever you talk to Ben?"

"He looks upset?"

"Umm-hmmm."

"Well, that's silly. I'm sure he realizes Ben and I just work together."

"But maybe he thinks you and Ben like each other."

"Ben?" Stacy laughed.

"Ahem. . . Thanks a lot, Stacy." Ben sounded embarrassed. "If you two insist on having a private conversation, then maybe you could turn off your intercom, since you're standing right next to each other."

"Sorry, Ben, if I offended you. You're a nice guy and all, but. . ."

Ben sighed loudly. "No offense taken. But, I'm going outside to take a little break. In case there's an emergency, call me. You all can pick on someone else while I'm gone."

Maddy and Julia could be heard giggling.

"So what are you going to do?" Courtney wanted to know.

"I told you. Nothing."

"You're just going to sit here and do nothing about the way she keeps looking at you?"

"What do you mean?"

"Haven't you noticed that she's noticed that he's watching you?"

"Yes, Courtney, but what can I do about it?"

"You can at least try to find out why she's upset with you. Did it occur to you that if he cares nothing for you, she wouldn't be jealous of you?"

"Okay." Stacy put her hands up, as if in self-defense. "Maybe. I'll call him tomorrow and try to find out what's going on."

"That's the spirit." Courtney patted her on the back.

"The bride and groom are ready to cut the cake and are coming your way," said Julia.

Courtney and Stacy moved aside to make room for the bride and groom.

"Where's the photographer?" Stacy asked.

"Here he comes," said Courtney.

"I'll be right back," said Stacy.

"Everything okay?" asked Courtney.

"I'm fine, but I need to use the restroom," she said. "I'll be back in a few minutes."

"See ya," said Courtney.

A few minutes later, just as Stacy was about to exit the restroom stall, Julia's voice came over the headset. "Stacy, don't answer me, because she'll hear you, but I just wanted to let you know that woman just followed you into the bathroom."

Oh, no. What am I going to do? "Lord, help me," she prayed softly and pushed the stall door open. The woman was standing in front of the sink, waiting for Stacy.

"Excuse me," Stacy said quietly, trying to get to the sink to wash her hands. The woman didn't move but stood glaring at Stacy.

A soft answer turns away wrath. Again, she said, "Excuse me, I just need to use the sink. I won't be in your way for more than a few seconds."

"I don't think so. We need to talk," the woman barked.

"Okay. . . ," Stacy said slowly. "Let's talk. Is there anything in particular you wanted to discuss?" She moved around the woman to the sink and began to wash her hands.

"Yes. I want to know why you're trying to steal my boyfriend." The woman stood with her hands on her hips, waiting for an answer.

Stacy wanted to explode. How could this woman be so cruel? She wanted to yell at the woman for stealing Max from her. Instead, she took a deep breath. "I don't even know your name," she said. "I'm Stacy." She held out her hand, but the woman didn't shake it. She just looked at the hand until Stacy withdrew it and nervously placed it at her side.

"I'm Vivianne," the woman said. "And I still want to know what you want from my boyfriend."

"Max?" Stacy asked.

"You mean you know him?" said Vivianne.

"Well, yes. I mean, we dated a couple of times."

"Oh, really?" Viv raised her eyebrows. "And when was this?"

"Almost two weeks ago. I would assume that was when he met you," Stacy said meekly.

"We did not just meet. I have known Max for almost a year, and I would know if he were seeing someone else. So I don't believe you."

"I don't see why you shouldn't believe me. We did date, and then. . .we didn't," Stacy said, not wanting to give Viv the details of what had happened between her and Max. "I'm sorry if you don't believe me."

"Humph," was all Viv said.

Then Stacy got a sick feeling in the pit of her stomach. "Are you saying that we were both dating Max at the same time?" So much for his look of sincerity, she thought sadly.

"Well. . . ," Viv hedged.

"Listen, I've got a job to do, and this isn't getting anywhere, so if you'll excuse me. . ." Stacy quickly walked to the door, willing herself not to let this woman see her cry.

"Wait a minute." Viv's eyes flashed. "Why don't we just ask Max?"

"I don't think so—" Stacy began.

"Don't you want to know?" Viv said.

"Yes, but this isn't the time or place," Stacy said wearily.

"Well, it might not be a good time for you, but it is for me," said Viv as she pushed past Stacy and left the restroom.

"Lord, I could really use some extra strength right now," Stacy breathed before heading out to complete the work that needed to be done.

As she resumed her work, Courtney patted her shoulder. "I heard what she said." Seeing Stacy's puzzled look, she added, "Your headset was on."

"Oh." Stacy nodded.

"What do you think?" asked Courtney.

"About what?" Stacy snapped. "Isn't it enough that Max never mentioned he was dating someone else? But now his girlfriend wants to accuse me of stealing him from her. So I don't need anyone to ask me what I think about all of this. I think I've been hurt enough as it is without having to answer nosy questions from my friends."

Courtney pursed her lips and was quiet. "Okay," she said, nodding. "I'm going to make sure the photographer is getting the candid shots of the reception that the bride wanted."

❧

Max could feel the tension building. Ever since Viv had returned from the ladies' room, she'd been fuming. Now she was giving him the silent treatment. He'd seen her follow Stacy into the restroom, and he wondered if they had talked. He knew he was in for some type of argument during the ride home. As soon as they finished their cake, Max suggested they leave.

"Are you in some type of hurry?" Viv glared at him. "The bride and groom haven't left yet, and she's going to throw the bouquet any minute."

"Well, I am kind of tired."

"I'm not." Then she lowered her voice. "I'm guessing you want to get away before your other girlfriend gets a chance to say something to you."

"Stacy?" Max asked.

"So she is your girlfriend?" Viv snapped.

"No! We just dated a few times. That's it."

"So why do you keep looking at her?"

Max exhaled deeply.

"I think we need to talk," said Viv.

"Then let's go home," Max said.

"No, not just the two of us, but you, me, and her." Viv pointed a finger in Stacy's direction.

"Now?" Max asked.

"Now," said Viv, following Stacy into the kitchen.

Max had no choice but to follow. *At least the rest of the guests won't be able to see us.*

Stacy was at the counter, ladling leftover punch into pitchers, with her back to Max and Viv.

As soon as they reached her, Viv began speaking. "I want to know what's going on with you and Max."

Angrily, Stacy whirled around and pointed the ladle at Viv. Punch sprayed into the air, landing on the floor, Viv's dress, and Max's shirt. Stacy's lips were pinched. "I think the logical thing to do would be to ask him." Then she turned her attention to Max. "Leave me out of your relationship problems. Did you date me only to make her jealous?"

"My dress!" Viv wailed.

"We're not even dating," Max said quietly.

"Well, then why on earth are you here with her?" Stacy's temper was getting the better of her. "I almost thought I could trust you, but that's a joke. I also thought you were a nice guy. Not the kind of guy who would date a woman like her and let her harass a nice person like me." Blinking back tears, Stacy quickly left the kitchen.

"Max, did you see what she did? She purposefully ruined my dress just because she's jealous of you and me."

"Well, maybe she didn't do it on purpose," Max began. He pointed to his own shirt. "Maybe it was just an acci—"

"So whose side are you on?" Viv put her hands on her hips, ready for an argument.

At that moment, one of Viv's friends poked her head in the door. Looking at them quizzically, she paused before speaking. "What in the world are you two doing in here? She's about to toss the bouquet. Aren't you coming?"

Viv took a deep breath and smiled. "Sure, let's go now," she said, walking toward the door, turning only to throw Max a withering glare.

Finding himself alone in the kitchen, Max hesitated for a moment, wondering what he should do next. As he left the kitchen, he saw Stacy and Maddy retreat into a small hallway. Half curious, half wanting to talk to Stacy, he followed them. As he neared, he could hear the two of them talking in hushed tones. He paused, hidden around the corner from where they stood.

"Don't cry about it. He's not worth it, Stacy," Maddy said.

Max slowed his footsteps. He felt terrible. Although he was hurt and upset himself, it hurt him even more to know she was in tears over the situation. The last thing he wanted to do was make her cry. Now was probably not the time to confront Stacy. She felt bad, and he was on edge. He needed to get back to Viv before she got suspicious and came looking for him. As for the punch, Stacy seemed to have a knack for klutzy moments, and he was sure it had been an accident. She probably felt terrible about it, and he didn't want to make her feel worse. As he turned and headed back to where the rest of the guests were, he heard Stacy's voice clearly.

"And that woman! If I'd known she was so mean, I'd have dumped the whole bowl of punch on her head. She deserved way more than the few splashes she walked away with!"

Max cringed inwardly as he walked. *So she had meant to spill the punch on us.* Another strike against the woman whom he'd so blindly fallen for. *I'll go to her office first thing Monday morning and get this settled. Since she did this on purpose, she deserves to pay both dry-cleaning bills.*

❧

That night, Stacy sat at home, replaying the events at the reception over and over in her mind. "I'm so embarrassed about the punch on her dress," she said to Maddy as they sat watching an old movie on TV.

"It's not like you did it on purpose or anything. And besides, she should know better than to sneak up behind people who have something liquid in their hands. Remember when we were little and Mom would tell us not to jump out and startle her when she was carrying groceries? It's the same thing," Maddy said while spreading a graham cracker with whipped cream. Then she handed it to Stacy. "I wouldn't feel too bad about it."

Stacy thought for a moment as she chewed. "You know, part of me wants to apologize, but I just can't. How could he do that to me? I mean, I feel like he's such a liar! I'm still not sure what his reason was for asking me out, but I'm positive it didn't have anything to do with his actually liking me. He needed something, and whatever it was, I guess he got it."

"Stacy," Maddy rolled her eyes and exhaled, "I'm not too crazy about Max right now either, but do you have to keep going back to the 'Guys only ask me out because they want something from me' theory? Maybe all you had was just a misunderstanding."

Stacy finished off another graham cracker. "If so, it was a pretty complex misunderstanding."

Chapter 9

Flyer 87: *It looks like things are finally starting to make sense now. But Kent's got a lot to do now if he wants to save the women.*

Leslie: *That Patrick Edger is despicable. What kind of man would have his own sister kidnapped?*

The Butler: *The kind of man who sends his sister to pretend she's the cousin of someone else. Debra knew what she was getting into.*

Lizzy: *Excuse me, Butler, but are you saying Debra deserved to get kidnapped?*

George: *My opinion on the matter is that Edger promised to cut Debra in on the deal if she would pretend to be related to Jill. She wasn't forced to do it, and she knows her brother. She knew what she was getting into.*

Ms. Drew: *I hate to say it, but Sherlock was dreadfully wrong. Sure, Debra knew what she was getting into, but maybe she had a change of heart and wanted out of the deal. That could be why her brother kidnapped her.*

Sherlock: *Ms. Drew, you've probably spoken too soon, as usual. We agree on one point. Debra was in on this from the beginning to help her brother find out who kidnapped his hostage out from under his nose. But as for Debra having a change of heart and getting kidnapped herself. . . No way. Kent's too smart to go looking for her. What he needs to do is find Jill.*

Ms. Drew: *Sherlock, I'm not catching your drift. . .which is not unusual, considering how vague you always are.*

Sherlock: *You'd catch my drift if you could, but I won't be too rough on you since I know it's hard for you to think so deeply. I'm thinking Debra kidnapped Jill away from her brother.*

Lizzy: *But why. . . ?*

Ms. Drew: *If she did, which I don't believe for one minute, it would be out of the goodness of her heart to save that girl from Edger.*

Sherlock: *But why is she still missing? Debra took her for the money that this Vita-Vitamin will make.*

Flyer 87: *Good point, Sherlock. I've considered that myself!*

Sherlock: *Thanks for your support. Ms. Drew seems to be turning everyone against my sound opinion in favor of her nice girly type guesses.*

Ms. Drew: *That's ridiculous! If Debra did the kidnapping, why would she go to Kent and ask him to find Jill? He'd have realized it was a scam by now, being the excellent detective that he is. And he wouldn't have fallen in love with someone he suspects committed the crime.*

Sherlock: Do I have to spell it all out? The reason Kent hasn't figured it out is because his mind is clouded with his feelings for Debra. She's a smart woman and, like too many women, dishonest and sneaky. (Grandma, Lizzy, and Leslie excluded from this generalization.) Anyway, she has tricked Kent into falling in love with her, only to keep him away from the truth. Kent's a nice guy—he wants companionship, and he meets a beautiful woman. Sure his judgment is a little shaky. Next thing you know, she'll be faking a cold on him while she runs off to Jamaica with the money the formula brings in. But I guess it's not her fault. She's a woman. She can't help it.

Ms. Drew: I don't know what you're insinuating about me, Sherlock, but I don't appreciate it one bit. You're probably the type to string along five or six women at once and then pit them against each other. With your attitude toward women, I'm guessing that you can't keep a girlfriend for more than a week.

Sherlock: I don't have to take this right now. I've had an unbelievably long and trying day—due to women, no less! Good night, everyone!

"Ooohhh." Stacy shuddered. "That man is worse than Max. Even after that fiasco at the wedding today." She waited for her computer to load the newest messages, but after a few moments, nothing new came up. "It looks like Sherlock went and scared everyone off, or was it just the two of us arguing?" She shrugged, then began typing.

Ms. Drew: I guess I shouldn't be surprised Sherlock is under the impression that he is the only one who has problems and the world must stop and pause when he's reached his limit. Isn't that just like a man? It's getting late, I'll be back tomorrow. 'Night all!

❧

Monday morning, Stacy was at the office, preparing a to do list for the wedding Courtney and Julia would be coordinating the next day. She and Maddy were taking the weekend off, as Courtney and Julia had done the week before. Ben had gone on vacation to visit his family in Texas right after the Wilson-Becker wedding, and he wouldn't be back for another week. As she bent over her work, she heard the bells that announced someone had entered the shop. She looked up and met Max's eyes.

Stacy stiffened and greeted him coolly. "Can I help you?"

Without hesitation, Max began. "Actually, you can. I think you might owe me an apology."

"Give me one good reason why I owe you anything," Stacy said angrily.

"Don't act so innocent, Stacy. First of all, you proved yourself to be dishonest the day you canceled our date claiming to have the flu. You didn't even have the decency to just tell me you had another date. I let it slide, thinking that I wouldn't bother with you anymore, but I know you spilled the punch on purpose."

Stacy was furious. "What in the world are you talking about? I did not spill that punch on purpose, and I was really sick. How dare you accuse me of lying."

"Stacy, I heard you tell your sister that you should have dumped all of the punch on Viv. And the night you canceled our date, I saw you and your sister out with two guys at two in the morning. Don't try to deny it."

Comprehension flooded over Stacy. "You saw us that night? What were you doing out that late?" she countered.

"I had a church basketball game. And what's your excuse?"

"You'll never believe it, but I'll tell you anyway," said Stacy. She told Max the whole story about how she'd had to leave the house that night, then waited for his response.

Max stood with his arms folded over his chest. "And what about the punch?"

"When you heard me say that, I was upset. I said something I shouldn't have, but I wouldn't do something like that on purpose to anyone."

Max unfolded his arms, and his eyes softened just a bit.

Unfazed, she continued in her defense. "The two of you should know not to sneak up on people who have something liquid in their hands. I even spilled a little punch on my dress. You surprised me. And furthermore, if you had really been so upset about the date, you'd have confronted me about this sooner. So I'm guessing that it not only wasn't that important to you, but it also shows that you have a knack for holding a grudge and then using it to start an argument when everyone's forgotten about it and no one really cares!"

"I believe you, Stacy," he said softly.

"I feel so vindicated now," she said facetiously. "And if you really wanted to look so much better than me, you wouldn't have admitted that you were eavesdropping on a private conversation." She marched over to the door and held it open. "Mr. Edwards, if you'll excuse me, I have work to do."

"Then, I'll be seeing you." Max grinned impishly, then walked behind the counter and sat in the chair she'd been sitting in. "It's a good thing that I came here so that you wouldn't have to close the shop while you ran errands."

Stacy frowned and shook her head. "Errands?" she asked.

Max smiled a wide, overly kind smile. "Yes, errands, or whatever it is you needed to do. You're the one standing next to an open door saying you have work to do." His tone took on a teasing note. "You could be a little nicer to me since I offered to watch your shop."

Stacy gasped angrily and hurried over to the counter. "Max, get out of my chair right now."

He stood slowly, feigning surprise. "You're not leaving?"

Her eyes were flashing now. "No, but you are." She held her arm out stiffly, pointing at the door.

"You would put a customer out?"

"I don't consider you to be a customer unless you buy something."

Max looked around the showroom, looking at the floral displays, cake models, china patterns, etc., before returning his gaze to Stacy. "All right then, what about this set of china?" he asked. Smiling, he pulled out his wallet.

"Why do you want china?"

He shrugged. "I don't really have any nice china. When I get married, my wife probably would appreciate being able to have dinner on something besides a Styrofoam plate." He smiled. Exasperated, Stacy turned away. She couldn't believe how cruelly he was acting. She turned to face him, her eyes flashing. "It's bad enough that you're marrying her, but do you have to come and throw it in my face?"

Max was puzzled. "You think I'm getting married to Viv?"

"Well—aren't you?" asked Stacy, her face growing warm.

Max smiled. "And you're jealous, right?"

"And you are rude and insensitive." Stacy glared at him for a moment then looked away.

He cleared his throat, then took a deep breath and exhaled. "Stacy, I'm sorry. Sorry for not believing you when you said you were sick." He took a step closer. "Sorry for not being mature enough to return your calls." He moved even closer. "Sorry for letting you think Viv and I are more than friends." He took one last step and gently held Stacy's hand. "I'm sorry that I've spent the past few weeks letting bitterness and mistrust come between us instead of getting to know you better. Can you forgive me?" His eyes were full of concern and tenderness.

Stacy felt like a heel. She closed her eyes and held back the tears that were threatening to flow. She nodded and tried to find her voice. "I forgive you. But you have to forgive me too." She paused to wipe the corner of her eye with her hand. "I've acted so horribly to you today. And at the wedding. I was jealous." She choked back a sob. "When I saw her, I felt betrayed and used. I'd trusted you, and it looked like you only needed me to make your girlfriend jealous." She looked at the floor so Max wouldn't see her tears.

Impulsively, Max reached out and hugged her. He held her more protectively as she continued to sob. He wanted to kiss her, but now wasn't the time. He needed her trust more than he wanted a kiss. "Stacy, I haven't had an actual 'girlfriend' in years. I rarely even date. I promise, you can trust me." He held her away from him and looked her in the eye. "I don't know how you've been treated in other relationships, but I promise I will treat you with the utmost respect. I would never intentionally hurt you. But I think that from now on, if either of us resents something the other one does, we need to talk about it immediately instead of letting it fester like this. Can you promise me that?"

Stacy was breathless. She hadn't expected Max's hug, and now she was overcome with emotion. Max had wrapped his arms around her protectively and held her so close she could feel his heart beating. She smelled his cologne and could feel the texture of his shirt and tie. Then he suddenly held her at arm's length and asked her to promise not to hold back anything that he did to upset her. The look on his face was so intense that, for a moment, she felt he might kiss her. She wanted him to kiss her, and she didn't want to ruin the moment by answering the question. So she waited.

Apparently, he didn't see her pause as an opportunity to kiss her, but instead must have been thinking she was deciding on an answer to his question. Stacy sighed. The moment had melted away like fog on a summer morning. But she appreciated his concern and so she answered, "Yes. I agree." Then she smiled. "Does this mean we're going to give it another try?"

Max laughed. "Only if you promise me you'll never go out in public with your eyes looking like that. At least not with me."

Stacy gasped and ran a finger under her eye. So much for waterproof mascara. "I must look pretty funny, huh?" she laughed.

"Or scary," Max supplied.

She put her hands on her hips. "Who asked you?" she said, trying to sound stern. Then she laughed. "Okay, I promise not to go out in public with mascara all over my face." Then her smile grew even wider. "At least not with you. What my eyes look like on my own time is none of your business. Is that a deal?"

"A deal," Max said, his face serious. Then he leaned over and kissed her.

Chapter 10

Stacy opened her oven and inhaled the scent that emerged from inside. It was the first day of November, and Max was helping with her traditional early decoration of her home for Christmas.

Stacy and Max had been spending so much time together that the summer and most of the fall had flown by. Maddy had gone back to school, promising to return to work the next summer if there was still a position open. She also begged Stacy to call her the minute Max did anything "really exciting—like propose!" Stacy had promised but had warned Maddy not to expect much. The two hinted to one another that they were interested in marriage, but there were no concrete plans made.

As she pulled the apple pie from the oven, Max came into the kitchen with tinsel and garland wrapped around his head and arms, singing "Deck the Halls."

"What in the world?" laughed Stacy.

"This decorating is hard work. Don't blame me if I act a little loony. What do you expect? I've been here for hours, and you haven't given me a crumb to eat," said Max as he eyed the pie.

"Don't be so dramatic," said Stacy, shooing him away from the pie. "We just had dinner an hour ago. This pie needs to cool."

"For how long?" Max asked pitifully.

"At least until you get the rest of that garland hung over the mantel," she bargained.

Max took one last look at the pie before heading back into the living room. "All right, but I'll only finish if you let me have a piece while I work. I deserve it. Remember, I helped you pick those apples at the orchard last week."

"Okay, okay. Get to work and I'll bring you a piece," said Stacy as she reached for a plate.

A few minutes later, Stacy handed Max a slice of pie. He sat down on the couch and took a bite. "Delicious. If you let me take it home, I'll cancel your bill for all the labor I put in today."

She playfully punched him in the arm. "What labor?"

He motioned around the room. "This. You people who use artificial greenery seem to think more is better. At my parents' house, we cut down the tree the day before Thanksgiving and hang a little garland. But you. . .you had to deck every inch of every hall and wall." He laughed. "Just 'cause it doesn't die, doesn't mean you should put it everywhere."

"You'll just have to humor me. Christmas is my favorite time of the year. I like to start celebrating early."

"Just think. This year will be the best Christmas you've ever had, because I'll be with you," he said, leaning down to kiss her.

"Are we a little conceited today?" she asked.

"No, just tired. Maybe delusional. Or is it delirious? At any rate, I think I might need more pie." He held out his plate to Stacy.

Stacy took the plate and was in the kitchen, dishing up another slice, when Max came in and wrapped his arms around her. Stacy relaxed into his embrace and sighed contentedly.

"I have a wonderful idea," said Max.

"About what?"

"Why don't you come to St. Louis and spend Thanksgiving with my family?" said Max.

"I don't know. . ." Stacy trailed off, pulling away from his arms.

"Why not? I'm spending Christmas with your family."

"Because. . .it's different. You see my family all the time. You go to my family dinners and activities. You know my family as well as you know me. But I don't know yours very well."

"Which is exactly why I want you to come and spend time with them."

"Your birthday was enough for me."

"That was almost two months ago. We'd barely been together for four months."

"So these extra two months are going to make that much of a difference?"

Max put his arm around her and led her back into the living room. "Come on, you didn't give them a chance. They were here for a whole week, but you spent all but one night working. I know you could have spared a little more time for them."

"Your parents are so intimidating."

"Only if you let them be that way. They just don't know you."

"But my family was much more receptive to you from the time we started dating seriously. And besides, that first night when we went to dinner, your mother kept making all those comments about how she was looking forward to spending time with you. I stayed away because I felt like I'd be imposing if I tried to see you again. Besides. . .that was just your parents. I haven't even met your brothers and sisters."

This time Max sighed. "Stacy, they want to meet you. They figure it's pretty serious if I'm not coming home for Christmas. Plus, I want to show you off. So think about it for me, okay?" he said before planting a soft kiss on her cheek.

"I'll think about it, but I'm not making any promises," said Stacy before returning his kiss.

"I must have been out of my mind to say yes," said Stacy as she searched through her closet.

"Out of your mind or not, you leave tomorrow, so you should finish packing," said her mother, looking at Stacy's empty suitcase and the clothes that were all over the room. "I don't know what you're worried about. I'm sure they'll love you the same way we love Max."

"They weren't that crazy about me when they came for his birthday."

"They just didn't know you, Honey," said her mom, patting Stacy's shoulder.

Stacy shook her head. "But you and Dad didn't know Max. You treated him like part of the family the minute you met him."

Berniece Thompson sat in the overstuffed chair in Stacy's room. She was a woman with a gentle spirit whose wisdom was highly evident to those who knew her. Her skin and hair were the same color as Stacy's, and they resembled one another very closely. In fact, Berniece's mother kept pictures of Berniece from infancy through her early twenties, and one could place those pictures next to pictures of Stacy at the same age, and they almost looked like the same person. Berniece, however, was a little taller than Stacy and wore her hair like Maddy's, except hers was sprinkled with strands of white.

Berniece sighed. "Stacy, I'm sure that once they get to know you, they'll love you. But sometimes you have to give people a little time. They haven't spent nearly as many hours with you as we've spent with Max. Their son lives in a different city than the rest of the family, and a mother feels inclined to be a little more protective of her kids when she doesn't get to see them on a regular basis. She probably wonders how you truly feel about Max."

"Mom, I understand all of that, but Max is not a baby. He just turned thirty-four. The real problem is that she thinks I'm not right for him because she wants him to marry Vivianne."

Berniece was surprised. "Vivianne from the wedding?"

"Umm-hmmm." Stacy began sorting through shoes to decide which ones she should take. "It was pretty uncomfortable. I tried to avoid them, but the one night I went to dinner with them, she made these comments about Viv and how sweet she is, and how mature she is, and how pretty she is, and on and on and on." Stacy sat down on the bed and shrugged. "Apparently, last Easter, Max's whole family came here and met her at his church. They all loved her. And they think I'm a poor substitute."

"Did you tell Max how you felt?"

"Yes. I didn't want to, but he knew something was bothering me and he reminded me of our promise to share our feelings with each other."

"What did he think?" Berniece was concerned. "I don't know if you should go this weekend if things are that bad. Why didn't you tell me?"

Stacy shook her head. "There wasn't that much to tell. Max says that they liked Viv but they didn't notice that he wasn't really interested in her. He thinks his mother and one of his sisters talk to her on the phone occasionally, but they'll be more courteous when I see them this week."

"Well, what if they're not?" asked Berniece. "Do you want your dad and me to come with you?"

"No." She shook her head. "That'll just make it harder, I think. Besides, you've got all the relatives from Dallas coming here. Don't worry about me. Max has promised that everyone will be on their best behavior."

"If you say so." Berniece stood and looked at her daughter doubtfully. "But I'll be praying for you, and if you need anything, just call—collect, if you have to."

Stacy laughed and held up her hands. "Mom, it might be a little uncomfortable at first, but I hope it won't be that bad! Max and I trust each other, and I know he cares about me as much as I care about him. In fact, the other day, he. . ." Stacy smiled and launched into one of her many little anecdotes about Max's chivalry.

At this, Berniece relaxed a little. Stacy called her with one of these stories several times a week since Maddy had gone back to school, and she listened intently as she and Stacy fell into the rhythm of packing and sorting items to be packed.

&

"Your younger brothers are the twins, Albert and Anthony, and Friday is their birthday. Right?"

"Right," said Max. "And my older brothers?"

"Umm. . .Otis and Jackson. The twins are single. Otis is married to Marva, and their kids are Annitra and. . .?"

"Otis Jr."

"Right. And Jackson and. . .Verna? are expecting a baby next month. Your sisters are Dana and Latrice—and Latrice is married to Donald, and their kids are Kaneisha and. . ." Stacy exhaled and looked at the clock. "We're an hour away from St. Louis, and you have so many relatives that it's impossible for me to remember all of them." She bit her lip, anxious.

Max didn't take his eyes off the road. "Latrice's new baby is Joyce. She's a month old. And don't worry, you're doing fine. No one expects you to remember everyone's name."

Stacy had a bad case of nerves and she was feeling a little snippy. "Well, I want to remember all of their names. Otherwise, I'll be subjected to listening to the story of how Viv remembered everyone's name after only a few hours."

Now Max was agitated. "Stacy, you're so nervous, it's making me nervous—and it's my own family. Don't get anxious over Viv. My whole family knows that Viv and I are not seeing each other. They know you and I are serious about each other." He squeezed her hand and winked.

"What did you tell them about Viv?" Stacy wanted to know.

"I told them we're just friends."

"Good friends?"

"Friends, Stacy. Just friends. Besides, Viv made it a point last Sunday to bring this guy she's dating to church to introduce him to me. She told the guy I was like her older brother. We rarely talk now. As soon as my family gets to know you, they'll love you."

Stacy shivered.

"Cold?" Max asked, reaching for the heat control.

"No." Stacy waved his hand away. "The temperature's fine. I'm just nervous."

"You've got to relax," said Max.

"I know, I know. I'm trying. Let's just go over the names again. Now Dana's your sister who's my age. She's the one I'm staying with, right?"

"You've got it. Now do you want to do the aunts and uncles?"

Stacy laughed, some of the tension melting away. "I guess I asked for it. Sure, why not?"

❧

"We'll be there in about two minutes," said Max as he maneuvered through quiet residential streets lined with big, old-fashioned houses and huge trees on every lot. "Are you okay?"

"Um-hmm. Uncle John is your mom's brother, and his wife is Daphne. Aunt Florence is your dad's sister, and her husband is Raymond. Who are their children again?"

"They're my cousins," said Max.

"No, seriously. What are their names?"

"It doesn't matter. Not right now. There will be seven or eight more sets of aunts and uncles here on Thursday, and along with them over thirty cousins plus their kids. I just told you about Florence and John because they'll probably be here tomorrow to help with the cooking. Oh!" He snapped his fingers. "I forgot to ask you. Mom asked if you wanted to help cook tomorrow. Is that okay with you or would you rather get out of the house?"

Stacy's eyes widened. "Your family starts cooking on Wednesday? My mom starts on Thursday morning. But, that's fine. I'd love to help."

Max's face grew worried. "Maybe you shouldn't. I could show you the city tomorrow instead. How about that?"

"Max, no. I've been to St. Louis dozens of times. Plus, I want to help. And it's not like I'm butting in. She asked you if I would help, right?"

"Well, yeah, but now that I think about it, I don't know what you'd really get to do."

"You said there'd be at least fifty people for dinner. There's got to be something I can help cook. Please let me do this."

He considered for a moment. "Okay, but be careful. Part of the reason they start cooking on Wednesday is because there are so many secret recipes. Everyone needs a little private time in the kitchen. Don't look over anyone's shoulder when they're measuring ingredients, and don't offer any suggestions, okay? Especially with Aunt Daphne's cranberry relish or Mom's special broccoli casserole, or

Marva's collard greens, or Florence's candied yams. And then there's Latrice's pineapple upside down cake and—"

"Max, okay. Point taken. But there's got to be some other stuff I can help with."

"Oh, sure. Especially tomorrow morning. The first thing they do on Wednesday is clean chitlins."

"Chitlins?" asked Stacy.

Hearing Stacy's questioning tone, Max asked, "You do know what chitlins are, don't you? You know, otherwise known as 'chitterlings' or pig intestines."

"Of course I know what they are," she said.

"And you know how to clean them, right?"

"Well, I. . ."

He waved his hand. "It's okay if you don't. Mom'll show you how. She's even made me help her clean them before. Here we are!" he said excitedly.

Stacy took a deep breath and fingered the door handle. She glanced at Max, her eyes worried.

"Don't get out yet," he said, reaching for her hand.

"Why not?" asked Stacy.

"Because we're going to pray. Okay?"

"Okay," said Stacy, feeling relieved as she let Max's hand envelop her own. She bowed her head, and Max began his prayer.

"Lord, we just want to say hello to You, and thank You for getting us here safely. Right now, we'd like for You to fill us both with Your peace and help us to remain calm and free of anxiety. Please comfort Stacy and help her to be herself and not feel pressured to meet any certain requirements this weekend. In Jesus' name we pray, amen."

"Amen," said Stacy, now smiling. "I feel much better already."

"And, Stacy," said Max as he opened the door, "they're not ogres. They're my family." He smiled. "They want to get to know you as much as you want to know them, okay?"

"Okay." She nodded.

At the front door of the house, Max gave Stacy's hand a warm squeeze as he rang the doorbell.

A man who appeared to be a younger version of Max opened the door and yelled, "Hey, everybody, Max is home!" before he and Max hugged. Within moments, the foyer of the family home was filled with men, women, and children, all either hugging Max, waiting to be hugged, or talking excitedly.

After the initial excitement, Max remembered Stacy, who was standing quietly to the side, observing the family reunion. Her peace was feeling a little shaky as she observed the dressy attire which everyone was wearing. She'd only worn a pair of jeans and a casual sweater, since she knew she'd be in the car for almost four hours. Even Max was wearing slacks and a nice shirt, something she hadn't noticed until now. She wished she'd stopped and changed before they'd arrived.

"Everyone, this is Stacy," he said. Then he looked at Stacy and said, "Sweet-heart, this is. . .everybody," and he laughed. "I'm sure you'll sort them all out sooner or later."

Stacy smiled and said, "It's nice to finally meet you all. And Claude and Mavis, it's nice to see you again."

Mavis Edwards, Max's mother, walked forward and laid a hand on Stacy's shoulder. She was a diminutive woman, whose skin was just a shade darker than Max's. Her silver hair denoted her sixty-eight years, but she moved with a light-ness of step and the energy of a woman half her age. Although she was very thin, she was not frail but carried herself proudly, with such dignity that she seemed much taller than her actual height of five foot nothing.

"We're glad you could make it. Max's friends are always welcome here," she said, turning to Max. "And speaking of friends of yours, I have a surprise for you," she said, smiling brightly. It was obvious that Max had inherited his good looks from his mother, including his beautiful smile. Turning to the room everyone had emerged from, which Stacy guessed to be the living room, she said, "All right Honey, you can come out now!"

Vivianne emerged from the room, wearing a purple V-neck cashmere sweater and a pair of flattering black wool slacks. Her hair was pinned up elegantly with several curls framing her face and the back of her neck. She wore simple diamond studs in her ears, along with a matching pendant on a gold chain. Her shoes were black leather loafers that perfectly accented her entire ensemble.

"Surprise!" she said and ran over to give Max a hug. Bewildered, Max re-turned the hug and glanced warily at Stacy.

Stacy smiled warmly, in an effort to prove that she wasn't bothered, but inside she was shaking, and soon she would be shaking visibly if she didn't get some time alone to compose herself. She glanced at the grandfather clock in the hallway. It was only five. There was no way she could pretend extreme fatigue and get a chance to turn in early for the night. She wanted to melt into the floor.

Chapter 11

Max sensed that all was not well and asked Stacy to come to the car to help him bring in some gifts that he had for his nieces and nephews. Thankful, Stacy agreed.

"Why did you bring me all the way here to deal with her for the next four days?" Stacy demanded as soon as they reached the car.

"Stacy, I promise, I didn't know she was coming. Honestly, I don't know what's gotten into my family. They're not cruel people."

"They might not be cruel to you or her, but they seem to have something against me," she said, her voice shaky.

"Oh, Stacy," Max said and wrapped his arms around her. "I'm so sorry. . ."

Stacy was not appeased, and she freed herself from his arms. "No," she said. "I am not allowing them the pleasure of looking out the window to see you trying to comfort me. As far as they're concerned, I'm not upset by her coming, and don't you act differently. I'm going to survive this weekend, but I doubt our relationship will."

She glared at him momentarily, then said, "Now let's go back inside and enjoy the holiday." She looped her arm through his and said, "Remember, I'm not upset, so don't try to pay special attention to me. If they can't accept me for who I am, then that's their loss. And why didn't you tell me everyone would be so dressed up?"

"I. . .I didn't even think about it," said Max weakly. He sighed. It was going to be a long four days.

❧

That evening seemed to drag eternally for Stacy. She didn't make any real progress getting to know Max's family; they were all too excited to see Max. During dinner, Stacy was seated on one side of Max, while Viv was seated on the other. Viv monopolized the conversation, while Stacy miserably pushed food around on her plate, trying to look happy.

By the time the meal was over, Max claimed to be too tired to sit in the family room to talk, and he said he assumed Stacy felt the same. Reluctantly, Mavis decided the evening should come to an end, due to all of the cooking that had to be done the next day. Stacy was sent to stay with Max's younger sister Dana, in her apartment, while Viv would room with Max's older sister Latrice and her family, who lived next door.

As Max loaded Stacy's bags into Dana's car, Stacy felt close to tears. Max seemed to be genuinely sorry for all of the problems that had occurred, but Stacy refused to speak to him. She wasn't ready to forgive him just yet. During the ride to Dana's, both women were silent. They were the same age, but Dana possessed a quiet, reserved personality and didn't seem to speak much.

At least I don't have to worry about trying to make conversation with her, thought Stacy. *At this point, if I have to say more than three words, I'll burst into tears.* When they reached Dana's home, she showed Stacy the guest room and the bathroom down the hall.

"You'll be coming to cook in the morning?" she asked.

"Yes," Stacy managed.

Dana nodded. "Then I'll wake you up in time to get ready," she said, then turned and retreated to her own bedroom.

Stacy spent the night alternating between tossing and turning and crying and fighting her conscience about the way she'd treated Max. She believed him when he said he knew nothing about Viv's coming, but she still felt betrayed. She seriously considered calling her mother to come and take her home, then decided against it. She didn't want to appear petty and immature. On the other hand, she held out hope that she would somehow be able to smooth things over with Max by the next morning. He was staying at his parents' home, so maybe he would have a chance to appeal to his parents on Stacy's behalf before the weekend was over.

At 4:00 A.M. she resolved to apologize to Max when she saw him again. She also prayed and asked forgiveness for her attitude that evening. Peace washed over her, and she felt safe and secure knowing that her heavenly Father would see to her needs. Soon afterward, she fell asleep from sheer exhaustion.

At five-thirty Stacy became aware that Dana was standing in her room, saying something. Taking a look at the clock, she sat straight up in bed. *Something must be terribly wrong for her to wake me at this hour.* "Is Max okay?" said Stacy, jumping out of bed.

Dana looked at her blankly. "He's fine. Why'd you ask?"

Stacy stopped searching for her shoes and socks to ask, "Then, why are we up so early?"

Dana shrugged. "I let you sleep kind of late, actually. We need to be at Mom's house in an hour. To cook, remember?"

At this point Stacy realized that Dana was fully dressed and ready to leave. "Oh, okay," she said. "How long do I have before we need to leave?" she asked.

"About half an hour, forty-five minutes at the most," said Dana. Then she flipped on the light switch and asked, "Are you okay? Your eyes are kind of puffy and red. Did you sleep okay?" She sounded genuinely concerned, which surprised Stacy.

Stacy shrugged. "I had a hard time getting to sleep," she admitted. "But I'll be fine." Dana eyed her closely before turning to leave. "You drink coffee?" she asked.

"Sure." Stacy managed a smile.

"Then it'll be ready when you are," said Dana.

Stacy speedily took a shower and got dressed. She didn't want to be late, but she wanted to look nice. She put on a pair of chinos and a yellow sweater twinset, then carefully applied makeup. When she walked into the kitchen, Dana looked up from her magazine in surprise. "Is that what you're wearing?" she asked.

"Yes. Is something wrong?" asked Stacy.

"Well. . .we're going to be cooking. I know you don't want to get your good clothes messed up," said Dana slowly. "Although you do look really nice," she added, noting Stacy's suspicious look. Dana looked down at her own clothes. "I just threw on these old jeans and a sweatshirt with a T-shirt underneath." She hesitated a moment. "If you didn't bring any old clothes, I could loan you something."

Stacy sat down at the table and poured a cup of coffee. "No thanks. I'm fine. I'm sure your mother has an apron around somewhere." She sipped her coffee. *Today, I am not letting Viv look like a model while I look like the maid.*

Dana shook her head. "If you say so."

After they were in the car, Dana forgot something and went back inside, returning a few minutes later with a brown paper bag which she placed in the trunk. After a few minutes on the road, Dana reached inside her purse at a stop sign and pulled out a small plastic bag filled with crushed ice. She handed it to Stacy, explaining, "Your eyes are still a little red." Then she added, "You probably don't want some people to think you've been crying."

Stacy was touched and surprised. She never would have guessed that Dana would be so sympathetic to her. "Thanks," she said, feeling a little choked up. "You don't know how much I appreciate this." She placed the bag over her eyelids.

"No problem," said Dana. "Just don't act so timid around Mom." She paused, letting her words sink in, then continued. "You don't think she wants her son to possibly marry a woman who can't stand up for herself and be a strong support to him and their kids, do you?"

Stacy considered Dana's words. "I guess I've never really looked at it like that. I've been so wrapped up in myself and how I felt. I know I've been really defensive, like she wants someone else for Max." She shrugged. "I don't have any brothers. I know what a mother wants for her daughter, but I never stopped to consider what a mother wants for her son. But why are you telling me all of this now? Why not last night?"

"I kind of figured you weren't in the mood for talking last night. Guess I was wrong."

"No, you were right about that," Stacy admitted. Then cautiously, she added, "So, are you saying you want to be friends?"

Dana laughed. "Girl, what are you talking about? Of course I want to be your friend! I think we could be good friends, if we try." Growing more serious, she added, "I'm the baby of the family, so I got lots of special attention. Sometimes I still do, even though I'm twenty-five." She laughed. "When I was in grade school, Max always looked out for me. I was little for my age, and he would walk me to and from school so the other kids wouldn't pick on me. We were really close to each other. Still are." She looked Stacy in the eye. "Listen, Stacy, I know my brother, and I know he's happier since he met you. So yeah, to answer your question, I want to be friends."

Stacy felt encouraged. Her eyes grew teary and she nodded her head. "Yes. I'd love it if we could be friends."

"Good. Now stop that crying and put the ice back on your eyes so you don't walk in Mama's kitchen with red eyes."

Stacy relaxed for the rest of the ride to the Edwardses' residence. She and Dana chatted amiably, and she felt encouraged that today she might be able to make similar strides with the rest of the family.

Chapter 12

In Mavis's kitchen, everyone bustled around at a brisk pace. For a moment, Stacy felt lost, until Dana nudged her in the direction of the big table that Mavis was covering with newspaper.

Mavis took a look at Stacy and asked, "Are you here to cook or look cute?"

"Well, I. . .to cook," said Stacy, confused.

"Hmmph," said Mavis, eyeing Stacy's outfit again. Then she handed her the stack of newspapers and said, "If you wanna help, finish covering this table and the floor around the table with these papers. Then you can go and ask Sheryl or Latrice to get you an apron."

Stacy began putting the newspapers down, and from the corner of her eye, she saw Dana wink at her. Stacy smiled back and wondered where Max was. With all of this noise, he couldn't possibly be sleeping. Looking around, Stacy noted that Max's sisters Sheryl and Latrice were there, and so were his aunts Florence and Daphne, along with Otis's wife, Marva. But Viv and Verna didn't seem to be around. *She's probably around here somewhere, waiting to make a grand entrance,* thought Stacy. Seconds later, her unspoken question was answered.

"Mama, where is Verna this morning?" asked Sheryl.

Mavis shook her head. "She wasn't too keen on cleaning chitlins this morning. Said the smell was bothering her. Plus, she's a little tired, what with the baby going to be here in a few weeks." Mavis smiled and waved her hand. "I sent her with Claude and Max and the twins to get the Christmas tree. She felt bad about leaving the rest of us to cook, but I told her we'd find a way to manage. Then Viv, bless her heart, volunteered to keep Verna company, so I let her go too."

"Do you know when they'll be back?" asked Dana, glancing at Stacy.

Mavis shrugged and threw her hands up in the air, a questioning look on her face. "Lord knows when they'll get around to coming back. But if I know my boys, they won't want to miss out on my pot roast, so I at least expect them back for dinner."

Stacy was stunned. "It's barely 7:00 A.M. Why would they leave so early to get a tree?"

Mavis turned from the sink where she'd been putting the chitlins in a plastic bucket. "Well, Honey, they have to drive two hours to that farm where the man sells the trees." She smiled, and a distant look came over her face. "We've been going to that same place for the tree for twenty-eight years, today. I measure the time by my twins. I don't even remember why we picked that place."

She shook her head. "You'd have to ask Claude about that. Once he gets it

79

in his head to do something. . .humph. I was eight and a half months pregnant and we had all the kids in the car. Otis was twelve, Latrice was ten, Jackson was eight, and Max was six. The rest of the kids weren't born yet, and if I'd known the twins were going to come two days later, I probably wouldn't have gone and suffered through all the squabbling that was going on in the backseat."

Stacy was growing more and more comfortable as she listened to Mavis's story. She was beginning to view her more as a mother than a foe. *Maybe I will be able to make friends with her.*

Mavis was walking from the sink to the table with the bucket. "Ladies, I got thirty pounds of chitlins here, and if we want to get the rest of our cooking done, we need to get started. Everybody take a seat and let's clean."

Stacy put on the apron Florence handed her and took a seat at the table and watched the women work. They worked at a comfortable pace, sometimes talking more than cleaning, but they were getting the job done. She wrinkled her nose at the strong smell filling the room and stared at the chitlins. *No wonder Mom never wanted to cook them,* she thought. She decided that although she had no idea what to do, she would try to fake her way through this, rather than let Mavis know she needed help. Stacy took a spoon and a piece of meat about eight inches long and tried to mimic what the other women were doing. After a few minutes of scraping the cold, wet piece, she put it into one of the three bowls the cleaned chitlins were placed in and moved on to another piece. Unfortunately, Mavis's eyes didn't miss much.

"Honey, what are you doing?" she asked, looking at Stacy. Everyone else looked too.

"Me?" asked Stacy.

Mavis stood up and walked to Stacy's spot at the table. "You're getting water on my table. When the newspaper gets soaked through, you need to put some more down." Then she leaned over to inspect Stacy's work. Stacy began working again, growing uncomfortable when Mavis didn't move away. Stacy glanced up at Mavis with a questioning look on her face.

Mavis was staring at her in utter disbelief. "Lord, have mercy," she said. "Child, have you ever cleaned chitlins before?"

Stacy didn't answer immediately, so Mavis motioned for Florence to get up from her seat next to Stacy. "The least you could have done was stop her before she got too far," she reprimanded Florence.

"Honey, I was talking to Daphne. I didn't even notice until just now," Florence apologized.

Mavis took Florence's seat and took the piece Stacy had been working on. "You know what chitlins are?" she asked Stacy.

"Pig intestines," Stacy said quietly.

"Now I know you know what's inside intestines," said Mavis.

Stacy nodded.

"So why are you cleaning the outside?"

Stacy looked as Mavis opened the piece she was holding. "I'm so sorry. I didn't know. . . I've never. . ."

"Um-hmm," said Mavis. "Now look here. These are already slit open. The stores do a pretty good job of cleaning 'em out, but you gotta use the spoon to scrape out any dirt and corn or knots or hair or. . .well, whatever. Otherwise. . .if you cook 'em like this, somebody might get sick. Not to mention they won't be tender. And I am known for my tender chitlins."

Mavis stood and let Florence have her seat back. "Somebody fish out the ones she already worked on so we can clean 'em for real." Turning to Stacy, she said, "Honey, any questions you have, just ask Flo here." She went back to her seat, still talking. "Daphne, I remember when Poppa used to slaughter the hog and we had to clean fresh chitlins. Now that was work," she said emphatically. "This is like a walk in the park."

"Um-hmm, Girl, I know that's right," said Daphne.

Embarrassed, Stacy returned to her task, this time really accomplishing something. Not to mention the fact that half an hour later, she and her clothes were wet and reeked of chitlins. Stacy looked around the table, noticing that no one else seemed to be getting as messy as she did. She sighed and kept working, determined to prove to Mavis she could do well.

A few minutes later, Dana patted her on the shoulder and handed her the brown paper bag she'd placed in her trunk. "Thought you might take me up on the offer for old clothes now." She smiled.

"Thanks so much," said Stacy appreciatively.

"And now that you've got the hang of it, you shouldn't get so wet," said Mavis, who had come over to inspect her progress.

Mavis was right. She didn't get nearly as messy, but the smell didn't go away. Two hours later, Mavis seemed satisfied that everyone had done their job to her specifications, and she put the meat in a huge pot with water, garlic, onions, and other seasonings to boil for the next couple of hours.

Stacy worked nonstop for the rest of the day. After the chitlins incident, everyone seemed a little wary of her ability to cook, so she was given small jobs, like chopping vegetables for the macaroni and cheese or measuring ingredients for cornbread and peach cobbler crust. Gradually they realized that she knew her way around a kitchen, even if she'd never cooked chitlins, and eventually she was even invited to help with the brisket and turkey.

Although Max's sisters and aunts seemed to accept her and began to include her in their conversations and jokes, Mavis still was not overly warm. As the day wore on, she watched Stacy closely. The closest she came to being friendly was when Mavis let Stacy make the rolls. Stacy sensed this was a test of some sort and knew she needed to pass it. As she worked on the bread, she was glad she had learned her mother's recipe by heart.

Mavis seemed impressed when she tasted the finished product and smiled thoughtfully as she said, "These remind me of the ones my grandmother used to make." Shaking her head, she remarked, "I've mastered a lot of things in the kitchen, but I never got my rolls to taste like this." Then she said she had to check on her ham and sent Stacy to help Sheryl with the chestnut dressing.

At four o'clock, Dana told Mavis she and Stacy needed to take a break. "We'll run home and shower and be back in time for dinner," said Dana.

Stacy was a little disappointed because Florence had offered to show her the special seasoning blend she used in the black-eyed peas, but she had to admit, she was tired. She didn't think she'd ever worked so hard and long in a kitchen.

"All right," said Mavis a little reluctantly. She put her hands on her hips. "I guess everybody wants to run off now, claiming to be tired and leave me here to work on Anthony and Albert's birthday cake."

"Now, Mama," said Latrice, leaning over to give her a quick kiss on the cheek. "We've been working for hours, and if you don't let us get some rest, we'll be nodding in our okra tomorrow. Plus, I left Donald with the baby today. I know he's probably ready for a break."

"I've got to check on my kids too," said Marva. "Otis Jr. picked Annitra up from school today, but I'm a little nervous about him getting his license only a month ago. He offered to go to the grocery store for me, but I think I'll call him and tell him I'll do it on my way home." She hurried off to use the phone.

"And besides," said Daphne, "you know you keep that recipe for the boys' chocolate cake a secret. I'll never forget the year you claimed I kept trying to steal your recipe." She rolled her eyes playfully and laughed.

"Oh, all right," said Mavis. "Get out, all of you," she said in a cheerful tone. Then she pointed to Daphne. "Especially you. I've got to work on my sweet potato pies now, and even if you did find out how I make the cake, you're not getting my pie recipe." The women laughed and began gathering up purses and coats on their way out the door.

After they got back to Dana's apartment, Stacy took another shower and got dressed again. After what she'd just been through, she was going to wear something comfortable. "I don't even care what Viv'll be wearing," she said as she looked through her bags. She settled on a nice pair of jeans with a soft, pink wool turtleneck sweater that accentuated her long, graceful neck.

"Wow," said Dana when Stacy met her in the living room. "You look pretty."

"I feel comfortable," said Stacy, sinking into the softness of the couch. "This is the first time I've been able to simply relax today, without worrying about how well I can cook something."

Dana laughed. "I think Mom was impressed. You're a pretty good cook. That kind of stuff is her hobby. I don't care for cooking much, but she made me learn. Anybody who can cook is a friend of hers."

"Has Viv passed the kitchen test?" asked Stacy dryly.

"Well, she helped make dinner last night. She's an okay cook, I guess, but not too creative with seasoning. Mom likes creativity."

Stacy tilted her head to one side. "I'm guessing I didn't score any major points in cleaning chitlins."

Dana giggled. "Not really, but Viv didn't either, since she wasn't there. I have to admire you for sticking around and showing determination."

Stacy laughed. "I might have been determined to clean them, but I don't have any desire to eat them tomorrow."

"It's an acquired taste, that's for sure. But Mom cooks them better than a lot of people I know. At least taste 'em." She laughed. "But we'd better get a move on. She won't like it if we hold up dinner."

When they got back to Mavis's house, Max and the others still had not returned. Stacy and Dana watched television in the family room with Latrice and her family, along with Uncle John and Uncle Raymond, while Daphne and Florence helped Mavis with the meal. The mood was relaxed, and Stacy felt like she was fitting in nicely. She was glad she'd had to spend her first day with the family without Max. Otherwise, she might have depended on him too much and not gotten to know everyone as well as she had.

Thirty minutes into the wait, they heard the sound of the van pulling into the driveway. Everyone bustled around, waiting to see the tree that had been brought home.

Claude was the first one in the door, followed by Anthony and Albert, who carried the tree. It was only about seven feet tall, but it was rotund and would take up a great deal of space, even in the large family room. Verna and Jackson entered, followed by Max and Viv. Stacy braced herself for whatever might happen next. Viv was dressed stylishly casual, much like Stacy, in an emerald green sweater and jeans and hiking boots. Her hair was up in a curly ponytail and her cheeks were flushed from the cold. Stacy had to admit, Viv was a very attractive woman.

Max, who was reaching out to hold baby Joyce, looked as handsome as ever. He wore jeans and a navy blue flannel shirt with a jacket. Stacy's heart did a flip when their eyes met. She loved him. Plain and simple. She didn't care about the way he'd been gone with Viv all day. She trusted him, and she felt secure. For all of these years, she'd been waiting for someone to love, and Max was the one. *I wonder if he feels the same way,* she mused as he handed the baby back to Latrice and made his way across the room to Stacy.

Stacy smiled and waved at him, but Max didn't smile. His face was serious. *He might be upset about the way I acted last night,* she worried.

As soon as Max stood in front of her, Stacy spoke. "Max, I'm really sorry about last night. I overreacted and—"

"Let's go outside," Max interrupted. Viv watched with sharp eyes as he gently led Stacy to the front door and outside to the swing that was on the porch.

Stacy's heart pounded. *He must be really upset. Maybe he's decided that he really likes Viv. Maybe he doesn't want to see me anymore. I don't know how I'll stand the rest of the weekend if he breaks up with me right now,* her mind raced.

"How was today?" he asked. "Did everything go okay?"

"Oh. Yeah, everything. . .it went pretty well."

Max sounded relieved. "Good. I've been a little anxious about how you were doing. I feel guilty for leaving you here by yourself all day like that."

She remembered the events of the day and smiled at Max. "I had a good time. Your sisters and aunts are really nice, and your mom—I think she's getting used to me." Stacy shivered, more from relief than cold. *He's not breaking up with me,* she thought. Continuing, she added, "But I do owe you an apology. I was out of line last night. I know better than to take my fears out on other people. I should have prayed instead of lashing out at you."

Max put his arm around her shoulders. "I prayed for you last night. I hope you aren't upset with me about this morning. Getting the tree today is a family tradition, and you'd said you wanted to cook. I wish we would have left later so I could have checked to see if you'd be upset about Viv's going, but Dad insisted on leaving early. Before we went for the tree, we went to breakfast, and then after the tree we had lunch, then Verna decided she wanted to show Viv around the city.

"I wanted to come home and check in on you, but I didn't want to be rude, and I knew I'd probably be in the way. And I kind of figured you might be able to fit in better if I wasn't hanging around all day. Plus, Dana promised me last night she'd take good care of you."

Stacy was surprised. She looked up at him. "She took excellent care of me. We're good friends now." Then, remembering her own promise to be honest with Max, she said, "I'll admit, I was a little upset this morning when you weren't here, but after we started cleaning chitlins, I was so busy, I didn't have time to be angry." She quickly explained some of the events that had transpired in Mavis's kitchen throughout the day.

Max was very amused. After laughing for several minutes, he grew serious again. "Stacy, I don't know what Mom feels about Viv, but I made it pretty clear to her today that she and I are just friends. I wasn't disrespectful, but I think I got the message across to everyone else who was with us." Then he grew thoughtful. After a few minutes, he took a deep breath and said, "You know what I realized?"

"What?" asked Stacy, smiling.

"I love you."

Stacy's mind raced. *He loves me,* she thought happily. He hadn't said it out of pity or for the purpose of manipulating her, like other men she'd dated had done; he really loved her. She answered him honestly, because she trusted him. "I love you too, Max."

Max put both arms around her and kissed her. Stacy could feel his heart beating again, like she had the day he'd held her while she cried. She kissed him back, enjoying their closeness.

A few moments later, Max kissed her one last time, then said, "We'd better go back in. It's probably time to eat."

"All right," said Stacy as Max stood up and reached for her hand. As he led her back inside, she felt as though her feet hardly touched the ground.

The rest of the night, Stacy was in a lighthearted mood. Viv was not especially warm, but Stacy didn't allow herself to get wound up over it. Instead, she prayed, *Lord, please help her to find someone who loves her. I know how she feels and it can be scary to be alone. Show her that You love her and that You have created someone for her, and You are waiting for the right time to bring them together.* A few minutes later, she added, *And, Lord, please let me find favor with Mavis. Show her that I'm not trying to steal her son away, but help her to understand that Max and I really love each other.*

Throughout the meal, Mavis seemed to be watching Stacy and Max and appeared to be in deep thought for most of the evening. Max and Stacy stayed close together, their faces glowing with joy. After dinner, the whole family helped decorate the tree, then everyone prepared to return to their homes to get some rest in preparation for the next day.

Max walked with Stacy out to Dana's car and gave her a quick kiss before she got inside. "I'll see you tomorrow," he said, stroking her cheek with his finger.

Chapter 13

Thanksgiving morning, Stacy and Dana slept in. At least it felt like sleeping in, in comparison to the time they'd risen the previous day. The two of them had stayed up late, laughing and sharing girl talk. Dana was genuinely happy for Stacy and said it was "Only a matter of time before we're really sisters." That remark put both of them into a dreamy mood, and they spent their remaining time awake talking about weddings. Finally, they both had to admit they were totally exhausted, and they went to bed, sleeping until almost ten o'clock.

To their surprise, it had snowed overnight, and the city was blanketed in six inches of wet snow. Ever since she'd been little, the sight of snow filled Stacy with an extra helping of Christmas spirit. The brightness of the snow and the feel of the icy air perked Stacy up a bit, and she looked forward to the rest of the day with even more optimism. They made it to Mavis's at one, and to Stacy's surprise, the street was lined with cars.

"Get ready to meet all the relatives," said Dana. "Only I'm warning you. . . some of them I see so seldom, I forget how we're related."

Inside, the home was filled with men and women, children and babies. Stacy found Max in the great room helping his brothers move all the furniture out in order to set up tables. Only the Christmas tree stayed in the room. The kitchen was also crowded. In addition to the food they'd prepared already, women were steadily bringing various salads, side dishes, and desserts. Mavis gave Stacy the job of helping Latrice set all of the food out, buffet style, in the hallway outside the great room.

Meanwhile, people steadily introduced themselves to her, and Stacy hoped she could remember at least some of their names. In less than an hour, it was time to eat. The family was assembling in the great room so Claude could say the blessing over the meal. Stacy and Latrice were two of the last to enter.

Stacy was looking for Max when Mavis drew her aside. "Honey, I have a really big favor to ask you, and I hope you don't think I'm out of line here." Mavis's voice was motherly, and Stacy was happy to see a change in her so soon. If it meant that Mavis would accept her, Stacy would be glad to do her a favor.

"Sure, what is it?"

"Well," Mavis twisted a corner of the dishtowel she held in her hand, "this morning, Latrice told me that Viv isn't going to be coming over today. I hear she's not feeling too good."

Stacy's heart fell. She had a feeling this favor wasn't going to be very pleasant.

Apparently, Mavis was bent on making Stacy work hard for acceptance. Gathering up all of her remaining determination, Stacy tried to sound concerned. "Does she have a cold?"

"I'm not exactly sure what's wrong. I guess she's just feeling under the weather. A pity. . .it being Thanksgiving and all. Everybody's over here, and she's probably feeling a little lonely. She doesn't have any family, you know."

Stacy's conscience pricked her. *It would be terrible to be truly alone, without any family.* "What do you need me to do?" she asked Mavis.

Mavis turned and motioned for Stacy to follow her to the kitchen. "I know you want to be here with Max, and I'm not trying to separate the two of you. But do you think you could run over and check on her. . .maybe take a plate to her? I'd do it myself, but I thought she might enjoy the company of someone her own age. . . ." Mavis trailed off. Noting the look of despair on Stacy's face, she quickly added, "You don't have to stay long, and I'll be sure to save you a seat next to Max."

Stacy knew she must have looked surprised because the next thing she knew, Mavis was seated at the kitchen table, patting the chair next to her for Stacy to sit in. "I guess I owe you an apology." She hung her head, then looked at Stacy. "I know I haven't been as nice as I should have. When I met Viv a few months ago, I just decided for myself that she was the woman for my Max. But I realized yesterday, when I saw how patient you were, that I hadn't really asked the Lord who He wanted for Max." Mavis sighed. "Sometimes I try to help Him out and I end up making a mess of things. So. . .I'm asking you to forgive me. Viv is a nice woman, and I know the Lord will bring her someone. In fact, I'll be praying for that to happen. But I can tell just by watching you two that you and Max are in love. That, and the fact that you sat there and cleaned those chitlins yesterday." Mavis laughed. "That's love if I've ever seen it."

Stacy was so happy she could cry. In fact, her eyes did get a little wet. Impulsively, she hugged Mavis. "I forgive you," she said. "I've been praying that we could be friends."

Mavis hugged her tightly and patted her back. "Now don't cry, Honey. Max will think I've done something to you, and I don't want him getting upset over nothing. Now what are we going to do about Viv?"

"I'll take a plate over and see if she wants some company," said Stacy.

"Good," said Mavis. She busily hurried around, putting food into containers. She placed all the containers in a picnic basket and handed the basket to Stacy. "There's enough food for both of you in here. Now don't be gone too long. I'll explain to Max, but I know he won't be happy if you're not back in time for dessert."

"When is dessert?" Stacy asked.

"Well. . .I'd say around five o'clock. After dinner, we all just kind of socialize, then Claude likes to read a passage of Scripture to everyone. Then we have dessert. So you have a few hours."

"I won't stay too long," promised Stacy as she opened the back door.

When she rang the doorbell next door, Stacy was surprised to find Viv the picture of health. She was up and dressed, and nothing about her seemed out of the ordinary except that her eyes were a little red. "Oh." Stacy smiled. "I see you're feeling better. In that case, why don't we go next door and have dinner with everyone?"

Viv hesitated. "I don't think so. . ."

"I guess you might not be feeling one hundred percent yet," said Stacy. "That's okay," she added, stepping inside. "We can have dinner here. Mavis sent over enough food to feed us both for a couple of days."

Viv shut the front door. "I know you don't want to be here. And I guess you've figured out that I'm not really sick. I just told Latrice that so I wouldn't have to deal with everyone today. So I'll just take this and you can go back over there and be with Max. But thanks for coming anyway." She opened the door and looked at Stacy.

Stacy sat on the couch. "If you don't mind, I'd like to stay here with you. I don't think we've gotten off to a good start."

Shutting the door, Viv wiped her eyes with the back of her hand. "You are the last person I'd want to see me crying." She walked to the couch and sat next to Stacy. "I know I've treated you terribly. I want you to know that I knew the punch on my dress was an accident. I was just being stubborn. I've been over here crying all morning because yesterday I realized Max doesn't care about me the way he cares about you."

She sniffed and reached for a box of tissues on the coffee table. "It's not his fault. He's been trying to tell me that ever since we met. But I kept trying to convince him. I even called Mavis a few weeks ago and sort of invited myself here this weekend because I knew he'd come home and I thought I might be able to. . ." This time she sobbed while Stacy rubbed her back and tried to comfort her.

Viv looked up. "I really don't have anything against you. I'm so embarrassed to say I'm a Christian after what I've done. I got saved two years ago after the rest of my family died in an accident. I'm still learning how to be godly, but that's no excuse. I just saw a handsome man and decided I wanted him. Then I met his family, and they reminded me of my own family. . . . I was so lonely." She burst into tears again.

"I can't imagine what it would be like to lose my whole family," Stacy said sympathetically. "But I'm not upset with you. I feel terrible about some of the things I've thought about you. So can you forgive me?"

Viv nodded. "Yes, I can. I don't want to be your enemy. You're pretty nice, and you've put up with a lot from me. The way you came over here today. . ." She shook her head. "I've read it a hundred times in the Bible, but now I really know what it means to turn the other cheek and go the extra mile. And I know it wasn't easy."

Stacy hugged the woman and let her cry. Eventually, she and Viv had lunch, and Stacy remained with her for the next few hours, lending her shoulder for Viv to cry on and praying for her. Later, she convinced Viv to come next door with her and have dessert with the rest of the family. When the two of them walked in together, everyone was milling around, preparing to listen to Claude read the Christmas story.

Mavis hugged Viv, then asked Florence to introduce Viv to some of the relatives. "She's my adopted daughter," she said, winking at Stacy. Then she hugged Stacy and whispered, "You'll be my daughter soon enough." She released her from the hug and said, "Thanks for going over there to work things out with her. I had a feeling she was more emotionally ill than physically. I knew I could count on you." Then she patted Stacy's shoulder. "Claude's about to start reading, so you'd better go find Max. The last time I saw him, he was getting mighty fidgety."

Leaving the kitchen, Stacy almost ran into Max in the hallway. He put his arms around her and kissed her. "Mom told me where you went. I'm so proud of you."

Stacy smiled and returned his kiss.

~

The next morning, the roads had grown icy, and Stacy and Dana carefully made their way to Mavis's. Max and Stacy were leaving after lunch, and they wanted to squeeze in as much time as they could with the family.

Viv left soon after Stacy and Dana arrived, needing to catch her early flight back to Kansas City. After a lively breakfast celebration for Albert and Anthony's birthday, the family moved to the family room to sit and talk. Claude announced he was going for his walk and started bundling up in his coat, along with a scarf, hat, and gloves.

"Now, Claude," said Mavis, "it's too cold and too icy to be out walking today. Why don't you just sit down and go for your walk tomorrow?"

Claude shook his head. "Mavis, I go for this walk every day. I went yesterday morning and it was still snowing. A little cold never hurt me—you know that."

Mavis's face was the picture of determination. "The only reason you went yesterday is because you sneaked out when I wasn't looking. Now what if you slip and fall? How are you going to get home?"

Claude stopped buttoning his coat. "Okay, I'll take Stacy with me. That way, if I slip and fall, which I won't, she can help me get home." He looked at Stacy. "Come on, get your coat."

"Now, Dad," said Max, standing. "Don't make Stacy go out in this weather." Motioning for Stacy to sit back down, he said, "Let me get my coat, and I'll come with you."

"Stacy, get your coat," said Claude. To Max, he said, "I didn't ask you to come with me, so you can just sit back down. I'll be out on the front porch," said Claude to Stacy as he turned to leave the room. "So hurry and get ready."

"Don't listen to him," said Mavis. "You don't have to go out there and freeze just because he's got it in his head to go on a walk. Let Max go with him."

Stacy stood up and patted Max's shoulder. "I'll be fine. I could use the exercise." To Mavis she added, "I'll make sure he doesn't walk where it's too icy."

"Thank you, Honey," said Mavis, relieved. "I've got a warm pair of gloves you can borrow," she said. "Could somebody look in my coat pocket and get my gloves?" she asked.

"I'll get them," said Max. "And I'll let you wear my scarf," he said, leaving to find the items.

In a matter of minutes, Stacy was bundled up and ready to go. "Now don't you let him drag you all over," said Mavis, opening the door. "When you get too cold, you put your foot down and tell him you have to come back."

"I will," said Stacy.

Outside, Claude was walking back and forth on the porch. "I was wondering what took you so long," he said. "Let's get a move on." As she followed Claude down the stairs to the sidewalk, Stacy thought, *I guess I still have to earn his approval. Please don't let me mess things up, Lord.*

For awhile they walked silently. For the first time that weekend, Stacy was able to really observe Claude. He was such a quiet man that she'd almost totally overlooked him during the midst of her quest to win Mavis's heart. Claude was tall and wiry. *And energetic too*, thought Stacy as she struggled to keep up with his long strides. His skin was the color of milky caramel, but he and Max shared the same dark brown eyes. He was totally bald on the top, and the hair that remained on the back of his head and around his ears was completely white. His face was long and thin, his nose and cheeks lightly dusted with freckles that were accented by thin gold glasses that sat upon his pointed nose.

After a few minutes, Claude abruptly stopped and turned around to face Stacy. "I've been waiting for you to catch up, Girl. Am I gonna have to walk slower for us to have a conversation while we walk?"

Stacy stopped and tried to catch her breath. As her breathing returned to normal, she nodded her head. "If you don't mind, I would appreciate it if you'd slow down a little. I'm not used to this pace."

Claude laughed. "Now that's what I like. A little honesty. Even my own kids won't tell me I'm walking too fast. I just hear 'em jogging behind me, gasping for air. When I ask if they want me to slow down, they barely have the breath to say, 'No, Dad, I'm doing just fine.' " Claude imitated the sound of someone gasping for air as he spoke. He shook his head. "They just don't like to be outdone by old folks, that's all." When Stacy joined his side, he slowed his pace and asked, "When are you and Max figuring on getting married?"

Stacy's face grew warm despite the frigid temperature. "Well. . .he hasn't really asked me yet."

"If he hasn't yet, I don't think it'll be too long before he does," smiled

Claude. "Especially now that you found a special place in Mavis's heart. I wondered how you'd do, but everything worked out fine."

Feeling brave, Stacy ventured, "I was so nervous at first. I couldn't figure out what she wanted from me."

"Well, you did okay, as I see it. Mavis is real particular about who her kids settle down with. She wants her sons- and daughters-in-law to be strong and supportive. We black folks need to have strong families, you know. I won't argue with that. Except sometimes, when Mavis starts holding her auditions, she forgets to pray about who should get the part."

Hearing the theater analogy, Stacy remembered Max telling her that his father had wanted to be an actor when he was a young man. He was good, but never got far, due to the lack of parts for African-American actors.

Claude continued. "Especially with Max. From the day I met Mavis back when I was fourteen years old, I knew she wanted to be a mother. We've been married for fifty-two years, and we've had kids for forty of those years. Mavis wanted to have a family, but she was patient and supportive of me while I tried my hand at acting. When I realized I couldn't make a decent living chasing that dream, I got a steady job and we started raising a family. But for those first twelve years, she worked and helped support us. She didn't complain and never once did she tell me like everybody else, 'Why don't you give up? You're never gonna make it nohow.'

"Nope, she stuck by my side and told me she knew I could do it, and that meant the world to me, just knowing she thought I could do it. But mothering has been her full-time job since the day Otis was born. She fussed over all her little ones, and she still does. When Max was born, he gave us a scare. He was born almost two months early, and stayed small and sick for the first ten years of his life. Even when he learned how to walk, he was always tripping and falling and getting banged up. When he was older, he'd protect Dana from bullies at school. One time I asked him why he didn't get one of his older brothers to help him and he said, 'Dad, I know what it's like to get picked on because you're little. Now that I'm bigger, I want to help Dana like Otis and Jackson helped me.'"

Claude laughed. "The funny thing was, he was still little for his age. He didn't really fill out until he went to college. Mavis didn't coddle him, because she said she wanted him to fend for himself. But she did spend plenty of time praying that boy would make it through the day without breaking a bone or falling on his head. He's always been real tenderhearted and wants to please everybody. We taught him not to let folks run over him, but he wants to make people happy and it bothers him when he can't. He and I are a lot alike. So you see, she didn't really have anything against you. She just wanted to be sure her 'tiny baby' gets blessed with a wife who will be there for him, like she was for me."

Stacy was quiet as she considered all Claude had said. She prayed that she could be all of those things and more to Max. Then she spoke to Claude. "I feel much better now, knowing all that."

"I thought you might," said Claude. "That's why I wanted to talk to you. But between Mavis and Max and Dana and everybody else, your time was pretty much monopolized. So I figured I'd take you somewhere where they didn't want to go." Putting his arm around her shoulder, he said, "Now let's head back to the house. It's too cold to be out in this weather."

Max and Stacy left that afternoon after they'd been hugged and kissed by all of the family members. As soon as she settled into Max's car, Stacy felt a wave of exhaustion sweep over her, and she promptly fell asleep, awakening when Max gently nudged her awake to tell her they were home. He walked her inside and helped carry her bags, then kissed her on the cheek and left, promising to call the next day.

Chapter 14

The next morning, Stacy awoke on her couch. She remembered fixing a bowl of soup and turning on the television. *I must have been totally wiped out*, she thought as she looked around her living room. Sure enough, the television was still on and the bowl of soup sat on the coffee table, untouched.

Stacy was in the bathroom splashing water on her face, thankful she didn't have to work that weekend, when the phone rang. "Hello?" she said.

"It's me." The sound of Max's voice made Stacy's heart flip-flop. "Do you have a wedding today?"

She smiled. "No, not today. For once, nobody's getting married—at least no one that hired me to coordinate their wedding."

"Lucky you. I'm at the office getting caught up on work. Do you think we could see each other tonight?" asked Max.

"Of, course. I'd love to," she said. "I miss you."

"Already?" he laughed.

"Yes, already," she said.

"I miss you too," he said softly. "Can I pick you up at seven?"

"That's fine with me. How should I dress?"

"It's up to you," he said. "Casual is fine. I thought I'd cook for you tonight at my place."

"Why don't I save you a drive and meet you there?" she said. She enjoyed spending time with Max at his home.

"If you insist. I'll see you at seven then?"

"Seven o'clock." Stacy smiled.

After ending her conversation with Max, Stacy had breakfast, then went to check her computer. Things on the discussion group were pretty quiet, something she attributed to the holiday weekend. In fact, Sherlock hadn't even responded to her last message. In actuality, there wasn't much to respond to. The two of them had been bickering over nothing in particular up until the day Stacy left to visit Max's family. The book discussion was complete for the time being because the book had ended, but the story hadn't.

It seemed Archer Mason had decided to write this book in two parts, and on the last page of the book, the hero, Patrick Edger, was about to burst into the building where Jill was being held. The new book wasn't due to come out for three more weeks, so the discussion group had almost come to a standstill, since all anyone could do was speculate and nitpick.

Stacy was disappointed in the way the book had left everyone hanging, but she was glad she had gotten away for a little while and hadn't argued with Sherlock for a few days. She could barely remember why she had disliked him in the first place. Deep in her conscience was the growing feeling that she started as many arguments as he did. *I didn't mean to,* she mentally defended herself. *It was just all of that stress with Max and our relationship, then Viv. . .and. . .he shouldn't just go around picking on complete strangers.*

The discussion group had become almost addictive to her. *Maybe I can get a handle on the time I spend there and the things I say while we wait for the sequel,* she thought as she checked her E-mail. She had to admit, she appreciated having an Internet connection on her computer. After Maddy had gone back to school, Stacy, not wanting to get behind on the discussion, had gone out and bought a new computer for herself. Not only for the discussion, she convinced herself, but also to be able to keep in touch with Maddy and others by E-mail.

Six unread messages sat in her mailbox now. One from Maddy, one from Grandma, one from Leslie, and three others from old college friends. She read her E-mail, then went through her snail mail. Several catalogs had come, and she pondered the question of what to get Max for Christmas.

She knew he liked to read, but he'd never told her exactly what kind of books he liked. She thought about getting him the new Archer Mason when it came out. *Maybe we could read it together,* she thought excitedly. *Then again, I've never told him about the discussion group. I'll tell him eventually, but not now. He's got a computer at home and I wouldn't want him to join the discussion group and find out how I've been acting there.*

She stood up and headed to the shower. "Nope," she said aloud. "I'll have to get him something else. I wouldn't feel comfortable knowing that he could see all of the rude things I've written. Besides, it's not just that I feel embarrassed. He might get upset with Sherlock for the way he treats me, and there could be real trouble."

≈

Max scurried around his house, picking up odds and ends and throwing them in his room. He wasn't a messy housekeeper, but he wasn't extremely orderly either. Everything had a place, only the place wasn't permanent. If he put it there, then it stayed there until he needed it and put it someplace else. . .wherever was convenient. However, he wanted the place to look nice for Stacy, so he took extra care to tidy things up, as he always did when she visited.

He was in the study, tidying his desk, when he thought about the book discussion. Things had quieted down a little while everyone waited for the sequel, but still he couldn't seem to get along with Ms. Drew. He knew he started a great many of the arguments they had, but she also had the uncanny ability to strike out at him the worst when he was having problems in his relationship with Stacy. They'd been together as a couple since their reconciliation after the wedding, but it hadn't been all smooth sailing. Stacy was still learning to trust him, and it was aggravating when they had a misunderstanding.

Take, for example, when Viv showed up at Mom and Dad's, he thought. Those were the types of things that made her distrust him, adding to his stress level. Sometimes, it felt good to vent his frustrations at Ms. Drew. Remembering back to when she first joined the group, he realized he probably should have ignored her and the rivalry wouldn't have come so far. But then again, he had just met Stacy and was trying to find a way to get her to accept him. Ms. Drew had chosen the wrong time to challenge him.

He knew it was no excuse. Shaking his head, he said, "I need to grow up and stop taking my frustrations out on that woman, however annoying she may be. Lord, forgive me," he said. "Help me to be able to bite my tongue—or my fingers—when I feel the urge to lash out at her, no matter what she says to me. In Jesus' name, amen."

At that moment the doorbell rang, and Max went to answer it. On his way out of the study, Max grabbed the Archer Mason books that were on his desk and shoved them in a drawer. He knew Stacy liked to read, and under any other circumstances, he wouldn't have minded sharing some of his favorite books with her, but he needed them for reference, and Stacy had recently bought a computer. If she decided she wanted to join the discussion group, she might not be too happy if she caught wind of the way Max, as Sherlock, had treated Ms. Drew. It might be hard for her to trust him if she knew how rudely he sometimes acted. *I'll tell her about the discussion group after I'm positive I'm able to ignore Ms. Drew,* he thought as he opened the door for Stacy.

❦

"I love this one," said Courtney, fingering a long, lacy gown.

Stacy shook her head. "Too frilly."

"What about this one?" asked Viv.

Stacy inspected it closely, then said, "I don't think so. I'm not wild about the big bow in the back."

"Me either," agreed Courtney.

"Is anyone hungry?" asked Stacy. "It's two-thirty, and I haven't eaten since breakfast."

"Come on, just a few more minutes," said Viv.

"All right," said Stacy, a little reluctantly. "I've got to get at least some of my Christmas shopping done today."

Max was on a business trip over the weekend, and Stacy, Courtney, and Viv were out spending an afternoon together when they had wandered into a small bridal boutique. Stacy was ready to leave for two reasons. First of all, although she and Viv were getting to be good friends and had spent a few afternoons together, she wasn't sure how Viv would handle all this wedding talk. Viv had recovered from Thanksgiving, but Stacy had been careful ever since to not bring up subjects that might hurt Viv's feelings. Second, it had been Courtney's idea to visit this shop, and Stacy didn't know if her own emotions would hold up very well. She and Max had been nearly inseparable during the two weeks since Thanksgiving, but he hadn't given any indication he wanted to get married. . .at least any time soon.

He had confided that he still would like for their relationship to one day develop into a marriage but had never formally asked her to marry him. She knew in her heart that the minute he asked, she'd accept.

As she gazed around the shop, her heart ached. Weddings were her life, but those were weddings for others. She'd dreamed about her own for so long that it now felt as though all she would ever do was dream of getting married. Seriously shopping for a wedding dress without a proposal seemed like going shopping without a checkbook. It was a mean joke to play on her heart. *If Max would only propose. . .*

She ran her hand across the smooth, cool material of another gown and sighed. Courtney and Viv were on the other side of the shop putting on veils and giggling like two schoolgirls. It appeared that Viv was doing fine. "I guess I'm the one I was worried about," mused Stacy.

"You don't have to look so mournful," said Courtney, as she and Viv walked toward Stacy. Patting Stacy's shoulder, she added, "I'm sure he'll propose soon."

Viv nodded in agreement. "I know he loves you. He's just been single for so long. He wants to be sure." Then she winked and added, "And we both know his family adores you."

"I hope you're both right," said Stacy. "But let's not dwell on it right now. Let's eat."

Shortly after returning from his business trip, Max left a message on Stacy's machine to let her know he'd gotten back safely. They usually saw each other several times a week, and when they weren't together, they communicated by phone, sometimes several times a day, even if only just to say, "I love you."

After a quick dinner of canned soup, Max logged on to the discussion group to see what was going on. After a few moments of browsing around, Max could tell that no one was posting right now, but several messages had been posted while he was away.

> **Leslie:** *I can't wait for the sequel to be released. But I don't know how much time I'll have to read it. Christmas is only twelve days away (that's the figure my children gave me this morning), and I don't want to spend the holidays with my nose in a book.*

> **The Butler:** *I know what you mean. All of my children and their children will be here to visit me in a few days. Since my wife died, I really look*

forward to spending time with them. I don't want my grandkids to miss out on time with me because I'm reading a book.

George: *My sentiments exactly. I want to know how the story ends, but I've got a lot of family gatherings to go to this year, since my wife's got so many relatives and friends. At least I finally hired two more employees. Otherwise, I might have to close the store!*

Booknut: *I'm feeling thankful to be happily single right now, but how are you enjoying the married life?*

George: *I love being married. . .even though it's only been a month! But I don't think my wife will appreciate my deserting her during our first Christmas to read a book. In fact, it might cause problems. She thinks I spend way too much of my (limited) free time here anyway. I tried to get her to join in, but she's not interested in sci-fi. She only reads romance.*

Grandma: *Tell her we'd be glad to have her here.*

Flyer 87: *Don't tell me you guys want to disband the discussion group!*

Ms. Drew: *I don't think that's what they mean. I want to be in on the discussion too, but I've got a special someone I want to spend my holiday time with.*

Lizzy: **gasp* Nancy! You've never mentioned this guy before. Is it serious?*

Ms. Drew: *I'm hoping. He seems serious enough but still no proposal. But I'm staying optimistic. :) I've even been checking out some wedding dresses!*

Grandma: *I'm happy for you, Nancy.*

Flyer 87: *Since everyone seems to be pretty busy, why don't we restart the discussion January 2?*

Leslie: *You have my enthusiastic agreement!*

Ms. Drew: *Mine too. I hope Sherlock sees that we're postponing the discussion. I feel kind of sorry for him, though. From the way he usually acts, I don't think he has many friends. It would be terrible for him to have to go through the holidays alone—not even having anyone to argue with here.*

Lizzy: *Where has he been, anyway? I haven't seen a post from him since a few days before Thanksgiving.*

Ms. Drew: *I hope I didn't run him off.*

Booknut: *I doubt it. Maybe he's just busy. It's really odd, though, how you and he don't get along. He used to be such an amiable person.*

Ms. Drew: *You can't be blaming his attitude on me!*

The Butler: *I don't think Booknut meant any harm, but Sherlock was a lot nicer before you came. Then again, you never know. Maybe it was because none of us ever really challenged his theories. He was right all of the time, and we just agreed with him. Plus, shortly after you came, I remember his saying he was having some problems with his girlfriend.*

Grandma: *I really hope you'll be a little easier on the poor guy, Nancy. . . if he ever comes back.*

Ms. Drew: Of course I will. But if things go well over the holidays, I might not be here as much anyway. Then he can have the place all to himself again. But I have to add that even though I've had problems in my relationship, I didn't take it out on people in this group. We've worked things out with mature communication.

Leslie: Don't leave, Nancy. Just try to make peace with Sherlock. After all, it is Christmas. Uh-oh! Sorry, everyone, but now I've got to go make peace between a couple of my kids. I think I hear them fussing about a peanut butter sandwich. Talk to you all after Christmas!

Grandma: I guess I should go too. I've got cookies in the oven.

Ms. Drew: I guess I'm done for now too. See you after the holidays!

Booknut: Same here. I probably won't venture back here until the discussion starts.

George: You guys better order your books early. People have been placing orders like crazy for this book in my store! It's already a bestseller, and it's not even out yet.

Max rubbed his eyes. It was late and he was sleepy. It was good to see what everyone was thinking. But he didn't appreciate the pity party Ms. Drew had started for him. He didn't need their sympathy. *I'm not having problems in my relationship with Stacy. We're getting along just fine.* He sat in front of his computer. His fingers were itching to type a response. *If I tell them I'm doing fine, that wouldn't necessarily mean I was going back on my promise to the Lord that I wouldn't let Ms. Drew upset me.* After several minutes of contemplation, he typed this message:

Sherlock: To Everyone & Ms. Drew—I have not left the discussion group. In fact, I've ordered the book on-line and it should be here in a few days. But I am not having problems in my relationship with my girlfriend! I really don't appreciate the fact that you have all been talking about me behind my back. Ms. Drew did not "run me off"—she shouldn't flatter herself. It's just that I would much rather spend time with my sweet and caring girlfriend than argue with Ms. Drew. In fact, I am going to ask her to marry me really soon.

I am glad to know that Ms. Drew has found some other poor fellow to pick on. I sincerely hope for his sake that she doesn't trick him into proposing to her. Before she gets married, she needs to learn how to treat other people with respect. But if he does propose, I can't help but feel relieved that she will probably want to spend all of her free time bothering him, and then maybe we can get back to decent discussions around here. Merry Christmas, everyone—I won't return until the discussion begins again.

Max smiled with satisfaction. *I didn't address my post directly to Ms. Drew so I didn't break my promise. In fact, I think I handled that pretty well.* He turned the computer off and left his study. But in the back of his mind, he had the feeling that all he had really succeeded in doing was making himself a loophole in order to have the last word against Ms. Drew.

Chapter 15

The next morning was a Sunday, and Stacy was just finishing the last touches of her makeup when the doorbell rang. Max had come to pick her up for church. Since they both had their own churches, when they decided to attend church together, they had a hard time deciding whose church they would attend.

"Since we aren't engaged," Stacy had pointed out, "it doesn't make sense for either one of us to leave our church." So the two had decided for the present they would alternate between both churches. This was the week they would attend Max's church.

During the drive to church, Max seemed quiet and distracted. Stacy tried her best to keep the conversation going, but Max seemed almost determined not to converse. Finally, she gave up and remained quiet for the rest of the ride.

Something must have upset him on his trip. But he seemed fine when he called last night to let me know he'd gotten home, she argued with herself.

Before her thoughts could get any further, Max's voice interrupted. "We're here. I'll drop you off at the front door so you don't have to walk through the cold. Just wait for me in the foyer, okay?"

Stacy nodded and exited the car when Max stopped at the driveway in front of the church. Inside the foyer, Stacy chatted with some of the people she'd gotten to know during her previous visits at Max's church.

"Hi, Stacy!" Viv was smiling brightly and waving to get Stacy's attention.

"Hi!" Stacy replied.

Then, conspiratorially, Viv leaned closer to Stacy and whispered, "Did he ask yet?"

Stacy shook her head. "No, not yet. Maybe I was wrong to think he would ask so soon."

"Well," said Viv, "I'm sure it will only be a matter of time."

"A matter of time for what?" asked Max, coming to join them.

Startled, both women turned around and exchanged glances. *How much has he heard?* was the unspoken question on their faces.

Viv spoke first. "Never mind." Then she said, "This week I'm working in the nursery during the service, so I'll see you two later. And don't forget my Christmas Eve party before the service Wednesday night. You promised to come!"

At Max's church, each Sunday school class held a Christmas Eve party before meeting at the church for the Christmas Eve service. This year, Viv was hosting the singles' class party.

"We'll be there," said Max.

"Good," said Viv. Then, with a wink to Stacy, she turned and was gone, lost in the crowd of people who were milling around.

"Let's go and sit down," said Max, gently taking Stacy's arm and leading her into the sanctuary.

⤜

During the sermon, Max fought the urge to squirm in his seat. He'd had trouble sleeping after he'd written that post the evening before, and his discomfort had now turned into guilt.

Max listened as Pastor Winslow read the text for the sermon, Psalm 19:7–14: "The law of the Lord is perfect, converting the soul: the testimony of the Lord is sure, making wise the simple. The statutes of the Lord are right, rejoicing the heart: the commandment of the Lord is pure, enlightening the eyes. The fear of the Lord is clean, enduring forever: the judgments of the Lord are true and righteous altogether. More to be desired are they than gold, yea, than much fine gold: sweeter also than honey and the honeycomb. Moreover by them is thy servant warned: and in keeping of them there is great reward. Who can understand his errors? cleanse thou me from secret faults. Keep back thy servant also from presumptuous sins; let them not have dominion over me: then shall I be upright, and I shall be innocent from the great transgression. Let the words of my mouth, and the meditation of my heart, be acceptable in thy sight, O Lord, my strength, and my redeemer."

Max's stomach churned. He glanced at Stacy, who sat next to him. Feeling his eyes on her, she turned her head slightly and smiled at him. *Now that I have her trust, I can't even trust myself,* he thought. He read verses 13 and 14 again: "Keep back thy servant from presumptuous sins. . . . Let the words of my mouth, and the meditation of my heart, be acceptable in thy sight, O Lord."

Max was enveloped with guilt. *I've spent all this time arguing with Ms. Drew, and now I can't resist the temptation. Instead of being so arrogant, I should have found a way to be a good witness to her. Maybe she doesn't know how to be a Christian, but there's no excuse for me,* he told himself. *I have to go back and apologize. . .and this time, it has to be for real.*

He bowed his head and repented again, this time in earnest. When he finished, he felt as though a heavy load had been lifted off his shoulders. From now on, he would do what was pleasing in God's eyes in his dealings with Ms. Drew. *Who knows, I might even be able to lead her to Christ.*

Stacy glanced at Max questioningly, and Max realized he had spoken his last sentence aloud. "What did you say?" she asked.

"Never mind," said Max happily as he kissed her cheek.

⤜

After Max took her home, Stacy was restless. She used her nervous energy to clean her entire apartment from top to bottom, then had a quick lunch. After lunch, she tried to sit down and unwind but realized she still felt uneasy.

"Maybe I'm just tired," she said. She went to her room and changed into her pajamas, in preparation to take a short nap.

After getting settled into her bed, she tried to drift to sleep but tossed and turned instead. After half an hour, she got up and made some herbal tea. As she sat at the table, sipping her tea, she puzzled over Max. He had acted so oddly on the way to church, but halfway through the service, she'd sensed a transformation come over him. His whole demeanor had seemed different. He'd been peaceful and much more talkative on the way home. He was a different man. . . happier somehow.

I wish the same thing would happen to me. Strangely, she and Max seemed to have switched attitudes today. She'd felt fine on the way to church, but during the sermon, she'd felt this restlessness come over her and she'd been trying to shake it ever since. Her eyes wandered across the table and fell on her Bible. She grabbed it and flipped to the psalm Pastor Winslow had taught from that morning.

After reading the passage through very slowly, she reread verse 14: "Let the words of my mouth, and the meditation of my heart, be acceptable in thy sight, O Lord. . . ." She trailed off, thinking about some of the things she'd written on the book discussion group. She'd never have said those things to another person's face, but somehow knowing she was completely anonymous made her feel brave enough to say those things. Sherlock gave her the opportunity to get back at all the men she'd dated but never had the nerve to tell off. She'd heaped her frustration at others on him. . .in the privacy of her own home.

"So I could get up the next day and go to work and church and still be the same nice, sweet Stacy," she mused. Then she groaned, thinking of the things she'd thought about writing, but hadn't, because they were too awful to write, even anonymously. "I guess the meditations of my heart have been anything but pleasing, huh?" she asked herself. "Lord, I need to repent. . .and apologize to Sherlock too," she said, remembering the tart holiday greeting she'd left for him. Stacy bowed her head and began to pray.

Almost an hour later, after a heartfelt conversation with her heavenly Father, Stacy lifted her head and wiped her eyes again. She made her way to her computer and turned it on. Sure enough, Sherlock had apparently seen her posts. Last night, he'd addressed a message to the entire group, and just a few hours ago, he'd posted a message specifically to her. Stacy decided not to read either one. Right now, it would be too much of a temptation, she thought. Instead, she sat down and wrote a sincere apology.

Everyone will wonder why I'm being so nice, she thought as she typed. *They'll think I'm being impersonated! But from now on, I am going to be a good witness on this discussion group. When everyone comes back after Christmas, Ms. Drew will be a changed person.*

Chapter 16

Two days before Christmas, Max stood in the jeweler's, nervous. He was waiting for the sales clerk to ring up his purchase. He couldn't wait to see the look on Stacy's face when he pulled out the ring!

He mentally counted the months he'd known Stacy. Nearly seven. But he'd just left a covert meeting with Stacy's parents, and they'd given their blessing for him to ask Stacy to marry him. Yesterday, he'd phoned home to tell his own parents, and they were in agreement with Stacy's parents. He and Stacy were spending Christmas with her family, and he planned to ask her after Christmas dinner.

"Thank you, Sir," said the woman as she handed Max the small package. "Merry Christmas."

"Merry Christmas to you too," said Max.

<hr>

"I can't believe Christmas is in two days. It feels like I went back to school for the fall semester just a couple of weeks ago!" Maddy said excitedly as she and Stacy walked through the mall, doing some final shopping. "Do you think I should get something for Max, since he's spending Christmas with us?"

"I guess you could, if you wanted to. Mom and Dad got him a sweater. And yesterday I got a package from his parents and his sister Dana."

"What did they send?" Maddy questioned.

Stacy shrugged. "I don't know. Both packages are marked 'DO NOT OPEN UNTIL DECEMBER 25!' But I sent their gifts to them last week. I got Mavis a cake platter, and I bought Claude a jogging outfit."

"What did you get for Max?" asked Maddy.

Stacy hesitated, then said, "A scarf."

"That's all?" Maddy asked, incredulously.

"Well. . .and gloves too," said Stacy.

"Oh, come on! I thought you guys were more serious than that. Almost every time I called home this semester, Mom told me about how all of you went to dinner or the movies or something. How you guys call each other 'sweetie' and 'precious.' You're telling me all you got him was a scarf and gloves? What if he asks you to marry him or something?"

Stacy abruptly turned to face Maddy. "Why do you say that? Do you know something I don't know?"

"Actually, no," she admitted, truthfully. "But I guess I was kind of hoping. Wouldn't it be so romantic for him to propose to you on Christmas?"

"It would be perfect," Stacy agreed. "I know he's pretty serious, I just can't tell for sure how much so. He's hinted about marriage, but I'm not sure if he was joking. Viv and I had this same conversation last week," said Stacy, as she inspected a small figurine on a display shelf.

Maddy's jaw dropped. "The Viv from the wedding?"

"Yeah, we're on speaking terms now. Didn't I e-mail you about Thanksgiving?"

"Well, yeah, but. . .I thought you just made up with each other. I didn't know you two hung out."

"The first time she called me, I was a little surprised too, but actually she and Courtney and I have had some fun times together. She's really starting to heal, and I'm glad we've gotten to be friends."

"If you say so." Maddy shrugged. "But I'm happy if you're happy. I just wish we knew more about Max's intentions. Now that I have no indication that he and I might be related sometime soon, how about I get him a hat to go with that scarf and gloves?"

<hr />

Early Christmas Eve morning, Berniece Thompson came into Maddy's room. "Maddy." She gently shook her daughter. "Max is on the phone. He wants to talk to you."

"Me?" asked Maddy.

"Yes," said Berniece. "He wanted to know what would be a good gift idea for Stacy. I figured you might know some of her hobbies better than I do, so I told him he could ask you."

Groggily, Maddy sat up. "He's just shopping for Stacy on Christmas Eve?"

"Well. . ." Berniece bit her tongue. This gift was a decoy gift, something for Max to give Stacy tomorrow morning when all the gifts were exchanged. But if she told Maddy about the ring, she would probably let it slip to Stacy before Max had gotten the chance to propose. Instead, she shrugged. "Your father always shops for me at the last minute, and I don't mind."

"I would," said Maddy as she leaned over to reach the phone that sat next to her bed. Before she picked up, she asked, "How did you know that? He's always made Stacy and me promise not to tell you about his last-minute shopping."

"Intuition," said Berniece as she left the room.

Picking up the phone, Maddy said, "Hello?"

"Hi, it's Max," he greeted her. "Sorry to bother you so early in the morning, but I've got a question. What do you think Stacy would like for Christmas?"

"You couldn't think of anything to get her?" probed Maddy. "I thought you two were pretty serious."

"Well. . ."

"I guess you're not that close," said Maddy. "If you were, you'd know about those books she likes."

"What books?" asked Max.

"I can't remember the names. They're science fiction adventure types. This guy's written like twenty of them and she has them all. Except for the latest one. It's a sequel. The book just ended at a really exciting part, and now everyone has to wait for the sequel."

"Archer Mason?" asked Max, excitement rising in his voice. "I love those books!"

"Yeah, that's him. Mason. And the only one she doesn't have is the new one. But you waited so late, I don't think you'll have much luck. She dragged me all over yesterday trying to find a copy, but it was sold out everywhere."

"I got a copy of it last week. Maybe I could give her that one and get myself another one when it's back in stock."

A used book!? He's not one for special gifts, is he? But I guess Stacy doesn't mind. . . although she could probably do better. Guess that's love for you.

To Max, she said, "I'm sure she'd love it. She was pretty disappointed because she's in this book discussion group, and she doesn't want to be behind when they start the discussion up next week."

"Discussion group?" asked Max, his excitement fading slightly.

Maddy exhaled impatiently. "Boy, you guys don't know that much about each other. It's an Internet discussion group, and she's been in it for months. From what she tells me, the discussions can get pretty heated," said Maddy, slipping her feet into a pair of socks.

Max's mouth went dry. *It can't be the same discussion group.* He cleared his throat and tried to talk. "Hey. . .umm. . .do you know what her handle is?" he said, sounding hoarse.

"You mean the name she uses for the group?"

"Yeah," said Max, trying to sound casual.

"Umm. . .yeah. It's like Miss Marple or Agatha Christie. Maybe Angela Lansbury—one of those mystery solvers, you know? Maybe it was. . ." Maddy paused, thinking.

Trying to sound casual, Max said, "Nancy Drew?" then held his breath as he awaited the answer.

Maddy considered for a moment. "Yeah, I think that's it. Only I think it might actually be Ms. Drew. Stacy's awesome at solving mysteries. Funny, huh?"

"Hilarious," said Max, his stomach starting to churn. "Listen, Maddy, I've got to let you go. But don't mention this to Stacy. I want her to be surprised."

"No problem," said Maddy. "See you tomorrow." She hung up the phone and headed downstairs to find some breakfast. As she walked, she said to no one in particular, "I hope he doesn't feel bad when she gives him that nice scarf and gloves and he has to pull out an old book. I'm glad I only got him a hat."

❧

Stacy spent over an hour getting ready for Viv's Christmas party. After she showered and put on her makeup, she put on a long black skirt with a red holiday sweater. For fun, she added a pair of earrings that were shaped like Christmas tree ornaments. Slipping on a pair of black pumps, she looked at her watch. It was nearly five after seven, and Max had said he'd be there at seven. *It's a good thing Max is running late, otherwise, he'd have to wait for me to finish getting ready.*

Ten minutes later, Stacy was ready, but Max still hadn't arrived. To pass the time, Stacy put on another coat of lipstick and made sure her makeup was still in place. As she was finishing, she heard the doorbell ringing. "I'm coming," said Stacy.

Irritated, Stacy peeked out the peephole. It was Max. *He must be in a big hurry to stand there ringing the doorbell over and over again,* she decided. She opened the door and smiled. "I'm sorry I couldn't make it to the door in time. Do you want to come in for a minute?" she asked.

He shook his head. "No, let's go ahead and leave now. We're late." He sounded upset.

Wonder why he'd pick Christmas Eve to be in such an awful mood? Stacy grabbed her purse and coat and hurried out the door. The silence on the ride to Viv's was awful. *I wonder what's gotten into him? When I talked to him last night, he was fine. Tonight, he's barely speaking and didn't even kiss me,* thought Stacy.

When they arrived at Viv's, Max opened the car door for Stacy but didn't hold her arm the way he usually did as they walked to Viv's front door. Just before he reached out to knock on the door, Stacy stopped him. "Max, is everything okay? Are you upset with me for some reason?"

He stared at her for a moment, his eyes tinted with an emotion she couldn't read.

At that moment, the door opened, and Viv greeted them happily. Max immediately strode to the living room and joined some of the men in conversation. Stacy stood in the front entrance, puzzled. Viv looked at Max, then at Stacy. Then she squeezed Stacy's hand and said, "If you don't mind, I could use some help in the kitchen."

Stacy smiled and said, "As long as there are no chitlins involved, I'd be happy to help you." She followed Viv to the kitchen, turning to glance at Max. His back was to her, and Stacy felt like turning around and running home. She shook off the impulse and joined Viv and some of the other ladies from Max's church in the kitchen, arranging finger foods on trays.

As she worked, Stacy mulled over the whole situation. Apparently, Max was very upset for some reason, but he wouldn't say why. As she carried a plate of petit fours to Viv's table, Stacy decided she would act as though nothing was wrong. She would try to have a good time, and on the way home, she and Max would work things out.

When she made her way to the living room, she stood at Max's side. He treated her almost like a stranger. Stacy glanced at her watch. It was eight-thirty.

The party would only last for another couple of hours before everyone left and went to the church for the Christmas Eve service. Hopefully, she could make it through the party, but if things got too bad, she might be able to get Max to drop her off at home on his way to the church.

❦

Three hours later, Stacy felt pleased with herself. She'd made it through the party, and now she was at church, enjoying the Christmas Eve service. She had managed to ignore Max's strange attitude and actually had a good time, talking with many of the people from Max's Sunday school class. She looked at Max, who sat next to her. She wished she could make things right with him, but she didn't know what to say. She had racked her brain but couldn't remember anything she might have done to upset him. At this point, she felt like she deserved an apology from him.

She felt his eyes on her again, and she turned and looked him in the eye. His eyes were filled with a mixture of anger and hurt that made Stacy's heart ache. If only he would open up to her and explain what was really bothering him. Determined to help him, Stacy gently placed her hand over his, hoping to ease the tension.

Max stiffened and quickly pulled his hand away.

Stacy felt angry now. She had tried everything, and nothing was working. Max was acting like a spoiled child. She started rationalizing. She'd seen other men, clients of hers, act similarly when the time drew close to their weddings. Maybe Max really would propose soon, and he was just getting cold feet about popping the question. She hoped that was why he was acting so strangely. It didn't excuse his behavior, but it was easier to believe than thinking he was really angry about something else.

❦

Max could not believe how innocent Stacy was acting. No matter how angry he acted, she seemed to ignore him. She actually appeared to be having a good time, even though he was clearly upset. But it made sense. This was exactly how Ms. Drew treated him. He couldn't wait for this evening to end. He wanted to go home and have some time to himself.

Since his conversation with Maddy that morning, he'd been troubled. Not only was he upset at finding out who Ms. Drew really was, he was afraid of how she would react when she learned he was Sherlock. They had treated each other terribly, and though he'd sincerely apologized on Sunday, he didn't know if their love for each other could stand this blow. He couldn't figure out a way to broach the subject with Stacy, and she wasn't helping matters any. She laughed and talked at the party with his friends from his church, and now she was singing Christmas carols like she didn't have a care in the world.

Worst of all, he was the only one who knew about her charade. Everyone else saw her as Stacy, the nice, kind person she pretended to be. It was like Dr. Jekyll and Mr. Hyde. . .Stacy and Ms. Drew. His friends chatted jovially with Stacy but gave him questioning glances and whispered to him, "Lighten up." Apparently they too, had been taken in by the gentle, sweet side of Stacy and were miffed at him for his dark mood.

If they only knew Ms. Drew, thought Max. And he still had to get through tomorrow with her family. He wanted desperately to cancel, but he couldn't come up with a good enough excuse. He had no choice but to spend the day as he had planned, with Stacy and her relatives.

I assume they all know about Ms. Drew. After all, Maddy was the one who told me about it. Maybe they all think it's kind of funny. They probably laugh at me behind my back. He wished his own family could be there with him. At least he wouldn't feel so odd. Suddenly, he had an idea. He stood up to leave the sanctuary. When Stacy looked at him questioningly, he whispered, "I'll be right back."

Chapter 17

The next morning, Stacy sat in her parents' living room with Maddy. Unable to sleep after Max had taken her home, she'd called Maddy and told her she was coming over to spend the night—at least what was left of it. She'd gotten there at one in the morning, and after tossing and turning until five, she got up and got dressed for the day. Maddy followed suit, simply because Stacy was making too much noise for her to continue sleeping. Now, at seven, they were waiting for their dad's relatives to begin arriving for breakfast. Their parents were in the kitchen, along with their dad's parents, Grandpa Luke and Granny Rachel.

Stacy was wrapping up the end of her story to Maddy. "So then he jumps up and leaves the service. A few minutes later, he comes back with this really smug smile on his face."

"Weird," said Maddy.

"Tell me about it," agreed Stacy.

"So is he still coming over today?" Maddy wanted to know.

"As far as I know, he is. When he took me home, he said, 'See you tomorrow.'"

"Something is definitely weird with him, Stacy. Maybe he's just so in love with you that he's beside himself, and he can't act rationally."

"Where'd you get that line from? A movie?"

Maddy shook her head. "No, this girl in my dorm said men act like that sometimes."

Stacy rolled her eyes. "I wouldn't go to her for advice on a regular basis. She seems to dish it out with quite a dramatic flair."

After thinking for a moment, Maddy said, "Maybe he's jealous."

"Nope. Impossible. There's no one for him to be jealous of."

"That's true. You guys are really faithful to each other." Then, lowering her voice, she said, "Have you told Mom and Dad yet?"

Stacy shook her head. "No. I hate to worry them. Especially in front of Granny Rachel and Grandpa Luke. You know how they all love Max. So I just told her that at the last minute, I decided to spend the night here."

"Well, you'd better tell somebody something. There are going to be a lot more people over here besides Granny and Grandpa today, and if Max is still in a weird mood, everyone will notice. That would be uncomfortable. Then how would you feel? The whole family expects you two to eventually get married."

"I know," said Stacy. "But I just don't have the heart to—"

Berniece interrupted her, peeking her head into the room. "Stacy and Maddy,

I need your help in the dining room. Max just called and said his parents and two of his brothers and his sister Dana came to town last night. He wanted to know if he could bring them with him. I need you to set more places at the table."

"This could be something important," said Granny Rachel, winking at Berniece.

Stacy and Maddy looked at each other.

"What's wrong with you two?" asked Berniece. "Stacy, I thought you'd be excited."

"I am," said Stacy weakly.

"So get moving," said Berniece, handing her a stack of plates and flatware.

Once they were in the dining room, Maddy shook her head. "Uh-oh. This sounds pretty strange. Stacy, if I were you, I would not let that man and his family in the door. What if he just goes nuts right here in the dining room? What if his whole family goes nuts too?"

"He is not going to go nuts, and neither is his family," said Stacy, as she set the table. "His family probably just surprised him this morning, and since he didn't do any cooking, he wants to bring them here."

"And you believe that explanation?" asked Maddy.

"For right now, I have nothing else to believe," said Stacy.

An hour later, Stacy's family, her grandparents, her dad's three brothers, and their families, along with Max, Mavis, Claude, Dana, Albert, and Anthony, sat in the dining room, having breakfast.

Stacy had lost her appetite. She was seated next to Max, and he seemed like a different man than he'd been last night. He was kind to everyone, including Stacy. She cast a nervous glance in his direction, and he smiled at her. However, it wasn't his usual smile. Something in his eyes seemed to be mocking her. In the back of her mind she held tightly to the theory that he might be experiencing pre-proposal jitters.

Mavis and Claude, on the other hand, were warm but seemed to be a little confused. The same went for Dana and Albert and Anthony. Before breakfast, Dana quietly told Stacy that Max had called their parents late last night and told them it was important that they be here this morning. She and the twins had come along because Mavis didn't want Claude to drive in the snow.

Stacy looked around the table. Everyone seemed to be expecting something to happen. Except Max. He seemed calm and relaxed as he ate his breakfast. Stacy cut yet another piece of the waffle she had no intention of actually eating and sighed. Whatever he had up his sleeve, she hoped he'd go ahead and get it over with.

After breakfast, the family settled in the living room to exchange gifts before the women began preparing dinner. Usually, each family gave a gift to another family, and the members of the individual families exchanged gifts among themselves. This year, Stacy's family had gotten the other four families porcelain nativity scenes. They had also gotten one for Max's parents, and Stacy was glad her mother had wanted to give it to Max today, instead of just mailing it to his parents.

From their uncles' families, Stacy's family received a fruit basket, a lace tablecloth, and a beautiful crystal vase. Mavis and Claude had brought the gifts Stacy had sent them and thanked her excitedly when they opened them. Stacy was also relieved that she'd remembered to bring their gifts with her last night. Dana had gotten Stacy a photo album.

"I know it's kind of unusual," said Dana, "but you might be able to put wedding pictures in it and pictures of your kids and stuff." She smiled. "In fact, to start it off, I put our family photo on the front page," she said, flipping to show Stacy the picture.

Stacy's heart lifted a little as she considered the gift. *If they think Max and I are getting married, maybe they have an inside track as to what's going on.*

Stacy had gotten Dana an espresso machine and a pound of gourmet coffee. She had learned over Thanksgiving weekend that Dana was a coffee enthusiast. Dana loved her gift and hugged Stacy. "Thanks, Sis," she whispered.

Max's parents couldn't wait for Stacy to open their gift. "It's from the entire family," they said, "but it was our idea," added Mavis.

Stacy's heart pounded as everyone in the room watched her open the gift. It was a beautifully bound leather Bible with her name embossed in gold on the front. Stacy gasped. The name on the front of the Bible read "Stacy Edwards." Embarrassed and speechless, she looked to Mavis, hoping for an explanation.

Mavis was beside herself with happiness. "We took the liberty of changing the name a little early," she said. "In a few months, I doubt it'll matter. We also filled in the family tree side for our family," she said.

Everyone wanted to see the Bible, so Stacy passed it around. She nervously glanced at Max. He was staring at her, but not so angrily as he had last night. Instead, he looked almost wistful.

"Well, what did you get me?" Max was asking her. It was now time for Stacy and Max to exchange gifts. Wordlessly, Stacy handed him the package she'd wrapped for him. She felt bad that she hadn't thought to give everyone gifts with such deep meaning as the gifts she'd been given, and now she felt even worse that she'd only gotten Max a scarf and gloves. *But what was I supposed to get him? What I felt like giving him was a poster that said, "Yes! I'll marry you. . .if you would hurry up and ask." But that would hardly be appropriate.* A smile formed at the corners of her mouth.

Max made a big display of shaking his gift before he opened it. "It doesn't sound like coal, so I guess I've been a good boy this year," he said, to the amusement of everyone. He opened his gift and held up the contents of the box for everyone to see. Everyone smiled and nodded approvingly, but Stacy could tell they were a little disappointed. But it wasn't her fault that she hadn't gotten him a more meaningful gift. She hadn't wanted to buy something presumptuous and scare him off.

Then it was time for Max to give Stacy her gift. She could tell by the size of it that it wasn't an engagement ring—not that she had any definite reason to expect one. Once again, the room was silent as they waited for Stacy to open her gift. And Max had that same funny smile on his face again. Again, she reflected on the question of the state of his emotions. What if this gift was some kind of practical joke? The last thing she wanted to do was open a present to have something jump out at her or make some kind of weird noise. Her hands trembled as she carefully removed the wrapping paper. Her heart pounded and she could feel beads of perspiration forming on her forehead. Just as she removed the final layer of paper, Maddy jumped up and practically shouted, "If it catches on fire, run and throw it in the sink, Stace!"

Alarmed at the loudness of Maddy's voice, and the thought of a flaming gift, Stacy jumped and threw the gift down on the floor. Looking down at it, she noted it probably wasn't going to burst into flames, considering it hadn't already after the impact of being thrown so hard. Stacy and Maddy looked at each other for a moment, then Stacy forced a shaky laugh. She had to explain something quickly before everyone thought she and Maddy were crazy. Everyone had shocked looks on their faces, especially Granny Rachel.

"Ha, ha!" laughed Stacy, searching her mind for an explanation. "Don't be upset, everybody. It was just a little joke," she said, looking at Maddy pointedly.

"Oh. . .yeah, we just wanted to lighten up the mood a little," said Maddy as she sat down. "We didn't. . .really think it would catch on fire," she said, a little sheepishly.

One might have been able to hear a pin drop. . .despite the fact that Berniece and Kyle Thompson had plushly carpeted floors. Finally, Granny Rachel chuckled. Everyone else joined in tentatively, not really knowing what else to do. Max joined in and laughed heartily, easing the bewilderment of all in the room.

"I don't get these young people's jokes," Grandpa Luke loudly whispered to Rachel.

"Neither do I most of the time," she whispered back. "But just the same, I try to laugh so they don't think I'm a spoil sport."

Max leaned over, picked the gift up, and handed it to Stacy. "Why would I give a gift that catches on fire?" he asked. Leaning over to kiss her cheek, he whispered so only she could hear, "Is your conscience starting to burn?"

Everyone assumed Max's private comment was whispered words of a man in love to the woman he loves. They smiled approvingly and waited to see the gift.

Bewildered at Max's last comment, Stacy unwrapped the rest of the gift and found, to her relief, it was only a book. A book she really wanted, she noted happily, as she took a closer look. "Thank you, Max," she said, genuinely pleased. "I've been trying to find this book. . . ." She trailed off, seeing the look on his face.

Max cleared his throat to get everyone's attention.

Whatever he's planning to do, it's going to happen now, thought Stacy.

Everyone looked at him expectantly. He kept his voice lighthearted as he said, "We should probably excuse Stacy now so she can retreat to a quiet corner of the house to read the book. She needs to be sure and get every detail right so she can dazzle her book discussion friends with her sleuthing ability," he said, his voice tinged with sarcasm.

Stacy's jaw fell. So he's upset about the book discussion? But why? And who told him? She laughed nervously and began an apology. "Max, I didn't know it bothered you that I'm in a book discussion group. If I'd known you'd be this upset, I would have told you. . .honestly, I would have."

Max's eyes held Stacy's for a moment. Then he said, "I had every intention of proposing to you today, Stacy. But my Sherlock and your Ms. Drew can't make it through a book discussion, let alone a marriage."

Stacy trembled as the total depth of the situation hit her. While everyone except Max sat around looking confused, Stacy got up and left the room. She went outside and sat on the front porch. The chilly air did little to cool the burning embarrassment she felt. Seconds later, the door opened, and Max stepped out and sat next to her.

"You're Sherlock?" squeaked Stacy.

Chapter 18

Yes," said Max, looking down at the ground.

"Well!" snapped Stacy, anger flooding through her. "Did you have to go through all that? Couldn't you have at least just said it straight out?" Then she answered her own question. "But no, that would be totally uncharacteristic of you. You enjoy treating me like that. I wouldn't marry you if you begged me to!"

His eyes grew wet, then he looked away. Turning to face her again, he said, "I figured you'd see it that way. I guess that's it, then."

She shivered. "I guess so," she answered, staring at her shoes. She wanted to cry. Her perfect man was her worst enemy. The one who had listened to her dreams and shared his with her, the one who had kissed her and held her in his strong embrace, was the same one whom she'd argued with for the past several months. As she thought about it, she willed herself not to cry. It was one thing for Max to see her cry, but Sherlock wouldn't care if she was hurting. She glanced at Max. He appeared to be going through similar turmoil. It was pretty ironic, actually. She tried to fight back a smile but couldn't hold it in. Instead, it became a small giggle.

"So you do think it's funny?" Max asked softly.

Stacy looked up at him. His warm chocolate eyes were wet with unshed tears, and she could tell he had taken her smile as a personal insult. She touched his arm softly. "Max, I'm not laughing at you. I'm laughing at our inability to honestly communicate with each other. It's all there in the archived discussions for the whole world to see. I never knew that you were Sherlock, but it was still wrong of me to act like that, regardless of who you were. It's not funny, but it's kind of sad. Just think about it. The fact that two adults couldn't resolve problems effectively between the two of us. When we got upset, we went to our computers and took out our frustrations on complete strangers, who just happened to be us."

"You're right," said Max. "It was not very Christlike, and I'm sorry, I really am."

Stacy's eyes lit up with remembrance. "And I accept. And I apologize too. But didn't you read my apology?"

"What apology?"

"Sunday, after church, I posted an apology for you and the whole group. If you don't believe me, go and see for yourself."

His eyes narrowed. "That proves nothing to me. All it tells me is that you saw my apology and felt guilty, so you decided to apologize too."

"Your apology? When?" it was her turn to ask.

"The one I posted for you Sunday right after church," he said pointedly. He rubbed his chin. "And besides, how could you post an apology for me, but not read the one I left for you?"

Stacy thought for a moment, then remembered something. "I did see you had posted two messages. One on Saturday night and one Sunday a few hours before I posted. But," she hung her head, "I didn't even read it because I assumed it would be a mean note to get me back for all of the things I'd said a few days earlier. I didn't want to get upset by reading it and end up too angry to apologize."

"Stacy. . . ," Max began, "I just—" He was interrupted by the sound of the door opening once again.

This time it was Mavis. "It's pretty chilly out here," she said, shivering.

"Mom, you should be inside. You don't have a coat on," said Max gently.

"Neither do you, and neither does Stacy. I just wanted to let you know that we all cleared out of the room. Half of us are in the kitchen and the rest of us are watching football. So if you want to come inside and finish, you'll be able to have a private conversation without freezing." She gave them a long look, then went back inside.

"I think the den would be a lot warmer," said Stacy, standing. "Why don't we go in?"

Once they were inside, Stacy waited for Max to finish the statement he had begun.

Finally, he stood and began walking back and forth. Then he stopped pacing and spoke. "It looks like we made a pretty good mess of everyone's Christmas morning. Either that or we put on a great comedy routine." He smiled sarcastically.

"Max," Stacy said as she walked to where he stood. "I love you," she said quickly. Before he could answer she added, "I don't want our relationship to end. I want to spend the rest of my life with you. . .I want to be your wife. Can you find it in your heart to forgive me? The only reason I never told you about the book discussion is because I was too embarrassed for you to see the way I treated Sherlock. I knew you would find my attitude toward him unattractive."

She waited for him to speak, but he didn't. A few minutes later, she added, "But why didn't you ever tell me you were in on the discussion group? I have the right to feel just as misled as you."

"I guess for the same reason you didn't tell me. I didn't want you to think I would ever treat you like I treated Ms. Drew. So I hid it from you. At least I thought I did."

"Do you think you'll ever love me again?" Stacy ventured.

Max laughed hesitantly. "Stacy, I never stopped loving you. I love you now just as much as I did when I bought this ring." He pulled a small jewelry box out of his pocket and stared at it. "Every fiber of my body wants to ask you to marry me." Meeting Stacy's gaze, he said, "But I don't think we can honestly put all of this behind us right now. It wouldn't be fair to either one of us. I think we should just back off until we've had time to think more clearly."

"But for how long?" asked Stacy, feeling scared.

He shrugged. "As long as it takes."

"I don't need any more time, Max. I know that I love you. I've already put all this behind me," she said, waving her hand.

"Stacy. . ." He sighed wearily. "I guess I'm the one who needs more time. I've spent all of this time wanting to be different from other men you've dated, but I acted just as bad, even worse. How can we trust each other after all of this? I know I need time to think about it. Putting this behind us is easier said than done, and you have to understand that."

Stacy's shoulders slumped. "I know. As much as I care for you right now, I honestly can't say that I trust you one hundred percent."

"That's what I'm talking about," said Max. "If we got married tomorrow, we'd be doing ourselves a grave injustice. We need time to pray about this."

"You're right, but it still hurts. I want us to be the same as we were a few days ago, but so much has happened, I know that it's not realistic to act like nothing happened. I'll leave it up to you to contact me," she said, wiping a tear from her cheek. "I still love you. And I won't stop until you come to me and say that you can't ever love me again."

Max wiped her tears with his finger. "Stacy, don't cry. This is really the best thing for both of us. We shouldn't force ourselves to make a decision about this right now. We might regret it later. I'm just trying to protect both of us."

"From love?" she sobbed.

Once again, Max held her as she cried. This time, however, Stacy felt more than comfort. Stacy fought the stirrings of her heart that made her want to kiss him and inhaled the scent of his cologne as if it were the last time he would ever hold her in his arms. As she listened to his heart beat in time with her own, she knew she belonged with Max, but the shadow of doubt had crept into both of their hearts. She forced herself to pull away from him.

She looked him in the eye. "You'll let me know when you decide?" she asked.

"I will. And I'll understand if you want me to leave now," he added softly.

"No." She reached her hand toward him but quickly withdrew it. Fighting tears, she looked at the ceiling and said, "I think it would be best for everyone if you stayed."

"But will you be okay?" he wanted to know.

"I'll be worse if you leave right now," she said.

"Then I'll stay. But let's not make ourselves miserable. Why don't you help our moms in the kitchen, and I'll hang out with the men." He squeezed her hand and kissed her tenderly on the cheek. Then he left, leaving Stacy alone.

After a few minutes, Stacy finished crying again and headed to the kitchen. His kiss had given her hope, and she wouldn't stop hoping until he gave her reason to stop.

Over the course of the day, everyone's spirits gradually lifted, even Stacy's. Max was kind to her but steered clear of being alone with her. Everyone looked on sympathetically, but no one said anything concerning the matter. That night, before he left, Max whispered to Stacy, "I'll be in touch, okay?"

Stacy nodded and blinked back tears for what seemed like the millionth time that day, and then he was gone. *Maybe for good,* she thought sorrowfully.

Chapter 19

S tacy spent the rest of the weekend at home, praying that Max would forgive her. Monday morning, she dragged herself to work, but she continued to fret.

Finally, Courtney said, "Stacy, you can't possibly sell weddings to people with that kind of look on your face. I don't want to be insensitive, but I've been trying to cheer you ever since you called me Christmas evening. If you don't think you'll feel better any time soon, I'm asking you to go home and not come back until you're better. At least for the good of our business."

Stacy, speechless, bit back her anger. How could her best friend treat her like this? Then she realized Courtney was telling the truth. After a few long moments, she said, "You're right. I'm being immature about this whole thing—again. I'll take off the rest of the day, but I'll be back in the morning, good as new."

"That's the Stacy I know," said Courtney. Then she chewed her lip, embarrassed. "And I'm sorry if I sounded harsh. If anything, I guess I was upset with myself for not being able to cheer you up."

"It's okay," said Stacy as she hugged Courtney. "I needed it." On her way out the door, Stacy grabbed a stack of papers. "I'll do some work on the Lane-Forrester wedding while I'm at home."

"See you tomorrow then," Courtney said cheerily.

~

At home, Stacy worked feverishly trying to keep her mind off Max. She had thought about calling him several times since Christmas, but a voice in her heart told her to wait.

"But, Lord," Stacy complained, "I need something to do while I'm waiting. I hate to sound like a spoiled little kid, but I thought for sure You had sent Max to me to be my husband. I'm going nuts just sitting around doing nothing, waiting for Max to make up his mind. It feels so unproductive."

A few minutes later, a voice seemed to say, "It is unproductive to not be prepared. Why not plan your wedding?"

"Plan my wedding?" Stacy asked aloud. "Lord, was that You? Or am I working too hard. . .at planning weddings?"

Suddenly, Stacy remembered a Scripture her pastor had spoken about in Sunday's sermon: "They that were foolish took their lamps, and took no oil with them. But the wise took oil in their vessels with their lamps. . . . And while they went to buy, the bridegroom came; and they that were ready went in with him to the marriage: and the door was shut."

Stacy shook her head. "Lord, I hate to sound like I am seriously lacking in the faith department, but are You asking me to take that Scripture literally. . . ? I'm sorry, but I really don't think I can." She sighed and closed the ears of her heart, plunging into her work with urgency.

Late that night, still working, she dozed off. She dreamed she was at her own wedding, walking down the aisle to meet Max at the altar. It was the most joyous day of her life, and all of her family and friends were there, celebrating with her. Max had just lifted the veil to kiss her when she heard. . .the phone ringing?

Instantly, Stacy shook herself awake and ran to answer the phone.

"Hello?" she said, hoping to hear Max's voice.

"It's me, Courtney," the voice on the line said.

Stacy sighed, exposing her disappointment. "Hi, Courtney."

"I guess you were hoping it was Max," Courtney said.

"I guess I was," said Stacy. "But never mind. I'm trying to keep myself occupied. What's up?"

"Actually I was calling just to see how you were doing. And also to let you know that a ton of catalogs came in this afternoon. I've been watching them pile up for weeks and putting them aside to sort out later."

"Bridal catalogs?" asked Stacy, still thinking about her dream.

"Yeah, gowns, cakes, reception favors, invitations, honeymoon destinations, you name it." Courtney sighed. "I guess you wouldn't want the fun job of sorting through all of it."

Stacy bit her lip, considering the job. Then she remembered that Scripture: "The bridegroom came and they that were ready went in with him to the marriage and the door was shut."

There's that verse again, she thought. Then she spoke to Courtney. "You know what? I'll do it."

"You will?" asked Courtney. "I thought you hated tedious stuff like that."

Stacy shook her head. "I don't know. . . . Maybe tedious is what I need right now. I'll start on it in the morning."

"Good," Courtney sighed with relief. "I'll see you in the morning then."

❧

The next morning, Stacy attacked her job with newfound energy, trying to ignore the thought that she should start planning her own wedding. She kept note of things they could suggest to their clients and threw out things they already had or couldn't use. But by noon, she was tiring of this assignment.

Courtney offered to run to a nearby bagel shop for lunch, and Stacy gratefully accepted the offer. Twenty minutes later, Courtney returned with bagel sandwiches and one of Stacy's favorite treats, a double chocolate chip muffin, topped with a generous dusting of confectioner's sugar.

While she ate, Stacy flipped through the gown catalogs. "Maybe we should branch out, open a gown boutique," she mused aloud.

"Here?" asked Courtney, looking around the crowded showroom.

Stacy shrugged. "The people who own the toy shop next door are moving to a bigger location in a couple of months. We could lease that space and put the gowns there."

"I thought you said gowns would be too much trouble, keeping the stock current and all."

"I guess I'm reconsidering. Or maybe it's just the part of me that likes to play dress up that's doing the talking. Oh!" Stacy gasped. "It's the dress!"

"What dress?" Courtney asked, coming over to investigate.

"The dress I wore at my wedding!" said Stacy, holding up the page for Courtney to see.

"But you've never been married," Courtney rationalized.

"But I wore this last night," explained Stacy.

"You got married last night," Courtney stated wryly.

"Well. . .I dreamed I did," Stacy defended herself. "I was wearing this dress."

"Hmmm. You had good taste in your dream wedding," said Courtney as she examined the dress. It was a long, ivory charmeuse princess gown, overlaid with sheer organza with Alençon lace and tiny rhinestones. Sewn to the thin tank straps of the stunningly simple bodice were long bell sleeves of organza that were hemmed with fine satin ribbon.

"If you were wearing this dress," said Courtney, "I hope that I, as one of your bridesmaids, which I know I was, got to wear this dress." She pointed to an ankle-length gown made of a pale silvery crepe that glowed with a hint of pink. Dainty cap sleeves and an empire waist were accentuated with a satiny silver ribbon that circled the bodice and formed a tiny bow in the front.

Stacy looked at Courtney and laughed. "I'm sorry, but I guess I was being a little self-centered, it being my own wedding and all. I really don't remember what the bridesmaids were wearing. But," Stacy said, suddenly rising to check the big wall calendar they used to keep track of the weddings, "I promise you that on February 14, you will be wearing that dress as one of my bridesmaids."

Courtney laughed. "Stacy, what are you talking about?"

Stacy put her hands on her hips. "I'm saying that I'm getting married on February 14 and you can either help me plan the wedding or stand there laughing at me."

"But. . .but. . .who?" Courtney sputtered. "What are you going to do, run an ad in the paper for a husband?"

"Believe me, the thought has crossed my mind." She laughed. "But no, I'm pretty sure it'll be Max."

"So he called you last night?"

"Not exactly, but I think he'll come around. I can feel it." Her eyes were shining with excitement.

"Stacy, I know you're feeling a little strange, but even if he had called last night and proposed, Valentine's Day will be here in just a little less than two months. That's not much time to plan a wedding. And even if we could, what happens if Max decides he wants to end the relationship for good?"

Stacy turned to her friend. "You know the parable of the Ten Virgins?" she asked.

"Yeah. . . ," Courtney said slowly, waiting for an explanation.

"Well, I'm putting oil in my lamp."

"Stacy, I hate to tell you, but. . .you can't take that parable literally!"

"I know, but I think that last night the Lord impressed it on my heart to do this. I think that He wants me to take it literally. . .for right now, at least."

Courtney knew it would be useless to try to talk Stacy out of it. Instead, she said, "Okay, but if nothing happens, where will you stop? Ordering invitations, a cake, booking the church? If it falls through, they might try to send you to the nuthouse! Are you telling me that God promised that Max will propose to you if you plan this wedding?"

Stacy threw her hands in the air. "I don't know!" she laughed. "Actually, it wasn't so much a promise that Max would propose, but more like an urgency to be ready for whatever happens. Or. . .whomever." She paused, deep in thought. "I may never marry Max. But what if the man I'm supposed to marry comes along February 12 or 13 and I'm not ready? For the sake of my own faith, Courtney, I have to try. I guess I'll take it one day at a time and see where the Lord leads me. And I'm starting by finding a dress shop to order this dress for me."

❧

Max put down the phone and frowned. He'd just had a twenty-minute conversation with Stacy but never got around to saying what he really wanted to say. It had been nine days since he'd seen her, and he missed her terribly. This was their second phone conversation, both of which he'd initiated. It was strange to talk to her on the phone, because they could never really find a comfortable topic of conversation. She seemed to be holding something back, and he knew he was holding something back. A rather big something. If he told her about it, he felt he'd be forcing her to make a decision, and if he didn't tell her, he'd end up feeling like a chicken. But then again, it was pretty farfetched and presumptuous.

He got out his Bible and decided to spend more time in prayer. He wanted more than anything in the world to approach Stacy with this surprise, but he needed to know that his heavenly Father was in agreement. He would wait on Him before he proposed to Stacy.

One thing is for sure, Max noted as he glanced at his calendar. *I hope He answers me pretty soon.*

Chapter 20

Two weeks later, Stacy was tired. She was tired of work, but mostly she was tired of waiting for Max while she planned this one-sided wedding. Those who knew about the wedding, including her family, her co-workers, and Viv, had promised not to tell anyone else about her plans. She knew they all believed she was off her rocker, but she didn't care. . .except it was now the middle of January and the only communication she had with Max was his twenty-minute phone calls two or three times a week.

They talked about everything but their future and how they felt about each other. It was almost like they were just meeting and getting to know each other from the very beginning, except they both seemed to feel uneasy about the barrier that was between them. But she couldn't very well tell him about the wedding plans. He might ask her to marry him out of guilt.

At this point, she was beginning to doubt if she had really heard from the Lord. She hadn't gone near the discussion group, not even to read Max's apology, even though she'd been tempted to do so, just to feel some type of connection with him. She hadn't even responded to the E-mail Grandma and Lizzy had sent her because she didn't know how to explain what had happened.

"What do you think of this rose?" asked Courtney, interrupting Stacy's thoughts. The rose she held was creamy white, with a sheer veil of pink. It was long-stemmed and in full bloom, its petals healthy and succulent.

"It's gorgeous," said Stacy.

Excitedly, Courtney continued. "You realize you haven't chosen flowers yet, right? These would be perfect—not only for your bouquet, but for centerpieces, and floral arrangements, and. . . ," she paused dramatically, "they would be perfect accents to the cake you chose. Since the cake itself is so simple, we can have the baker use these roses to fill the spaces between the cake tiers."

"I guess we could," said Stacy dubiously.

"Is it my idea that you don't like, or. . ."

Stacy waved her hand, dismissing the statement. "No, I love the idea. It's perfect. I'm just getting cold feet about actually continuing these plans."

Courtney sat in one of the chairs in the office. "Okay, Stacy. You can't give up hope now. You've dragged the rest of us into it, and we're starting to really have fun. Maddy called and told me the dress we sent her fits perfectly, and Viv and I went for one of our final fittings yesterday. It's your dream wedding, Stacy, on Valentine's Day to boot! Everything is going so well, I'd have a hard time believing it's all a mistake. The colors are breathtaking—all of the white and pink and silver and ivory. And what about the fact that the wedding we had for that day was postponed until April? You know I'm right. It's been one miracle after another!"

Stacy stood up. "You're right. I need to stop being so worried." She leaned her head to one side, "Although, a miracle groom wouldn't be so bad right now." She held up a small envelope. "This is an invitation—with my and Max's names on it. I'm just waiting for a good reason to send these out. They're all addressed and they need to be sent within the next week or two. Later than that would be pushing it."

"Why don't you send one to Max?" Courtney suggested.

"I've been thinking about it," laughed Stacy. She looked at her watch. "It's about closing time. I'm going to stay late and finalize my order to the caterer. If you need to, you can go ahead and leave for the night."

"Thanks, Stacy. I'm exhausted." Courtney grabbed her coat and dug her keys out of her purse. "And don't worry about the roses. I've ordered more than enough. They'll be all over that church!"

"Thanks, Courtney," said Stacy. "Did I ever tell you you're my best friend?"

"Not nearly enough," she said as she turned and left.

Stacy worked for another hour and finally closed up shop. When she walked outside, the sun had just set, and a light snow was falling, adding another layer to the several inches that still covered the ground since Christmas. She shivered as she searched her purse for her keys. *I know I just locked the door to the shop, so I didn't leave them in the car.* Panicked, she set her purse down on the hood of her car and began pulling items out. She heard a car pull into the parking lot, but she wasn't frightened because many of the neighboring shops were still open and a steady stream of people was coming and going.

"Stacy," said the masculine voice behind her.

She recognized his voice instantly. "Max!" she gasped. Tears rose to her eyes. It had been so long since she'd actually seen him!

"I didn't expect you to cry." He smiled.

"I'm sorry, I just. . ." Stacy couldn't think of a word to say.

Max bent to pick up an object in the snow. He stood up smiling and dangled her keys in the air. "You just lost your keys?"

"Oh, thank you," she said reaching out for the keys.

He shook his head and put the keys in his pocket. "I don't think you can be trusted with these, Miss Thompson. I guess you're going to have to marry me so I can keep track of them for you." The look in his eyes grew more intense. "Stacy, I know what I want to say, but I don't really know how to say it. If you've been through one-tenth of what I've been through. . ." He rubbed his chin.

"I knew even on Christmas Day I wanted to marry you, but I felt like I owed it to you to give you time to think about the whole situation. I misled you about the discussion group too. Ever since I met you, I've wanted to spend the rest of my life with you, but my own insecurity kept leading me to believe that you were trying to get rid of me, you were just playing games with me.

"I blew my top when I found out you were Ms. Drew because I wanted you so badly, but I wasn't sure you felt the same. I could tell from your attitude on Christmas that you loved me and had already forgiven me, and I knew in my heart I'd forgiven you, but I was hesitant to go ahead and propose without giving us some time away from each other. I was really scared that you might say no. I wanted to leave myself a window of opportunity. Looking back on things, I made myself look really immature."

He took her hand and held it between his hands. "But now I'm asking you to be my wife. Forever." He stood silently, waiting for her response.

"Oh, Max," was all Stacy said as she flew into his open arms. She was where she belonged. . .finally.

A few minutes later, Max gently pulled back from their kiss and spoke. "Stacy, I know you're a wedding coordinator and all, and I don't want to force you to work a wedding miracle or anything, but. . ."

"Yes?" she asked, her eyes dancing.

"I've done something really impulsive and presumptuous." He shifted his weight from one foot to another, and Stacy could tell he was nervous. Finally, he blurted out, "I booked us on a honeymoon cruise."

"Max, that's not terrible. It sounds wonderful!" she squealed.

He shook his head. "The only problem is, we have to leave on February 15!" He shrugged his shoulders and put his hands in the air. "I really just called to find out some prices, and they started pitching me on this Valentine's Day package. Before I knew it, I had bought it, without even stopping to think about planning a wedding. It was such a good deal and I'm willing to get married at City Hall tomorrow morning, but I know you want a big wedding." He had a pitiful look on his face. "Do you think you could get your dream wedding together by then?" he asked quietly.

"Max Edwards," said Stacy. "You. . ."

He steeled himself for the coming argument. But instead, Stacy began laughing. She laughed for a good minute, until Max begged her to tell him what was so funny.

"Max Edwards," she said as she reached up to kiss him. "You are the most wonderful man I have ever met." Taking him by the hand, she led the way back to her shop. "If you think the cruise is something, let me show you what I've been up to!"

Epilogue

February 16

    To Grandma, The Butler, George, Flyer 87, Booknut, Leslie, and Lizzy: Sorry we haven't been around since the discussion picked up again. But don't worry, we're reading the sequel together. A funny thing happened on Christmas Day. We'll explain when we get back. Right now we have nine more days to enjoy before the end of our Caribbean honeymoon cruise! Thank you all for your friendship. We miss you all. Keep the discussion going for us.

Sincerely,
Sherlock and his new bride, Mrs. Drew–Sherlock
(no kidding—we got married!!!)

    Leslie: *Am I mistaken or did Sherlock and Ms. Drew. . .get married?*

    Grandma: *Now, that's the best ending I've seen in a long time. From the way those two carried on, I wouldn't have believed this even if I'd read to the end of the book!*

    Flyer 87: *I agree, Grandma. I guess you might say love itself is a mystery!*

    The Butler: *A mystery that the two best sleuths on this board couldn't figure out.*

    Booknut: *Nope, they never saw it coming!*

    Lizzy: *And I suppose you did?*

    Booknut: *I've been reading between the lines with those two, and it didn't take rocket science to see they were crazy about each other.*

    Lizzy: *READING between the lines?!!? To see that coming, you'd have to TYPE between the lines. There might have been some attraction there, but anyone could see this was more coincidental than anything else.*

    George: *Booknut and Lizzy—Better watch out! I hear wedding bells calling your names!*

THE WIFE
DEGREE

Chapter 1

Madison Thompson yawned, stretching out on the chaise lounge in her parents' sunroom. As the warm, cozy May sunshine spilled in from all sides, Maddy closed her eyes and considered taking a long, delicious nap. "After all, I deserve it," she said to herself. She'd just completed her last semester at Texas Southern University, and now she was back home in Kansas City for good.

She opened her eyes and sighed comfortably, pushing away the nagging feeling that she should really be unpacking all of the boxes she'd brought home from school yesterday evening.

Her eyelids were growing heavier by the moment, so she reached for one of her mom's comfy couch pillows and snuggled into position for a nap. The boxes could wait. . .the nap couldn't.

"Maddy?" her mother, Berniece, peeked in the room. "Dad and I are going to do a little shopping. We'll be back in a couple hours. Do you need anything?"

Maddy opened her eyes. "As long as you get back in time for dinner, I'll be fine. If you leave it up to me to cook, it'll be something like lunch meat sandwiches or canned soup," she laughed.

Her mom laughed too. "It's your dad who's the slowpoke shopper, but I'll try to get him to speed things up a little by reminding him that we have a hungry daughter waiting for dinner."

"Thanks, Mom. If the house seems really quiet when you get back, don't worry. I'll probably be in here sleeping."

"Thanks for the tip, but you're forgetting that we're used to it being quiet ever since you went away to school. The only time it's ever noisy anymore is when you're home on vacation."

"I guess you're going to have to get used to the noise again because it looks like I'm back for awhile," Maddy joked.

"Don't worry about us. We're as happy as can be right about now," Berniece said as she left the room.

Maddy closed her eyes again and listened to the garage door going up, then down. As the sound of her parents' car driving away grew faint, Maddy felt herself drifting to sleep.

Not even five minutes later, she heard a dog whimpering. She groaned and put the pillow over her head to mask the sound.

Much to her disappointment, the whimpering didn't stop but grew even louder. Maddy sat up and looked around. Apparently, the sunroom was too close to the great outdoors for her to get a decent nap. She stood up and decided to go to her room to finish the job she'd started. As she walked past the door that led out to the deck, a movement in the corner of her eye caught her attention. Startled, she turned to get a better look and saw a muddy golden retriever puppy with his paws on the door. When she moved closer, it began wagging its tail at a frenzied pace.

Maddy put her hand on the doorknob, then hesitated. She was not a big fan of pets of any kind, especially muddy ones. And her mother would not be happy if this little ball of energy got loose in her sunroom. Plus, it could be rabid or just plain mean. Maddy tilted her head and looked at the little dog again. He looked harmless, so she decided to slip outside and see if he had any type of identification she could use to return him to his owner.

Cautiously, she opened the door a crack and slid outside, keeping the puppy from getting inside. Then she knelt down and tried to get a look at his collar. "Calm down, you little mud puddle," she said as she reached for his neck. The dog jumped up and down, yipping excitedly.

Maddy sighed. "Well, I can't let you in my parents' house, and I can't take you home if you don't sit still."

As though he understood what she was saying, the puppy sat still long enough for Maddy to check his collar. Maddy checked once, then twice, but the results were the same. No tags. "A lot of good that did," she said.

She stood up and looked around, hoping to see the puppy's owner nearby. The puppy jumped up and left his muddy signature on her legs. She looked down at him. "Rule number one—keep your paws off my legs," she told him. The puppy sat down, tilted his head sideways, and lifted his floppy ears.

Maddy walked down the deck stairs and around to the front yard with the puppy at her heels. Mrs. Myston, a neighbor who lived across the street, was outside working on her flower beds. Maddy waited to make sure no cars were coming before she crossed the street, knowing her new friend was right behind her.

The puppy bounded across the street ahead of her and headed right to Mrs. Myston's newly planted impatiens. Mrs. Myston chased him away from the flower beds and said, "Oh, no, you don't. I just replanted the ones you dug up last week." She smiled at Maddy and said, "Hello, Madison. Your mother told me you were getting home some time this week. I saw you got in last night."

"I sure did, and I'm glad to be home for good." Maddy smiled. Mrs. Myston saw everything that happened on the block. She acted as though it were her job to know all the goings-on of the neighborhood.

Mrs. Myston returned her attention to the puppy, who was sitting still for the moment. She shook her head and exhaled. "Now why on earth did you bring him over here, Madison?"

Maddy put up her hands to plead her innocence. "I found him on our deck. I was wondering if you knew who he belongs to."

Mrs. Myston pointed across the street to the house next door to Maddy's. "The Sanders. Actually, he belongs to their son. . .you remember Jordan, don't you? The one who had all the girlfriends in high school." ·

Maddy nodded. *How can I forget him?* she thought. Jordan Sanders had been the only boy she'd ever truly had a crush on. She'd decided in the second grade that he was the most handsome boy she'd ever seen, and from then on, her infatuation had grown. To put it simply, he was tall, dark, and handsome. Years of playing basketball had produced muscles on top of muscles on his six-foot-three frame. His skin was a deeply bronzed shade of mahogany, and he'd always worn his hair so closely shaven that from a distance, he appeared to be bald. His face was almond-shaped, enhanced by a broad nose, full lips, and dark brown eyes. Maddy sighed. She hadn't seen him in at least two years, maybe even three, and she could still remember exactly what he looked like.

Yes, I remember Jordan, she silently answered Mrs. Myston. She'd spent the past few years trying *not* to think about him, alternating between hoping he would be there whenever she came home for vacation, and praying that she'd never have to face him and listen to his taunts again. She hadn't even been home a full twenty-four hours and Mrs. Myston was asking her if she remembered him.

Mrs. Myston continued. "But for some reason he seems to leave the puppy there an awful lot."

"So this is Jordan Sanders' dog?" Maddy asked, glancing at the puppy, who was happily digging in an empty flower bed.

"Um-hmm, and I wish he'd take it away from here. I've been chasing this little mischief-maker out of my yard for the last two weeks." Mrs. Myston smoothed a lock of silvery white hair away from her face, leaving a smudge of dark earth on her maple-colored forehead.

"Well, I guess I'll take him over there now. Sorry about your flowers, Mrs. Myston."

"I'll get over it, Madison."

Maddy smiled inwardly. For as long as she could remember, Mrs. Myston had insisted on calling everyone by their full name because she absolutely detested nicknames.

Maddy waved good-bye to the woman and beckoned for the puppy to follow her. "The party's over, Muddy. I'm taking you home."

"Just hope he doesn't think your yard is his new playground," Mrs. Myston said as she got down on her knees to continue working.

As Maddy stepped into the street, she turned around to make sure the puppy was still behind her. "Muddy, you shouldn't make life so hard for Mrs. Myston," she scolded. "She'd probably be really nice if you left her flowers alone." Maddy smiled as an old memory came back to her. "Although, I will admit that I used to get into a lot of trouble with her when I was younger. There's just something about her flower beds that makes you want to reach in and pick a few. But you're going to have to get your habit under control, otherwise—"

Maddy's speech was cut short as a dark blue SUV sped up the street and suddenly stopped in front of her house. The driver's side door opened and a very handsome man whom she instantly recognized as Jordan Sanders jumped out and looked straight at her. His shoulders had gotten a little broader and his skin was darker due to the sun, but everything else was the same.

Maddy's heart fluttered like it had back in high school whenever she'd seen him. *For once it looks like I have Jordan's total attention.*

"Where do you think you're going with my dog?" he asked abruptly as he stepped over to scoop up the puppy.

Maybe not his full attention, she thought. Maddy turned around and looked for the dognapper. Then she realized he was talking to her. "Excuse me?"

"I said, where are you taking my dog?" His forehead was wrinkled in accusation, and his crescent-shaped eyes narrowed to slits.

Maddy inhaled and exhaled while contemplating an answer. Putting her hands on her hips, she said, "For your information, I found your little trouble-maker on my back porch. He left his muddy paw prints on our back door and on my legs. In spite of that, I attempted to do the honorable thing by trying to find his owner. I took him across the street and while I was asking Mrs. Myston if she knew who he belonged to, he proceeded to dig up her flowers. At this very moment, I was taking him to your house, when you jumped out of your car and accused me of trying to steal him. If that's the thanks I get, then I'm sorry I didn't leave him on my back steps, whining and barking."

Jordan shifted from one foot to another. Several moments passed while he stared at her. Maddy grew uncomfortable, realizing he was probably thinking up one of his famous one-liners. The puppy whimpered and struggled to get down, but Jordan acted as though he didn't hear him. Mrs. Myston had abandoned any and all semblance of gardening and was now watching the confrontation with an amused look on her face.

Finally he opened his mouth and retorted, "For your information, this is my parents' house."

"Whatever, Jordan," said Maddy as she walked toward her house.

"Do I know you?" he asked, sounding confused.

Maddy rolled her eyes without even turning around. Her pride had just received a considerable blow, but if he didn't remember her, she wasn't going to make matters worse by trying to jog his memory. *What would I say?* she thought. *You remember. . .I live next door. You used to tease me and call me Madison the Librarian because I made good grades. When I was a sophomore and you were a senior, you told all your friends on the basketball team that I had a crush on you. They started writing me secret admirer notes that appeared to be from you, and when I approached you about it, everybody had a good laugh at my expense. I cried for a week. Now do you remember me?*

THE WIFE DEGREE

"No way am I bringing any of that up," Maddy grumbled. That particular memory never failed to sting a little, even a full six years later.

Just as she opened the front door, Jordan spoke up again. "Hey," he said, a note of surprise coloring his voice.

Maddy gathered up all of her courage and turned to look at him. A look of realization was spreading across his face.

"Madison?" he said, sounding very puzzled. He put the puppy down and jogged across her yard toward the door.

Maddy was flustered. *What does he want now? Is he really about to start teasing me again, after all this time?* Just as Jordan began walking up the porch steps, she slammed the door.

Chapter 2

Maddy sat down on the floor, put her hand over her mouth, and listened as Jordan rang the doorbell repeatedly. Right now she was about half a second away from a good cry. She'd been rude, and he probably felt pretty silly, but she didn't know what else to do. If nothing else, Mrs. Myston was probably being entertained.

She knew she couldn't ignore the ringing doorbell. Her conscience was pricking her and she realized she had to do something. She stood up and opened the door. Jordan stood on the porch, his finger still on the doorbell. He cleared his throat and shifted his weight back and forth. Maddy had never seen him look so unconfident. She glanced across the street and, sure enough, Mrs. Myston was unashamedly still watching.

"Um, Madison, I mean, Maddy, I. . .didn't recognize you. You must be taller or something. And you don't have your glasses anymore."

Maddy arched her eyebrows, waiting for the punch line. Confusion flickered in his fudge-colored eyes.

Jordan put his hand up, as if to stop her from saying anything. "Not that glasses are a bad thing. I wear contacts myself. So. . ."

"So?" Maddy said, waiting for him to finish.

"So. . .well. . ." Jordan shrugged and remained quiet.

"So. . .you're telling me that you can't make up the rest of the joke. Is that it?"

"No. . .Maddy, let me explain. I wasn't very mature back then, and I—" The phone began ringing.

"I'd better get that," said Maddy, reaching out to shut the door.

Jordan held out his hand to stop her. "Are you expecting an important call?" he asked.

"Well. . .maybe," Maddy hedged.

"Then I'll wait for you to answer it," he said in his usual confident voice.

Maddy opened her mouth to tell him to just come back later, but the strong set of his jaw told her he was determined to wait, so she hesitantly left the door open and walked into the living room to answer the phone. *I don't care if it's the wrong number. It's an important call as far as I'm concerned,* she decided.

"Hello?"

"Yes, my name is Arnold and I'm calling from American Best Long Distance Company," the voice said.

A sales call. Disappointed, Maddy hesitated, trying to decide what to do.

"Hello?" the man said again.

Maddy glanced toward the front door where Jordan was still waiting. *This is too convenient.* She smiled broadly. "Arnold!" she said happily. "I'm so glad you called." She smiled and paused, hoping it would appear to Jordan that this was an important call.

"Ma'am?" said Arnold, sounding puzzled.

"Arnold, would you hang on just a minute?" she asked pleasantly. "Someone is waiting for me at the door—"

"Excuse me?"

Maddy ignored his comment and continued. "No, no. . .no one important." She emphasized the last word and looked at Jordan, who was listening very carefully. "Just give me a second and I'll be right back." Maddy put the phone down and walked to the door.

"It looks like I need to take that call," she said.

"I guess so. I'll come back later," said Jordan.

Maddy just smiled. "Yes, that would probably be best for me."

"And Arnold, apparently," said Jordan.

"Who?" said Maddy, puzzled.

"On the phone," said Jordan.

"Oh, yes, Arnold. He's probably wondering what happened to me," she said.

"Then I'll come back later," said Jordan.

"You do that," Maddy muttered under her breath as she shut the door.

Relieved, she sat down on the floor once again and breathed a sigh of relief. "Saved by the bell," she murmured. Then she remembered Arnold. Maddy jumped up and ran to the phone, trying to figure out a way to explain all this to him. Hopefully she wouldn't have to change her parents' long distance provider just to make it up to him. When she reached the phone, she found that Arnold had hung up.

She chuckled. "I'll have to keep that technique in mind the next time someone calls trying to sell something I'm not interested in," she said.

She thought about Jordan again, and the tears she'd been trying to hold back started flowing from sheer emotional overload. Then the phone rang again. "Oh, no," said Maddy. Apparently Arnold didn't give up easily.

Maddy shut off her tears and picked up the phone. "Listen, Arnold, I can explain," she said in a rush.

"Um, Maddy, who's Arnold?" She recognized the voice of her older sister, Stacy.

"Oh, never mind, it's a long story."

"If you say so. You sound upset. Is everything okay?"

"Give me a few minutes to decide and I'll let you know," said Maddy.

"Okay. . . . So how's the new graduate?"

"Fine. Exactly like I was when you came to my graduation. How's the newly-wed?" she asked.

"Maddy, it's been three months. I'm not exactly a newlywed anymore," said Stacy.

"I personally would consider five years newlywed since you did promise to spend the rest of your lives together," said Maddy. "What's five measly months versus the rest of your life?"

"Whatever you say." Stacy laughed. "I'm not up for any philosophical arguments right now."

"Hmm. . .well, since you insist the honeymoon is over, is there anything I should know about?"

"I never said the honeymoon was over, so what in the world are you talking about?"

"Do I have to spell it out? I don't have a summer job yet, so if I need to start buying presents for, say, a niece or a nephew. . .I'll need a little advance notice, if you get my drift." Maddy smiled.

"No babies on the way, if that's what you're referring to." Stacy laughed. Then she grew serious. "But enough small talk. What's this Arnold business? And why do you sound like you've been crying?"

"What makes you think I've been crying?" Maddy tried to sound more cheerful.

"The same way I always know you've been crying. Your voice is all croaky. You sound like a frog."

"Thanks a lot, Stacy."

"So what's going on?" Stacy was insistent.

"I don't even know where to start." Maddy's voice began to waver.

"Then don't start now. Why don't you come over for dinner? Max is out of town on business and won't get back until tomorrow. Meanwhile, I'm desperate for company."

"Okay, that sounds like fun," said Maddy. "Just give me a few minutes to freshen up. I've got mud all over my legs, and I need a quick shower."

"Mud?" asked Stacy.

"I told you it is a long story, and you'll hear the whole thing when I get over there."

"I can't wait," said Stacy.

Maddy quickly got some clothes together and was just about to jump in the shower when the phone rang again.

"Hello?" she said.

"Maddy, it's me," said her mother. "Are you really hungry right now, or can your dad and I get a little more shopping done?"

"Hi, Mom. Shop all you want because I'm going to Stacy's for dinner."

"Oh. In that case, we might catch a movie or something."

"That's fine. Do you mind if I take the car?"

"Go right ahead. Oh, and Maddy, I forgot to tell you. Sometimes the

Sanders' puppy gets loose and sits on our porch. He can get pretty noisy, and I didn't want you to think he was an intruder. All you have to do is call them and they'll come get him."

"Don't worry, Mom. It already happened and I handled it just fine," she told her. Inwardly, she winced, dreading the thought of having to face Jordan again.

❧

"You played like you knew the phone salesman?" Stacy howled with laughter as Maddy related the events of the afternoon. The two of them were sitting on the couch in Stacy's family room before dinner.

"Well, I had no choice," Maddy said, failing to find it all quite so funny. "It was either stand there and be ridiculed again like in high school or find an excuse to make him leave."

"So what do you think he was going to say?"

Maddy shrugged. "Obviously nothing nice. He had that look on his face."

Stacy rolled her eyes playfully. "What look?"

"The look he always had when he was making fun of me. You know, the 'Maddy's-from-Mars-all-she-ever-does-is-read' look."

Stacy looked sheepish. "You remember all that stuff he used to say?"

"Yes, I do. Don't you?"

"Not really. I was already away at college by that time. All I really remember about Jordan is that he was the bad little kid who lived next door. I think he was a freshman when I was senior."

"But you knew that I had a crush on him for years. Even when I was in the second grade."

"Well, yeah. How could I not know? But you told me you were over that by the time he graduated and left for college. Besides, how can you fall in love in the second grade?"

Maddy rolled her eyes. "Okay, you have a point there. But I had a crush on him all through high school too."

"But when was the last time you saw him?" Stacy pressed.

Maddy shrugged. "I think two or three years ago. I was home on Christmas break." She wished Stacy would stop probing now, because she didn't want to admit what she thought she was feeling.

Stacy leaned forward. "You still like him? You haven't even seen him in two or three years."

Maddy grew defensive. "Of course not. But I am curious about what he's been doing since I last saw him."

Stacy put her hand on her forehead and reclined on the couch. "If you don't like him, then why are you so interested in what he's been doing?"

"I can't be curious about my neighbor?"

"You can be curious about your neighbor, but I don't think it's wise to be curious about an old crush who has a history of making fun of you."

"I guess you're right." Maddy was quiet for a moment, reflecting on what Stacy had said. It made perfect sense, but she was having a hard time ignoring all that had occurred. Then, she remembered something else. "Stacy, he didn't even recognize me!"

"So?"

"So?" Maddy stood up and did an imitation of a model on a runway. "That means I must look totally different to him."

"Is that a good thing?" Stacy lifted her eyebrows.

Maddy sat down, discouraged. "You are no fun, you know that?"

A timer went off in the kitchen. "What did you want me to say?" Stacy stood up. "I think the pasta's done. Come on in the kitchen and help me with the rest of dinner."

Maddy frowned. "Are you kidding? You know I don't cook. I'll wait right here for you."

Stacy playfully put her hands on her hips. "Shall I refresh your memory with the story of the Little Red Hen? Or do you want me to paraphrase my point directly from Scripture: If you don't work, you don't eat."

Maddy folded her arms. "Then I'll order pizza."

Stacy sighed. "Forget it. Just come in here and talk to me, at least," Stacy said, beckoning Maddy to follow her.

Maddy stood up slowly. "Fine. If you insist, Betty Crocker," she said sarcastically. "But the second you ask me to stir something, I'm back in the family room."

"Lord help the man you marry," said Stacy, as she opened a jar of spaghetti sauce.

"I'm not planning on getting married any time soon. I have a great career ahead of me, and when I do get married, I'm not going to be some man's cook, or laundry woman, or gardener, or secretary. We'll be equal partners," Maddy shot back.

"You can only be equal partners if you are willing to do things equally," Stacy said quietly.

"What are you implying?"

"I'm not implying. I'm saying that Max and I are equal partners, but we both cook. We both do laundry. We both do errands for each other. We're not experts at everything. He's better at laundry and I'm a better cook. You don't cook or do laundry. You don't have many domestic skills. How can you expect to be equal?"

Maddy frowned. Stacy could be so frustratingly bossy sometimes. The bad thing was, she was making a lot of sense right now. "Mom and Dad don't care," she retorted.

Stacy shook her head. "No, they just gave up after you flunked home ec."

"So? That was the only time I flunked anything. I made straight A's in all my math and science classes. Even physics and calculus."

"They just figured you would eventually come around. But I know Mom's concerned about it."

"Enough." Maddy put her hands over her ears. "I know I need to learn someday. And I will. Just not now."

Stacy shrugged.

Maddy grew uncomfortable because Stacy looked smug. But they had pretty much called a truce and she didn't want to push things, so she changed the subject. "So are you going to tell me what Jordan's been doing lately?"

"As far as I know, he graduated from art school in New Jersey a couple years ago. There was something about him almost getting kicked out of school, but I guess that all got cleared up."

"Kicked out? Who told you that?"

"Mrs. Myston. But I didn't let her go into all of the details. You know how she can get. Plus, I don't think she knew the whole story. I guess his parents didn't want to discuss it, and she was asking me if I knew what happened."

"Oh." Maddy understood. If Mrs. Myston didn't know the whole story, she would ask around until she found out. Maddy was actually a little surprised Mrs. Myston hadn't asked her about it. "So then what happened?" she asked Stacy.

"Then I heard he moved to New York and worked, but then decided to move back here six or seven months ago. I think he started his own business."

"Really? What does he do?"

"I don't know. Art, I guess. Someone told me he paints murals for people."

Now Maddy lifted her eyebrows. "Hmm, you seem to be on top of things. How do you know about this?"

"Well, Mrs. Myston told me about the college thing. And one of my clients who got married about two or three months ago filled me in on the rest. We were at the rehearsal and I asked if she knew who painted the murals on the walls in the hallways. She told me it was one of the guys who went to church there, and she mentioned his name. I told her he used to live next door to me, and she told me what I just told you."

"So Jordan goes to church now? Are you telling me he's a Christian?"

"I don't know. I assumed he was. And if you're even remotely interested in him, you'd better make sure he is before you start getting all emotionally entangled."

"Stacy." Maddy was sarcastic. "You sound like Mom." She paused, then continued. "Of course I'm not going to date a guy who's not a Christian."

"I just wanted to make sure before this whole thing went too far," Stacy said apologetically.

Maddy nodded and was silent a few moments. Then she spoke up again. "Stacy?"

"Yeeeessss?" Stacy singsonged, then sighed. "This subject is getting boring to me so let's wrap it up soon, okay?"

"Okay. My question is: Do you think I look prettier than I did in high school?"

"Maddy, you've always looked pretty to me. Since the day they brought you home from the hospital. A little wrinkly, but still pretty."

"No, Stacy, this is important. Don't give me a 'sister' answer. Tell me from a non-relative point of view."

"Okay." Stacy took a deep breath and looked at Maddy for a few minutes. "I guess the contacts make a difference. And. . .you're not so skinny anymore. You've gotten kind of curvy in the right places. But you're still short." Stacy's voice took on a teasing tone. "I hate to break it to you, but I don't think you'll ever hit five feet. You're still about half an inch too short."

"And I wear makeup every once in awhile, and I don't wear jeans and tennis shoes every day," Maddy finished. "I even own a few dresses that I like to wear."

"Yeah, I guess. So is this about Jordan?"

"Kind of. I think I was somewhat of a tomboy when I was younger. And in high school I was a total bookworm. So now maybe I've just blossomed, and Jordan finally sees me as a woman, instead of the skinny girl with glasses who lives next door and always has a book with her."

"Maybe he does, Maddy, but there's nothing wrong with any of those things. You were beautiful back then too. Jordan just didn't notice, so it was his loss, not yours."

"That's what you think."

"Fine," Stacy laughed. "Have it your way. But I'll tell you something else that used to get Jordan's attention."

"What?" Maddy smiled.

"Cookies. Homemade. The way to that man's heart was definitely through his stomach. Now tell me how you intend to remedy that? I think he might be a better cook than you."

"I don't need to remedy the situation. I see it as a perfect match. He'll cook, and I'll wash the dishes."

"Is that so?" Stacy teased.

"Yeah." Maddy wiggled her eyebrows up and down and stuck her tongue out.

"Then I'll let you brush up on your dishwashing skills after dinner."

Both women burst into giggles.

"But I'm warning you," said Maddy. "Don't use your best china unless you have rubber floors. You know I hold the record for the most broken dishes."

Chapter 3

Jordan Sanders sat in his parents' living room and looked out the window for probably the fifteenth time in fifteen minutes. He couldn't believe the beautiful woman he'd inadvertently started an argument with was Madison Thompson. Madison the midget, he'd called her in high school. That and a host of other names. He grimaced at the thought. She had grown maybe an inch since high school, but he was still well over a foot taller. Who would have guessed she'd turn out to be so. . .gorgeous?

Jordan closed his eyes and tried to remember what it was about her that had first caught his attention this afternoon. Everything. Her smooth, glowing skin reminded him of pure honey mixed with shimmering gold dust. Madison's round face was gently framed by dark, glossy hair that just brushed her shoulders and moved as gracefully as she did. Her hazel eyes had grown fiery and bright when she'd fussed at him about the puppy. He didn't remember ever noticing her eyes before. As he stood on her porch and tried to apologize, it seemed like she'd turned to stone. Her wide eyes grew cool, and he searched her round face in hopes of seeing the tiniest trace of emotion somewhere. He hadn't been 100 percent sure, but he thought her eyes seemed to be unusually wet, and it tore at his heart to think he might have made her cry. When had she stopped being the wiry kid with the glasses who had followed him around adoringly and blossomed into the woman with the round lips, softly curving figure, and the chip on her shoulder?

Five years ago, she'd had a huge crush on him. When he would leave on the weekends to go on dates, he would sometimes see her peeking out of a window. He hadn't cared back then and had laughed at her. Girls had lined up to go out with him, and Maddy had hardly been his type.

Now the tables had turned. Not only had he waited for her to come back so long he had missed the singles' Bible study at his church, but he was also literally staring out his window waiting for her return. She'd left over two hours ago; he'd told her he was coming back over. She obviously didn't care. It was a Friday evening and she was probably out on a date with Arnold, laughing at him.

I wonder how serious she and Arnold are? he thought.

"Jordan?" his mother called.

"I'm in the living room," he answered.

"Are you staying for dinner?" His mother entered the room and looked at him. "Are you okay? Why don't you turn the lights on?"

Jordan shook his head and stood up. "No, Mom, I don't think so. And I'm feeling fine. I'm just really tired."

"Well. . ." His mother stared at him doubtfully. "Are you sure? I made collard greens. . .and your dad and I can't eat them all. Why don't you take some home?"

"Nah, I'm not too hungry. But I'll probably be back tomorrow."

"Two days in a row? I might just have to bake a cake for you," she laughed. "To what do I owe this honor?"

He leaned down and kissed her on the cheek. "Mom, you act like I never come to visit. I'm here once or twice a week."

"I know. We just get lonely for you sometimes."

"Okay, okay. You'll see me tomorrow, and thanks again for keeping the puppy for me."

"You're welcome, but I have to tell you that dog gets into more trouble. It's only been a couple weeks, but the neighbors are starting to get upset. The next time you decide to impulsively buy a dog, please make sure there aren't any rules against having pets where you live."

Jordan sighed. "I'm really sorry about that, Mom. I hope he's not too much trouble for you and Dad. I'll be moving to a new apartment in another month or so, and then I'll take him with me."

His mother sighed dramatically. "Of course, we really don't mind having him around. Especially since he's the closest thing to a grandchild we have right now. We'll just shower all of our grandparently love on him for the time being."

Jordan laughed heartily. "Mom, I don't think 'grandparently' is a real word."

"Of course it isn't." She laughed. "I just needed to come up with something fast, and 'grandparently' was the only word I could think of to get my point across."

Jordan chuckled. "I've got to get home, but how about you and dad joining me at church on Sunday? We could go for brunch afterwards."

His mother sighed. "Honey, you know I'm glad that your religion seems to have helped you through. . .some difficult times in your life, but it's not for me right now. And you know how it upsets your father when you mention your being—" Jordan figured she was probably trying to think of a word besides "fanatical," as his dad liked to say. After several moments, she looked back toward the kitchen where his father was. With a pleading look in her eye, she shrugged. "You know what I mean," she said, lowering her voice.

Jordan lifted his eyebrows. "Saved?" he asked, vocalizing the word she couldn't bring herself to say. It was frustrating not being able to comfortably discuss his Christianity with his family.

His mother spoke slowly. "If that's what you want to call it. But, no, we won't be coming with you to church. We can still do the brunch if you'd like." She smiled hopefully.

Jordan's heart sank. This was the way it always went. If he invited his father to church, the conversation erupted into a bellowing lecture from his dad about Jordan being weak. If he asked his mother, she politely refused, citing that religion was "not for her."

Jordan walked to the door. "I'll let you know, okay? And please say good night to the puppy for me."

"We will. And Jordan?"

He turned around, ready to answer her question. "Yeah?"

"It would be nice if you would give the dog a name. We hate to go around just calling him 'puppy.' "

Jordan slapped his hand to his forehead. "I keep forgetting. I'll try to come up with something this week, okay?" He waved good-bye and headed out to his car, noting that no one seemed to be at home next door.

&

The next morning, Jordan got up bright and early in order to stop by Maddy's before he went to work. On his way there, he stopped by the grocery store and bought a card. As an afterthought, he also purchased a single yellow rose. He'd heard yellow roses symbolized friendship, and he wanted to give Maddy a token of peace. He pulled in front of her house, hoping his parents didn't get upset that he hadn't stopped in to see them first. As he walked up the driveway, he took a deep breath, hoping she would be in a better mood today.

He rang the doorbell and waited. Nothing happened, so he rang it again. Maybe they were all asleep. It was just a couple of minutes after seven, but it was also a Saturday morning. He'd hoped they might at least be stirring around. Apparently, they were still sleeping. Or maybe not. He fidgeted nervously and wondered if Maddy was still too upset to talk to him. For all he knew, she could be looking through the peephole and laughing at him. He shrugged and started walking toward his car.

He knew in his heart he was sorry for the way he'd acted years ago, and God knew too. If Maddy didn't want to hear his apology, then the Lord would just have to heal her heart without Jordan's help.

He'd only taken three steps away from the porch when he heard the front door swing open. Jordan turned to see Mrs. Thompson standing at the door in a fluffy periwinkle robe with a puzzled look on her face.

She covered her mouth to mask a yawn. "Jordan?" Mrs. Thompson blinked several times.

He cleared his throat. "Hi, Mrs. Thompson. Is Maddy home? I just wanted to talk to her for a second."

Berniece looked at him with a sharp expression on her face. He knew the look. It was a look of distrust, and he didn't blame her. He wouldn't trust himself either, if he were Maddy's mother or father.

They had politely endured his mischievous antics in grade school, and at that time had even been somewhat friendly to his parents. But when his high school years rolled around, which included his endless teasing of Maddy and the parade of girlfriends he collected, her parents had even stopped speaking to his parents, except for the customary neighborly wave and hello and good-bye.

He knew for a fact that since he and Maddy had gone to college, their parents had been able to take steps toward a friendship once again, although his parents complained that the Thompsons were too religious. He'd secretly been hoping that the Thompsons might be able to convince his parents to take steps toward salvation, and now he wondered if he might be messing things up again. It would hardly come as a shock to him if Maddy's mother decided to chew him out right here and now. He looked across the street. *And wouldn't you know it, Mrs. Myston is working in her flower beds at this hour of the morning,* he thought.

Beginning back when he was in the fourth grade and had developed a habit of running through her flower beds and immaculate yard, Mrs. Myston had warned Jordan about his getting a comeuppance for his deeds someday. However, that particular bad habit had ended by the ninth grade. But by then, she'd switched from harping about her yard to lecturing him about his reputation for having a different girlfriend every week or so. And though he never admitted it to her, the thought of being punished worried him, because punishment was something he heard about only from other kids or saw parents dish out to their children on television sitcoms.

Most adults and even some of his peers said he was spoiled because he was an only child, and not only did he agree with that, but he was proud of the fact. He had no siblings with which to play and therefore had no need to ever share anything. For the first seven or eight years of his life, he'd begged and pleaded for a little sister or brother, and his parents bought him toys to make up for the missing siblings. By the time he accepted the fact he would always be an only child, he decided it was for the best. He was the sole beneficiary of his parents' total attention, both emotional and monetary.

On occasion, he felt touches of loneliness, but there were always plenty of kids at any given time who were more than willing to put up with his selfishness and moodiness in order to play with his multitude of toys. When they grew too old for toys, the same kids wanted to ride in his new car, and girls didn't mind being seen with a guy who had a huge wardrobe of expensive clothing. And although he'd never had to share anything in his life, he'd learned that it paid to use his generous allowance to buy flowers and gifts for his dates. Back then, he never gave without the intention of being paid back.

He scratched his head and thought about Mrs. Myston again. He hadn't thought about her warnings in a long time, and he had pretty much gotten over the fear of what his punishment might be. But as it looked, in a matter of minutes, he *was* going to get his comeuppance. Mrs. Myston, who'd predicted there was going to be such retribution, had seen the first of it yesterday and would be fortunate enough to see part two this morning.

Mrs. Thompson looked beyond him and waved to Mrs. Myston. Then, to his surprise, she opened the door wider and waved him in. "I guess we overslept a little today, but I'll run up and see if Maddy is awake. Why don't you come in and wait in the living room."

Jordan hurried inside and stood in the entry hall, trying to think of something to say. For the second time in two days, he was speechless, and that in and of itself was somewhat terrifying. He'd lived most of his life possessing a back pocket full of quick, although not always polite, comebacks to everyone.

The more he'd let Jesus into his thought life, the more these answers seemed to evade him, which was a little refreshing sometimes, except when he was standing in someone's front entry hall, his mind racing but leaving his mouth at a loss for words. Mrs. Thompson looked down at the card and flower he held, reminding him that he still held them.

"It's for Maddy," was the only thing he could think of to say.

"Oh," she said, lifting her eyebrows slightly. When he didn't answer but merely nodded his head, she pointed toward the living room and said, "Why don't you go in there and have a seat. I'll go get Maddy." As he started to move to the living room, she turned and went up the stairs.

Jordan sat down on the oversized ivory sofa and looked around. He didn't remember actually ever having been inside the Thompsons' house. The color scheme consisted mainly of different shades of white complemented with varying hues of green, ranging from celadon to forest green. He suddenly felt underdressed and wished he'd worn something besides his old jeans and T-shirt. Soon after he'd started art school and begun to focus on his painting rather than dating, he'd given up expensive clothing in favor of clothes he could actually work in.

Still, it was a little unnerving to be on such unfamiliar turf wearing clothes that were really only suitable for getting paint splattered on them. He wished Maddy would just come downstairs so he could apologize and get it over with. *I wonder what's taking her so long?*

The thought occurred to him that Mrs. Thompson might have gone to get her husband to yell at him instead of going to wake Maddy. He guessed he probably deserved it. He also remembered his clothes had several paint stains on them and he began to wonder if, somehow, the stains might have gotten on the furniture. He quickly stood up and checked the sofa. It was as clean as a whistle. Just to be on the safe side, he decided to remain standing while he waited.

After almost ten minutes, he decided she wasn't going to come down and talk to him. And it didn't seem like anyone was going to inform him of Maddy's decision either. They were going to let him sweat it out. And he was already starting to do so.

Then an idea hit him. He could just leave the card and flower and she would see it when she was good and ready. He set the items on the end table next to the sofa and headed toward the front door. However, he underestimated the distance between his foot and the table leg, and as he turned to walk away, he tripped over the small round table, knocking it over, along with the phone that had rested on the tabletop and the items he'd just placed there.

At least they have wall-to-wall carpeting, Jordan thought. The table had merely made a muffled *thump*, but the phone seemed to fall a bit harder. Or it could have seemed loud only because he was so nervous. Jordan looked around, expecting one of the Thompsons to come running in. When they didn't, he set the table upright and placed the phone back on top. This was the same phone Maddy had picked up yesterday when Arnold called. As he put his card and the now-beginning-to-wilt rose back on the table, he wondered about Arnold. *What kind of name is Arnold, anyway? Somehow, I can't imagine Maddy being stuck with some guy named Arnold.* He shook the thoughts away. It was time to get out of here. He'd done his job. *So why am I standing here, staring at the Thompsons' phone, wondering what kind of guy Maddy's boyfriend is?*

"Ahem."

Jordan looked up and saw Maddy standing in the entrance of the room. She looked even prettier than she had yesterday, wearing a long turquoise sundress that complemented her brown skin. Now he realized why she'd taken so long. How thoughtless of him to barge in on a woman first thing in the morning. No way was she going to jump out of bed and run downstairs to see the man who'd made fun of her personal appearance for years.

He wished there was a way for him to tell her how attractive she was without putting her on the defensive or making her suspicious that he was up to something underhanded.

He took a deep breath and smiled. "I was beginning to wonder if you were going to come."

She smiled back, looking much more at ease than she had yesterday. "And I was beginning to wonder how our phone found its way to the floor."

"Oh." If it was possible for a man to blush, Jordan figured he would fit into that category at this moment. "I was just about to leave when I accidentally knocked the table over," he explained. "I didn't hear you coming."

Maddy laughed. Her laugh was as refreshing as a cool breeze, in contrast to the reception he'd been expecting. "I guess not, considering all of the noise you were making knocking things over."

"Sorry," was all Jordan said. *If only I could stop sweating,* he thought, as he reached up and casually wiped his forehead. Somehow, it felt strange for her to be teasing him. He was here, after all, to apologize for his own teasing. *Can't she cut me a little slack?* He wiped his forehead one more time and hoped she didn't notice.

"Well, here I am," she said cheerfully. "You look a little warm. Is it too hot in here? We could go outside."

Jordan looked toward the front door and thought about Mrs. Myston, who was probably waiting for him to get tossed out on his ear. He'd rather pour sweat in the Thompsons' living room than have Mrs. Myston witness what might be ahead. He shook his head. "I'm okay."

"Are you sure? We could go out to the sunroom. There aren't any gardening neighbors out there," she said.

Jordan laughed. This might not be so hard after all. Maddy had a pretty healthy sense of humor. And she apparently understood his not wanting Mrs. Myston to see and hear what he had to say. "The sunroom sounds great," he said.

Maddy turned and led the way past the family room, through the kitchen to the sunroom. Her parents were sitting in the breakfast nook, and when he smiled at them, they managed to smile back.

The entrance to the sunroom was in the kitchen. The back wall of the kitchen was a series of glass panels, and even though the kitchen and sunroom were two separate rooms, they were separated only by a wall of glass. He sighed, realizing he'd jumped from the frying pan into the fire. He didn't know what was worse, Mrs. Myston or Mr. and Mrs. Thompson. He swallowed hard and had the fleeting thought that the lump he'd just forced down was probably his pride. He stopped in the middle of the kitchen. Maddy opened the door to the sunroom and waited for him to follow.

Jordan stood his ground. *Since I have to do it, I might as well do it right,* he decided. "Actually, I can say what I have to say right here." Mr. and Mrs. Thompson looked at him with surprise and expectancy on their faces. He wiped his forehead again. Maybe he'd spoken too soon. He felt another lump build in his throat. Pride was a stubborn pill to swallow.

"We don't mind you using the sunroom," said Mrs. Thompson. She looked like she felt a little sorry for him.

"No." Jordan put his hands up to quell any further arguments. He made eye contact with Maddy and started talking before he lost his nerve. "Maddy, I just came over to apologize to you and your family about the way I used to tease you. I could make an excuse and say I didn't know better, but that wouldn't be the whole truth. My parents let me get away with a lot, but I knew in my heart that I was hurting your feelings. I became a Christian about three years ago and I knew the Lord didn't appreciate what I'd done." He shrugged. "I'm just sorry it took me so long to tell you." He quickly strode over to Maddy and handed her the flower and the card. She looked stunned. "And I'm sorry I yelled at you about my dog yesterday. I'd had a bad day at work, but it didn't make my actions right."

Maddy looked at the card and then at him.

"It–it's not a love note or anything," he stuttered. "I just wanted to write down how sorry I was and how I hope you'll forgive me."

Maddy nodded and solemnly said, "I forgive you."

Jordan sighed in relief. It was done. Except it felt like something in his heart had suddenly opened when she'd spoken to him. She had allowed him to come into her home and in spite of the past had managed to sincerely treat him with trust and understanding. With a sudden rush of unexplainable emotion, his heart felt relieved of a burden. *She's the one,* he thought.

Jordan pushed the thought away as he grew aware of an awkward silence that had settled in the room. It would be best for him to leave, but. . .he knew he had to do something in order to see her again. Only, with the apology being complete, he had absolutely no reason to see her again.

The reality of that thought was not very appealing. He took what felt like his hundredth deep breath in the last ten minutes and decided to plunge ahead and say what he felt like saying before he lost the nerve. "We don't have to talk ever again if you don't want to. But I would like to be your friend. The decision is up to you."

No one said anything. He figured he'd said too much. And he had the feeling he'd sounded incredibly. . .unmasculine. He hurried to get himself out of the hole he'd just dug. "But you don't have to say no or even yes right now. You can think about it, okay?"

"Okay," Maddy said slowly.

"So I guess I'd better go. I'm gonna be late for work," he said.

"Oh, I'm sorry," said Maddy. "I'll walk you to the door." She led the way and he silently followed. She opened the door and moved aside for him to leave.

He walked to his car feeling confused and a little embarrassed about his impulsive request. Was it asking too much to want not only forgiveness, but also friendship?

Jordan reached his car and opened the door with a heavy heart. Forgiveness was all he'd come for and he'd gotten it. Anything more he really didn't deserve from her.

As he pulled away, he casually glanced at the doorway and was surprised and encouraged to see her standing in the doorway waving to him. While he returned the wave, he prayed.

Thank You, Lord, for letting her forgive me. And if it's Your will, please let there be a way for me to be her friend. . .and eventually maybe more.

Chapter 4

Maddy stood in front of the mirror and eyed her reflection. Nervously, she smoothed nonexistent wrinkles out of her ankle-length, fuchsia matte jersey dress. She hoped she looked professional enough.

Today was her second interview for the position of computer instructor at the Ernst Mevlom day camp for teens who were academically advanced in the field of communications. She'd gone to the first interview during her spring break. During her second semester, she'd kept in touch with the head administrator, Mrs. Calvin, who had nearly promised her the job. This second interview was more of an open house for the board of directors and alumni teachers to meet those who had applied for teaching positions.

Still, she couldn't help but feel a little jittery. *What if they decide I'm not the person they're looking for?* Her sister, Stacy, had offered her a job working in the wedding planning business, but Maddy had done that last summer and the hours were erratic. Plus, she wanted her weekends to be more free, which was almost impossible in that line of work, since people seemed to always get married on weekends.

Taking deep breaths to calm down, she slipped on a light jacket over the dress and headed outside to her car.

As she put her seat belt on, she heard a tapping on her back window. Looking behind her, she was startled to see Jordan standing behind her car.

She smiled, happy that he'd come over to see her. It had been a little over a week since his apology, and she had been wondering if she'd even get a chance to really thank him. She had figured he had gotten too embarrassed and decided not to come over again.

While she rolled the window down, Jordan walked around to her side of the car. Maddy grinned. "I wondered if I'd see you again."

Jordan leaned down and looked into the car. "Well. . .I thought you might need a little time to think about it," he said. He smiled.

"So do you think nine days was enough time?" Maddy said in a teasing tone.

He lifted an eyebrow and said, "Why don't you tell me?"

"Hmm. . . ," said Maddy. She paused and waited to see his reaction.

Jordan's smile disappeared as he stood up and put his hands in his pockets.

"Actually, five minutes was enough time," replied Maddy. "I know it took a lot of courage for you to apologize like that, and I really appreciated it. And if the offer still stands, I can always use a friend."

"You're not just saying that?" asked Jordan.

Maddy shook her head. "No, I might have been pretty upset with you, but I wouldn't joke about something like that."

He grinned and playfully exaggerated wiping his brow.

Maddy cleared her throat and looked at her watch. It was a little after eight-thirty. "I hate to ruin this friendly moment and all, but I need to be somewhere in about twenty minutes, so. . . ," she trailed off, not quite knowing how she should end the conversation.

"Hey, sorry about that. I've actually got to be somewhere too. But if you're not busy later on, do you want to get together and do something tonight?"

Maddy's eyes widened. "Are you asking me out?"

He shrugged. "I guess so."

Maddy tilted her head to the side and lifted an eyebrow. "In what sense?"

"What do you mean?"

"In what sense are you asking me out? As in a date or as friends?"

Jordan considered for a few seconds. "As friends. Is that acceptable?"

Maddy smiled halfheartedly. "Sure. What time?"

"Is eight o'clock okay?"

"Yeah. Where are we going?"

"Actually, I don't know. This is all off the top of my head."

"Oh, really?"

"Um-hmm, but here's what we'll do. I'll tell you what I thought of tonight, and if you don't like my idea, you can pick something. Deal?"

"Deal." Maddy turned the key to start the ignition. "Now if you'll excuse me, I have to get to an interview."

Jordan stepped back to allow her room to leave. "I'll be praying for your interview to go well," he said.

"I can use it." Maddy laughed as she backed out of the driveway.

On her way to the interview, she replayed the scene between her and Jordan in her memory. She was happy about seeing Jordan again, but something about the whole conversation was gnawing at her thoughts. She really had figured he wouldn't come back, and she had even considered going over to his parents' house to find out how to get in touch with him, but since he'd come back today, she wouldn't have to go that route. And now, Jordan Sanders, her old crush and arch nemesis, had asked her out.

Although, she reasoned, *it's only a friendly date.* Maddy frowned. That was the part that bothered her. He had hesitated when she asked if it were a date. Sure, she wanted to be his friend, but her old feelings for him were more apparent, even after years of trying not to dwell on them. *I'd be so hurt if he really just wants to be my friend,* she thought.

Was he only doing this to further make amends for his actions in the past? She didn't want him to start regarding her as a pity case—someone he wouldn't normally be friends with but felt compelled to be nice to.

Maddy shook her head. *He has to feel something,* she told herself. *I just don't see Jordan Sanders as the type of guy to go out with someone he can't stand.*

As she pulled into the parking lot of the Mevlom Institute, she decided to stop worrying and spend the next few hours focusing on securing her job. As far as Jordan was concerned, she'd think about him later.

❧

Jordan placed the small square of fabric next to the strip of cardboard he'd just finished painting. He squinted for the umpteenth time, trying to determine if the shade of paint he'd just blended matched the fabric sample from his client's sofa. Judge Margaret Wilbrieg had requested a toned-down lime green as the main color of the abstract she'd hired Jordan to paint. So far, the paint stores had been unable to mix a color to suit Judge Wilbrieg's tastes. Jordan had stopped running from store to store and had spent the better part of the morning trying to mix the color himself.

Things were going slower than they probably should have since he'd been thinking about his conversation with Maddy. Was it his imagination or had disappointment shaded her face when he said he was asking her out as a friend? He wasn't sure. But he was inclined to chalk it up to his imagination, due to the fact that she obviously had a serious relationship with that guy Arnold. If anything, she was probably just making sure he had only feelings of friendship for her since she was already dating someone. In all likelihood, she was probably glad she didn't have to inform him that they could only be friends. Why should she be disappointed that he wanted to be just friends if she was happy with Arnold?

He walked around the room slowly, trying to see if the paint sample stayed true to the color of the fabric square in different lighting. As he walked, his thoughts strayed back to Maddy. *Is she really happy with Arnold? Of course she is. Remember the way she smiled when Arnold called her that day? She just accepted my invitation because she wanted to make me feel better about my apology. So we'll just go out as friends, and that'll be the end of it. She has Arnold, and I don't need to embarrass myself by trying to suggest anything more than friendship to her.*

At that moment, Judge Wilbrieg walked into the room. "Jordan, I'm heading to the office, and I'd appreciate it if you could get that color matched up sometime today. I want that mural to be done before my annual barbecue, and June 13 is only three weeks away."

Jordan held up the sample he'd been studying. "How does this look?"

Her eyes widened and she smiled with approval. "That's perfect. I'm so relieved that we have the color." She walked to the wall where the mural was to be painted. "I know at first I wanted it to be abstract, but now I've changed my mind. I still don't want it to be symmetrical, but maybe a little more sedate. Maybe some big sweeping strokes here, with a touch of some other color like marine blue or purple to fill in." She gestured excitedly as she spoke.

Jordan cleared his throat. "Okay. . .but are you sure you have time? Didn't you say you were heading to work?"

She shrugged. "In a minute, but first I want to take a look at the other colors again. I'm really starting to have second thoughts about the fuchsia."

Jordan sighed and tried to follow her rapid stream of suggestions on how he should paint the wall. Glancing at his watch, he noted it was just eleven o'clock. He couldn't remember a day when eight o'clock had seemed so far away.

⁓

It was a little after two o'clock when Maddy left the Mevlom Institute, her stomach growling slightly and her feet starting to ache. After she and the other applicants had watched a short film about the work of the institute, Mrs. Calvin had taken them on a tour of the massive building. After that came the informal brunch with the returning staff and the board of directors. After that, the board retreated to an office to interview each applicant again.

Maddy waited with the others outside the room while each applicant spent an average of half an hour in the interviews. While she waited, she had prayed to keep from getting too nervous. After their interviews, the other applicants each left until Maddy was the fourth and final one to be interviewed. She entered the room and tried her best to answer all the questions flung at her. She thought she had done well. The message she'd hoped to convey was the fact that she really felt she had a lot to offer both the institute and the teens at the Mevlom day camp.

They assured her they were impressed with her, but they had to choose carefully since they had only three positions to offer and four applicants to choose from. When her interview ended, Mrs. Calvin told her she would be contacting all of the applicants later in the day to inform them of the decision.

Maddy inhaled the fresh air, happy to be outside. She hoped she could find a way to occupy her time until she received a phone call from Mrs. Calvin. Hopefully, she would have good news for her. If not, it was back to weddings and those all-day work schedules on Saturdays. Maddy concentrated on selecting what she would wear tonight when she went out with Jordan.

When she pulled up to the house, she noticed Mrs. Myston outside in her garden. Jordan's puppy sat in her yard, watching her as she worked. After parking the car, Maddy walked over to Mrs. Myston.

"Hello, Madison," said Mrs. Myston.

"Hello, Mrs. Myston," she answered. Pointing toward the puppy, she remarked, "I see your little friend is back."

Mrs. Myston shook her head in exasperation. "The Sanders aren't home, so I can't get rid of him. Might as well keep an eye on him."

Maddy laughed. "It doesn't look like he's a threat to your garden anymore."

"That's what he wants you to think," replied the older woman. "He's just waiting for me to turn my back so he can undo what I've been doing out here."

Mrs. Myston glared at the puppy. The puppy tilted his head to the side and wagged his tail.

Maddy tried to hold back a smile. "So what are you going to do with him after you get done?"

Mrs. Myston shrugged. "I don't plan on leaving him out here, that's for sure. I guess I'll just keep on working until the Sanders get back."

Maddy grew concerned. The air was starting to get warm, and she didn't think it would be too healthy for Mrs. Myston to work in the sun for so long. Mrs. Myston's forehead was beaded with sweat and her skin was looking a little flushed.

Maddy looked at the puppy, and he gazed back at her with brown eyes. He stood up and trotted over to her. He tried to jump up on her legs, but Maddy backed away. This was why she had never wanted a pet. They were too messy. But she couldn't let Mrs. Myston stay outdoors for who knew how long until Jordan or his parents came to claim the puppy.

She took a deep breath and hoped she wouldn't regret what she was going to say. "It's getting pretty hot out here. Why don't you go inside and cool off? I'll watch the puppy for awhile."

Mrs. Myston's eyes lit up. "Thank you so much, Madison. I've been out here for almost two hours, and I didn't really know how much longer I could stay out here. I just hated to see my garden get torn up again."

"Well, it's not a problem, really. Since he's not too dirty, I'll just put him in the sunroom until Jordan comes. . . ." Maddy trailed off, realizing she'd inadvertently told Mrs. Myston that Jordan was coming over.

"I guess you and Jordan have everything worked out?" said Mrs. Myston.

Maddy didn't feel like answering a lot of personal questions about her relationship with Jordan. Mostly because there wasn't any relationship to discuss. Jordan had made it clear he wanted only to be her friend. Mrs. Myston would find out soon enough that Jordan wasn't romantically interested in Maddy. "I guess so," she said slowly.

"Going on a date tonight?" Mrs. Myston continued.

"Oh, no. . .just a little friendly get-together. But I should probably get home. I'm waiting to hear the results of an interview I had this morning, and you probably want to take a break."

"It is getting warm out here," Mrs. Myston agreed. "I'll talk to you later, Madison, and I hope you get the job."

"Thanks," said Maddy. She called the puppy and walked back to her house. She didn't want to risk him messing up something, so she led him to the sunroom by way of the backyard.

"Now, you've got to stay in here until Jordan comes," she told him. "And if you break something, don't think I won't make him pay for it." The puppy wagged his tail. When she turned to leave, the puppy started whimpering. *Oh, great. A whining puppy is not my idea of a good houseguest.* Maddy sat down and tried to think of a way to get him to be quiet. She had planned to take a short nap, but she didn't think she would be able to tolerate hearing him whimper for the next few hours. Then she noticed that he had grown quiet. "Good," she said, standing up. "I'll be back to check on you in a little while, and I meant what I said about you breaking stuff."

When she opened the door, the puppy started whimpering again. Maddy groaned. "Are you saying you want me to stay here?" The puppy wagged his tail. "I guess I could sit out here for a little while. Just let me go change my clothes." Maddy hurried to her room and changed. Sure enough, even upstairs, she could still hear the puppy loudly protesting the fact that she had left him alone.

On her way back to the sunroom she stopped in her mother's craft room and found her mother stenciling colorful animal designs on a small wooden footstool.

"Mom, I thought you might be in here. What are you up to?"

Her mother looked up. "I promised to paint six of these for the church nursery by Sunday."

"They look good so far," Maddy said as she glanced at two that were already finished. "I just got back from my interview, and I'm still waiting on a call to find out if I got the job."

"I'm sure you did fine. But what is that noise?"

"Oh, I volunteered to keep Jordan's puppy out of Mrs. Myston's flower beds until Jordan arrives or his parents get home."

Berniece nodded. "Just make sure you keep him in the sunroom. I saw Jordan stop you on your way out this morning," said Berniece. "Is everything okay?" Her mother's eyes crinkled with concern.

Maddy could hardly contain her smile. "It's better than okay, Mom. He asked me out."

Berniece smiled and looked relieved. "Well, that sounds like fun. I'm glad you two seem to be getting along."

Maddy nodded. "I'm just glad that he came over today. And he says that he's asked me out as a friend, so there's no pressure for us to decide if we really like each other, but I kind of think he might be slightly interested in more than friendship."

"Honey, the best thing I can tell you is to keep the Lord with you every step of the way. He knows how this will all turn out, and if you remember to ask Him before you make your decisions, He won't let you take a wrong turn." Berniece dipped her paintbrush in a container of water and swished it around.

"I know, Mom," Maddy said. She leaned over and kissed her mother's cheek. "But I've got to get back to that puppy before someone cites us for disturbing the peace."

Her mom chuckled. "He does seem to be getting louder. And tonight your dad and I are going out to dinner with Stacy and Max. You're welcome to come along. We'll probably be leaving around seven."

Maddy shook her head. "Sorry, Mom, but I already have a date with Jordan, remember?"

"That's right. If you have a change in plans, you can still come with us."

"Thanks, Mom," said Maddy. She turned and headed toward the sound of the barking and whining. As soon as she stepped into the sunroom, the dog instantly quieted.

Maddy grabbed the television remote and sank down on the couch, thankful for a moment of rest. She flipped the television to a news station and stretched out on the couch. The puppy sat right in front of the television, but Maddy didn't move him because he was too short to block her view. After a few minutes of stock quotes, the puppy was fast asleep, and Maddy felt herself drifting off to sleep. Just as she closed her eyes, the phone rang. Maddy sat up and grabbed the cordless from the coffee table.

"Hello?"

"Hello? Could I speak with Madison Thompson, please?" the woman on the other end asked.

"This is she."

"Madison, this is Mrs. Calvin at the Mevlom Institute. I just wanted to let you know that you got the job."

"Great! When do I start?"

"The camp doesn't start for two more weeks, but we have faculty orientation next week, starting Monday. We'll spend most of the time going over the curriculum so the teachers can get their lesson plans together. Just show up at the institute on Monday at nine, and we'll go from there."

"Thanks so much."

"We're glad to have you aboard. You have your work cut out for you." She laughed.

"I'm looking forward to it."

"Well, if you don't have any more questions, I'd better get to the rest of my calls."

"No, I'm fine for now. If I need to reach you before Monday. . ."

"Just give me a call here at the institute. If not, I'll see you Monday morning."

"All right." Maddy hung up the phone and reached down to pet the puppy, who had been awakened by the ringing of the phone. "You can go back to sleep now," she told him. Maddy yawned and stretched out again, then fell asleep.

An hour later, Maddy awoke to the sound of a ringing phone. Groggily, she opened her eyes and reached for the receiver. "Hello?"

"Maddy? This is Jordan."

"Oh." Maddy sat up, fully awake. "Hi. You'll never guess who I've been baby-sitting all afternoon."

"I give up," he said.

"Your puppy," Maddy answered. "And, by the way, you never told me his name."

"Oh, I'm sorry about that. Actually, he doesn't have a name yet."

"Oh, really?"

"Yeah, I've been trying to think of one, but nothing sounds good yet. No pets are allowed in my apartment, so my parents are keeping him until I can move somewhere else."

"Well, unfortunately for Mrs. Myston, your parents weren't home today. When I got home a few hours ago, she was planning to stay outside until someone came to get him, because she thought he would wreck her garden. I didn't think she should be out in the heat that long, so I took him for awhile."

Jordan sighed. "I'm really sorry to put you through all of this, but I'll take him to my parents' when I come tonight."

"That's fine with me. He hasn't been too much trouble so far. By the way, how should I dress for tonight?"

"That's the reason I was calling. I was having trouble thinking up something really fun to do, so I thought for tonight we could cook for ourselves and just talk for awhile."

Maddy felt her heart rate pick up suddenly, and she put her hand on her chest as if she would be able to still the thumping in her chest. "Cook?" she asked.

"Yeah. How about it? I'll bring the food and you supply the kitchen?"

Maddy considered what she should say. On the one hand, she didn't want to put his idea down, especially since he *had* said "for tonight." That implied that he might want to get together again, so she didn't want to offend him and ruin any chance she had of seeing him again. On the other hand, she didn't want to relive her home ec days either. They'd taken the class the same semester and he had used her kitchen mishaps as the topic of many jokes. Was he trying to embarrass her again, even after his big apology? Maddy shrugged. She might as well be up front with him and see what he would say.

"Actually, I'm not so sure about that, Jordan. I can't believe you've forgotten how bad I was in home ec. I don't think I've really progressed too far beyond that stage, so I don't think I would be much help to you, as far as dinner goes."

Jordan laughed heartily. "Oh, come on, Maddy. Everybody learns how to cook in college, if only of necessity. You can't be as bad as you were back then."

"I'm serious," Maddy said.

"I'm sure you're joking, but if it makes you feel any better, I'll do most of the cooking. I'll be the head chef and you can be my assistant. Is that better?"

"Okay. . . ," she relented. "But I'm telling you the truth. Just don't be surprised if I can't do too much," she said.

"Okay. Just have the kitchen ready, and I'll do the rest," he said.

"That sounds like a plan. What time should I expect you?"

"I'd say around six-thirty or so. We should be eating by eight, at the latest."

"Do you know what we're going to be cooking?" she asked.

"Not really. I'll just have to see what grabs my attention at the market," he said. "And will your parents be eating with us?"

"I don't think so," she said. "They're going out for dinner with my sister and her husband."

"Then I'll see you in a couple hours," he said before hanging up.

Maddy hung up the phone and tried to calm the nervousness that was rising in the pit of her stomach. "What have I gotten myself into?" she asked the puppy. He just wagged his tail and licked her toes. She sighed and reached down to pet his fluffy head. "Stacy was right," she told him. "I don't know the first thing about cooking, and Jordan's not going to be too impressed with that. Stay here and be quiet," she told the puppy. He seemed to understand and stretched out on the floor as if he were about to take another nap.

Maddy headed upstairs to ask her mother for advice. This time she found Berniece curled up in an overstuffed armchair reading a book.

"Mom?" said Maddy.

"Yes?" Berniece closed the book and looked at Maddy expectantly.

"I have a slight change of plans. Jordan's coming over tonight. He wants to cook."

Berniece nodded. "That's fine."

Maddy sat down on the floor next to the chair. "He wants me to *help* him cook. I don't cook."

"Just tell him you're a little rusty in that area. I'm sure he'll understand."

Maddy shook her head. "I tried, but he thinks that I'm exaggerating."

"Well, in that case, I think you're going to have to tough it out. Cooking's not that hard, as long as you follow the directions, you know." Berniece smiled. "And I don't think it's a really big deal. If you have a question, just ask him. I'm sure he's no gourmet chef. Just stick with the recipe and you'll be fine."

Maddy groaned in frustration. "I have a bad feeling about this."

Berniece laughed. "Just be honest and don't worry about it." She glanced at her watch and stood up. "It's almost four-thirty and I need to decide what I'm wearing tonight. And after all that painting today, I think my fingernails could use a coat of polish." She looked down at Maddy, who still sat on the floor. "Don't get too upset about it, Sweetie. If he really likes you, he's not going to care about you not learning how to cook. And if it still bothers you, it's never too late to learn. Think about it. With your computer work, you have to follow a lot of directions. Cooking's not that much different." Then she turned and headed to her bedroom.

Maddy stayed seated on the floor. *Maybe Mom is right. It's not too late for me to learn.* Feeling the effects of her newfound determination, she stood up and headed to her room to fix her hair and get dressed. While she waited for Jordan, she would look over her mother's cookbooks. *I'll try to at least familiarize myself with some cooking jargon.*

Chapter 5

Almost two hours later, Maddy was surrounded by cookbooks in the kitchen, when she heard the garage door open, signaling that her dad had gotten home from work. When he entered the kitchen, his eyes widened.

"Don't make any jokes, Dad," she warned playfully.

"Okay, I won't. But what's with all the cookbooks? Didn't Mom tell you that we're going out for dinner tonight?"

"You and Mom are, but I'm staying here because Jordan is coming over and I'm helping him cook dinner tonight."

Her dad arched an eyebrow and said, "Jordan?"

"Yes, Jordan."

"When is he coming?"

"He should be here in a few minutes."

Her dad laughed. "And you're trying to take a speed course in cooking before he gets here?"

Maddy shrugged. "Kind of, but it's pretty hard. I don't know if any of it is really sinking in." Before she could say more, the doorbell rang. "That's him," said Maddy. She quickly began putting the cookbooks back on the shelves.

"I'll get the door," said her dad. "Do you want me to stall him while you hide your textbooks?"

Maddy playfully rolled her eyes. "No, thanks, I'll be finished by the time he gets in here."

Her dad laughed even harder this time as he left to answer the door. "Even so, I'll walk really slowly," he called back to her.

Maddy finished putting the books up and looked over the kitchen. At least it was clean. *I might not be the greatest cook, but at least I know how to clean a kitchen.* She rested her hands on the island and tried to look casual as she waited for her dad to come back with Jordan. *Lord, please let him be planning to cook something relatively simple. . .like spaghetti.*

The two men entered the room, each carrying a brown paper bag of groceries.

"Hey, Maddy," said Jordan. Looking around the kitchen, he remarked, "I guess you're ready to get started."

"Ready as I'll ever be," she said, forcing herself to smile. Meanwhile, her stomach flipped while she wondered what type of cooking duty she would be given.

"I guess I'll let you two get started. I don't want to hold up the meal," said her dad as he set the bag on the island. He waved good-bye and left Maddy and Jordan in the kitchen.

Jordan set his bag down also. "When I pulled up, I saw the lights on at my parents' so I guess I'll take the puppy over there before we get started. Could you show me where he is?"

Maddy pointed to the sunroom. "He's out there. The door in there leads to the backyard."

"Thanks." Jordan walked toward the sunroom.

"Oh—what about the food? Should I put it somewhere? Like the cabinets or refrigerator?" Maddy asked him.

Jordan shrugged. "You can lay everything out, but I don't think you need to refrigerate anything, except the fruit and the yogurt, unless you really want to. We'll just pull it all back out, since we're about to get started."

"Oh," she said, feeling a little silly. "Right. I'll just lay everything out."

As soon as he left the room, Maddy began emptying the bags. First, she pulled out a couple tomatoes. *Good. Tomatoes are in spaghetti. Maybe I can pull this off after all.* Then she pulled out vinegar, olive oil, and a can of sun-dried tomatoes. Next, she found a can of artichokes, a jar of red peppers, cherry tomatoes, green onions, and garlic. *What's with all the tomatoes?* She was starting to worry. She'd emptied one bag and so far she hadn't seen any pasta or tomato sauce. Maybe it wasn't spaghetti after all.

She moved on to the next bag. There she found cherry juice, strawberries, raspberries, mozzarella cheese, vanilla yogurt, cranberry juice, a lemon, a loaf of sourdough bread, and cheese tortellini. Maddy suddenly felt tired. This was obviously beyond spaghetti. *How am I going to keep up?* She rubbed her aching temples.

Jordan came back through the door, carrying several assorted cuttings of green plants. He grinned. "Let's get started, because I'm starving." He handed Maddy the plants and said, "I guess you'll need to rinse them off. I just pulled them from my mom's garden." Looking around, he said, "I'll need a few pots and pans."

Maddy pointed to the cabinet where her mom kept all the cookware. While Jordan was busy getting a pot of water to boil, Maddy puzzled over the plants she was holding. *What an odd gift,* she thought. Never could she remember having received a bouquet of plants instead of flowers. But Jordan was not the average guy. He was an artist. . .so maybe he thought plants were nicer than flowers. *Still, it would have been nice to have a few flowers mixed in with these.* She leaned over to smell them and was pleasantly surprised. They were highly fragrant and almost smelled good enough to eat.

Smiling, she went over to the sink and rinsed them off as Jordan had directed. She also couldn't remember having to rinse off a bouquet of flowers. She ran the plants under some cool water and set them on the counter while she looked for a nice vase to set them in. A few moments later, she found a medium-sized vase and partially filled it with water. She looked in the pantry and found the aspirin her mother kept for flowers and crushed a couple. She added the aspirin to the water and then tried to arrange the plants to look pretty. After she was done, she stood back to admire her work. It was certainly unusual, but it would make a nice centerpiece for the table. She went to put the vase on the dining room table, then returned to the kitchen where Jordan was busily chopping the onions.

Mustering all of her courage, she asked, "What can I do?"

Jordan looked up from his work and smiled. "Let's see. How are you with vinaigrette?"

"Excuse me?" she asked.

"I need a tomato vinaigrette for this salad," he said.

"Oh. Well, just tell me what I need to do and I'll do my best. By the way, what are we making?"

Jordan laughed. "Sorry about that! I haven't even told you what we're having. For dinner we'll make a tortellini salad with tomato vinaigrette along with bruschetta with roasted peppers and mozzarella. For dessert, I thought we'd have fruit smoothies."

Maddy blinked. She hoped the panic she felt didn't show on her face. How in the world was she supposed to make a vinaigrette? "Wow. That sounds like something we'd have at a restaurant. I didn't know you were such a good cook."

"Well, I went to cooking school for two semesters in New York," he said. "And I also worked at a restaurant for a little while. So I can't say it came naturally."

"Now about this vinaigrette. . ." Maddy managed what she hoped was a lighthearted chuckle. "It's been awhile since I've made one, so you'll need to refresh my memory," she fibbed.

He handed her a grater and a bowl. "This is a tomato vinaigrette, so you'll need to cut the tomatoes in half and rub them over the grater until there's nothing left but the skin. Then add a little minced garlic, a couple of tablespoons of vinegar and olive oil, and whisk it together. Got it?"

Maddy nodded. "It's all coming back to me now." This she could handle. While she worked, she struck up a conversation. "So what do you do exactly?"

"I paint. Mostly murals." Jordan stirred the tortellini, then resumed slicing the roasted peppers. "Right now I'm working on three. Two for churches and one residential."

"So you must really enjoy it?" Maddy questioned. She slowly rubbed the tomato back and forth on the grater. Hopefully, if she went slowly enough, she would be able to do this for the entire time Jordan cooked.

"Oh yeah. I love it. Right now the ones in the churches are for a nursery and a Sunday school class. It's basically kind of a big Bible picture book theme."

"What about the residential one?"

Jordan sighed. "It's supposed to be a big abstract in really bright colors. The lady is having me paint a whole wall of her living room in neon colors."

Maddy's eyes widened. "Neon?"

"Yeah."

"You don't sound like you're enjoying that one too much."

"I guess I am. The problem is, she wants to tell me how to paint it. I think she would be more satisfied if I handed her the brush and let her do it herself." He laughed.

"How do you find work?"

"Sometimes by word of mouth, especially with the residential projects. Then I do a lot of advertising and handing out business cards wherever I go."

"Sounds like fun. So what's your next big project?"

"Actually, my next project is going to be the most exciting one I've done yet. I've been looking for a place to move where I can keep my dog, which was why I hadn't been able to get back over here sooner."

Maddy nodded. "Did you find a place?"

He grinned. "Actually, I was more successful than I'd expected to be. I'm trying to decide between three places."

"Are any of them near here?" she asked.

He shook his head. "No. I wouldn't be able to find what I want in south Kansas City. I've been looking downtown, near the City Market."

Maddy raised her eyebrows. "The City Market? What are you looking for? An old warehouse?"

Jordan's eyes lit up. "Pretty close. I've narrowed my choices down to three loft spaces downtown."

"Really?" she asked. "That's pretty interesting. For a long time I didn't even know we had loft space in Kansas City. It seems so. . .New York, or something."

"I know. I rented a loft when I lived there, but I didn't do too much to it in the decorating sense. But now that I'm getting settled here, I wanted to take a huge open area and really take the time to decorate it the way I want. So I've spent the last two or three weeks checking out different spaces, and I think I'm pretty close to making a decision. I'll probably move within the next month or two."

"That's pretty soon. Are you all packed?"

He laughed. "Not really. But I don't really have too much stuff. I could move with one truckload. I've been holding off buying a lot of furniture until I could find a more permanent place. And now, it looks like I'm almost there."

"Well, I've never been inside a loft, so once you get settled, you'll have to let me come over and take a look," she told him.

"I will," he said.

Her parents entered the kitchen. "Hi, Jordan," said her mother.

"Hello, Mrs. Thompson," he replied.

"Everything smells delicious. I hate to miss out on this," said her dad.

"We'll save you a taste," Jordan promised.

"We're headed over to meet Max and Stacy," said her mother. "We have the cell phone, so call if you need us."

"Okay," replied Maddy. Her parents glanced at her bowl of tomatoes with raised eyebrows but didn't comment before they left.

She and Jordan worked in silence for the next few minutes, until Jordan spoke up. "How's the vinaigrette coming?" he asked her.

"It's coming," she said brightly.

He turned to the stove, lifted the pot of tortellini, and carried it to the sink where he drained it, then rinsed it under running water.

Maddy completed her grated tomatoes. She couldn't remember how much oil and vinegar she was supposed to add, and Jordan was busy mixing the tortellini with the other ingredients he'd chopped, so she just guessed.

She remembered that Jordan hadn't used any measuring spoons or cups, so she decided to try to eyeball the measurements like he had done. She lifted the bottle of olive oil and poured a steady stream of it for about ten seconds. She stirred it, but it looked a little too thick to her. In addition, the oil kept separating from the tomatoes. When she added the vinegar, she put in twice as much vinegar as the oil, hoping to thin the mixture out a little. What resulted was a pink, blotchy mess that wouldn't blend together. In addition, the vinegar smell was really strong. She stirred vigorously, trying to make the oil blend in better.

A few moments later, Jordan looked up. "What's that smell?" he asked, his nose twitching.

Maddy's cheeks started to burn. She decided to act like she didn't understand what he was talking about. "I don't smell anything." She pointed to the area where he was working. "It might be the onions."

He sniffed. "No, it smells like vinegar," he said, looking toward her mixing bowl.

"Oh, that." Maddy swallowed. She covered the bowl slightly and turned away. "I just added the vinegar to my sauce."

"How much?" he said.

Maddy was at a loss for words. "Why don't you work on your dish and I'll work on mine." She abruptly turned and headed to the walk-in pantry, taking her bowl with her. In answer to his raised eyebrows, she said, "I need to add some of my special vinaigrette ingredients."

Once she was safely inside the pantry, she tried to decide what to do. Obviously, the vinegar was too strong. Should she add more tomatoes or try to tone down the vinegar some other way? She looked around frantically. *Maybe more olive oil.* She shook her head and tried to think what her mom would do if this happened. As she scanned the shelves, she had a dim memory of someone saying to put a potato in something if it got too salty. She found a potato and left the bowl in the pantry while she went back in the kitchen to rinse and slice it.

Quickly, she rinsed, sliced and chopped the potato, then added it to the mixture, wondering how long it would take to absorb the extra vinegar. She dipped a finger in the mixture and tasted it. It was so sour it burned her tongue. Making a face, she realized the potato was not going to be enough. As she scanned the shelves again, her eyes rested on a bag of sugar. *That should do the trick.* She quickly poured a generous amount of sugar into the bowl and stirred it. Now it was a grainy, pink liquid with big chunks of potato that still smelled like vinegar.

Maddy frowned. Even if the sugar cut the vinegary taste, Jordan would probably realize that it was too pink. She'd had tomato vinaigrette before and it was much redder. She looked around until she found a box containing small boxes of food coloring. One held a green liquid, another held blue, and two held a red liquid. Maddy grabbed one and poured in a fair amount of the reddish liquid. When she stirred it, it turned pinkish orange. "What in the world?" She looked at the bottles again, and realized she'd used the *yellow* dye instead of the red.

"Oh, great," she said. Then Jordan knocked on the door. "Maddy? Are you okay in there?"

"Um, yeah. I'm coming right out." Maddy opened the door and came out without her bowl.

"Where's the vinaigrette?" he asked. "I'm almost ready to put it on the salad."

"I'm leaving it in there for a few minutes. To let it sort of. . .mesh," she told him. "Is there anything else I can do?"

"You could work on the bruschetta. I've already made a spread, so you just slice the bread, put the spread on it, add a little mozzarella, and put it in the oven."

"I'll start on that now," she said.

"Oh, and Maddy, where are the herbs?"

"The what?"

"The herbs. You know, the basil, oregano, rosemary. . ." He looked at her expectantly.

"Oh. They're in the pantry. I'll bring them right out. You just stay right here." Maddy rushed to the pantry and quickly gathered several bottles of dried herbs. "Here they are," she said when she returned to the kitchen.

"Not these," he said.

"Not these?" she repeated.

He shook his head. "I was talking about the fresh ones I brought."

She looked at him blankly. "I don't know what you're talking about."

He laughed. "C'mon, Maddy. Don't joke with me. Remember, I brought over some fresh herbs from my mom's garden. I handed them to you."

Maddy gasped. "Oh, *those* herbs."

He nodded, grinning. "Yeah, those. Where are they?"

Maddy wanted to melt into the floor. So far, she'd ruined a vinaigrette and mistaken fresh herbs for a bouquet of greenery. She pointed toward the dining room. "They're in there," she said quietly. "On the table."

While Jordan went to get the plants, Maddy wondered how she would explain why she'd arranged fresh herbs in a vase.

Jordan came back a few seconds later with a grin on his face. "I got the herbs. And I must say, it's too bad we have to eat them, because they look so pretty like this," he said. "Can you tell me what this white stuff in the water is?"

Maddy wordlessly turned and went into the pantry. She grabbed the bowl of what had started out as vinaigrette and showed it to Jordan. "Okay. I have a confession. I've never made a vinaigrette. In fact, I can't cook. The only work I ever do in a kitchen is washing dishes."

"And the herbs?" he asked.

Maddy closed her eyes. "I thought they were a gift for me. Like flowers, except without. . .any flowers. So I put some aspirin in the water to help keep them alive. I didn't realize what they were."

Jordan appeared to be trying to refrain from laughing for a few seconds. Then he finally said something. "Don't feel bad. Anyone can make a mistake," he told her.

"You're not going to tease me about this?" she asked.

"Not the way I would have in high school. I can't promise you I won't crack a few smiles over it. I can't even promise that I'll never mention it again, but I won't do it in a mean way."

"Okay," said Maddy. "What do we do about the vinaigrette?"

"It looks like I'll start over. And you can just. . .watch." He leaned over and stirred the mixture in the bowl. "I'm not even going to ask what's in there."

"Good. Because I wouldn't tell you anyway," she said firmly.

"Listen, I'm going to run over to my parents' and grab some more herbs. You just wait here, okay?"

"Okay." Maddy sat down on one of the stools that her mom kept at the counter, while Jordan opened the door.

"Don't cook anything while I'm gone," he called over his shoulder.

❧

Jordan chuckled as he snipped herbs for the second time that evening. Maddy had been so cute, trying to impress him with her cooking skills. He was just glad she hadn't tried to act like nothing was wrong and asked him to eat it, because he didn't think he would have been able to swallow it.

He had figured something was going wrong when he had started smelling the excess vinegar that she had very liberally poured into the bowl, but he didn't know what she could have done to it while she was in the pantry. By the time she shut herself in the small room and then tried to slip out to rinse off a potato, he'd had to bite his tongue to keep from making a joke that might have hurt her feelings.

He had to walk a fine line in his newly cultivated friendship with Maddy for two reasons. Even though most of his friends knew him as a really easygoing guy with a penchant for humor, he still had trouble deciding what type of jokes were funny and what cracks were mean. When he was younger, it hadn't mattered— he had just wanted to get a laugh. But now that he was a Christian, he was keenly aware of the fact that at the end of his life, he would have to answer to the Lord for everything he had done, thought, and spoken. And he didn't want to stand at the door to heaven trying to explain away some of the harsher humor he had let slip out. Secondly, with Maddy, the last thing he wanted to do was verbally tear her down. If anything, he wanted to build her up, to help her see how special she was. She seemed unsure of herself sometimes, and he wondered if any of his teasing in high school had an effect on how she viewed herself.

Too many times he saw someone he had gone to high school with, and during the conversation, the person would tense up, trying to brace himself for more teasing. Five years ago he might have said, "It's just a joke. Lighten up a little." But he'd experienced an event that had taught him what kind of damage verbal abuse could do. And it didn't have to be done in a mean-spirited way. Jokes could scar a person's soul just as badly as a loud, angry tirade spewn forth by an abusive bully.

Harper Blackston. The name came to his mind out of nowhere. . .and everywhere. Reflexively, Jordan squeezed his hands into fists, his fingernails digging into the flesh of his palms. The name was one he'd tried to erase from his memory, and yet it somehow had seared itself into everything that he did. He couldn't forget it. He couldn't hide it. He couldn't escape it. Jordan stood up so fast that he felt dizzy for a second. He put his hand on his forehead and wiped away beads of sweat.

"Therefore, there is now no condemnation for those who are in Christ Jesus," he whispered. Romans 8:1 had been the first Bible verse he had learned, and the one that he now leaned on the most.

The man who led him to Christ had shown him that verse, and Jordan prayed the prayer of salvation because he liked the hope the verse offered. In fact, it had been one of the main reasons he had accepted Christ. He hadn't become a Christian simply to gain entrance into heaven after he died, or even to be able to worship at Christ's throne for all eternity, because those things had not even entered his mind at the time.

Instead he had taken hold of salvation because he had experienced a fleeting moment of reality. Frankly, he had had to admit to himself that he knew very little when it came to matters of eternity, and he'd been scared. But Jordan had been in awe of the fact that God wanted to grant man forgiveness so much that He let His only Son be the sacrifice for all of man's sins, both reckless and premeditated. Since the forgiveness was his for the asking, Jordan had eagerly asked and received.

Almost ironically, his faith in the truth of that verse was put to the test. And for a long time, his faith failed. During that period, Romans 8:1 alone hadn't seemed enough. And he'd nearly drowned while being tossed in the sea of horror his conscience had created for him. Then, when he'd given up almost any hope, an unexpected ally had tossed him a lifeline, leading him back to Romans 8, in addition to Isaiah 43:25, which had comforted him almost instantly. At first, it had been almost unfathomable to imagine that God would blot out his sins and not even remember them. But he'd finally accepted and believed it.

Yet, even today, nearly three years later, he was keenly aware of another fact. While God might wash his sins as white as snow, Jordan could still remember them. Unless someone came up with a pill to make the mind successfully dislodge unwanted memories, he was stuck with the memory of the part he'd played in the whole ordeal.

He would never forget. And it haunted him. . .teased him. Worse yet, he couldn't talk to anyone about it. His parents didn't want to hear it anymore. The people at his church might react any number of ways, and Jordan didn't want to take the risk of finding out what they would say. And Maddy—he couldn't risk destroying their friendship so soon by telling her. It was his own solitary burden to bear. It was between him, God, and Harper Blackston, who would never speak to a living soul again.

"Jordan?" Maddy's voice drifted to him over the fence. "Where are you?"

He looked around to see her standing on the deck of her house. "Over here," he said as he made his way back to her yard. The sunset was in the beginning stages and the warm glow of the sun spilled across the yard, enveloping them in elegant gold sprinkles.

His heart caught in his throat for a moment as he stared at Maddy. She was smiling at him, and he couldn't recall ever seeing her smile like that. She smiled at him as though he had never said a mean word to her. Just like that, she had forgiven him, and he found it hard to believe. With God, he could understand, but he never really believed that another human being would be able to offer forgiveness so freely. He had apologized to others just as sincerely as he had to Maddy, but they hadn't responded with the same warmth Maddy had extended. She was beautiful, and he couldn't deny that he felt a stirring in his heart when he thought of her. But even if she weren't in another relationship, he didn't think she would let herself ever develop romantic feelings for him again, and even if she did. . .she wouldn't want to be involved with him if she knew what he had done.

Still, he couldn't restrain himself from breaking off a small branch from his mother's lilac tree. When he reached Maddy's porch, he presented her with the lilacs.

"Thanks," she said, leaning over to sniff the light purple blossoms. "You really didn't have to."

"I did it because I wanted to," he said in a really bad imitation of a southern accent. He deepened his voice a notch and said, "It was unchivalrous of me not to bring you flowers tonight in the first place."

Maddy laughed and batted her eyelashes. In a high-pitched southern accent that was only slightly better than his, she said, "Then I'll just add these to the fragrant greenery you gave me earlier." As she turned to head inside, he grabbed her hand and pulled her back.

In response to the questioning look on her face, he said softly, "You have something on your cheek." He lifted his hand to her face and brushed away a small tomato seed that had glued itself to her face. He marveled at the softness of her cheek and left his hand on her face a second longer than was necessary. As he considered kissing her, she closed her eyes and leaned toward him slightly.

Jordan sighed and removed his hand from her cheek. She had looked at him with such trust that it nearly broke his heart. He was going to have to put a stop to things before they got started. He cleared his throat. "I guess we should go ahead and finish up so we can eat. I'll do the vinaigrette, and you can do the bruschetta, okay?" With that, he opened the door and strode into the house, and Maddy wordlessly followed.

≫

Maddy could have cried, but she didn't. If she wasn't mistaken, Jordan had been about two seconds away from kissing her, but had apparently changed his mind. *What did I do?* she wondered as she spread Jordan's roasted pepper paste on the slices of bread she had cut.

Since they had come back in the kitchen, he had barely even looked at her again. *Am I that unattractive? "Maddy the mutant."* Maddy blinked in surprise as she remembered the familiar chant. A visual memory of Jordan laughing and teasing her sprang up in her mind's eye. Was that how he really felt about her? Was she imagining the almost kiss, or had he planned it that way? Did he feel attracted to her even a little or was this some sort of elaborate joke?

She finished putting the mozzarella on the bread and put the baking sheet in the oven. When she finished, she turned around and caught Jordan staring at her. She smiled at him and he gave her a stiff grin in return, then busied himself with the tortellini salad. *Lord, what's going on here? Am I doing something wrong, or does he like me and he just feels unsure of what to do?*

At any rate, she was determined to make the evening less uncomfortable for both of them, so she decided to strike up a conversation. "So tell me more about your puppy," she said brightly.

Jordan looked relieved and said, "There's not too much to tell. He doesn't have a name yet because I can't think of one. He's two months old, and he manages to escape from my parents' yard every day, wreaking all manner of havoc in all of our neighbors' yards, yet he doesn't touch a single plant in my mother's garden. How's that for an interesting pet?"

Maddy laughed. "I think he's acting out because you're neglecting him. Maybe you should try to spend a little more quality time with the poor thing," she quipped.

Jordan laughed in response. "Maybe you're right. I'll take him to the park next Saturday. I'd take him this Saturday, but I've already planned to work. Why don't you to come with us?"

"Only if I wouldn't be imposing," she replied.

"Of course not," he said. "We'd love to have you come. How about it?"

"I wouldn't miss it." She smiled. She pulled the bread out of the oven and sighed with relief. Everything seemed to be normal again.

Chapter 6

The next week passed in a blur for Maddy. She spent her days in training sessions for her new job as a computer instructor at the Mevlom day camp, and she spent her evenings settling back into her parents' home. She unpacked all of her boxes from school and found that she had accumulated quite a collection of things in her dorm room. So much, in fact, that her room at home wasn't big enough to hold all of her mementos and belongings from both her elementary through high school years and college.

In the evenings she sorted everything out, deciding what to keep, what to throw out, and what to store. The items she threw out were few and far between. She ended up cramming the room as full as she comfortably could and boxed up the rest, claiming to her protesting parents that she was "storing it all in the attic for a little while until I can think of what to do with it all."

In the back of her mind, she had a feeling that she would probably never throw away any of it, and when the time came for her to move out on her own, she'd probably end up carrying all that stuff with her wherever she went. But she didn't mind. It was part of her history, and that type of thing had always been important to her.

The highlights of that week were the few evenings when Jordan stopped to see her. One night they went to get ice cream, and the next evening they took his puppy for a walk around the neighborhood. That evening, Maddy had just gotten home from work, and when she stepped out of the car, the puppy jumped up and placed his muddy paws on her cream-colored slacks. She'd become furious and fussed at the puppy for a few minutes, and Jordan had offered to pay the cleaning bill. By then Maddy had softened a little, and she jokingly suggested that he name the puppy "Muddy," since he was covered in mud most of the time.

Jordan thought it was a good choice, but joked that he didn't want to name the dog "Muddy," because it started with the same letter as Maddy's name, and sooner or later, he would probably start mixing them up. So he decided to name the dog John Hancock, and Hancock for short, in keeping with the same general idea of how the puppy was always leaving his signature, or "John Hancock," on people's legs.

Friday evening, she had reluctantly gone to play laser tag with the singles' group at her church. She had really wanted to stick around the house and see if Jordan might stop by, but her best friend, Laina, had insisted Maddy come along. The two of them had been best friends since they met at vacation Bible school in the second grade. Although Laina had gone to college in Kansas City, and Maddy had chosen Texas Southern, they had kept in touch and had remained close.

Maddy had been neglecting Laina in favor of Jordan since their first date, and Laina made her feel more than a little guilty for it. "I don't know what's going on with you, but I get the feeling you're trying to avoid me," she had gently teased. "But if you don't come tonight, I'll come over there myself and find out what's going on." She laughed.

"Okay, okay, I'll go," Maddy conceded. Laina had been there for her during her ill-fated crush on Jordan in high school, and the last thing she wanted was for Laina to come over while she and Jordan were visiting. Maddy had been pretty quick to forgive him, but her best friend knew how much he had hurt her. Knowing Laina, she wouldn't be so trusting of Jordan's apology.

So she went with Laina and had a good time, while opting not to mention Jordan just yet. Her parents had also been gone for the evening, so Maddy had no way of knowing if Jordan had stopped by.

When Maddy awoke on Saturday, she spent most of the morning in a flurry of excitement in anticipation of spending the afternoon at the park with Jordan and Hancock.

When Jordan pulled up to the curb that afternoon, Maddy went outside to meet him, and a few moments later, Hancock came trotting up the street, his paws covered in his favorite medium.

"He's been at it again," said Maddy.

"Oh, no," Jordan groaned. "What have you gotten into today?" Jordan asked the puppy, who jumped up and planted his paws on his legs.

"I don't know," answered Maddy, "But if we wait a couple of minutes, I'm sure one of the neighbors will probably come over and let us know."

"I guess they can tell my parents the extent of the damage," said Jordan. "So let's go to the park."

They decided to go to Jacob Loose Park, which had a small lake and a big area where Hancock would be able to run around.

When they got there, Maddy was surprised that Jordan had packed a small lunch. "I could've put something together, if you had asked me," she remarked as he began pulling items from a picnic basket.

"Well—" He looked at her uncertainly. "It wasn't too much trouble, and I figured you were probably too tired from your first week at work to go through any extra trouble."

Maddy stopped pouring the glasses of lemonade and stared at him for a moment. "Translation," she said sarcastically, "is that you don't think I'm a good enough cook to be entrusted with making lunch."

Jordan wiggled his eyebrows. "No comment there. Now, are you ready to eat?" He held up two bags of potato chips. "I got regular and salt and *vinegar*. . . in your honor."

Maddy arched her eyebrows. "Ha, ha, ha, *so* funny." Taking the lid off of a container, she said, "This smells really good."

Jordan shrugged. "It's just grilled cheese. And it's not even hot anymore."

"It smells delicious." Maddy took a bite and found it tasted even better than it smelled. "Umm. . .I like it. And it's not your run-of-the-mill grilled cheese. What's in it?"

Jordan turned to Hancock, who was edging closer and closer to the blanket and the food. "Sit still, boy. I've got a treat for you." He opened up a bag of doggie treats and tossed a few to the puppy. Then he answered Maddy's question. "Smoked Gouda on jalapeño and sun-dried tomato focaccia."

"I assume you baked the bread yourself."

"No," said Jordan. After a short pause he added, "I've been too busy to bake this week."

Maddy playfully tossed a chip at him. "My goodness, aren't you feeling a little conceited today?"

"Hey, a man shouldn't be ashamed if he's got skills in the kitchen, right?"

"I guess not. I just wish I had a little more culinary knowledge," she grumbled.

"Don't worry about it, okay? Some people have it and some. . .don't." Jordan rubbed his hand across his smooth scalp and grinned.

Maddy rolled her eyes. "Oh, goodness." She laughed.

For a few minutes, neither of them spoke. Jordan finished his sandwich, wiped his hands on a napkin, then asked, "I came over to see you last night, but nobody was home. You and your parents go out to dinner or something?"

Maddy shook her head. "My best friend, Laina, was after me to hang out with her, so we went to play laser tag with the singles' group at our church."

He nodded, wordlessly.

"I would have invited you if you had come over sooner."

Jordan waved his hands. "Nah, I wouldn't want to come barging in on you and your group."

Maddy laughed. "Oh, come on. You wouldn't be barging in. You would be my guest."

"That's really okay," he said firmly. "Besides, I hang out with the singles' class at my church sometimes too."

Is he trying to give me a hint or something? Shyly, she asked, "Are you seeing someone at your church?"

"Me? Nah. Why else would I be spending so much time with you?"

"You said we were seeing each other just as friends," reminded Maddy. "I distinctly remember you telling me you only wanted to be friends." *Is he getting ready to ask me out on a more serious basis?*

"Yeah. . .I haven't forgotten about that," he said slowly.

Maddy's heart dropped. *What kind of game is he playing?* Her mind raced back to their dinner together last week. Out on the deck, she was certain he had wanted to kiss her, and then his demeanor had totally changed. And now, he had almost acted a little jealous of her going out with her church group, and then he had admitted he only wanted to be friends. From now on, she wasn't going to make herself so vulnerable to him. If he wanted to know how she felt about him, he'd have to be a little more honest about his own feelings.

Reaching over to pet Hancock, who was starting to whimper, Maddy said, "Why don't we go for a walk? He's been pretty good to sit here while we ate."

Jordan held up the empty bag of doggie treats. "Are you kidding? It took these to keep him from snatching our lunch off our plates." He stood up and stretched, and Maddy tried not to stare at his long, muscular arms.

She stood up and folded the blanket and handed it to Jordan, who went to put it in his car along with the basket before they took a walk around the park.

When he returned, Maddy was busy trying to keep Hancock from jumping up on her.

"Hancock! Sit!" ordered Jordan. The puppy grew still and sat down. Jordan held up a leash in his hand. "I probably should have put this on him a few weeks ago. But I think now's probably a good time to start," he said. They spent the next few minutes trying to keep the wriggling puppy still long enough to fasten the leash to his collar.

Finally, they began their journey around the park. After a rough start, Hancock got used to the leash and happily strayed as far as the long cord would let him. Whenever they got close to another group of people, Jordan would gently shorten the leash, giving himself a little more control of the puppy's wanderings.

As they drew closer to the park's famous rose garden, Jordan suddenly asked, "So what about you? Are you seeing somebody?"

Maddy looked at him out of the corner of her eye. *Not even twenty minutes later, he's at it again,* she thought wryly. *This time I'm not going to be so transparent.* She shook her head and shrugged. "No," was her simple answer.

"Oh, really?"

"Really," she nodded.

"Not even someone at your church?" he questioned.

Maddy tried not to smile. *So that was why he kept asking about where I'd been last night.* "No one," she said. *If that doesn't answer his question, I don't know what will.*

Jordan furrowed his brow. "So who all was there last night?"

"Why in the world are you asking me all of these questions?" Maddy wanted to know. "It was just a bunch of friends from church. You probably wouldn't know them."

Jordan shrugged. "Try me. So who was there?"

Maddy rolled her eyes. "Let's see, my best friend Laina, Gabriella, Vincent, Luke, Tisha, Rakim, Autumn, and Tiffanee. Do you know any of them?"

Jordan frowned. "I kind of remember your friend Laina. Didn't she go to high school with us?"

"Yeah." Maddy nodded. It was a nice feeling to hear Jordan refer to the two of them as "us."

"Was anybody else there?"

Maddy groaned. "Wow, you sure are being thorough all of a sudden. JaShandra, and Cole. . .and Arnold, of course."

Arnold Jenkins and his wife, Patty, had been in charge of the youth group for as long as she could remember, and they had recently decided to start up a singles' group as well. Unfortunately, Patty hadn't been able to make it last night, because she had twisted her ankle during an aerobics class. Maddy smiled, thinking of how miserable Arnold had looked last night. Laser tag was obviously not his idea of a good time. For a couple in their sixties, Patty and Arnold tried to plan activities that appealed to the young members of the group.

"Oh, really?" said Jordan. "So you were holding out on me the first time?"

Maddy giggled. "Okay, so sue me. I forgot a couple of names."

"Some important names, I might add," said Jordan. His jawline grew firm and he was quiet.

"What are you talking about?" Maddy was bewildered.

"You didn't mention Arnold the first time around," he said tersely. "I would consider him an important name."

Maddy tried to figure out what was going on. "Okay. . .yeah, I guess you could say Arnold's pretty important to the group."

"And to you? What do you think about him?"

"Huh?" Maddy was puzzled. She figured she must've told him about Arnold and Patty starting the group, but she couldn't figure out why he was making such a case out of it.

"Would you be there if Arnold wasn't there?" he continued.

Maddy shrugged. "I guess not," she admitted. "I mean, it was basically his idea to get together and everything. He's the one who keeps the group together."

"So what do you and Arnold talk about?"

Maddy chuckled. "What, are you kidding? I've known Arnold for almost as long as I can remember, but we don't exactly have really long chats. He might call occasionally to let me know if something's going on, but other than that. . . " She shrugged, not knowing what to say. "He's way too busy to sit down and just talk to me for no reason," she finished lamely. "Besides, he usually has Patty to talk to."

They had now reached the outer edges of the rose garden, and Maddy heard the familiar strains of Pachelbel's Canon in D. It sounded like there was a wedding in the rose garden today. Maddy smiled, remembering some of the pleasant memories she had from working with Stacy and the many weddings she'd helped coordinate last summer. "I think it would be so romantic to get married out here in the rose garden," she told Jordan, hoping to ease some of the tension.

He looked at her and seemed to soften a little. "Yeah, I guess that's pretty cool. Right now I bet they're just glad it's not raining."

Maddy lowered her voice because they were getting closer to the ceremony. Small weddings of fifty guests or so were common in the rose garden, and it was also common for people who weren't even guests to stand around and quietly watch the ceremony. In fact, it was expected, due to the fact that both the park and the rose garden were public grounds. "Let's get a little closer," she whispered. "I want to see the bride's dress."

Jordan nodded and they reached the outskirts of the pavilion just as the "Wedding March" began. They were as close as they could possibly get without taking a seat next to one of the guests, but they were hidden from sight by several stone pillars that were covered in vines, in addition to a pretty dense covering of assorted rose bushes.

"Where's the music coming from?" Jordan whispered.

"Probably a CD player. There are electrical outlets in some of these pillars. We did that when we did weddings here last summer."

Jordan nodded.

Seconds later, the bride made her entrance. She was beautiful in a long gown with a satin bodice and a wide, fluffy tulle skirt. As Maddy watched the bride make her way down the aisle, she told Jordan, "You might want to shorten Hancock's leash before he walks into the wedding uninvited."

At that moment, the music cut off abruptly. The bride had only made it halfway down the aisle, and she stood there for a moment, confused. There was a general murmur that rippled amongst the gathering of guests, as Maddy realized what was going on. Instantly, she dropped to her knees and began moving among the columns trying to find out where the cord to the CD player needed to be plugged in. Seconds later, she found Hancock tangled up in not only his leash, but also the cord to the CD player. Quickly, Maddy disentangled the cord and plugged it back in and the "Wedding March" came back on again. Again, Maddy heard a murmuring run through the crowd. *What now?*

Suddenly, Jordan was kneeling next to her. He quickly unplugged the cord, and when she started to protest, he put his hand over her mouth. "Shhh. Never mind the music," he whispered. "The bride just walked down the aisle in silence and they went ahead and started. When you started the song back up again, they got really confused."

"Oh, sorry," Maddy said sheepishly.

"Let's just get out of here," said Jordan, starting to crawl away.

When they were a safe distance away, they stood up and quickly moved in the other direction.

When they were out of hearing distance, Maddy said, "I can't believe we just messed up a wedding."

Jordan laughed. "I just wish you could've seen the look on the groom's face. I think he might've thought it was a sign or something."

Maddy playfully swatted his arm. "What are you talking about?"

"I've been in a couple of my buddies' weddings, and I was standing there in the bathroom while they lost their lunches five minutes before the ceremony. Believe me, they were having second thoughts. One of them prayed for God to give him a sign if he shouldn't get married." Jordan stopped and bent over from laughing so hard. When he stood up, he finished the story. "What he didn't know was that a friend of ours was hiding in one of the stalls. The guy had been planning some kind of practical joke on me, but when he heard that prayer, he flushed the toilet just to see what we would do."

Maddy put her hands on her hips. "So what happened?"

"Calvin thought God was speaking to him. We didn't know Drew was hiding in there, and we couldn't see his feet, so we figured the toilet was flushing by itself. My buddy jumped up and was about to call the whole thing off until Drew came running out to stop us."

"And did the wedding go on?"

"Yeah. . .after about a thirty-minute delay. The pastor had to pray for him to calm down. That was four years ago. To this day, Calvin's wife still won't let him invite Drew over to the house."

Maddy groaned. "That is so pathetic. I worked at almost thirty weddings last summer, and all of the grooms showed up."

"And you're telling me not one of them got nervous?" Jordan stopped walking and looked at her incredulously.

"Well, all of them had cold feet to a degree, which is understandable, because marriage is a big commitment; but I will add that none of them canceled the wedding."

"Well, it happens," Jordan countered. He started to grin again. "And I know the look. Believe me. . .that man's feet were blocks of ice. If you had messed with that music one more time, he would've bolted." He held his sides from laughing so hard.

"Funny, funny. One day it'll be your wedding, and you might not have so much to laugh about," she scolded.

Jordan seemed to sober instantly. He cleared his throat. "Nah. . .I'll be fine."

"Is that so?"

"Yeah. I'm not going to ask a woman to marry me unless it's God's will. And if He never gives me the go-ahead, then I'm not going to force it."

Maddy turned and faced him. "Don't you ever want to get married?"

"Yeah. To the right woman. I'm just willing to wait on the Lord's timing is what I'm trying to say."

"Oh," said Maddy.

"What about you? I noticed you seem to get pretty excited about weddings."

"Of course, I want to get married," she told him.

"But you're not dating anybody," he said. He took hold of her hand and gently held it. "Why not? Hasn't somebody at least caught your eye?"

Maddy didn't know what to say. She didn't really feel comfortable putting her emotions on the line by just telling him that she was interested in him. *Maybe I could just hint, and see if he gets it,* she reasoned. But the problem was how to phrase what she said without obviously just saying, "I like you." She furrowed her brow and tried to put together a string of sentences to answer his question.

Jordan stopped walking and looked at her carefully. "You still haven't answered my question, you know."

"I know, I just didn't know what to say."

"Just say what you feel."

"Okay." She took a deep breath and started. "I *am* interested in this guy. I don't really know how he feels about me. Sometimes he's really attentive, and sometimes. . .I don't know. I don't really think I'm his type. And I get the feeling that he might be somewhat interested, but. . ."

"But what?" Jordan wanted to know.

"I'm not really sure. I think he's trying to determine for himself if he could ever be in love with me." There. She'd said it. That practically summed up what she thought about Jordan, and if he couldn't read between the lines, it was his own fault.

"Why not?" he asked. "Why wouldn't he be interested in you?"

Maddy sighed. "I don't know. He's older, and. . .I'm younger. I act a little silly sometimes. I can't cook. I've never kept house." She shrugged in frustration. "I'm just not the 'wifely' type, and I think he's looking for someone who is—someone who would obviously be a good wife and mother." Maddy's eyes unexpectedly filled with tears as she put into words her fears about her budding relationship with Jordan. She blinked several times and turned away.

Neither of them said anything as they made their way back to the car. After they rode a few minutes, Jordan spoke again.

"Maddy, those things are not that hard to learn. All you need is a little practice. And I think you would be a good wife and mother. Maybe you should just take a chance and tell him how you feel," he said gently.

Maddy shook her head. Thankfully, Jordan had allowed her to regain her composure, so she wouldn't have to start crying in front of him. "I don't think that would be the greatest idea," she told him. "It just wouldn't be practical. We get along fairly well, so I think it's just best to let things stay the same and not try to rock the boat."

Jordan shook his head. "I can't say that I agree. Maybe you should just tell him. You never know what he might say."

"Maybe he should just tell me how he feels about me," she countered. "Believe me, I've thought about it, and I'm not going to just tell him."

Jordan's mouth spread into a grin. "There's a verse in the Bible about that, you know."

"Tell me," Maddy said.

Jordan cleared his throat. "John 8:32. 'Then you will know the truth, and the truth will set you free.' And it sounds like you could use a little freedom with this situation. It feels really good to get things like that out in the open."

Maddy's stomach felt like someone had dropped a rock on top of it. He was right, but still. . .she couldn't imagine trying to tell him after this whole conversation that he was the guy she was talking about. It would be too awkward for both of them. She turned to face him. "I see your point, but it's not something I can work up the nerve to do right now."

"Nerves?" Jordan asked.

"Exactly," Maddy answered.

"If you ever need help, you can practice on me," Jordan said helpfully. "That way, you can have a trial run at it. Since I'm your friend, it won't be so uncomfortable."

Maddy stifled a groan. Why on earth would she *practice* telling Jordan to his face that she might be falling in love with him? It was embarrassing to even think about it. "I'll keep that in mind," she said. "But for now, I'd really like to drop this subject." She looked out the window and watched the scenery pass in a blur. It was becoming too unnerving for her to sit here indirectly discussing her feelings for Jordan to his face.

He sighed. "Okay, you know the situation best, so I won't say anything else. But if you ever need to talk to a friend about it, I'm a good listener." He smiled and patted her hand.

A thought popped into her head and before she even seriously considered it, the words came tumbling out of her mouth. "How about helping me learn how to cook?" she asked. Embarrassed, she pursed her lips and started hoping he hadn't heard her.

"What?" He lifted his eyebrows, looking confused.

She sighed. There was no way she could take back what she'd just said. "If you want to be such a good friend, I'm asking you to help me learn how to cook," she repeated.

"I don't mind helping you out, but if you don't mind my asking, how is that going to help the situation?"

She shrugged. "It'd give me a little more confidence to approach him and eventually tell him how I feel about him."

Jordan slowly nodded, his forehead wrinkled. Finally, he spoke. "So you're saying you want me to help you learn how to cook to impress some guy who doesn't know you exist?"

"That's a little harsh, don't you think? He knows I exist. . .he just doesn't know that I like him. And if I told him now, he'd laugh at me. I just need a little time to—"

"Time to make yourself into the kind of woman he thinks you should be," Jordan interrupted her.

"I get the feeling you don't think it's such a good idea," Maddy said, not really sure whether or not she should be disappointed. Even she had to admit, it was kind of a silly plan.

Jordan shook his head. "Not really." They turned onto Maddy's street and he slowed the car to a stop in front of her house before he continued. "I mean, what if he decides he likes your cooking, but he decides you would be even more attractive if you were five inches taller and had red hair instead of brown? Would you try to please him then?"

Maddy merely murmured in agreement. In fact, she was kind of glad that the subject hadn't gone much further. It was best to let it drop and move on. If things between her and Jordan were going to get more serious, it would have to happen on its own.

"But I guess I could lend a hand, if you really wanted me to. I did say I would help you out, if you needed me to." Jordan's voice broke into her thoughts. "Sooo. . .when do you want to get started?"

She stared at him, blinking several times while she thought of something to say. *Now what should I do?* she wondered. It wasn't actually a bad plan, once she really thought about it. And if nothing else, it would give her more time with Jordan. And depending on how things went, she would eventually work up the nerve to tell Jordan how she felt about him, if he hadn't already figured out that he was the guy she had the crush on. "How about Monday evening after I get home from work?"

"Okay, that sounds like a good start. But before you get your hopes up, I don't think I've ever seen one of these Cyrano de Bergerac schemes work out according to the plan. I'll do my best to help you in any way I can, but if it doesn't work out, you have to promise me that you won't be upset with me."

Maddy laughed. "Okay. I won't be upset with you. But I have a feeling that this time around, the outcome is going to surprise you." She impulsively squeezed his hand, then jumped out of the car. As she walked to the door, she whispered, "Yes, this time I think you'll be very surprised."

❧

Jordan's stomach tightened. Again. His stomach had acted strangely the entire ride back to Maddy's house. Trying to shrug it off, he waved good-bye to Maddy, who was standing at her front door, then he walked next door to his parents' house. They weren't home, so he deposited Hancock in the backyard, making a mental note to call his parents later to make sure they knew the puppy was out there. As he started the drive home, he reflected on what had turned out to be an eventful day. He had been excited about having the afternoon free in order to spend time with Maddy and to let the puppy burn off some of his boundless energy.

But there was an uneasy feeling in his stomach that had been bugging him since he'd brought up the subject of relationships. He was angry with this guy Arnold, who seemed to be playing with Maddy's heart.

The man was all wrong for her. Jordan couldn't understand why this guy

Arnold didn't see what an altogether lovely woman she was. And at the same time, he was relieved that the two of them weren't really a couple.

But beyond that, his emotions were a twisted jumble of *maybe. . .what if I* and *I probably shouldn't.*

Would it be entirely rude of him to say to Maddy, "Forget about Arnold. I'm really attracted to you. How do feel about me?" Or would it be more practical for him to take a stance as a friend in whom she could confide about the whole thing? And would it be fair to himself to try and divert her attention from Arnold when she was feeling so vulnerable? Would she momentarily make herself believe that she had feelings for him, then come to her senses later, realizing that she still cared for Arnold?

Jordan drummed his fingers on the steering wheel and shook his head. That wouldn't be fair to himself. He would be crushed if that were to happen.

He sighed. If he had taken the time to get to know her years ago, maybe this wouldn't be happening now. For all he knew, they would have dated throughout high school and college and been married by now.

Married. The thought had a nice ring to it. But why was he even getting his hopes up? Especially now, with this whole situation about the cooking lessons. But the more he thought about it, the more he realized it was what he really wanted.

He wanted Maddy to be his wife. And thanks to his big mouth and constant teasing back in high school, he'd lost out on winning the woman of his dreams. If he'd only been mature enough to recognize it back then. . .back when she had been interested in him.

It was too late to go back and undo the past. But it wasn't too late to be there for her during this situation with Arnold.

As long as Arnold didn't realize what a jewel Maddy was, Jordan was happy to spend every moment he could with her.

All he could do now was hope and pray the Lord would show him a way to show Maddy how much he cared for her without trying to force her to give up on Arnold.

He had wanted to tell her how he felt about her right there in the car, but then she had come up with the plan for him to give her cooking lessons.

Looking back, he figured he should have said no and then stuck to it. But he realized that no matter how silly he would feel if he went along with it, it would give him the perfect opportunity to spend more time with her. And that seemed like the perfect plan for him. Until now. Taking a clearer look at the situation, he knew this was no way to win a woman's heart. Arnold's shadow would always be hanging over him.

Jordan remembered the dreamy look that Maddy had when she talked about Arnold. Would she ever get that look in her eyes when she thought about Jordan? Jordan shook his head. "Not until she gives up on Arnold," he grumbled. He felt like telling Maddy he'd changed his mind about the cooking lessons, but he had already committed himself. And given his past experiences with Maddy, the last thing he wanted was to break his word.

"I guess I'll have to turn it over to You, Lord," he prayed quietly. "I just hope I have enough faith to let You keep the ball in Your hands, even if I start to feel desperate."

Chapter 7

M addy patiently waited for the students to file out of her classroom. Her first day at work had come to a close. *So far, so good,* she told herself. The students seemed to get along with her well and, except for one student, none of them had really given her too much trouble. However, that one student, a girl named Trina, had given Maddy enough problems to rival the rest of the students' willingness to cooperate. It wasn't as though the girl didn't like the classes. In fact, she seemed to enjoy her work, and learned quickly. She spent a good deal of her time questioning everything Maddy told the class to do, making wisecracks, passing notes, and flirting with the guys in the class. And most infuriatingly, whenever Maddy asked her a question, she would say she didn't know the answer. Yet, Trina answered those questions and more on the pop quiz for the day, and had been the only student in the class to get a perfect score on that quiz.

During the lunch break, Maddy had asked Mrs. Calvin about Trina's academic records. Maddy learned that not only did Trina have some of the top grades of any of the students who had applied to the camp, but she had also just graduated as her class valedictorian. Trina had attended the camp the previous year and won numerous awards for her performance. But when Maddy had consulted Irena Phelps, who'd been Trina's instructor the year before, Maddy learned Trina had been somewhat of a problem student back then.

After the last student left the classroom, Maddy gathered her purse and walked to the parking lot. The camp was being held on a small college campus, which was comprised of no more than ten academic halls connected by scenic, winding pathways. The Mevlom Institute was using only three of the buildings for its camp, and Maddy had seen only the building where she taught her class and the smaller building that housed the campus cafeteria.

As she walked, she noticed a group of students who had been in her classes, including Trina. As she got closer, they suddenly grew quiet and kept casting glances in Maddy's direction. Maddy felt the tiniest sinking sensation in her chest.

Just four years ago, she had been the same age as these students, and there was no way they would have reacted to her then as they just had. Now she was out of the loop, no longer a peer, but an authority figure. *And I'm not even that old,* Maddy thought. *On the other hand, maybe it's a good thing they see me as being so much older. That way, I get more respect when I'm trying to teach. Yes. I'm not here to hang out with them. I'm supposed to be their teacher.*

"'Bye, Ms. Thompson," said one of the students, a girl named Stacia. Then several of the others in the group followed suit, echoing a chorus of "'Bye, Ms. Thompson."

Maddy nodded and waved, hoping she was acting in a mature manner. "Good-bye, students," she said, internally wincing. When did she ever really talk like that? In trying to act maturely, she ended up feeling ridiculous. Maddy's cheeks began to grow warm, so she quickened her pace and passed the group, not wanting to overhear what they might say about her.

"Hey, Ms. Thompson?" asked an all too familiar voice. Maddy held back a shudder, realizing there was only one student she knew by voice after her first day on the job. She paused and turned around to see Trina break from the ranks and walk toward her.

Maddy stood and waited for the girl to come closer. But Trina only covered half of the distance between them. Then she all but shouted, "The guys want to know how old you are," as she gestured to some of the boys in the group, who were standing in poses they probably assumed were mature and macho, but actually looked comical.

Maddy didn't know what to say. Why did all the problems develop after classes were out? She vaguely remembered that some of the guys in her own high school had developed crushes on female teaching assistants and substitutes from local colleges. The girls had been jealous of them, and the guys had swooned when the female teaching assistants walked into a room. The same concept applied to male college students who worked as teaching assistants. The guys got jealous, while the girls had thought they themselves were falling in love.

Maddy had always thought the concept was pretty ridiculous. Some of those college students were only two or three years older than the students they were teaching. And now, she was in the same boat. She frantically dug into her memory to recall what those assistants had done to halt any student's crushes. Unfortunately, she didn't remember. But she knew she had to come up with an answer. Soon.

"I don't think that's really important," she told the students. "What's important is that I'm your teacher for the summer and that means—"

"Did you go to college?" interrupted Trina, who was walking closer to her.

Maddy swallowed and lifted her chin a tad higher. "Yes. And I graduated also." *That sounded pretty silly.*

She heard one of the kids say, "Oooh, she graduated." The others snickered in response.

What she wanted to do was run to her car, but she couldn't exactly run away from a student, so she stood her ground as Trina grew closer.

When Trina finally got within three feet, Maddy cleared her throat and asked, "Is there something you need?"

Trina turned and looked at her friends, who now seemed to be engrossed in conversation. "Um. . .do you think I can talk to you before class on Wednesday?"

she asked in a low tone.

Maddy shook her head before she even said a word. She needed to set boundaries before things got out of hand, and the first thing she needed to do was make it clear to Trina and the others that she was in charge. "I really don't think so," she told the girl.

"What about after class then?" The expression on the girl's face had grown serious, almost pleading, and her eyes mirrored the same emotion.

"Well. . ." Maddy had the feeling whatever she wanted to discuss was important, and she didn't want to turn her down. While she deliberated a moment, she noticed Trina kept turning around to glance at her friends.

Finally, Trina sighed and said, "Never mind. I just thought you meant what you said this morning about talking to you if we needed help and everything. If you don't have time, then I'll talk to somebody else." She turned around to go back to her friends.

Maddy felt terrible. What kind of teacher was she? "All right," she relented before the girl got too far away. "I can stay for fifteen minutes after class on Wednesday. Okay?"

Trina just nodded and jogged over to her friends.

As Maddy resumed the walk to her car, she heard one of the students call out, "Hey, Trina, what'd you say to Ms. Thompson?"

Maddy heard Trina laugh in response and say, "I just told her that her clothes were out of style." The group burst into loud, raucous laughter.

Maddy quickened her pace. That girl was impossible. The second she'd started to feel like she was making a connection, the girl turned around and mocked her in front of the rest of the students.

And, she thought, looking down at her black crepe pantsuit, *this outfit is not out of style. It might be a little dressy, but it's not outdated.*

When she reached her car, she was thoroughly upset. Before she even fastened her seat belt, she took five minutes to pray and calm down so she wouldn't let her emotions affect her driving. When she began to relax, she buckled up and started the car. By the time she got closer to home, she wasn't upset; but she was pretty disheartened and had serious doubts about whether or not she would be able to teach the rest of the summer.

Her mother was out in the front yard, digging in her flower beds, and Mrs. Myston was helping her.

Maddy parked in the driveway and walked around to the front to say hello.

"How was work?" her mother asked.

"Okay, I guess. I had a little trouble toward the end, but it'll be under control by the end of the week, I'm sure."

Her mother nodded in agreement. "Just give it a little time. I'm sure you'll do a great job."

"I hope so. Otherwise, I might have to find a new job next week."

"If you got the job, I'm sure you can do it. Otherwise, they wouldn't have hired you," her mother said.

Mrs. Myston shook her head. "No offense, Madison, but aren't you a little young to be teaching high school students? What could the people who hired you have been thinking?"

Maddy bristled but tried to remain calm as she asked, "What do you mean?"

Mrs. Myston patted Maddy's arm in what she probably thought was a comforting manner. "You're just a child yourself. And a nice, well-mannered one at that. What can they expect you to do for those hooligans?"

Maddy wondered if she'd just been insulted. She decided to shake it off, since she knew Mrs. Myston meant well. "Mrs. Myston, these kids are not hooligans. They're some of the brightest and smartest at their schools. I just probably need better teaching skills."

Mrs. Myston shook her head. "You be careful, Madison. I watch the news and I know that smart doesn't always mean 'nice' when it comes to these kids nowadays. You never know what they might be up to."

No one said anything for a minute, then Mrs. Myston brightened and said, "But I do think it's nice of you to try to look for the good in all of your students. That's a good start as long as you don't let your guard down."

"That's true," said her mother. "Maddy always seeks out the best in people," she said, smiling.

If only you knew how I feel about Trina right now, Maddy thought. "I guess I'll go in and change. I'll see you later, Mrs. Myston."

"Oh, look, Madison. Your gentleman friend is here," reported Mrs. Myston.

Maddy turned around to see that Jordan had pulled into his parents' driveway. He got out of his car and jogged over, carrying a grocery bag. He handed the bag to Maddy and said, "I'll be over in about ten minutes. I just need to say hi to my parents. But don't peek in the bag."

Maddy stared at the brown paper bag. "What's in here?" she called to Jordan.

Jordan stopped and smiled. "Lesson one. Wife class 101. Don't tell me you forgot."

"Oh. No, I didn't forget, I just didn't realize the semester was starting today." Maddy laughed.

"Wife class?" echoed her mother and Mrs. Myston. The looks on their faces were priceless, and if she hadn't had such a hard day, Maddy might have had a good laugh.

"It's a long story," said Maddy. "And kind of a joke, that I didn't think he would take seriously. But basically, he's teaching me how to cook. So I'd better get inside and make sure the kitchen is clean."

Maddy left the two women out on the lawn and hurried inside to give the kitchen a once-over. She transferred a few items from the sink into the dishwasher and wiped down the counters for good measure. Just as she was finishing, Jordan came through the back door.

"I didn't think you were really going to help me out," Maddy told him.

"I promised I would, didn't I?"

"Well, yeah, but I thought you did it just to make me feel better. To be honest, I'd pretty much forgotten about it."

Jordan looked a little disappointed. "If you really don't want me to stay, I don't have to."

"No, no. It's okay. I'm ready to learn," said Maddy as she took a seat at the kitchen table.

"Are you wearing that?" Jordan asked.

Maddy looked down at her outfit for the second time that day and sighed. "You think it's outdated too?" she asked Jordan.

"No, it looks great on you. But it might be a little fancy for cooking class," he said.

"I'll change," said Maddy.

She ran to her room and changed into a T-shirt and pair of shorts, then returned to the kitchen where Jordan had set out several bowls.

He looked up at Maddy. "From now on, I'll let you get all the utensils and things out, but since you were tardy today, I had do it myself," he said in a mock stern voice.

Maddy smiled. "Sorry, Mr. Sanders. I won't be late next time."

Jordan laughed and opened the bag. "Now, the first thing about cooking is you have to follow the directions. If you follow the recipe, it should turn out perfectly. So. . ." He reached into the bag and pulled out a bag of chocolate chips. "What I want you to do is read over this recipe," he said, handing her the bag.

Maddy took the bag and glanced at the recipe on the back. "We're making cookies? That's it?" she said.

"I thought we'd start off with something easy," he replied.

"Jordan, I thought this was supposed to be beneficial to me. You know, 'wife class' and everything. What man would want to eat cookies for dinner?"

He shrugged. "I would."

Maddy tilted her head and lifted her eyebrows in response. "Every day?"

"If that was all my wife knew how to cook, I would happily eat cookies day after day after day." He laughed.

"Seriously. I'm sure I can pull off a batch of cookies. When do we get to the harder stuff?"

"After we make these cookies. And I hope for my sake that you can pull this recipe off, because I need these to take to my church's singles' group meeting tomorrow night."

Maddy looked up at him, surprised. "I didn't know you went to your church's singles' group meetings."

He shrugged. "I told you I hang out with them sometimes, but I usually don't make it to the Tuesday night meetings."

"So you're starting now?"

"When I can. They're having a barbecue tomorrow and I'm signed up to bring cookies, so I hope you do a good job, or they'll think I'm an awful cook."

"I'll try my best; but isn't it unethical to try to pass your student's work off as your own?"

"Why don't you tell me?" he laughed. "Between the two of us, you're the one who gets paid to teach."

"Okay, let's get off the subject of teaching. I'd rather not think about it. What do we do first?"

"First, you read the recipe over thoroughly and then get out all of the ingredients. But since they're my cookies for my meeting, I went ahead and bought the ingredients, so all you need to do in this case is take everything out of the bag. However, we will need to use your oven, bowls, and things like that."

"You can be sure I'll deduct the cost from my tuition," she told him. Maddy read the recipe and measured the ingredients while Jordan watched.

Thankfully, the recipe was not very difficult. It actually turned out to be pretty simple, leaving her to wonder why she had previously thought cooking to be some great mystery.

Cooking was turning out to be a combination of math and science, with certain amounts of particular ingredients combining to create edible results. It reminded her of chemistry. Cooking was something she could learn if she really tried.

The only thing that bugged her was the fact that Jordan was taking *her* cookies to his church meeting. *Was he interested in a woman there? And what was he going to tell her about the cookies? "My cooking student, who has a crush on me, made these. She's not a very good cook, so eat them at your own risk."*

The thought of it made Maddy a little queasy. But before she became too ill, Jordan interrupted her thoughts.

"So how was your first day at work?"

"It was okay until it was officially over. I had one problem student, but she didn't really get out of hand during class."

"So what happened afterwards?"

Maddy related the events with Trina and the other students and waited for Jordan to respond.

"That was it?" was all he said.

"What do you mean 'it'?" she asked.

"That's not too awful."

"Maybe it's not to you, but to me it is. I have a student who makes fun of me and challenges me in front of the others, and some of the boys have a crush on me."

Jordan gasped loudly, then put his hand across his forehead and clutched the countertop as though he might fall down. "Oh, no! The world is ending! Half of

Maddy's students are in love with her and the other half are laughing at her! What to do, what to do!" he said in a high-pitched voice.

"Oh, be quiet," Maddy said, as she playfully tapped him on the arm with the spoon she was using to stir the cookie dough.

"Oops!" Maddy exclaimed, realizing she had gotten some cookie dough on his arm and the sleeve of his shirt.

Jordan instantly sobered. "Hey. This mix is supposed to go in the oven, not on my arm."

"You deserved it."

"I did?"

Maddy nodded.

"Then, I think you deserve this," he said as he wiped some of the dough off his arm and spread it over her nose.

"Very funny," Maddy said. She picked up the spoon and held it in front of her like she was wielding a weapon. "If you want any of this dough to end up in the oven, I suggest you refrain from smearing any more on your student's nose."

"Okay, okay." Jordan backed away in retreat with his hands in the air. "So tell me more about this camp," he said, changing the subject. "I get the feeling it's not your typical summer camp with cabins, mess halls, and macaroni necklaces."

Maddy shook her head. "It's a mix between an internship and a specialized summer camp for high school juniors and seniors who want to go into communications. Some want to work at newspapers, some want work for radio or television, and the camp tries to match them up with businesses in those different fields. They either attend classes or work for eight hours a day, depending on which day it is. Seniors attend the classes Monday, Wednesday, and Friday. Tuesdays and Thursdays they work at the places where they're required to intern. My job is to teach different computer skills that they might need for these kinds of jobs. It's not really complicated, since so many of them have worked with computers a lot. But, every once in awhile, I manage to come up with something they don't know. On Tuesdays and Thursdays, I teach the juniors. Wednesdays and Fridays they work at the places where they're interning."

"So what do the juniors do on Mondays?"

"They have the option of either auditing the senior classes or just taking the day off. I only saw two juniors today."

"That's a pretty intense way to spend the summer. Do you think they're having any fun?"

"Probably. I did a similar program during my junior and senior summers. I liked it better than school because I got experience working at big companies, and I didn't have to study subjects I didn't really care for."

"Like home economics," Jordan supplied.

"Yeah."

"Plus, it's not really for the entire summer. The session ends the second week of August, so they have a little time to unwind before school starts."

"So that's why I never saw you around during the summertime," Jordan said.

"Were you looking for me? Or looking *out* for me to avoid me?" Maddy teased.

"Oh, that's harsh," Jordan said. "Let's get these in the oven." He handed her a cookie sheet.

He noticed I wasn't around in the summer. I wonder what that means. Maddy wanted to press the question a little further, but Jordan didn't appear to be very talkative at the moment, so she focused on rolling the dough into perfect little balls, then placing them on the baking sheet.

A few minutes later, Jordan spoke up. "You always were so smart, Maddy. Even though I was older, I felt stupid next to you a lot of the time. I barely concentrated in high school and I have the grades to prove it, even though I probably could have done better if I'd worked a little harder." He laughed. "I guess we're total opposites. You liked math and science and hated the other subjects. I liked anything that didn't have absolutes and right and wrong answers, things that change and things that are open to interpretation."

"Like art," she said.

"Exactly. I mean look at us, even now. You're rolling the cookie dough into perfect spheres, and I'm flinging it on the sheet any kind of way."

Maddy looked down at the cookie sheet and chuckled. He was right. "I guess you're right. But even with all our differences, we still get along pretty well, don't you think?"

"Yeah. I guess that's the part I didn't understand back in high school," he said softly.

Before Maddy even realized what he was doing, Jordan leaned over and gently kissed her on her forehead. She looked up at him and held his gaze for a long moment, hoping for some type of profession of love from him. He said nothing but continued to look into her eyes. Maddy placed her hand on his arm. "Is everything okay?" she said quietly.

Jordan grinned and seemed to return to his usual joking self. "I guess we need to finish these cookies," he told her. Quickly, he picked up the cookie sheet and put it in the oven. He stayed at the stove for a few minutes, checking the temperature, while Maddy reflected on the kiss. It had happened so fast she wasn't even sure if it was real or if she had imagined it.

What was going on? How could he act like nothing had just happened? Somehow, she was going to have to get some answers from him. And the sooner, the better. After a few minutes of shaping more cookie dough, she finally worked up the nerve to look at Jordan, who was now busy running water into the sink to wash dishes.

He turned around and flashed her a quick smile. "Now comes the fun part. The cleanup. Do you want to wash or dry?"

"It doesn't matter to me," she said.

"Then you can dry." He turned his back to her and started washing the dishes they'd used.

Maddy silently dried the dishes, and by the time they finished, the first batch of cookies was done. Half were perfect little circles and the other half were wildly abstract shapes.

"Mine look better," said Maddy.

"They look better to you. I think mine have lots of character," he said.

Jordan suggested they take some out to Mrs. Myston and her mother.

"But what about the rest of the dough? I've already started shaping it," she told him.

"Oh, yeah. I guess we should make the rest of them."

"Why don't you take some outside, and I'll get the second batch started," she suggested.

"Good idea. Are you sure you can handle it?"

Maddy rolled her eyes. "I just did these, didn't I?"

"Right." He placed a few cookies on a plate and bounded out the door with a relieved look on his face.

Once again, he seems glad to get away from me. Maddy recalled the night out on the porch after she'd messed up the vinaigrette.

Maddy put a dozen more cookies on the sheet and checked the temperature of the oven. She set the timer on her watch and went outside to see how everyone liked the cookies.

"Maddy, these are good," said her mother.

"Thanks," Maddy replied, smiling.

"These are delicious, Madison," said Mrs. Myston. "Jordan must be a good teacher to get this kind of result in only one lesson."

Maddy nodded. "He is a good teacher."

The two women complimented the cookies for a few more minutes, then launched into a discussion about the hedge roses they'd planted the week before.

Maddy and Jordan sat and quietly listened while the two women talked. Jordan still seemed a little uncomfortable, so Maddy stayed quiet to see if he would initiate a conversation.

When the timer on her watch sounded, Maddy jumped up and rushed to the kitchen. The cookies were perfectly browned, so she took them from the oven and put another batch in, after making a slight adjustment to the temperature.

Just as she was about to head back outside, the phone rang. "Hello?"

"Maddy, it's Laina. What are you doing?"

"Baking cookies."

Laina laughed. "No really, what are you doing?"

"I am making cookies. . .with Jordan Sanders," Maddy said, checking to make sure Jordan wasn't within earshot.

"How did this come about?" Laina wanted to know.

"It's a long story that I'll have to tell you about later."

"Like when?" she persisted.

"I don't know. The next time I see you."

"How about tomorrow night?"

"Tomorrow?"

"Yes. Some of the people in our Sunday school class are going out for dinner. We can ride together and you can fill me in on the way."

Maddy frowned. "I don't remember hearing about any of this in church yesterday."

"You didn't. Patty just called me about maybe getting some of the class to help plan a surprise party for Arnold's birthday. So some of us are going out to dinner for a little planning session."

"Oh, I see. I guess I could try to make it," Maddy said, remembering that Jordan probably wouldn't stop by because he was going to the party with his friends from church.

"You won't *try* to come. You will come. Okay?" said Laina.

Maddy decided to tease her friend a little. "I guess I could show up. But it's not really you I want to see. I'm only coming because it's for such a good cause."

"What's the good cause that means more to you than seeing your best friend who you've blatantly avoided since you got home from college?"

"Arnold's surprise party, of course," Maddy laughed.

"Ahem," Jordan cleared his throat.

Maddy turned around to see him standing by the door. "Oh, I didn't hear you come in."

"I wanted to check on the cookies," he told her.

"Oh. They should be done by now."

"Already?" he asked.

"Yeah. The recipe said to bake at three hundred degrees for twelve minutes, so I turned it up to broil and figured they should be done in about six minutes." At that moment, the timer on her watch went off. "See? I bet they're ready now."

Jordan just stared at her.

To Laina she said, "I've got to let you go, but I'll see you tomorrow. Just be sure you let me know what time you're picking me up." Maddy hung up the phone and opened the oven door. Thick, black smoke poured out from the interior.

Maddy inhaled smoke and started coughing. "Oops," she said to Jordan.

Jordan grabbed the pot holders from her and pulled the cookie sheet from the oven.

The cookies were blackened on the bottoms and around the edges, while the top center portion was still raw.

"Hmm. . . ," said Jordan. "What was that theory you had about the temperature again?"

"Logically speaking, I figured if I doubled the temperature, the cookies would be done in half the time. So I made a mistake," she defended herself.

Jordan shook his head. "This is not algebra, Maddy. It's cooking. You have to follow the directions when you don't know what you're doing."

Maddy felt herself growing angry. She made one little mistake, and now he was treating her like she was a two year old. Not to mention the fact that he'd acted like she had the plague after he kissed her. She grabbed a spatula and started scraping the burnt cookies off the cookie sheet. "I know what I'm doing. . .I just made a miscalculation. I'll buy you some cookies for your party, just stop talking down to me. I'm an adult, you know."

"You're right. I'm sorry," he said, his voice taking on an edge. "But maybe if you hadn't been so engrossed in planning Arnold's surprise party, my cookies wouldn't be burnt."

"You had no right to eavesdrop on my phone conversation. And I think you should leave Arnold out of this. He's one of the nicest people I know. Besides, he didn't burn your cookies. I did. And I promise you that you won't have to go to your party empty-handed." Maddy went to the pantry and started pulling out ingredients for more cookies. Thankfully, her mother had everything she needed. She turned to Jordan and said, "I can handle this. Why don't you come back in two hours and I'll have them ready for you?"

"I'll be next door if you get done earlier," was all he said before he left.

"Good riddance," Maddy grumbled after he left. "I'll have your cookies ready for the party, Mister. You just watch. I'm sure your girlfriend will be impressed."

Chapter 8

Jordan stared in the direction of the television set, but his eyes weren't focused on the show his parents were engrossed in watching.

He had really messed things up now. For one thing, what had he been thinking to kiss her like that? And why hadn't he been more sensitive to her feelings about the burnt cookies? Or better yet, why did he overreact when he heard her discussing Arnold's surprise party?

Although he'd known this was going to happen, it just didn't seem fair that Arnold should get all of Maddy's romantic attention, while he had to settle for a cooking-class relationship.

Jordan stood up and walked to the kitchen. He lifted one of the sections in the blinds and peeked out the window. He saw Maddy's outline in her kitchen, moving around. He chuckled softly. She really seemed determined to make those cookies.

Jordan opened the refrigerator and poured a glass of milk. Sitting down at the kitchen table, he thought, *I probably should go and apologize to her.* Otherwise, they would both be upset and nothing would be resolved. He took another swallow and rubbed his hand over his head. Yes, he would go over and apologize, although it would be nice if she would come and apologize to him.

He bowed his head and prayed that he would be able to control his emotions and not get bent out of shape about the little things so much. After all, a few burnt cookies were not the end of the world. And no matter how much he hated to admit it, a party for Arnold wasn't exactly cataclysmic either. But he didn't want to destroy his somewhat fragile friendship with Maddy.

Suddenly, the light flickered on. Jordan looked up to see his dad standing over him.

"What in the world are you doing, sitting here in the dark?"

Jordan hesitated. Whereas his mother was slightly more open to hearing about Christianity, his dad was way more resistant. Did his dad really want to know what he'd been doing? Jordan swallowed and decided to be honest. "Actually, I was praying," he told him.

His dad snorted. "Did it help anything?"

"God listens to all of my prayers, Dad. And He answers them too."

Jordan could tell his dad was already upset about something else and he braced himself for what might be coming next. When his dad got in this mood, he was always ready for a good shouting match about why Jordan had chosen to become a Christian. The two of them would go at it for hours, Jordan trying to make his dad become a Christian, and his father putting down everything Jordan said.

But lately, Jordan had realized it was absolutely hypocritical to yell at his dad about how Christianity had changed him. If he had changed so much, why was he yelling about it? It only infuriated Martin Sanders all the more when Jordan wouldn't yell back at him.

His dad sat down across from him and smiled without warmth. Jordan felt like he was the opposing attorney at one of his dad's trials. When he'd been in high school, many of his friends had been envious of the material things his family owned. But they didn't really know what it had been like to grow up as the only child of Martin Sanders, the champion prosecutor. They didn't know what it felt like to live in a house where everything was conducted like a trial. And they certainly didn't know what it had felt like to tell his dad that he didn't want to follow in his footsteps and go to law school. His dad had ignored him for a week when Jordan had announced his intention to go to art school.

Just when it seemed Martin had starting accepting the idea of his son being an artist, Jordan had come home and announced that he had asked Jesus into his heart. That's when the real opposition had begun.

Jordan sat up straighter and waited for what was coming.

"I notice you're spending a lot of time next door."

Jordan nodded.

"Would you like to share the reason why?"

Jordan swallowed. "The Thompsons' daughter, Maddy. She's a friend of mine."

"Since when? You made fun of her in high school."

"And I apologized, and now we're friends."

"So this was another one of your mercy missions?"

Jordan frowned. "I don't know what you're talking about. Maddy is my friend, plain and simple."

"I thought you Christians are supposed to tell the truth, but here you are telling me you've forgotten all about Harper Blackston?"

Jordan's throat felt like it was swelling. "You didn't ask me about Harper Blackston. You asked me about Maddy. And no, I haven't forgotten about Harper."

"Well, what are you doing with her, Jordan? Is this little project something I'm going to have to write a check for when you come crying to me in the middle of the night?"

Jordan stood up. "You have no right to throw that back at me. It was my own money—"

"You listen to me." His dad had stood up and now stood directly in front of him. "It wasn't your money yet," he yelled. "It was mine, and I made a big mistake when I wrote that check. So whatever you do now, make sure you paint enough Noah's arks in church hallways to cover any more checks you might feel obligated to write."

"I won't ask you for another cent, you can be sure of that," Jordan said, his voice growing louder.

"While you're at it, why don't you pray and ask for those nightmares to go away? Why don't you pray and ask for that *Christian* counselor to send me back some of the money I shelled out—"

He was interrupted by a knock on the kitchen door.

Jordan hurried over to open the door. Maddy stood outside, holding a plastic bag full of cookies.

"I'm sorry I'm a few minutes late but here they are," she said, holding out the bag. She peeked around Jordan and waved to his dad. "Hi, Mr. Sanders," she said. "I hope I didn't come at a bad time."

"No, of course not," said his dad. "Those cookies look delicious. I hope Jordan will let me taste a few."

Jordan was irritated with the way his dad always acted like the model father when other people were around. He smiled at Maddy and said, "I'm sorry I got upset about the burnt cookies, and I really appreciate you making these."

"Oh, it's okay." She smiled. "I needed the practice."

Jordan felt his dad's eyes on him and couldn't think of anything to say. Maddy shifted from foot to foot. "Well, I guess I'll see you later?"

"Are you busy tomorrow night?" Jordan asked.

"Actually, I'm supposed to help plan Arnold's party. And I thought you had a barbecue?"

"Oh, that's right. Maybe sometime later this week. I'll give you a call, okay?"

"Okay," Maddy said, flashing him a tiny smile.

Jordan shut the door and turned around to face his dad. "I'm pretty tired. Is there anything else you need to say?"

His dad shrugged. "You've heard it before, but I'll say it again. I don't like seeing my only son running around being a do-gooder. There was no reason for you to get involved in all this religion stuff. What happened was not your fault."

Jordan let out a weary sigh. "Dad, I know you don't believe it, but being a Christian got me through what happened. I don't know what would have happened to me if I hadn't. . . ." He trailed off, not wanting to pursue the subject anymore. He leaned over and hugged his dad, who instantly stiffened. His dad had never been the hugging type. "I'll just say this. I love you and Mom, and I'll pray for you until the day I die. Jesus is just waiting for you to say yes, and when you do, you'll know true peace."

His dad said nothing, but instead turned out the light and left the room.

Jordan quietly left and drove home. He hadn't really gotten to apologize to Maddy the way he'd wanted, but he had done the best he could, given the circumstances. What made him restless were the memories his dad had exultantly dredged up and waved in front of him like a trophy.

That night, he tossed and turned, unable to rest. When he did surrender to exhaustion, his sleep was plagued with a montage of guilt and anguish.

Chapter 9

Wednesday afternoon, Maddy walked to her car after work. Unlike Monday, she didn't see any sign of her students, and she was relieved. They had been a little more difficult today, and she was glad to be going home. Maddy opened the back door of her car and threw her bags on the back seat. Just as she opened the front door, she heard a voice.

"Hey, Ms. Thompson!"

Maddy turned around and saw Trina running towards her.

As the girl came closer, she slowed down a bit. "You said you would talk to me today after class, Ms. Thompson."

Maddy looked at her watch. "I promised you fifteen minutes. As it stands, classes have been out for almost half an hour. I was waiting in the classroom for you to show up, but you never did. I assumed you had changed your mind." Maddy tried to look pleasant, but she was frustrated that the girl still wanted to have this discussion.

Trina looked down at the ground, then back up at Maddy. "I kind of forgot, okay? So can we talk now?"

Maddy held back the enormous sigh she wanted to release and pointed to a small wooden bench a few feet away. "Over there," she told Trina. "But I still only have fifteen minutes."

Once they were seated, Maddy asked, "Now, what was it you wanted to discuss?"

Trina suddenly seemed hesitant to speak, which Maddy deemed to be uncharacteristic of the girl, even after having been her teacher for a short time. Usually, she seemed to be the center of attention.

Finally, she said, "I just wanted to ask you, well. . .how did you get along with people in college?"

Maddy was surprised. All of this for such a simple question? "Well, I guess I got along with everyone pretty well."

"But how did you make friends?"

"I just. . .did my best to be myself, and tried to reach out to people. Especially my freshman year. Everyone is trying to make friends then, so it's not too hard." She smiled at Trina. "Are you worried about making friends this fall?"

The girl shrugged. "A little. I don't have too many friends right now."

Maddy was surprised. Every time she saw Trina, she was with a large group of the other students. Cautiously, she said, "It looks like you're getting along with the kids here at camp."

Trina shrugged. "Not really. They like it when I make jokes or help them with their homework. Nobody ever calls me up and invites me to go anywhere. The boys will flirt with me for awhile. The girls will be jealous because the boys are interested in me. Then the boys will find out I'm smart and back off. The girls might be nicer to me after awhile, but they don't ever really count me as a friend."

"Is that why you pretend you don't know the answers in my class?"

Trina nodded. "Most of the people here this year are new, and they've never met me before. At least they'll be friends with me for a little while."

Maddy bit the inside of her lip. She knew that feeling all too well. But she didn't think she'd experienced half as much as Trina had. Although Jordan and his friends had teased her mercilessly, she'd still had plenty of other friends, both male and female. From what she could tell, most of Trina's peers had alienated her. Maddy was at a loss for words. She knew that she couldn't honestly tell Trina, "I know what you're going through." But she couldn't just say, "I'm sure everything will work out someday" either.

Quickly, Maddy prayed before she spoke. *Lord, please help me to say the right thing. I don't know exactly how she feels, but I have an idea. Show me how to tell her about You and how You care for her.*

Trina was staring at her, waiting for an answer. She seemed like a different girl than the one Maddy had dealt with during classes. She was serious, mature, respectful. . .and hurt.

"You know, Trina, I think at college you'll be able to have a fresh start. But I don't think you should try to reinvent yourself, even temporarily, just to make people like you."

"But nobody will talk to me if I don't, Ms. Thompson."

"I think that if you let people know you're smart and you're not ashamed of it, they will learn to respect you, even if they are a little jealous or intimidated."

"They never have before," Trina said.

"Well, that was their loss. I think you should concentrate on trying to be yourself instead of trying to be what you think people would like for you to be."

Trina shrugged. "But what if they still don't like me after that?"

Maddy took a deep breath. "Trina, did you know that Jesus loves you? Even if you feel like no one else cares, Jesus does."

Trina stood up. "Listen, Ms. Thompson. I came to talk to you because you're not much older than me and you're really smart. I thought you might be able to help me out and give me advice about making friends. What I don't need is a Sunday school lesson. I thought you were pretty cool, but you sound like a preacher." With that, Trina walked away.

Maddy wondered whether or not she should chase Trina, but she decided against it. She didn't know if she had broken any kind of rules by witnessing to Trina, but it might make matters worse if she went running after her, so she just prayed that Trina would be okay until Friday. Maybe then she would have a chance to talk to her again.

Maddy waited for several more minutes in case Trina came back, but she didn't return. Reluctantly, Maddy got in her car and drove home. She decided to watch her mother cook dinner in order to gain a little cooking practice. After dinner, she graded some of the students' work and prepared lessons for the next week. She tried to relax by reading a book, but she felt restless.

After almost an hour of rereading the same page of the novel, she decided to call Jordan and see what he was up to. She hadn't seen him since Monday night, and she didn't get to talk to him for very long after she finished the cookies because he had been having a discussion with his dad. Or maybe it had been an argument. What she did know was that she could hear the shouting even in her own backyard.

She searched around in her room for his phone number and then dialed. The phone rang four times, and just as she was going to hang up, he answered.

"Hello?" His voice sounded groggy, almost as if he had been asleep.

"Hi, Jordan, it's Maddy."

"Hi." He sounded a little down. "Is there something you need?"

"Well. . .not really. I was just calling to say hello. I hadn't heard from you in a couple of days, and I was just wondering if you were okay."

He waited a long time before answering. Finally, he said, "What do you mean by okay?"

"I–I overheard your dad yelling the other night."

"What did you hear?" he wanted to know.

"Nothing, really." Maddy was a little embarrassed. She probably shouldn't have said anything. She'd be embarrassed if someone overheard her parents fussing at her. "I didn't hear anything. I just heard loud voices," she told him.

Jordan sighed deeply. "I don't know if I've told you this before, but my parents aren't Christians. So every once in awhile, my dad decides to prove how wrong I am about being saved."

"Oh, Jordan, I'm really sorry. I don't have any idea how that might feel."

He was quiet. "Be glad you don't know what it's like. It's not much fun."

"Is there anything I can do?" she asked, feeling helpless.

"Just pray."

"Consider it done," she told him.

"Are you busy Saturday?" he asked.

"Not that I know of."

"Then let's do something."

"Like what?"

"How about I surprise you?"

Maddy laughed. "That sounds like fun. What time should I be ready?"

"How about ten?"

"In the morning?"

"Yep. In the morning."

"I take it you're already formulating some type of plan," she said. "Can you give me a hint?"

"I don't know. I don't want to give it away."

"Come on. . .just a little clue?"

"Okay. You might want to bring a camera."

"That's it?"

"That's all the hints you get. You won't find out anything else until Saturday." Maddy laughed. "Okay. I guess I'll just have to wait until Saturday."

A few moments later, Maddy ended the conversation and hung up the phone. She exhaled softly. Jordan was trying terribly hard to pretend that he was okay, but he wasn't. She could tell something was bothering him, but whatever it was, he didn't want to talk about it.

Lord, please give him peace about what's bothering him and heal what needs to be healed.

Chapter 10

Saturday morning, Maddy awoke early and patiently waited for Jordan, who came to her house five minutes early. His surprise turned out to be a "tour" of sorts, during which they visited several of Kansas City's many fountains. At each fountain, they took pictures of each other, and when they reached the final destination, the famous J. C. Nichols Fountain on the Plaza, they sat in the grass and had a picnic.

Maddy invited Jordan to join her at her church on Sunday, but he seemed to grow uncomfortable and declined, saying he'd prefer not to. Monday morning she returned to work and found that Trina was no longer being disruptive in class. In fact, she had become the total opposite. She was quiet and withdrawn, and during free periods, she no longer spent time with the other kids. Instead, she would retreat to a corner and just sit or read a book. Maddy noticed that the other kids seemed puzzled at first by Trina's behavior, but as time passed, they began teasing the girl, calling her names.

Maddy was shocked to see that the kids had turned on Trina so quickly. Just a few weeks earlier, she'd been the center of attention, and everyone had seemed to enjoy her company. Now, it was just the way Trina had complained about to Maddy. When she showed the other kids that she was intelligent, then they didn't seem to think she was much fun.

Maddy instantly identified with how Trina must have felt, but when she tried to talk to the girl, Trina told her to stay away from her. "I don't need you feeling sorry for me, Ms. Thompson. I already told you it would happen," she said. From then on, she seemed to purposefully avoid Maddy and rarely even made eye contact with her.

As the rest of June unfolded, Maddy was happy that Jordan seemed to spend more and more time dropping by her house in the evenings. They spent hours cooking. And while Jordan proved to be a patient teacher, Maddy felt she was a good student. He complimented her many times on her ability to pick up on things quickly. She made mistakes on occasion, but she rarely made the same mistake twice.

Over the Fourth of July weekend, Jordan traveled with Maddy's family to St. Louis where her brother-in-law Max's relatives lived. Max's family was a lot of fun, and their holiday get-togethers were very lively. She and Jordan endured lots of good-natured teasing about the status of their relationship. Soon everyone lost interest when Mavis, Stacy's new mother-in-law, along with Maddy and Stacy's own mother, brought up the subject of Max and Stacy starting a family.

Although Maddy could tell Stacy wasn't thrilled with all of the attention, Stacy and Max took it in stride. Maddy was just glad the focus had shifted from herself and Jordan, because the last thing she wanted was for Jordan to feel pressure about their relationship. And as far as she could tell, he didn't get upset. He continued coming over to visit, and the two went on several outings together, although Jordan assured her they were going just "as friends." It wasn't exactly the most romantic summer of her life, but Maddy didn't complain. She kept praying and waiting for an opportunity to tell Jordan how she really felt about him.

But shortly afterward, Maddy had to deal with more pressing concerns. Trina's grades started dropping dramatically, and the girl began skipping classes. On the rare occasion that Trina did come to class, she totally avoided Maddy and the other kids. Finally, Maddy reported to Mrs. Calvin what was going on, but her supervisor advised Maddy not to get involved in students' disagreements. "We're not here to make everyone get along," the older woman told Maddy. "Our job is to teach. Kids have arguments all of the time. Chances are, next week Trina will be back in the group, and they'll all be teasing some other kid. We can't spend our time trying to make kids like each other. They have to learn to solve their own problems in a mature way."

Maddy tried to explain that she knew how Trina was feeling, but Mrs. Calvin just waved her off. "As long as she's not a problem in the classroom, it's not really your problem, Maddy. If she does something that warrants discipline, then we can do more. We might be able to call a conference with her parents or something, and get more insight into what's going on at home. But remember, we're not psychologists, we're teachers. If we spent our time trying to reach out to all the kids who have felt rejected at one time or another, we'd never get any teaching done. It happens to almost everyone at some time or another."

And it can hurt for a long time, Maddy thought. But in her heart, she knew Mrs. Calvin was right. Most kids in school felt like outcasts at some time or another, but eventually they resolved their problems. And even though she had only been hired to teach, Maddy's heart ached for the pain Trina was feeling, and she wished she could do something to help the girl.

⋘

A few days later, during one of her cooking sessions with Jordan, Maddy mentioned the situation with Trina.

When she told him about the other kids making fun of Trina, Jordan seemed to grow uneasy.

Frowning, he said, "Does she seem like she's angry at the other kids?"

Maddy shrugged. "I don't think so. Hurt is more what I'm thinking. I just keep wondering if there's a way I can help her. Maybe I was too unfeeling the day she came to me for advice. I basically just threw out some pat answers at her and told her to be herself, because eventually, someone who cares about what's inside will come along and be her friend." Maddy looked at Jordan and said, "I think I felt like her sometimes in high school, and I used to get so tired of hearing people say, 'Eventually somebody will like you for who you really are.' And now, I've gone and told someone else that same answer. I feel like such a hypocrite."

Jordan crossed his arms and leaned against the wall. "You know, hearing this from you makes me feel pretty bad too. I know I've apologized for my teasing, but I can't apologize for the people who teased you because they heard me do it. I feel so responsible for how hurt you felt."

Maddy chuckled softly. "Jordan, I appreciate your honesty and remorse, but I don't hold any of that against you. Sure, you might have given some other people the idea to tease me, but whether you made fun of me or not, somebody was probably going to pick on me at some time or another." She paused, then finished. "And as much as I'm embarrassed to admit it, I did my own share of teasing people who I figured were lower on the totem pole than myself. I don't think anyone is innocent of that, but I really wish people would think more about the consequences before they ridicule someone else."

"Yeah. . .the consequences," Jordan murmured. He tilted his head to the side and asked, "You don't think she wants to get back at the other kids, do you?"

"No, I think she'd rather just disappear so they won't have anything to say about her. I just keep thinking that there's something I could do to help her."

Jordan shook his head vigorously. "Promise me you won't get involved with this, Maddy. Just like your boss said, you're just a teacher, and it's not part of your job to fix your students' arguments."

Maddy frowned. "Jordan, I don't think you're being very sensitive to how she feels. If I can figure out a way to help her, I will."

"No! Just stay out of it."

Maddy was stunned. In all the years she'd known him, he had never yelled at her. Even all of his teasing had been done in a lighthearted tone of voice. She didn't know what to say, so she waited for him to speak.

Jordan walked over and stood directly in front of her. "You have to promise me that you will stay out of this. Let the kids work it out themselves."

Maddy was too shaken by his previous outburst to argue with him. Silently, she nodded.

Jordan sighed with what seemed to be relief, but he still seemed uncomfortable. He fixed himself a glass of water, then sat down at the kitchen table.

Something was still disturbing him, and he didn't appear willing to share it with her just yet. But it didn't look like he felt like continuing their cooking lesson either. Maddy nervously cleared her throat and Jordan looked at her expectantly. "You know, I'm a little tired from work," she said. "Would it be okay with you if we finish this tomorrow?" She looked around the kitchen. So far, they had only measured out dry ingredients for a loaf of focaccia. It would keep just fine until tomorrow.

Jordan nodded in agreement. "If you don't mind, I think that's a good idea." He stood up and moved toward the back door. "But I just remembered that I can't come tomorrow. Remember, I'm moving in two days and even though I don't have that much stuff, I've still got to pack it."

"I don't envy you one bit," Maddy said, hoping to lighten the mood. "It took me long enough to get everything packed to bring home from school. You need any help?"

"Nah. I'll be done in a couple of evenings, I think. And don't you have to get ready for Arnold's party this weekend?"

Maddy shrugged. "Yeah, you're right. In fact, I'm baking the cake, so pray for me. I'll be really embarrassed if it doesn't turn out right."

"Hey, you've been a good student. You make me proud."

"Thanks" She grinned. "But I'm looking to brush up on my painting skills, so when you decide how you're going to decorate your loft, I'll be glad to lend a hand."

Jordan eyed her carefully. "So now you want this guy to know that you're a skilled wall painter?"

Maddy didn't answer for a minute. Jordan had a habit of bringing up this guy she had a crush on and making her feel flustered. She couldn't tell if he knew she was referring to him and he was gently teasing her, or if he thought she was referring to someone else. Either way, she didn't want to just blurt things out one day. She was going to have to tell him. . .eventually.

"Ahem. Maddy, I'm willing to let you help me, but remember I have to live there, and paint can be kind of expensive. Plus, the place has wood floors which I prefer stayed unpainted. So let's try not to relive any of your early kitchen mishaps in my apartment."

Maddy grinned widely. "I'm not clumsy, you know. I just have little accidents sometimes. But I promise I'll be very careful with your paint and your precious hardwood flooring. So when do we start?"

"I'm moving on Friday. Give me a few days to get settled in. How about a week from today?"

"Okay, I'll have to check with Stacy or Laina and see if one of them can come. If one of them can, we'll see you next Wednesday."

Jordan lifted an eyebrow. "Stacy or Laina?"

"Mm-hmm. I know we're just friends and everything, but that's been my little personal rule all through college. If I'm going to a guy's house, I need to have someone there with me. You understand, right?"

"Oh, yeah. I totally understand. And that's a good idea. I should have been the one to think of that," he said. He opened the door to leave and said, "Next Wednesday, then. I'll probably give you a call sometime before then."

"Okay." Maddy waved as he left.

For the next few minutes, she puttered around the kitchen, putting up the ingredients they'd measured. As she worked, she hummed a little tune, smiling to herself. Things with Jordan were going well. He was proud of her progress in the cooking department, and soon she was going to show him that she could be a good homemaker.

The only troublesome spot in her plan was the fact that he kept questioning her about the guy she'd previously admitted to being interested in. He kept dropping hints that he was willing to help figure out what she should tell the guy. Sooner or later, she was going to have to fess up. The only problem was, she didn't want to tell him until she was a little more proficient at becoming more wifely.

As she looked around the room, trying to figure out what to do, the huge calendar on the refrigerator caught her attention.

In a week, July would be over, and Maddy still hadn't worked up the nerve to tell Jordan about her crush on him. She felt boxed in—unwilling to tell him—but frustrated with herself for feeling so nervous about it. Maddy remembered a Scripture Jordan had mentioned several weeks earlier.

The truth will set you free. "You seem like you could use some freedom," he'd joked. And he was right. She wasn't going to experience freedom as long as she kept her mouth shut. Yet, never had there been a moment that seemed like the right time.

"You have to tell him the next time you see him," she admonished herself.

Hopefully, he would take it well. If not, she had only three weeks until her teaching job at the camp ended. If Jordan couldn't stand her, maybe she could move away and get a job in a different city to spare herself the embarrassment of occasionally running into him.

≈

Jordan assembled yet another box and tried to stifle a yawn. It was one o'clock in the morning, and he was supposed to move in another seven or eight hours.

Unfortunately, due to some unforeseen complications on one of his projects, he'd had to put off packing until now. And if he was going to get any rest before morning, he needed to finish soon. Looking around the small living room, he was amazed to see how much stuff he'd accumulated in the few months he'd been living there. And even more amazing was the amount of time it was taking to pack it all up.

At this point, he was simply throwing things into boxes with no set pattern of organization. He would just need to unpack everything pretty soon to make sure he could find all of his essentials.

As he worked, he thought about the conversation he'd had with Maddy a couple of nights earlier. For a moment, he could have imagined that *he* was the guy she had been working so hard to impress. When he'd asked about the mystery man for what seemed to him like the millionth time, something in her eyes had illuminated, causing him to recall the dreamy-eyed look she used to give him in high school. Until then, he hadn't seen that look from her since their reconciliation, unless they were discussing the mystery guy.

At times, he was tempted to believe that the attraction he felt toward her was returned, but most of the time, she was all business. She had a goal in mind, and he still couldn't figure out the exact purpose of the cooking lessons.

And when she'd mentioned she'd be bringing a chaperone to his apartment, he was surprised. At first he thought she might be hinting that she felt some attraction to him, but his hopes had been dashed when she'd told him she had to stick to her rule even though they were "just friends." She wasn't really afraid of being alone with him, because they'd been out dozens of times. But they had always been in public places. And at her house, at least one of her parents was usually around.

She was just politely letting him know that even though she didn't feel anything for him, she just wanted to make sure there was no "appearance of evil" as long as they were at his place.

Probably so Arnold doesn't think she's got a boyfriend or something, Jordan thought.

This Arnold business was getting out of hand. The more time Jordan spent teaching Maddy how to cook, the more equity she was investing in her future with Arnold.

Jordan shook his head. His relationship with Maddy was turning out to be pretty one-sided. Apparently, he was the only one who was emotionally involved. Something had to give. The next time he saw her, he was going to have to start winding things down. She had developed into a more than adequate cook, and he had already promised that she could help him paint his apartment. But after that, he was going to put an end to all of their time together.

Soon, he would start pressing her to tell Arnold how she felt. And the sooner the better. If Arnold returned her interest, Jordan could gracefully bow out before he got any more emotionally involved with her. And if Arnold didn't. . .Jordan would be there to pick up the pieces.

Yes, that's the way to handle it. The only thing that still concerned him was Maddy's desire to help her wayward student. The eerie similarity of that situation sent chills down his back. Maddy had seemed frightened when he'd suddenly yelled at her, and he'd been too embarrassed to explain his outburst. But if she grew too insistent in trying to reach out to that girl, he was going to have to tell her about Harper Blackston.

He had dreaded doing so because, given his own rocky past with Maddy, he wondered whether she would be able to forgive him for the part he'd played in the whole ordeal.

Jordan set his jaw grimly. As things stood, there was probably no future for him and Maddy, and he was already coming to terms with that. But if he needed to protect Maddy's safety, he'd tell her the whole story without worrying about whether she would think less of him. Her life was too important to risk his own discomfort.

Chapter 11

Wednesday evening, Maddy drove downtown with Laina to Jordan's loft. Laina was hardly thrilled with the prospect of coming along since lately she and Maddy rarely saw one another outside of church events, due to their busy work schedules and Maddy's many friendly get-togethers with Jordan.

The only image Laina held of Jordan was of the cocky, teasing flirt he'd been in high school. And now, whenever Maddy brought up the subject of Jordan, Laina changed the subject. Maddy had hoped bringing Laina along for the evening would show her friend what a different person Jordan had become. And secretly, Maddy had decided that Laina would probably be good moral support when she told Jordan the truth about her crush on him.

In the car outside of Jordan's, Laina crossed her arms. "How long do you think we'll be staying?"

Maddy groaned. "I don't know. And if I'd known you were going to be so pouty about this, I wouldn't have asked you to come."

Laina stared at Maddy pointedly. "You knew I didn't want to come and watch you swoon over your old crush, but you had to bring me anyway, because Stacy was busy."

Maddy opened the car door and got out. "I am not swooning over Jordan anymore. We are just friends." She walked briskly toward the entrance of the building.

"But you still like him."

"What if I do?" Maddy challenged.

"I don't want you to get hurt all over again."

Maddy stopped walking. "How many times do I have to tell you that he has changed?"

"It's too soon to really tell," Laina insisted. "In high school, he dated so many girls, it made my head swim. And he never felt any remorse about breaking a girl's heart."

"Don't worry about my heart," Maddy reassured her. "He already broke it once, and I will not give him the opportunity to do it again. So just try to be nice to him for my sake, okay?"

"I'll *try*," Laina grumbled.

As they rode the elevator to Jordan's apartment, Maddy contemplated the situation. Bringing Laina along had not been the wisest idea. Instead of making her confession to Jordan, Maddy would have to work to keep the peace between Laina and Jordan. So, her confession would have to wait for another day. Maddy smiled, feeling very relieved. Yes, she decided, she would have to come clean with Jordan some other time. Maybe. If only she could figure out when.

Seconds later, they stepped off the elevator and walked a few feet to Jordan's apartment door. As Maddy was about to knock, he swung the door open. Hancock squeezed his way past Jordan and jumped up to greet Maddy in his usual manner.

"Sit, Hancock." Maddy laughed. "At least your paws aren't all muddy. I think the indoor life is a good thing for you," she said, while ruffling the puppy's ears.

"You're five minutes late," Jordan said, smiling.

"Sorry about that," said Maddy. "We had technical difficulties during our walk from the car to the door." She looked pointedly at Laina. "But everything's fine now."

Turning to Jordan, she said, "Do you remember my friend Laina?"

"Oh, yeah. When I teased you, she was always right there with you to glare at me." He glanced over at Laina, who was standing silently with her arms folded. "And it looks like she's only gotten better at it."

"Laina," Maddy pleaded.

Jordan held out his hand. "C'mon, let's call a truce. I'm a changed man. Really. You don't have to worry about me." Hancock lay on the floor near Laina's feet and rolled over on his back. "See, even Hancock likes you," Maddy said, trying to break the ice. "Please, Laina?"

Laina eyed Jordan awhile longer, then reluctantly held out her hand. "I hope you're telling the truth," she told him.

Jordan shook her hand and smiled. "Don't worry, I'll be on my best behavior."

Hancock sat up and barked as if to concur with Jordan. Laina managed a small grin.

Jordan wiped his hand across his brow and said, "Whew." Maddy and Laina stared at him questioningly. Jordan shrugged. "It's pretty nerve-wracking to know somebody who can't stand you is going to help you paint your apartment. Especially if you have floors this beautiful."

Maddy and Laina laughed along with Jordan.

"I think he's the one you'll have to worry about." Maddy pointed at Hancock. "How are you going to keep him out of the paint?"

Jordan grimaced. "Oh, no, I hadn't thought about it. The loft is one huge space, so I can't put him in another room. Come on in and I'll figure out something," he said, waving them inside. Jordan offered Maddy and Laina some tea while he set up a temporary furniture barricade to keep Hancock away from the painting. Laina played with Hancock while Jordan moved furniture, and she seemed to be having a good time—with the puppy, at least.

Inwardly, Maddy was relieved. Jordan had managed to talk Laina into a truce, making things easier for all of them for the evening. But, she still didn't think now was the time to open her mouth about her crush on him. She'd have to do it sometime when she and Jordan were alone.

As Jordan went off to a corner to collect some cans of paint, Maddy looked around. The room was the size of a basketball court. The apartment was currently nothing but a huge, wide-open room. In addition, there was a small upstairs loft area that was partially hidden from view by a half wall that ran the length of the area, with the exception of the entrance at the top of the short flight of stairs. The walls had probably once been bright white but had faded and were pretty dingy. The hardwood floors, though, were a beautiful shade of honey brown and had been sanded, stained, and varnished to perfection.

Boxes were stacked in a haphazard fashion throughout the room, and several pieces of furniture sat in the middle of the space, forming the puppy barricade. A kitchen area occupied another corner.

Jordan came and stood next to Maddy as she finished her perusal of his home. "So what do you think?"

"It's beautiful. It really is. I love the natural light."

Jordan nodded. "That's part of the reason I picked this place," he said, gesturing to one of the walls lined with huge windows.

"So how are you planning to arrange your furniture?" Laina wanted to know.

Jordan shook his head. "I'm not quite sure yet. I guess I'll have to find out after the paint dries. Part of the fun with a loft is trying to figure out how you want to divide the living area." He walked to one end of the room and Maddy and Laina followed. He waved his hand toward the kitchen. "As you can see, this is the kitchen, and I plan to leave that space open, instead of walling it off. Right over there, I plan to put the dining area, and over here," he said as he walked toward the middle of the room, "is where I want the main living space to be. Kind of a great room type of area. And then, that big space over there will be my office and studio work space." He grinned. "That way, I'll be able to work on some of my bigger paintings at home."

Maddy smiled. "I bet you're pretty excited about that."

"Definitely."

"But how are you going to divide the areas so they look separate?" Maddy asked. "Right now it still just looks like one big room."

"That's where I get to use my imagination. And paint," he added, grinning. "Eventually, I want to use murals to create a feeling of separation between the spaces. But before I go painting huge pictures, I've got to get the walls painted plain old white. So let's get started, okay?"

"Okay," Maddy agreed.

For the next hour, the three of them worked to ready the walls for painting by taping off the moldings and ceiling, then securing newspapers to the first few feet of floor that extended out from the wall. After that, they got out the paint rollers and proceeded to apply a coat of bright white paint to the walls, with the exception of the one wall that was totally brick.

Maddy had never painted a room in her life, and she discovered it was hard and somewhat messy work. However, she didn't mention her complaints to Jordan because she didn't want him to think she was a wimp.

An hour and a half later, the first coat was complete. Although it was dark outside, Maddy could still see that the new paint was a huge improvement over the dull white the walls had been earlier. She glanced at her watch and realized it was getting late. She would have liked to stay a little longer, but she had to work the next day and she knew Laina had to do the same. She grabbed one of the wet towels Jordan had set aside to use for cleaning and rubbed some of the fresh paint splatters off of her hands.

"Jordan," she said, "I hate to paint and run, but we've got to get home. But I'd love to come back and help again. I'm curious to see what's next."

Jordan paused from painting for a moment. "Thanks. I'm glad you guys helped me. This is a huge room and I really didn't expect to get a whole coat done today." He returned the roller to the rolling pan and walked Maddy and Laina to the door. "And you two are welcome to come back and help out again. I figure I'll let this dry for two or three days, then put the next coat on. After that, we'll have to touch up around the baseboards and the ceiling. Then we paint the trim."

"Sounds like we have lots of work cut out for us," said Maddy.

"Oh, joy," Laina said dryly. At first, Maddy was concerned that Laina wouldn't be willing to come back with her, but as she glanced at her friend, she noticed a playful sparkle in Laina's eyes.

"And thank you, Laina, for helping out, even though I know you'd rather have been somewhere else."

"Oh, it was no problem, really," she said. "Maddy gave me a choice of whether or not I could come." Continuing, she added, "She said I had to come or she wouldn't be my best friend anymore. Naturally, I wanted to keep my best friend, so I came," she deadpanned.

Maddy exhaled loudly in exasperation. "Laina, it wasn't exactly like that," she scolded playfully.

"Maybe not in your memory." Laina laughed. "But it was, and I forgive you for using the ultimatum."

Maddy sighed. "I think it's about time for us to be going. I'll give you a call in a couple of days and see what's going on, okay?"

Jordan nodded in agreement. When Maddy and Laina left, he walked with them to Maddy's car.

On the way home, Laina spent most of the time talking about Jordan's transformation and was so enthusiastic about his new attitude that Maddy almost felt like her best friend was beginning to develop a crush on Jordan.

But Laina, ever so intuitive, reassured Maddy that she didn't have to worry about that. "I'm just relieved to know that you're not involved with the *old* Jordan Sanders," she told Maddy.

"We're not really involved. . .yet," Maddy felt compelled to explain. "Right now we're just getting to know each other. But you never know what might happen," she said.

"Knowing you. . .you never know," Laina agreed. "But what was all that he kept saying about your mystery crush?" Laina wanted to know. "Is this some sort of secret you haven't told me?"

Maddy sighed. "No, you know who my mystery crush is, but Jordan doesn't. And now it's gotten a little out of hand. I just haven't found a good way to tell him." Briefly, she explained the conversation she and Jordan had shared that day after leaving the park. "Now he thinks he's helping me learn to cook to impress some guy, and I'm not really sure how to tell him that I did all this to impress him. The only thing is, I figure if I tell him too soon, he'll be upset with me and he won't want to be even my friend anymore."

Laina was silent for a good while. When she spoke, she said, "You're telling me that the reason you spend all this time with Jordan is because you're enrolled in a sort of. . .wife school with Jordan as your teacher?"

"Basically." Maddy nodded.

"And he's only going along because he thinks that you're doing this for some other guy?"

"That's where I'm not so sure. Sometimes I get the feeling he's a little jealous of the other guy. And sometimes it's like he doesn't really care."

Laina let out a long sigh. "You are the only person I know who could get into a mess like this."

"Well, what am I going to do to get out of it?" Maddy wanted to know. "I was going to tell him tonight, but you saw how well we get along. What if he gets so confused that he won't give me a chance to totally explain the situation? What if he tells me to stay away from him forever?"

Laina shrugged. "I don't know. I've never heard of anything so odd in my whole life. But I think you're going to have to tell him the truth. And soon."

"You're right. I'll call him in a couple of days and set up a time to see him. Then I'll tell him."

❧

Jordan wearily tugged on Hancock's leash. Although he liked being able to keep his dog with him, instead of at his parents' home, the daily walks were beginning to become somewhat of a chore. Actually, it wasn't the walk itself. Both he and Hancock enjoyed that part. The hard part was trying to get Hancock to go back home. The dog seemed to have an inner sense about when Jordan decided it was time to head back to the apartment. He would suddenly get extremely stubborn and try to pull Jordan in the opposite direction. The past couple of evenings, Jordan had practically dragged the puppy back to the apartment.

The few people who had happened to witness the tug-of-war had tsk-tsked and pointedly informed Jordan that people like him shouldn't be allowed to own pets if they were going to mistreat them. Jordan had tried to explain that he wasn't trying to hurt the dog, but they had refused to listen. One man had gone so far as to threaten to call the Humane Society to report him.

Today, Jordan had decided to take an easier route. Instead of trying to drag an unwilling puppy home, Jordan had simply picked the puppy up and carried him home, rather than risk an embarrassing scene. Unfortunately, the puppy had proven to be much heavier than he looked. By the time Jordan reached his building, he was grateful that the building had an elevator.

As soon as Jordan opened the apartment door, Hancock ran over to the couch to claim his favorite seat. Jordan followed suit and wearily closed his eyes, still huffing and puffing from the exertion of carrying Hancock. A few seconds later, Hancock moved over and began licking Jordan's face. Jordan petted the puppy for a few minutes before starting dinner.

A few moments after he began looking through the refrigerator for inspiration, the phone rang.

"Hello?" Jordan questioned.

"Hello, Jordan, it's Maddy," was the cheery response on the other line.

"Oh, hi. What's up?"

"Not much. I was sitting here in the kitchen looking at the recipe for the focaccia we started last week, and I decided to finish it myself."

"So how did it turn out?"

"I'll let you know when I take it out of the oven."

"You'll have to save me a piece," Jordan said. He closed the refrigerator and sat down on one of the stools he kept at the kitchen island. "So how's work?"

"Pretty good. The students are really into their internships right now, so they're pretty interested in what I have to say in my classes. They take what they learn in the classes back to their jobs."

"How's your problem student?"

"Not too bad. She's still pretty withdrawn, but she's not causing any problems. In fact, she actually asked me about the Bible today after classes."

Jordan was quiet, unsure of what to say.

"I know I told you I wouldn't get involved," Maddy said, "but how can I refuse to share the gospel with someone? The last time I mentioned Jesus, she ran away, but now that she's asked again—without me forcing it on her, I can't ignore her."

Jordan exhaled loudly, then asked, "What did she want to know?"

"Well, several weeks ago, I told her that Jesus loves her, no matter how other people are treating her. She got upset and said that I didn't understand. That was when she started avoiding me."

"So what did you tell her today?"

"I told her that Jesus does love her. I invited her to come to church with me."

"You what?"

"I invited her to come to church with me."

Jordan closed his eyes. "Maddy, don't you think you're hiding behind rose-colored glasses here?"

"About what?"

"About. . .this." Jordan's words came out in a rush. "I know she needs to hear the gospel, but don't you think you're getting her hopes up a little?"

"How would I be doing that?"

"You know how kids can be. What if she goes to church with you, gets saved, and goes back to class and finds out the kids still don't like her? Aren't you just a little bit worried that she might take it out on you?"

Maddy's voice sparked with indignation. "No, I'm not. The Bible tells us to share the message of salvation with others. When we do that, we run the risk of people being upset with us. But I feel like the Lord allowed me to get this job, and I'm not going to be ashamed of Him, just because you think things won't work out with Trina."

"Maddy, you're right, we have to share the gospel with people, but we have to be careful about how we approach them. Just use common sense."

Maddy was silent for a moment, then she spoke up angrily. "What makes you the expert? You were no saint yourself, but somehow you managed to get saved. I'm assuming someone shared the gospel with you while you were at college. And judging from the way you used to act toward Christians, I doubt you were very receptive at first. Am I right?"

Jordan had to tell the truth. "Right," he said quietly. The memory of how he'd taunted anyone religious burned in his mind as he listened to Maddy.

Maddy seemed to understand his discomfort. When she spoke again, she was more compassionate. "But what if no one ever said anything to you because they were scared of how you might treat them?" she questioned.

Maddy was right. No matter how many times he had teased Christians, they still seemed to always pop up, handing out tracts and inviting him to church. And thanks to them, he knew where to turn when he was ready to make a change. But what about people like Harper Blackston? Where did they fit in? What about Pastor Maneskroll?

Jordan wiped his forehead and took several deep breaths. It was time to tell Maddy the whole story behind his conversion. "Maddy, I need to talk to you. In person. Can I come over?"

"Jordan, I'm sorry I upset you. But I'll be okay. You don't need to come over and give me a speech." Her voice was kind, but firm.

"It's important." He was pleading, but he wasn't ashamed. He needed to get this off his chest.

"Oh, all right. But don't try to change my mind about inviting her to church, because I already asked her. She's going to call me on Saturday to let me know if she's coming."

"I'll be there in half an hour." Jordan hung up the phone and left the apartment. In the car, he tried to concentrate on the road and prayed, "Please let me say the right words to Maddy, Lord. Please keep her safe. And please help this girl Trina by bringing her to You without causing any harm to come to anyone else."

Chapter 12

Maddy heard Jordan's car pull up just as she finished straining a pot of tea. She didn't know why she was making hot tea in the middle of July, but Jordan had sounded so stressed on the phone that she figured a cup of herbal tea might help him feel better.

When the doorbell rang, her dad said, "I'll get it."

From the kitchen, she heard her dad greet Jordan. "Haven't seen you around here for awhile. How's the new place?"

"It's coming along."

"I heard Maddy and Laina gave you a hand with painting. Did they give you any help or did you have to spend the whole time cleaning up after them?" her dad asked as he and Jordan entered the kitchen. He winked at Maddy, so she knew he was just kidding with her.

"Dad, please." She smiled. "Of course we helped him. Didn't we, Jordan?"

Jordan's smile was strained, but his eyes sparkled as he added, "I was pretty worried about my floor at first, but it came out looking no worse for the wear."

"That's good," said her dad. "So what's on the menu for tonight? Maddy already made some kind of fancy bread for us."

"Focaccia, Dad," she reminded him.

Jordan shook his head. "No cooking for me today. I just came over to talk."

Maddy's dad eyed Jordan closely. "You okay, Son?"

Jordan shrugged. "I think so."

Her dad opened his mouth, then closed it. "I'll be upstairs with Berniece. If you need anything, just let me know." He patted Jordan on the back and headed upstairs.

Jordan stood in the middle of the kitchen with his hands in his pockets. Maddy's heart went out to him. She could tell that whatever was upsetting him was serious. She was glad she hadn't refused to let him come over. But she was at a loss for what to say to comfort him. "Would you like some tea?" she asked, gesturing toward the teapot.

"Sure," he answered.

While she poured the tea, Jordan sat at the kitchen table, silent.

A few minutes later, Maddy joined him. She sat quietly, waiting for him to start talking.

He gazed up from his teacup and looked her in the eye for a moment. "Maddy, only a few people know about this. It's just such a terrible thing. . .I haven't even told anyone at my church."

Maddy's heart started beating wildly. Suddenly, she was uncomfortable with the idea of Jordan confiding anything this serious in her. She reached out and put her hand on top of his. "Then you don't need to tell me. If it's really upsetting you, I can just pray for you."

Jordan hesitated for a moment, as if he were about to agree with her. Then he shook his head, gently pulling his hand away. "No. I need to tell you." He took a deep breath, then began. "When I went away to college, I was the same Jordan you used to know. I wasn't mean, but I teased people—a lot. You know how I was, and you know how the things I said hurt."

Maddy nodded, saying nothing. The way he'd treated her was obviously still bothering him, and she didn't want to add to his trouble by saying too much.

"Well, I acted the same way at college. I was popular, and I teased anybody who seemed. . .I don't know." He shrugged, apparently looking for the right words. "Anyway, there was this guy, Harper Blackston. He was pretty quiet. Really smart. And even back then, I knew he was a brilliant artist. Maybe I was even a little jealous of him. I felt insecure around him, because I knew he was better than me at the time. But he was kind of eccentric, just small things, mostly, so I would try to make myself feel better by teasing him. I wasn't the only one who made fun of him—lots of people did—but I did more than my share. He lived in a dorm room across from mine for the first three years."

Jordan sipped his tea. "Whatever anybody said never seemed to bother him. He just ignored us. He made good grades. He didn't really hang out with a lot of people, so we figured he had friends somewhere else. And the fact that he didn't seem to get upset when we teased him. . .I think it just egged us on. We kept jabbing and digging, just to see what it would take to make him get mad. We thought he was some kind of robot or something. . .he never really paid much attention to us. I wasn't a Christian then, and I know I said some pretty rough stuff, so bad I can't even repeat it now."

Jordan's eyes suddenly grew watery. Looking into his cup, he said, "There was this preacher. His name was Malcolm Maneskroll. He wasn't too much older than all of us, just in his early thirties. He really had a heart for college students."

He looked Maddy in the eye now. "You were a Christian when you went to college, so you probably saw all the bad stuff that went on, but had the sense to stay away from it."

Maddy nodded slightly. She'd made her share of mistakes, but Jordan was right. The support she had from her parents and her church had helped her to steer clear of much of what went on.

Jordan shook his head. "Well, I didn't. But it seemed like this preacher was always popping up somewhere. It was a small college town, and he would stand on the corners in the party district of town, if you could call it that. He would hand out tracts and invite us to his church. I went probably once or twice during my first three years there, and all I did was make fun of him."

Jordan got really quiet and held his head in his hands. Maddy moved closer and patted his back. She had never, ever seen him cry, and she didn't know what she could do to help him. Maddy was a little scared and didn't know if she wanted to hear the rest of the story.

Abruptly, Jordan sat up straight.

"Jordan, you don't have to tell me this."

"Yes," he said. Wiping his eyes with the backs of his hands, he started again. "By the time my senior year started, this pastor, Malcolm, had led several students to Christ. And he was working on several others. The college-aged members of his congregation would go out with him and help hand out tracts and witness to people in broad daylight, in the middle of the street. They were really excited about the Lord." Jordan smiled slightly, as though he was recalling a happy memory.

"One of the people he was helping was Harper Blackston. Most of us didn't know it, but the summer before our senior year started, Harper had tried to commit suicide. Not many of the students lived there year-round, but Harper had lived there all his life. His father had died before he was born, and his mother had raised him. She was an alcoholic and a drug addict and had been sentenced to two years in prison for drug abuse, but none of us knew that either. Anyway, Harper called Malcolm after he took all the pills, and Malcolm took him to the hospital. When Harper got better, Malcolm started witnessing to him. Harper wouldn't go to church, though. He was too embarrassed to go, because even some of the people at the church still made fun of him sometimes. But Malcolm was persistent. He invited Harper to his house and let him meet his wife. Harper apparently felt comfortable with them, and he started spending a lot of time there.

"One day, right after Christmas break ended, I was walking downtown to go to the store, and I saw Malcolm. It was early in the morning, and hardly anybody else was out on the street. He stopped me, and he said, 'Jordan, Jesus is waiting for you to make up your mind.' I laughed at him, like I normally did. I told him that since he was always telling us that Jesus was going to be around for eternity, that Jesus could wait another day for me. Then he grabbed my arm, and he got really serious. He said, 'Jordan, if you died today, give me one reason why Jesus shouldn't let you go to hell?'

"I don't know what it was, but I finally listened to him. I think he scared me. Nobody had ever put it to me like that before. We sat down on a park bench, and he read me these Bible verses. He asked me if I believed Jesus was the Son of God. I said yes. Even though I didn't know exactly why I was saying yes, I knew in my heart that Jesus was God's Son, and I knew He had died on the cross for me. Even though I had never thought much about it before, I also knew that Jesus had risen from the dead and was back up in heaven. But then I thought about some of the things I'd done.

"I told Malcolm, 'I've done some pretty bad things. I don't think God will really forgive some of the stuff I've done.' He told me that Jesus would wash my sins away, and give me a clean slate. He read Romans 8:1 to me and I just felt so relieved. That sounded good to me, and even though I had my doubts, I went ahead and prayed this prayer with him. When we finished, he hugged me and said, 'Welcome to God's family.' He told me I needed to come to church and make a public profession of my faith. I told him no at first, but he just smiled and said, 'I'll see you Sunday.'

"The rest of the morning I felt like I was floating on air. I was smiling so much, I felt like my face was going to get stuck. People kept asking me what was making me so happy, and I just kept saying, 'Jesus loves me.' A lot of people thought I was making fun of the Christians on campus because they were always saying stuff like that.

"I didn't care what they thought about me, and I didn't try to explain it to anyone. I knew I was feeling better than I had in a long time, and I wasn't making fun of somebody to make me feel happy. My roommate was a Christian, and I remember locking myself in the room later that day and borrowing his Bible. I kept reading those same verses Malcolm had shown me, trying to make sure he was telling me the truth. When my roommate came up after dinner, I started asking him all these questions. I had hardly talked to the guy since he'd gotten saved, but Malcolm had already told him I'd gotten saved, and he was just as excited as I was. He suggested we go out and celebrate at this coffee shop where he was supposed to be meeting Malcolm and some of the other students for a Bible study.

"We left the dorm, and right outside we saw Harper. I wanted to apologize to him, but all I could think to say was, 'Hey, Harper, Jesus loves you.'

"He had never, in three years, said hardly anything to me when I had teased him, but just then, he pushed me up against a concrete wall. He was a big guy, and he could have beat me up any day, but I never realized it until then. I was scared because he was choking me.

"He said, 'Are you telling me Jesus loves you too?'

"I barely whispered 'yes' before he let me go and just gave me another shove. I had a small cut on the back of my head, where he pushed me against the wall, but I didn't even notice it until later. 'Don't give me that,' he said. He took off running in the other direction. My roommate was pretty shaken up too, and by the time we got to the coffee shop, he asked everybody to pray for Harper.

"Malcolm wasn't there yet, so they just started praying for Harper. They seemed to know he had been going through a rough time, and even though he got along with Malcolm pretty well, he was leery of the rest of them.

"They were all happy that I'd gotten saved, and they told me that they had been praying for me for a long time. I was shocked that they even cared about me that much, since I'd never been that friendly to any of them."

Jordan stopped and cleared his throat. "Malcolm never showed up that night." He looked at over at Maddy. "Do you recognize this story yet?"

Maddy's stomach started flip-flopping. Something about Jordan's story was making her uneasy. The names he'd mentioned seemed familiar. Then she remembered something from the news a few years ago. She remembered Stacy mentioning that Jordan had attended art school in New Jersey. But somehow, she never connected his name to that school. . .or that story.

She impulsively hugged Jordan. "Oh, Jordan, I'm sorry. I never knew you— I'm sorry." Maddy tried to stop herself, but she started sobbing. Not long after, Jordan was crying along with her. Minutes later, he pulled away.

"An hour later, we left the coffee shop and walked to Malcolm's house."

Maddy held up her hand. "I don't know why you're telling me this, but you don't have to. I know."

He shook his head and continued. Tears were still streaming down his face. "There were police cars everywhere."

Maddy closed her eyes. This much she knew from the news. Harper Blackston had killed Malcolm, and then himself. Malcolm's wife had hid in the bedroom and later escaped through the back door.

Jordan was still talking. ". . .Malcolm's wife said Harper had been upset because of what I'd said. He didn't believe that Jesus could love me *and* him. It was my fault."

Maddy was silent. She knew Jordan blamed himself, and she could understand why. But surely, he hadn't been carrying this around for all this time?

"I went to Malcolm's funeral. It was on a Sunday. I didn't want to go, but I remembered how Malcolm had wanted me to come to church that Sunday. I just felt like I couldn't let him down. The other students tried to be nice to me, and even though no one ever came right out and said it, most of them blamed me. I thought they had a right to. I never made my profession of faith in Malcolm's church. In fact, I never went back after his funeral. My roommate avoided me whenever it was possible, and even the non-Christians avoided me. The police took me in for questioning, and I couldn't think of anything except how I was responsible."

"Jordan," Maddy said gently. "The news reports. . .most of the students I saw who were interviewed said they felt responsible. They said everybody teased him. They all said they felt bad."

Jordan shook his head. "I know. But I shouldn't have said anything to him that night. He was upset about me."

"Jordan, he was on medication. He'd tried to commit suicide at least two other times. His doctors said he was unstable."

"Maybe. But maybe not. We'll never know."

"So what happened to you?" Maddy's question was barely above a whisper.

"I couldn't think. I wanted some help. I felt like I had canceled out my salvation, but none of the students who went to the church would give me the time of day. I stopped going to class. The school threatened to kick me out. My dad threatened to sue the school. He was just embarrassed that his son had anything to do with that situation.

"Finally, one day, I was packing up to go home. I didn't know what I was going to do, but I couldn't stay there. My roommate came in with Malcolm's wife. I started crying and begged her to forgive me. She said it wasn't my fault. She said that Harper would get into yelling sessions with Malcolm about other students who laughed at him, even the ones in Malcolm's church.

"The only thing that had been different that time was that Harper had brought a gun. She told me that I was welcome to come to the church, but I refused. I felt too guilty. She gave me one of Malcolm's Bibles. I told her I couldn't take it, but she told me that he had already set it aside to give to me that morning after I'd prayed with him.

"It was an old, worn Bible, and she flipped to Isaiah 43:25 and told me that God had already forgiven me, but as long as I blamed myself, I wouldn't *feel* truly forgiven. She told me that she even struggled with her own guilt concerning Malcolm. She'd felt that she might have been able to prevent it if she had not allowed Malcolm to invite Harper to their home in the first place. Then she gave me the card of this guy who was a Christian counselor and I called him. I started meeting with him, and he helped me understand God had forgiven me. I was able to stay at school and finish my degree.

"My dad hated the fact that I needed counseling, and even more, he couldn't understand why I wanted a Christian counselor. He blames the school for me becoming a Christian. He thinks they should have put Harper out of school before he did so much harm." Jordan smiled slowly. "We still don't see eye to eye. He hates it when I talk about Jesus. Right before I graduated from art school, I talked him into taking half of the money out of this trust fund he had for me. I wasn't supposed to get the money until after I finished college, but I told him that if he wouldn't take the money out, I would when I was able. I gave it to a fund that Malcolm's wife started for kids who wanted to go to Bible college. My dad was furious. He thinks the counselor brainwashed me into giving my money away. He keeps saying that the Bible turned me into mush." Jordan smiled again, then said, "Basically, he thinks Jesus stole some of his money. Every once in a while, he gets really heated up about it."

"What about your mom?" Maddy asked.

"She's not into religion, but she's glad I found something to help me feel better. She just doesn't want to say anything to set my dad off. So as long as I keep quiet about Jesus, things are okay at their house."

Maddy sighed sympathetically. She couldn't imagine what Jordan had gone through, but even more importantly, she couldn't imagine not being supported by her own parents in her decision to be a Christian. They had set the example for her, and when she was four years old, she had made the decision to accept Jesus for herself.

"Jordan, I'm so sorry," she said again. "Are you okay?"

He gave her a half smile. "Most of the time. Sometimes, I get bogged down with guilt, and it takes me a little while to recover. Being around you is sometimes hard, because of how I used to treat you. But I had to tell someone. Only the people I went to school with, my parents, and my counselor know about this. I haven't told anyone here. Not even the people at my church."

Maddy didn't know what to say. While she was still pondering all that he'd said, Jordan spoke up again. This time, his face grew intense and he held her hand as he spoke.

"Maddy, to be honest with you, I admire you wanting to witness to that girl in your class, but I had to tell you this to make sure you understand the seriousness of something like that. When people have been hurt, you never know exactly how they might react, even to people who genuinely care about them." He looked away for a second. "The three years I've been saved, I've never been able to witness to anyone. I've been too scared. I know it's wrong, but I walk in the other direction. I'm glad you're not afraid to, and I'm even a little jealous. I feel like a coward. I'm a grown man, over six feet tall, and you're more that a foot shorter than me, yet you have more courage than I do. I witnessed to one person, and look what happened after I did."

Maddy was still shaken. She could understand Jordan's fear. In his happiness over getting saved, he'd told Harper that Jesus loved him, and it had been taken the wrong way.

"That's why I started painting murals," Jordan went on. "It's my silent way of telling people about Jesus. One day I'll be able to open my mouth and tell people, but until then, this is what I can do."

Maddy nodded. "I don't know what to say. I know it took a lot for you to tell me all of this, and I appreciate it." Nervously, she added, "But I still think I need to invite Trina to church. And I'm sorry about what I said about someone having to witness to you. I didn't know the whole story. But if Malcolm hadn't stopped you that morning, where would you be now?" she asked gently.

Jordan shook his head. "I've asked myself that question a million times. I'm glad he stopped me, but if he hadn't, he might still be alive today. . .or maybe not."

Jordan stood up. "I've kept you up too late. I'd better go."

Maddy stood up and followed him to the door. "Thanks for trusting me enough to share your story. I really appreciate it. Is there anything I can do?"

Jordan smiled. "I can always use prayer. I'm not perfect yet."

Maddy bit her lip, unsure of how to phrase her next question. "Will you be upset with me if I still talk to Trina?"

Jordan exhaled loudly. He looked down at the floor for a long time, then said, "No, I won't. I know that you'll do what the Lord tells you to do. Sometimes I just feel like I need to protect you from what could happen, even though I might be wrong. As long as you follow the Lord's leading, you'll be doing the right thing, I think. The more I think about it, the more I know that Malcolm stopped me just in time." He reached out and enveloped Maddy in a hug.

Maddy leaned against his chest, listening to his heartbeat. She knew Jordan didn't see this as a romantic hug, but just for a moment, she let herself believe that he was hugging her because his love for her was deeper than just friendship. Reluctantly, she pulled away.

Looking him in the eye, she said, "I will pray for you, Jordan. I promise."

"Thanks, Maddy. You don't know how much I appreciate it." Slowly, he opened the door and walked outside. Right before he got into his car, he turned and smiled. "See you later."

Maddy waved as his car disappeared down the street.

Chapter 13

The next day at school, Maddy felt jumpy. On Thursdays, she taught the juniors, so she didn't expect to see Trina, but nonetheless, no matter how brave she'd tried to be for Jordan, his story had shaken her.

Was Trina someone to be afraid of? Maddy couldn't tell. She tried to not be afraid, but with little success. By the time classes were over, Maddy practically flew out of the building. Her heart pounded as she walked to her car, and only when she was out of the parking lot did her pulse slow back to its normal rate.

When she got home, she found her mother in the kitchen and poured out the whole story that Jordan had told her the night before.

When Maddy finished, she asked her mother, "Do you think I did the wrong thing by inviting Trina to church?"

Berniece Thompson was quiet for a long time. She stared at her hands, deep in thought. Finally, she said, "We raised you and your sister not to be ashamed of your faith. Both of you witnessed to your friends all throughout school, and your dad and I are proud of you. Earlier this summer, when you first started telling us about Trina, I was happy that you were trying to reach out to a student in need."

She paused and looked Maddy in the eye. "I can't say that Jordan's story hasn't scared me. But not every situation turns out like that. What we can do is pray about this. The Lord will show us what His will is for her, and whether or not He wants you to get personally involved. I do know that even if we don't say anything directly to certain individuals, we can always pray for them. And sometimes prayer is the route God wants us to take. Other times, He wants us to be more vocal. Why don't we pray about it right now?"

Maddy murmured her agreement. She and her mom bowed their heads right then and asked God for guidance about Maddy's role with Trina.

When they finished, Maddy said, "She said she would call me tomorrow if she was going to come to church. What should I say if she calls?"

"If she wants to come, I think she should," her mother said slowly.

"I feel the same way too," Maddy agreed. "I guess we'll just have to wait and see what happens."

❧

Later that evening, Maddy went bowling with some of her friends from church. "Did you tell Jordan that you have a crush on him?" Laina asked.

Maddy slapped her hand to her forehead. "Oh, no. I totally forgot."

Laina gave her an I-don't-believe-you stare.

Maddy returned the look. "Trust me, Laina. I saw Jordan yesterday, and I really did forget."

"You can't expect to build a relationship on lies," Laina countered.

Maddy sighed in exasperation. "I know. But. . .I really don't think there is any hope for a relationship anymore."

Laina frowned. "Why not?"

"I can't tell you all of the details, but when he came over last night, he told me some things. I really did forget to tell him about my crush on him, and I'm glad I did, because it wouldn't have been the right time. And now I don't think I need to."

"You're not making any sense."

"I know. What I'm trying to say is, Jordan has changed, but he really is being my friend because he feels so awful about how he used to treat me. I think he's satisfied to keep things the way they are, and I'm not going to push things further by telling him I've liked him all these years. This whole summer I don't think he's even briefly considered more than a friendship with me."

"Are you sure?"

"Almost one hundred percent positive. To Jordan, being my friend is sort of a step of faith. A test to see if I would really forgive him for how he treated me. And all I can say is I'm glad I accepted his apology. I think it would have hurt him if I hadn't."

"So that's it?" Laina asked.

"Yeah."

"But wait—doesn't he think you have a crush on some other guy?"

Maddy shrugged. "Maybe. But I never did. I had the crush on him. When I see him, I'll tell him the crush is over."

"Is it really?"

"I think so. I still care for Jordan, but I can't tell what's real, mature love from my old schoolgirl crush, or just wanting to help him with what he's going through. Now is not the time to cloud things up by being impulsive."

Laina's eyes softened. "You know what I think?"

"What?"

"I think that you're on the right track. You can't make a decision like that based on how you feel from day to day. Like Arnold and Patty are always telling us, lasting love is based on what you know, not what you feel."

"Yeah, good old Arnold and Patty," said Maddy. "I wish Jordan could meet Arnold. I think they'd get along pretty well. Unfortunately, Jordan seems to get really upset when I mention Arnold. I can't figure it out."

Laina laughed. "Maybe he thinks Arnold is your mystery crush," she said, wiggling her eyebrows.

"Oh, right." Maddy laughed. "Jordan is jealous of the married man who leads the singles' group with his wife?"

"You did tell him Arnold is married, didn't you?"

"Yes. . .well, I think I did." Maddy grew silent as she thought back to the day she and Jordan had taken Hancock to the park. That was the first day she'd ever mentioned Arnold. She couldn't remember whether or not she'd told Jordan that Arnold was married. Then her mind flashed back to the day of Jordan's apology. She'd been so rude, trying to get away from him and—"Oh, no! The guy on the telephone," she groaned.

"What guy?" asked Laina.

Maddy swallowed. "It's a long story, but the first time Jordan tried to apologize to me, I got scared. I thought he was going to start teasing me. He was standing at the front door, asking to come in, but I wanted him to go away. The phone rang and it was this guy selling long-distance services. His name was Arnold, and I played like I knew him. I exaggerated a little, and Jordan must have thought that I had a crush on some guy named Arnold. And then whenever I mentioned Arnold from church, Jordan got really tense. Especially when I told him we were planning a surprise party for Arnold." Maddy covered her face with her hands. "I can't believe I didn't put the two together all this time."

"Me either," said Laina. "How could you not remember?"

Maddy tried to remember. "A lot happened that day. By the time I saw Jordan again, he was apologizing, and I totally forgot about my little telephone episode."

"Yikes," Laina said. "I'd say you should tell him the next time you see him. You can't have him walking around, mad at Arnold any longer."

"You're right. But for other reasons, I don't want to burden him by telling him I had a crush on him. He has a lot to think about now."

"Do what you have to," said Laina. "But just get it done."

❧

The next morning, Maddy awoke to the sound of the phone ringing. Groggily, she leaned over and picked up the phone. It was probably Trina.

"Hello?" she said.

"Hi, it's Jordan."

Maddy sat up. "Hi."

"Are you busy today?"

"I don't know. I figured I'd wait around for awhile in case Trina calls, but my parents should be here if she does. What did you have in mind?"

"Do you want to ride out to Powell Gardens with me?"

Maddy thought for a moment. Today would be a good day to talk to Jordan. "Sure. What time? I'd prefer to leave in the afternoon sometime, if you don't mind."

"How's two o'clock?"

"Two is fine. I'll see you later."

During the morning, Maddy did a little housecleaning. By noon she was done and she restlessly sat waiting for Trina to call. While she waited, she got out her Bible and began to pray. At first, her prayers were about Trina. As time went on, her prayers shifted to Jordan.

Lord, please show me what to say to Jordan. I don't think now is a good time to tell him about my crush on him, but I want to be honest. Is he the husband You've chosen for me? And if he isn't, how should I treat him? I hate to pull away from him right now, after everything he's told me, but I don't want to keep going, not knowing what he's feeling. I don't want either of us to get hurt, but right now I feel more scared for myself than for Jordan. I think I care about him way more than he does for me. Please show us both Your will. In Jesus' name, amen.

Maddy opened her eyes and wiped away tears. It was in the Lord's hands now.

Jordan came at exactly two o'clock. Maddy was outside talking to Mrs. Myston when he pulled up.

"Where is that dog of yours, Jordan?" Mrs. Myston asked, looking around suspiciously.

Jordan put his hands out in front of him. "I had to leave him at home. You can't take pets to Powell Gardens."

"Oh. Powell Gardens is such a pretty place. Be sure and stop by the chapel. It's beautiful." She smiled.

"Are you ready?" he asked Maddy.

"Sure. Let's go. Good-bye, Mrs. Myston," she said, waving to the woman.

"Take care, you two," she returned.

"We will," said Jordan.

In the car, Maddy decided it was a good time to get her confession out. Powell Gardens was a good forty-five-minute drive out Highway 50 in Kingsville, Missouri.

"Ahem. I have something to tell you," she told Jordan after they'd been riding for almost ten minutes.

"I have something to tell you too." He grinned, looking across at her.

"Oh? Who goes first, then?" she asked.

"You. I'll tell you later on."

"Okay. Well. First off. . .I think we have had a miscommunication." Maddy went on to tell Jordan the story of the two Arnolds and how she didn't have a crush on either of them.

"I see," Jordan said. "So I was all worked up over the wrong guy."

"And about the mystery crush," Maddy went on. "It's over. I was never really clear about my feelings for the guy, so. . .I put it all in God's hands for now. I'm not going to worry about it anymore."

Jordan just nodded. "So you're not going to tell me who he is?"

Maddy shook her head. "I don't think it's all that important right now."

"I see," he said. Abruptly, he changed the subject. "So did Trina call you today?"

Maddy shook her head. "She may call later on, though."

"Yeah," said Jordan.

Silence enveloped them for a few minutes before Maddy decided to strike up another conversation. "So how's Hancock doing? Is he still refusing to come home after his walks?"

Jordan laughed. "Yeah. And he's getting way too heavy to carry. I enrolled him in obedience school. He starts in two weeks."

"Good idea," Maddy said.

Once again, the conversation lulled, but this time neither of them made any attempt to restart it. The rest of the ride was continued in silence.

When they reached Powell Gardens, the parking lot was crowded. Apparently, lots of people had decided to come out to enjoy the place.

Maddy and Jordan entered through the visitors' center, paid the admission fee, then stepped outside, where the garden walkways began.

"Which way do you want to go?" asked Jordan. "The rock and waterfall garden or the chapel first?"

Maddy glanced at the small map she'd picked up inside. It had been years since she'd been to Powell Gardens. She remembered the place was big. It spanned over eight hundred acres and had been originally purchased by George Powell, Sr. Later it was used as a dairy farm, a Boy Scout camp, and a natural resource center before it was converted to a botanical garden open to the public in 1988.

"How about we walk to the perennial garden, by way of the rock and water-fall garden? Then we could work our way to the chapel and see the wildflower meadow on the way," Maddy suggested.

"Good idea," Jordan agreed.

As they walked, they were quiet, content to watch others enjoying the garden. Many families had come out, and it was amusing to watch toddlers and little kids stopping and examining everything that was growing, even down to blades of grass.

After they crossed the bridge from the island in the middle of the lake, they headed to the rock gardens. They spent quite some time walking through the shaded garden, enjoying hydrangeas, dogwoods, and other shade-loving flowers and shrubs. "I hear that it's really beautiful in the spring when all the azaleas are in bloom," Jordan told her.

"I bet it is gorgeous," Maddy said. "Listen to the sound of the water. Isn't it peaceful?"

"It is."

They shared an amiable silence as they walked through the perennial gardens, which were aglow with color. This garden was actually a series of different gardens, ranging from woodland gardens, a secret garden, a butterfly garden, and prairie gardens, in addition to a garden of flowers familiar to the Kansas City area.

As they headed past the wildflower meadow to the chapel, Jordan joked, "Have you seen enough flowers yet?"

"I think so." Maddy laughed. "It's all starting to blur together. What was your favorite?"

"I liked the butterfly garden, actually," said Jordan.

"I did too," said Maddy. "But I think my favorite was the fragrance garden."

"That was nice too."

A few moments later, a family came from the opposite direction on the path. Three children walked a few feet ahead of their parents. The two older boys, probably around six or seven years old, were laughing and giggling. Just behind them was a darling little girl who looked to be about two years old. Smiling shyly, when she passed by Maddy and Jordan, she paused for a moment, looked up into their faces, and shyly said, "Hi."

Maddy and Jordan stopped and said hello to the girl and her parents, who were a few feet away.

"She was adorable," Maddy said after the family had passed.

"I know. It's amazing how little kids are so trusting. They'll stop and talk to complete strangers and not even be afraid."

"I know. Look, there's the chapel," said Maddy. She began to walk at a quicker pace until Jordan stopped her.

"Hey, slow down. I'm too tired to go that fast. We've been walking for miles."

Maddy closed her eyes, then opened them. "Miles?"

Jordan pulled out his map of the grounds. "According to this map, by the time we finish touring all of the attractions, we will have walked over a mile and a half. In case you haven't noticed, it's pretty hot out here. I'm trying to conserve energy."

"Okay, I'll slow down," Maddy apologized. Jordan was right. It was pretty warm out.

As they walked, she concentrated on the chapel, which was getting closer with every step they took. The chapel was a small, angular structure that sat at the far edge of the lake, bordered by woodlands on one side. The other sides were bordered with water, an extension of the wildflower meadow, and natural grasses.

Part of her rush to get to the chapel was wanting to find out what Jordan had to tell her. He had said he would tell her when they reached the chapel, and her curiosity was getting the better of her. *Be patient,* she reminded herself.

Jordan's steps seemed to be agonizingly slow, but Maddy had a feeling he was carefully considering what he wanted to say, so she didn't rush him.

Surprisingly, no one was in the chapel when they got there. Once they were inside, Maddy forgot her impatience. The wood bracing that comprised the walls cast diamond-shaped patterns and shadows all around them. Although it was man-made, the structure blended well with its natural setting. It was simplistic, but beautiful. Maddy sat on one of the benches, just staring at the elaborate patterns of surrounding timber.

It was noisy, but quietly so, with the sound of the wind and birds echoing through the small room.

Jordan sat down next to her. She heard him take a deep breath, and she knew the time had come for what he wanted to share.

Maddy looked him in the eye and saw an intensity and determination that she hadn't ever seen in him. She braced herself for what might be coming.

Jordan began without pomp or ceremony. "The other night, after I left your house, I couldn't sleep, thinking about Malcolm and everything that had happened. I felt like I had left some loose ends there. His wife had written me two or three letters, letting me know what was going on with church, but I never answered them. The next day, I got another one of the letters and decided to give her a call. She told me that the church has really grown, and they were getting close to finishing a larger building. There's a new pastor now, of course, and she recently remarried. This month they've been putting the finishing touches on the new church, and next week they're having a service each night to dedicate the new church. She said she'd thought about asking me to come, but she didn't want to upset me. But when I called her, she decided to go ahead and ask. She wanted to know if I'd come and give a small speech one of the nights, since I donated a lot of the money to the church's college fund. She thought I might want to meet some of the students who've benefited from it."

Maddy closed her eyes in relief. She hadn't known what Jordan was going to say, and not knowing made her nervous. She turned to face him. "Are you going to go?"

He nodded slowly. "I think so. I feel like I need to. I never made a public profession of faith. I feel like the Lord wants me to go."

Maddy nodded understandingly. "Then I think you should go. How long are you going to be there?"

"I thought I'd catch a plane early on Monday and stay until the main service on Sunday morning."

"That's over a week," Maddy said gently. "Do you think you'll be okay?"

He didn't answer at first but looked toward the front of the chapel, out the big windows that overlooked the water. Finally, he said, "I think I won't be okay if don't go."

"I understand," Maddy said. And she did. It was something he needed to do for himself, and she knew he would feel bad if he didn't do it. Part of her was a little disappointed. She'd all but made it clear that she wasn't dating anyone, and she wasn't interested in anyone. She'd been hoping that now Jordan would ask her out, but his words had put an end to her hopes and sealed her convictions about their relationship. He viewed her as someone to confide in about his past, and it was her duty as a friend to support him as he continued to heal.

"I knew you'd understand. My parents were far from thrilled about it when I told them last night, but I think they'll understand someday."

Maddy just nodded. Apparently, she was less of a confidante than she had thought she was. He'd told his parents before he'd told her. They sat for another ten minutes or so, each of them lost in their own thoughts, until Jordan stood up. "You ready to head back?"

"I guess so."

As they stepped out of the chapel, Jordan took hold of Maddy's hand. She was surprised but didn't say anything. When they reached the car, he finally let go of her hand.

"Are you hungry?" he asked, once they were on the highway headed home.

Maddy checked her watch. It was nearly six o'clock, but she didn't have an appetite. "Not really," she said apologetically. She figured Jordan was probably pretty hungry.

He looked at her with concern. "You look pretty worn out. I probably shouldn't have kept you out in the sun so long. Do you want me to take you home?"

"I think so. I've got to substitute teach a friend's Sunday school class in the morning," she told him. "And you know how it is with little kids. You can't afford to look tired because they'll pick up on it and get the better of you before you realize it," she joked.

When they reached her house, Jordan walked her inside and made her promise that she would drink lots of liquids, in case she was a little dehydrated.

Maddy laughingly agreed, and she felt touched by his concern. Before he left, he gave her a quick hug, and then said, "Thanks for being so understanding, Maddy. I know I might have seemed a little self-centered today, and I'm sorry you had to put up with my being so quiet. The gardens are such a good place to think, but it was good to have you there with me."

"Don't worry about me," she told him. "I did my own share of thinking today too."

"So you're not upset with me?" he questioned.

She shook her head. "I guess I'm just starting to feel a little more. . .contemplative myself. Is that a real word?"

"I think so." He laughed. "I'll either call you before I leave or after I get there Monday, depending on what time my flight is."

"Okay, I'll be waiting," she told him.

Chapter 14

The rest of the weekend passed quietly for Maddy. Monday morning, she waited as long as she could to hear from Jordan before she left for work, but when he didn't call, she assumed his flight had been an early one. As she walked into her classroom, she wondered what she would say to Trina, who had not called on Saturday or come to church with her. To her surprise, Mrs. Calvin was waiting for her.

"Good morning, Ms. Thompson," said the woman.

"Hi, Mrs. Calvin. How was your weekend?"

"Good, and yours?"

"Mine went well," answered Maddy.

"I don't have a lot of time for conversation, Maddy," the woman said. Her forehead was wrinkled with concern. "I'm actually here concerning one of the students."

"Which one?" Maddy asked.

"Trina Sheppard."

"What's happened?" Maddy was instantly alert.

Mrs. Calvin shook her head. "We don't know. Apparently, she's run away from home."

"When?" Maddy breathed.

"Saturday, we think. Her parents are really worried. They figured she'd come home in time for classes, but she didn't. They told me she mentioned you a lot at home, and I knew you tried to help her. They were wondering if you'd heard from her."

Maddy sat down at her desk, feeling deflated. "No, I haven't," she said, shaking her head. "Did they really think she'd contact me?"

"They had hoped so, but I guess she didn't. I'll go call them now."

"Please, let me know if you hear anything," Maddy requested.

The rest of the day went by in a blur. Right before Maddy left for home, she stopped by Mrs. Calvin's office, only to learn that Trina still hadn't contacted her parents.

That evening, Maddy's parents had dinner at her sister's house, but Maddy stayed home in case Trina or Jordan called. While she waited, Maddy prayed for both Jordan and Trina.

At nine-thirty, she still hadn't heard from either of them. Refusing to allow herself to worry, Maddy went to the kitchen to make some tea. Just as the water started boiling, the phone rang. Anxiously, Maddy grabbed the phone. "Hello?"

"Hi. It's me, Jordan. Are you okay?"

Maddy relaxed a little. Jordan had finally called. And she was touched to know that he could sense everything wasn't okay.

"I think so," Maddy said hesitantly. She didn't want to subject Jordan to any stress by launching into an explanation of what was going on with Trina.

"Do you want to tell me about it?" he asked.

Maddy shook her head, even though he couldn't see her. "No. But how was your day?"

"It's been pretty rough at times. But I'm glad I'm here. The church has grown so much over the past few years. Most of the congregation came to the prayer service tonight, and I'd say there were at least two hundred and fifty people there."

"Wow," Maddy said.

"The service wasn't really that long. It was just about an hour or so, and it wasn't really structured or scheduled. The pastor just stood at the podium, prayed, and then encouraged everyone to spend a few minutes praying silently on their own. I got down on my knees and before I knew it, the pastor was standing up, praying the closing prayer. It was really special. I feel—I don't know. But I feel better somehow."

"I'm happy for you."

"I saw Malcolm's wife this morning," Jordan said. Maddy heard the tone of his voice grow more serious. Instead of replying to his statement, she waited for what he would say next.

"She seems really pleased that I decided to participate in the dedication services. I told her that I felt like I had been running from something since I'd left. And even though it was hard to come back, I felt relieved, somehow, to be there."

"Really?"

"Really. I don't know what it is. I also met the new pastor and his wife. After the service, I went to their house and told him my story in a nutshell. He wants me to give my talk at the service on Sunday."

"So you are staying the whole week?" Maddy asked. She was happy for Jordan, but the thought of having to deal with Trina being missing while Jordan was away for a week made her feel alone, even though she knew she could talk to her family or Mrs. Calvin about it. She just didn't want to tell him the bad news over the phone.

"Yeah. And I'm really nervous about it. I wish I could do it tomorrow or something and get it over with. I feel like I might freeze up or start crying in front of all those people."

Maddy's heart melted, knowing that it was very uncharacteristic of Jordan to admit to being afraid of something. Yet, within the space of a week, he had chosen to voice some of his most personal fears and worries to her. She knew she couldn't take his words lightly. "I know you'll do fine. And if you want, I can pray for you."

Maddy could almost see Jordan smile. "That would be great," he said. "I was hoping you'd say that."

"No problem," Maddy answered.

"But that's enough about me. How did things go with Trina today?" Jordan inquired.

"Actually, I didn't see her," Maddy told him. Then she quickly gave him a brief explanation about what had happened.

Jordan's voice grew more concerned. "I was worried that something like this might happen. I just wish I were there with you."

"Jordan, don't be silly. There's nothing you can do about it now, except pray," Maddy told him, trying to sound more confident than she actually felt.

"I really don't like the way this sounds," Jordan persisted.

"Neither do I, and I'm worried for her." Maddy sighed. "She doesn't seem like the type of kid to just run away, and I don't think she has many friends to turn to. I just hope nothing has happened to her."

"I guess you're right. There's nothing I can do," Jordan said.

"Exactly. Don't worry about me. But do pray for Trina."

"I will. And I'll try to call you back tomorrow or maybe Wednesday. And if you can, would you stop by my parents' house sometime this week and visit Hancock? They're keeping him while I'm gone, but I bet he'd be glad to see you."

"Sure. And I'll let you go since you're calling long distance," Maddy told him. "Talk to you later."

" 'Bye," said Jordan before he hung up.

Tuesday morning, Maddy left for work early and went straight to Mrs. Calvin's office before she went to her own classroom. She could tell by the look on the woman's face that there was either no news or bad news.

"Nothing yet?" Maddy asked disappointedly.

"No. I'm sorry, Maddy," Mrs. Calvin said gently. "But if I hear anything. . ."

"Thanks, Mrs. Calvin, and I won't keep bugging you about this. I'll just keep praying."

Mrs. Calvin nodded soberly. "That might be the best thing."

Maddy left the office with a heavy heart, determined to keep her attitude upbeat and positive for her students' sake.

When she got home after work, Jordan called to tell her he was on his way to the Tuesday evening service. Their conversation lasted less than five minutes.

Maddy helped her mother cook dinner but started feeling restless soon afterward.

"Didn't you tell Jordan that you would play with his dog?" her mother asked in an attempt to take Maddy's mind off Trina.

"Yeah, I did. I think I'll go over now."

"You could take him to the park or something," her mother suggested.

Maddy nodded in agreement. "I think that would probably be good for both of us. In fact, I'll call Stacy and see if she wants to come."

"Good idea," said her mother.

Twenty minutes later, Maddy was in her car on the way to her sister's house, turning around every two minutes to tell Hancock to stop trying to jump into the front seat. Once, he jumped into the front seat anyway, landing partially in Maddy's lap. Between trying to drive and getting the exuberant dog into the back seat, Maddy nearly had a fender bender with the rear bumper of the car in front of her at a traffic light. "When I tell Jordan about this, you're going to be in big trouble, buddy," she told him, trying to sound as stern as possible. Hancock didn't seem to mind her warning, but he didn't try to jump in the front again for the rest of the ride. Still, Maddy was a little shaken from the near miss, and by the time they reached Stacy's house, Maddy was relieved.

Getting out of the car, she warned Hancock to stay where he was, and he whimpered in reply. Stacy came out to meet her. Maddy asked, "I think we have a slight change of plans. Would you mind if we played with Hancock in your backyard?"

Stacy glanced at the huge dog in Maddy's backseat. "That's fine. But why are we skipping the park?"

Maddy groaned. "Because I don't think my nerves will last that long." She then told Stacy about Hancock's antics on the way over. "Jordan's putting him in obedience school next week, and it's not a moment too soon."

Maddy got Hancock out of the car and kept a firm hold on his leash while they walked through Stacy's house on their way to the backyard. When they were safely away from anything breakable and within the confines of the small, grassy yard, Maddy let the dog run free. For several minutes, she and Stacy took turns throwing a ball for him to retrieve.

"So tell me how things are with Jordan. Mom told me some of what happened with him at his school. That's pretty tough."

Maddy nodded. "Yeah, he's had a hard time with it. But from what I can tell, he's glad to have the chance to go back."

"That's good," Stacy commented. "But what about you and him? Is there more than a friendship?"

"No." Maddy shook her head.

"Why not? Mom said he spends enough time at the house to be an extra kid. Hasn't he dropped any hints?"

"Maybe. Maybe not. I'm not really sure. Or maybe I don't know how to read hints anymore. For awhile I thought he might be interested when he thought I had a crush on someone else. But when I told him there was no other guy, I think he might have lost interest."

Stacy eyed her incredulously. "You're telling me that all this time you haven't told him you were interested in him?"

Maddy nodded.

"That's not going to get you anywhere," Stacy said.

"I know. The thing was, I was all set to tell him, but first I had to make sure things were okay between him and Laina. She was still upset with him for the way he used to act. By the time that was settled, I was ready to tell him, but then he told me about the terrible tragedy at his college. All of a sudden, my confession didn't seem that important anymore. And besides, if I told him and he wasn't interested, I'd feel like I was putting undue stress on him when he's already going through so much. He might feel like he has to return my interest, just because I've listened to him and tried to be supportive when he's having such a struggle."

"You're right about that," Stacy agreed.

Both women were silent for a few minutes, while they watched Hancock chase his tail.

Suddenly, Stacy spoke up again. "Would you tell him if you didn't think he'd feel pressured to be more than friends?"

"I'd love to," Maddy confessed. "But I seem to time it wrong."

"I suggest you jump in and just say it the next time you see a safe opening. Otherwise, you're stringing yourself along. He has no idea what you feel about him and vice versa."

"You're right. I don't want to just blurt it out, without any preface. I do stuff like that way too much and it gets me in trouble. Like the day on the telephone with that other Arnold." Maddy sighed and hugged her knees to her chest. "I just wish I could make it more special."

"Like how?"

Maddy shrugged. "I don't know. Like cook him dinner or something—now that I know how to cook," she joked.

Stacy smiled. "I really can't believe he taught you how to cook."

"It wasn't that hard. I don't think it was so much that I couldn't learn. . .I think I was just *ready* to learn."

"You're probably right. But it's still funny that he actually came over and gave you lessons. What a way to get to know the guy you have a crush on." Stacy laughed.

Maddy arched an eyebrow. "Hey, it worked, didn't it?"

"Too bad you didn't have a graduation."

"Yeah too bad," Maddy agreed. "I don't know what a ceremony for that would be like, though."

"Instead of walking across the stage, you'd just stroll across the kitchen floor," Stacy quipped.

"Yeah, and instead of a diploma, he'd hand me a rolling pin," Maddy laughingly added.

"And instead of one of those long robes, you would have to wear an apron," said Stacy.

"And a chef's hat!" Maddy added. The two dissolved into giggles at this last image, laughing until their stomachs hurt.

Several minutes later, after they had suppressed most of their laughter, Maddy stood up. "I'd better get Hancock home before it gets too late," she told her sister. "I don't want him jumping into my lap if it's dark outside."

"Well, thanks for coming over. Maybe by the time Jordan gets back, he'll be feeling better so you can tell him."

"Hopefully."

"Maybe you can even have that ceremony."

"Yeah, sure." Maddy smiled. "Or maybe we can have the 'practice' conversation," she joked.

"Practice conversation?" Stacy asked.

"Yeah." Maddy laughed. "Jordan is always bugging me to let him help me figure out what to tell the guy. He wants me to 'practice' the whole conversation on him."

Stacy said nothing but lifted an eyebrow. "You know," Maddy continued, "come to think of it, he might not have such a bad idea. Sometimes I've wanted to practice the conversation on him, and then end up by telling him that he's the guy." She glanced over at Stacy and laughed. "What do you think? Should I do it? I could even cook him dinner."

Stacy thought for a moment. Finally, she said, "It might be workable. . . although it is a pretty roundabout way of doing it."

"Yeah. He might think I was totally nuts by the time I finished," Maddy said.

"Might?" Stacy laughed.

Maddy gently shoved her sister. "All right, that's enough. I know it's a silly idea. But hey, at this point I'm willing to try it."

"Are you serious?" Stacy asked incredulously.

Maddy stood up. "Actually, I'm really considering it. I can't say for sure, but it's the closest I've come to an actual plan so far."

Stacy shrugged. "Whatever you feel comfortable with. Do you need any help?"

Maddy put her hands on her hips. "Oh, sure. Ms. Wedding Coordinator always wants to plan everyone else's party."

"I do not!" Stacy laughed.

"Yes, you do." Maddy giggled. "But if I decide to do this, I might give you a call—but only for a little advice. I don't want you taking over."

"Just let me know what I can do," Stacy persisted.

"I will. And there is one thing you can do for me right now. Pray for Trina. I hope she's somewhere safe."

Stacy instantly sobered. "I will." She hugged Maddy and said, "I think she's going to be okay, but I'll keep praying."

That night, Maddy tossed and turned as she had the night before. Not only was she concerned about Jordan and Trina, but she kept trying to decide whether or not she should have the dinner for Jordan.

After several hours, Maddy sat up and turned on the lamp next to her bed. It occurred to her that after nearly four months of being in a semi-relationship with Jordan, she was more confused than she'd been in the beginning. Constantly trying to protect her feelings from the pain of rejection had led to a dead end. Stacy was right. It would be better to just get things out in the open. Otherwise, she and Jordan could go on for months and months, maybe even years, not knowing where the other stood.

Lord, should I tell Jordan how I feel about him? Before she could even finish praying, a Bible verse came to her memory. *The truth will set you free.*

"I guess that's Your answer, Lord," she said. Almost instantly, a feeling of peace washed over her. *Now, if only telling Jordan would be so easy.*

Maddy sighed, knowing she would spend the next few days gathering all her courage. But it was time. She valued her friendship with Jordan, but if the Lord didn't want there to be more, she had to do something soon; otherwise, she would be deceiving herself. And there was no escaping the wisdom of God's word. Telling the truth would make her free, whether or not Jordan decided he loved her more than as a friend.

Chapter 15

Wednesday evening, Maddy had just gotten home from work when the phone rang. Hoping it would be Jordan, Maddy ran to the phone. "Hello?"

"Um, Ms. Thompson?" The voice of the girl was familiar.

"Yes," Maddy replied, trying to put a face with the voice.

"This is Trina," the girl said.

"Trina! Where are you? Your parents are so worried about you."

"I know. I'm home now, but Mrs. Calvin asked me to call you after my parents told her I was back."

Maddy remained silent, not knowing what she should say.

"I'm sorry I didn't call you back about going to church," said Trina.

Maddy felt tears of relief coming to her eyes. "That's okay. Just don't run off like that again." Then she added, "And the invitation is still on, if you want to come."

"Well, actually, that's what I wanted to tell you about. I don't want to take up too much of your time, but I wanted to tell you what happened."

"Go ahead, I'm listening." Maddy sat down on the sofa and waited. She heard Trina take a deep breath.

"I didn't mean to run away. I went out Saturday to one of the clubs that some of the kids at my school go to. I met this guy there, and he seemed really interested in me, and he invited me to a party at one of his friends' houses. It was really late, but I decided to go anyway. I was just feeling so bad about myself, and I decided that I was going to do whatever I needed to do to make friends. Everyone at the party was older than me; most of the people were in college, so they had drugs and alcohol. I didn't want to get drunk, and I've never done drugs, so I kept refusing whenever anybody offered me some. The guy who'd invited me started teasing me because I wouldn't, so I decided to leave. But I felt so depressed that I got on the road and just kept driving. I drove most of the night and I just didn't want to go home. On Sunday morning, it seemed like I kept passing by all of these churches, and I kept thinking about how you invited me to go to your church. Finally, I think I was somewhere in the middle of Kansas, and I saw this little church by the side of the road. I don't know why I did it, but I pulled over and sat outside of the window and listened, because I was too ashamed to go inside.

"The preacher was talking about some of the same things you told me about—how Jesus loves us no matter how other people feel about us." Trina stopped talking and Maddy could hear she was sobbing.

"Trina, do you want to call me back and tell me the rest later?" Maddy asked gently. "I'll be home all this evening."

"No. I want to finish telling you. He talked about praying this prayer to ask Jesus to forgive me of my sins and come into my heart, but I didn't feel ready to pray that yet. I got up and walked over to my car. I tried to drive away, but the car wouldn't start. So when everyone came out of the church, I was sitting in the parking lot, with a car that wouldn't go anywhere. The pastor and his wife came over to me and invited me to their house for dinner. I couldn't believe they did that because they didn't even know me, but I felt safe. They told me that the Lord told them to invite me. So I went to their house, and that's where I was until this morning."

"Why didn't you call?" Maddy asked, starting to feel a little angry. "We didn't know if you were safe or not."

Trina sighed. "I don't know. The pastor's wife kept asking me about my family, and I lied and told her I didn't have any family. They reminded me of my grandparents, and I didn't want to explain to them why I had run away, since I wasn't even sure why I'd done it in the first place. They said they didn't believe me, but I could stay with them until I got a job and earned some money to get my car fixed, as long as I went to church with them."

"So then what happened?"

"I stayed there, and they kept asking me if I knew Jesus. I told them I knew about Him, but I still didn't want to pray that prayer. Then Tuesday night I went to a Bible study with them. This lady stood up and gave a testimony about all of the bad things she had gone through before she finally got saved. I knew then that if I didn't do something, I could end up like she did and maybe worse. So when they asked if anybody wanted to pray the prayer and get things straight with Jesus, I went to the front of the church and prayed."

"Oh, Trina, I'm so happy for you!" Maddy exclaimed.

"Thanks, Ms. Thompson. And I feel happier than I have been in a long time. This morning I told Pastor Walston and his wife that I needed to call home, and my parents drove out to pick me up. Then two other things happened. First, my parents got saved. Then, when my dad tried to start my car, it started perfectly. I think God wanted me there for a reason."

"So where are you going to go to church now?" Maddy asked.

"My parents and I agreed to start going to churches beginning Sunday until we find one we like. And I've decided to stay here my first two years of college instead going away right now. I think my parents and I can get to know each other better now that we're all thinking alike."

"I'm glad. I think you're making a good decision," said Maddy. "So will I see you in class Friday?"

"Well. . .no. I told Mrs. Calvin that I'm quitting the program. There's only about a week and a half left to the camp, and school starts in another couple weeks. I need to get everything in order since I have to apply to a different school this fall. But maybe we'll visit at your church someday."

"I'd like that," said Maddy. "And I understand about your quitting. But thanks for calling to let me know what happened. I've had a lot of people praying for you the past few days."

"Tell them I really appreciate it," Trina said. "And I want to thank you for not giving up on me even when I was being so rude. I'm really sorry, and I didn't mean it, but I know better now."

"I forgive you." Maddy's reply was sincere. "And I'll be praying for you when you start school."

"Thanks. I know it might not be easy to make friends, but just like you said, it's better to be myself and make friends instead of trying to be someone other people want me to be. I don't want to mess up again trying to be someone I'm not. If Jesus can love me, I'm sure I can find some other Christians who'll treat me like you did."

Maddy swallowed. It felt good to know that she had done the right thing. And she was glad the Lord had intervened before things got any worse for Trina. "I'm so happy you feel that way, Trina," Maddy said.

"Me too. But I've got to get off the phone. My parents need to call some other people and let them know I'm okay. But maybe I can call you sometime?"

"Sure. And if I'm not home, just leave a message and I'll call you back as soon as I can."

"Okay. 'Bye, Ms. Thompson."

"Good-bye, Trina." Maddy hung up the phone and smiled. Apparently, God hadn't wanted Trina to visit her church Sunday. But, judging from the outcome, things couldn't have turned out any better. She was just about to go tell her parents the good news when the phone rang again.

❧

"I should have called sooner," Jordan told himself as he hung up the phone. His conversation with Maddy had left him feeling disabled by mixed emotions. At the time he'd made the call, it had seemed like a good idea, but now things had seemed to take a turn in a direction that didn't suit his plans. He'd been both happy and relieved to hear that Trina had returned and was starting to make some changes in her life. Looking back, he felt that he had almost certainly over-reacted about Maddy's initial zealousness to reach out to the girl. God had a plan for Trina, and if Maddy hadn't listened to the Lord's leading, things might have ended differently. Or maybe not. Jordan couldn't say for sure. God has a way of getting someone else to do the job if another person refuses, as Jordan's pastor had a habit of saying. But the news about Trina was not what was concerning him at the moment. It was the dinner.

The day had been ideal until Maddy had told him of her latest plan. He'd spent the morning and afternoon walking around, trying to put his feelings into perspective. He'd known almost since the moment he and Maddy had met again that he had feelings for her. As the summer had progressed, Jordan had felt it would be pretty safe to wait and see how things panned out with her mystery crush. And he'd felt certain that his efforts and prayers had been rewarded when Maddy had confessed at the gardens that day that she no longer had any feelings for the guy. Right then and there he'd wanted to drop to his knees and propose to her, but he hadn't because he knew it would be too sudden for her. He couldn't expect her to transfer her feelings over to him at the drop of a hat. And he knew that he needed to come back here to settle his own feelings about his past before he considered a serious relationship. The emotions and fears he'd experienced here had still been very much alive, although hidden beneath his cheerful exterior. But he knew that he needed peace. It would not be fair to carry that type of turmoil into a marriage.

And so far, he was finding a way to put all of the negative memories behind him. He was prepared to forgive himself for good and move on. He'd planned to take Maddy somewhere and tell her all of this as soon as he returned home. She knew what he'd been through, and she understood why he needed to come here. He'd figured that once he explained that he loved her and wanted to spend the rest of his life with her, she'd—

She'd what? Jordan sighed and leaned back in his chair. He hadn't exactly expected her to fall into his arms and declare that she still liked him; that, in fact, she loved him after all of these years. But he had hoped there was still some emotion on her part—that she would be willing to give a relationship with him a chance. . .without him having to be a tutor while she worked to catch another guy's attention. He wasn't exactly planning a proposal—that would be too sudden. Maybe. Maybe not. They'd known one another forever, and over the course of the past few months, he'd grown closer to Maddy than he had to any other woman he'd dated. But in his heart, he knew. He'd been praying and struggling with his emotions for several weeks now. And he knew that given just the slightest encouragement from Maddy, he'd ask her to be his wife in an instant.

But it was too late for any of that. Maddy had been almost giddy with excitement as she'd told him about her own plans and her feelings for this man. And now, she felt sure of what to do. Not only was she going to finally tell the guy, but she wanted Jordan to listen to what she planned to tell the guy. When she'd asked for his help, Jordan had been too stunned to say anything but yes. It was his own fault, really. She told him that he himself had given her the idea. And he had. Only, he'd never really expected her to take him up on the offer. But she had. And upon his return on Monday night, he would have to sit down and listen to Maddy as she rehearsed with him how she would finally pour her heart out to another man.

After all of his prayers, he'd felt confident to have a heart-to-heart with

Maddy and tell her he loved her. But she said she'd been praying too, and she thought it was time to tell this guy how she felt about him.

How could this be happening? Both he and Maddy had based their decisions on their own prayers and what they felt the Lord had instructed.

Jordan frowned. Somehow, between him and Maddy, one of them was not hearing from the Lord correctly. And he had the sinking feeling that it might be him. Glancing at his watch, he realized if he didn't leave soon, he was going to be late for church.

I'm not going to give up unless You tell me to, Lord, he prayed as he left his hotel room.

❧

Sunday morning Maddy awoke bright and early. She'd spoken to Jordan the night before and he'd mentioned that he was still a little nervous about having to speak in front of the whole church. She called his hotel room, but there was no answer. She figured he must have left early.

But before she got ready to go to church, she got down on her knees and prayed.

"Lord, I just want to ask that You will wash Jordan with Your peace this morning, and take away any fear he has about sharing his story. I know it will be rough for him, so please hide him under the shadow of Your wings and let him feel Your protection. And I ask the same for myself for tomorrow. I know I need to have this conversation with Jordan, but I'm still a little jittery about it. Please give me the courage I need to make it through. And if Jordan doesn't feel the same about me, please help me not to feel too hurt about it, and don't let him feel any guilt. In Jesus' name, amen."

When Maddy got up from her knees, she felt calm and unafraid. She smiled. "The truth has made me free," she told herself. "Well. . .almost."

❧

Maddy stared at the table one last time. The day had been ideal. Classes had gone well, and all the students and teachers had been in cheerful moods since it was the last week of the camp.

She'd been able to leave on time, and when she got home, she'd immediately set about preparing dinner for Jordan. First, she'd roasted a chicken with a rub of *herbs de Provence*, a mixture of basil, fennel seed, lavender, marjoram, rosemary, sage, summer savory, and thyme. Next, she oven-roasted a spaghetti squash, which she knew was one of Jordan's favorites. She also prepared a simple Greek salad. For dessert, she'd made a raspberry sorbet the night before. The menu was simple, but she knew that Jordan really liked each of the dishes, because he'd said so when he'd taught her how to make them.

Now, she stood at the window, waiting for Jordan to arrive. It was ten after eight, and even though he was only a few minutes late, she was starting to worry that he might not come after all. Finally, she saw his SUV round the corner to her street. She ran back to the dining room and lit the candles on the table. Just as she was going back to the door, the phone rang.

Maddy sighed and hurried to pick up the extension in the living room. "Hello?"

"Maddy, it's me," her mother said. Her parents were having dinner at Mrs. Myston's house. "I just wanted to let you know that Jordan just pulled up."

Maddy laughed. "Yes, Mom. And I know you want to know what's happening, so I'll make it easy for you. I'll open the blinds in the dining room. That way, you can watch us eat dinner from Mrs. Myston's living room. Mrs. Myston won't even have to get out the binoculars."

Her mother laughed. "You don't think we would spy?" she asked in mock indignation.

"I didn't think you wouldn't," Maddy said. At that moment, the doorbell rang. "I've got to answer the door, Mom. I'll get back to you later."

"Okay, Sweetie. And Mrs. Myston told me to tell you that Jordan is all dressed up in a suit and tie, so it's a good thing you decided to wear your long turquoise dress. But I better let you go. Your dad says that if you don't open the door soon, Jordan's going to get suspicious."

"Then I'll go now." Maddy laughed.

She put down the receiver and went to the front door. Jordan stood on the steps, holding a single rose, surrounded by a variety of herbs. Holding them out to Maddy, he said, "I thought I'd bring these by for old times' sake. You can either cook the herbs or put them in a vase. The rose. . ." He tilted his head to the side. "I don't suggest cooking with the rose."

Maddy laughed and took the flowers and herbs. "Come on in," she said. Jordan stepped inside. Just before Maddy closed the front door, she caught a glimpse of her mother and Mrs. Myston in Mrs. Myston's living room window. Maddy shook her head and smiled to herself. If things didn't go well, she could count on them to be there for her in a matter of seconds.

Jordan was standing in the hallway, looking nervous.

"Why don't we eat dinner first?" she suggested. "That way you can tell me about yesterday."

Jordan nodded in agreement. "Let's get the easy part out of the way."

While they ate their dinner, Jordan told her what had happened.

"I was so nervous Saturday night that I got up early in the morning. I ended up leaving much earlier than I needed to, so I decided to walk around town. While I walked, I just prayed and prayed. After about an hour, I started to relax, and before I knew it I had made my way to the campus. While I walked, I thought about Malcolm, and I thanked God that Malcolm hadn't let me walk away from him that morning. I feel like it was truly God's hand on Malcolm that directed him to ask me that question. And I am so thankful that he didn't ignore me just because I'd already turned down the gospel so many times. And by the time I made it over to the church that morning, I wasn't nervous anymore. In fact, I couldn't wait for my turn to speak.

Maddy didn't interrupt but waited for Jordan to finish.

"I had to wait for the entire sermon to end. Finally, right before the altar call, the pastor called me up to the podium. Malcolm's wife and her new husband introduced me, and I almost lost my courage while I stood there waiting for them to finish. But finally, it was my turn. I started out by telling everyone that I needed to make my public profession of faith. And then I just told them everything, pretty much the same way I told you. I started crying, and when I looked around, lots of other people were crying too.

"By the time I finished my story, I felt totally bold. Before I even realized it, I started giving an altar call. And even though I had never, ever really witnessed to anyone, I started asking these people if they knew what their relationship with the Lord was. I told them that it was important to not waste any time when our eternity is at stake. I don't even know where I got the words from." He stared at Maddy and shook his head in disbelief. "The words just came to me. And before I knew it, people were coming to the altar and praying. And I'm no preacher. But I'm so glad that I was able to get up there and talk yesterday. Hopefully, somebody will remember my courage and be able to tell other people." He hung his head. "I'm just embarrassed that it took me so long to do it. But I'm glad I went. And I feel more encouraged to keep witnessing to my parents. Hopefully, one day they'll actually listen to what I have to say instead of getting upset with me."

Maddy smiled. "I do too. I'm so proud of you. And it looks like your testimony definitely had an impact on some people." She didn't say anything else, because she was starting to feel a little jittery about what she still had to do.

They spent the rest of the meal discussing different subjects, such as Maddy's job and Jordan's apartment. Finally, Jordan finished the last bite of his sorbet.

He looked down at his empty bowl and said, "Well, Maddy, the dinner was delicious. At least this guy will know you can cook." Then he asked, "Are you going to cook this same dinner for him too?"

Maddy swallowed. It was time to start confessing. "Well. . .this dinner was planned for you since you like these dishes so much."

Jordan looked relieved. "I have to be honest with you, I didn't want you cooking my favorite dishes for some other guy."

Maddy was surprised. Was this an answer to her prayers? Was Jordan about to reveal that he had feelings for her? She paused, expectantly. Neither of them spoke for several moments.

Finally, Jordan said, "I guess it's your turn. Do you want to do this in here or the living room?"

"In here," Maddy said emphatically. "Is that okay with you?"

"Sure. I'll just sit here and play like I'm the guy. Go ahead and say what you need to say." He smiled but looked uncomfortable.

Maddy swallowed. "I guess the best way to start is to just jump in. Please don't interrupt me. You can say whatever you want when I'm finished."

"Sounds fair to me," Jordan said stiffly.

Maddy cleared her throat and began. "It says in the Bible that the truth will set me free. And I'm telling you this because I need to be free. I started out trying to get your attention by learning how to cook. I thought that if I knew how to cook, it would make you take notice of me. But what I didn't realize was that I was only attracted to a small facet of you. And as I worked to impress that facet, I realized there was more of you I didn't really know. A good friend of mine kept telling me that a man should love me for who I am, not who I can make myself to be, but I didn't believe him." She paused and smiled at Jordan.

"The funny thing was, I found myself telling the same thing to one of my students. And I got so frustrated with her when she didn't believe me. Ironically, she told me a few days ago that I was right. The only thing was, I realized that I wasn't practicing what I was preaching. I was telling her one thing and doing something totally different.

"So I've asked you here tonight so that I can be honest with you. A long time ago, I fell in love with my next-door neighbor. At least, I thought I was in love. But when I met him again, he wasn't the same person. I plotted and schemed about how I could get him to notice me, and I came up with the idea of getting him to teach me how to cook. But like I said, he wasn't the same person. And even though I thought I loved my next-door neighbor, I fell in love with my cooking teacher." Maddy stopped and drank a sip of water, while avoiding eye contact with Jordan.

"My cooking teacher is a great guy. He's a Christian. He's a very patient teacher who supported me, even though he thought I was making a mistake. And he became my friend, trusting me enough to share some very personal things with me. We pray for each other, we laugh and have fun together. When I realized I was falling in love with him, I started praying about it. I was scared to open up and be honest, but one day I was praying, and I remembered the verse that says the truth will set me free. I've been trying to hide it and deny it, but now I know for sure. And even though I don't know how he feels about me, I know I have to say this." Maddy took a deep breath and looked across the table, locking gazes with Jordan. "I love you, Jordan Sanders," she said simply. She held her hands to stop them from shaking.

Jordan opened his mouth, then closed it. Finally, he cleared his throat and said, "Are you sure?"

Maddy nodded, tears filling her eyes.

He exhaled loudly, then stood up and walked around to her side of the table. He pulled out the chair next to her and sat down. "Maddy, you don't know how happy I am that you told me this. I've spent this whole summer being jealous of your mystery crush. And it was me the whole time?"

"Yes," Maddy said, wiping her eyes. "How do you feel about that?"

He grinned. "I feel relieved. I've been praying and praying about how I feel. When you told me you were going to tell the guy, I felt like God hadn't heard any of my prayers. All day long I kept wondering how in the world I was going to react to your telling me that you were in love with some other guy." He took her hands and stood slowly, gently drawing her out of her chair.

The two stood for several moments, gazing into one another's eyes.

"So does this mean. . .?" Maddy trailed off, not quite knowing what to say.

"It means, Madison Thompson, I love you too. Would you marry me?" said Jordan.

Maddy burst into tears mingled with laughter. "Of course. I was just getting nervous because it was taking you so long to ask."

He took her in his arms and kissed her. When he pulled away, Maddy grinned. "So did I graduate?" she asked.

"Graduate?" he repeated, confused.

"From wife school," she reminded him.

"Oh, yes, wife school," he said. His face grew serious and he was quiet for a few moments. Slowly, a smile spread across his face. "Yes, you've earned your wife degree. How about another kiss?"

Maddy put her hand in front of her face. "Not so fast, Mister. What was my grade?"

"Hmm. . .I'd have to say A minus," he said as he leaned toward her.

"A *minus?*" she challenged. "Why not a solid A?"

Jordan lifted an eyebrow. "Surely you haven't forgotten those double-the-temperature-half-the-time chocolate chip cookies?"

"Oh," said Maddy. "I guess you're right. I'll have to settle for the A minus." She lifted her face to him and let him kiss her again.

When the kiss ended, Jordan said, "I think you just earned that A, Miss Thompson."

"That's more like it, Professor Sanders." She laughed.

PRIDE AND PUMPERNICKEL

This book is dedicated to everyone who ever had a List.

Chapter 1

Dana Edwards sat at a booth taking notes on the general state of things around her. The early Saturday morning breakfast rush slowly ebbed, and while employees stood behind the service counter, the restaurant itself looked a little neglected. Several customers searched for an empty place where they could sit, but they were understandably reluctant to sit at an unkempt table.

With a sigh of understanding, Dana stood up and began clearing the tables the staff hadn't been able to reach. Plates, trays, cutlery, and plenty of assorted crumbs graced far too many tables and booths. In addition, many nearly empty cups of coffee, juice, and milk added to the mess. Several minutes later, Dana glanced at the service counter, where several of the teenaged weekend employees engaged in friendly banter. Since no customers waited in line at the time, Dana signaled for a few workers to come out to the eating area.

Two girls approached with guilty looks on their faces, and Dana forced herself to remain calm. After all, they had done an excellent job serving the customers.

"Okay, guys," Dana said, smiling to relieve any tension. "You're doing a great job with the folks coming in. Nice attitudes, fast service, the works. I'm putting down good things in my report."

They appeared to relax as she spoke. "Thanks, Miss Edwards," said the girl who wore a name tag that said "Marcy."

"You can call me Dana," she told them, hoping to ease any remaining fears they might have. She knew what it felt like to be a teenaged employee on the receiving end of a correction from the boss. "We do have a slight problem," she continued. "To be more specific, the eating area needs some TLC. You've got to find a balance here." She indicated the expanse of the room with her outstretched arm. "After receiving fast, pleasant service at the counter, the customers still need a clean place to sit down and eat their bagels or drink their coffee."

The girls nodded.

Dana pointed to a table behind them. "See that one right there? Now tell the truth. Would you eat at it?"

"Not really," said the other girl, shaking her head.

"Neither would I. I've been watching the customers, and they don't like the looks of it either," said Dana in a firm, but gentle, manner. "I want you guys to clean up what's out here right now. Is there some type of system to make sure things don't pile up like this when the place gets busy?"

The second girl shrugged, while Marcy shook her head, indicating the answer was no. "Kim keeps reminding us, but we forget sometimes."

Dana made a mental note to include this issue in her talk with Kim, the store's full-time manager. "I understand," she told the girls. "But something more will have to be done. I'll talk to Kim and see if we can't come up with a workable solution. Remember, Grady Bakeries are a family-owned business, and Mr. and Mrs. Grady want their customers to know that even though we have two new locations, the quality of service they've enjoyed since the first store opened will not be compromised."

"Okay," said Marcy. "We'll try to do better."

"Good. Thanks for cooperating." Dana returned to her table. She gathered her notebooks and purse, then went back to the kitchen. Hopefully Kim had finished receiving and inventorying an early morning shipment of supplies so they could have a short meeting before Dana had to get to the next store.

On her way to the back, she refilled her coffee mug. The past week had been a blur, consisting of a never-ending series of driving back and forth among the three locations of the Grady Bakery stores to observe operations. This morning she had rolled out of bed at five o'clock in order to get here by six, and at eight A.M. her energy reserves were dwindling rapidly.

Dana inhaled deeply, energized by the scent. The coffee made the often long hours she worked more pleasant. Grady Bakeries had great blends, and she loved walking into one of the stores first thing in the morning to be greeted with the heavy aroma of gourmet brew.

As she rounded the corner, she nearly ran into Kim, who hurried out from the back. "Whoa!" Dana tried not to spill the contents of her mug.

Kim grinned. "Whoops, sorry."

"It's okay." The mug had only been half-full, so she hadn't lost a drop.

"The last thing I want to do in the middle of a performance review is spill the boss's coffee." Kim laughed. "Especially a boss who we all know *needs* her morning coffee."

"You're right about that," Dana added, teasing her good friend and coworker. She and Kim had previously worked together here at the original bakery location, where Dana had been the manager and Kim, the assistant manager.

When Mr. and Mrs. Grady opened the two new stores six months earlier, the two women received promotions; Kim as the manager of this first location in the small city of Clayton, and Dana as the general manager of operations for all three stores.

"Your hair looks so cute. I love the French twist," Kim said while they walked back to the office.

"Thanks. I spent twelve hours getting it braided last week. Sitting in that chair feels like torture sometimes, but it works for me in the long run. All I have to do at night is wrap them. In the morning, I either wear them down or put them up, like today."

"I'm thinking of getting braids this summer," said Kim. "You'll have to give me your stylist's number."

"No problem. My sister Latrice does them. She's the family hair artist."

"I'll definitely give her a call then. Now, about the review. . .how did we do? Or do you have time right now? What's your schedule like for the rest of the day?"

Dana glanced out of the big windows that lined the front of the store. The recent weather in the St. Louis area had been unpredictable. Several storms blanketed the city in nearly a foot of snow, though the streets were now clear. Right now, a smattering of flakes gently fell from clouds that promised even more snow, and Dana knew maneuvering through traffic might prove to be difficult. Glancing at her watch, she told Kim, "I think we can go over a few things, but I need to be at the Kirkwood store from ten 'til two."

Kim shrugged. "You've got plenty of time. Kirkwood is twenty minutes away."

"On a good day, but with this snow and traffic, I'll have to add another ten minutes to the drive."

Kim laughed. "That's right. I forgot you drive like my grandmother." She led the way to her office, and Dana followed.

The small, brightly lit room felt much warmer and cozier than the rooms in other parts of the building. Dana thought of her own office above the new store in the city of Creve Coeur and sighed. In the six months since she'd taken her new job, and the accompanying office, she hadn't done a thing to beautify her workspace. The walls remained a generic, new-construction white, and the only furniture items were her desk, chair, and file cabinets. In a word, the room felt and looked bland, and she really disliked being there.

Kim, on the other hand, had taken a nondescript room and infused it with color. She'd painted the walls a cozy yellow and stuffed warmth into every nook and cranny, using colorful accents and figurines, along with a green-and-gold area rug. The crowning jewels of this space were the overstuffed armchairs Kim bought for a song at a garage sale. Kim always had an eye for potential and expertly reupholstered the chairs herself, using colorfully patterned chenille. If jealousy weren't sinful, Dana might easily be quite envious about Kim's beautiful office and her natural gift for interior decoration.

"It's eight o'clock now, and you have about an hour and a half before you need to leave for Kirkwood," Kim announced once they were seated. "So tell me your initial thoughts. How did my folks do out there during the rush?"

Dana began a detailed report of what she witnessed and pointed out small glitches and major problems, including the table mess problem. Kim dutifully took notes, and she and Dana spent a good length of time dialoguing about how to fix things.

At nine-fifteen, Kim glanced at the clock on the wall. "Well, we've got a lot to work on, but don't worry about my staff. We'll have things going smoother in no time."

"I know you will, and I'll be sure to tell that to the Gradys when I meet with them tonight," Dana promised.

Kim leaned back in her reclining armchair. "You have a meeting with them tonight?"

As Dana nodded, a now familiar sense of worry momentarily gripped her. Hoping Kim hadn't noticed her sudden change in demeanor, Dana forced a big smile and changed the subject. "So, what's new with you?"

"Uh-uh." Kim shook her head. "I saw that look on your face. What's going on with the Gradys that you don't want me to know about?"

"Nothing," Dana replied in a firm voice.

Kim's eyes narrowed. "Dana, I know you. We've worked together for two years. Something is wrong, and it's about work. Am I right?" She paused, then added, "You don't have to pretend with me. Everyone is talking about it."

Dana let out a resigned sigh. "Okay. Yes. I mean, no. Actually, I don't know, but I have a feeling I might find out soon."

Kim tapped her pencil on the edge of the desk, a habit Dana had often seen surface whenever her friend grew nervous. Kim stared across the room for a moment, then looked back to her. "I know the Gradys are concerned about profit since the new stores have opened. Craig, the manager at the Kirkwood store, mentioned he heard Mr. Grady say he had some regrets about moving so quickly. Is that what's really going on?"

Dana pursed her lips, considering what she *could* say. Finally, she admitted, "I am aware of some financial concerns."

Fear marked Kim's expression. "Are we going to lose our jobs? Are they going to close the stores?"

"That's the last thing they want to do. But that's also why I've been reviewing procedure at the stores so carefully this month. Of course they expected to lose money after opening two brand-new stores. Still, they are pretty concerned about the figures they're seeing. Hopefully, after tonight's meeting, we'll have some kind of preliminary solutions. I have some ideas I've been thinking over that I'd like to discuss with them."

"I hope so," Kim remarked. "I just bought a new car. I really can't afford to lose my job."

"Same here. My car isn't all that reliable, but I've been waiting to buy something newer until I have more answers."

"My mortgage payment isn't all that cheap either," said Kim. "I mean, my two sisters and I split the bill three ways, but it wouldn't be a picnic if one of us couldn't pay for a few months. If I get fired or laid off, it'll affect them until I can find another job."

The alarm on Dana's watch went off, indicating the time had come for her to head to her next stop for the day. She gave Kim an apologetic nod. "I know; it's a little scary. But pray. And pray hard. This will get worked out."

Kim walked Dana back down the hallway, through the kitchen, and out to the public area of the bakery. "Drive carefully, and call me as soon as you know anything."

"Don't worry, I will. I won't see the Gradys until this evening around six, so I might end up calling you tomorrow."

"That's fine."

Dana opened the door and waved good-bye to Kim. As she walked to the car, she wrapped her scarf around her neck to form a more effective shield from the icy cold winds. She hurried the last few steps to her car and waited a few minutes for the engine to warm up. On her way to the next store, her thoughts were troubled. When it snowed, she usually enjoyed looking at the scenery, but today she couldn't seem to find much joy in the steady sifting of fluffy snowflakes. Kim's concerns were valid, and many others in the company shared the same fears.

Grady Bakeries were in serious financial trouble, and so far, there hadn't been any plausible antidotes. Dana needed to entertain the very real possibility that her job could be in jeopardy. The idea was a scary one, not only for her—with the opening of the two new stores, the Gradys had tripled their employee base, and many of those workers were adults with families who counted on the paychecks and benefits they received.

Dana thought about Kim's comments and knew many others would have trouble making their car or house payments. A feeling of relief washed over Dana because she had waited to shop for a new car until after her work situation became more stable. She had given up her apartment to lease a small house which belonged to the Gradys. They had given her a more than generous deal. In the event that they would have to raise the rent or cut her salary, Dana doubted she would find a better bargain, but she could probably move in with her parents for awhile.

Dana pulled the car to a stop at a red light and briefly closed her eyes to pray. "Lord, please send the Gradys some help. I want to keep my job, but I don't want to see others lose their jobs, and I don't want the Gradys to lose the company they've been building for almost thirty years. I know it's all in Your hands, so I'm praying that You would be merciful to all of the people who are depending on this company for their livelihoods."

Chapter 2

At the next store, Dana definitely sensed low morale. When he saw her come into the store, Craig, who stood behind the counter talking to one of the employees, motioned for Dana to go on back to his office.

Dana took a short detour to the coffeepot for some of the warm brew and headed toward the office to wait for Craig. A few minutes later, he came in. At only eight past ten in the morning, Craig looked tired and didn't seem to be his usual happy-go-lucky self.

Dana pasted on a smile and tried to sound positive. "Looks pretty busy out there. Has it been like that all morning?"

He shook his head. "Unfortunately, no. Things just picked up about ten minutes ago. I had seven people scheduled to come in at six o'clock, and things were so slow, I sent three of them home at nine. I hated to do it, but we were just bumping into each other with nothing to do."

Dana sat down in one of the chairs facing Craig's desk. "I don't understand how this can be happening. When we had just the one store in Clayton, we never seemed to have a lull in activity. Now, the traffic pattern is pretty sketchy. All three stores are getting a minimal number of customers. What's going on?"

Craig made a mumbling sound and began digging through his desk drawers. He pulled out a shiny, colorful flyer and handed it to Dana. "This is what the problem is. They're taking our customers."

Dana grabbed the paper and took a good look at it. The ad touted the virtues of a new bakery called The Loaf, and although she had seen their flyers and advertisements before, she hadn't paid much attention to them. She shook her head. "I don't think so. People love our bakery. Who can resist wholesome organic baked goods that have been well known in the community for twenty-six years?"

With a guilty look on his face, Craig pointed to a half-eaten muffin resting on his desk. "Even loyal customers have short memories when certain stores have Banana Macadamia Mania Muffins and we don't."

Feeling shocked, Dana glanced from the muffin to Craig then back to the muffin. There were no "rules" preventing Grady employees from eating food from other stores, but the idea that Craig had brought food from a competitor's store *into* a Grady bakery unsettled her. "That's not one of ours?" She examined it more closely.

He grimly shook his head. "Don't get me wrong—I like our food, but I thought I'd do a little research. You know, scope out the competition." He shrugged. "To be honest, I actually bought the first one a couple of weeks ago. I know it doesn't look very loyal, so I'm trying to break the habit."

Dana couldn't think of a word to say. She'd come for a routine performance review, only to meet a manager confessing he loved the competitor's muffins. She opened her mouth, then closed it, deciding that this definitely qualified as one of those times when less was more.

Craig suddenly snatched up the remaining portion of the muffin and tossed it into the trash can, looking very proud of himself. "There," he said, shaking his hands emphatically. "I'm sorry. It won't happen again."

Dana cleared her throat, wondering how the day could take a turn for the bizarre at such an early hour. She took off her coat and placed it over the back of the chair, then stood. "I think I need a refill on this coffee. I'll run out front to grab some, then we can discuss operations when I come back."

Craig nodded, his gaze drifting toward the trash can. "Okay, I'll wait for you," he said.

Dana grimaced while she walked to the coffee machine. The way Craig had eyed that trash can, she wondered if other customers felt the same way about that new bakery. When she returned, Craig seemed much more like his normal self. He sipped from a glass of water, and he had several folders out on the desk for Dana to review.

"Well," she said, taking a seat again. "You know how these reviews go. I check all of your review files, and I need to sit and observe how things are going from the customers' point of view. Before I head out there, are there any things that really concern you about business in general?"

"For one thing, I'm hearing all kinds of rumors that the Gradys are going to shut us down." He stopped, then nodded. "Yeah. That concerns me. If they're closing the stores, I need to know now. We're a single-income family, and my wife home schools our kids, so I don't want her to work."

Dana nodded in agreement. "I know how you feel, and I've been hearing rumors over at the corporate office myself. Unfortunately, I don't have any definite answers. There are problems, but the Gradys don't want to close the stores. I have a meeting with them tonight, and we'll hopefully get to discuss it. I have several ideas I think could help turn things around."

"Okay. But if it looks like things are getting bad, I'm telling you I want out as soon as possible. I know the bakery business well, and The Loaf is hiring managers. If things are going sour here, I'd like to make a fairly quick transition."

Dana blinked. "You had an interview with them?"

"Not yet. Exactly. But it's only fair to me and my family, you know?"

"Of course." Dana leaned back in her chair, thinking. Maybe the lagging sales at Grady stores had more to do with that new bakery than she had allowed herself to believe. "Okay, Craig. You think The Loaf is taking our customers. Tell me why."

Craig didn't hesitate before he answered. "Dana, our food is good, but it's, well. . .old. It's not exciting. Customers are fickle, and the menu at The Loaf is interesting." He shrugged. "I can't entirely blame the customers. Everything on our menu sounds. . .boring." He winced. "Did that sound too harsh?"

Dana frowned. His comments were far more blunt than she had expected, yet his honesty made her respect him that much more.

"No, no," she said, shaking her head. "In fact, I'm glad you told me. These are things I'll need to discuss with the Gradys tonight. I'm sure they are aware of The Loaf, but it's good to have input from your perspective as well. This could be an important factor in what they decide to do."

Craig sighed, looking relieved. He ran his hands through his sandy blond hair, rumpling it. "Um. . .you know, if you do tell the Gradys, would you mind keeping me anonymous? I do like my job here, and if they don't close things down, I don't want them upset with me."

Dana laughed. "Craig, your muffin revelations startled me, but I know the Gradys well. They go to my church, and they're nice people. They are also very business minded, so they *want* to know things like this. They're not going to fire you for telling them how you feel."

"Good." He leaned back, looking satisfied. "Then you can use my name."

"Thank you." Before Dana could say more, the phone rang, and when he answered, one of the store's suppliers instantly drew him into a conversation that looked to be lengthy. He cupped his hand over the receiver and mouthed, "This won't take long."

Dana waved her hands to show that she didn't need to talk to him at the moment. "I'll take these papers and go and set up out front," she whispered. "When I'm done, I'll come back to talk with you."

He nodded and waved back, still carrying on with his phone conversation. Dana grabbed her coffee and headed to the dining room, where she spent the next two hours silently observing and taking notes about what she saw. Afterwards, she reviewed her findings with Craig for another half hour before leaving for her last review at the remaining store.

As she drove, she grew increasingly concerned about the competition. Why hadn't she paid more attention to The Loaf four months earlier when they first entered the market? "I could have at least gone in and checked them out," she muttered to herself.

The seed of an idea took root and rapidly grew. Maybe she *should* stop by one of their stores and take a look. Dana shook her head, even though she only argued with herself. It just didn't seem right. "I am a manager, not a spy."

Then again, what could it hurt? She had as a much of a right as anyone else to stop at a bakery and look at the menu. Realizing that she could get to one of the stores in under five minutes, Dana acted on impulse and decided to go ahead and pay The Loaf a visit.

Feeling very much like the key player in an espionage film, Dana circled the crowded parking lot several times before finally taking a space far away from the front door. She had two reasons for doing so; the first being she would be completely mortified if someone she knew recognized her car, and second, because no other spaces were available. The latter offered her no comfort, and she considered fleeing the scene; but her curiosity had been tickled, and she simply had to find out what kind of magnet behind those doors consistently pulled in such large crowds.

She quickly made her way through the cold air to take shelter indoors. She pulled open the massive, eggplant-colored doors and instantly relaxed after catching a whiff of the decidedly cozy aroma of baked goods and brewing coffee.

The long line snaked down the length of the counter, toward the door, and spilled into the eating area. The bright, modern décor matched perfectly with the lively music playing over the intercom and the cheery rumble of voices in the background.

Part of her felt like a traitor, but the more decisive part of her needed to stay and see what they were selling. Several people came in behind her, and since she hadn't exactly gotten in line yet, they rushed ahead of her to secure a spot in the long line.

Dana reluctantly edged closer to the back of the queue, wondering how long this would take. She had already sacrificed her lunch hour to come here, and she hated the idea that this trip might spill over into her working hours. She couldn't, in good conscience, visit this place on company time. Dana stopped and looked at her watch, noticing that one o'clock lurked around the corner, poised to make an appearance in less than ten minutes. Her lunch break officially lasted for an hour, but since Dana rarely even left the office for lunch, she decided that today she would splurge a little and stick this out.

Before she could take another step closer to the back of the line, another man swooshed past her and got in place. These people were serious about their bread, Dana decided, hurrying to get behind the man before someone else got in front of her.

While she waited, Dana looked around. Built very recently, the interior of the store still sparkled. The two new Grady bakeries had never boasted such a high-gloss look, not even at their grand openings. They were clean and new, but the décor was much more simple and the atmosphere far quieter. Dana had always liked the look of the Grady bakeries, but now she wondered if the simple, charming look had been a major mistake.

The man in front of her seemed to be doing a great deal of rubbernecking as well, and Dana wondered if the place awed him as much as it had her.

She studied him as he glanced around. He seemed vaguely familiar, but she couldn't be sure if she had seen him before or just known someone who looked like him. His appearance was not incredibly spectacular, but he did seem to stand out.

He towered at least ten inches over her height of five feet two. He had medium-toned skin and a short haircut. Dana had seen probably a million other men with similar features. What caught her attention about this man was his clothing. He dressed impeccably. The long, black overcoat he wore seemed almost an exact match to the one she and her sister-in-law, Stacy, bought for her brother, Max, this past Christmas—a single-breasted cashmere blend that turned out to be a great deal pricier than she or Stacy expected it to be.

Moments later, the stranger unbuttoned the coat and loosened the long cashmere scarf wrapped around his neck. Dana caught a glimpse of his ensemble, which consisted of a turtleneck, a charcoal blazer, and matching slacks.

A small sigh escaped her lips. She had never considered herself to be picky about a man's outward appearance. She always assumed that she would most likely end up with someone average looking who got dressed up like this no more than ten times after their wedding, but she suddenly realized there was something to be said about a man in a suit. *Something positive, that is.*

The man smiled down at her. Dana quickly shifted her gaze away, embarrassed to be caught staring. The line moved forward at a good pace, and she prayed it would move faster. In her peripheral vision, she could see him watching her, and she felt somewhat uncomfortable.

As she took a few more steps forward, she allowed herself another peek at the man. Even though his looks were average, he had a nice profile with his sculpted jawline, strong forehead, and well-shaped nose.

Stop it! she told herself. *No one pays any attention to things like that. Leave the descriptions to people who write novels.* The man glanced at her again, and Dana looked away, feeling ridiculous. *Stop overacting,* she chided herself.

Maybe because the men I work with rarely ever put on a dress shirt, let alone an ensemble like this guy. The bakery business could hardly be called a pristine, easy job. Though many of the people she worked with were men, whenever she saw them, they generally seemed to wear some of the baking ingredients. . .mostly flour.

Dana couldn't imagine this guy setting foot in a kitchen, unless he wanted to tell his kitchen staff what he'd like for dinner. He definitely looked like the type of man who'd have servants and maybe a manor on a hill somewhere. Someplace grand like. . .like where? A Mediterranean villa or a Caribbean mansion? *Nah. . .not this guy. He'd live somewhere like. . .* She tilted her head to the side and considered. Finally, she had an answer.

"Pemberley," she blurted out. For some reason, he reminded her of Mr. Darcy, from the Jane Austen novel. She didn't know if he might be as conceited as the infamous Mr. Darcy, but he certainly had a stately demeanor that reminded her of the character. Unfortunately, she had neglected to confine her imaginative thoughts to her mind, where no one else would hear them.

"Excuse me?" the man asked, turning around to face her.

Chapter 3

Dana's throat went dry. How could she have allowed herself to say something so. . .silly. . .and fictional? And out loud, at that. Pemberley, the home of Mr. Darcy, didn't really exist outside of Jane Austen's novel, *Pride and Prejudice*.

The man, still waiting for her to answer, cleared his throat softly. "Did you say something?"

"No," she answered quickly, feeling her face grow warm. She couldn't tell a lie. "I mean, yes. But I was just talking to myself."

"Oh," he said, lifting his eyebrows. "If that gets too boring, you can always just talk to me. I don't think I would be terrible company, and the conversation wouldn't be one sided."

Dana smiled politely in an attempt to collect every remaining ounce of her dignity and to refrain from leaving the store immediately.

"So, do you come here often?" he asked, seemingly determined to embarrass her further.

"Do you?" She hated answering questions posed to her by strangers.

He shook his head. "Actually, I'm new in town. Just transferred here for a job. I hoped you might be willing to tell me your favorite things on the menu."

Aha! Dana thought. He was a new customer as well. She should probably try to win him over to Grady Bakeries. "I never come here," she said matter-of-factly. "I usually get all my baked goods at another place."

He looked amused. "So if you never come here, why are you here. . .now?"

Dana took a deep breath. Obviously, he was one of those people who took everything literally, but he did it in a rather charming way. "I guess I just wanted to check out what they have. Thought I'd try something new, but now I don't know. . . ." Dana paused and shook her head. Craning her neck to look toward the front of the line, she sighed. "It doesn't even seem like this stop will be worth it. If we don't start moving, I'll go to my usual bakery."

"You have my attention now," he said. "Tell me about the other place."

"Oh." Dana waved her hand dismissively. "I know you've heard of it. Grady Bakeries? They serve excellent food, and they've been a part of the community for years and have three different locations." He didn't look very convinced about the virtues of Grady Bakeries, so she continued. "Now this place here, The Loaf, it's only been open a few months. And you know how that can be. They could just be a fad, a flash in the pan. They might not last the year." She tried to look sympathetic.

He grinned. "I doubt it, judging from the crowd here. They have plenty of customers, but if what you said is true, it's a good thing you came here before they start boarding up the windows and trying to sell the place. Otherwise, you might never know what you missed."

Dana fought the urge to frown. She felt absolutely childish trying to convince even *one* customer to stop visiting this place. If he wanted to shop here, she had no power to stop him.

"But," he said, "I'm planning to check out that other store you mentioned while I'm in town."

"Good. I think you'll probably like it." Not bothering to hide her curiosity, she asked, "So where are you from?"

He shook his head. "Most recently, I'm from New Jersey, but that's just the latest stop in the string of places I've lived. I'm originally from New York, but I'm in St. Louis for a job interview."

"So you'll be moving here?"

He nodded. "I think so. I have a meeting tonight with my potential employers, but I think I have things pretty well set." He winked. "From what I can tell, I think they need my help."

Part of Dana felt a tad irked by his extreme confidence, which she felt bordered on an over-inflated ego; but at the same time, she began rapidly accumulating a list of questions about him. She wanted to ask his name, what type of work he did, and where he had lived before New Jersey, but she held her tongue in check.

Beyond what he had told her, she knew nothing about him, and if she started asking too many questions, he would probably feel slighted if she didn't reciprocate with information about herself. She didn't feel comfortable giving out so many of her own personal details to a total stranger.

They were very close to the front of the line now, and Dana lifted her gaze to examine the menu, hopefully in order to put an end to their conversation. While he seemed nonthreatening, and she didn't feel afraid of him, she knew she couldn't be too trusting. He seemed to take the hint that she didn't want to keep talking and turned around.

Next in line, he stepped up to the counter to place his order. He had a melodic but deep voice, and he spoke articulately. He also proceeded to request one of nearly everything on the menu.

Dana wondered what in the world he would do with all of that food. Not only did he buy loaves of bread, but in addition, he got cookies, pastries, and bagels. Maybe he was shopping for a party.

Realizing that she was staring at him again, Dana forced herself to concentrate on the menu. Overwhelmed by the wide array of options, she didn't know what to choose. When one of the people behind the counter called on her, she stepped up and ordered a loaf of wheat bread and a Chocolate Raisin Oatmeal

Buddy muffin. She didn't know why she picked those two items, but she felt a tremendous amount of pressure to not hold up the line when she'd had nearly fifteen minutes to make her decision.

When the clerk handed her the bag, Dana quickly paid for the items and headed to the door. So much for espionage, she thought. How in the world had she picked such mundane items? When she reached the exit, she noticed that the man from the line followed directly behind her. If he hadn't looked threatening before, he appeared even more harmless now, with his arms full of bags of bread.

Since he would probably have a hard enough time getting his car unlocked, Dana held the door open for him.

"Thanks," he said.

"No problem."

They walked silently for a few more steps until he reached his car, parked conveniently close to The Loaf's front door. He put several of the bags on the hood while he got his keys, while Dana continued toward her own car. "Hey!" he called.

She turned around to see what he wanted.

"I don't know your name."

She shrugged helplessly. "Sorry, but I don't feel comfortable giving you that kind of information. I don't know you."

He looked disappointed. "Okay," he said slowly. "What if I tell you my name?"

She considered it for a minute. She really didn't know this guy, and as much as she might like to get acquainted, she heard warning signals going off in her head—signals that sounded exactly like her parents and seven overprotective siblings. The baby of her family, Dana had been a very outgoing child—so outgoing that her parents feared for her safety sometimes, due to her tendency to strike up conversations with complete strangers.

Her five brothers and two sisters, ever vigilant and highly bossy, had taken it upon themselves to serve as Dana's acting parents when their parents weren't around.

Unfortunately, her siblings, not being *parents*, did not approach these warnings with the same tact and gentle firmness with which her parents had. Their method of choice had been to frighten Dana with images and stories of the worst possible things that could happen to her. Of course, this had been very convincing to her as a young child, but still to this day, she sometimes got nervous chills when she met people in uncontrolled environments, outside of places like church or work.

Like now. She shook her head. "Sorry, I don't think so."

He looked even more disappointed, and Dana considered granting his request. After all, telling him her name hardly compared to giving out state secrets.

Before she could answer, he brightened. "Maybe I'll see you at that other bakery."

"Maybe," she said cautiously.

"Any chance you might tell me which one you usually go to?"

Dana grinned. This, she could handle. If he came to the bakery, she would feel more secure in that environment—on her own turf, so to speak. "I go to all three."

He nodded. "Then I'll be on the lookout for you."

"I'll be on the lookout for you too." She hurried to her car because the wind made it way too difficult to just stand around talking. If she ever saw this guy again, the Lord would have to arrange the details.

❧

Dana left the office early in order to go home and freshen up before her dinner meeting with the Gradys. She also sampled the muffin she'd gotten at The Loaf. Actually, the people at The Loaf had elevated the pastry above mere muffin status by naming it the Chocolate Raisin Oatmeal Buddy. Dana couldn't understand the name, but then again, the entire menu had been riddled with odd phrases and combinations. The muffin itself felt cold and hard from sitting out in the car for hours, but she remedied that by microwaving it.

Sitting at her tiny kitchen table, Dana cautiously nibbled the first bite. As she chewed and swallowed, she realized Craig had been right. Absolutely right. The Loaf had excellent muffins. As much as she hated to admit it, their muffins were far tastier than the ones sold at Grady Bakeries.

Dana's stomach churned, and she put the muffin down. If their muffins were this good, the rest of their bakery items could probably walk circles around the stuff sold in Grady stores. Dana reached for her cordless phone and dialed Kim's number.

Kim answered and sounded hesitant when she realized Dana waited on the line. "Is this about work? I just got home five minutes ago, and I wanted to have a long soak in the tub. You don't want to know what happened with me and a batch of sourdough starter five minutes before we closed."

Dana instantly envisioned several scenarios, all of them equally sticky. "Sorry. I just wanted to ask you something."

"Go ahead but be quick. Besides, don't you have a meeting tonight with the Gradys?"

"Yeah, and that's why I'm calling." Dana paused, wondering how she should proceed. Since Kim said she had little time, Dana decided not to beat around the bush and just ask the question. "Have you ever bought anything from The Loaf?"

Kim kept silent.

Dana waited.

Kim said nothing.

Dana cleared her throat. This felt like a replay of her discussion with Craig this morning. "Kim, this isn't an interrogation. I'm not going to fire you for buying something from them."

Kim let out a sigh. "Okay. Listen, this is what happened: My sisters brought home some Danishes once, the Cherry Cream Cheese Caper."

"The what?"

"Don't ask. All of their food has long names."

"Oh, don't get me started on the names," Dana said. "I bought a chocolate chip muffin, and I nearly ran out of breath trying to recite the name while I ordered it."

"So you go there too?" Before Dana could answer, Kim continued. "I'm glad to hear this from you. I felt like such a traitor because after we ate the danishes, I went back to get more and discovered those Dill Fennel Drama baguettes. They're terrific with tuna salad. And now I feel much better knowing that you go too." Her words spilled out in a rush. "I guess I'm just tired of eating our stuff at work. It doesn't have the same pizzazz. I go to The Loaf almost every day to pick up something, and I've tasted pretty much everything they sell. So," Kim slowed down, "what's your favorite?"

"Um. Well, I don't know. I've never been there before today," Dana said pointedly.

"Oh. I see. This was a trap, huh? You got me to spill my guts about my secret trips to the other bakery so you can tell on me at your meeting?"

Dana shook her head, even though Kim couldn't see her. "No, that's not it. I've been wrapped up in my work and hadn't realized our competition is formidable until this morning when Craig mentioned it. I went there this afternoon and bought a couple of things."

"So what do you think?"

"I think we're in trouble," Dana said without hesitation.

"You just said we couldn't get fired for eating at another bakery. Why the sudden change?"

"No, not 'we' as in our jobs. At least not right now," Dana admitted. "But I think The Loaf is a big reason that our business has been down."

"I know," Kim said. "To think—I've been chipping away at my own job by eating stuff from that place. I promise I won't go back. Not even for one of those Cilantro Parmesan Peace bagels. I won't let my sisters go either. You can count on it."

"Thanks, but that's too little too late. Even if none of our workers shop there, people will still go in droves. We have to do something, and I plan to talk to the Gradys about this tonight."

"Good. We do need to do something. They've had the same menu since the bakery opened, and I was a little kid then. We need change."

Dana didn't think that qualified as the solution. "There's something to be said for classic simplicity, Kim. I don't think we need to go out and copy The Loaf's menu."

"Copy? No," Kim agreed. "Update? Yes, yes, a thousand times yes."

"I never thought I would hear someone who likes antiques criticize something for being *old*," Dana quipped.

"Classic simplicity is great for furniture but a waste of time and money when it comes to the food business. People want new and exciting, and if you don't give it to them, they go where the action is."

Dana still didn't agree, but she decided not to make an issue of it. She would take her concerns to the Gradys, and since they had developed the first menu, she felt sure they would see her point. They needed more publicity right away. The menu wasn't as hip as the one over at The Loaf, but trends were always coming and going. Grady Bakeries had the benefit of time and experience on their side, and Dana remained confident they would prevail in the end. To Kim, she said, "We'll see what the Gradys think."

"Good idea. I'll be praying," Kim assured her. "Call me when you know something. I'm on pins and needles about this."

"Me too. I've got to run and get ready for dinner, but I'll probably be sending out a memo Monday morning."

"Or, you could just call me tonight. It's not like I'll be asleep or anything. Who can sleep when her job is up in the air?"

"Okay," Dana agreed. "If it's not too late, I'll call you tonight."

"Define your idea of 'too late.' I have a feeling we have differing opinions on the matter," Kim persisted.

"Kim. . . ," Dana said. "Just let me go and get ready, okay?"

"All right."

Dana hung up and went to her closet to decide out what she would wear for her dinner meeting. Since they were dining at a small, somewhat formal place, she decided on a black matte jersey tunic with a matching pair of comfortable pants.

She flipped open her compact of pressed powder, ran the sponge over her face a couple of times, then applied a quick touch of mascara, put on a touch of the deep reddish lipstick she saved for special occasions, and grabbed her coat.

❧

The restaurant was located in downtown Clayton, only ten minutes away from her bungalow in Richmond Heights, but the temperature had dropped, and she didn't want to speed on roads that might possibly be a little slippery. Dana arrived ten minutes early, just as Mr. and Mrs. Grady were arriving.

Mrs. Grady got out as soon as her husband stopped the car. She made a beeline toward Dana and ushered her into the restaurant. "It's too cold to stand out here talking." They waited inside the doorway for Mr. Grady, then were led to their table.

As soon as they were seated, Dana reached into her oversized shoulder bag and pulled out the notebook she'd been carrying around.

Mr. Grady took one look at the book and shook his head. He gently took it, closed the cover, and set it aside. "Let's at least order appetizers first."

"Besides, Ethan isn't here yet," said Mrs. Grady.

Dana looked from Mrs. Grady to her husband. "Who's Ethan?"

Mr. Grady smiled. "Let's order something, then I'll explain."

Dana didn't feel very hungry, but Mr. Grady made it clear that he wanted to eat soon, so business matters would have to wait for a bit. They discussed the weather until the waiter arrived with iced tea and a platter of portabella mushrooms stuffed with a cream cheese and crab mixture.

After a few bites of mushroom, Mr. Grady glanced around the room, looking worried. "I wonder what's keeping Ethan so long?" Patting his wife's hand, he added, "We should have stopped by his hotel and driven him over."

Mrs. Grady nodded. "He must have gotten lost."

Mr. Grady looked at Dana. "I guess you're ready to talk business. Why don't you tell me how the reviews went today?"

Dana agreed and began her narrative of how things had gone. She concluded with a lengthy statement concerning the competition from The Loaf.

To her surprise, Mr. and Mrs. Grady not only agreed but also indicated they were well on the way to finding a remedy for the problem.

Mrs. Grady sighed. "I guess our menu is a little dated, but until The Loaf opened, people seemed to like what we were selling. Now, we have no choice but to make some rather extensive changes."

Dana wrinkled her forehead. She had already indicated to Kim that she felt Grady Bakeries could make a recovery without trying to copy The Loaf's strategy, but it didn't appear that the Gradys felt the same as she did. "What do you mean by changes?" Dana ventured cautiously.

Mr. Grady grinned. "We're going to give our entire menu a makeover," he said, speaking in low tones, as though the competition sat at the next table.

"The whole menu?" Dana asked, shocked. She loved that menu. Solid and dependable, it never changed, and Dana felt its real beauty lay in true simplicity. "How?"

"We're hiring someone who knows what people really want," said Mr. Grady. "And you're going to help him."

Mrs. Grady clasped her hands together, looking excited. "His name is Ethan Miles, and he's a very experienced chef. He's lived all over the world, so he knows all of the latest trends."

Dana blinked. They were trying to get ahead by copying the competition and somehow needed her to lend a hand in all of this. She shook her head. "But I'm not a baker. I'm not even part of the marketing department. I'm just the general manager. How am I going to help?"

"You're going to be Ethan's assistant," Mr. Grady said. "I am spending a great deal of money to revitalize our image. He will need someone to introduce him to the workers, get him acclimated to the city, and help him go over the records to analyze what items sell best. You'll also have to help organize product development and testing, then help the stores integrate the new items and phase out the old as seamlessly as possible."

Dana couldn't talk. Her job currently devoured more overtime hours than she preferred to count, and now Mr. Grady had essentially suggested she work the equivalent of two jobs. She did her best to hide her displeasure. She felt slighted that they hadn't asked her opinion before deciding to make her play secretary to an overpaid baker while doing her regular duties.

This was downright ridiculous! She began gathering ideas to voice her complaint, but before she could say anything, Mr. Grady stood up and beckoned someone over to the table. Dana sat with her back stiff, unwilling to acknowledge this troublemaker right away. She inhaled deeply, trying not to let her temper take over.

To put things simply, she felt wronged. She hadn't been shown the respect her position afforded her. She should have been a part of the decision-making process instead of having the news thrust on her five minutes before she met her new "boss." Normally, she took charge of things at work. She told the other employees what to do and answered directly to the Gradys and no one else—until now.

"Learn to be a servant of all. . . ." The words seemed no louder than a whisper, a glimmer of one of the Bible verses Dana had memorized as a little girl. She sighed, realizing the truth of the verse. In order to be great in God's kingdom, a person first needed to learn how to serve others, just like Jesus had. Still. . .it didn't feel good. She had always imagined that if she were ever in this position, it would somehow feel more noble. This didn't feel noble. It stung her pride. *"Pride goes before destruction, a haughty spirit before a fall."* The verse echoed in her ears. Dana closed her eyes.

Okay, Lord, she admitted. *I'm trying to learn what it is You're trying to teach me.* She opened her eyes and turned around to find herself facing the man from the line at The Loaf.

He smiled, almost as if he were amused to find her here.

"Dana," said her boss, "this is Ethan." Turning to Ethan, he said, "Ethan, this is—"

"Dana," Ethan said, interrupting him. To Dana, he said, "I didn't think I would find out your name this soon."

Dana blinked. She couldn't think of a single word to say, but she was well aware her three tablemates were waiting for her to comment.

Chapter 4

Suppressing a grin at Dana's sudden silence, Ethan picked up the conversation, explaining to the Gradys how he had run into Dana earlier at The Loaf. "I asked for her phone number, but she wouldn't give it to me."

"Dana is our operations manager, so you don't have to worry about her phone number. I imagine you'll see enough of each other at work," Mr. Grady supplied with a chuckle.

Ethan felt pleased. He'd had a sneaking suspicion earlier that the woman he'd met at the bakery might somehow be more than just a dedicated Grady Bakery customer. Smiling at the Gradys, Ethan added, "It's nice to know that I'll be working for a company whose employees are so *committed* to finding ways to win new customers."

Dana's eyes widened at his statement, and Ethan wondered if she thought he might be making fun of her.

She cleared her throat. "Well, I'm glad you're supposed to be the marketing genius. It seems that my plan to infiltrate the customer line at The Loaf would be far too time consuming." She gave him an overly sweet smile, then turned her attention to the menu.

Ethan tugged at his collar, feeling vaguely uncomfortable, as if he'd wandered into the midst of a battlefield while the opposing sides reloaded their weapons. The calm before the storm.

Resolving to keep quiet until he knew more about the situation, he grabbed his glass of ice water and quickly gulped down enough to give him a momentary headache.

Mr. Grady cleared his throat. "In our earlier conversations, you mentioned needing an assistant to help with your research and development."

Ethan nodded. "Yes, and you said that you didn't know if you had the finances to create another position so suddenly. Have you made any decisions either way?"

Mr. Grady nodded slowly, glancing across the table at Dana. She sat with her back as straight as a rod, her chin lifted high.

"I'm going to be your assistant," she informed him, her mouth forming a smile that didn't look very happy.

Now Ethan knew the origin of the problem he sensed. For reasons that remained unknown, while Dana had seemed interested in him personally, she didn't seem particularly thrilled with the idea of being his assistant. He hoped to prolong eye contact, but she once again turned her attention to her menu.

Just then, the waiter came around, ready to take orders. Ethan quickly decided on a pasta dish flavored with an herb and cream sauce.

While the rest of the table ordered, he thought about the situation with Dana. Should he tell the Gradys that he could do the job without her? If he did, where would that leave him? He *needed* an assistant. Of course, if absolutely necessary, he could do the job alone, but it would take longer and end up costing the Gradys more money.

Ethan wondered if Dana would get a pay increase to do this job and if she would still be expected to do her previous duties in addition to being his helper. She still remained very quiet, and Ethan had a feeling this new job had come as a surprise to her.

After the waiter left, Mr. Grady asked Ethan if he felt ready to give any details of his ideas for the company. Ethan relaxed somewhat. Talking about work seemed far more comfortable than wondering how to smooth things over with his new—and apparently unwilling—assistant.

He related what he bought and tasted from the menu at The Loaf. In the end, he concluded that their food boasted a new and exciting look and taste; he held no doubt that he could formulate a competitive menu for the Gradys.

Ethan explained his thoughts to the Gradys, then added, "But on Monday, I'd like to give your menu the same going over. I'm not quite convinced that we should have to throw everything out. If what you already sell has been successful this long, then maybe it's not totally done for. In my experience as a pastry chef, people are always looking for something new; yet, after the new has worn off, they tend to gravitate back to familiar favorites."

Dana seemed to perk up at this statement, and Ethan felt relieved that his image could be improving in her eyes. In his opinion, Dana's approval would be a good thing. After their initial meeting that afternoon, he'd been very disappointed that he'd not even learned so much as her name.

During the ride back to his hotel, Ethan had worked to burn her image into his memory. A petite, captivating beauty, Dana was the total package.

Her round cheeks, wide, velvety brown eyes, full lips that showcased pretty white teeth, and cassia-toned skin all combined to form the most memorable face Ethan had ever seen. Barely over five feet tall, she was built like a Normal Woman, with a capital N.

Ethan had realized he had no reason to be so concerned with remembering how she looked. To put things simply, Dana was unforgettable.

After mentally kicking himself for not finding a way to continue their conversation, Ethan's disappointment had threatened to cloud his entire day. After a good half hour of trying to figure out what he should have said and done to get more information, he'd given up and turned the whole issue over to the Lord. "If You want me to see her again, then I'm ready to let You arrange things," he had prayed.

Even though he had been sincere, he didn't expect much to come of his request. The sight of her this evening jolted him. Just as he'd been ready to conclude that the Lord did indeed want him and Dana to meet again, his excitement deflated after he encountered Dana's hesitance.

Now, instead of being enthusiastic, he felt confused. He wanted to tell the Gradys that he would do the job alone but then worried that Dana might feel he had belittled her ability to do the job—and he didn't want that to happen.

Was the fact that Dana would be working with him a mere coincidence, or did the Lord really have something more in mind?

～

Dana felt out of kilter. Earlier this afternoon, this man seemed charming and attractive. Now, despite the fact that he hadn't really done anything to her, she fought the impression that he could almost be an enemy. *At least, not yet.* Already, she'd be forced to rearrange her work schedule in order to help him.

Dana glanced at Ethan, wondering what qualified him to succeed at this job. His appearance didn't seem to suggest he could resolve the situation. Dana considered his ensemble this afternoon to be quite dressy, but this evening his attire appeared even more formal.

Wearing a black dinner jacket and matching pants along with the same cashmere coat and scarf, Ethan had made his entrance in the restaurant smelling of new clothes and looking as unwrinkled and glossy as a magazine photo. This image didn't mesh with Dana's image of the traditional chef.

In spite of her reservations, Dana couldn't deny that the opportunity to work with him did interest her. At least he didn't need to change everything. Perhaps, given the opportunity to work side by side with him, she could be influential enough to prevent him from disturbing too much of the company's foundation.

During the remainder of the meal, Ethan and the Gradys plotted and planned their new marketing schedule. Dana stared at her dinner and did her best to look cheerful, her feelings a strange jumble of expectation and dread. When the meal ended, she declined to stay for coffee and cheesecake and left early, pleading fatigue.

～

The weekend passed too quickly for Dana. After church on Sunday, she spent time with her family, who had gathered at her parents' home to celebrate her nephew's birthday.

Her mother noticed that something troubled Dana. After Dana finished explaining the situation, Mom didn't offer any direct advice.

"I think you'll have to decide what you need to do," said Mom. "Pride can be a tricky thing, and we have to be sure to react to a situation for the right reasons. Otherwise, we might let our own notions of how we should be treated take over and start to control us."

Dana pursed her lips. This wasn't the type of advice she'd hoped for. "Okay, I understand that, but don't you think the Gradys were a little unfeeling about this?"

Mom shrugged her shoulders, and Dana knew she didn't see this situation the same way. "Honey," Mom began, "I don't think the Gradys meant you any harm by asking you to work with Ethan. But I do know their business is in trouble, and without their business, you wouldn't have this job. I can't tell you what to do, but I think if I were in your shoes, I'd work as hard as I could to help the company—and my job."

Dana knew her mother spoke the truth, but she couldn't help feeling a little sorry for herself. Most everyone else in her family tended to side with Mom's point of view, and Dana felt herself growing more frustrated.

Sure, she needed to give her all to help the company; but somehow, she felt they weren't willing to give her as much as she planned to devote to them.

Monday morning she arrived at work, her heart heavy with the realization that she would indeed have to do her best to stick this out. Still, she wasn't looking forward to the job. After filling up her mug of coffee, she trudged into her office, hoping to get a few minutes to brace herself for Ethan's arrival.

Instead, she found him sitting at her desk, apparently waiting for her to arrive. Dana stopped abruptly in the doorway, accidentally sloshing some of her coffee over the sides of the mug. "Ouch!" she exclaimed, as the hot liquid trickled over her fingers.

Ethan jumped up, grabbed the mug from her, and set it down on the corner of her desk. Before she could say a word, he took her hand and examined it. Too stunned and embarrassed to protest, Dana stood there.

As he checked over her fingers, Vanessa, from the marketing department, walked into the office. She stopped, her eyes widening at the sight of Ethan holding Dana's hand. Before Dana could explain, Vanessa backed away. "Sorry, I didn't mean to interrupt. It's nothing important, so I'll come back later."

Dana snatched her hand away from Ethan, who gave her an amused look. "No harm done," he said. "But if I were you, I'd run it under cold water for a bit."

Dana shot a glare at him and practically ran down the hallway after Vanessa. The last thing she needed was for the rest of her coworkers to get the idea that she and Ethan were. . .well, anything more than two people working on a plan to help the company.

She located Vanessa in the break room, putting butter on a bagel and chattering to other workers. When Dana entered the room, Vanessa suddenly hushed.

Dana wanted to groan. News could certainly travel fast. Gathering all of her dignity, she held up her injured hand, which still dripped convincingly with coffee. "I spilled my coffee," she informed the entire room.

A few people nodded their heads and made sympathetic sounds.

As she headed toward the wet bar in the corner, Dana kept talking. "Ethan said I should run cold water over it to make sure it'll be okay." No one said anything. Determined to nip any rumors in the bud, Dana made a big show of running cold water over her hand. When she finished, she went to the bagel box and grabbed one.

"So," she said to Vanessa, "what did you need to talk to me about?" Trying not to sound or look desperate, Dana split the bagel and slathered cream cheese over it.

Vanessa gave her a blank stare.

Dana sighed. "Remember, you were just in my office?"

A look of realization came over Vanessa's face. "Oh, that," she said. "I just wanted to check with you about some of the new ads we've been working on. Mr. Grady came in earlier. He said that before we run the new ads, we should check with you since we're going to be taking some things off of the menu."

Dana felt mildly pleased. At least Mr. Grady hadn't come in and announced to everyone that Ethan now ran the show. Suddenly, she frowned. Mr. Grady never came into the office before eleven—on the days he did come in to work. "Mr. Grady was already here this morning? Before I got here?"

Vanessa nodded. "He brought Chef Miles in and introduced him to everyone."

"Oh." Dana's heart sank a bit. She put the two halves of the bagel back together and lifted it to her mouth. Before she could take a bite, Vanessa held up a hand.

"Yes?" Dana asked, somewhat irritated.

Vanessa shrugged. "I thought you hated pumpernickel."

"I do."

Vanessa looked pointedly at the bagel Dana had just prepared.

Dana took a deep breath and looked at the piece of bread. Sure enough, she held a pumpernickel bagel. Dana wanted to groan. By now, everyone had gone back to quiet chatting, but they were still discreetly watching her.

Dana laughed nervously. Might there be any way to fix this without making herself look even sillier?

"Oh, pumpernickel—my favorite," said someone from behind her.

Dana didn't have to turn around to recognize that the voice belonged to Ethan. "Is this for me?" he asked, gesturing toward the bagel she held.

Dana shrugged. "If you want it."

"Thanks," he said, sounding really pleased. "I waited and waited for you to come back. How's the burn?"

"It's fine," Dana said firmly, moving away before he could grab it again. Now, everyone had dropped all pretense of conversation in order to watch the exchange.

He smiled. "Hey, this is a good system. I look over your scalded hand, and in return, you fix me a bagel. Think you could spill coffee every morning?"

Dana forced a smile. She supposed she could be happy that Ethan had just confirmed that she had, indeed, suffered a burn. However, that victory had been undone when he'd suggested to everyone within hearing that she had just skipped down to the break room to fix him breakfast.

Only about a tenth of all the employees were in the break room, but Dana knew how the account of her conversation with Ethan would travel once they left the room.

Rumors could spread around an office as quickly as news of a picnic moved through an anthill, and her efforts to quell any false ideas had probably only succeeded in furthering them.

Giving up on the idea of setting things right, Dana headed toward the doorway, while Ethan carried on a conversation with the others.

Before she could leave, she heard one of the women say, "Chef Miles, when do we *all* get to call you Ethan? Or do we have to be working directly with you for that privilege?"

Several others chuckled, and Dana winced, realizing she had made yet another mistake by using his first name when explaining about the burn.

Back at her office, she wearily sat down at her desk. She reached for her coffee, which now held an unappetizing chill. While she waited for Ethan to finish his breakfast, she alternated between wanting to laugh and cry. In some respects, this morning's incident might be funny, but right now the humor wasn't all that prominent.

While trying to prepare for Ethan to return, she moved her coffee aside and tackled some paperwork she had left on Friday. She prayed that the menu issues could be resolved quickly so Ethan could go back to New York, and her life and job could return to normal; but in the back of her mind, Dana had a feeling she would be in this for the long haul.

Chapter 5

H mm," Ethan mumbled, chewing yet another bite of bread. He swallowed and took a drink of water. Glancing at the platter in front of him, he took a deep breath and reached for another piece.

"What do you call this one?" he asked Dana, who sat across the table.

"Oatmeal wheat."

"Just oatmeal wheat?"

Dana lifted her eyebrows slightly. "That's what it is," she said, both sounding and looking quite terse.

Shrugging, Ethan popped the small square into his mouth and chewed. This ranked as one of the best he'd tasted. As he swallowed, he reached for his notebook and jotted down some impressions, as he had done with each previous piece he'd tasted. Oatmeal wheat should stay the same. . .maybe a few revisions—it could probably be more moist. *Mostly needs a name change,* he scribbled.

As he finished, he could sense Dana leaning ever so slightly toward him—and his notebook. Ethan hated the feeling of having someone watch him so closely. He shut the book, and Dana eased back, looking quite uninterested.

Ethan held back a grin, realizing that Dana seemed terribly interested in what he wrote. Ethan supposed he could share his observations, but quite honestly, he didn't feel comfortable doing so. There would be no way to guess how she might react. He'd hoped to get started on better footing with her this morning, but she'd spilled coffee all over her hand and gotten upset with him when he'd tried to help. After that, in the break room, she snubbed him in front of everyone present—all but ignored him, as though he didn't exist.

Since then, she had stayed as silent as a stone—only talking when he asked her a direct question. She was extremely knowledgeable about all aspects of the company, and he understood why the Gradys chose her to help him. If they had picked anyone else, his time would have been wasted, as he probably still would have ended up asking Dana everything he needed to know.

She had a great head for business—exactly the type of person he would choose to run the administrative side of his restaurant if he ever got around to opening one, rather than simply helping other people fix theirs. Correction, he decided. He'd like to work with her if he could get some assurances that she was actually a real person instead of some sort of robot who had no idea of how to interact with other people.

Ethan looked at his watch. "It's a little after noon," he announced to Dana. She nodded in agreement but didn't reply.

Ethan closed his eyes briefly. *Lord, help me through this. I can't imagine spending the next few months or even hours with this woman if she's going to act like this the entire time.*

"How about lunch?" he suggested.

Dana opened her mouth and closed it. From the look on her face, she almost seemed unsure of whether there would be any benefit to getting away from work if she still had to be in his company. Ethan supposed if they went their own separate ways for lunch, she would probably be much happier. The idea of suggesting they do just that crossed his mind, but Ethan decided against it. Although his plan to get to know his assistant had not failed, it had been subject to numerous delays. Even though she seemed bent on making his workday miserable, he didn't yet want to throw in the towel.

"How can you be hungry? You've been eating bread all morning."

He shrugged. "I need to clear my palate before I can finish the rest of these samples, so I want to eat something besides bread for lunch."

"Oh, the trials of being a chef," Dana said, not sounding at all sympathetic.

Without waiting for her to agree with him, Ethan stood up, retrieved his coat from the chair, and waited for her to do the same. "We'll have to take your car, of course, so you can pick the place."

Dana actually smiled. "Sure, I think that can be arranged. And I'm feeling generous, so I'll treat."

The sentence sounded like an oxymoron. The words "Dana" and "generous" didn't seem to go together. Ethan supposed he should feel wary of her sudden cooperation, but he felt too hungry to give it much thought. Besides, maybe she just needed awhile to warm up to him.

As he followed her to the car, he wondered where they would be dining. His mouth watered at the thought of a big, juicy hamburger and thick, homemade French fries, and he hoped she would pick a place that served a good burger. But he couldn't very well offer to let Dana pick the place, then change his mind— especially since she had offered to pay.

Oh well, he decided. The least he could do was be gracious, since she seemed to be making an effort to be nice.

Dana drove a short distance and pulled into a parking lot of a small diner. The place didn't look fancy by a long shot. Instead, it reflected years of wear and tear. Although some people he knew would do their best to stay away from eateries like this, Ethan didn't mind. He'd learned a long time ago that some of the less elaborate establishments had some of the best food. Besides, the parking lot was full, and a steady stream of people came and went. That had to count for something.

Dana pulled into a parking space but didn't make a move to get out of the car.

Ethan cleared his throat. "So, is this the place?" He tried not to sound overly enthusiastic, not knowing if Dana would think he might be trying too hard to be friendly.

At first, she didn't seem to have heard him, but just as he opened his mouth to speak up again, she glanced over at him with a strange look on her face. She shook her head. "No. . .I took a wrong turn. I pulled in here to turn around." Dana shifted the car in reverse and quickly pulled out of the parking lot.

Ethan felt more than a little disappointed. The smells coming from that place were wonderful, and he hated to leave it behind. Apparently, the diner didn't suit Dana's style. He'd have to remember how to get here on his own sometime.

Finally, after several more minutes of driving, they arrived at a small, quiet café. Ethan felt like groaning. No way was he going to find his hamburger here. The heartiest thing he found on the menu was a chicken salad. Although it turned out to be rather tasty, the salad wasn't as filling as he had hoped it would be.

Ethan tried not to let his disappointment over Dana's choice of a restaurant show for two reasons. At first, he'd thought she really wanted to be on friendly terms with him. Although moments of quiet did settle over them, the tone was different. The silence Ethan endured all morning had been stony, but now it had become amicable. Second, Dana seemed really anxious of his opinion of the place. For some reason, whether or not he liked this place seemed very important to her. He could tell by the hopeful look on her face, and though he probably wouldn't want to dine here every day, he'd enjoyed it well enough.

When the check came, Ethan offered to go half and half with Dana. Places like this were not exactly inexpensive, and he didn't want her to feel financially pressured on his account. Dana firmly, but kindly, refused his help. At least, at first she did. She tried to write a check, but the waiter informed her that they did not accept checks.

"But I don't have any cash with me."

The waiter shook his head. "Perhaps a credit card?"

Dana nodded and began searching through her purse. Less than a minute later, she came up empty handed. "I'm sorry, but I don't have my credit card with me. I usually leave it at home unless I know I'm going to be using it for something specific. Couldn't I just write a check just this once?"

The waiter lifted his eyebrows. "Madam, we accept cash or credit."

A look of sheer mortification washed over Dana's face. Other customers were beginning to glance in their direction.

Ethan pulled out his wallet and handed over his credit card. "My treat this time," he told Dana. He hated to sound as though he were taking over like a rescuing knight, but really there had been no other choice.

Apparently, Dana agreed. "Thank you," she whispered as the waiter carried away his card to process the receipt. "I'm so sorry about this. I'm just so embarrassed. I should have realized this place didn't take checks."

Ethan frowned. "I thought you came here often."

Dana sighed. "Not really. I actually prefer much simpler fare, but I worried that you might want something fancier, since you're the famous chef and all." She leaned closer and lowered her voice a notch. "Remember that diner we went to at first? I actually wanted to take you there just to spite you. I figured Mr. 'I need to clear my palate' wouldn't enjoy that place."

Ethan leaned back and laughed, not caring if others were watching. "So how'd we end up here?"

Dana looked down at the table. "My conscience got me at the last second," she admitted. "I drove away as fast as I could and didn't look back. I repented all the way here."

Ethan laughed again, then leaned closer toward her. "I'll let you in on a little secret of my own. I could have cried when we left that diner. The smells in the parking lot were fantastic."

Dana's eyes widened. "You mean, you wouldn't have minded eating lunch there?"

"No, and I insist we go there next time."

Dana looked relieved. "Good. And I'll treat. They do take checks there."

The two of them shared a laugh before Ethan decided to broach a more sensitive topic. "Dana," he began, "I have no idea why things have been strained between us, but I want us to be friends. If you can't commit to that, I'd like for us to at least be civil. I think that will be an important part of the probability of us succeeding at this job."

She nodded slowly. "I agree. I haven't been all that fun to be around, and I'm sorry. Will you forgive me?"

Ethan nodded. "Sure. Would it be too tacky of me to ask why you've been upset with me?"

A startled look passed over Dana's face, and Ethan hurried to clarify his question. "I'm not trying to prod where I shouldn't. My only concern is that I've done something to offend you, and I don't want to do it again."

"I see. . . ."

Before she could answer, a woman walked up to their table.

"Excuse me," she said cautiously. "I hate to interrupt, but aren't you Ethan Miles, the chef?"

Ethan nodded, and the woman smiled. "Oh, I love your cookbook," she said. "In fact, I wish I had it with me so you could autograph it. Remember the dinner party recipes you had when you were featured in *The Household Chef's Magazine?* I have to tell you, they turned out fabulously. I made them for a garden party last summer, and everyone just raved."

"Well, thank you," Ethan said. "I'm always glad to hear that someone enjoys my recipes."

"Oh, of course," said the woman. "I'm hoping that you'll have a cooking show again sometime soon. Why did the network cancel it?"

"Well, actually, my contract ended, and I didn't feel ready to renew," Ethan explained. "I liked doing the show, but it took away from my regular schedule.

Right now I'm doing freelance work for independent restaurants and bakeries in addition to writing my next cookbook. Maybe later I'll be able to juggle all that with a cooking show again."

"I certainly hope so," the woman agreed. "But in the meantime, I'll be looking forward to your next cookbook. When can I find it in stores?"

"I'm still writing it, but it should be on the shelves around this time next year. Next February at the latest."

"Perfect," the woman said. "I don't want to take all of your time, but thanks for chatting with me."

"And thank you for your comments about my cookbook."

As soon as the woman left, the waiter returned with the receipt. "I guess we should get back to the office," Ethan told Dana. "We've got a plate of bread just waiting to be tasted."

In all honesty, he wanted to finish their previous conversation, but he wasn't sure if this would be a good time for the question he'd been on the verge of asking. The last thing he wanted to do was cause Dana to feel pressured. Maybe in a few days the topic would come up again.

❧

"What a day," Dana sighed, as she unlocked the door to her house. Ethan had handled the situation at lunch graciously, and although she still had her doubts about whether his influence would be good for the bakeries, she had gained more respect for him.

She still felt remorse for giving him the silent treatment that morning, and she hated to think of what her mother would say if she heard how Dana had behaved. *I'm acting like a spoiled little kid.* Dana shook her head. "This has to stop," she said firmly. "Tomorrow I'm going to go in and do my job. If his influence will hurt the company, I'll trust the Lord to fix whatever goes wrong."

The aspect of leaving all of her uncertainties to prayer lifted a weight from Dana's shoulders. With a smile, she headed to the kitchen to fix dinner.

❧

"What do you think of adding cranberries to the raisin bread?" Ethan asked.

"Well," Dana paused and put her hand over her mouth to mask a yawn, "I don't know. You're the chef, right?"

Ethan shrugged. "But you're my assistant. You know the market; you know the customers." He stirred a few spoonfuls of yeast into a bowl of warm water and set it aside. "Tell me how you think it will taste."

Dana opened her mouth, only to let another yawn escape. Mortified, she apologized as she continued to fiddle with the apron strings she still struggled to fasten behind her back. When had she ever worn an apron? At any rate, the women on old sitcoms from the fifties made tying an apron look so easy. Then again, they'd worn decorative, frilly little aprons, while she stood draped in a huge white cloth that could have doubled as a small bed sheet.

"Let me help you with that." Ethan crossed the room. "You don't have to tie it behind your back. Wrap it around and bring it back to the front, then tie it."

Dana nodded and did as Ethan instructed. Of course, he got to wear a chef's jacket, not an apron. When she finished, she caught a glimpse of her reflection in one of the windows. "This thing is not exactly figure flattering," she murmured.

Taking a seat on a barstool, Dana yawned again. "Tell me again why we're here at five-thirty in the morning."

"We need to use a fully equipped kitchen to test the recipes. If we come any later, we'll be in the way of the bakers who work here, so we had to come early."

Dana nodded. "So why didn't we use the kitchen at the main office so we could come in to work during normal hours?"

"Mr. Grady said the floors and countertops are being redone. The contractors wanted to start right away, or else they would take another job. So we're stuck here with early hours until that kitchen gets done."

Mr. Grady had been trying to schedule that remodel for a few months now, and it was just Dana's luck as a definite allergic-to-morning person that the work would have to begin at this hour. Most days she counted herself fortunate to be alert by nine. Anything before that seemed to be a blur. "Okay, what do I need to do?"

"Take notes for now," he said. "I need help, but I'm picky about measuring everything myself when I'm creating."

Dana didn't argue. Taking notes suited her just fine. At least, it would *after* she made her coffee. "Can I interest you in coffee?"

Ethan, engrossed in examining the current raisin bread recipe, nodded absentmindedly.

Dana powered up the small kitchen coffee maker and located some coffee beans. This wouldn't be as good as the stuff they made in the huge commercial machines for the customers, but at this early hour, she couldn't be picky. While the drink brewed, she returned to her chair, notebook in hand.

"Ginger!" Ethan said.

"Excuse me?"

Ethan gestured toward the notebook. "Write that down. Ginger. I need ginger in this bread."

"Okay," Dana said, making a note of it. "Anything else?"

"Not yet. . .but keep your ears open. If I say something, just jot it down. It'll help for later reference."

Dana had a feeling this might turn out to be a long baking session. She was used to spending hours in the kitchen making holiday meals with her family, but she'd never put in that many kitchen hours at work.

While measuring cups of flour into a bowl, Ethan glanced at Dana. "You feeling okay?" He looked concerned.

"I don't look okay?" Dana asked, only half joking. She smiled and waved his concerns away. "You must be more of a morning person than I am."

Before he could answer, the timer on the machine went off, signaling the coffee had finished percolating. "Stay there. I'll get it," Ethan said. In moments, he had poured two mugs and set them on the counter. Taking a seat next to her, he took a long sip. "This is good coffee."

Dana took a drink and murmured her agreement. After another sip, she said, "I'm ready to work now."

Ethan shook his head. "Let's finish our coffee." After a short pause, he added, "Maybe we can talk—you know, have a conversation."

Laughing, Dana ignored the uncertain look in his eyes. "I see where you're going, and I'll just apologize for yesterday again. I was in a silly mood that I don't really want to talk about. However," she took another drink, "it won't happen again."

Ethan looked relieved. "I'm glad. Now we can get to know each other." His smile was warm and genuine.

Dana felt at ease. She could get used to this. Sitting in a kitchen while a handsome chef baked bread. . .

Oh, quit it. Just yesterday you couldn't stand the sight of the man; now you're practically swooning. Before her thoughts could wander any further, she spoke up. "So tell me about you."

He took a deep breath. "I'll give you the condensed version, since we have to get to work today." He set his mug down, a thoughtful look on his face. "Well, I'm twenty-nine years old. I'm originally from Chicago, and I wanted to be a fireman since I was five years old." He stopped and looked at Dana. "Are you sure you really want to hear all this?

She nodded. "Yes. So how did you end up as a chef?"

"When I was in the tenth grade, my class took a tour of a fancy restaurant. We got to watch the chefs make crème brulee and bananas foster." He laughed. "That hooked me. I'd never seen a dessert you had to set on fire, and from then on I was convinced that I too was called to set perfectly good desserts on fire instead of dousing burning buildings.

"I went to a culinary institute in New York and graduated with honors. I've written two cookbooks, worked at famous restaurants, had a cooking show, and now I do independent consulting."

"Wow," said Dana. "I think I've seen your cooking show once or twice. I knew you looked familiar, but I couldn't put the pieces together until that lady at the café mentioned it yesterday." She quirked an eyebrow. "I just hope the Gradys can handle the bill for your services."

He laughed. "I'm doing this job at a cut rate. I'm not charging half of what this is worth."

"Why?" Dana asked, curious.

"I like to help people, and I'm scouting the country, looking for the ideal place to open my own establishment. This is a good way to travel, get a handle on regional restaurants, and keep from digging into my savings to pay for it."

Dana blinked. He certainly exuded confidence. Yesterday she might have rankled at this statement and thought him rather conceited. In all honesty, she did her best to remain positive even now, as he spoke.

It somehow bothered her that he referred to the Gradys as an almost charity case. One half of what his services were worth, her foot! Hadn't Mr. Grady said Ethan's bill was rather sizable? If this were a discount, she'd hate to see the regular price.

Ethan gave her an odd look. "Did I say something wrong?"

Dana sighed. He seemed sincere enough. Maybe he was one of those people who couldn't help boasting every now and then. He'd probably meant no harm. Besides, in all honesty, she knew nothing of what this type of consultation would be worth. She merely worked for a restaurateur and still had a lot to learn about the business.

She smiled and assured Ethan she was all right. "So what have you enjoyed the most about your job?"

He didn't answer right away. "I don't know. Every day has so many little rewards. If I had to pick just one thing. . .I'd say. . .designing and baking my sister's wedding cake." He shrugged. "I know it sounds silly, but it actually gave me a chance to feel like I was a part of the whole thing. My dad paid for the wedding, my mom and sister planned it, so the cake was my humble contribution."

"That's so sweet," Dana said, impressed. "Now that I know a good baker, I'll have to put your name down in my wedding planning book."

Ethan blinked, a surprised look on his face. "Oh. I didn't know you were engaged."

Dana watched his gaze travel to the bare ring finger on her left hand. "Congratulations," he said, his voice sounding flat. He picked up his coffee mug and headed back to the bowl where he'd been mixing bread.

Dana, understanding his assumption, laughed, feeling a tad sheepish. "Well, thanks, but I guess I have to admit that congratulations aren't in order yet. I'm not engaged."

He looked up from the mixture he stirred. "Oh? Just waiting for him to pop the question, huh?"

Dana cleared her throat and set her mug on the countertop. "Actually, I'm not seeing anyone. I just like to keep notes for wedding ideas so when the right guy comes along. . . ," she trailed off, feeling embarrassed. Why had she told him all of this?

Dana decided to try again. "My sister-in-law is a wedding coordinator, and she always tells people that if they have more than a general idea of what they want for the big day, it will make things easier when it's time to sit down and plan."

Although he seemed to be holding back a smile, he replied, "She's right. I've seen people dissolve into tears just trying to pick a cake. If you're not careful, planning a wedding can be stressful."

"So I guess I'm on the right track," she said, ready to put the topic behind them. Talking to a complete stranger about her wedding dreams made her a little uneasy. "What about you? Are you married, engaged, anything like that?" As soon as the last sentence left her mouth, Dana cringed inside. *Anything like that? What was that supposed to mean?*

Unfortunately, Ethan hadn't missed her awkward question and decided to answer it. "No to married. No to engaged." A thoughtful look came over his face. "I don't understand the last question. 'Anything like that?' If you explain it, maybe I can come up with an answer."

Dana chuckled. "Okay, okay, it was a silly question. It just means, what about you? Are you attached?" She could feel her face burning as she asked the question.

He stopped stirring and let the spoon rest on the side of the bowl. "Does someone want to know?"

Dana tried not to lose her composure. "No one I know," she informed him in a matter-of-fact tone.

He nodded and resumed stirring. "Tell 'No One' that I'm as single as can be."

Dana couldn't think of a word to say. This was not good. Now he probably thought she had a more than friendly interest in him. Not good at all. She changed the subject. "I guess I should tell you all about me now," she suggested.

Ethan shook his head. "Nope. We've got work to do."

Relieved, Dana reached for her notebook. Work she could do. It was constructive and would keep her from thinking about Ethan's expressive brown eyes. She returned to her seat and stared at her paper.

"Why don't you tell me all about you this evening? Over dinner?"

Dana looked up at him, and their eyes met. He waited for a response, but she couldn't decide. "Dinner?" she repeated.

"Yes. Remember, I'm also visiting restaurants when I'm not working. That's my own project, research for my eventual restaurant. I hoped you could suggest a good place."

"Oh," Dana said. He wasn't asking her out on a date. Her emotions were a mixture of relief and disappointment. He just wanted her to pick the restaurant. "I guess that would be okay," she said slowly.

"Good. And don't pick that café we went to again," he said, not looking up from the spices he measured.

Dana simply nodded. This was doable. It was nothing out of the ordinary. She would go on a business outing with a chef tonight. Not a date. This was business related. And that was acceptable. Right?

Sure, it's fine, she reassured herself. *So why do I feel butterflies in my stomach? Only because he's a single, handsome, slightly egotistical chef who I have to work with for the next few months, that's why,* she scolded herself.

"Anise," said Ethan. "Write that down, Dana."

Dana wrote the word "anise" three times, thinking about how special her name sounded when Ethan said it.

Chapter 6

"It's your turn now," Ethan said after he and Dana ordered their meals. She gave him a puzzled look.

"My turn for what?"

"To tell me about yourself," he reminded her. He took a drink of water and waited.

Dana smiled. "Right, it's my turn. Unfortunately, there's not all that much to tell."

"I'd still like to hear it."

"Okay," she said. "I'm the youngest of eight kids. Otis, Latrice, Jackson, Max, Albert, Anthony, Sheryl, then me." She laughed. "Believe me, we never had a dull moment at our house."

"Seven brothers and sisters?" This surprised him. Dana seemed so serious and almost old for her age, unlike other people he'd met who were the youngest in their families. He couldn't imagine having that many siblings, especially ones older than himself. "Wow, how did it feel to be the youngest?"

Dana grinned and, without hesitation, replied, "Like I had nine parents instead of two."

Ethan laughed. "Sounds like your brothers and sisters took their jobs seriously."

Dana shook her head. "I don't think they were always that enthralled with the job. I was the little one, so after the initial newness wore off, they realized they were stuck with me."

"So they tried to dodge you?"

Dana shrugged. "Sometimes. It just depended on what kind of mood they were in. I'll admit I got my share of babying—especially from my brother Max. Even when the rest of them got sick of me, he generally took up for me. He's still the most tenderhearted of the bunch."

"Really? What's the age difference between you two?"

"Eight years. When he went to Kansas City for college, it broke my heart. I was only ten, so I thought he might be mad at me and left me behind on purpose."

The waitress arrived with their food and interrupted the conversation for a moment. After they began eating, Ethan picked up where they had left off. "Are you and your brother still close?"

Dana tilted her head to the side. "Not as much, I guess. He got married last year. He and Stacy will celebrate their first anniversary in a few weeks."

Ethan nodded. "Any nieces, nephews?"

Dana nodded. "Lots. I'd bore you if I started telling all of my 'Aunt Dana' stories. The oldest, Otis Jr., will be going away to college in the fall, and the youngest won't be here until June."

"Boy or girl?"

Dana shrugged. "Max and Stacy don't want to know, so it'll be a surprise. They told us at Christmas, and they're so excited."

"Sounds like you're a busy aunt."

Dana laughed. "Yes, only three of us are still single—me and the twins, Albert and Anthony. That means we are the ones the rest of them can count on for free babysitting. And my house is the destination of choice for impromptu sleepovers." She grinned, her eyes sparkling. "Word has gotten around with my nieces that I have a pretty nice makeup collection, and I don't mind letting little fingers play with my lipstick. It's also known that I like to spend some time at the Galleria on the weekends."

"The Galleria. . . So you're a fan of shopping malls, huh?"

"You bet," said Dana.

"I guess there's no contest between spending the night at your house or with your two brothers?"

She shook her head. "Only for the girls. Albert and Anthony have a major collection of video games, and they will invent something to do before they step foot in a mall, so the boys gravitate toward their house."

"Hey, I like video games myself," Ethan said. "Where do they live?"

Dana sighed impatiently. "Oh, please, not you too. My dad teases that the only reason they're still single is because they would have too much difficulty dividing up all of their games if one of them got married."

Ethan laughed outright. "I have to confess, whenever I travel, I usually pack my system and a few games in my suitcase. It helps me to relax, gives me something to do besides think about work."

Dana shook her head and laughed. "They have the opposite effect on me. I concentrate too much on trying to work all of the buttons, and I never have fun since the other person always wins."

Ethan nodded. "My sister does that. I'll have to teach you how to play and enjoy yourself at the same time. Besides, it's not about winning. It's just for fun."

Dana gave him a wry smile. "Tell that to Albert and Anthony."

After they finished, the waitress reappeared, wondering if they'd like to order dessert. Dana decided to pass, but Ethan wanted to taste their flourless chocolate cake, so she decided she would have coffee while he had dessert. Ethan ordered and asked for two forks.

"Sure you don't want a bite before I start eating this?" Ethan asked before he tasted it.

Dana shrugged. "Okay, maybe a bite." She reached for the extra fork and took a tiny piece. "It's delicious," she admitted.

"Sure you don't want to share it?"

"I'm sure. But thanks for offering."

Later, as they walked to his car, the January wind whipped around them, blowing Dana's scarf to the ground. Ethan bent down to retrieve it.

His fingers brushed hers as he handed the scarf to her. Dana's hands were little and cold to the touch. "Shouldn't you be wearing gloves in this weather?"

Dana blinked. "I must have left them at home."

Ethan reached into his pocket and handed her his own gloves. "Then wear mine. It'll take the car a little while to warm up."

"Thank you," Dana said quietly. The smile she gave him made up for the fact that his own hands were freezing.

"I feel bad taking these from you," she said, lifting up her hands, now engulfed in his gloves. They were so baggy on her tiny hands that Ethan wondered if they would do any good.

"Are you sure you don't need them? You're the one who has to touch the steering wheel, and I know how much I hate driving without gloves."

"I'll be fine. But if you insist on helping me, I do need to ask a favor." He opened the passenger's side door for Dana. After she got inside, he hurried over to his own side and got in.

The steering wheel felt brutally cold, as Dana had predicted, but Ethan tried not to show it. He gripped the wheel as if it might even be warm. As he maneuvered the car out of the parking lot, Dana reminded him of his earlier question.

"So, what's the favor?"

He hesitated. He'd been trying to work up the nerve to ask this for the past few days at work but hadn't decided if his request might be too intrusive. Maybe he had spoken too soon and should wait until later. The last thing he wanted to do was ruin the friendship he and Dana seemed to have forged over the past day.

He shook his head. "Never mind."

Out of the corner of his eye, he saw Dana purse her lips together and tilt her head to the side. He tried to change the subject.

"What about sports?" he asked. "I hear a lot about the Blues. Maybe we should take in a game sometime. You know, so I can get the full St. Louis experience."

Dana laughed. "Sure. I'm not a big hockey fan, but we can go to see the Blues. And if you're still here when baseball season rolls around, we can go see a Cardinals game."

"Anything else I'm missing that I need to experience as a temporary St. Louisan?" he asked, smiling.

"Lots," Dana told him. "Since you're into tasting the area cuisine, you'll have to visit Ted Drewes's; but you'll have to wait a little while because they're only open February through December, so in a couple of weeks, I'll take you there. You should see all of the people lined up outside in the summertime, waiting to order frozen custard."

Ethan grinned. "I'll make it a point not to leave until I've had some."

"But you didn't trick me, Mr. Ethan D. Miles," she teased. "You're changing the subject. Now about that favor. . ."

Ethan sighed. He hadn't gotten off the hook with that one. He should have kept his mouth shut. "All right, if you must know," he began.

Dana nodded, waiting for him to continue.

"I hate to ask you this because I don't want you to feel like I'm pushing my way into your weekend, but I know you're a Christian, and I need a place to go to church while I'm here. I already missed going this past Sunday, and I thought I'd see if you would allow me to attend your church."

Dana was quiet for a moment, then burst into laughter.

"What's so funny?"

When Dana finally stopped, she answered, "As if I could keep someone out of a church. Churches don't belong to people, Ethan, they belong to God."

"I know that," he said. "Still, I wondered if you would dread working with me all week, then have to see me on Sundays. Saturday would be the only day you could escape me."

"Me?" Dana asked in an overly innocent voice. "Why would I want to escape you?"

This time it was Ethan's turn to laugh. "You're kidding me, right? Let me refresh your memory. Remember last Friday night when we met at dinner? And Monday morning when you treated me like I had the plague in front of everyone at the office? How about the lunch date when you tried to take me somewhere I'd hate on purpose? For what reason? I don't know, since you refused to tell—"

"Okay, okay." She laughed. "I get the picture, and I apologize again. But, no, I won't be upset if you come to my church. I go to the same church as the Gradys anyway. . . ," she trailed off, midsentence. "Wait a minute. Didn't you think of asking them where they went to church?"

Ethan shrugged. He realized that not much escaped Dana's notice. "I guess I could have asked them," he began. "But maybe I decided I'd rather attend the place where my charming assistant goes."

A long moment of silence settled over them before Dana finally answered, her voice flat. "Oh, I see. The charming assistant. I hope you're not expecting me to take notes about ingredients during the sermon."

Ethan glanced over at her. She stopped smiling, turned away from him, and stared out of the window. They were now rounding the corner to her block, and Ethan struggled to find the right words to say. Knowing Dana, she would hop out of the car, leaving him feeling awkward and in the dark about what he'd said to upset her.

Not knowing how to proceed with the conversation, Ethan opened his mouth and started talking. "About church on Sunday," he said. Dana didn't respond, but he continued, grasping at straws. "Since I really don't know my way around that well—I mean, I know how to get to my apartment, work, the grocery store, and now your house. But would you mind if I. . ." He paused, slowing to a stop in front of her house.

Sighing deeply, Dana nodded. "That's fine. You can meet me here and follow me."

Ethan had a feeling he might be treading on thin ice, but he spoke up anyway. "I was hoping we could ride together. I'd be willing to drive."

"Well, I'd prefer to drive myself—"

"Then I'll ride with you," he finished. "But I'll chip in money for gas."

Dana sighed again. "Fine." She opened the door a crack, then turned to face him. "Thank you for dinner." The stoic look in her eyes melted away for a moment. "I. . .I had a good time."

"So did I. Thanks for coming."

"Thank you for asking me." She gave him the tiniest of smiles and hurried out of the car.

Ethan watched her make her way to her front door and waited until he determined that she got safely inside before pulling away from the curb.

As he thought back over the events of their evening, he smiled. He'd had a good time, even if it hadn't been an official date. Dana could call it whatever she wanted, but it was as good as a date, in his opinion. And now, he'd managed to arrange to ride to church with her Sunday. He might even be able to take her to dinner afterwards.

❧

Dana closed the front door with a sigh. What had happened here? If Ethan didn't feel the need to remind her that she was nothing more than the *assistant*, she might be able to have a few hours of uninterrupted fun with him. He was humorous, he was charming, he was good looking. . .he was a Christian. He was perfect. Maybe.

But why did he constantly have to assert himself as The Boss? Wasn't this evening supposed to be a nonwork event? Even he had called it a date during their conversation at dinner.

Dana trudged up the stairs to her bedroom without bothering to take off her coat. She put on her pajamas and applied a beauty mask. The label claimed the mask would do an amazing number of miracles, including cleanse her pores and help her to relax.

Shrugging, Dana turned off the overhead light and flipped on one of the floor lamps because it gave off a soft, dim glow. As she sat in her overstuffed armchair, she leaned back with her eyes closed, waiting for the mask to do its work. While she rested, she became increasingly aware of a familiar scent—the scent of Ethan's cologne, to be exact.

Somewhat startled, she sat up straighter, trying to determine if her imagination had grown a tad overactive. As she looked around the room, she saw no clue that explained the woodsy fragrance. After a few minutes, Dana decided that she had probably been thinking about Ethan a little too much. After all, hadn't she just seen on the news the results of a research project that explained how people were likely to link certain smells and foods to memories? That explained it. Thinking about Ethan made her imagine his cologne.

Dana chuckled, wondering if anyone would ever be able to invent a way to imagine something like chocolate or ice cream and be able to taste it without actually ingesting any.

Closing her eyes, she leaned back in her chair again, but this time her rumpled coat, which she had tossed over the back of the chair, made it hard for her to relax.

Dana swiftly tossed the coat clear across the room, aiming for her bed. She'd learned this trick from watching Albert and Anthony clean their rooms in a hurry. Living with so many brothers had its drawbacks, but she'd definitely picked up some interesting housecleaning tips from them. At least she didn't just throw clothes into her closet the way they did. She still utilized hangers, whereas they liked to toss shoes and other items inside and quickly shut the door.

Before she could close her eyes again, Dana noticed something on the floor. Two large black objects lay on the other side of the room, near the foot of the bed. With a shriek, she jumped up in the chair too scared to turn toward them again. Whatever they were, they hadn't been there a few minutes ago. In the dim room, they looked particularly ominous, and she wished she had left the ceiling light on instead of the floor lamp.

Forcing herself to take deep breaths, she tried to remain calm. The first thing she needed to do was determine what those *things* were, then get out of the room and call one of her brothers to come over and remove them.

Frowning, Dana wondered if this might be another one of Anthony or Albert's jokes. They lived a five-minute drive away and had a key to her house for emergencies. They knew she hated critters of any kind, even ants or ladybugs, and she kept her house exceptionally clean to discourage any little visitors from taking up residence.

Her brothers, on the other hand, had collected bugs, worms, and pets, causing her no small amount of distress during her girlhood years. Sliding a frog or hamster into her bed had been a great source of entertainment—and ultimately punishment—for those two.

She remembered once asking her mother why Albert and Anthony had to be *twins*, instead of just *one* boy. To her six-year-old reasoning, contending with only one of them would have been much easier.

Dana hopped down from her chair, swooped up the cordless phone from the table a few feet from the chair, and jumped back to her perch, still safe from her intruders.

She hit a button on her speed dial and listened to the phone ring several times. Apparently, her brothers were trying to pretend they weren't even at home!

While she stood on the chair, waiting for someone to pick up the phone, Dana had a horrifying thought. What if those things crept off while she talked on the phone, making a plea for help?

A vision of sliding her feet into an expensive pair of shoes, her toes meeting a dead—or even worse—a live critter made Dana grimace. That did it. She would stay in the room while she waited for backup. If those things wandered somewhere, she'd at least have a good idea of where they went.

Before she could give the idea more thought, Anthony answered the phone. "Hello?" he said, sounding somewhat groggy.

Dana's teased-little-sister instincts kicked in. She could imagine the two of them sitting on their couch, just waiting for her to call, and eventually answering the phone, pretending they had been asleep in order to prolong the joke.

"Oh, please," she replied, her voice dripping with sarcasm. "I know you are not *even* asleep. Get over here and get these things out. Now!"

Anthony sounded more awake. "What?"

"You heard me," Dana said, her voice alternating between quavering and yelling. "I want you two to get over here and get these things out of here. It's not funny!"

In the background, she could hear Albert asking what was going on. Anthony explained, still pretending he didn't know what she was talking about. She sighed heavily.

"What things?" Albert asked, taking the phone from Anthony.

Dana's temper flared. She could be in danger, and they were taking this too far. "You know good and well what they are. Those. . .black things! The ones you put in my bedroom. Come get them now, or I'm calling Mom and Dad!" Before they could say another word, she clicked the phone off. The twins would have to go some great lengths to make peace with her after this. She should be in bed, getting her rest. As it stood now, she would have a hard time falling asleep, wondering if they had accidentally forgotten some of their other creatures.

Remembering her resolve to watch the creatures to make sure they didn't escape, Dana slowly turned around and took a quick look. A sigh of relief escaped from her lips. They were still there, in the exact same position.

Weird. Why haven't those things moved? She twisted a bit to get a better view. They were still there. And now they didn't look like things at all. They looked like. . .

"Oh, no," Dana groaned. She got down from her chair, feeling like an absolute ninny. They weren't live critters; they were Ethan's gloves, and they must have fallen out of her coat pockets when she tossed it across the room. They also accounted for the smell of Ethan's cologne.

The screech of tires interrupted her thoughts. She heard car doors open but didn't hear them slam shut. Albert and Anthony. How in the world would she explain this to them? Next, she heard the front door creaking open, then loud footsteps rumbling up the stairs.

Seconds later, her brothers entered the room, both wearing pajamas, one holding a baseball bat and the other wielding a golf club. The intense expressions on their faces made Dana burst into laughter.

"Where is it?" Albert shouted, his voice full of worry. Dana felt instant remorse. She'd gotten them out of bed, yelled at them, and scared the daylights out of them, all for a pair of gloves. She seriously doubted they would find her explanation amusing, but she tried anyway.

After several moments, they lowered their impromptu weapons. Albert, the more easygoing of the pair, reached out for the gloves. "So you went on a date with this guy, he loaned you his gloves, they ended up on the floor, and you thought we had played some kind of trick on you."

"You *mistakenly* thought," Anthony supplied in a mock fatherly voice.

"Yes. I'm really sorry for getting you out of bed. It's been a long night, so why don't you go home, and we can all go to bed?"

Anthony grinned. "No way. This is too good. Tell us more."

"More? Why?"

Albert shrugged. "Because we want to hear more. It isn't every day our sister has a date."

Dana put her hands on her hips. "This is none of your business. So go home. Now." She made a shooing motion to emphasize her point.

Anthony shrugged. "You know, we could argue that you owe us—that maybe you even set us up, having us rush over here, with just enough time to throw on boots and grab our keys. Maybe you didn't have a date. Maybe you put that stuff on your face and tried to scare us, looking like some kind of alien."

Dana touched a finger to her cheek and stared at the greenish-brown residue on her finger. She'd forgotten all about the mask. "Ha, ha, laugh all you want. It was an honest mistake, and you know I don't play practical jokes."

"These are a man's gloves," Albert said to Anthony, as if that proved her point.

Anthony grabbed the gloves away from his brother and sniffed them. "Yeah, and they're covered in cologne. Where does this guy work? The cologne factory?" Anthony wrinkled his nose and held the gloves away in an exaggerated fashion.

Dana shrugged apologetically. "Look, you guys, I'm sorry to put you out, but I'm too tired to talk right now. Maybe tomorrow or Sunday."

"So when do we get to meet him?" Anthony asked.

"Never," Dana said in frustration.

Her brothers exchanged knowing glances.

"What?" Dana wanted to know.

"What's this guy like?" asked Albert.

"He's a nice guy," Dana said, not wanting to have them conduct a brotherly evaluation of Ethan, especially since he'd made it clear they had a working relationship and nothing more.

"Nice, huh?" said Albert.

"And it's over between you two?" added Anthony.

"Yes," she answered.

"So why'd you go out with him in the first place?" Anthony asked.

"Because. . ." was all she could say. What else could she say without embarrassing herself? *He's ideal husband material, and I like him, but he doesn't like me?*

No, she didn't want to put that on her brothers' shoulders right now. Pests that they were, they would still be a little upset with any guy who they thought wasn't treating her well.

"Because what?" Albert pressed.

Dana groaned. Why couldn't they drop this already? "Because. . .I don't know. Nothing clicked, okay?"

"But he's nice," Anthony stated. He and Albert exchanged that look again.

"Yes, yes, yes, he's nice. So go home now, okay?"

Her brothers obediently turned and headed back down the stairs. Dana followed and locked the door behind them. Through the window, she could see their car, parked at a crazy angle, the doors wide open. They would have a cold ride home. Even with all of their pestering, Dana was grateful that they lived nearby and were willing to come to her rescue. A close-knit family provided such comfort in so many ways. Still, she longed to have her own family like so many of her other siblings now had.

Dana trudged back upstairs and began the process of washing the now-crusted mask off of her face. Hopefully her brothers would just let the memory of this escapade fall by the wayside.

No, this one would probably go in the history books as far as Anthony and Albert were concerned. She only had herself to blame. If she hadn't been in such a daydreaming mood after getting home, she would have realized the mysterious things were just gloves long before making the phone call to her brothers.

After settling in under her warm comforter, Dana's last thoughts were about her dinner with Ethan. Too bad she had gotten her hopes so high about Ethan, but he wanted a business relationship with nothing more than friendship. She could deal with that. Hopefully.

Chapter 7

Dana didn't even see the ice. She *did* see her foot, enclosed in a sensible black pump, flying up in the air as the rest of her landed on the ground. Next, she saw Ethan leaning over her. "Wow! Are you okay?"

"My pride is going to sting for awhile." She took hold of Ethan's extended hand and regained her footing. *Thank goodness I wore the long wool skirt this morning.*

"Are you hurt?" Ethan asked.

Dana took a tentative step forward, relieved that she had miraculously escaped a sprain or, even worse, a broken bone.

"I'm okay," she assured him. Her cheeks burned as she felt the curious stares of her fellow church members. She would have preferred to enter the church without having her dignity undermined by a very visible spill in the parking lot. At least she could blame her fall on the ice, saving herself the embarrassment of tripping over her own feet or nothing at all.

Calm down, she told herself. Her nerves had been aflutter since the moment Ethan arrived at her door, eager and ready to attend church.

During the short drive to church, they'd chatted about work, and though Dana didn't like to think about her job on weekends, she felt relieved that the topic of conversation hadn't been more personal.

Torn between wanting their relationship to be more, yet wishing she still had her old position at work, Dana couldn't quite put her finger on how she felt about Ethan. The same went for him asking to attend church this morning. Did he really just need a good church to attend or did some part of him want to spend more time with her?

Not knowing how he felt was the hard part. The easy part was having Ethan hold her arm firmly as they entered the church. Even if they were only friends, she could still pretend they were something more. Her pretending lasted all of fifteen seconds.

"Hi, Aunt Dana." Seventeen-year-old Otis Jr. stopped directly in front of Dana and Ethan. Junior, as the rest of the family called him, gave Ethan the once over, then shifted his gaze back to Dana, plainly curious as to the stranger's identity.

Dana quickly introduced her nephew and Ethan, adding, "He came to work for the Gradys recently and wanted to visit different churches, so I invited him to come here."

Apparently satisfied with this explanation, Junior shook hands with Ethan, then disappeared into the throng of people.

"Your nephew, huh?" Ethan said.

Dana nodded. "The first grandbaby. I was the only aunt in the third grade," she added, laughing.

Ethan gestured in the direction her nephew had disappeared. *"Grandbaby?* He's an inch taller than I am," he said, laughing. "He looks like an ad for a protein drink—you know, the ones that say, 'Drink this, and you'll look like a bodybuilder in a week.'"

"He's the star of his high school football team," added Dana, "and built exactly like my brother Otis. We're not sure how that happened. My mom is shorter than I am, and my dad is a few inches taller, but both of them are as skinny as beanpoles."

"So Otis is your oldest brother?"

"Yeah," said Dana. "But he's a nice guy."

Ethan let out a mock shudder. "I'm just glad this isn't one of those moments like in the movies where I meet your entire family for the first time, and we announce we're getting married."

Dana laughed but sobered quickly. "Well, you're partially right."

Ethan shot her a quizzical look. "Partially?"

"Yes, partially. My whole family goes to this church, and they'll want to meet you; but, like you said, we're just friends, so they won't be extremely critical."

"Your whole family?" Ethan repeated.

Dana nodded.

Ethan stood still. "What do you mean by extremely critical?"

Dana shrugged. "It doesn't matter. We're just friends so relax."

Ethan wiggled his eyebrows, looking very much like a mischievous schoolboy. "Suppose I meet them today as your 'friend,' but by this time next week, we decide we're in love and want to be married. Would I have to 'meet' them all over again?"

Dana swatted his arm with the church bulletin. "To be perfectly honest, that scenario has never occurred, as far as I know. We'd be the first."

"Then I'd better get on their good sides now. You never know what the future may hold."

Dana didn't know whether he was still joking or somewhat serious. She didn't have much time to think about the idea because they had entered the sanctuary. Her sister Latrice caught sight of her and began gesturing for Dana to come over to the pews the Edwards clan occupied.

"That's my family," Dana told Ethan as they headed closer. From the way everyone's attention focused on Dana and Ethan, she guessed Junior had already reported that she had brought a "friend" with her this morning.

"The whole pew?"

"All three of those pews," she corrected.

"Wow!"

Because the service would begin shortly, Dana made a quick round of introductions. Everyone was obviously interested in knowing exactly who Ethan was, but thankfully, the organ music began, signaling that church had started. Their curiosity would have to wait until later. Because she arrived later than usual, she and Ethan had to squeeze in on the third pew, right next to Junior and his sister, Annitra.

The service lasted a little over two hours, during which Dana's assorted relatives turned and cast what they probably thought were surreptitious glances at her and Ethan. She had the feeling her mother would invite Ethan to Sunday dinner, and she didn't know if that would be a good idea.

They would undoubtedly be somewhat disappointed when they learned she and Ethan weren't dating, but if they liked him well enough, they might get the idea to "help" her and Ethan along into something more. Not only would that be embarrassing for her, but Ethan would wind up feeling totally uncomfortable.

After church ended, Dana had no choice but to finish making the round of introductions to the rest of her family and several curious friends who wanted to meet the visitor. Although Ethan seemed to be handling the attention well, she felt guilty for not having given him more warning about the interest his presence would create.

Her parents, who still hadn't formally met Ethan, were across the sanctuary chatting with a neighbor, and Dana decided she would try to get Ethan out to the car before they had the chance to invite him to dinner. She could rush home and get him back to his car, then make it to Mom and Dad's alone.

Unfortunately, she and Ethan were not of the same mind. He either didn't catch her hints that they needed to leave, or he was flat out ignoring her by talking sports with Otis and Jackson. When she finally managed to convince him that she needed to leave, they exited the sanctuary, only to run right into the Gradys.

"There you are!" Mr. Grady exclaimed. "It's good to see you this morning, Ethan."

Ethan's grin expressed his pleasure at having so easily found a church to attend. "I knew I couldn't go wrong when Dana told me that you attend here as well."

"Does that mean you'll be coming back?" asked Mrs. Grady.

"I think so," Ethan said with a smile. "Everyone I've met has made me feel so welcome. In fact, I'll probably have a hard time leaving when my work here is done."

"We'll miss you too, Ethan," said Mrs. Grady.

This topic caught Dana off guard for a moment. He was right. This church family was warm and close-knit, and Ethan fit in like a long-lost friend. The church members wouldn't be the only ones to miss him when he left. While his absence might return things to normal at work, she wondered if it would also leave an emptiness in her heart.

"We're heading out to dinner soon," said Mr. Grady. "Would you two be interested in joining us?"

"Oh, no you don't." Dana didn't have to turn around to match the good-natured voice to a face.

Dana's mother and father had apparently overheard the Gradys extend the invitation to dinner. "Phil and Nora, I'll have to ask you to take that invitation back. I've cooked plenty for the rest of the family, and I want Dana and her friend here to come and eat with us today," announced her mother. "Of course," she added, smiling, "you two are more than welcome to come too."

Phil and Nora nodded. "That sounds like a good idea to me," said Mr. Grady. "I never turn down good home cooking on a Sunday afternoon."

"Great," said her father. "We'll be glad to have you." He turned to Dana and Ethan. "Young man, I don't think we've met yet." He reached out to shake Ethan's hand.

"Mom and Dad, this is Ethan Miles. Ethan, these are my parents, Mavis and Claude Edwards. Ethan is the new chef I told you about last week. I'm helping him with the menu changes at work."

"Oh, yes," said her father, recognition spreading over his features.

Ethan shook hands with both of her parents and laughed. "Actually, Dana and I are approaching this as more of a joint project."

Dana lifted her eyebrows. She didn't ever remember hearing her job described in this light, even if he had worked hard to keep peace between them at work. Was this a bit of a show for the Gradys and her parents? To her surprise, he continued.

"And I've got a hunch that if Dana told you all about me last week, I might not have gotten a glowing review; but I've had all week to make up for past wrongs, and I think I'm doing a pretty good job." He turned and casually put his arm around Dana.

Her parents gave him a tentative smile, while the Gradys beamed. Dana felt like melting into the floor. This man had just blatantly flirted with her in front of their boss and her parents. . .in a church of all places!

Without being too obvious, Dana gently eased away from his touch. Had he lost his senses? He had all but declared they were in a dating relationship, when they really weren't. Now she knew she had to get him out of the building before he did any more damage.

"You know, I don't know if Ethan is free to come this afternoon," she said, hoping he would take the hint. "Didn't you say you were going to be going over recipes this afternoon?" she asked in a last, and probably desperate-sounding, attempt.

Ethan blinked, looking innocent and confused. "Well, yes, but that won't take me all day. Besides, are you going to dinner?"

Dana sighed. "Yes, I am, but I didn't think you would be interested."

He shook his head and cast a magnanimous smile at her. "I'd hate for you to have to drive all the way back to your place to get me to my car, then have to head back to your parents' house. I'll just come with you to make it easier." As if that weren't enough, he added, "We rode here together," for the benefit of Dana's parents and the Gradys.

Phil, Nora, Mom, and Dad all exchanged glances. Dana knew that look. It could be interpreted as the this-boy-is-serious-about-this-girl look. Under other circumstances, she wouldn't have minded the look; but since Ethan's apparent interest had seemingly "blossomed" within the last few minutes, she couldn't help being a little suspicious.

"Oh. Okay," she said, feeling defeated. Dana didn't doubt that by the time they actually arrived at her parents', the whole house would be abuzz with the account of his apparent attraction to her. She hadn't seen much of Albert and Anthony today, but she wondered if they would be able to place Ethan as the owner of the mysterious gloves from the other night.

"Well, then we'd better get going," she told Ethan.

"The same goes for me," said Mom. "Reverend Brown and his wife will be joining us too, so I've got to run home and get this show on the road. We'll see you there," she said before heading away, Dad right behind her.

The Gradys said their temporary good-byes and left, mentioning they wanted to talk to one of the Sunday school teachers about something.

Dana didn't stop to talk to anyone else but made her way to the parking lot, Ethan hurrying along behind her. As soon as they were in the car, away from curious eyes and ears, she turned to him, ready to give him a piece of her mind. "What in the world were you thinking?" she asked, not sure if his explanation would cause her to laugh or cry.

❧

Ethan couldn't quite pin down the meaning of the look on Dana's face. It wavered somewhere between laughter and tears. He felt certain he had done something to distress her and tried not to sound antagonistic. "What do you mean?"

Dana let out a sarcastic laugh. "Are you kidding me? I'm talking about that whole act you put on in front of my parents and the Gradys. What is going on?"

Ethan wasn't exactly sure himself. Maybe he *had* laid on the charm a little too thick. Maybe not. What he did know was that he liked his new job, his employers, this church, and all of the people he'd met there. Maybe most importantly, he liked Dana.

Of course, he'd not yet told her about this new detail. But then, he too had been hard-pressed to understand this growing attraction he felt. When he arrived at her house this morning, he'd been prepared to be patient—and give her time to decide how she felt about him. At least, that had been his original plan; but when he realized he would get to meet nearly her entire family, he decided he needed to meet them as a man who was interested in her—not merely a friend or coworker. First impressions were important, and he didn't want to spoil his chance with the Edwards family. He had gone wrong by not making Dana aware of how he felt, and he could understand how she would be confused. She apparently thought he had made a major mess of things.

A glance at Dana confirmed that she still waited for his explanation. Ethan took a deep breath, still wondering exactly where he should start.

"I'm sorry. I just wanted to make a good impression on your family, and I got carried away."

Dana gave him a look that spoke volumes—she wouldn't let him off the hook so easily. Would telling her his feelings right now be a good idea? They'd only met a little over a week ago, and that wasn't enough time to go around proclaiming to have fallen in love with someone.

One or both of them could end up hurt if he spoke too soon. For all he knew, she could be in love with someone else. Or he might realize two hours from now that his feelings for her weren't as strong as he'd thought them to be.

He sighed deeply. The only option would be to keep his mouth shut and see how things developed. "Look, I'm really sorry," he tried to explain. "I just messed up. Will you forgive me?"

Her features softened somewhat. "I guess so," she said after a moment. "But now my whole family will be expecting to hear that we're actually dating or something like that."

"Something like what?" Ethan tried to lighten the mood.

Dana's face relaxed a tiny bit more, and Ethan guessed she might be less upset than she had been minutes earlier.

"We don't have to disappoint them, you know. We are dating," Ethan interrupted. "Sort of," he said with a shrug.

Dana gave him a blank look.

"Remember? Dinner the other night? And lunch together nearly every day?" He searched her face carefully for any sign that she had enjoyed their time away from work together as much as he had.

Dana spoke again, her voice laced with caution. "Every time we went somewhere, you always mentioned how you were getting a lot of research done for your future restaurant, or you called it a working lunch. You never said we were dating, and you certainly didn't act like we were dating."

Ethan felt like his heart had gone tumbling down the stairwell of a ten-story building. Sure, he'd tried to give the impression that they were going out on business, but surely she realized after a few days that they weren't really discussing business during those times together.

While he contemplated how he should reply to this latest comment, Dana started the car. "Forget it," she told him. "If we don't get there soon, they'll have to wait dinner for us. Trust me, you might have made a good impression on my brothers this morning, but if you hold up dinner, they won't be amused."

Ethan wanted to finish the conversation, but it seemed Dana wanted to drop the subject, so he felt content to let the topic rest for the time being.

The street in front of Claude and Mavis's home was lined with cars on both sides. "Did I happen to come on family reunion Sunday?"

She laughed and shook her head. "No, it's like this every week. The whole family, and whatever friends and neighbors Mom and Dad invite, converge on the house every Sunday after church and stay for the afternoon."

Ethan got out of the car and hurried around to open her door. While they walked to the house, he casually reached out and took hold of her hand. As they had been the night he and Dana had gone to dinner together, her small hands were cold. He'd lend her his gloves, except she hadn't yet returned them. He wanted to tease her about still having his gloves, but he didn't want to ruin the moment.

This marked the first time he and Dana had truly held hands. They'd brushed fingers on occasion, and this morning he'd briefly held her hand as he helped her up from her fall on the ice, but he now reached out with the intention of staying connected with her. To his surprise, she didn't pull away from him.

Instead she gave him a relaxed smile. "You've done it now, you know. I can tell you that at least one person inside that house has noted the fact that we're holding hands."

"So?" Ethan asked, not willing to let go. Her hand fit his perfectly. The simple act didn't feel awkward or forced, but totally comfortable. He hoped this could be a sign of a possible change in the way she felt about him and, ultimately, about *them*.

"So they'll be talking about it. Wondering. Asking questions."

Ethan shrugged. "I don't mind, if you don't."

Dana didn't say anything, but she didn't remove her hand from his. Surely more than chance had put them together. He remembered the first day he had seen her, just over a week ago. She'd intrigued him from the start, and he'd prayed for the opportunity to meet her again. To his surprise, he had. Talk about answered prayer!

A nagging thought popped into his head. Would the Lord have answered his prayer, only to show him that he and Dana weren't meant for each other? The idea seemed unlikely and even borderline cruel, but Ethan wasn't willing to take a chance on pushing God out of the picture just because things were going well at the moment.

Lord, am I moving too fast for Your will? he prayed as they stepped inside the Edwards household. *Am I doing the right thing?*

❧

Lord, this feels right. But am I getting ahead of You? Dana prayed as she and Ethan stepped inside the house. Holding Ethan's hand felt. . .she couldn't describe the feeling with one word. "Right" was too cliché. "Comfortable" was too bland. "Nice" was too unimaginative.

Whatever this indescribable feeling eventually turned out to be, she hated to see it end, but she had to let go of his hand in order to help her mom and the other women get dinner on the table. The sound of the men and boys laughing and teasing echoed from the direction of the living room, while the clanging of pots and pans rang out from the kitchen.

Holding Ethan's hand might be nice, but if the two of them stood in the front hallway for much longer, the entire family would be making jokes at their expense. Dana gave Ethan a little squeeze to let him know she didn't want to run away from him, then let go.

"I've got to help out in the kitchen, but you can stay here and talk with the guys."

Ethan nodded, and Dana steered him in the direction of the living room. As soon as they came to the doorway, Mr. Grady and a few of the others called for him to come join them.

Once she felt Ethan was settled, Dana headed to the kitchen to lend her help. Her mother usually did most of the cooking, although many times her sisters and sisters-in-law brought a dish or two.

Her sister Sheryl took the lead in peppering her with questions about Ethan.

"Isn't that the same guy you complained would undermine your position at work?"

Mrs. Grady, in the corner buttering rolls, looked surprised to hear this. "I didn't know you felt like that, Honey."

Dana cringed inwardly. Didn't Sheryl realize she couldn't just blurt things out when her boss's wife stood nearby? Since everyone seemed to be waiting for her answer, she nodded. "Yes, he is the same guy, but things at work haven't been as bad as I thought." Silently, she added, *Of course, things could have been better, but no way am I going to let Mrs. Grady think I'm whining.*

Dana's admission that things weren't so terrible after all brought on gales of laughter from the others.

"I'll say," said Verna, Otis's wife. "He's not bad on the eyes either."

Dana had to smile. Her family members always teased and joked around with each other like this. Over the years, she had done her fair share of teasing. Her moment to be on the receiving end of the ribbing had come, so she couldn't get upset.

"Really, you guys, we've only known each other a little over a week," she explained. "So don't get carried away."

"I fell in love with Donald in a week," supplied her sister Latrice.

"Ahem. . . ," said Aunt Florence. "The first time you clapped eyes on Donald, you were in the first grade. If you're younger than eighteen, it doesn't count."

Everyone burst out laughing again, pausing long enough for Latrice to defend herself. "Speak for yourself—but mind you, I never said he fell in love with me that same week."

"Yes," said Aunt Daphne. "But what was the boy supposed to do, what with you chasing after him all those years?"

"Umm-hmm," added Florence. "By the time you graduated from college, the boy just got plumb wore out. He married you because that was the only way he could get a break."

Latrice playfully tossed a dishtowel at Florence, then hugged the woman.

While everyone laughed at the latest exchange between Latrice and Florence, Dana took advantage of her moment off the hot seat to grab a stack of plates and head to the dining room to set the table.

There were actually several tables of varying sizes and shapes packed into the oversized dining room, and Dana couldn't remember a time they had just one table in use for Sunday dinner.

Years ago a new neighbor had made a snide comment about the "disheveled décor" in the room.

Mom, not missing a beat, had answered that she collected tables and chairs like some people collected dolls or coins. She then asserted that her collection might be more useful because it helped make room for friends and family.

"Whenever I get a new table, I never seem to have any trouble finding people to come over and sit down to dinner," she had told the woman, effectively putting an end to the topic.

Now that woman attended on Sundays at least once a month, and she never complained of not having a good time, despite the so-called disheveled décor.

The huge Victorian style house had been built nearly ninety years ago, and large rooms were one of the greatest advantages of the place. Her mother always seemed to find new spots to put things, and while the furnishings needed some updating, the interior was a comfortable jumble of the things her parents loved and refused to part with. And while Mom and Dad sometimes grew weary with the constant upkeep on the house, they liked the charm of the place and refused to move away.

Of course, her parents were more apt to keep the house as long as Latrice and her family lived just next door. Having someone reliable nearby gave Dana and her siblings tremendous comfort.

Albert and Anthony were the last to leave the nest. Still, Dana and her siblings visited their parents quite frequently. Daughters, daughters-in-law, and granddaughters helped Mom with the interior, while sons, sons-in-law, and grandsons helped Dad with the exterior.

Someday Dana hoped for the opportunity to bring her own little ones to visit Grandma and Grandpa. A wave of wistfulness washed over her. While her sisters had married and begun families with ease, the mysterious path leading toward her own husband still remained stubbornly hidden.

Her thoughts were interrupted when her sisters entered the room, bringing food to place on the tables. In a matter of minutes, everything was in place for dinner to begin.

After everyone assembled in the dining room, Dad prayed over the meal, and the assortment of guests sat down to dinner.

Dana and Ethan sat at a small, square table with the Gradys, and to her dismay, most of the conversation revolved around work. All traces of the sentimental man who gently held her hand just an hour ago disappeared during the discussion. He had been replaced with Ethan-the-Chef.

When the Gradys expressed concern over whether or not customers would eat bagels flavored with beets and saffron, Ethan-the-Chef actually had the nerve to tell them he really needed complete control of the project to make it a success. "I know what people like," he assured them. "I've done this dozens of times, and I really do think I have the recipe for success." Smiling, he added, "No pun intended."

His voice carried a tone of absolute confidence that irked Dana more and more as the meal progressed. What made him so certain he could waltz into town and, in a little over seven days, decide what the customers would and wouldn't like?

Dana felt that as the district manager, she had a better idea of what the customers would like. And while they might not be storming the store to pick up loaves of oatmeal wheat bread, her intuition told her that saffron-beet bagels would probably send them *running* to The Loaf.

Ethan's problem came from the fact that he had yet to go out and talk to a customer. Dana spent her fair share of time at the main office behind a desk, but she'd put in a good many hours behind the counter as well. She thrived with the hands-on approach. Ethan liked to create from feeling and ideas.

When he mentioned he had an idea to put basil and mint in the house cornbread recipe, Dana decided he had gone far enough.

This had gotten downright ridiculous. There needed to be a balance between his creativity and her sensibility, or one of them would get frustrated. . . and that someone would likely be her, since Ethan considered himself the authority on projects like this.

"I have an idea," Dana said before she could lose her nerve. The three of them turned to face Dana, who had been largely silent during the conversation.

"Yes, Dear?" said Mrs. Grady.

Dana suddenly felt self-conscious. How could she say this without attacking Ethan's creativity or sounding like she needed to defend her ego? "Well. . .I just wondered if we might be moving along too quickly. Or maybe even taking drastic steps we don't need to take."

"How so?" asked Mr. Grady.

"For instance, this mint and basil cornbread. Do you really think people are going to love it?"

Mr. Grady shrugged. "I like plain food myself, so it doesn't appeal to me. But Ethan's right about folks nowadays wanting to eat fancier dishes. I think we'd lose more ground to the competition if we didn't compete."

"But The Loaf has plain cornbread with a fancy name," Dana countered. "Maybe people just like the name. What if they hate our mint basil cornbread? What if they stop coming because we added too many distracting ingredients to everything on the menu?"

Ethan cleared his throat. "Dana, I've really tried to be patient, but just because you want things to stay the same doesn't mean the Gradys do. They've hired me to help change things, so if I left things as they are, I'd be letting them down and taking their money for no reason."

Dana bit her lip. He had a point, but then, so did she. She looked to Mr. Grady for help. He himself had admitted that Ethan's recipes sounded a little far out for his taste.

Mr. Grady looked torn for a moment. Finally, he spoke. "I wish I had something to offer, but I don't. I've lost touch with what people want, and that's why I hired Ethan." Almost regretfully, he turned to Dana. "I've got too much money tied up in this to just give up and leave things the same."

Dana felt like the wind had been knocked out of her. Mr. Grady had sided with Ethan and basically told her to mind her own business.

"I think I have a suggestion," said Ethan. "Maybe we should set some boundaries. I know I said I needed an assistant in developing and testing the recipes, but maybe things would go smoother if I could work with someone else. That way Dana could get back to her old job."

Mr. Grady nodded cautiously. "Sure, I think we could do that. But when it's time to get the food to the stores, you'll still need to let Dana know how you're progressing, since she's in charge of the other managers. She'll need to have a fair lead time to work with the advertising department to get the word out. Then she'll need to know how you want to phase things in so the employees in the stores will be ready."

"That works for me," said Ethan. Looking at Dana, he asked, "How about you?"

Despite the fact that she still didn't like Ethan's approach, Dana felt satisfied with this arrangement. She was back in charge again, and Ethan would have to find another assistant. "Works for me," Dana said cheerily.

Before they could discuss things further, they were interrupted when Otis Junior came to the table, balancing four small plates with pieces of Mom's famous, gooey butter cake.

"This is delicious," said Ethan, taking a bite. Laughing, he added, "Is this a St. Louis specialty?"

Mrs. Grady laughed. "You could say that. It's pretty popular here, but everyone has her own twist on how to make it."

Dana bit into her cake, but the pieces felt like sand in her mouth. She knew she should feel victorious at having the opportunity to go back to her old routine. No more early mornings watching Ethan measure flour and chop herbs. No more writing down different ingredients when he got an idea. No more being called the assistant.

But that also meant no more workdays spent at Ethan's side. Had this decision been a win or a loss?

Chapter 8

Two weeks later, Dana arrived at work a little earlier than usual. The kitchen remodel at the main office had finally been completed, and that meant Ethan would be able to move his testing facility away from the other kitchens where people actually worked.

On her way to her own office, she took a detour by way of the kitchen to see if Ethan had arrived. Truth be told, she was excited to see him. Ever since their decision to work separately, she had not seen much of him. Apparently, he'd been spending every spare moment testing recipes and had actually started working from the kitchen at his condo because there he wouldn't get in anyone's way. The only exception to this was church on Sundays. But he now drove his own car instead of them riding together as they had done that first Sunday. And while he came to dinner at her parents' after services, he tended to spend a lot of time talking with her father and brothers, especially Albert and Anthony.

This abrupt interruption of their time together had also pushed aside any inkling of what had seemed to be a budding relationship between them, and Dana wondered if she had imagined that he had ever held her hand. Their conversation in the car about whether or not they were really dating didn't even matter anymore. How could dating be an issue between two people who rarely even saw each other?

≈

Dana didn't know where their relationship stood, but she wanted to find out. Waiting in the hallway outside of the test kitchen, she could see Ethan through the large plate glass windows. He kneaded dough, while his assistant dutifully chopped some greenish herb.

Not wanting to interrupt, Dana tapped on the window to get his attention. He looked up, not missing a beat in the constant motion of kneading. With a smile and quick nod of his head, he motioned for her to come inside.

Dana opened the door and walked in. Something smelled a little. . .odd, but she decided not to mention it. There would be no sense in starting an unnecessary argument with him.

"I wasn't sure you were here, but I guess I should have known you'd already be hard at work by now," she said cheerily.

His laugh reminded Dana of how much she had missed seeing him every day. She took another step toward the table where he worked. She wanted to talk to him but didn't want to yell across the room so his assistant would hear every word.

He must have understood her reticence. "Andrea, why don't you go ahead and take that coffee break?"

The young woman smiled gratefully, and Dana returned the smile, remembering the few days she'd worked with Ethan in the kitchen. The man had boundless energy. He liked to start work before the sun came up and continued working well into the night hours. Ethan was the only person Dana knew who would fit the description of both an early bird and a night owl.

"Haven't seen you in awhile," said Ethan. He shaped the dough he'd been working into a round ball and put it aside.

"I know. We've been working too hard, I guess."

He moved toward a cooling rack where several loaves of bread rested. "I want you to taste something."

Dana nodded and waited while he cut a slice of still-warm bread. She chewed and swallowed. The bread didn't taste bad, but whatever he put in it made it hot—as in spicy. Dana had tasted chili that didn't burn this much.

Ethan waited for her opinion with an expectant look on his face. "What do you think?"

Dana grimaced, fanning her mouth. "It's spicy."

Ethan grinned. "I know. Cayenne, mustard, and anise. Do you like it?"

She shrugged. "I'm sure someone will. I'm sorry I can't be more helpful, but I just don't care for spicy food."

"Oh." He put the bread away, while Dana fixed herself a glass of water.

"I just wanted to see how things were going with the new recipes," Dana told him. "Mr. Grady mentioned that you were ready to get some into the stores."

"Yes, that's right," said Ethan. "Why don't we discuss this at lunch?"

"That's fine with me. I'll be free after twelve-thirty or so."

"Then I'll come up to your office and get you when I'm ready."

"Okay, I'll see you then." As Dana left the kitchen, she couldn't keep the smile off her face. Now that she and Ethan had spent some time away from each other, it seemed that their friendship had gotten back on track.

Ethan knocked on the door to Dana's office.

"Come on in," she called.

He entered to find her at her desk on the phone. She motioned for him to sit down. While she talked, Ethan waited patiently for her to finish her conversation. Apparently, she was speaking to someone in the advertising department about how to introduce the new menu items.

Ethan realized he did feel a bit impatient for their lunch meeting to begin. While he supposed it had been a good idea for them to work at their own separate jobs, he hadn't realized just how much he would miss Dana. Seeing her on Sundays had come to be the highlight of his week, and now that they were beginning the next phase of the project, they would be able to spend more time together. Of course, the closer they moved to the completion of the job, the closer he came to leaving for another assignment.

Dana finally hung up the phone, and minutes later they were on their way to a nearby café.

During their discussion, Ethan told Dana about the recipes he wanted to introduce first. He sensed she still had issues about the flavors being too unusual, and it disturbed him. He was in charge of the creation process, and her job was to get his food into the stores. Knowing that she didn't totally agree with his ideas still bothered him.

He'd poured his heart into his recipes. If Dana didn't accept his work, it would feel like she rejected a part of him.

Ethan blew out a sigh. There was obviously something about him she didn't like or trust. He'd sensed it from their first meeting with the Gradys. Although she hadn't said exactly what upset her, until the issue got out in the open, there would be no way their friendship could grow stronger. He decided to ask her exactly what was going on before it grew too late.

"Dana, I'm getting the feeling that you don't like something about me or my work," he said. Dana looked at him with surprise, but she didn't object, confirming his feelings. "Now I know we're working toward the same goal here, but this sidestepping the issue has to stop. What is going on?"

She didn't answer right away. After a long pause, she nodded. "Okay, but not here. There's a lot to this, and I don't have time to go into all of the details right now."

Ethan shook his head. "I don't think it will be good for the company if we wait much longer. I almost get the feeling sometimes that we're working against each other instead of with each other."

"I do too," she answered. "But really, I think it would be better if we waited until after work. I've got a million things on my to-do list for today. So could we talk about this tonight?"

"I can't tonight. I'm going to the Gradys' for dinner, but I'm free tomorrow night. How about then?"

"I can't. I'm babysitting for Jackson and Marva."

"Wednesday?"

Dana shrugged. "That might work. But I'm supposed to help with the youth group at church. They're rehearsing for the Easter play, and I'm the assistant director. Afterward, I'm going to Mom and Dad's for a late dinner, so you're welcome to come along. Maybe we can talk on the way there."

Ethan's spirits lifted when Dana extended the invitation. She seemed relieved that he wanted to get this conversation out of the way. Maybe then they could move forward with their friendship. "Wednesday it is. Maybe we could go out for a bite to eat after work. I'll be starving if I have to wait that long for dinner."

Dana laughed. "To tell you the truth, I'm usually pretty hungry by then too. How about you get to my house at five, then we can get food and be at the church by six-thirty?"

"Perfect."

Just then, the waitress came with the check, and Dana insisted on paying. "I have cash with me today."

After paying the bill, they headed outdoors to Ethan's car. While they rode, Ethan debated asking Dana out on an "official" date. His new next-door neighbor was an actress and had given him a free pair of tickets to her newest play, set to premiere Friday at a local theater. At first he'd refused the tickets, since he wasn't especially interested in theater; but when she'd persisted, he'd accepted, thinking he might be able to persuade Dana to go with him.

Now his plan had hit a snag, since he'd wanted to get their work discussion out of the way before pursuing any type of romantic relationship with her. The play opened two days after their conversation would take place. If he asked Wednesday night, he'd be risking the chance that she'd already have plans. He wondered if Dana was one of those women who flat out refused a date if the guy didn't give at least a week's notice. If he asked now, and the conversation on Wednesday didn't go well, then he'd have the unpleasant task of backing out on the date, something he felt would be tacky.

As Ethan mulled over the options, Dana spoke up, interrupting his strategy planning session. "Ethan? I need to ask you something."

"Sure."

"I may be doing this all wrong, but I'm a little confused. Sometimes I get the feeling we're heading toward a more than friendship-type of relationship, and sometimes it feels like we barely know each other. I guess I want to know if you're feeling the same way."

He exhaled softly. "I do, but if we get into that, we'll have to open that can of worms you wanted to put off until Wednesday night."

They had reached the parking lot of the Gradys' main office, and Ethan pulled into an empty space. "I'll tell you what I feel, and you can decide if we should finish this conversation later as well."

Dana frowned slightly, small wrinkles forming above her brows. "Okay, I think I know where you're heading with this, and I think we shouldn't put it off. How much time do you have right now?"

He shrugged. "I'm flexible, but I thought you had a desk overflowing with stuff to do."

"It can wait a little while," she said. "So let's talk."

"Okay. To make a long story short, I'm interested in a romantic relationship with you. I felt attracted to you when we met in line at The Loaf. I got the feeling that you felt the same way. I hoped we'd run into each other again, and I prayed about it. I was so glad to see you that night at dinner, but you treated me like. . ." Ethan trailed off, unable to put his thoughts into words. "I just got the impression that you were upset with me."

Dana didn't answer right away, but when she spoke, her words poured out. "You're right; I did get upset. I'll be honest with you. Ever since I was a little girl, my family has gone to Grady Bakeries. I worked there as a clerk in high school. I worked as an assistant manger during my last two years of college. After I graduated, they promoted me to be the manager of one of the stores. Then, last year, I got this promotion.

"First of all, I worried that your being here and my having to be your assistant made it seem like my opinion didn't matter. I felt like I'd been demoted.

"I've worked hard for this job, and the thought of the company going out of business scares me." She shook her head, then continued. "Really, I'm not trying to work against you. But I feel like we have to be careful in how we go about changing the Grady Bakery image. I like your creativity, and I like most of your recipes—but that's beside the point."

Dana grinned and placed her hand on top of his. "Face it, Ethan, you're probably the only person who's going to like all of your recipes. You shouldn't take that as a personal offense."

Ethan chuckled. "Am I that transparent?"

Dana quirked an eyebrow and grinned. "Actually, I just guessed. This is my whole point: I know you probably think I'm fighting tooth and nail to discourage you, but I'm the last person who wants the bakeries to close. I love my job.

"We're not some fancy gourmet place, and we've never pretended we were— at least, not until now. We're just an organic bakery that has been around for years and years. We've done well selling simple, wholesome, tasty foods, and it's worked for us. Sure, the customers haven't been as faithful as they have been in the past, but that's no reason to alienate the ones who still like the menu exactly the way it is. I'm convinced that our problem doesn't have one all-encompassing explanation.

"Lack of variety plays a part, but things change. Customers move away. Maybe people have forgotten about Grady Bakeries. Or maybe new folks in town don't even know about us. I don't think we've explored these avenues enough." She shrugged, then grew silent.

Ethan had to admit that Dana had a point, but this was not his territory. He'd assumed these points had been covered long before he'd come on the scene. What did she expect him to do about it? He couldn't very well tell the Gradys to fire him, try other options, then contact him later if they didn't work.

He shook his head and looked into Dana's eyes. She was obviously upset; near the verge of tears. "Okay, I see your point—but what am I supposed to do about it? I'm here to do a job, and I can't not do what they've asked me to."

Dana wiped a tear away from her cheek with the back of her hand, leaving a trail of mascara on the side of her face. Then, a steady stream of tears began to fall.

Ethan didn't know what to do. He hadn't expected her to break down like this. "Don't cry," he said, fumbling around in his jacket pocket for a tissue. After locating a clean handkerchief, he gave it to Dana.

She accepted it and proceeded to bury her face in the cloth as she continued to weep. After a few moments, she looked up from the handkerchief. "What if your 'recipe for success' fails? Then what happens? The Gradys will have to close the bakery, and I'll lose my job—and so will everyone else," she said between sobs. "But that won't matter to you. You'll be off at your next job, trying out your recipes until you decide to open your own restaurant."

Ethan felt helpless and somewhat defensive. She had all but accused him of doing only what he wanted instead of coming up with something that would work for the Gradys.

Still, no matter how much he wanted to brush off Dana's concerns, he couldn't totally ignore her point. Although she had never done his job, he supposed maybe he sometimes did put his ideas ahead of the agenda for this job.

There remained the possibility that he had been right, and Dana was wrong. Then again, maybe she'd been right and he stood in the wrong. Judging from past experience, Ethan guessed that neither one of them was 100 percent correct, and the solution most likely lay somewhere in the middle. The only way to find out would be to get the new breads into the stores and see how the customers reacted.

Ethan started to say so but bit back the words, realizing Dana would probably take his observation as a challenge.

There needed to be a way to let the customers decide—but how? His job required him to get the food into the restaurants, then his work would be done. He hadn't planned to stick around to see how things went after the fact.

As he mulled this over, a glimmer of an idea took root in his mind and started to grow. Turning to Dana, he put his plan into words. "What if we introduced the new foods but didn't set anything in stone?"

"What?"

"What I mean is, we can do surveys, have the customers fill out opinion sheets, things like that. If one recipe seems to be a total failure, we ditch it or tweak it. If they get totally disgusted that one of the old breads is missing, then we bring it back."

A hopeful look crossed Dana's face for a millisecond, then disappeared. "But that will take time and more money because we'll need more employees to do the surveys. I doubt Mr. Grady will go for that."

Ethan considered her words for a moment. Dana was right; the Gradys didn't have the money or time this would take. Unless. . .

"What if you and I do the work? I could stick around for an extra month or so and not charge any additional fees. If you can rearrange your schedule, you and I can rotate between the three stores, conduct surveys, and find out exactly what people think of the new menu."

"And then what?" Dana had stopped crying and folded the handkerchief.

Ethan looked her in the eye. "We do what it takes to get business thriving again. I promise I won't leave until I get it right. I'll do everything I can to keep the Grady Bakeries alive." As he spoke the words, a weight like a rock settled in Ethan's stomach. Was this plan too ambitious? What if this company was really on its last leg? Then what would he do?

"Really?" The light returned to Dana's eyes. "You promise?"

Ethan swallowed. He might be in way over his head, but right now, reassuring Dana mattered the most. "I promise," said Ethan.

Dana smiled. "Then I have work to do. I should probably get back to the office." She sounded almost apologetic.

Ethan cleared his throat. "So should I."

Once inside the building, before they went their separate ways, Dana held up his handkerchief. "I don't suppose you want this back right now?"

"No, I don't think so. Since we're still on for Wednesday, you can give it back to me then."

"Sure." Dana hesitated. "But I thought we just had the big discussion."

Ethan shrugged. "So, who says we can't hang out? I mean, is there any reason that you don't want us to get to know each other better?"

Dana looked him in the eye yet didn't speak right away. "I don't exactly hate the idea. Still, I don't think we should get too serious since you're not planning to stick around after everything is in place here."

"Okay," Ethan said, trying to look cheerful. He guessed she had taken the logical point of view, but he didn't feel too happy about it. "So. . .you're saying that we can only be friends?"

Dana looked at her shoes, then somewhere behind him, just above his head. "I guess so. I mean, both of us are happy with our jobs, and we're pretty settled into our routines." She shrugged. "I guess I'm saying that if we did get serious, we'd have a lot of reorganizing to do. You like New York, and I like St. Louis, so who would have to pack up and move?"

Ethan didn't think her reasoning made much of a difference. After all, wasn't love supposed to conquer all? He couldn't imagine distance being able to suppress true love. He didn't argue. Instead, he gave her a half-hearted nod.

"Okay. If that's how you want to approach things, we'll be friends. But if we start feeling differently, I don't think we should let distance be a factor. There's always the chance that God created us just for each other."

Dana lifted an eyebrow. "So what's your point?"

"My point? God doesn't make mistakes. If He planned something, we're the only ones who can mess up His plan by not doing what He wants us to. So, if He wants us to be together, do you think He's looking down here saying, 'Oops, they live in different cities. Better scratch that one.' "

Dana gave him an incredulous look for a long moment. Then she broke into laughter. Shaking her head, she said, "Okay, you're right. So we'll just spend time together and keep praying to see what the Lord's will is for us. If that means more than friendship, then I won't argue with Him."

"Good. Neither will I," said Ethan.

Dana pointed toward the stairway. "I need to get back to work, so I'll see you. . ."

"Later," Ethan finished.

"Later," said Dana. As she headed for the staircase, she looked over her shoulder. "And I love your idea about the surveys." The smile on her face reminded him of liquid sunshine. "Thanks for sharing it with me. I promise to do my best to make sure it goes well." She gave a little wave and walked upstairs.

Ethan stood watching until she disappeared at the top. "Lord," he said quietly, "I really like her. If I can't help this bakery stay in business, I think she's going to be really upset with me, so I'd appreciate all the help You can give us."

Dana tossed and turned for a long time that night, unable to sleep. Instead, she kept replaying her conversation with Ethan in her mind.

Had her imagination worked overtime, or had they really discussed everything from work to a possible relationship?

Ethan's words about "God creating us for each other" weighed heavily on her mind. Was there such a thing as a perfect mate for anyone?

Dana had no clear answer. Of course, ever since she was in high school and old enough to understand the importance of choosing a good mate, she'd prayed regularly about her future husband.

Some of her friends prayed for God to send them "The One," and Dana had always written them off as people who were too obsessed with fairy tales.

There had been a time when she had looked forward to a fairy tale romance, but the way things had been going lately, she wondered if she would end up perpetually single. That is, before Ethan came along.

She dated off and on, but never seriously. The men she'd gone out with were nice, but not her ideal.

What *was* her ideal? Without a doubt, he was part fairy tale, part romance novel hero. Her freshman year of college, Dana and several of her friends had written down their description of the perfect husband. Dana's hero would be dashingly handsome, gentle, and sensitive, but confident and strong. He would like animals and children and abhor all evil. If the need arose, he would be willing to drop everything just to be there for her.

Of course, *he* had never appeared. And Dana's friends who were now married had eventually marked more than a few qualifications off their own lists.

Naively, Dana had once shown her list to Latrice, and within twenty-four hours all of her siblings had heard about it. They had teased her mercilessly, especially the twins. Her mother finally came to her rescue, gently reminding them that they shouldn't make fun of Dana for having high standards but admonishing Dana that God knew what was best for a person, and He would give her the mate He knew she needed.

After three years of carrying that wish list around, Dana finally put it away, even though she could still remember every word of it. After graduating from college, Dana decided that since Mr. Right hadn't come around, she would concentrate on work until he put in an appearance.

She began her career as one treading water; her job served as merely something to do until Mr. Right showed up. In the meantime, she chalked his absence up to reality.

Obviously, life didn't work as smoothly as a fairy tale, so she had to think more practically. And her list of ideals probably needed to be adjusted, not abandoned. After all, it was entirely possible that Prince Charming's horse simply had a broken leg.

After a year or so, she'd given up treading water in favor of a tentative dogpaddle. Mr. Wonderful hadn't yet appeared, and the first promotion had all but fallen in her lap. Another advancement propelled the dogpaddle into a more vigorous motion. Thoughts of Mr. Wonderful had taken a back seat, and Dana perfected a full out breaststroke, moving as one training for the Olympics. Who needed a Mr. Wonderful when she had a medal within her reach?

Things had worked out well until Ethan had appeared. In her opinion, she all but had that medal in the bag. She stood at the top of her game, in a position of authority and prestige. No more treading water, no more dog paddling. Dana was on her way to the podium. Mr. Wonderful would have to catch *her*.

Ethan's arrival had knocked her out of the deep water and back into the shallow kiddie pool, where even treading water was out of the question. No longer the boss, she took directions instead of giving them. Thankfully, Ethan had been wise enough to suggest that she return to her old job while he did his. He still held a position of prestige, but once he returned to New York, she would be able to regain her ground.

Dana punched her pillow, searching for a more comfortable position. "And that's where it gets confusing," she said aloud to the empty bedroom.

Yes, she wanted to be at the top of her game again—but she didn't want Ethan to leave so quickly.

Lately, her thoughts of career were constantly competing with dreams of marriage and family. Dana wondered if this might be some type of internal diversion tactic; a way to disguise her frustration with her change of role at work.

Or might the simple truth lay in the fact that she had fallen for Ethan and didn't care that every minute she spent with him seemed to chip away at her intense career ambition?

She didn't know. She couldn't come up with anything to compare this feeling with. This certainly wasn't a fairy tale. Or a book. Or a movie.

In the majority of these fictional scenarios, the heroine was tall, thin, and beautiful. Her voice rang out in a flawless soprano, and she never had bad hair days. The hero was handsome, dashing, and brave. He knew exactly what he wanted—the heroine—and nothing stopped him from pursuing her.

Dana's life did not fit that description in the least. At five foot two, the last time she had been tall was at birth, measuring twenty-two inches long. She had been the "tallest" baby in the nursery at the time. And thin was relative. Every few months, she embarked on a new plan that never seemed to get rid of those extra ten pounds. The theory of relativity applied to her hair as well. She'd experimented with many ways to work with the texture God had given her, and currently the easiest option was to spend several hours in a chair while Latrice painstakingly braided her hair into hundreds of tiny braids.

So, she wasn't the typical heroine, but she had yet to meet the perfect man. While Ethan might be tall and dark, he still wasn't extremely handsome. In addition, he possessed his own puzzling collection of foibles. One minute, he held her hand. The next, he fluffed his ego, bragging about his "recipe for success." Never mind the fact that if customers didn't like his gourmet creations, the Gradys would be back in trouble again. He had obviously missed the day at school when they discussed the Customer Is Always Right rule.

Dana shook her head. Sometimes she had the feeling that Ethan couldn't see the forest for the trees. Yet, in an instant, he had reversed her opinion of him with his idea about surveying the customers and his offer to stick around longer to get the job done correctly.

Then, he'd amazed her again, hinting about a possible romantic relationship.

What had happened? Dana didn't know, but she no longer counted down the days until Ethan left. Was there any reason why she shouldn't just relax and see how things developed? The question had only one answer.

"Lord," Dana prayed, "I feel so confused. I'm alternating between feeling like meeting Ethan is the best thing that's happened to me, then wishing I had never met him.

"I guess the thing I need to do is stop relying on how I feel and find out what You know. Please show me how I should approach my relationship with Ethan. Should I treat him like a coworker, a good friend, or a future husband?"

Chapter 9

The next morning, while Ethan worked in the test kitchen, Mr. Grady stopped in to speak with him.

"What's this I've been hearing about customer surveys? How much more is this going to cost?"

"Any extra costs will be minimal. Basically, we're only going to need to write up a survey sheet and make copies."

Mr. Grady shook his head. "You never mentioned any surveys before. I thought you had a foolproof plan."

Ethan nodded. "Well, we think it wouldn't hurt to double check. Dana wanted to make sure that the customers really like the new items and find out if we need to bring back some of the older ones. The only way to be certain is to actually ask, so that's what we're going to do."

Mr. Grady gave him a dubious look. "And this is all right with you? I thought you two were working separately."

Ethan waved away the man's concern. "I assure you, we're both in agreement. The reason we're working together is that we know how it needs to be done. Plus, you won't have to hire more people to do it."

Mr. Grady brightened at this new aspect. "Sounds like a good plan to me. Tell Dana congratulations for coming up with such a brilliant plan." With that, he turned and left.

Ethan refrained from correcting the notion that Dana had come up with the plan. It really belonged to him, but he supposed it didn't really make that much of a difference. Who cared who owned the idea, as long as it proved to be helpful?

❧

"Mmm. . ." The woman bit into the scone again. As she chewed, she hummed appreciatively. "Oh, yes, these are really good. Are you going to keep these?"

Dana decided to let Ethan answer that one.

"If they go over with everyone else the same way they have with you, then yes, they'll stay on the menu."

The woman distributed the remainder of the scone between her two children. "Well, I definitely like the Orange Cranberry Raisin scones a lot better than the plain raisin ones you had before. These seem more moist and buttery. I mean, I could serve these at a tea or something."

"Well, thanks so much for your comments," said Dana.

"Oh, it's no problem for me," said the lady. "I just can't wait until you start selling these behind the counter. Do you think it will be long before you're done testing?"

"No, Ma'am, we don't anticipate longer than a week or two to get an item in the store after it's been tested. Within a couple of months, we should have the entire new menu in place," Ethan explained.

"Good," she said. With that, she shepherded her children away from the sample table and toward the counter to place her order.

A few customers later, Dana looked at her watch. "It's about closing time for us."

Ethan agreed. "Yeah, we only have about half a dozen scones left. Do you want to take them home with you?"

Dana laughed. "No, thanks. I've been smelling them all day, so it feels like I've eaten a dozen. Why don't we leave them here for the workers?"

"Good idea."

As Dana gathered up her purse, coat, notebooks, and other work materials, she and Ethan laughed and joked about their day. This had been the third day in a row of testing customer reactions to the new scones, and the decision appeared to be pretty straightforward.

"Looks like the orange scones are here to stay," said Dana.

"Looks that way. Of course, we'll have to check over all of the written surveys to be sure; but if everything goes well, I think I can get the bakers in the kitchen this weekend to teach them how to make these."

"I'll see you in the morning," said Dana. "We're going to be testing the parmesan tomato bagels, right?"

Right," agreed Ethan. "Are you going anywhere tonight?"

Dana stopped and smiled at him. "Are you asking me out?" Last Wednesday Ethan had accompanied her to the Easter play practice, and on Friday they had gone to his next-door neighbor's play. Sunday he'd come to dinner at her parents' home, and yesterday evening they had gone to dinner after work.

He grinned. "As a matter of fact, I am. Don't you have to help with the Easter play again tonight?"

"I do. I will every Wednesday until after Easter, but you're welcome to come along."

"I'll meet you at the church," he said. "And while I'm at it, do you have plans for Saturday? I thought we could spend some time together."

Dana shrugged in apology. "I'm being 'Aunt Dana' for the day and taking a few nieces and nephews to the Magic House."

"Magic House?"

"It's a children's museum. They have all kinds of hands-on stuff to keep kids busy for the day."

Ethan nodded. "I see. How about Saturday night?"

"We have plans for pizza and that new cartoon at the movies."

The expression on Ethan's face revealed his disappointment. As far as Dana knew, he'd not done many activities outside of work and church, and she wondered if he might feel homesick or even lonely. "Why don't you come with us—if you don't mind spending the day with little kids."

He brightened. "Just let me know what time I need to show up."

"I'll give you a call later this week." Dana noticed Kim standing behind the counter and realized she needed to check in with the manager to let her know how the product testing had gone over with the customers. "See you at church tonight." She waved good-bye to Ethan.

As soon as Ethan left, Kim came out from behind the counter. "I loved those scones. How are customers liking them?"

"They're wild about them," Dana admitted. "I think we'll be able to get them behind the counter sometime next week."

"Wow, that's fast," said Kim.

Dana nodded. "We don't have much time to waste. We need to get this company back on track as quickly as possible."

Kim took a seat at an empty table and gestured for Dana to sit as well. "It looks like things are kind of serious with you and the chef."

Dana chuckled softly. "I thought you wanted to talk business."

Kim arched her eyebrows. "Well, he is a fellow employee. I had a meeting with Mr. Grady the other day, and he talked about you and Ethan constantly. He told me that Ethan goes to your church now."

"He needed a church to attend while he's here," Dana explained. "Don't get carried away, okay?"

Kim pushed out her lower lip and frowned in an exaggerated fashion. "Now I know you're not telling me something, Dana. Ever since he got here, we never talk anymore."

"Hey, I have a job to do," Dana said in defense. "I don't have much time for chitchat lately. I thought the greater issue here was to keep the bakeries in business."

Kim gave her a penetrating look. "Fine, Dana. I won't pry."

Dana sighed. "Okay, Kim. Ethan and I have been spending some time together. You could call it dating, but I don't want it to get blown out of proportion. He's only been here a month, and as far as I know, he'll be leaving as soon as he's done with his job."

Kim looked puzzled. "So, you're saying you're dating, but it's not serious?"

"We're not sure. We're praying about it. We just don't want to force a relationship that we know will have to end. If the Lord wants us to continue the relationship, He'll make a way for us. Other than that, we're basically just getting to know each other."

"Do you think you know each other pretty well?" Kim wanted to know. "I mean, like, little things. His favorite color? His mother's name? His favorite time of year?"

Dana shook her head. "I am not about to answer your pop quiz questions."

Kim wiggled her eyebrows comically. "Why not? Are you telling me you think he's perfect?"

Dana giggled. "I never said Ethan is the perfect man. We've had our share of disagreements, but I do enjoy spending time with him."

Kim laughed. "I do enjoy spending time with him," she mimicked in a high-pitched voice. "Forget the quiz. I can tell you like him, Dana. So does this mean you've given up that silly list of requirements?"

Dana put her finger to her lips and made a shushing noise. "Why do you have to bring up the list? I don't even know where I put it."

"Yeah, right. Like you don't have it memorized. I'm just glad you came to your senses. No man is ever going to meet all of those requirements, unless you hire an *actor* to be your husband."

"Yeah, I know," said Dana. "Even though Ethan's not perfect, I don't feel like I'm missing out on anything I put on the list. And I figure most men probably feel the same way."

"What do you mean?"

"I'm saying, I know my brothers have an ideal woman they'd like to end up with, but the ones who've already gotten married say that their wives have qualities they never even thought about."

Kim gave her an incredulous look. "Your brothers had lists?"

Dana shook her head. "Not exactly, but they had a general idea of what their perfect wife would be like. Now that they're married, they say the wives God gave them were better than any woman they could have imagined."

Kim nodded, a serious expression on her face. "I think your brothers may be right. I know that I've prayed about different things with a certain result in mind, and when the Lord answered my prayer, I didn't get exactly what I wanted. So many times, the result ended up better than what I had originally asked for."

"Same goes for me," Dana added. "I think what we sometimes forget is that God really is our Father, and He knows what's best for us even better than do our physical parents. Remember when we were little, and we would ask for things, and our parents would give us what we *needed* instead of what we *wanted?*"

Kim nodded. "I hated that. Like getting me three pairs of reasonably priced jeans instead on one pair of really expensive ones. My mom did stuff like that all of the time, and it drove me nuts. But she really taught me a lot about budgeting. In the long run, it made me more responsible."

"I think that's what I'm learning about my 'list,' " said Dana. "I may have something in mind, but I'm willing to let God work out all the details. I know I'll be happy with the man He wants me to marry. I've just had to learn to trust Him."

Kim agreed. "Yeah, I know it seems hard to give up your ideals, but really, we have to accept that God will make the right choice. Parents want their kids to be happy, and God feels that same way about us.

"There may be times when we experience discomfort, but He has a perfect plan. Remember when our parents took us to get shots to keep us from getting sick? The shots weren't exactly a picnic, but they protected us in the long run."

Dana nodded thoughtfully as several customers came inside the building. Kim stood up and looked toward the growing line. "I guess that means my break is over. We're a little understaffed today, so I need to help out."

Dana smiled. "Thanks for the talk. I needed a few minutes to just chat with a girlfriend."

"No problem," said Kim. "And I know we just had that whole conversation about praying and everything but. . ." She hesitated.

"What?" asked Dana. She could tell by the glimmer in Kim's eye that her friend was in a joking mood, but she decided to play along with it.

"Just don't rush things with Ethan," said Kim. "You may think the quiz is silly, but it has some valid points."

"Like what?" Dana asked.

Kim shrugged. "I'm not sure. Personally, I would never agree to marry a man unless I knew if he liked kids. Oh, and I'd need to know his middle name."

"Why those two things?"

Kim laughed. "I don't know. Probably because I love kids and want to have at least seven and because I hate my middle name."

Dana thought for a moment. "You know, I don't think you've ever told me your middle name. What is it?"

Kim shook her head. "No way. I hate it, and I'm never telling anyone."

Dana laughed. "What if the man you want to marry just has to know before he proposes?"

Kim cocked one eyebrow. "We'll have to see about that." She turned to walk away, then stopped. Over her shoulder, she remarked, "You know how we talked about our parents wanting the best for us?"

"Yeah."

Kim shook her head and wrinkled her nose. "I think middle names are one of those things that they seem to mess up on more than other things. Maybe we should outlaw them altogether."

Dana laughed. "Oh, Kim, it can't be that bad."

Kim pursed her lips and nodded. "Oh, yes, it can. See you later."

Dana waved good-bye. "Okay. We'll be here Monday with some new bagels."

"Can't wait to taste them," said Kim. "And I'm glad you came up with this idea for the surveys. Mr. Grady is so pleased that the menu won't be set in stone until after the surveys are done."

Dana blinked in surprise. "Actually, Ethan came up with the idea. I'm just doing the organizational part of it."

Kim gave her a look that suggested she didn't believe her. "Dana, you don't have to let him take all of the credit because you like him. Mr. Grady told me you developed the plan."

Dana shook her head. "It's not all mine. It's a joint idea."

Kim shrugged. "Never mind. I guess it's not a big deal as long as it gets done."

"Right," Dana agreed. "See you later."

As Dana drove home, she thought about her list once again. Kim was right. The list didn't matter as long as God did the choosing.

Once she got home, she planned to do a massive search for that list, and if she found it, she would burn it. The time had arrived for her to take a back seat in the search process and let God be in charge.

❧

Ethan watched as the basketball swished right through the hoop.

Anthony laughed and patted him on the shoulder. "That's another win for me and Ethan."

Ethan laughed as Albert and Jackson immediately began negotiating a rematch. He and Dana's brothers had spent the better part of the morning playing two-on-two at the indoor court at the gym, and Albert and Jackson had lost five of the six games they'd played.

Ethan held up his hands in surrender. "I think I'm played out for now. I'm out of shape from standing around in the kitchen all day. I need to get to the gym a little more."

Jackson scoffed, "You don't have to brag that you're out of shape when you've beaten the socks off of us."

Anthony dribbled the ball. "He's right. If I weren't on his team, he'd have lost too. I could beat the three of you by myself."

Albert and Jackson spent several moments grumbling about Anthony's boasting.

"Yeah, right," said Jackson. "We'll see who's the best when it's warm enough to play golf. Anybody can put this big ball into a basket."

"Yeah, anybody but you," quipped Anthony. "Golf? Bring it on."

Ethan laughed. His golf skills were more developed than his basketball game, and he looked forward to getting out on the course again. He hoped he would still be here by the time they were ready to hit the links. After having bonded with these guys, he tried hard not to think about the possibility of moving on.

"Let's get some lunch," suggested Albert.

"Yeah," agreed Ethan. "Why don't you guys come over to my place, and I'll fix something to eat?"

"Sounds good to me," said Jackson. The twins agreed and after showering, the four men headed to Ethan's condo.

Over their lunch of turkey sandwiches, Albert first brought up the topic of Dana and Ethan. "Looks like you and Dana have gotten pretty serious. Want to talk about it?"

Ethan nearly choked on the water he sipped. No, he didn't want to talk about it, but from the looks on their faces, they did. He shrugged. "Maybe."

"Does she know you're not going to be here after you finish the work for the Gradys?" asked Jackson.

"Of course she does," Ethan told them.

Anthony took a more direct approach. "So why are you dating her?"

Ethan studied the three men, his gaze moving from face to face. They were serious. He held up his hands in defense. "Look, I didn't force her to go out with me. We know there's a possibility that I will leave eventually, but we decided that we'll just pray about it. In the meantime, we don't think it'll hurt to spend time together."

"So, you're saying that if you leave, you'll still continue the relationship?" asked Jackson.

Ethan took another bite of his sandwich. "We haven't really discussed that. It could happen. Or one of us could end up relocating."

Anthony shook his head. "Dana would never move away. She loves St. Louis. Plus, she's not the type to drop her entire life for some guy."

Albert chuckled. "Especially if he doesn't line up with the list." His brothers laughed and began eating their sandwiches again.

The list? Ethan had a feeling Dana had probably not told him about this for a reason, but his curiosity forced him to ask, "What are you talking about?"

"Nothing, Man, don't worry about it," said Anthony.

"Yeah, it's a girl thing. No big deal," added Albert.

Ethan chuckled and shook his head. "Uh-uh. You can't do that to me. I want all of the details."

The brothers stopped eating and looked at each other. Suddenly, they seemed hesitant to say anything.

"Look, we shouldn't have even mentioned it," said Jackson. He gave the twins the look of a disapproving older brother. "It's Dana's thing, and if she wants to tell you about it, she will."

Ethan pushed his plate aside, his appetite gone. "Thanks a lot. If my relationship with Dana goes wrong, I'll spend the rest of my life trying to figure out what part of the list I didn't line up with."

Jackson frowned, then seemed to take pity on him. "Okay, I'll tell you this. It's Dana's list of what the ideal guy would be like. We used to tease her about it because it was so long."

"And impossible," added Anthony. "No man could be like that, so don't worry."

"Yeah, she's probably forgotten all about it," said Albert.

"Wait a minute. Back up," Ethan said, shaking his head. "What do you mean, 'No man could be like that'?" He leaned back in his chair. "Can't you give me a hint so I can at least try?"

Albert and Anthony didn't say anything. Apparently, Jackson would make the decision.

After several moments, Jackson shook his head. "Trust me, you don't want to be like this list. For one, she wrote it a long time ago. And second, a man who acted like this would have some serious problems. Nobody would like this guy."

"What?" Ethan said, feeling even more confused.

Jackson shrugged. "I don't even know how to explain it." He tilted his head toward his brothers. "You tell him."

Anthony nodded. "Here's the deal. The other day I babysat Annitra, and she wanted me to read this book to her. It was called *Anne* something."

Albert nodded. "I've had to read those books. *Anne of Green Gables*. It seems like there's at least ten of them. They never end, and she always wants to read one of them."

Anthony nodded. "Yeah. Anyway, we get to this one part, and Anne is talking to her mother or something, and she's disappointed because her friend is getting married. It's not that she doesn't want her friend to be happy, but she thinks the guy is all wrong for her. She goes on and on about how the guy wasn't wicked or wild enough.

"So then her mother says, 'Do you want her to marry some bad guy? Or would *you* want to marry a wicked man?' She thinks about it, then says, 'Well, no. But I'd like to marry somebody who could be wicked and wouldn't.' Now," Anthony crumpled up his napkin and set it down on the table for emphasis, "what in the world does that mean?"

Albert nodded. "Women want you to be all sensitive, right? But if you're too good, you're boring."

Jackson nodded and pointed at Ethan. "But if you're not nice enough, tough luck. There's no balance. If you tried to act like that, people would think you were insane. Especially women."

"So you're saying Dana's list is like that?" Ethan asked.

Anthony leaned his head to the side and thought about it for a long time. "Sort of," he said finally. "It's just a long rambling list of things she thought would be cool. But some of them aren't really practical."

Jackson laughed. "But a lot of guys who liked her got dumped because they were too different from the list. We would ask what happened to them, and she said it just didn't work out."

"Yeah, she'd say, 'Oh. . .he's nice, but. . .'" Albert shrugged. "It didn't matter. We never saw them again."

Anthony continued. "It's like, why do women get all swoony over men who act like that in books and movies? Like that *Pride and Prejudice*. What's up with that? That Darcy guy is such a jerk for so long, but women love him." He shook his head.

"Dana loves that book," added Albert. "And so do Mom, Sheryl, and Latrice."

"My wife does too," said Jackson. "Verna drags that movie out every Christmas, and it takes forever to watch it. Man, it's long."

Ethan laughed. "Seriously? Darcy?"

"Yeah, do you know him?" Anthony said, laughing.

Ethan shrugged. "You don't even want to know how much my mom liked that book, but I've never read it or seen the movie." He looked around the table. "Do you guys want to rent it?"

They shook their heads emphatically. "You can do that on your own time," said Jackson. "Just make sure you don't have anything else to do for several hours."

The men moved on to a different subject, but they no longer had Ethan's full attention. His thoughts were about Dana's list.

Before the men left, Ethan had another question for them. "So what does Dana think of me? Did she describe me as. . .*nice?*"

Albert and Anthony exchanged a look, and Albert answered first. "Yeah, she did, but only back when she first met you."

Jackson clapped a hand on Ethan's shoulder. "A word of advice. Forget about the list. Please don't try to pretend you're Mr. Darcy. She's outgrown it."

"Are you sure?"

"Positive," said Anthony. "If not, you'd be history by now." He and his brothers laughed their way down the driveway to their cars. Ethan stood in the doorway, hoping they were right.

He knew many women had an ideal in mind for potential husbands, but being up against some mysterious checklist made him nervous. He'd been feeling pretty secure in his relationship with Dana, but for the first time in a few weeks, he felt genuinely worried.

Lord, he prayed, *I know this is in Your hands, but if Dana's got a list, I can't compete with fiction. Please help me to do the right thing and let You guide our relationship.*

❧

"Are you sure about this?" Ethan gave Dana an incredulous look. As he hesitated, a woman with two toddlers moved past him, through the entrance gate.

Dana laughed out loud. "Yes, I'm sure. It's just a carousel, so what are you afraid of?" Shaking her head, she handed over two tickets to the operator. Without waiting for Ethan to voice any further doubts, she took hold of his hand and pulled him through the gate.

"So what's your pick? Horse, camel, or sleigh?" she asked him.

Ethan shrugged. "I don't know. I haven't been on a carousel since I was a little kid."

Dana led the way to a sleigh that would seat both of them and sat down. Patting the seat next to her, she said, "We'll ride here the first go round to get you acclimated."

Ethan shook his head. "Hey, I'm not a baby. We don't have to ride in the sleigh. It doesn't even move."

Dana grinned. "I was hoping you'd lighten up." She pointed to a nearby white horse decorated in soft pastels. "I'll ride that one."

"Then I'll take the camel next to your cotton candy horse." His voice sounded slightly gruff, but Dana could tell he was in an amiable mood.

After all of the riders were settled, the calliope music began, and the massive carousel glided to a start. After a few revolutions, Dana asked Ethan if he enjoyed the ride so far.

He smiled. "I guess so. I'll admit, this is a pretty unusual activity. I've never even seen an indoor carousel before. How old is this?"

Dana thought for a moment. "I'm not exactly sure. If I remember correctly, it was originally built in the early 1900s. It used to be kept outdoors at a different park, but eventually they moved it here."

"This is pretty cool," Ethan said. "It moves so smoothly that it's hard to imagine it's an actual antique."

"This thing was definitely built to last," Dana agreed, gently patting the brass post that protruded from her horse's back. "Isn't it kind of interesting to think that we're touching something that other people back in the 1920s touched? The world has changed so much since then; it almost seems impossible that we have this merry-go-round in common with an earlier generation."

"That's true." Ethan looked down at his clothes. "I doubt they'd be wearing jeans and tennis shoes like we are."

Dana shook her head. "Definitely not. More like suits and dresses."

The ride coasted to an end, but when Dana got ready to leave her perch, Ethan shook his head. "I'll be right back," he said, before hurrying off to talk to the ticket seller. Moments later he returned, a mile-wide grin on his face. "Pick another seat. We're good for the next five rides."

Dana laughed. Minutes ago, Ethan had grudgingly stepped on to the carousel; now, he'd bought tickets in advance.

Dana exchanged her horse for a camel. "The next five, huh?"

"Yeah. This is actually pretty fun." Ethan clambered up and took a seat on the horse next to her camel.

"Did I ever tell you I sometimes get motion sickness?" she teased.

"No, you didn't. Maybe we should sit in the sleigh."

"I'm just teasing."

"Just to be sure, let's take the sleigh this time around." Ethan cupped her waist and pulled her down, then gestured for her to step into the sleigh first. Settling in next to her, he added, "This seat doesn't go up and down like the others."

Dana giggled. "Okay, we're sitting where you want to. But, just for the record, I don't get motion sickness. I would have been fine on the camel."

As the music began and the carousel cruised to a start, Ethan reached for Dana's hand and held it. He winked. "And just for the record, I know that. I just thought it would be more romantic if we sat here together."

Dana felt her stomach flutter and took a deep breath to steady her emotions. Ethan might be stubborn about business, but he definitely had a soft side when it came to relationships—especially theirs. The way he'd looked at her made her heart melt. She'd never dated anyone else who really seemed to make such an effort to do the things she enjoyed, like riding this carousel. Ethan seemed to understand when things really mattered to her and gave his best effort to enjoy them as well.

Dana wondered to what extent she should continue to guard her emotions from any possible hurt. Glancing sideways at Ethan, Dana realized she could do little about that now. She'd already fallen in love with him—for better, or for worse.

If he were to propose to her at this very moment, she had a feeling she'd accept without hesitation and think things through later. Given their sometimes rocky interactions at work and the fact that he still planned to continue his freelance business around the country, she wondered if she'd been too careless with her emotions. Did he feel the same way? Did he have any doubts about ending their relationship as soon as he completed his contract with the company?

Dana stole another glance at his profile. Ethan was too busy examining the architecture of the carousel to look at her, but he gave her hand a little squeeze, almost as if he knew she needed reassuring.

With a small sigh, Dana gently leaned her head on Ethan's shoulder. By now, his scent was familiar and comfortable—an unusual blend of earthy cologne and bread dough. Feeling content, Dana closed her eyes long enough for a silent prayer.

Lord. . .I think I know what it feels like to have found the person I'm supposed to spend the rest of my life with. For that, I'm really thankful and honored that he's turning out to be so special. Even though there are a lot of things that seem overwhelming about making this relationship permanent, I'm trusting You to help us work out the details.

❦

Ethan drummed the steering wheel, humming softly to himself. Normally, he hated being stuck at this particular stoplight, but today the wait at the intersection of Whispering Pines and Olive didn't feel long at all. A glance in the rearview mirror confirmed what he already knew—he practically grinned from ear to ear.

The light changed again, allowing only a few more cars to escape the growing line of traffic. Ethan inched his car forward, still content to wait. As he glanced at the small business card on the dashboard, he wondered if this most recent chain of events had simply been a coincidence.

The night before, he'd stopped to chat with his landlord. Dave occupied the condo next to Ethan's. During the course of their conversation, Ethan had jokingly mentioned that he'd been considering opening his future restaurant in the St. Louis area.

Without hesitation, his landlord had suggested Ethan get in touch with his cousin, who just happened to be a real estate agent specializing in commercial properties. "Shari might have something she can show you," Dave said enthusiastically.

Ethan nodded agreeably but didn't give the idea of going much thought. Half an hour later, Dave phoned to inform Ethan that not only did Shari have a property listed that he might want to see, but she could show it the next morning.

Ethan tentatively scheduled an appointment yet did some intense prayer that night. In the morning, he awakened feeling confident that he wanted to keep the appointment.

After calling work to let Mr. Grady know he'd be a bit late, he rushed off to make his appointment with Shari. She'd ultimately shown him half a dozen different properties that could easily meet his list of requirements.

In the past, he'd always assumed that he'd have to build his own restaurant, but now he felt a surge of excitement. Purchasing an existing building would put him that much closer to his goal.

The light changed once more, finally allowing Ethan to get back in motion. Continuing toward work, he again pondered the idea of remaining in St. Louis. The notion to stay here had crossed his mind more than a few times, especially now that he and Dana were so close.

He'd always envisioned starting his business somewhere closer to New York, but he knew Dana loved her hometown as well. Might there be some room for a compromise? If so, who would be the one to relocate?

Even though he'd just looked at potential buildings to house his restaurant, Ethan didn't feel 100 percent sure that St. Louis was his ideal location.

He thought back to the previous week when he and Dana had ridden the carousel at Faust Park. Six months ago, he'd have had a hard time imagining himself on a merry-go-round nine times nonstop. After the first few times, the motion had become a little monotonous, but he didn't care. Watching the pleasure on Dana's face and being able to hold her hand for so long had been worth the wave of dizziness he felt when he set foot on solid ground after the ride ended.

The truth was obvious. He loved Dana, even though he couldn't pinpoint the exact moment he lost his heart to her. At some point in time, attraction had become admiration, which in turn developed into respect. Respect had expanded to include friendship, and without his giving much thought to the progression of friendship, Ethan had been led to the brink of falling in love.

"So now what?" Ethan asked himself aloud. Returning to New York would be difficult, but he missed his home, family, and friends. Though there was a chance Dana might want to leave St. Louis, he had a feeling such a drastic move would not meet with a favorable reception from her family.

The last thing he wanted to do was try to convert their relationship into a phone and E-mail romance. But were they close enough to move beyond simply dating one another? Had the time come for a deeper commitment?

Ethan slowed his car to a stop at yet another light. Shaking his head, he contemplated his choices. No matter how much he avoided the facts, his time in St. Louis rapidly drew to a close. He could either propose to Dana and see what happened or go back to New York and try to continue the relationship as best he could.

Ethan drummed his fingers on the steering wheel again and waited for the light to change.

Too much had happened in the past twenty-four hours for him to make a coherent decision. He needed to be sure that when he made a choice, he made the right one.

"I don't want to mess this up," he rationalized. After several more moments of consideration, Ethan decided to take an entire week to devote some serious prayer time to his concerns.

"Lord, I know I've asked You to show me Your will before, but if I ever needed to make the right choice about something, now is definitely the time."

As soon as the words left his mouth, a feeling of contentment washed over Ethan, giving him the reassurance he so needed. There was no mistaking that sense of peace. As long as he didn't put his own feelings over God's plan, he knew he was definitely on the right track.

Chapter 10

H mm. . . What's the special occasion?" Dana asked. Ethan stood in the doorway of her office, holding a bagel with cream cheese smeared on top. He had jabbed two small candles into the top, and as the flames danced, melted wax slid down into the cream cheese. Ethan held the bagel out to her, but Dana shook her head. "I'll pass. I'm not into eating wax."

"At least blow out the candles."

Dana quickly blew and returned her attention to the inventory sheets she'd been studying.

Ethan cut the bagel in half. "Sure you don't want a piece? It's pumpernickel."

Dana wrinkled her nose. "How many times do I have to tell you, I can't stand pumpernickel?"

He shrugged. "It seems weird that two people so perfect for each other can be so different. I still can't believe you don't like pumpernickel."

She shrugged. "Well, I don't. And a couple can hardly find out if they're perfect for each other in a few weeks."

"Eight weeks," said Ethan. "That's the special occasion. Today is the two-month anniversary of the day I got here."

Dana glanced at the calendar on her wall. "Wow, I didn't even realize it. Time is moving so fast."

Ethan cleared his throat. "I know. I wanted to ask you something."

Dana nodded and forced herself to remain calm. Lately, the question of whether or not Ethan would return to New York had been weighing heavily on their minds. She knew more than ever that she didn't want him to leave, but Ethan had to make the final choice. If he felt the Lord wanted him to return home, she couldn't argue with that.

She gave Ethan her bravest smile and waited for him to say what he'd come to say.

"I love you," he said simply. "I know two months shouldn't be enough time to fall in love, but that's what happened." He reached for her hands and held them in his. Looking into her eyes, he continued. "I'd feel pretty relieved if I knew how you felt about me."

Dana laughed, still trying to appear calm. Inside, her stomach turned somersaults as her brain replayed Ethan's sentence over and over again.

I love you. Those were the words she'd been waiting to hear. Of course she loved him too. As much as she'd prayed for guidance, she felt at peace. Surely, this was God's will.

Ethan had confirmed what she'd been feeling, and she couldn't ever remember being happier. Without a second thought, she reached forward and hugged him. "I love you too."

Ethan pulled away from her. "Are you sure about that? I don't have a test to pass or anything? I don't have to give up pumpernickel bagels?"

Dana shook her head. "I'm sure." As she looked at him, she knew this was what it felt like when prayers were answered. Everything fell into place perfectly, and there were no rough spots. The Lord's fingerprints were all over this.

"I think this means I also have an answer about moving back to New York," Ethan told her. "I've been praying about it, and I really think I want to open my restaurant here."

Dana felt so happy, she could hardly speak. She'd been praying about this as well, and she never felt the Lord leading her to leave St. Louis. Knowing Ethan wanted to move here was a great comfort. "That sounds wonderful."

"Of course, I'll have to do some hard bargaining with Mr. Grady so I can hire you to work for me," he laughed. "And don't worry, I won't be bossy. It'll be a real partnership, husband and wife working side by side. I'll let you do your thing with the business side, and I'll be in charge of cooking."

Dana hesitated. His sudden talk of marriage caught her off guard. Of course, she had expected nothing less than a marriage proposal, but he had merely jumped from "I love you" to "husband and wife." Though they were in love, she hadn't expected a proposal from him this soon.

In Ethan's mind, she had quit her job, married him, and agreed to manage his restaurant.

Ethan must have noticed the look on her face. "Hey, what's wrong? I thought you'd be happy."

Dana swallowed as she tried to think of how to explain how she felt. "I'm fine. It just seems like everything's moving so fast without much warning."

"I know, I know—but we don't have to approach this at the speed of light. I just thought we'd need to make sure we feel the same."

Ripples of relief melted over Dana. "I agree. And I think we should still keep praying about this—just to be sure," she explained. "I mean, it's way too early to think about marriage. We still don't know each other that well."

Ethan folded his arms. "What do you mean? I think we know each other pretty well."

Dana struggled to find the words to answer him. At a loss for an explanation, she fell back on Kim's reasoning. "What's my favorite color?"

"Yellow," Ethan said, not missing a beat.

"My favorite time of year?"

Ethan grinned. "Winter. You love snow as long as you don't have to drive in it."

"My middle name?"

"Marie." He leaned forward and spoke in a mock whisper. "So do I pass the test?"

"It's not a test. . . ," Dana said. She had to admit he had learned a lot about her. Likewise, she knew he loved spring, the color green, and his middle name was. . . Okay, she didn't know his middle name yet. Dana could see room for improvement.

She tilted her head to the side, thinking. Finally, she said, "We still need to get to know each other better. I don't know your middle name yet. What is it?"

Ethan shrugged. "You're kidding, right? The last time I checked, middle names weren't the magic word to get to the altar. In fact, I thought I just needed to say, 'Will you marry me?' "

Dana sat very still for a moment. "Are you asking me to marry you?"

"Not quite," said Ethan.

So what did he mean? "Then what are you saying?"

Ethan stood up. "I'm saying I *will* ask you to marry me soon, but I'm not so unromantic that I'm going to ask you while we're at work and you're sitting at your desk surrounded by a million papers."

Dana laughed. He had artfully avoided her middle name question, but she didn't mind letting her almost-fiancé off the hook for now. Maybe, like Kim, he hated his middle name. "Thank you for the warning."

"You're welcome," said Ethan. "I hate to cut this visit short, but I need to get back to the kitchen and check on my banana muffins."

Dana lifted an eyebrow. "You're making plain banana muffins? That's a first."

"Actually. . .they're banana pineapple with chocolate chunks and coconut. Sort of tropical with chocolate thrown in for the fun of it."

Dana's stomach growled at that instant. Had dinnertime come so soon? "I may be down to have a sample later on."

"You'd better hurry," he warned. "Everyone wants to taste these, and I might not have any left if you wait too long."

"I'll do my best. I've still got the surveys from yesterday to look over."

"Oh, right. Let me know how the bread pudding went over. If it's still not working, I have another idea. I'll see you later." Just before he left, he blew her a kiss.

Dana caught it and blew one to him in return. Her first kiss from Ethan just happened to be one that didn't feel like anything. At least, the feeling wasn't *tangible*—but if she could bottle the emotional high that accompanied the airborne kiss, she'd be a millionaire. She could see it now, lined up neatly on shelves at major department stores, in fancy bottles.

Airborne Kiss, by Dana, the bottle would read. She would become rich and famous.

Dana laughed aloud at the idea. "For one thing, it wouldn't be sitting on the shelves. It would be flying out the door," she said, grinning. Being in love was fantabulous.

As Dana considered this feeling, her gaze landed on a stack of recent surveys, and a deep sigh escaped her lips.

While being in love felt amazing, telling Ethan he would have to cut one of his recipes from the menu would be the total opposite. The challenge lay in finding a way to break the news gently. The way she felt right now, she would rather ignore the problem, but in her heart, she knew it must be done.

The majority of the recipes had done well with the customers. Although some of the recipes had needed some extensive adjustments, Dana had been forced to eat her words a number of times. At least, until Ethan invented the bread pudding.

The pumpernickel-walnut-cherry bread pudding, to be exact. The first time they'd offered it to people, the majority of customers had agreed that it just wasn't something they would buy.

Ethan had persisted, feeling confident that he could tweak the recipe to make it more appealing. He'd returned to the test kitchen and emerged with virtually the same dish, with the addition of ginger and caramel.

She and Ethan had returned to the stores and asked people to taste it again. This time, people had been a tad more reluctant. Again, to Ethan's dismay, the response had not been good.

Instead of giving up, Ethan went back to the kitchen and returned with a brand new dish that Dana had considered to be more of a monstrosity than a dessert. The already overly flavored pudding now boasted coconut, raisins, lime zest, and dried cranberries.

"Have you even tasted this?" Dana asked Ethan.

He became instantly offended and barely spoke as they conducted the surveys. By this time, most people tried to pretend they didn't see the sample table. They practically had to beg people to come and taste it, and as Dana had expected, the response turned out to be far from favorable.

Dana took a look at one of the most recent questionnaires.

I can't imagine why you would put so many flavors in a dessert. I can't even tell what this tastes like, one sampler had written.

Another wrote, *What is this supposed to be? Surely not bread pudding?*

The others were pretty much the same, ranging from eloquent and tactful: *This is not really something I'd like to serve to guests. I think dessert should be a time for simplicity instead of another excuse to overload the taste buds,* to simple: *It tastes terrible! Sorry. . . .*

Poor Ethan. He was obviously proud of this recipe and wanted very much for it to remain on the menu. In Dana's opinion, and according to their agreement, it had to be cut. No one seemed interested in eating or buying it, and with the amount of ingredients it called for, it would be a major waste of the bakers' time and the company's money.

Dana leaned back in her chair and tried to determine how in the world she would break the news to him. He really seemed attached to whatever he created, and when faced with criticism, he sometimes took it as a personal insult.

She decided not to think about it right now. She would let a few days pass and see if he focused his interest on a different recipe. Maybe by then he would be more willing to let go of that awful bread pudding.

〰️

"Hi there," said Ethan, as he entered Dana's office. "I got your voice mail. What did you need to talk about?"

An unreadable look crossed her face. "Could you sit down for a minute?"

Ethan sat down, trying to fight the apprehension that settled over him. Pasting a smile he didn't feel on his face, he asked, "Anything wrong?"

Dana spoke quietly. "Actually, yes. Remember our agreement about the recipes and the survey?"

Ethan nodded. "Yeah."

"Okay. I think it's time to get rid of the pumpernickel bread pudding."

Ethan laughed, feeling relieved. "You're joking, right? You're just kidding because you hate pumpernickel." Dana didn't answer. "Right?" Ethan prodded.

Dana gave him an apologetic look. "I'm sorry, but I'm really not kidding." She shook her head. "We just can't put it on the menu."

"Hey, wait a minute," he argued. "We agreed that I could tweak things to make it better, remember?"

Dana shook her head. "You've tweaked twice, and now people are practically running from it. With all of the ingredients you have in it, I'm not surprised. It bears a striking resemblance to fruitcake."

Ethan winced. He realized it hadn't exactly gotten rave reviews, but he refused to believe it had been that terrible.

Dana continued. "We just can't keep wasting time and money on it."

Ethan tugged at his collar. Had Dana done this just to prove that people wouldn't like all of his recipes? So far, the response for everything else had been good, and he felt confident he could fix the bread pudding. "Give me another chance."

Dana shook her head. "Look, Ethan, Mr. Grady is wanting to get this menu in place. We still have to test your new muffins and those croissants. Let's just cut our losses on the pudding, okay?"

"I don't think so. People might not recognize it, but that dish is a gourmet masterpiece. It might not take off right now, but give it a few months."

Dana sighed. "Ethan, please don't make this harder. I know I've been really supportive about your changing the other recipes. We both know I didn't think many of them would work. Do you think it felt good to eat my words time and time again?"

Ethan didn't answer. This was his favorite recipe, and he couldn't believe she had decided to be so unreasonable.

Dana spoke up again. "Plus, it has a million ingredients and will cost a fortune to make. It'll just get moldy sitting there and never being sold."

At that moment, Mr. Grady came into the office, waving a glossy magazine. "Look! Grady Bakeries is mentioned in this month's issue of *Restaurant Owner.*"

"Wow," said Dana. "I hope they said good things."

Mr. Grady grinned. "You bet. And it's all because of Ethan." He whipped his reading glasses out of his pocket, put them on, and began to read.

"Chef Ethan D. Miles, culinary genius and knight in shining armor for countless numbers of failing restaurants, has left New York to focus on the Heartland for the time being. Miles is applying his know-how to making over the menu at the St. Louis-based Grady Bakeries.

"If his previous record is any indication of how he'll fare, Grady Bakeries will be back on track immediately. It's still anyone's guess as to when Chef Miles will settle down and apply his creativity to his own restaurant. Until then, stop by one of the Grady Bakeries to get a taste of his latest ingenuity."

Mr. Grady closed the magazine emphatically. "This is excellent. I've dreamed about getting a mention in this magazine. This is an answer to prayer."

"That's excellent," Dana agreed. "Ethan, you really do know what you're doing."

The glowing review pleased Ethan. He'd heard a great many compliments concerning his work, but this had come at a time when he really needed the encouragement. Turning to Dana, he said, "Now will you let me keep the bread pudding on the menu?"

Dana's jaw dropped. "We had an agreement. You promised."

Mr. Grady interrupted. "What's this about bread pudding?"

Dana shot Ethan a glare, and he didn't say anything. He hadn't expected Mr. Grady to get into the disagreement.

"Mr. Grady," Dana began, "Ethan and I agreed when we decided to do the surveys that if anything just didn't seem to work with the customers, we would get rid of it."

"But we also agreed that I could work with the recipe for awhile," Ethan added.

"For how long?" argued Dana. "All you've done is add things to it."

Mr. Grady frowned. "Dana, I think the least we can do is let Ethan work with it. Even if the pudding doesn't sell immediately, word may get around that Ethan's created the recipe, and that might boost sales."

Dana was incredulous. "Do you really think putting Ethan's name on that thing will pick up sales?"

Sighing, Mr. Grady said, "In times like this, every little bit helps."

"That's my point exactly," said Dana. "Every bit does count, and this recipe is too expensive to make. It has a thousand ingredients and won't be cost effective unless we charge an exorbitant amount per serving, and people buy it right and left. As of now, people don't even want to taste a free sample."

Ethan realized Dana did have a point, but since Mr. Grady seemed to be on his side, he didn't want to look a gift horse in the mouth. He had complete confidence he could fix this recipe.

"Dana," Ethan said, trying to think of a way to calm her down, "when I came up with the plan to do the surveys, I only wanted to help you feel better. You didn't think people would like my ideas, so I tried to think of a way to make the menu more comfortable for you—but I still have the final say in this."

"You thought of the survey?" asked Mr. Grady. "I thought that was Dana's idea."

Dana shook her head. "No. Ethan came up with it, and I did the organizing."

Crossing his arms, Mr. Grady frowned deeply. "Dana, I'm disappointed. All along I've been thinking you came up with the concept, and I was proud of Ethan for agreeing to it." He shook his head. "But this is appalling. You're telling me that Ethan, who's done this job time and time again, came up with the idea to appease you? I remember how you complained that no one would buy his recipes, but I thought you'd gotten over it."

Ethan had never heard Mr. Grady like this before. He actually sounded angry. Dana looked absolutely flabbergasted, and Ethan wanted to jump in and smooth things out, but he didn't. If he let Dana have her way now, the bread pudding would be permanently shelved.

"Mr. Grady, please let me explain—" said Dana.

Mr. Grady pursed his lips and shook his head. "I'm afraid it's not up for discussion, Dana. I'm the one who has the final say, and I want that bread pudding in the stores along with everything else he's created for us."

Tears welled up in Dana's eyes. Ethan felt like his heart had been torn in two. Should he pick Dana over the bread pudding?

She nodded slowly. "I see." She opened her desk and began pulling out several items.

"What are you doing?" Ethan asked.

Dana looked at Mr. Grady. "I'm sorry, but as the overseeing manager of Grady Bakeries, I can't stand by and watch this man waste your money over something so ridiculous. If you want to know how people feel about that pudding, take a look at these survey sheets." She gestured toward a stack of papers. "I have forced myself to be humble when I'm wrong, but he refuses to admit defeat on a bread pudding." Juggling the armload of items she'd removed from her desk, she reached for her purse.

"Please accept my resignation, effective immediately. If Ethan knows my job so well, I suggest that he take my place." Without another word, she sailed through the doorway and disappeared into the hallway.

Ethan was too stunned to talk.

Apparently, Mr. Grady felt the same way. Mr. Grady didn't say a word, but after several moments, he jammed his hands into his pockets and left the office.

Ethan remained in the room alone, feeling like he had been hit in the chest with a rock. What had he done? Was Dana only upset about work, or would this disagreement spill over into their personal relationship? Had he just allowed his ego to ruin the chance to spend the rest of his life with the woman he loved?

∼

Stay calm, Dana told herself as she walked to her car. She unlocked the door and got inside after tossing her belongings on the passenger's seat.

Before she started the car, she took several moments to take deep breaths, in hopes of subduing her emotions.

Did I really just quit my job?

She wanted to cry. Dana had poured her heart and soul into that job, and she walked away from it. She needed to find a new job and house, since the Gradys owned the small house she now rented. But Ethan's attitude upset her the most. Talk about prideful! The way his nose tilted in the air, he would drown if it rained.

Pumpernickel bread pudding indeed! What would it take for him to admit that it hadn't been appetizing in the least?

With a groan, Dana started the engine. In all likelihood, men would walk on Mars before Ethan admitted defeat.

Looking toward the building, another thought occurred to her. If Ethan really cared about anyone's feelings other than his own, he would have come after her by now. Obviously, he was too far gone to change. And she didn't know what to think about Mr. Grady's behavior. Apparently, he had sold her out for a magazine article.

Dana tuned the radio to the classical music station as she drove. She wished the sound of the music would erase the pain she felt. Her relationship with the man she loved—or, at least, thought she loved—was over. It looked like Ethan wasn't Prince Charming after all.

∼

The phone rang, jolting Dana out of her sleep. "Hello?" she asked groggily.

The person on the other end sighed. "Dana, it's me."

"Yes, Ethan?" She held back the emotional stream of questions she wanted to ask him.

"It's nine-thirty, and you're not in the office. I need to know what's going on with you."

Dana cleared her throat. Of all the nerve. . . "In case you weren't paying attention, *Chef* Miles, I resigned yesterday. Therefore, I have no need to be at work today."

"Dana, come on. Don't be childish about this—"

"I'm not the one being childish," Dana cut him off. "You're the one who can't admit your recipe stinks. It's only one measly recipe, so what difference does it make?"

He hesitated, and Dana tried to imagine the look on his face. Was it at all possible that he felt torn between her and his precious bread pudding?

"Dana, really, the Gradys need you here. Mr. Grady is in utter shock, and everyone is speculating about what's happened. Please come back."

Tears rolled down Dana's cheeks. She hated the fact that she had walked out on her job. That type of action wasn't typical of her at all. She felt terrible about leaving the Gradys at a time when they were so vulnerable—but that hadn't stopped Ethan from taking advantage of a struggling company.

"I can't. Really." Wasting no time, she hung up the phone before Ethan could reply. Dana cried herself to sleep again. Ethan still hadn't mentioned their relationship. Did that mean it had ended? Would he change his mind and go back to New York now?

❦

Ethan gave up on calling after a couple of days. After explaining the situation to Albert and Anthony, they assured him that he should just let Dana have some time alone instead of continuing his hourly pleas for her to come back to work.

"By Sunday she'll be in a better mood," Anthony assured him. "Come to dinner at Mom and Dad's, and you can talk to her then."

"I don't know if that's such a good idea," Ethan hedged. "I seriously doubt she'll invite me."

"Then I'm inviting you." Anthony's tone let Ethan know he saw no problem with the idea. "You need to talk to each other, and if she won't pick up the phone, you can find a way to have a conversation then."

Ethan continued his quest to get Dana to return his calls, but it didn't work. Instead, he poured out his heart to the answering machine, but to no avail.

He tried going to her house, but she wouldn't answer the door. By the end of the week, she had left her house to spend a few days with her parents, according to Anthony.

At work, things headed toward shambles. The survey system ground to a standstill because Dana had been the one in charge of running it. Orders, inventory sheets, and requisitions constantly came in from the three stores. Mr. Grady, along with the rest of the staff, was doing his best to divide Dana's duties. To put things simply, no one realized how much she had done until she wasn't there to do it any longer.

Mr. Grady tried calling her, but he met with the answering machine as well.

At church, she avoided Ethan like the flu. When he sat next to her on the pew, she didn't even turn to look at him. That had really stung.

Still, Ethan wanted to attend dinner at her parents' in hopes of trying to speak to her.

After checking with Anthony to see if the invitation still stood, Ethan steeled himself and decided to go. Hopefully, Dana would respond better if they were face-to-face. At least it was worth a try. The worst that could happen would be that she would just choose not to talk to him.

At Mavis and Claude's, Ethan patiently waited for the right moment. First, she disappeared into the kitchen to help with the meal. Afterwards, she washed dishes, then played with her young nieces and nephews. Finally, when she went to the kitchen to cut one of the neighbors a piece of Mavis's butter cake, Ethan saw his chance and jumped at it.

He followed her into the kitchen, then started his speech. "Dana, please come back to work. We need you there. Mr. Grady is so embarrassed that he yelled at you. He didn't mean it, and he wants you back. I want you there. So does everyone else."

Dana didn't look up from the cake she was cutting. "So what's going on with the new recipes? Are they in the stores yet?"

"Not yet. We've hit a few snags, since you were the one coordinating all of that."

Dana pursed her lips. "And the bread pudding?"

Ethan didn't answer. She had made this too personal. Now he owed it to himself to get that recipe figured out.

Dana sighed and picked up the saucer. "It looks like you all are handling things just fine without me."

Ethan touched her arm to keep her from running away. "You know that's not true. Don't do this."

Dana shook her head. "I have an interview tomorrow morning at The Loaf. It's a little trendy for my taste, and I won't be district manager, but I think I'll get the job." Her eyes took on a hurt look. "I'd rather not talk about this again. I'm really trying to put it all behind me."

Ethan nodded. She had made up her mind, and arguing about it would do no good. "What about us?" he asked hopefully. "We were about to get engaged."

Pain danced across Dana's face. She bit her lip, then looked at the floor. "I don't know. I need some time to pray."

She eased away from him and headed back to the living room. She might as well have just said, "It's over." Feeling crushed, Ethan quietly retrieved his coat and gloves and left. He couldn't stand being in the house with her if she wouldn't talk to him.

❧

Dana sat in the parking lot outside The Loaf's regional office. She had aced the interview and would start Monday as the manager of one of the suburban stores in Chesterfield—but did she really want to take this final step away from all she'd worked for at Grady's?

She didn't know. Instead of trying to decide, she took a drive. As though her car were on automatic pilot, she ended up in the Grady headquarters parking lot. From the exterior, everything looked the same as it had been when she'd left. She wondered if things inside were still favorable.

Had Ethan been exaggerating when he'd said they were willing to take her back?

Dana leaned her forehead against the steering wheel and prayed. "Lord, I don't want to go back in there, but I gave the Gradys my word that I would do my best for them. I don't feel right about leaving now, but I don't feel thrilled with the idea of working with Ethan either.

"He's so wasteful and arrogant, Lord. Even though I love him, I don't know if we could really ever be happy together. He has to have his way, even when someone might get hurt.

"I miss him, but he really confused me last week when he stood there and said nothing about his part. Meanwhile, he shut his mouth while Mr. Grady blamed me. I didn't mess things up, Lord. It's not my fault. I'm not the one who needs to have a better attitude. I'm not the one who has the ego problem."

Aren't you?

The thought was startlingly clear. Dana sat up and looked around, convinced someone had spoken the words aloud.

"Am I, Lord? Is it my fault?"

A man's pride brings him low, but a man of lowly spirit gains honor.

The verse was Proverbs 29:23, and she had learned it in high school. Why had it popped into her mind just now?

Dana took a long look at her situation. In all honesty, she had to admit that she felt pretty low right now. Try as she might to blame Ethan, he still had his job, his house, and his dignity. She, on the other hand, had lost these things by storming out of the building in a huff.

Ethan wasn't the only one causing problems. She'd spent time focusing on his ego problems, failing to realize she had her own struggles with pride. She thought she'd overcome it when Ethan's recipes had become such a success, but she'd only been fooling herself. God knew her pride had merely lain dormant, stewing, bubbling, and waiting for a crack in the surface.

Dana had felt bad for Ethan concerning his bread pudding, but the sense of vindication had quickly overtaken any genuine sadness. She had been happy to see Ethan fail for once. She couldn't wait to hear him admit that he'd been wrong. All along, *she'd* been wrong. What difference did it make to her if he never apologized or admitted his attitude had been bad?

She wasn't his judge. The only One who deserved to hear apologies from any human being was God, the Creator of earth and everything on its face and within its depths.

Dana leaned forward again and sobbed. "Oh, God, please forgive me. I've been doing this all wrong. I am not Your instrument to exact correct behavior from other people. Help me to mind my own business, Lord."

Dana remembered one of her mother's favorite phrases. "If everybody really minded his own business, the world would be a much quieter place. We wouldn't have time to do anything else. As far as God is concerned, we have enough personal business to keep us occupied from the day we get here until the day we leave this earth."

Dana never paid attention to this statement before, but now she saw just how accurate her mother had been.

Suddenly, she knew exactly what she needed to do. She would apologize to Mr. Grady and Ethan and get her job back. She'd given her word and wasn't about to go back on it.

Her dignity stung at the thought of the task ahead, but Dana ignored the feeling. It had already gotten her in more than enough trouble.

Chapter 11

"Coming!" Dana ran downstairs to answer the doorbell. She hadn't been expecting any company and was pleasantly surprised to see her mother on the other side of the peephole.

"Hi, Mom." Dana reached out and gave her mom a hug and a quick peck on the cheek. Her mother carried a picnic basket on her arm, and judging from the looks of it, it was heavy. "Is everything okay?"

"It will be when I'm done." Mom headed for the kitchen without even removing her coat. "I brought you breakfast."

Dana hesitated before following. This did not seem like a good sign. The "traveling breakfast buffet," as her siblings had called it, meant Mom was up to something serious. Most likely, her mother had a specific discussion in mind, and Dana wasn't so sure the topic would be an easy one.

When she reached the kitchen, Mom had pulled nearly everything imaginable from that basket. Preserves, bacon, biscuits, fruit, and lots of other little items came from the depths.

Dana's stomach did a little flip-flop. Was she in trouble? Had she done something to upset her mother? Rather than pry and run the risk of making things more difficult, Dana decided she would let Mom take the lead.

Only after they filled their plates and sat down to eat did Mom get down to business.

"You know I'm proud of you for going back to your job, don't you?"

Dana nodded. "That means a lot to me. But I needed to do it. I couldn't just leave them in the lurch."

Mom nodded. "You're a good worker, and they appreciate you. Mrs. Grady told me that just yesterday."

Dana smiled. Hearing second-hand information that her bosses still liked her felt good. In fact, it was a major relief. Mr. Grady had been rather quiet after she'd returned two weeks ago. He was probably trying to figure out what had made her fly off the handle in the first place, but not knowing exactly how he felt still made Dana a little nervous.

"And how is Ethan?"

Aha! Dana held back a smile. The real reason for the breakfast buffet became clear. Her mother wanted to see how things were with Ethan.

Dana picked at her scrambled eggs, choosing her words carefully. "I guess he's doing okay. I see him at work occasionally and at church."

"Your brothers said you and Ethan have stopped dating. Is that true?"

"Basically. It's the only thing we can do right now. Besides, there's a lot going on at work. The new menu is almost in place, but it's still pretty busy around the office."

"How long has it been since you had the falling out with that boy?"

"Three weeks yesterday."

"And you don't mind having your relationship up in the air like this?" Mom prodded.

"Well, it's no picnic, but I can't force him to change. He's too arrogant for his own good and being around him so much makes me act worse. I'm really doing my best to stay away from him."

"Why?"

Dana blinked. "Because it's hard for me to separate my personal feelings from business. I want to, but it's hard."

"Last week you said you were working on your own attitude," reminded Mom. "So I guess you're back to trying to fix him, right?"

Dana winced. Her mother was right: she had slipped into old habits rather quickly. She took a deep breath. "I'll pray about it."

"Good. And maybe you should talk to Ethan."

"Not while he's still gloating about his bread pudding making it into the stores. I, for one, have checked with all three stores, and it isn't selling." Dana sighed deeply. "The whole thing is frustrating."

Mom just nodded. They finished the rest of their breakfast, then washed the dishes. Dana relaxed, realizing she was off the hook now. Her mother had made her point, and Dana didn't have to worry about what might be coming next.

At least it seemed that way. "How about a movie?" asked Mom as she put away the last of the dishes.

"Like what? There's not too much to see at the show lately."

Mom shook her head. "I meant on video. I brought my copy of *Pride and Prejudice*. Do you want to watch it with me?"

Dana didn't particularly feel like watching a movie, but she decided to please her mother. Besides, as long as the movie played, she didn't have to worry about anything else. She might even be able to relax for a few hours.

As she watched, Dana forgot her own problems and became immersed in the plot of the movie. When it ended, Dana and her mother sat on the couch and talked for awhile.

"Dana," said her mother, "I won't try to tell you what to do, but I think you're being a little hard on Ethan."

"I think he went a little hard on me. I feel so betrayed that he would jeopardize our relationship for something so trivial."

"I know, Honey, but nobody's perfect. Think about the movie we just watched. It took Elizabeth and Mr. Darcy awhile to get on the same page, but eventually they did start to understand each other. Both of them had their faults, but they did love each other."

"Mom, you really can't compare real life to a movie," Dana countered. "Besides, if Ethan really wanted to sort this out, he wouldn't be clinging to that silly bread pudding. He would try to understand how I feel."

"I don't want you to get bitter about this. That's why I'm concerned."

Dana smiled. "Thanks, Mom. I promise I won't be bitter about this. I'm trying to work on forgiving him, but for now I need to stay away from him. Otherwise, it just hurts too much."

Mom leaned over and hugged Dana. "Honey, I'm so proud of you. I was concerned about how you were handling all of this, but I feel much better after our talk."

Dana chuckled. Her mother did sometimes have the tendency to go overboard with worry, and Dana felt glad her mother was relieved.

After another half hour of chatting, Mom left to go home.

"When you don't know what else to do, pray," her mother reminded her. "Actually, just pray—even when you think you know what to do. You can never go to the Lord too much."

"I know, Mom. I don't want you fretting about me. If the Lord wants Ethan and me to start our relationship again, He'll let us know."

After Mom left, Dana decided to get outside for a little while. Her mother was right about one thing—she'd spent far too much time closed up in the house. It was mid-March, and spring waited just around the corner.

Dana spent the rest of the day working in her yard, pulling weeds, and digging flowerbeds in preparation for planting in another month or so.

By the time she went in for the day, she was thoroughly exhausted but in good spirits.

❧

Dana's resolve was put to the test the following Monday. As she conducted her progress report at the store Craig managed, she was pleased and relieved to find that business had picked up.

Craig and his employees were also breathing a sigh of relief. "This menu is excellent," he told Dana as she completed her report. "It's fresh, new, and it tastes good. The customers are glad to see something different, but they're also happy that we kept some of the old favorites like the honey oatmeal and the old-fashioned raisin bread."

Dana nodded, pleased to hear that things were going well. "Any suggestions I can take back to Mr. Grady?"

Craig shrugged. "I know I shouldn't say this, but I think we need to ditch that pumpernickel bread pudding. It's a pain to keep warm, and it's just taking up space since it's not selling well."

You don't say? Dana thought. *Why doesn't that surprise me?*

"I could put out more cinnamon rolls in the same space and sell them all before lunch."

Dana made a note of Craig's idea and tried to remain objective. "I'll let Mr. Grady know," she said. It was all she could say to keep the lid on what she really felt about the issue.

"Thanks," Craig agreed. "If you want, I could call Mr. Grady and tell him so myself."

Dana shrugged. "You really don't have to. It's my job to report the managers' concerns back to him, so don't worry about it."

"Hey, don't get offended," Craig told her. "I just thought it might be easier for you." He paused, as if deciding if he should say more. Finally, he added, "Because, you know, there are a lot of rumors going on about you walking out on the company, and everyone's pretty much blaming that chef Mr. Grady hired. We think he's done a great job overall, but we're behind you one hundred percent on this bread pudding thing. It's a total bomb."

Dana felt quite elated that others were on her side as well. They were basing their opinions on what happened in the stores—something Mr. Grady had not yet noticed.

Still, she couldn't get too involved in this issue because she wanted to remain loyal to Mr. Grady. Furthermore, her conscience would be on red alert if she got involved in gossip.

Realizing Craig waited for her answer, Dana smiled and took a deep breath. "Thanks, Craig. Like I said, I'll give this information to Mr. Grady. I know we all have our frustrations, but the company is in a vulnerable position right now, so I think it's best if we all throw our support behind Mr. Grady so we can be united.

"Talking about things behind his back won't really do anything but create a lot of tension, so I can't share my opinion with anyone but him. It's not the easiest thing to do, but it's really best for the company. He'll be paying close attention to sales records for the next few months, so if something just isn't working, he'll notice the figures."

Craig nodded. "Hey, I understand. And I'm not trying to start any trouble or anything. I want this company to get better too."

"Good." Dana peeked back out front where the midday crowd started to pour in. "It looks like we're on the road to recovery," she told him.

❧

Ethan paused outside the door to Dana's office. He could hear her on the phone, talking with one of the suppliers. Apparently, there had been a sudden spike in the price of flour, and Dana wanted to get to the bottom of the matter.

Ethan grinned. That was classic Dana, always frugal, always looking at the bottom line. But she had a soft spot for making people happy, even if it meant spending a few extra dollars here and there.

He lightly rapped on the door, deciding that it would be easier to go in there while she spoke on the phone. They hadn't had a real conversation in the three weeks since she'd come back to work, and he needed to talk to her before it was too late.

She smiled when he entered, and she seemed genuinely pleased to see him. She held up five fingers, indicating she would be off the phone shortly. Ethan waited patiently, trying to decide exactly what he should say to her.

He had completed his assignment, and after the day ended, he would no longer be employed by Grady Bakeries. The menu was in place and doing well in the stores—for the most part. He'd done more work on the bread pudding and felt confident that it would start selling soon. Sometimes things took time, and thankfully, Mr. Grady had offered to give the dish the extra chance that Dana had refused him.

He'd been surprised when she'd quit her job, but he'd been even more amazed that she'd actually come back to work, apologized, and picked up like nothing had ever happened.

Even more admirable was her general attitude about the ordeal. She still avoided one-on-one conversations with him, but she went out of her way to be polite to him. He hadn't heard a single negative comment about the bread pudding escape her lips, and that puzzled him. Actually, it made him nervous. He had the impression that the Lord wanted to show him something, but Ethan wasn't quite ready to listen.

Why could she handle this better than he? If he'd been in her shoes, he'd be inclined to quit and never come back. In the event that he came back, he'd have demanded that his opinion be heard.

Dana hadn't done any of those things. She was obviously very committed to her job and loyal to the Gradys—one of the things that had attracted him to her. Didn't everyone want to fall in love with someone so intensely loyal?

When she got off the phone, she looked at him expectantly. "Hi, Ethan."

"Hi, Dana. How have you been?" He tried to ease into conversation.

She shrugged. "Busy. Very busy, but that's a good thing because it means business is going well."

"Exactly," Ethan agreed.

"Did you need something? I'm not trying to rush you, but I'm scheduled for a business lunch with Mia down in advertising."

"Oh," said Ethan. "I wanted to ask you to lunch with me."

His words seemed to surprise her because she didn't say anything for a long time. "Maybe tomorrow?" she asked. "Would that work for you?"

"Well, no," Ethan told her. "Mr. Grady and I met this morning, and we decided that today will be my last day to work here."

Dana's eyes widened. "Oh? Already?"

He nodded. "Yeah, it looks like things are going well, and I won't be needed unless there's a problem with something."

Dana opened her mouth, then closed it. She sat up straight and clasped her hands together on the desk. He had a feeling she was trying hard to keep from mentioning the bread pudding. Again, her level of self-control amazed him.

"So what happens next for you?" she asked.

"I'm flying back to New York in the morning."

Dana nodded and gave him a tight smile. "Oh. Well, I'll be sad to see you go."

He chuckled. "You don't have to be so mournful. I'm just going to check on some things and take care of business. I'll be back in a week or so."

"Are you. . .still moving here?"

"I think so. I need to look for possible locations and things like that. It's still in the beginning stages, but I'm pretty sure the Lord wants me to stay in St. Louis."

When Dana didn't say anything, he leaned forward. "I've been praying about us. I miss you."

"I miss you too," she said without hesitation. "But where does that put us?"

Ethan sighed. Breaking up might be hard, but making up was plain old confusing. "I guess that's up to us. I still love you, and we have some things to sort out, but I don't think it's impossible."

Dana nodded slowly. "I'm willing to think about it. Why don't you call me when you get back, and we'll talk?"

"Sure." He grinned. "It'd be nice if you'd pick up the phone instead of letting the answering machine do the dirty work. I promise I'll be on my best behavior."

Dana laughed, and Ethan realized how long it had been since he'd really heard her voice, let alone a laugh. This reunion had turned out to be good for both of them.

"If I'm at home, you'll hear my voice and not the machine. I promise."

"I'll call," Ethan repeated as he got up to leave.

"Take care."

Ethan left the building feeling better than he had in weeks. He was eager to visit his parents and sister but sad to be leaving the place he had come to love as home.

His life was going well and would only get better if he could repair his relationship with Dana. For the present, he couldn't do a thing about it besides pray. This was something he'd have to address when he returned.

❧

Dana watched Ethan drive away, her mind taunting her with thoughts of what might have been. Was he really going to come back? Did he really want to continue their relationship?

At least she had managed to keep her mouth shut about the bread pudding.

The more she thought about it, the sillier the whole disagreement seemed. There was no reason why two adults should get so worked up over something so trivial. If they really loved each other, they should be able to forget it and move on. She was ready to. Did Ethan feel the same?

❧

"I'm having a tea for my Sunday school class this Tuesday," Ethan's mother told him. "Do you think you could make a dessert for me?"

Ethan chuckled. He'd been home less than twenty-four hours, and already his mother wanted him to cook something. In her circle of friends, it was a well-known fact that Hannah Miles loved to entertain but hated to cook. Consequently, anytime she held an event in her home, whatever she served was usually prepared by someone else.

"Sure, Mom. What do you want me to make?"

She grinned and pinched his cheek as though he were a baby and not a twenty-nine-year-old man. Ethan did his best to smile. Mothers.

"Make whatever you want, Sweetie. I've been having lemon bars and chicken salad lately, so they'd probably appreciate something different."

Chapter 12

Dana scanned the long hallway, searching for Ethan. She'd volunteered to pick him up from the airport, but to her dismay, she arrived fifteen minutes late. *He's probably wondering if I did this on purpose.* She eased past a group of travelers who had stopped moving, apparently unsure of where to go next.

"Dana!"

She turned around and caught a glimpse of Ethan, waving to get her attention. She returned the wave and began making her way back toward the other end of the terminal.

The terminal at Lambert Field was especially crowded this morning, and as Dana moved through the throngs of people, she imagined herself and Ethan as characters in a movie. She was the heroine, and Ethan was the hero, finally reunited after a long separation. Once they reached each other they would fall into each other's arms, and all would be well.

Predictably, her reunion with Ethan ended up distinctly anticlimactic. There was no falling into one another's arms. Ethan shifted his luggage to his other shoulder and said, "Hi."

"Hi. Sorry I'm late. I got caught in traffic."

"That's okay," he assured her. "I just finished claiming my bags, so it worked out fine."

"So where do I need to take you?"

"My condo. The lease is about to run out, and I need to sign a new one."

This certainly seemed like encouraging news. "So you are staying?"

"Let's walk and talk," Ethan suggested.

"Can I carry something?"

"No, it's not that heavy. Which lot are you in?"

"Follow me," Dana said.

"To answer your question, I am staying. You didn't think I would come back?"

Dana smiled. "Not really. I figured once you got back to New York, you would decide you really preferred to be there."

"No way. I like too many things about this place." He gave her a meaningful look. "I'm here to stay."

They were silent for the remainder of the trek to the car, and Dana tried to think of some way to fill in the awkward gap in conversation. They were sidestepping the real issue, but she didn't want to bring it up and run the risk of sounding pushy.

"Have you had lunch yet?" Ethan asked.

"No. How about you?"

Ethan shrugged. "Plane food, but that's about it. Do you want to stop somewhere?"

"Okay. I need to get back to work in a couple of hours, but I haven't left the office for lunch all week."

"If they need you, they have your pager number," Ethan said. "On second thought, you keep everything running so well, they probably don't even notice you're gone."

Dana lifted her eyebrows. "I hope that's a compliment. It almost sounds like you're saying they don't need me."

Ethan laughed. "You know good and well that's a compliment. You really are good at your job."

Dana smiled at him. She could get used to his praise. "Okay, Ethan, you don't have to flatter me. I think we both want to pick up where we left off, so there's no need to try and butter me up."

Ethan actually looked hurt, and Dana wanted to take the words back. Maybe he'd actually been saying those things just to be nice.

She sighed. "You know what? I'm making a mess of this. I don't know if you feel this too, but I'm just at a loss for words ever since. . .you know."

Ethan nodded. "Yeah, it's almost like we don't know how to talk to each other anymore."

Dana felt relieved. "At least I'm not the only one who feels like that."

"I'm sorry about my attitude," Ethan said. "I've been trying to justify how I acted, and the Lord isn't letting me get away with it."

Dana nodded, willing herself to be quiet so she wouldn't say something to get herself in trouble. Although she felt like asking if he still thought his bread pudding should remain in the stores, her conscience prevented her from doing so.

"So will you forgive me?"

"I've already forgiven you, Ethan. I know I've been avoiding you, but it's only because I've been working on my own struggles. I tried to hide it, but every time one of your recipes passed the survey test, it was hard for me. I guess my idea of what the customers wanted was pretty different from what they ended up liking."

"You were right about a lot of things. Remember, several of the recipes went back to the test kitchen for extra work."

Dana pulled the car into the lot of a small restaurant. "Is soup okay with you?"

"I don't really have a preference. But before we go in, I want to make sure everything is back to normal."

Dana shook her head. "No, we can't go back to normal. Because if I go back to the way I used to be, I'll still have the same problems. We have to grow and change all throughout our lives. Sometimes going back to the old way is comfortable but not necessarily the right thing to do."

Ethan nodded quietly. "I guess that's what I meant. I'm changing too. I can't promise that I won't get on your nerves sometimes or that I'll always say or do the right thing. But I have been working on some things lately. I don't want to ruin this relationship again."

Dana was pleased to hear him say that. Looking back, she could see they both had come a long way.

"Tell me, Dana, are you willing to continue this relationship? I still love you."

She bit her lip, hesitating. On the one hand, she was happy Ethan still loved her, but she didn't feel entirely comfortable picking up where they had left off. They almost needed to be reacquainted.

Ethan picked up on her silence and reached out for her hand. "Dana, you have to tell me what's wrong. Is it the list? Am I not close enough to your ideal?"

Dana blinked. How did he know about that? "What?" she asked him.

Ethan looked chagrined, and she realized he hadn't meant to let her know that he knew.

"How do you know about the list?" she questioned again.

"Well. . .I wasn't supposed to tell you."

"You're not even supposed to know I had written one. The least you can do is tell me how you heard about it."

"Your brothers. We were talking one day, they mentioned it, and I got them to tell me the whole story. I worried that you weren't very serious about me, and they made some jokes about your ideal."

"Oh." Dana paused, thinking. She didn't even have to ask to know that Albert and Anthony were in on this. They would be the main culprits. She wondered exactly what they had said.

"So exactly what did they tell you?"

"Do I have to answer that?"

"Yes," she said. When he didn't reply immediately, she poked him in the arm with her finger. "I'm waiting." Ethan looked so embarrassed, she felt like laughing.

"They didn't really go into specifics, but they told me that your notions were pretty confusing. They told me you wanted to marry somebody like Mr. Darcy from *Pride and Prejudice.*"

"They what?" Her brothers certainly had managed to confuse things. "I never said that. I never even wrote that. I have no idea where they got such a crazy idea."

Ethan shrugged. "Maybe they didn't understand the list."

Obviously, they hadn't. "You can say that again. I liked some qualities in Mr. Darcy, but I would never be happy to end up with someone exactly like him. At least, not the way he acted early in the book. I wanted a husband who could be sweet and kind, but I need him to be strong and a good leader. He would be. . ." Dana trailed off. Ethan was hanging onto her every word, and she didn't want to contribute to this mess any further. "Never mind. The fact is, I outgrew the list.

It doesn't make any difference anymore."

Ethan grinned. "You're sure about that?"

"Positive," Dana said emphatically. "It's not about a list; it's about who God knows I'll be happy with. If I met a guy who had every quality I ever dreamed of, I'd still have to make sure God wanted us to be together. If He said no, my plans would not have done me a bit of good."

"So if Mr. Darcy came knocking on your door one morning, you'd turn him away."

Dana grinned. "Well, let's not be so hasty. I'd at least let him come in and have some tea."

Ethan laughed. "Aha! What happened to the prayer?"

"I'd pray while I made the tea," Dana said in her defense. "I couldn't just let Mr. Darcy himself get away."

"Yeah, I'll bet. Somehow, that doesn't surprise me."

"Laugh all you want." Dana opened the car door. "But I'm going in to get some soup. You can either sit out here and make jokes about Mr. Darcy, or you can come in and have lunch with me."

Ethan followed. "I'll come inside. We can always talk about Mr. Darcy later." He continued laughing as they entered the restaurant.

Dana shook her head. Her brothers were going to have some serious explaining to do for divulging her silly high school secrets like that.

❧

The next day, Mr. Grady stopped in Dana's office early one morning and said, "It's time to do the award for Manager of the Year. The annual employee appreciation dinner is in two weeks."

"Wow, time has really flown by this year," said Dana "Who's the lucky manager?"

"Kim Penn. She has an excellent work ethic, and her employees are so productive. She really knows how to get the best out of people." He shrugged. "She's a lot like you."

Dana smiled. She was so thankful that Mr. Grady had forgiven her for her outburst. He had apologized for overreacting but stood firm in his decision to support Ethan's bread pudding until it could be determined whether or not it would eventually be productive in terms of sales.

"What do you think? Will Kim be excited?"

Dana grinned. "She'll be thrilled." Kim had spent the entire year going after this award. Of course, it wasn't exactly a major distinction in terms of the outside world, but within the Grady Company, the achievement was greatly respected.

"So you'll see to it that the certificate is drawn up?"

"Of course," said Dana.

"I also have more news," he said, taking a seat. "I got a call from Ethan this morning. He got back in town yesterday."

Dana nodded. "Yes, we had lunch together."

Mr. Grady smiled approvingly. "We had a long talk, and I thought you'd be interested in knowing that he's asked me to remove the pumpernickel bread pudding from the menu."

Dana was shocked. "He what?"

Mr. Grady shook his head. "He's asked me to remove it from the menu. He says he hasn't worked with it enough and doesn't think it's a good fit for our stores."

Dana tried to find her voice. She had to be careful not to gloat. "Well, Sir, if that's the way he feels. . ."

Mr. Grady laughed. "Dana, you don't have to pretend with me. I've been hearing from customers, managers, and my wife about the dish. I've been watching the sales records, and to tell you the truth, I'm relieved he called me. You were right; it was an unwise use of time, money, and display space. I planned to call him next week and tell him we needed to pull it."

Mr. Grady stood up. "You've got a good head on your shoulders, and I'm proud to have you working for us. Thanks so much for sticking it out with us, even when you were unhappy with me."

He shook his head. "I guess we all make our mistakes, and I just got so thrilled to be mentioned in *Restaurant Owner* that I took leave of my senses for awhile. Thanks for cutting me and Ethan some slack."

Tears came to Dana's eyes. "Thank you, Mr. Grady. It's really been an honor to work for you, and I look forward to many more years of the same."

Mr. Grady shook his head and waved her comment away. "Nonsense. I know pretty soon Ethan will want you working at his restaurant—especially since you two plan to get married. We'll be sorry to see you go, but we'll send you off with our best wishes." He turned and left the room before she could even answer him.

Dana sat at her desk, thinking about several things. First, she was thankful Ethan had been brave enough to pull his recipe. She still felt curious about what had prompted the decision, but there was no way she would pry into his business.

The second thing that puzzled her was Mr. Grady's remark about her getting married. While they had talked about marriage since Ethan's return, he still had yet to propose to her.

Could he be planning something? Dana smiled, wondering how he would try to surprise her.

Before she could get too wrapped up in her own thoughts, Dana remembered her promise to Mr. Grady to take care of Kim's award. She needed to have a certificate done, along with a plaque with Kim's name engraved on it.

She made a call to Betty, who was in charge of all employee records, and asked to have something with Kim's name on it sent to her office. The last thing she wanted to do was have Kim's name misspelled on the award.

Twenty minutes later, Betty delivered a piece of paper with Kim's name on it. At least it was supposed to be Kim's name. According to this paper, Kim's full name was Kimetra F. Penn.

Dana stared at the sheet. Kimetra? And what did the "F" stand for? Remembering that Kim wasn't particularly fond of her middle name put Dana in a dilemma. Would Kim want the plaque to read Kim or Kimetra? Would she want the middle initial totally omitted, or would she prefer it remain there since it was a special award?

The more Dana thought about it, the more confusing it became.

Finally, she decided to give Kim a call. She might have to give away the surprise about the award, but she would rather let the cat out of the bag than put the wrong name on the plaque. She dialed the number to Kim's office. Kim picked up on the third ring.

"Hi, it's Dana," she said.

"Hi, Dana. I'm surprised you caught me at my desk. You wouldn't believe the crowd we've had this morning."

"Excellent," said Dana. "That's good news."

"No kidding," Kim agreed. "There was a time I thought I'd go nuts if I heard another customer complain that his sandwich was all wrong, but I'll tell you, after some of the slow days we had during our slump, customer noise is music to my ears."

Dana laughed. "I won't keep you long, but it's come to my attention that your full name is Kimetra F. Penn."

Kim didn't say a word.

"Hello? Kim, are you still there?"

"Dana, who told you that?"

"Actually, I had Betty look up your file—"

Kim inhaled sharply, then interrupted her. "Dana, I can't believe you went snooping in the files to see if you could find my middle name. I'm actually pretty offended right now."

"Kim, please hear me out. I would never do that, and I can't go into details because you're not supposed to know this yet, but I needed to know the correct spelling of your name for something concerning work."

"What?"

"When I saw your name here in the file, I realized you probably didn't want your entire name on this work-related thing, so I called you to check on your preference."

Kim didn't speak for several moments, then she let out a squeal. "Oh, you're kidding! I'm Manager of the Year? Is that it?"

"I'm not allowed to tell you that, but I do need to know your name preference. And I'm pretty curious as to what that 'F' stands for."

Kim squealed again. "You know what, Dana? You have made my day. And if you have them put plain old K-i-m P-e-n-n on my plaque, I will be eternally grateful."

Dana decided to tease her friend a bit. "Exactly how grateful?"

Kim groaned. "I'll tell you my middle name if you promise never to reveal it."

Dana smiled. "Really? I was just kidding, you know."

"I know I don't have to tell you, but I'm in a pretty good mood. First, I will warn you that I have no idea what my parents were thinking."

Dana shrugged. "It can't be that bad."

"Yes, it can. They wanted to pick something that flowed into my last name, so they figured the perfect choice of a middle name was. . ."

Silence sounded from the other end. "Come on, Kim, you can't change your mind now. I'm hanging on your every word."

"Hold your horses, Dana. I was checking outside the door to make sure no one is listening."

"Oh. So what is it?"

"Fountain."

"Fountain? That's not so bad."

"Could you a be a little quieter, Dana? You don't have to go tell it on the mountain."

"I'm not talking that loud," Dana protested. Suddenly, the effect of Kim's full name sank in. "Fountain Penn?" Dana felt an attack of the giggles coming on, but for Kim's sake, she held them back.

"Yeah," Kim grumbled. "Kimetra Fountain Penn. They thought it sounded graceful."

"Wow," was all Dana could say without bursting into laughter.

"Listen, Dana, I've got a crowd out front. Don't ever mention this again, and please make sure there is no hint of my full name on the plaque. Got it?"

"Got it," Dana agreed. "And don't worry; my lips are sealed."

"They'd better be," Kim warned playfully. "And I'm sorry for overreacting earlier. I should have realized you wouldn't try to embarrass me on purpose. I'll talk to you later."

As soon as Dana hung up the phone, the giggles escaped. She couldn't believe Kim's middle name was actually Fountain. Talk about parents with a sense of humor!

Still, she felt glad her own parents hadn't opted to give her such an unusual middle name. Plain old Marie worked fine for her.

As she wrote Kim's name preference on a sheet of paper to send to the engravers, she started laughing all over again.

"Did I miss a joke?"

Dana would know that voice anywhere. She glanced up to find Ethan standing in her doorway.

"Hey, what brings you here this morning?"

He shrugged. "I had something I needed to do." Taking a step closer, he asked, "So what is so funny?"

Dana shook her head. "Just something Kim told me. Mr. Grady came in a little earlier." He nodded, and Dana chose her next words very carefully. "That was really understanding of you to pull the bread pudding. I know how much it meant to you."

Ethan sat in the chair in front of her desk. "You don't have to pretend I'm that gallant. The truth is, I convinced myself you hated that recipe because you don't like pumpernickel. When I went home, I made it for my mom's Sunday school tea. That's when I realized it wasn't working.

"Nobody wanted to be rude, so after everyone tasted it, my mom said they all suddenly remembered they were allergic to one of the ingredients. And my mom, who likes everything I make, confessed she had to force herself to swallow the one bite she tasted.

"She sent me to the store to buy some shortbread cookies, and by the time I got back, all traces of that dish had disappeared. My mom threw the entire thing out." Ethan shook his head. "She said she couldn't pin down any one flavor, and it seemed too complicated."

Dana smiled. "I'm glad she was honest with you."

"So am I," Ethan agreed. "I guess I had been a little egotistical because no one has ever flat out said that something I made tasted horrible." Shrugging, he added, "I guess there's a first time for everything."

"We all mess up sometimes," Dana said, trying to console him. He still seemed a little miffed, and she didn't want to rub his nose in it.

"I told my mom what had happened with us, and she gave me a piece of her mind. She sent me back with her own apologies that you had to put up with me."

Dana nodded. She could remember days in the not-so-distant past when she couldn't wait for Ethan to see the extent of his wrongs. Now that he had and was genuinely sorry, it hurt to see how badly he felt.

"Ethan, really, it's all been forgiven. I mean that. So how about putting this chapter behind us? I mean, we can't say we'll never make mistakes again, but at least we won't repeat this whole fiasco."

"I like the sound of that," said Ethan.

"We've both had our problems with pride, but we're working on getting our noses out of the air."

"Right. And we'll put the pumpernickel behind us too," said Ethan.

"You don't know how much I appreciate that." Dana laughed. "Who would have ever guessed bread pudding would cause such a ruckus?"

"Now that we've left pride and pumpernickel in the past, I want to talk about our future," said Ethan.

He got out of his chair and came around to her side of the desk. He stood awkwardly next to her for several moments, then dropped down to one knee.

Dana instantly knew what he would say, and this time she was ready. Ethan wasn't the perfect man, but she wasn't the perfect woman. With God's grace, they would be able to see past their differences.

Thank You Lord, for sending Ethan to me. Who needs Mr. Darcy, anyway?

Ethan reached for her hand and cleared his throat. "Okay, I'm going to warn you beforehand that I won't be able to do this as well as Mr. Darcy, but I will get straight to the point.

"I love you, Dana Marie Edwards. And I know I've caused some problems by being stubborn, but like you said, we've put all that behind us. That said. . ." He paused and reached into his pocket and pulled out a small jewelry box. "I'd be honored if we can move forward with our lives together. Would you marry me?"

Tears came to Dana's eyes, even as she thought of all the times she had promised herself she would not cry when her future husband proposed to her. She fanned her eyes with her free hand trying to stop the tears before they started rolling down her cheeks.

"I will," she said and hugged Ethan.

In the midst of her tears, she noticed the sheet of paper with Kim's name on it. Kim's advice about marriage trivia popped into her head, and Dana chuckled. Pulling away from Ethan, she cleared her throat. Trying to sound serious, she said, "Wait a minute. Before I can commit to this, I need to know something."

Ethan looked puzzled. "You're changing your mind?"

"It depends. . . ," she said mysteriously.

"On what?" The look on his face was priceless, a mixture of panic and confusion.

Doing her best to keep a straight face, she said, "I have to know your middle name."

Ethan shook his head. "You don't want to know my middle name."

Dana couldn't believe he was actually trying to get out of the question. It was so simple, and after all, he knew her middle name. "Yes, I do, Mr. Ethan D. Miles."

He sighed. "Fine. Did I ever tell you how much my mother liked *Pride and Prejudice?*"

Dana nodded. "I remember you saying that once or twice."

"Well, she really. . .really liked it."

"You're changing the subject. Now tell me your middle name. I demand to know."

Ethan leaned closer to her until his face was inches away from hers. He leaned forward a bit more, and Dana knew he would kiss her.

She moved away, shaking her head. "No. No middle name, no kiss," she laughed.

Ethan groaned. "I can't believe you're making me tell you." He put his arms around her again. "Ethan Darcy Miles."

Dana blinked. "Did you say. . .Darcy?"

Ethan nodded. "It's a horrible name for any little boy, especially when you're in the third grade and some of the older kids start teasing you about it. We will never give that name to any of our children."

Dana giggled, but Ethan shook his head. "Furthermore, I have guarded this name for years, and no one outside of my immediate family knows what the D. in my name stands for."

"I won't tell," Dana grumbled. This was too good to be true. She was in the arms of her own living, breathing Mr. Darcy.

Ethan shook his head. "That's not good enough. Since you know my secret, you have no choice but to marry me now."

As he leaned in to kiss her, Dana answered, "Gladly. . .Mr. Darcy."

WHOLE
IN ONE

Dedicated to Mike and Aya Ford,
my dad and sister. . .
who patiently answered all of my golf-related questions.
I love you both!

Chapter 1

Evette Howard brushed a stray curl away from her forehead and shoved it back into her ponytail. The sticky feeling from the heat and humidity was so bad that it almost took the fun out of practice. Almost.

She found it amazing that late April weather in St. Louis could get so warm. Still, given her family's line of business, she would take hot temperatures over cold any day of the week. The cooler the climate, the less likely people would be to go out and do anything related to golf.

Evette removed another ball from the bucket and positioned it on the tee. As she began her preshot routine, a soothing breeze rushed through, easing the intense heat for several moments.

As she prepared to hit the ball, her brother Craig's voice rang out over the intercom. "Evette, we need you inside, ASAP."

Taking a deep breath, Evette nodded and quickly hit the ball. She peeled off her glove, attached it to her bag, and replaced the driver. After counting her clubs to ensure she didn't leave one behind, Evette swung the bag over her shoulder and carried the bucket of balls inside the pro shop, where her dad and three brothers waited.

"Sorry to interrupt," said her dad. "Craig and Drew are supposed to go on lunch break, and Trevor and I have lessons to teach. We need you inside to watch the shop for a couple of hours."

"No problem. It's a little warm out there anyway. This air feels good."

"How'd you do?" asked Drew.

Evette shrugged. "Pretty well, I guess. Only got about halfway through, so I might hit more later. I wanted to put in a little time before I start lessons at three."

"Looks like my student is here," Trevor said, noticing that a car had just pulled up outside.

"I think I'll head out to the range and hit a few balls until Roger Stenson comes for his lesson," said her dad. "Are you ready to take over in here? Things shouldn't get too busy at this time of the day."

"I'll be fine. Just let me run to the ladies' room and freshen up." Evette headed off to splash a little cool water on her face, apply some perfume, and put on a touch of powder and lipstick. She didn't mind getting hot and sweaty out on the driving range, but she didn't want to mind the shop looking disheveled.

After her father and brothers left to teach their lessons and take lunch breaks, three customers entered the store in rapid succession. Two men wanted to try out different putters, and Evette pointed them in the right direction.

Then she spent time helping a woman on a mission find a birthday present for her husband. This proved to be a trying experience as the woman had no idea what he would like. After fifteen minutes of suggesting items ranging from golf balls to divot repair tools to a nice shirt, Evette convinced her to purchase a gift certificate in order to let her husband pick what he'd like.

She'd settled into her cove behind the desk to read over the latest industry magazines when the bell on the door jangled, announcing the entrance of another customer.

Evette instantly recognized him as Anthony Edwards, a member of the sizable Edwards clan who attended the same church she did. He had a twin brother named Albert, and both men were identically handsome. They shared the same height, muscular build, close-shaved haircuts, and skin the color of suntanned honey. The only reason Evette could tell them apart was because Anthony sported a small scar over his left eyebrow, a casualty of an accident during a game of touch football at a church outing a few years back.

As far as she knew, neither one of the brothers golfed. In the twelve years her family had operated the golf center, she couldn't recall either of them taking lessons or even stopping by the store to purchase golfing paraphernalia.

Anthony stood inside the doorway, apparently looking for something or someone.

Evette gave him a polite smile and asked if she could help him find something in particular. "You're Anthony Edwards, right? We go to the same church."

He nodded and moved a step closer. "And you're—Eve, right?"

"Evette," she corrected. "But when I was younger, everybody called me Eve."

"You used to be in the youth group, right? That's probably why I remembered you as Eve." He hesitated a moment, then said, "You know, it's been awhile since I've seen you at any of the activities or meetings."

Evette bit her lip, not sure what to say. She felt so uncomfortable whenever anyone asked why she was no longer involved in church activities. Going to Sunday morning service was about all the religion she could stand for a week. "I guess after I went away to college, I got out of the habit of going more than once a week."

Anthony looked thoughtful. "If you get the chance, you should come to Sunday school sometime or maybe to one of the singles' get-togethers. We have a regular group of almost twenty people."

Evette wrinkled her nose and gave a noncommittal shrug. Through occasional conversations with people from church, Evette gathered that Anthony was Mr. Church himself, always seeming to have his hand in some committee or other. From the youth basketball team to the choir and the church beautification committee, the man apparently loved being involved. "Maybe. We'll see."

An awkward moment passed between them, and Evette realized the look on her face suggested she had no plans of getting more involved. Anthony probably thought her a terrible heathen. She could almost see his wheels spinning, as he imagined some way to win her back into the fold. Weren't church people all the same?

He opened his mouth, and Evette braced herself for a sermon, feeling a twinge of frustration. Why couldn't people mind their own business? Wasn't it enough that she dragged herself out of bed early every Sunday morning and faithfully gave her tithes and offering every two weeks like clockwork? She always dressed appropriately, smiled at the pastor and his wife, and returned any hugs she received, especially from the elderly church mothers.

When Anthony spoke, he didn't mention church. "You're engaged to—Justin—Justin somebody, right?"

Evette swallowed hard. Even hearing his name still sometimes brought on a sick feeling in the pit of her stomach. "Justin Greene."

"That's right. I haven't seen him around, but he went out for the pro golfing tour, didn't he? How's he doing? You two set a date yet?"

Evette didn't know which of Anthony's rapid-fire questions to answer first. Ignoring the bad taste in her mouth, she cleared her throat and managed to put together a string of answers. "We're not engaged anymore. He did go out for the tour, and he's doing okay. Still on the semiprofessional circuit, trying to win enough money to get his membership card for the PGA—you know, the Professional Golfer's Association." Before Anthony had a chance to reply, Evette hurriedly changed the subject. "So—you must have come in here for a reason, and I'd hate to waste your time with chitchat. How can I help you?"

Anthony blinked, and Evette realized her transition to the next topic must have seemed abrupt. She felt a bit embarrassed, but she hadn't been in the mood to go into further detail.

Anthony moved on, seemingly giving the incident no further thought. "Actually I talked to Craig on Sunday about some golf lessons. He told me to come in and sign up."

Evette breathed a sigh of relief. This she could handle. "I didn't know you played golf."

"I don't. I can hit the ball a little, but not much more than that. I played with my sister's fiancé last week and totally embarrassed myself. This fall he wants to get all of his groomsmen out on the course the week of the wedding, and I need to have some skills by then."

Evette smiled, holding back the urge to laugh. It was no secret that Anthony excelled in whatever he played, from basketball, to volleyball, to football, and she could well imagine how he might have been irked to find he couldn't master the links in one afternoon. "I see. Well, Craig's on lunch break now, but if you want to leave your number, he'll be back in an hour or so, and I'll have him call you."

"How about I just come back later today?"

"That's fine. I'll tell him you came in."

"Thanks—I appreciate it." Anthony turned and headed toward the door then paused. "And don't forget—you said you'd think about coming to church more."

Evette pasted a smile on her face. The man did not give up. "I'll think about it."

The phone rang, ending Anthony's inquiries about her church attendance. He flashed a grin, then left without another word.

Evette decided to find a reason not to be in the store when Anthony returned.

❧

Anthony stared at the blank screen on his laptop. He needed to write the third installment of his weekly sports commentary for the newspaper, but he couldn't stop thinking about Evette.

At one time, several years ago, they'd been friends—or at least acquaintances. They were the same age and had been active in the church youth group in high school. They'd both gone to college here in St. Louis, but Evette's involvement at church had dropped off drastically over the past several years. She now put in an appearance only on Sundays.

Anthony wondered why she seemed to have such a distasteful attitude toward church. It made his heart twinge when he realized longtime acquaintances had slipped away from the church family without his noticing. Evette wasn't the first person he'd known to fade into the shadows. Nevertheless, he'd seen this scenario enough times to realize Evette most likely teetered on the brink of leaving and not ever looking back. Sure, she came faithfully once a week, but her habit was to slip in just before the service began and leave as soon as the benediction ended.

Her parents and brothers came every week as well, but none of them seemed to be involved in any further fellowship. Anthony didn't think being involved in church fellowship was mandatory, but he'd noted many who didn't get involved seemed much more likely to leave or attend more and more sporadically.

He'd been the same during his youth. In high school, going to church and being a part of the youth group had simply been a way to meet girls whom his parents would approve of his dating. And he supposed that if Evette hadn't been involved in such a serious relationship with Justin, he might have put more time into getting to know her.

In fact, if she hadn't had a boyfriend, he had no doubt he would have pursued her. She had a beautiful smile—when she smiled—and her complexion gave off an almost rosy glow. Her skin was the same color as his, maybe a shade lighter, and her hair fell to her shoulders in a thick mass of tiny gold and bronze ringlets.

For a woman she stood tall—at least five-ten, give or take an inch. With three brothers as her only siblings, she'd spent a lot of time outdoors, playing sports. While she had been on the skinny side back in high school, her figure was now healthy and athletic—not curvy and by no means willowy, but muscularly toned and strong.

Yes, if Evette and Justin hadn't been an item, Anthony knew he would have talked to her a lot more. But he hadn't, preferring to spend the bulk of his time with girls who were unattached and, therefore, had potential as girlfriends.

Anthony grimaced, remembering that phase of his life. He'd done his share of meeting and greeting and, ultimately, dating, keeping his social calendar full throughout high school and most of college. Yet, when he looked back at those years, he considered all of that mingling almost a waste of time.

At twenty-nine years old and striding down the corridor to thirty, he remained single, with no prospects in mind for a wife. Now that his baby sister, Dana, was engaged, his family turned their attention to the still-single twins: his brother, Albert, and him. The two of them had vowed to stand together and fight any attempts to make them panic at the thought of becoming permanent bachelors. It was a good plan—they were able to encourage each other if one of them felt a little impatient.

But Albert had been spending more and more time with Brienne Miller, a young woman who had recently joined the church. Anthony could already tell from the look in Albert's eye and the new bounce in his step that his brother found this girl pretty special.

So much for standing together. Anthony was on his own, with a bull's eye on his back that marked him as the last single person in his family.

Returning his attention to his computer, Anthony halfheartedly pecked out a few more sentences, but his thoughts were not on his work. He kept wondering what he might have done to keep Evette a part of the church family. If only he hadn't been so shallow about the manner in which he'd picked his friends. His mother would say there was no use in thinking about "what-ifs," and Anthony usually agreed. But he saw something in Evette's eyes to suggest that her outer demeanor of indifference didn't exactly line up with her true emotions.

With a sigh Anthony closed his word-processing program and shut down his computer. If his thoughts were correct, he wanted to do something about it.

Chapter 2

W hat do you mean, you can't take any more students?"

Craig gave Evette one of his I'm-the-big-brother looks. "I mean, I can't take any more students."

"But, but you—"

Craig put down the inventory sheet he was holding. "But what?"

"You told Anthony Edwards you would give him lessons."

"So? Why are you concerned about me teaching Anthony?"

Evette watched her brother's lips turn up at the corners. Oh, great. He had shifted to his teasing mode.

"Now." Craig folded the newspaper and laid it aside. "Are you sure you're telling me everything? How is it that my sister, who usually could care less about most people at church, has an unusual interest in the fact that some guy from there wants a golf lesson?"

Evette gave her brother a no-nonsense stare. "Don't tease me. You know good and well I don't care anything about him personally. But I do think it makes our business look bad with you telling him to come in for lessons, all the while knowing you can't take on another student."

"I never told him I would teach his lessons. Correct me if I'm wrong, but you, Dad, Trevor, Drew, and I all teach golf. We'll get your young man some lessons." Craig patted her on the head in a fatherly fashion, something he'd done for as long as she could remember.

Evette decided to ignore the "your young man" comment. Craig *wanted* her to jump on it, and twenty-six years of being a little sister had taught her to leave certain comments alone. "Okay, then. Who?"

"Who, what?" Craig looked mildly amused.

"Who's going to teach him? Trevor works with the youth camps all summer, so he can't take regular students. And Dad and Drew have full student loads, like you."

"So you can teach him. You've got at least six or seven slots open for new students, don't you?"

Evette sat on the chair behind the register. "True. But, in case you've forgotten, we've tried this route before. I teach all of the women who want lessons because men don't want to learn golf from a woman."

Craig sighed deeply, a sign he had tired of this topic. "Then Anthony will be the first. Besides, you're a better golfer than Trevor and Dad, and your teacher skills are better than Drew's. Any student of yours should be honored to have such a good instructor."

Evette basked in the glow of this uncharacteristic compliment from the brother who didn't waste accolades on undeserving recipients. "Really? Do you think so?"

"I know so." Craig picked up the newspaper again, a sign he was finished with the conversation.

"You didn't mention yourself in that group."

Craig looked up from his paper. "What?"

"You mentioned everyone but yourself. So where do I stack up compared to you?"

Craig leaned back and let out a hearty laugh. "You've got to go a ways to beat me, Little Bit."

Evette groaned at the use of his childhood nickname for her. "Oh, please."

"Please what?" he asked, looking wide-eyed at her.

Evette glanced out of the front window and noticed that Anthony had returned, as promised. Smiling sweetly at Craig, she said, "Please tell Anthony why you're not going to be his teacher." She paused, then added, "I take it you explain things better than I do too."

Craig chuckled. "Whatever you say, Little Bit."

Evette picked up a box of raincoats. "Don't call me Little Bit in front of our customers. I'll be in the clothing section if you need me." Without glancing back she headed to the corner of the store where they displayed the golf attire. She was close enough to hear the conversation at the register but far enough away so she wouldn't have to contribute anything to it.

While she worked, Evette alternately listened to her brother and Anthony, then fumed about why she had to be the one to teach him. She had never, ever taught a man how to play golf. And she had a feeling that a guy as into sports as Anthony would not take kindly to a woman as his golf instructor.

She smoothed the wrinkles from a lightweight jacket and slipped it on a hanger.

"So I've signed you up to take lessons from Evette. I know you wanted to take from me, but we've had a big jump in our enrollment since I talked to you last week. I'm putting you in good hands. She's an excellent golfer and an even better teacher. If you're willing to pay attention and do what she says, you'll learn the game well."

Evette turned her head toward the two men and held her breath waiting for Anthony to answer.

"No problem. I'm ready." Anthony shook his head. "I'll tell you one thing. This game is a lot harder than I thought it would be."

Evette exhaled, her impression of Anthony growing more favorable by the moment. Any other time Craig had tried to assign her to a man, things hadn't gone well. One middle-aged gentleman had actually stomped his foot and started yelling for the manager when she stepped out on the range and informed him she was his teacher. Craig had come outside then and used his negotiation skills on the man to no avail. Eventually he ended up transferring one of Trevor's younger students to Evette's roster to appease the irritated customer. Even that hadn't worked out smoothly. The boy Evette inherited from Trevor was only thirteen years old and resented the fact that he had to learn golf from a "girl." Evette could still remember the way he said *girl* with such disdain.

"Evette," called Craig, "could you please come over here and schedule Anthony?"

Evette set the box down with a sigh. Craig knew full well her available class times were in the book, next to the time-table of classes and teachers. Calling her over to do it herself was his brotherly way of getting under her skin. Before she could point out that Craig could have done this on his own, Anthony spoke up.

"Hey, sorry to interrupt your work."

His grin disarmed her, and Evette returned the smile as she rummaged through the desk for a pen. "That's okay. I hate folding clothes anyway."

"I'll finish up the display," Craig said, heading off to the opposite end of the store.

Evette curiously watched her brother's retreating form. Funny how he was so eager to leave the scene. If she'd been dealing with Drew or Trevor, she might have suspected the matchmaking virus. Craig was different—the ever practical sibling who usually left such silliness to the younger ones. Still, he did nothing without thinking the matter through from top to bottom and side to side. Though she wasn't sure why, he definitely seemed to be up to something.

But she didn't have time to think about it now since Anthony was waiting to settle his lesson time.

"Did Craig go over the rates yet?"

Anthony nodded. "Yeah. And we decided I should start with three classes a week."

Evette blinked. "Three?" Now she knew without a doubt Craig was up to something. The most they ever suggested for beginners was twice a week. More than two lessons would be too intense for someone simply trying to learn the game for recreational purposes.

Anthony leaned forward, craning his neck to get a look at the grid of open class times. "Do you have enough time for three?"

Evette tapped the pen against the desk, thinking. "No, that's not it. I just think three lessons per week might be too much to begin with. You don't want to get overwhelmed. I think once or twice would be better."

Anthony looked disappointed. "Are you sure? I mean, I really want to have this down by the time the wedding rolls around."

Evette couldn't hold back a laugh. "I can't promise you'll be a good golfer even if you take two classes a day every day until then. But if you want to come to the driving range on days you don't have a lesson, that might work well for you."

"Fine. Let's get this started. What days can I come?"

"I'll try to work around your schedule," Evette told him. "You're a sportswriter, right? So if you report on a game, you wouldn't be able to have class that evening."

Anthony frowned. "You're right. Does that mess things up?"

"No, not really. What we'll do is set your times at the beginning of the week to make sure you don't have a conflict."

"Fine with me. Can we start tomorrow?"

"Sure. How about five-thirty?"

"Good for me. An hour?"

"Correct." Evette marked Anthony down for the agreed-upon time.

"Good. I'll still have plenty of time to get to Bible study."

Bible study. Evette willed herself not to look up from the notebook.

"You know, if you don't have other plans, you might like to come along with me."

Evette blew out the breath she'd been holding. "I think I'll pass. I usually work on my own game after I'm finished teaching."

Anthony nodded. "Okay. See you tomorrow."

"Tomorrow," said Evette, her stomach already twisting with dread.

While she had been relieved to hear he didn't mind her as a teacher, she'd let her guard down. She'd been willing to believe his attitude suggested he might be interested in her.

What a joke. She now realized he must see her as some type of evangelism project. He hadn't even waited until his first class to invite her to a church function.

As soon as Anthony was out the door, Evette stalked over to Craig, who was nonchalantly folding polo shirts in the corner.

"You set things up?"

"Don't play innocent with me. Why did you tell him he needed three lessons a week?"

Evette put her hands on her hips and summoned her most effective glare.

"What's wrong with you? He's the one who wanted three lessons. I told him to try two, but he insisted on three." Craig shrugged. "He's a nice guy, you know, and he's still single."

Evette groaned loudly and held up her hands. "Don't you start with me. I don't need anyone. I'm fine, okay?"

An expression of guilt washed over Craig's face, and he stared at her for a long time. He folded a few more shirts then, ignoring Evette as she fumed.

"Fine, Evette. But what do you do besides work and practice golf? Do you think it would hurt you to spend a little more time with him? What's so horrible about going to a Bible study anyway?"

Evette blew out a sigh. Not only had he tried to set her up, he'd eavesdropped as well. "It's none of your business, Big Ears, so just be quiet."

"Hey, what's going on out here? We can hear Evette yelling in the back." Her dad emerged from the storeroom, with Drew right behind him.

Evette chewed the inside of her lip, feeling as if she were five years old again. Craig wouldn't tell on her, but he'd let his disapproval be known if she failed to be honest.

"I'm sorry. It was my fault. I got a little upset about something Craig did to me," Evette said pointedly. Her mom had laid down the no-tattletale law long ago, but there were ways to get around it without actually telling what the offender had done.

Her dad looked skeptical. "Look—I hope you two are acting like this only because there aren't any customers in here."

"Sorry, Dad," said Craig.

Her dad still looked unconvinced and cleared his throat. "It's been a slow night. I'll come out and watch the store, and Trevor and Drew will run the driving range. You've been here most of the day, so why don't you both take off early? Like now."

"Thanks, Dad," said Evette. Even though her dad had given them the adult equivalent of a timeout, she could already feel the stress of the day melting away.

On the way to their cars Evette attempted to make things right with Craig. "I didn't mean to explode just then." She gave him a sideways hug.

"I know you didn't. I shouldn't have gotten in your business like that. We'll both feel better in the morning."

"I hope so."

"We will." Craig hesitated then spoke what was on his mind. "Just try to relax a little, Evie. I know you're still hurting over this thing with Justin, but you have to—"

Evette shook her head, blinking back tears. "Please don't tell me to get over it or let it go. I'm hurt, and I have a right to be. How would you have felt if Lisa had canceled your wedding with no warning?"

Craig didn't answer but patted her on the shoulder. "I know. . .I know."

Evette pulled away, wiping her eyes with the back of her hand. "See you tomorrow."

"Drive carefully, okay?"

She nodded her head as she stepped into the car. She had a feeling her brother would take the long way to his house to follow her and make sure she made it home all right.

Evette buckled her seat belt, eager to be on her way. Today had not been the greatest of days, and she needed to unwind. She knew her mother would be willing to lend a sympathetic ear.

Chapter 3

Evette from church is going to be your golf teacher?" Albert asked. He and Anthony were sitting in the living room, watching television. As usual, Albert seemed to take delight in clicking the remote faster than Anthony's eyes could adjust to each image on the rapidly passing channels.

"Will you quit that?" Anthony pleaded.

Albert grinned. "Quit what?"

"You know what I'm talking about, Speedy Fingers. Now pick a channel and try to stay there for at least a minute."

"Fine." Albert switched to a sports channel and laid the remote on the coffee table.

"Now pass the popcorn and tell me more about Evette."

"There's not much to tell. You know her about as well as I do."

Albert popped several pieces into his mouth and chewed. "That's it? Nothing else?"

"Nothing else." Anthony reclaimed the bowl.

"You know, I hardly see her anymore. It's like she dropped out of sight when she graduated from high school. And isn't she engaged to that one guy—Justin—I can't remember his last name."

"She was, but not anymore."

Albert ate a few more kernels while he digested this information. "She's pretty," he said after awhile.

Anthony laughed. "What's that supposed to mean?"

"I don't know. You seem really excited about these classes. Does the fact that she's single have anything to do with it?"

"No. I'm thinking of a way to try to get her involved in church things again. I kind of get the feeling she might be a little lonely."

"Hmm." Albert grabbed more popcorn.

"Hmm, what?"

"Hmm, I think you're approaching this the wrong way. If you're interested in her, don't lie to yourself or Evette about it. Just ask her out. If you play Mr. Holy, trying to bring Ms. Lonely to church to meet more people, it'll probably backfire."

"What makes you the expert? For weeks you haven't talked about anyone but Brienne, and now you want to give me a speech about my golf instructor."

"I know what I'm talking about. I made that mistake with Kelly Pierce. While I tried to think of a way to get to know her better, she and Bill Hodge decided they were soul mates. And I was the one who spent all that time inviting her to come to different events."

"I see your point." Anthony snatched the bowl away from Albert, who was devouring handfuls at record speed. "If I decide I feel differently about Evette, I'll be sure to speak up."

"Good." Albert stood up from the couch and stretched. "I'm going to bed."

"That sounds nice, but I still have a column to write." As Albert trudged off to his room, Anthony flipped his laptop open and forced himself to concentrate.

⁓

"Okay, try again." Evette stood back and watched Anthony hit a few more shots. The first ball took flight to the right. The second went far to the left. The third ball bounced off the mat and ricocheted off the railing between the individual tee boxes. Evette ducked as the ball flew over her head and finally landed a few feet away. The past forty-five minutes hadn't been much different. Anthony was right. He was a terrible golfer.

He heaved a sigh and put the club down. "Sorry. I don't know what I'm doing wrong."

"Don't worry about it. If you were perfect, you wouldn't need lessons."

Anthony nodded his agreement and prepared to hit another ball. Evette grimaced, wondering how much longer she could watch him do this. Raising her hand, she said, "Hold on. I think you do need a change of pace. Why don't we head over to the putting green for the rest of the lesson?"

"You think I'm that bad, huh?"

Evette smiled tolerantly. "No, but you're getting more frustrated with every bad shot you hit." *That means all of them.*

"The more frustrated you are, the less you concentrate. To minimize the chances of someone getting hurt with an errant ball, I'm going to use my authority as your instructor and end this lesson with an exercise that doesn't involve an airborne ball."

Anthony followed her to the practice green, where she explained the basics of putting. To her relief, he did much better. He possessed a natural flair for reading greens, and Evette watched him sink ball after ball.

When the lesson ended, Anthony was more positive, but his face still held a look of disappointment. "It's too bad I can't hit the ball worth beans."

"Don't be so hard on yourself. There are lots of professionals who would love to putt like that."

Anthony shook his head at her compliment. "A lot of good that'll do me if I can't hit the ball straight. I'll be way over par before I even see the green."

"Some people hit the ball well off the tee but can't putt at all. Even though it might not look that way, the short game is really a big percentage of the entire strategy."

"I hope you're right." Anthony leaned on his putter and grinned. "Thanks for the lesson. I'll see you again Thursday."

"Five-thirty," Evette reminded him.

"Sure you don't want to come to Bible study with me tonight? Starts in an hour."

Evette felt her stomach tighten. "You know, I think I made myself clear yesterday. I'm not interested." As soon as she finished talking, Evette wished she hadn't sounded so harsh.

"Hey, I didn't mean to offend you. I just thought—" He didn't finish but picked up his clubs. "I'll see you Thursday."

After Anthony left, Evette went inside to freshen up. She was still upset that Anthony had invited her. She wished she could forget all about the discussion, but now she couldn't stop wondering if she should have agreed to go.

The fact that she didn't need his invitation to go irked her all the more. She was a member of the church as well and had a right to attend any of the functions without being invited.

I belong there as much as he does, but he's obviously asked me to come because he thinks I need spiritual guidance or something.

Evette strode into the pro shop.

"Your lesson go well?" asked Trevor.

"I guess. He'll be back on Thursday so maybe we'll have more progress on the driving range." Evette sat on one of the bar stools in the register area. Several customers came through, but not so many that the store was full.

"Where's Craig?"

"Out getting sandwiches for dinner," said Drew.

"And Dad?"

"Went home early since he didn't have to teach."

"Would you guys mind if I left early? Like now?"

Drew lifted his eyebrows. "I don't have a problem with it. You have to go somewhere?"

"Sort of." Evette grabbed her purse and keys. "Thanks. See you in the morning." She got into her car and, without even thinking about where she was headed, made her way to the church fifteen minutes later.

When she stepped out of the car, Evette realized she didn't have her Bible with her. Great. Anthony probably already thought the worst of her. Walking in without a Bible would only make him think he was right.

Evette stood with her hand on the car, debating her next move. The parking lot was filled with well over thirty cars, so she supposed she might be able to sneak in unnoticed and leave as soon as things ended. That way Anthony would have no further reason to hold her nonattendance over her head.

Her other option would be to forget it and go back to work. At least she wouldn't have to worry about facing any uncomfortable questions about why she hadn't come in so long. Clearly, the latter would be easier.

Evette stared at the church door, remembering how much time she'd spent here in her youth. Getting out of the habit had been so easy. Missing a Bible study here, a Sunday school class there, and conveniently working at her summer job during singles' meetings. Not to mention all the time she'd spent with Justin.

Her commitment to attending church had fallen apart so slowly at first, like an old hand-knit scarf she used to have. At first it had been easy to tuck in a few loose threads here and there, but one day it became entangled on something in the washing machine and ended up looking more like a pile of yarn than anything wearable.

The same went for the time she'd injured her Achilles tendon playing soccer and had to quit the team. At first she'd kept up her fitness routines the best she could, but after awhile, looking at the time she'd lost from soccer, getting back in shape had seemed impossible. She'd already missed a big part of the season. So she quit working out.

But a month later Evette realized that not working out would only hurt her more the next season. And she still wanted to play with the volleyball team and run track. Unwilling to lose sight of her goal, she forced herself to resume her workouts. The first week had been the hardest, but she was able to get past that by focusing on the reason she was there—the love of the sport.

In all honesty the same reasoning should have applied to church. But she'd been away from this type of fellowship for much longer than a month—more like six years of months.

Why didn't I go back? Her soul was not in mortal danger—she'd asked Jesus into her heart when she was eight. After she died she knew she would live in heaven for eternity.

I try to obey the Bible. I give money to the offering. I put in a respectable amount of Sundays in church. I buy calendars from the annual fundraiser.

Something about those actions felt dry and empty. Spending time at church didn't have the same appeal as the thrill of victory she experienced upon her return to soccer. She had resumed her workout routine because she missed it. Soccer, volleyball, track, golf—they were a part of her she couldn't bear to let go. She needed them.

But did she need church? Apparently not. Unlike sports, she had no misgivings about staying away from church.

Does that mean I think I don't need God?

The thought made Evette wince. Something about that seemed terribly irreverent, and she was glad she hadn't spoken the words aloud for someone to hear.

She managed to still her trembling hands long enough to open the car door and step back inside. After a long moment she put the key back into the ignition. Coming tonight had been a mistake.

The knock on the window nearly startled her out of her seat. "You made it," Anthony said from the other side of the window.

Evette opened the window cautiously. Now she was stuck. Why hadn't she left sooner? "I can't stay."

Anthony gave her a puzzled look. "Why?"

"I—I forgot my Bible." A lame excuse. There were probably a hundred spare Bibles inside. She took a deep breath and stepped out of the car.

Anthony chuckled and steered her gently toward the church entrance. "Don't worry about it. I'm sure we can find one for you."

Evette tried to hide her discomfort as she and Anthony entered the classroom. She recognized many of the attendees and noticed a few newcomers. Or maybe they weren't so new. After all, she hadn't attended in years.

The study leader, Tim Wilson, made sure a round of introductions took place for Evette's benefit, then began the lesson, mercifully shifting the attention away from Evette.

Tim and Anthony had located a Bible for her, and Evette kept up appearances by dutifully flipping to the appropriate chapters and keeping her eyes on the pages while the verses were read.

Other than that, she had trouble concentrating. The discussion was about showing God's love to those who didn't know about Him, and Evette wondered if Anthony had known about the topic in advance. She couldn't get past the suspicion that she was the guinea pig, the object lesson.

She half expected Anthony to get up and announce, "See—it worked on Evette. Two days ago she didn't want to come, but I kept praying, and she finally decided to come."

To her great relief he did no such thing. She felt defensive, though, by the time class ended. She couldn't ignore the curious stares from the other attendees. Some seemed surprised. Others seemed to give her the prodigal-has-returned look—an odd expression of pity and curiosity. She didn't need their sympathy.

I am just as saved as every one of you. Evette kept her head up and refused to feel intimidated.

She couldn't help imagining, though, what would happen if she jumped up and honestly spoke her mind. *I'm not your target! I come here every Sunday. Go help somebody else—you don't need to waste your energy on saving me!*

As soon as Tim prayed to close the meeting, Evette headed out the door, not bothering to wait for Anthony. She was still angry with him for dragging her here under these circumstances. She wanted to tell him exactly what she thought of his trick, but she didn't trust herself not to burst into tears. It didn't matter. She'd deal with it at his next lesson—if he had the nerve to show up.

As soon as she reached her car, Evette had to search in her purse for her keys. When she finally located them, they fell on the ground, just as Anthony burst out the door.

"Is everything okay?" His voice was the perfect mix of innocence and concern—obviously well practiced.

She held up her hand to stop him. "Don't go there. I thought you were a nice guy."

Ignoring her hand, Anthony took a few steps closer. "What are you talking about?"

She swallowed back the lump in her throat and blinked to keep her tears at bay. "This. You set me up." Putting her hands on her hips, she continued. "So what prize did you win for bringing me in?"

Anthony laughed. "Prize?"

Evette didn't see how he could keep up this confused act. "Yeah, prize. I know how these things go because I used to participate in them. Bring the most friends and get a gift certificate or something. Maybe a new Bible. You know, a gift in exchange for a poor, lost soul."

Anthony's face lit up with understanding. "Okay, Evette. Sometimes we do have things like that. But I promise you, that wasn't why I asked you to come."

"Then why did you ask me here?"

Emotions Evette couldn't read flickered across his face. Anthony opened and closed his mouth several times, and she knew he was trying to construct an answer.

"Don't bother." Evette opened the door and stepped into the car.

Anthony rushed over and begged her to roll the window down. Evette wanted to drive off and leave him standing there, looking as embarrassed as she felt, but she couldn't.

All right. She rolled the window down to the halfway point.

Anthony peered down at her, his fingertips resting on the window, as though that would prevent her from closing it before he finished explaining.

"I'm sorry you're feeling hurt. I honestly didn't know we were going to have that discussion tonight, and if I had known, I. . ." His voice trailed off.

Evette waited for Anthony to say he wouldn't have invited her if he had known what the topic was, but he didn't. Instead he took a different approach.

"I'm sorry if you felt uncomfortable, but my intention wasn't to hurt you."

"You thought humiliation would be a better method?"

"No. I promise you. I just wanted you to come. I thought you might have fun."

Evette chewed the inside of her lip. She couldn't stay here all night, arguing over Anthony's true intentions. "Well, I didn't have fun."

She started the ignition and gave Anthony a pointed look. "Now will you get your fingers out of my window?"

Anthony stepped back, his shoulders drooping. Evette drove away without looking back, her emotions careening back and forth between disappointment and hurt.

Chapter 4

I told you."

"Do you have to say that?"

"I guess not, but it felt good."

Anthony kicked off his shoes and put his feet up on the coffee table.

Albert wrinkled his nose and gave Anthony's feet a shove. "Hey, we agreed. No feet on the table. What if we have company? Nobody wants to put a drink on a table that smells like feet."

Anthony scowled at his brother. "You could at least make an exception for stressful situations."

Albert was adamant. "Then eat some ice cream. But no feet on the table."

"Evette thinks I asked her to come to church so I could show her how much she needs to repent."

"Did you?"

"No. And yes. She kind of dropped out of the church population, and I think it would be good for her to come back."

"Maybe you should let her decide when she needs to do that."

"I guess you're right. But I didn't hurt her feelings on purpose tonight. It happened before I realized what was going on."

"So apologize and let it go. Obviously she's not ready."

Anthony couldn't let the matter drop. "I know she wants to be there. I can see it in her eyes."

Albert shook his head. "I think you're barking up the wrong tree. And you sound like Mom or Aunt Florence with that see-it-in-the-eyes business. If Evette said she doesn't want to go, then what makes you think you know better than she does?"

Anthony couldn't explain what he felt. That same feeling—the feeling that he was about to witness another friend and believer drift away—was back, and this time his heart felt even heavier. "I can't make you understand what I feel, but I know she wants to. For some reason she can't—or won't."

Albert stared at him hard then finally said, "Do what you think you need to do, but I'd stay in prayer about it. And if you think you like her, then that'll confuse the lines even more. You have to make sure you're doing this because God wants you to and not because you think she's wife material."

Anthony sighed. Albert had a point, and he'd considered this since his confrontation with Evette after the meeting. He was attracted to her, and that did confuse things somewhat.

He laced his fingers together and leaned back, placing his hands over his eyes. Albert referred to this as his "praying position," and praying was exactly what he needed to do right now.

※

Evette awoke the next morning with a stomachache. And a headache. Along with a sore throat and stuffy nose.

Nothing unusual, considering she'd spent half the night crying.

Her dad left early for work and advised her to come in when she felt "up to it."

Her mother also got an early start to her day as a volunteer at the community center's literacy classes, so Evette was on her own.

After she showered and ate breakfast, Evette mulled over the idea of going in to work. She didn't like the idea that she had special privileges, but she also didn't relish the idea of spending the entire day with her dad and brothers watching her like a hawk.

As she went over the pros and cons of whether or not to go to the shop, the doorbell rang.

The visitor turned out to be a florist deliveryman, bearing a small arrangement of colorful wildflowers.

"For Evette Howard," the man said, reading from a clipboard.

"Me?"

"Sign here, please, right next to the X," he said, handing her a pen and sheet of paper.

Evette signed hurriedly, anxious to see who had sent the bouquet. She hadn't received flowers since—well, not in a long time.

She shut the door and ripped open the envelope. The note was short and simple. *I'm sorry—Anthony.*

It wasn't long, eloquent prose or even a love note, but Evette felt tears come to her eyes. Maybe she had acted too presumptuously last night. Even through her anger, she'd had a hard time believing Anthony had invited her to make her feel bad.

Maybe I should call him and let him know I'm not upset anymore, she wondered. Or maybe not. After all, he had a lesson tomorrow; she could tell him then.

※

Later that afternoon Evette was ready to head out to the range for her four o'clock lesson when Anthony stopped by the pro shop.

"Did you get my note?" he asked.

Evette grinned at him. "Yes, and the flowers were beautiful."

"I'm glad you liked them."

Craig and Drew, who were standing at the register area with her, wandered off to a different part of the store, giving Evette and Anthony a little privacy.

Evette stared down at the desk and bent a corner of a sheet of paper, trying to formulate her thoughts into words. "I guess I should be the one to apologize. I shouldn't have lost my temper like that. Will you forgive me?"

"Definitely." Anthony cleared his throat. "And I guess I have a confession to make."

Evette studied him carefully. He'd already admitted he didn't want her to get hurt, so what could he possibly be about to admit?

"You see, I did want you to come to church, but part of the reason was because I wanted to see you again. Soon. Maybe I should ask you to forgive me too."

"Oh." Evette didn't know what else to say. The sentiment was both flattering and frightening. Considering the circumstances with Justin, she wasn't quite sure she felt confident enough to jump into another relationship.

Anthony must have sensed her reticence, because he backed away from the counter. "So is the lesson still on for tomorrow?"

Evette swallowed and forced herself to talk. "Yes. I'll see you then?"

"Five-thirty," Anthony said, heading toward the door.

As soon as he left, Evette exhaled and realized she'd been holding her breath. A million emotions washed over her at once.

Anthony's attraction wasn't one-sided, but she didn't know how to approach a relationship with him. Would he ultimately turn out similar to Justin, or was he truly different?

The question nagged at her for the rest of the day, and that evening she went home utterly exhausted.

She tried not to think about Justin or Anthony, but her resolve crumbled. Long after she went to bed, she still lay awake, wrestling with her feelings.

She could remember the last time she had spoken to Justin. He'd called on a Monday morning, just before she headed off to work.

"Sweetheart, it's me."

"Hi, Justin. I'm sorry about the tournament yesterday. I prayed for you, but maybe you'll do better at the next one."

"Yeah, I hope so." He didn't bother to hide the defeat in his voice.

Evette felt the tension growing over the phone, and she struggled to keep the mood light. "I'm just about to leave for work. Did you get your flight arranged? What time should I pick you up at the airport?"

Silence from his end of the line roared in her ears, and Evette knew something wasn't right. "Justin? Please don't tell me you're not coming home again this week?"

He cleared his throat. "Sweetheart—I don't know how to say this."

"Oh." Evette had her answer. He had decided to forgo coming home, yet again.

Another heavy sigh from his end. "Evette—you know how important golf is to me."

Evette nodded and tried to find her voice. Of course she knew how much golf meant to him. He had talent, and with more experience he could do well as a pro.

She felt the tiniest bit frustrated that he had insinuated she didn't know how much the game meant to him. Wasn't she his biggest fan? The one who had encouraged him to keep trying even when he didn't do well in a tournament?

"Sure I do. We both know." Evette licked her dry lips and tried to keep her voice from cracking.

"I just think I need to spend more time going after this. I'm not getting a feel for things when I keep leaving and coming home for long stretches. The guys out here who make strides are the ones who stick with it and play more tournaments."

Evette knew then where he was taking the conversation, and she felt tears pool in her eyes. "So you're going to play full time?"

"Yeah. That's my plan—I hope you understand."

"I do—I understand. I mean, you'll be gone a lot when you make the tour so I guess I should get used to it. So—any estimate on when I'll get to see you again?" She tried to keep her voice light because she didn't want him to know how upset she felt.

When they first agreed he should play the preprofessional tour, Justin had committed to playing one or two tournaments a month, then working at her dad's range and pro shop the remaining weeks.

"I don't know yet," he finally answered.

Evette felt herself growing impatient with his nonverbal mood. Trying to talk to him when he got like this was like pulling teeth.

"Then when will you be home? Tell me what you're thinking. Dad's counting on you to work at least two weeks out of the month, and he'll want to know when you'll be home. And what about your students? It's difficult for them to be juggled between you one week and Craig the next. Plus, it's not fair to Craig. He already has enough students—"

"Evette. Don't stress over it. I might be home only one or two weeks this summer so it's obvious I can't teach anymore. I'll split my students between your brothers."

"But—"

"I'll call your dad and explain it to him myself. We'll work it out between the two of us."

Evette felt as if the wind had been knocked out of her. With those words she knew he had begun to cut her away from him. But she was determined to salvage this relationship. She hadn't given Justin the last eight years of her life for no reason.

"Look—I know how you feel about the tour, but don't you think it's a little inconvenient to spend so much time on the road right now? We're supposed to be planning the wedding and looking for a house. I thought we decided you wouldn't pour all of your time and money into this right now."

"No, Evette, that's what you decided, and I didn't argue because I didn't want to upset you. I'm so close I can almost taste this. I'm getting closer but making silly mistakes—losing by a few strokes. I need to keep my focus, and the only way I can do that is to play more successive weeks."

Evette counted to twenty to keep from losing her temper. Their wedding was set for December, and if Justin stayed on the tour for longer than four months, pulling off a wedding would be difficult at best. "So when will you be home? I guess I'll have to plan most of the wedding by myself."

"That's the other thing I wanted to discuss."

"The *other thing?* What on earth are you talking about?"

"Let's postpone the wedding, Evette. Please."

"Why?"

"Because I can't have it hanging over my head. I need to make the tour, and it's already July. If I'm going to make enough money to get my card, I need to be consistent over the next few months. If I'm close, but not close enough, I won't want to break my momentum for the wedding."

Evette was stunned, but she was determined to keep calm. "So the wedding is off for how long?"

"Indefinitely."

"I see."

"Evette, don't be angry with me."

"I'm trying not to, but it's hard. Twenty minutes ago I had a definite future, and now you've pulled the rug out from under my feet. What would you do if you were in my shoes? Honestly."

"I'd be upset. But this might be a good thing."

"A good thing? How is that?"

"I don't know. Think about it. We've been a couple since the eleventh grade. Eight years is a long time, and even though we're adults we've been connected to each other for so long. Maybe it's time we learned how to be independent of each other."

Evette didn't understand what he meant, but she tried to be understanding. "Maybe we should talk about this later. May I call you this evening?"

"I'll have to call you. I've got a flight to Arizona in an hour for this week's tournament."

Evette blinked. The deadline for entering the tournament had already passed. Obviously Justin had entered several days ago and had neglected to tell her until now. There was nothing more to say. He had broken their promise to be honest with each other, and that hurt more than anything else he'd said.

"I see," she said flatly. "Then we'll talk when you have time to pick up the phone."

"As soon as I get settled, we'll talk."

"All right. If I'm not home you can call the store."

"I'll do my best. But it might not be until tomorrow afternoon. I've got a bunch of other things to take care of since I'm going to be on the road so much."

Even as they said their good-byes, Evette still held on to the hope that she could convince him not to postpone the wedding.

⌇

Remembering that conversation made her cry. Ten months had passed, and the pain still existed as a dull ache she felt every day.

Things had only gone downhill from that point. He didn't call that day, or the next, but waited a full five days. That call had been even shorter, and most of the conversation centered around how he felt he would do in the tournament.

Evette had to watch the televised games to get a glimpse of him, and as his phone calls grew less frequent she hoped to see him in interviews just to hear his voice.

The ironic thing was that ever since then Justin's game had become more and more erratic. He'd struggled to keep his game consistent and hadn't won a single tournament. In fact, his best finish had been tied for tenth with six other people.

That September he at least had the decency to come home long enough to break up with her in person. "The pressure of having a relationship is too much for me to handle right now. I need to be free and not feel tied to any place or anyone right now."

Evette felt like yelling, "What relationship?" They talked once a week, at best, for no more than ten minutes, and he seemed more and more like a stranger.

Justin also announced he was moving to Texas to work with a coach he'd met. He'd already secured a job to teach at a golf academy during the off-season. "By the time the tour starts again, I'll be ready. I've learned how things go, and I know more about competing." Flashing his biggest smile, he said, "I'm on my way to the real deal, Evette."

He seemed so excited that Evette had to remind herself he had just dumped her. She had the feeling that their relationship had been over for months in his mind.

The last thing he said to her as they stood on her doorstep was, "Please be happy for me, Eve. You're the only one who really understands how much I want this."

Evette nodded and went inside as he walked away. She didn't need to watch him leave. Emotionally they had drifted apart long before then.

Some of her friends and relatives had speculated about whether or not he had another girlfriend, but Evette preferred not to pursue that angle. She'd already resigned herself to losing out to the game of golf, but she didn't think she could stand knowing whether or not another woman had been involved.

Now she felt vaguely relieved that the relationship was over. The pain and hurt were still there, but Justin had been right about one thing. She was learning how to be an independent person again.

Letting him make decisions and decide where they should go had been so easy. If he wanted to go out to dinner, they went. If he wanted to play golf, she followed along. Even when she was tired and wanted to stay home, she agreed to his suggestions to show him how much she loved him.

Now she sometimes reveled in the fact that she could plan her own evenings and weekends. No, she didn't want to be single forever, but she was enjoying this new season in her life.

Which was precisely the reason she needed to be cautious with Anthony.

Chapter 5

That's it—try it one more time."

Anthony inhaled deeply and took a close look at the green. The ball was near enough to the hole that he didn't need to apply a great deal of pressure to the putter. He swung the club gently, being careful to imitate the motion of a pendulum on a grandfather clock. The ball responded by rolling directly into the center of the cup.

Anthony glanced at Evette. "So? That was like twenty out of twenty-five. That's better than my last lesson."

"You definitely have a feel for putting. It takes some people ages to get it down, and others pick it up immediately. I'd put you in the second category."

Anthony laughed. "So am I ready for the pro tour yet?"

A strange look passed over Evette's face, but she seemed to recover from it quickly. "I think your short game skills will have to be 150 percent to make up for all the wayward drives you hit off the tee. You can't putt your way out of the rough, you know."

"Yeah." Anthony sighed heavily, remembering some of the more absurd shots he'd hit at the practice range. "I guess I need to spend more time working on my swing."

"Don't be discouraged." Evette replaced her clubs in her bag and headed back to the pro shop, rolling the bag behind her. "Everyone always has something about the game they want to improve. And maybe you're just thinking too hard about your swing." She stopped walking and tilted her head to the side. "How would you feel if we took your next lesson to an actual golf course?"

"Yeah, right." Anthony shook his head. "No way I'm leaving the practice range until I can play."

A smirk tugged at the corners of Evette's mouth. "I hear a touch of egotism."

Anthony lifted his eyebrows and smiled. "Hear whatever you want. I know this much—I'm not going out to let every other man see how bad I play. It'll take me forever to get the ball to the green, and whoever's in the group behind us will get impatient."

She shrugged, apparently not seeing his point. "So we'll schedule a time when the course is relatively clear, and if someone behind us gets antsy, we'll let them play through."

Anthony considered that for a moment. Her idea did make sense. And he would just have to pray nobody he knew saw him out there struggling to learn the game.

"Okay. But the course has to be clear."

"I'll do my best to make sure relatively few groups are out there, but no promises. I'm thinking about a weekday, maybe around ten in the morning. And we won't play one of the more popular courses. Something small and simple to get you started."

"Good. I can deal with that."

"And, of course, I'll be sure I remember to bring my Caution: Golf Lessons in Progress sign."

"What?" Anthony couldn't believe what he'd just heard. "A sign?"

"Yeah, I use it for all my students. It's about"—she gestured with her hands, indicating an expanse of about three feet by five feet—"yea big, and it has bright orange lettering. It's mounted on a pole, and I'll stick it in the ground so people will be more understanding. It's the same concept as the student-driver sign you see in the back of some cars."

"No. I'll play, but we are not using that sign." Anthony could envision the scenario. Not only would he run into probably a dozen people he knew, but they'd see him hacking away at the ball, not making any progress, with a bright orange sign and a woman teacher to boot.

"Why not? I'm getting the feeling you've embellished your golfing ability to your friends, and you don't want them to find out you're just learning."

Anthony held his hands up in defense. "Hey, what was I supposed to say? Ethan and some of the guys at work are forever bragging about the low score they shot and how they have some new gadget that's taken five shots off their game. And I'm a competitor by nature. Did you think I could admit I didn't know a five iron from a sand wedge?"

"Ahem." Evette cleared her throat. "Doesn't that fall under the category of—lying? Tsk, tsk, Mr. Bible Study."

Anthony sighed in frustration. It definitely stung to be reprimanded by Evette, especially after his zealous and disastrous attempt to get her to come back to church more often. She had taken his apology well, but he sensed she still felt a bit put off by the whole thing.

Had he been conversing with anyone else at this moment, he might have argued his point a little longer, but he knew it was probably best to confess right now. "Okay, I lied. And I have repented. And I will tell everyone I lied to that I messed up. But before I put my nongolfing skill on display for the world in general to see, I want a guarantee from you that you will leave that sign at home. Or else I won't go. I can confess my lie. I can deal with having a woman for a teacher. But the sign will be too much for me."

Evette widened her eyes. "And now the truth comes out. You don't like having a woman for a teacher."

Anthony felt as if he were falling deeper into a hole and wondered if he'd be able to dig his way out of it. He looked at Evette, hoping he could find a way to apologize yet again, then noticed something that put him at ease.

The solemn expression on her face couldn't mask the glint in her eye. She was teasing him.

The two of them burst out laughing at the same time. "I couldn't help giving you a hard time," she admitted. "You fell right into it, and the temptation was too hard to resist."

Anthony nodded, still chuckling. It was nice to see Evette return to her usual good humor—even if the change came at his expense. Her laugh was one of the most melodious he'd ever heard. He could sit and listen to the sound for hours on end, even years.

A fleeting memory of his conversation with Albert wiggled into the corners of his conscience. He had to watch himself now. Otherwise he'd look up and find he'd fallen in love with this woman and not even remember when or where it had happened. Be careful.

Anthony cleared his throat and swallowed the leftover laughter. "So about this sign—"

"For the record there is no sign." She smirked again. "But now I kind of wish I had one. You looked so mortified."

"I felt even worse. Boy, am I happy to hear you were kidding."

Evette reached up and patted him on the shoulder, and he caught a whiff of her floral perfume. "Come on," she said. "You didn't think I was that cruel? I wouldn't try to embarrass any of my students. My job is to help build confidence, not rip people to shreds."

Anthony struggled to think of a profound or meaningful reply to her statement, but when no inspiration came he decided to let the moment pass in silence.

After they went inside the pro shop, Anthony said good-bye, and Evette promised to set up a tee time for one of the next week's lessons.

He stopped at the exit and ventured a final question. "I'll see you at church on Sunday?"

"I know you see me as a total heathen, Anthony, but I do go to church every Sunday. I think I'm as much of a Christian as you are, but I don't feel the need to be in that building every waking hour to prove it." The edge maneuvered its way back into her voice again, and Anthony wished he hadn't said anything at all.

Before he could speak, she apologized. "I was out of line. Yes, I'll be at church, and I'm looking forward to seeing you there."

Anthony wondered at her sudden change of tone, but he decided it would be a mistake to ask her and useless to spend too much time thinking about it. "Talk to you later, Evette." He waved and walked outside.

On his way to the car Anthony felt like whistling. Something was different about Evette, and that was an answer to his prayers.

≈

Evette set her alarm for Sunday morning a half hour earlier than usual. Anthony might have an infuriating way of pointing things out, but some things he said made sense.

Getting to church on time hadn't been one of his suggestions, but Evette figured the least she could do was show up on time, instead of slipping in after praise and worship and leaving before the altar call.

It wasn't as though she were pressed for time. Her Sunday morning routine was just that—a routine, designed to keep her interaction with other churchgoers to a minimum. At first it had felt good to escape their prying questions and supposedly well-meaning comments. But now it made her feel plain old lonely. Out of the loop.

Evette had spent the past few days reflecting on the breakdown of communication between other churchgoers and her.

As she began her young adult years, many people had approached her with comments and suggestions about her relationship with Justin. Some of those statements were merely irritating while others were downright hurtful. She rebelled by sidestepping them as best she could. Statements like "We missed you last Sunday" or "Haven't seen you around much lately. Is everything okay?" or "Just because your boyfriend doesn't like church doesn't mean you shouldn't come" she answered with shrugs and noncommittal phrases.

Part of her knew they spoke the truth while the other part of her chafed at the fact that they couldn't keep their mouths shut and just pray for her.

Evette quit attending church altogether for awhile, using the excuse that the Christians were too nosy and hypocritical. Now she was beginning to see the immaturity in her line of reasoning. Although people had the tendency to say the wrong things at the wrong time, she couldn't blame that on the fact that they were Christians.

She'd had customers in the store say harsher things, and she hadn't even batted an eye. People who went to church were simply imperfect people, hoping to grow in their relationship with the Lord, who went to church to fellowship with others like them.

By sheer mathematics someone was bound to say the wrong thing now and then. Evette knew she wasn't perfect, and she had been wrong to hold them to a higher degree of perfection than she could attain. Some of them probably should have kept their observations about the beginning and demise of her relationship with Justin to themselves, but the root of their concern had been valid. She and Justin, although Christians, had slowly begun to drift away from the church.

Yes, she was prepared to mend her rift with her church family. Anthony's persistence upset her at first, but the mere fact that he had not lost patience with her after the Bible study impressed her.

After slipping into a buttercup yellow silk jacket and skirt, Evette spent fifteen minutes coaxing her curls up into an attractive style. She swept on a light dusting of powder and blush then finished with a natural tone of lipstick and mascara.

Giving herself a final glance in the mirror, Evette was pleased that Anthony would get to see her looking more feminine and refreshed than she did during his lessons.

She felt certain he would notice the difference, but at the same time she wondered if he would think she had gone out of her way to impress him. Although the two of them had barely begun a friendship, Evette couldn't ignore the growing attraction she had for Anthony. Was it wrong she wanted to put her best foot forward?

With a shrug she gathered her purse and went downstairs. Her parents were having breakfast and were not yet dressed for church.

"Evette, Honey, you look so nice and fresh in that yellow," her mother said.

"I've always thought that was a nice color on you," added her dad.

"Thanks, Mom and Dad," she said, feeling pleased that her extra effort had already been noticed.

"I made waffles for breakfast. Are you hungry?"

"Sounds delicious, Mom, but I have to get going, or I'll be late," Evette said.

Wearing a puzzled frown, her mother asked cautiously, "But where are you going?"

Evette tried to appear nonchalant. "I thought I'd go to Sunday school this morning." She shrugged. "I think Anthony said it still starts at nine-thirty."

"Anthony?" Her dad picked up on the name. "The one who signed up for golf lessons?"

"That's him."

Her dad nodded then turned to her mom. "Claude and Mavis Edwards's son."

"Oh, yes. One of the twins."

"Right," Evette said. "Now I need to leave, or I'll be late."

"Don't you want to take your Bible, Honey?" asked her mother.

"Great." Evette pressed her hand to her forehead. "Thanks for reminding me."

She put her purse aside, then kicked off her heels before she ran back upstairs to retrieve her Bible. After five minutes of searching, she located it under a pile of clothes. She vaguely remembered setting it there last week after church. Perhaps it was also a good time to start reading it on a regular basis again.

Evette ran back downstairs, hobbled into her shoes, grabbed her purse, and waved good-bye to her parents.

The streets were not too congested so she arrived at the church as the clock on her dashboard flashed nine-thirty. People were still arriving. She was relieved she wouldn't have to walk in by herself.

Evette parked her car. By the time she grabbed her things and locked the door, another car pulled alongside hers.

She looked over to find Anthony in the passenger's seat and his brother at the wheel. Anthony flashed her a grin, and Evette waited until he stepped out of the car before she headed over to say hello.

She might have been mistaken, but he seemed a bit more spruced up than usual. Instead of the polo shirt and slacks she often saw him wearing, he was dressed in a pinstripe suit and colorful necktie. Did he have somewhere special to go after the service, or was he dressed to impress as well?

Anthony spoke before she could give the matter any more thought. "You know, that yellow is pretty on you."

He noticed! Evette was so tickled that she couldn't hold back a smile. "You look nice yourself." Keeping the mood light, she said, "I bet you're surprised to see me here so early."

He seemed to consider her statement a few seconds. "Actually I am. But I promised myself I wouldn't ask any inane questions and make you feel uncomfortable."

Albert spoke up. "That means he wants to know why you came, but he won't ask. If any explanation is given, you'll have to give it yourself."

Anthony playfully elbowed his twin. "Will you let me talk for myself? Last I checked, my tongue still worked."

Albert burst out laughing and shook his head. He draped his arms over Anthony's shoulder. "Hey, I'm just trying to be a good big brother."

Anthony wriggled away and countered with, "Three minutes does not constitute a big brother. In fact, three minutes barely gives you the right to claim you're older than I am."

Anthony stopped walking and stared in the direction of the church doorway. "Hmm," he said, a mysterious ring to his voice.

"Hmm, what?" said Albert, still laughing.

"Hmm, I think I saw Brienne laughing and talking to Ray Jenkins."

"Really?" Albert glanced toward the door and quickened his pace. Then he stopped and turned back. "Hey, Evette, it's nice seeing you again. Excuse me while I run in here and prove my little brother needs some serious glasses."

"Glasses?" Anthony countered.

"Yeah, 'cause I think you're seeing things."

"Whatever. I guess your brain didn't convince your feet, because you're still running inside, aren't you?"

Albert shook his head but moved even faster.

Evette giggled. "Who's Brienne?"

"The woman my brother's falling in love with."

"Did you really see her with another guy?"

Anthony wiggled his eyebrows. "Actually I did. But he doesn't have to worry. She likes Albert as much as he likes her."

"You are so mean. You got him all worried for no reason," she said, smiling.

"I wouldn't say 'for no reason.' I got him out of my hair before he had the chance to embarrass me."

"I know all about that," Evette agreed. "I have three older brothers, remember?"

"So you definitely know what it's like."

They were a few steps from the entrance when Evette said, "I'm curious—what exactly did you think Albert would say to embarrass you?"

"And I'm curious about why you decided, out of the blue, to come to Sunday school," he answered. "Do you feel like explaining?"

"Um, not yet." Evette wanted to tell him about her tentative change of heart, but she wanted to be certain she could keep her resolve before she went into great detail.

"And I can't tell you why Albert was teasing me. At least, um, not yet," he said, mimicking her.

The first step inside the classroom proved to be the hardest. The curious stares were back and even more weighted with unspoken questions than last Wednesday.

Evette hesitated for a millisecond, but when Anthony took her hand in his and kept walking, she had no choice but to follow.

The class seemed to drag on for the first few minutes until the teacher started tossing out Scripture references to look up and take notes on. Evette soon forgot her discomfort and immersed herself in the lesson.

After the class dismissed, several people came over and said hello and told her they were happy to see her again.

Evette tried not to view their comments in a negative light and took them at face value—as genuine happiness to see her again.

During the service she sat with her parents, and afterward several more old acquaintances stopped to say hello. Most of them invited her to come back for Wednesday Bible study and prayer, but Evette decided not to commit until she had given the idea more thought. For the time being she felt uncomfortable taking anything more than baby steps—like coming to Sunday school this morning.

After several minutes of greeting and hugging people, Evette realized her parents had already left. She worked her way through the crowd, heading for the nearest exit, and had just stepped outside when Anthony called her name.

Evette turned and waited for him to come over.

"Some of us are going to lunch, and I wondered if you wanted to come."

Evette rubbed her temple. As much as she wanted to join him and his friends, the earlier start to the day and the anxiety of getting reacclimated had taken its toll on her. Although it was only half past noon, she felt drained. The idea of a large crowd at a noisy restaurant gave her a headache. "I don't know—"

Anthony seemed to sense her discomfort. "Come on—you'll have fun. It'll be just you, Albert, Brienne, and me. If you don't come, I'll be the third wheel with those two."

Evette decided a group of four was much less intimidating so she agreed. "Should I drive?"

He shook his head. "No, we'll all take Albert's SUV, and afterward we'll bring you ladies back to the church to pick up your cars."

Chapter 6

F ore!" Evette shaded her eyes with her hands and tried to follow the path of yet another errant shot from Anthony.

"You know, there's no one else out here, so you don't have to yell. It's not like either one of us is surprised I messed up. Again." Anthony sighed and rubbed his hand over his head, wiping away beads of sweat.

"Yes, I do. It's part of the rules. You never know when someone might have stepped out on the course." Evette sighed as they trudged forward to locate where the ball had landed.

Anthony looked as frustrated as she felt. He still had seven holes to play, but Evette wished they could quit now. The high temperature, combined with humidity, made her wish desperately that she could be swimming instead of out on a golf course.

Anthony stopped, pulled a towel from his bag, and mopped his face with it.

Evette kept walking, intent on finding the ball. When Anthony caught up, she pointed to it and waited for him to take another shot.

With any other student she might have called out a few pointers as he prepared to swing, but she had given that up three holes earlier. Anthony claimed her incessant tips were making him nervous, so she took the hint and said nothing more. But she felt a bit irritated with him at the moment. She was the teacher, and she could see at least ten mistakes he made each time he played a shot. If anything, he was worse since the ninth hole.

As Anthony moved through a rather sloppy preshot routine, Evette closed her eyes, unable to watch. After she heard the sound of the club head smack the ball, she waited for him to groan or complain.

But he didn't. Instead he let out an excited yell. "Oh, yeah!"

"What happened?" Evette opened her eyes and moved next to him.

"I'm on the green!"

"You are? From here?" Evette was happy for him, but she had a feeling he was mistaken. It would be difficult for even the most seasoned golfer to play a shot from this spot to the green. "Why don't we go make sure?" she suggested.

"Ha! You don't believe me, but it's there. Trust me." Anthony hurried ahead, apparently having caught his second wind. Evette did her best to keep up, but the heat made her feel like a wilted piece of lettuce.

Sure enough, Anthony was correct. Not only had he made it to the green, but the ball was less than a foot from the cup. He made the putt with no problem.

He leaned against his putter, looking so pleased with himself that Evette decided not to mention he had still shot an eight on this hole.

Besides, she was counting down the minutes until this round ended. She planned to go home and take a long, cool shower, then relax on the couch with a pitcher of iced tea.

Anthony looked thoughtful. "You know what?"

"I'm too tired to guess," she admitted.

"I think I'd like to end on a positive note. Let's call it a day. How about we stop for ice cream on the way back to the shop? My treat?"

Evette grimaced. "Honestly, I'm not even going to work the rest of the day. You're my only student, and my brothers have the store covered. I'd love to have ice cream with you, but not like this. I'm pouring sweat."

He nodded. "Same here. And I have a column to finish."

"You could come over later this evening," she suggested. "I mean, if you're not too busy."

He seemed to consider this then agreed. "Okay. Sounds good to me. Around eight?"

"Excellent."

After the short ride to the shop Evette didn't even go inside. If one of her brothers saw her, no doubt they'd ask her to stay and help with something. She was not one to dodge her job, but she was too worn out to do anything right now.

After a long, refreshing shower, she helped her mother cook dinner. Her mother seemed happy to learn that Anthony would be over later and kept asking why Evette hadn't invited him to dinner as well.

"Mom, it's okay. We can do that another day. Besides, he has a column to write. I know he'd come if I asked, but then he might be in a time crunch with his assignment."

"You know he'd come? It's getting that serious, is it?"

Evette laughed. "Okay, not that serious, but we do enjoy spending time together. Even when we're tired and annoyed, like today out on the course."

Her mother sat down at the kitchen table and motioned for Evette to join her. She reluctantly followed, but her mother's questions and willingness to listen put her at ease. Before she knew it, Evette found herself pouring out the details of her afternoon with Anthony.

Anthony arrived at Evette's house at eight o'clock on the dot. He hadn't been sure what kind of ice cream her family liked, so he'd brought three flavors—chocolate, vanilla, and à la mode. The third was his favorite—vanilla ice cream with real apple pie mixed in.

After Anthony was introduced to Evette's parents, they all gathered around the dining room table to have dessert.

"I told Evette she should have asked you to dinner," Mrs. Howard said. "Maybe you can join us next Sunday after church," she suggested.

Anthony agreed to come and chatted with Evette and her dad while her mother dished up the ice cream. Just as they began to eat, the doorbell rang. "I'll get it," said Mrs. Howard.

Evette and her dad were discussing a new floor display at the shop. Anthony was listening, but he could hear her mother conversing with someone at the door.

"Trevor! What are you doing here?"

"I wanted to talk to Dad. Is he here?"

"Well, yes, but Evette has company. Can it wait until tomorrow?"

"Actually, it's kind of important."

By this time Evette and her dad had stopped talking and were listening to the conversation at the front door. "Well, don't just stand there," her dad called. "Trevor, come in here and say what you have to say. Your mother's ice cream is melting."

"Ice cream? Now that sounds good."

Evette shook her head. "Mom, make him go home, please. All he ever wants to talk about is the store."

Anthony chuckled. Trevor was only a year older than Evette, and she had told him many stories about their close friendship and rivalry. Anthony leaned toward her. "It's okay," he whispered.

He tried to stay positive for Evette's sake since he knew she had hoped for a quiet evening. Apparently the evening wouldn't be as quiet as she had wanted, but Anthony didn't mind. He came from a large family and had seen many of his siblings' dates and parties similarly invaded—and many times he had been one of the intruding offenders.

Trevor strode through the hallway toward the dining room, still talking. "As a matter of fact, I have someone out in the car who wants to talk to Dad, so I can't stay long. Evette, I know you won't like it, but I think this'll be great for business." He stopped short when he entered the dining room and saw Anthony.

Evette stood up. "Okay, spill it. What won't I like?"

Trevor blinked slowly, seemingly deep in thought. "Well, maybe you won't mind, since you have your new boyfriend here and all—"

Evette flushed a deep pink. "Trevor, he's not my boyfriend. We're just good friends. And what does that have to do with whether or not I'll like what you have to say?"

Trevor grinned. "Oh, yeah? This looks kind of serious to me. It's a Tuesday night, Mom's all dressed up, Dad's not watching baseball, and you're sitting around the dining room table eating ice cream out of the fancy bowls." Trevor crossed his arms over his chest, looking amused by his analysis of the situation.

"Dad, will you tell him to go home?" she pleaded.

"Trevor, go home. But first tell me this important news about the store."

Trevor glanced at Evette, who gave him a withering stare. "You know, maybe this can wait until tomorrow."

"After all this fuss, tell me now," his dad commanded.

Trevor stood his ground. "Trust me, Dad. It will have to wait until later. Now is not a good time."

Evette's mother sighed. "Honey, was it worth all of that fuss? Why didn't you let it drop earlier?"

He shrugged. "I guess I got carried away with—oh, man! I gotta get back to the car. He—I mean, my friend is going to wonder what happened to me."

"What friend?" his dad asked.

"An old family friend who wants to talk to you about the store. But not now, Dad. I'm serious."

"Trevor, you are not making any sense," Evette said. "First you just had to talk to Dad, but now the big news isn't so important. What's up that you don't want me to know about?"

He held up his hands in defense. "Nothing. Sort of."

Before he could say more, the front door creaked open, and another voice called out. "Hey, Trevor? Mr. and Mrs. Howard? Is everything okay in here?"

Evette gasped and sat down in her chair.

"Justin?" her mother said. "Is that you?"

Her father stood up. "Why did you bring him here? Why not to the store in the morning?" He glanced back at Evette then gave Trevor a stern look.

"Dad, I didn't know she had—company. He called me an hour ago and wanted to know if I thought you'd give him his old job back. I just suggested we should come over and ask. . ." His voice trailed off as Justin appeared in the doorway.

"Hi, Mr. and Mrs. Howard—Evette—and—" He cast a puzzled glance toward Anthony.

"Anthony Edwards." Anthony stood and extended his hand. "I think we've met a few times."

Justin nodded slowly. "I think I do remember your face."

Anthony felt the tension rising moment by moment. He knew Justin and Evette had broken their engagement, but from the reactions of Evette and her parents he had the feeling it hadn't been a mutual agreement.

Evette stared at the curtains while Justin focused on the wall. Neither one seemed willing to make eye contact with the other, and everyone else in the room remained silent, probably trying to think of something to say.

Trevor spoke first. "We came at a bad time, Justin. You'll have to talk to Dad tomorrow."

"Oh, I'm sorry if we interrupted—something." He glanced at Anthony. "I was a little impatient and talked Trevor into bringing me over tonight."

"I'd actually like to discuss this now." Mr. Howard stood, motioning for Justin and Trevor to step out of the room. "You go ahead and start dessert without me," he said to Evette's mother after the other two had left. "I'll handle this in my office."

Evette sighed quietly. "What are you going to do?"

Her dad shrugged. "I guess I'm going to sort this out and find out why he's back and needs a job."

"You aren't going to hire him, are you?" This came from Evette's mother, her brow creased.

"Well—obviously I won't take him back if the other employees at the store have objections."

"You don't have to worry about me, Dad." The steadiness of Evette's voice didn't match the distressed look in her eyes. "If he needs a job and Craig and Drew want him back, then I'm okay. Obviously Trevor agrees, and I know you've been wanting to cut back your hours."

"Are you sure?"

"Not really. I don't feel good about him being around again, but I can work around his hours, and—things should work out fine."

Anthony felt increasingly uncomfortable. He'd accidentally been cast into the midst of a very personal family situation, and now he wanted nothing more than to get out. Fast.

Part of him wanted to stay and comfort Evette, who was obviously hurt, and another part of him wondered why her father and brothers seemed so willing to welcome this scoundrel who was responsible for her emotional damage.

Evette's mother started clearing away the dessert dishes, apparently having forgotten that the ice cream hadn't been eaten.

Anthony cleared his throat softly, and Evette jumped a little in her chair, as if she suddenly remembered he was still there. She leaned across the table and shook her head. "I'm sorry about this."

"It's not your fault; you don't need to apologize." What else could he say? Should he leave now or stay and pretend nothing had happened?

His thoughts returned to Justin, and he felt himself growing angry. He wanted some answers. Frowning, he spoke. "I don't know all the history here, so maybe I shouldn't say anything—"

"You're right," Evette cut in. "You shouldn't say anything. It's a long and confusing story. The gist of it is this: Justin and I were engaged, and he called off our wedding in a very tacky way. But before we dated, he was Drew's good friend, and he worked at our store for years. He spent so much time with our family that he seemed like one of us, and by the time we started dating, that just tightened the bond we had with him. As much as he hurt us, we are happy to see him—to my dad I think it's like having one of his own kids return. What can we do? Send him packing? Even you have to admit it wouldn't be very Christlike."

Anthony didn't know how to digest this piece of information. He certainly didn't want to try to determine how this would affect his friendship with Evette or her newfound desire to deepen her relationship with the Lord and with the people at church.

If anything, he remembered that in the past her time spent with Justin had kept her away from church, and he found it ironic that just as she'd decided to make this change, the situation appeared ready to repeat itself.

After Evette recovered from her initial shock of seeing Justin, he had the impression she was glad to have him back. Was she planning to rekindle their relationship? Did Justin have similar ideas? Anthony's stomach twisted painfully. He needed to think of a way to leave quickly, without offending her.

Evette rubbed her forehead. "I'm getting a terrible headache. Would you take a rain check for tonight?"

"Sure." Anthony stood up and followed Evette as she led the way to the front door. "I may need to cancel my Friday lesson. I have to cover the Cardinals' game."

I sound as if I'm trying to dodge her, he admitted to himself, feeling uncomfortable. *And maybe I am. Having her ex-fiancé here puts me in a strange position, and I'm sure she'd understand how I feel.*

Anthony cleared his throat. "I found out about Friday just before I came over," he added. In fact, he had planned to ask Evette to come along. Now that didn't seem like such a good idea.

Evette opened the front door and smiled. "We can reschedule the lesson. When do you have some free time?"

"I—don't know. Baseball's in full swing now, and my editor has the entire department working overtime. I may even have to attend a few out-of-town games."

Evette's smile faded, making him feel even worse. The last thing he wanted to do was hurt her feelings or make her upset with him, but he needed some time to think about what had just occurred. He wanted to protect her from the hurt Justin had caused, but he also wanted to run away.

Anthony stepped outside the threshold of the door and stood face-to-face with Evette. There must be something he could say to end the evening on a light note.

"Well, thanks for coming," Evette said. "I wish. . ." Her voice trailed off, and she looked down at the ground.

Go home now, he told himself, but his feet refused to move. Even as he drew Evette into a hug, Anthony had second thoughts about the action. At first Evette seemed frozen, but after a moment she returned the embrace. Seconds later he pulled away, pausing as their faces were inches apart. Evette closed her eyes and leaned a fraction closer while he did the same. Myriad emotions swirled in his heart, but he couldn't be sure love was one of them.

Do I love her, or do I only want to win her away from Justin? The echo of that thought hammered in his brain and held him back from kissing her. Anthony smelled the perfume he loved and felt her breath on his face, but he couldn't, or wouldn't, move a muscle toward her.

He took a step back.

Evette blinked and moved away as well.

"I'll be praying for you," Anthony said then turned and hurried down the stairs as fast as his feet could take him.

He reached his car and fumbled with the keys, wondering what in the world Evette would think of him now. "I'll be praying for you?" he repeated in a whisper. "What kind of good night is that?"

He's running away. And literally at that moment he was running. *I'm not surprised.* Evette watched through the front window as Anthony dashed to his car and sped away.

With a sigh she steeled herself to face the reality of what had happened. Dad, Justin, and Trevor were still in conference in the den, the door shut tight. Mom was in the kitchen, clanging dishes around and running water.

Evette decided to elude all worried glances and questions for the rest of the evening and go to bed early. Trudging up the stairs, she recalled Anthony's last words: "I'll be praying for you."

Not very romantic, that was for sure. And what was the deal with the kiss-that-didn't-quite-happen?

Maybe I have something stuck in my teeth. On the way to her room Evette took a detour to the bathroom and did a quick mouth check. Fresh breath, nothing green stuck anywhere. *So why did he run?*

In her room she put on her pajamas, turned off the lights, and did her best to fall asleep.

After several minutes it became apparent that Sleep had forsaken her and left his enemy, Questions, behind to keep her awake.

There had to be something behind the sudden return of Justin. Had he given up on the golf dream? Or was he truly repentant? He had to be sorry. Why else would he come *here* looking for a job? Even if he didn't play at the pro level, he was skilled enough to teach at any other academy.

And what about Anthony? No sooner had they taken tentative steps to a relationship than things became confused. At first he seemed puzzled, then upset. By the end of the evening he was obviously making excuses about why he couldn't reschedule his lesson. A baseball game—how convenient. Then there was the business with the kiss—or nonkiss.

Did he think she was being too forward? Something had made him stop abruptly. Then all he could manage to say was he would pray for her. The old suspicion that he had begun the relationship only to evangelize her returned.

Maybe he had never seen her as more than a friend. And now that she had an interest in being more involved in church, he was satisfied and ready to move on to his next project. The hug had been a mistake, a miscalculation on his part. Anthony's heart held no romantic emotions for her. He had proved this by his not-so-subtle attempt to steer the conversation to prayer.

Now that her analysis was complete, Evette felt relieved. At least Anthony had the decency to back out before she fell in love with him. As much as it hurt to admit she was disappointed, she could count him as a true gentleman, unlike Justin. Despite her attempts, Evette couldn't convince herself that Justin had made any significant changes.

Chapter 7

I n spite of how you feel, I think you did the right thing. About the kiss—or the nonkiss."

"Easy for you to say. You have a girlfriend." Anthony dunked a sponge into the bucket of soapy water and wrung it out. On a beautiful Saturday afternoon he had nothing more exciting to do than wash his car. This was pretty pathetic. Heaving a deep sigh, he concentrated on cleaning the car as well as he could.

"True. But I spent a lot of time thinking and praying before I asked Brienne to be in an exclusive relationship—and relationships are not about kissing. There should be some serious commitment before you jump into physical contact like that. For example—"

Anthony hated to be a spoilsport, but he didn't think he could stand to listen to Albert waxing poetic once again about his wonderful girlfriend. All he could think about was Evette and how much he missed her.

"Hey!" Albert yelled. "I get the feeling you're ignoring me."

Anthony looked at his brother. "What now? Please don't tell me the story about when you sent the roses to her at work and all of her friends gushed about how sweet you were. I don't think I can stomach it today."

"I just wanted a clean sponge." Albert waited, his hand extended.

Anthony handed his brother the sponge and resumed working.

"You may want to call your car insurance guy." Albert stood with his arms crossed, looking close to laughter.

"Why?" Anthony gave the car a once-over. "It looks okay to me."

"I think you're going to need a new paint job."

"You can't be serious."

"It's that one spot there that looks a little faded," Albert said, pointing.

Anthony leaned in to examine the area more closely. "Don't see it."

Albert shrugged. "You will if you keep rubbing the same spot all day."

"Oh, give me a break." Anthony groaned and flicked the sponge at his twin.

"Hey, watch it. I think I'm going to wear these jeans tonight. Speaking of tonight—you sure you don't want to come with us? We're not doing anything fancy, just burgers and a movie. You might feel better if you come. I mean, Dana and Ethan are going too."

Anthony shook his head. "At the risk of sounding like a grumpy old man, I really don't want to go see a romantic comedy with two couples—one of which is engaged and the other doomed to follow in their footsteps."

Anthony's younger sister, Dana, had been engaged for a little over a month, and already the word wedding was a permanent and repetitive focal point of her vocabulary. Wedding this, wedding that—talking with her and Ethan reminded Anthony of a conversation with a toddler who had just learned a new word.

"And what will you be doing tonight?"

Anthony shot his brother a silencing look. "Man, your car is done. I can finish mine by myself. Don't you have somewhere to go?"

Albert didn't take the hint. "I hate to be pesky, but I don't want to come home and find my dear twin brother on the couch, with his eyes glazed over from an excess of chips, soda, and video games."

Anthony said nothing but hurried to finish rinsing the car. Albert was being way too annoying, and Anthony was ready for some quiet time.

"Maybe I should call Mom—leave an anonymous tip that one of her babies is having a hard time. I'm sure she'd come over and keep you company."

"Don't do it, Man. You *will* be sorry if Mom gets all worried about me."

"Look—I just want to make sure you're okay before I go anywhere tonight. Can you at least tell me what your plans are?"

"If you must know, I am going to church. The singles' group is planning to play volleyball in the gym, and I decided I might as well go."

"Good for you. I think you'll have fun."

"I guess. It would be even more fun if Evette would come too. Justin's been back here for only two weeks, and already she's skipped Sunday school and Bible study."

"But she came to Sunday morning service," Albert reminded him. "If you want to see her, why don't you go and set up another golf lesson?"

"Didn't you just say I did the right thing by not kissing her?"

"Yeah, but I didn't say you should never talk to her again. Have you prayed about it?"

Anthony shrugged. "Sort of. Every time I start praying I imagine her and that Justin together. That's what they both want, you know. I could tell by the way they looked at each other. I predict they'll be engaged again by June."

"That's next month."

"Really? I think we should sign you up for genius school."

Albert chuckled and held up his hands in defense. "Okay, that didn't make much sense. I was only trying to keep the conversation going."

Albert glanced at his watch. "Dana and Ethan went shopping for wedding stuff, and I'm supposed to pick up Brienne and meet them in an hour. I'm going to change shirts and leave now. I hope you're in a better mood when I get back."

"I do too."

"Just don't let your thoughts about Evette and Justin stop you from praying. Look at all the examples in the Bible. Moses and David and Joseph and Gideon— what if they had given up because things looked or felt impossible?"

Anthony nodded. "I know you're right. I guess I needed a nudge in that direction."

Evette arrived at church a few minutes early. Not surprisingly she struggled to ignore the butterflies in her stomach.

Coming to the singles' event was a step of faith for her. She'd given in only after several reminder calls from Kaycee Hall, a woman on the hospitality committee.

Glancing around the parking lot as she headed inside, she couldn't help but search for Anthony's car. In the two weeks since Justin's return, she had been too embarrassed to attend Sunday school or Wednesday night services. The circumstances of her parting from Anthony that night at her parents' made her feel uncomfortable, and since she didn't know any of the others in the singles' group that well, she had opted not to go. When he never showed up to schedule another lesson, Evette had simply accepted the fact they weren't meant to be a couple.

But Kaycee had kept after her about the volleyball outing. Yesterday evening Evette hadn't been home when Kaycee called. Her mother had taken a detailed message, though, and almost insisted that Evette go.

"Even if you and Anthony don't ever speak again, why should that keep you away from church? You should go and make other Christian friends," her mother urged.

Evette chose to come this once to give herself a break from her mother's worrying.

She paused outside the gymnasium door and fought the urge to turn around and run home. Strangely enough, she had worked alongside Justin for the last ten days and had not been a bit distracted or angry or even wistful. Yet the possibility that she might see or speak to Anthony tonight made her knees feel weak.

Evette gave herself a quick pep talk. *Don't be silly. You're imagining these emotions. Anthony doesn't care for you like that. He's just glad you're back in church. In fact, he probably thinks of you as his little sister or something.*

Yes, that was it. Wasn't there a verse in the Bible somewhere about that? Something about men treating the women in church like sisters. Evette made a mental note to look it up when she got home. Perhaps that would explain Anthony's intentions.

Feeling momentarily strengthened, she swung the door open. Several people were already inside, and Anthony was not one of them.

Evette exhaled the breath she didn't realize she'd been holding. "Thank You, Lord," she whispered.

"What was that?"

Evette didn't have to turn around to know that Anthony had heard her quiet prayer of relief.

"Um, I was only praying." She felt her face grow warm and willed herself not to turn around until after she stopped blushing.

"Let me get that for you."

Anthony rushed forward to hold the door she had already opened.

She stepped inside the gym, and Anthony followed. "Praying about what?" he asked.

"I'd rather not say. Sometimes prayers are just between you and God, you know."

He let out a chuckle. "Yeah. I actually don't know why I even asked. Forget I said that, okay?"

Evette nodded. Anthony looked as handsome as ever, and she felt a pang of regret that things had gone sour between them. She prayed once more, this time taking care not to say anything out loud. *Lord, help me to get over him quickly. I'd like to have fun tonight and not keep going over what-ifs.*

They stood side by side, not speaking but watching the action on the court for several seconds until Kaycee came running over.

"Evette, I was beginning to think you had changed your mind. And, Albert, I thought you said you couldn't come."

"Actually, I'm Anthony," he corrected. "Albert did have another engagement, but I decided to come here."

Kaycee leaned forward and peered at Anthony curiously. "Oh! I guess you are Anthony." Shaking her head she added, "I can never tell you two apart. You should wear name tags or something. Of course, you and your brother are such practical jokers that I wouldn't put it past either of you to pretend to be the other." She giggled then gestured toward the center of the floor. "That game will be ending in a few minutes; then we'll start a new one. Why don't you two come on over and mingle with everyone else?"

"Sounds good to me." Evette followed Kaycee to the other side of the room. It was high time she got to know some of the other people her age who attended this church. Some of them she knew from her younger days, but reestablishing these friendships would still take time.

Although Anthony followed, they spent much of the evening apart, fellowshipping in separate groups.

After the meet-and-greet session, several games of volleyball, and a banana split buffet, everyone sat down on the floor while Gene Harris, the group leader, gave a short lesson.

At first Evette had trouble concentrating. Anthony sat right next to her, and her thoughts jogged back and forth between the man sitting beside her and the content of the lesson.

"Let's all turn in our Bibles to Matthew 22:37," said Gene.

Chagrined, Evette realized she had forgotten her Bible, but Anthony had his and offered to share.

"I'll try to keep this short, so why don't we all read aloud? That way I'll know I have everyone's full attention." Gene laughed, indicating he was trying to keep the mood lighthearted, but Evette wished she could melt into the floor. Was it that obvious that her mind had been wandering?

Feeling her cheeks flame yet again, Evette cleared her throat and read along with the others. "Jesus replied, 'Love the Lord your God with all your heart and with all your soul and with all your mind.'"

Gene closed his Bible. "That's all. Any questions or thoughts you'd like to discuss?"

Evette watched the others in the group. Everyone else seemed as surprised as she felt about the brevity of this lesson.

After several moments and no response from anyone, Gene chuckled softly. "I guess everybody's in shock, since I'm notoriously long-winded."

The crowd laughed in response, and Gene continued. "I guess I could be obliged to add more to my talk. I wanted to address a problem, or concern, that I'm certain many of you have struggled with from time to time.

"Some of us who are not married enjoy being single. Others are anxiously counting the days until we find our mate. Whether or not they mean to, those around us have the tendency to bring up the topic more often than we'd wish."

Gene paced back and forth, stopping now and then to emphasize a word or phrase. "Even the most steadfast and content singles have days where we feel pangs of loneliness. Usually this group won't seek after romantic relationships but will sit back and see what happens. If someone comes along, good; if no one comes along, then we can deal with that as well. We'll sometimes think back on previous relationships and wonder if we were mistaken when we chose not to pursue marriage earlier in life.

"Then there are some of us who jump from one relationship to the next, searching, second-guessing, analyzing, and often not getting anywhere. These will probably more often feel the pain of breakups and misunderstandings, and sometimes even betrayal."

Evette swallowed hard. She'd had only one real boyfriend, but she could fully sympathize with the agony of what Gene had mentioned. She had given Justin her all, and he had thrown it away. The gaping hole left by what she'd poured into their relationship still ached at the most inopportune times, no matter how hard she tried to ignore it.

Gene's voice broke into her thoughts. "We love Jesus and want to serve Him and give Him our best. I know you've heard that now, while you're still single, is an excellent time to put your all into serving the Lord. Although singleness can seem burdensome at times, the amount of flexibility and freedom you have at this stage can allow you to give more of your time than you could if you were married and raising a family."

Evette had heard this before, and while it made sense, it didn't bring much comfort. She never felt called to preach in foreign lands or quit her job to take on a full-time mission position. Even though she enjoyed her life as a single woman, she couldn't deny that she sometimes felt a longing for marriage and a family. Sometimes she daydreamed of ironing shirts, planning meals, and even changing diapers.

Though her days were no longer consumed with sorrow regarding the end of the engagement, Evette still felt something was missing.

She glanced at Anthony and wondered "what-if" one more time. He must have felt her gaze on him because he turned and gave her a smile.

The fluttery feeling in her stomach returned. But now was not the time for romantic daydreams. Evette pushed the thoughts away and tried to regain her concentration. She glanced up as Gene made eye contact with her.

He must have sensed I wasn't paying attention, Evette decided, feeling sheepish.

Gene cleared his throat and kept going. "My point is simple. Maybe you feel that while you are single you're only a fraction of a person. You hope you'll feel whole—that whatever is missing will magically materialize when you find the right person. I know I've wrestled with these same emotions." He paused and took a drink of water.

Evette shifted slightly and sat up straighter. She didn't want to miss a word of this. She had been mulling over the same thoughts.

"Folks," said Gene, "don't let this idea run your life. You are a whole person. Now don't get me wrong—when you do get married, you will feel another kind of completeness. But to imagine and be concerned that you must meet someone in order to be whole is not correct.

"Love the Lord your God with everything in you—your entire heart, your entire mind, your entire soul. It's not as easy as it sounds. But I can guarantee you this—once you get going, you'll wish you had done it sooner."

He stopped pacing and shrugged. "So you don't have a significant other yet. Don't despair about it. Choose now to serve Jesus with all of your energy. Love Him. He makes you whole. He saved you, He redeemed you, and He loves you. He loves you with all He has, and you can do the same for Him. Give Him your all. Remember those worries about being a fraction of a person?"

Gene shook his head. "Love Jesus with all your mind and don't give those thoughts any room. Does your heart ache sometimes? Open all the empty spaces in your heart, fill them with love for Jesus, and the ache will disappear.

"Be whole in Him. I promise—you'll be so much happier. Even if you don't think you're unhappy, you'll notice the difference. Besides, this is an attitude you want to have in place before you say 'I do.'

"If you don't, Miss or Mr. Right will come along, and you'll feel better for awhile. You'll think he or she was the missing piece. You'll go merrily along, thinking the puzzle is solved. But what happens the day you have a disagreement? Or when the other person disappoints you? What if one of you says something hurtful—and you don't even mean it?

"All of a sudden you might feel that hole open up again, and this time it'll be bigger. You'll be discouraged and may even wonder if you should have stayed single.

"This is when you'll need to realize that no person is perfect and people will fail you. You'll be able to pick up, forgive, and move on with your mate. We all make mistakes.

"So don't put all your trust in people. This doesn't mean you can't have deep and intimate relationships with other people. It simply means you shouldn't look to them to make you feel complete. Please give your all to the One who can make you whole. Make that choice and live it now. Do it while you have the opportunity to practice and grow at it. Pretty soon it'll be second nature to you."

Gene quickly ended in prayer and called the evening to a close.

Evette somehow got to her feet and made her way out to the car, but she didn't remember how. Her mind was still replaying bits and pieces of Gene's lesson.

He had hit the nail on the head—at least for her situation. She had been prepared to let herself believe she'd fallen in love with Anthony because she felt incomplete. Not that he wasn't a nice guy—a solid Christian—good looking. But she wanted more than anything to find some way to plug the crater that had formed when Justin left.

Evette shook her head as she fumbled with her car keys. No, that crater had existed before Justin left. It had existed in college, even in high school. Then one day she had looked up and felt a void, a tiny sinkhole of nothingness. Not long afterward, Justin had asked her out, and she accepted happily. The chasm was gone. Sort of.

Gene was right. Time with Justin had filled the gap. But when they argued or were apart for long periods of time or when she mistrusted him, the hollow came back—even bigger.

The time spent in getting over the breakup had caused the cavity to swell so large that Evette sometimes wondered if it would grow big enough to swallow her.

The delight of getting to know Anthony and a hint of his attraction to her began the cycle once again—a temporary fix for the hollow that quickly faded once she realized her assumptions were incorrect.

Evette located the correct key and unlocked the door. Footsteps sounded behind her. "Evette?"

It was Anthony. She put on a brave smile. "Hi."

He leaned closer. "Are you crying? Is everything okay?"

Evette blinked. She hadn't noticed the pooling tears until Anthony mentioned them. She rubbed her eyes with the back of her hand, thankful the sky was nearly dark. How embarrassing to be caught crying, of all things. "No. Just—watering, I guess. Pollen, maybe."

"Oh. One of my sisters has bad allergies, so I hope you feel better soon." He shifted from one foot to another but didn't say anything.

Evette cleared her throat and looked around. People spilled out of the church, some headed directly to their cars, some in groups of two or more, laughing and talking.

She sensed that Anthony had more he wanted to say, but she wasn't certain she was ready to hear whatever it was.

"Well," she said, taking care to keep her smile intact, "I guess I'll see you at church tomorrow?"

"Yeah. I'll be here. And I was wondering if you wanted to have lunch afterward?"

Evette shook her head. She had too many feelings to sort out. "I don't think so."

"It'll be at my parents' house. We usually all get together for dinner a couple of Sundays out of the month. I know they'd like to meet you." Anthony still sounded hopeful, and she hated to let him down.

"In fact, I know I can't. It's my brother's birthday, and his wife is planning a big party tomorrow afternoon. I really shouldn't miss it." Evette was grateful for the excuse, but declining the invitation still felt bittersweet.

"I see."

Evette slid into her seat. She decided that if he had anything else to say he would spill it before she drove away. As she was closing the door, Anthony spoke up.

"About last week—when I came over. I didn't mean to be rude or harsh when I left. And you're right—I don't know the entire situation, so it's not my place to opine about how Justin should be treated."

Evette didn't know how to read this comment. Did this mean he felt differently about her? She also noticed he had failed to mention the attempted kiss.

"Well, I'm glad you feel that way. Because he's working at the store full time now."

Anthony swallowed then took a deep breath. "I guess I never did reschedule my lesson. Can you fit me in some time this week?"

"Definitely." She smiled. She couldn't help but feel excited at the prospect of spending more time with him. "My schedule is even more flexible right now because Justin's almost always available to work in the shop. Of course that's because he doesn't have many students yet, but for now I can work around your calendar since you've gotten so busy lately." Evette stopped talking and reprimanded herself for rambling. That was a sure sign she was nervous.

"I'm free on Monday. How's two o'clock?"

"Perfect. I'll make a note of it in my planner."

Anthony rested his arm on the roof of her car. "I guess I've kept you standing out here long enough. I'll see you Monday."

Evette smiled. It felt as if things were returning to normal between them, and that was a relief. "I'll see you tomorrow—at church. Remember?"

He laughed. "Oh, yeah. Tomorrow. And if you change your mind about coming to my parents' just let me know. I'll give you a rain check, and you can redeem it whenever you want."

"Will do." Evette closed the door and started the car as Anthony walked away.

The wistful feeling wrung at her heart again. He would make a perfect boyfriend. . .soul mate. . .husband. In a flash she could picture them at their wedding, decorating a home, taking their kids to the park.

Her thoughts returned to Gene's lesson, and she firmly pushed the images away. The ache of emptiness had resurfaced.

Evette closed her eyes and breathed a silent prayer. *Lord, I want to be whole. And not because I have somebody. Show me how I can let You fill those hollow places— because I can't handle the weight of it on my shoulders again.*

Chapter 8

The jangling of the doorbell signaled that someone was entering the shop. Evette looked up as Trevor and Craig strolled in.

"Hey, Sis, we're back from lunch," Trevor announced.

Evette laid her paperwork aside. "Good, because I'm famished."

"I suggest the Caribbean chicken salad at Grady Bakeries," said Trevor. "That's what we had."

"I'll keep that in mind."

"How's business?" Craig wanted to know.

"Brisk. This nice weather has given lots of people golf fever. Since you two left, almost everyone who walks in the door has bought balls or gloves or tees."

"Where's everybody else?" Trevor glanced around the shop.

"Dad and Drew are in back rewrapping grips and fitting clubs. I think a couple of people left some clubs to have the shaft changed, and Dad said he'd let one of you handle it."

"Where's Justin?"

"He had his first lesson." Evette glanced at her watch. "He should be finished any minute now."

"Well, good for him. He's a great teacher, and I knew it was only a matter of time before people started beating down the door to study with him," said Craig.

"Yeah," Trevor agreed. "I'll have to watch my students and make sure they don't migrate over to him. I guess that makes him the resident pro around here."

"That makes who the resident pro?" Justin's voice sounded from the back of the store.

Trevor grinned. "Hey, you caught us talking about you. I don't want to look up and find out you took all my students."

Justin laughed. "I don't think we have to worry about that. I'm relieved I finally got one student. I was beginning to wonder."

Evette shook her head. "You didn't have to worry. You're a great teacher. As soon as word gets out, there'll be a throng of people at the door trying to get some range time with you."

"You think so?"

"I know so." Evette's heart did a familiar flip-flop. She had tried very hard to keep her distance from Justin, but that proved more and more difficult when she spent six or eight hours a day in his presence.

He seemed different somehow. Her father and brothers knew more about the reasons behind Justin's sudden return, and she had decided not to ask too many questions. The less she knew, the less she thought about the situation, and that helped her cope with his being around again. But Craig had confided that Justin's failure on the tour had humbled him considerably. His new vulnerability made Evette want to reach out to him and somehow cheer him up. The fact that he had a new student seemed to help considerably.

"Well, since I have this first lesson behind me, I want to celebrate. Who wants to go to lunch with me? It's my treat," said Justin.

"Sorry, but Craig and I just ate," Trevor announced.

"Dad and Drew will probably work through to get those orders filled, so you'll have to do the celebration lunch another day," said Craig.

Justin's shoulders drooped. "Well, what about you, Eve? Have you eaten yet?"

"I was going to run out and get a sandwich, and that's not very festive. Craig's right—you should celebrate another day when everyone can come. An evening would probably be best for everyone."

"Haven't you guys ever heard of spur-of-the-moment? Come on, Eve— don't make me have lunch by myself. I know you can't be upset with me still—I thought we agreed to let bygones be bygones. I know a great restaurant, and we'll be in and out in an hour."

Evette's brothers and Justin were silent as they waited for her answer. True, they had agreed to let the past remain in the past, but that didn't involve going to lunch with him. Still, she supposed it would be harmless, and she hated to be a party pooper when his confidence had a boost.

"Okay, I'll go. But I need to be back by two because I have a lesson."

Justin jingled his keys and glanced at his watch. "Hey, that's almost two hours. Believe me—we have plenty of time."

Before she knew it, Evette found herself in Justin's car as they zoomed toward the restaurant. One thing she hadn't missed about her ex-fiancé was his tendency to drive way too fast. Taking a deep breath, Evette checked the tension on her seat belt and prayed they would be safe. She hoped they wouldn't be in the car too long. When Justin entered the freeway, Evette's heart sank. The last thing she needed was to be in midday traffic on Highway 40 with a wannabe race car driver.

"Where are we going?" she ventured.

"This nice little café in the Central West End."

"Central West End? Are you kidding? It takes a good half hour to get there from this part of Chesterfield. I thought you said we'd be in and out in an hour," she protested.

"I changed my mind when you said you needed to be back by two. We have a little extra time so we might as well make the most of it."

"Isn't there anywhere else we can go?" she pleaded.

He considered for a moment. "I guess we could go to Clayton or Soulard."

Evette leaned back in her seat. She had also forgotten Justin's love for out-of-the-way places. She had once considered this trait romantic, but now she dreaded being in the car with him for more than ten minutes.

Considering her choices carefully, Evette decided the much farther ride to Soulard would fray her nerves too badly. Though Clayton was a bit closer, Justin would probably be upset she didn't want to visit his intended restaurant. "Never mind. We can do the West End."

"Good," said Justin. "I think you'll like it."

They didn't talk much for the remainder of the ride, except for Evette's many warnings for Justin to slow down or look out.

By the time they reached their destination, Evette was grateful Justin had the decency to open her car door. Her legs felt so wobbly from his risk taking that she didn't think she could stand if he *hadn't* taken her arm.

"Are you okay?" he asked.

"Honestly, I don't know. I think you drive even worse than you did when we—" She stopped midsentence, not wanting to say the word engaged.

Justin merely laughed and gave her a quick hug. "Nah. You just drive so slow that you forget what it feels like to go the speed limit."

At least twenty retorts ran through her mind, but Evette held her tongue. After all, this was supposed to be his celebration lunch. She only had to smile and say encouraging things and everything would be fine.

Once they were seated and had ordered their meals, Justin's easygoing demeanor changed somewhat. He grew very serious and leaned across the table to take her hand in his. "Remember what I said about bygones back at the store?"

Evette resisted the urge to pull her hand away. "Yes," she said cautiously.

"I didn't really mean it."

Evette blinked in surprise. Surely he wasn't about to blame her for the entire breakup? In her opinion the fault rested solely on *his* shoulders.

"Don't get me wrong," he explained. "I mean the part about putting the painful things behind us, but I wonder—"

Evette shook her head and took a sip of her water. "Don't wonder. Let's try not to think about it. There's nothing to wonder about."

"Come on, Eve—I know you. I still have feelings for you, and sometimes I can tell by the way you look at me that you do too. I messed up—made some big mistakes, but—"

Evette did pull her hand away. "No. I mean that. My family hired you to work for us, not to pick up where you left off. I don't dislike you, but I have feelings, emotions. I spent all this time trying to rationalize why you left. There's no way we can just—start again."

Justin leaned back in his chair and stared out the window.

Evette suddenly felt cold. "Justin, please. This is supposed to be your big celebration. Let's not be angry with each other—why don't we try to talk about something positive instead?"

After several moments of silence he finally spoke. "You're right. It's been hard for me to be around you every day. I keep thinking about how I ruined everything, and I wonder—you know, if we'd gotten married, next month would be our six-month anniversary."

Evette twisted the napkin in her lap. "Can we please change the subject? Reminiscing about what could have been may be fun and nostalgic for you, but it's not my cup of tea." Her brave front wasn't completely honest. Despite her words, Evette had a difficult time suppressing the image of herself as a bride, headed down the aisle to meet Justin.

Justin held up his hands. "No problem. What do you want to talk about?"

"Anything." Evette placed the napkin on the table. "Tell me about life on the tour."

His features darkened. "There's not that much to tell. I couldn't cut it. I'm not the worst, but I'm far from the best." He shrugged. "I was silly to throw myself into it like that. I should have come home, trained some more, married you, and then gone back to give it a shot. I was too impatient, and the more I tried to fix my game, the more it fell apart."

The pitiful expression on his face nearly moved her to tears. It was so easy to be unconcerned about him when he wasn't sitting right in front of her. "Then I'm glad you came back. Who knows—maybe you can try again in another year or so."

"Or maybe not. I'm not so sure that's what I want." His voice was urgent, almost pleading. "Maybe I'm meant to be a teacher, not a pro. I think I want to settle down, raise a family, you know."

The sound of Justin talking about raising a family rendered Evette speechless for the moment. Was he intentionally trying to make her cry?

"Are you okay?" he asked for the second time since they'd arrived.

Evette closed her eyes for several moments to hold back the tears. They weren't tears of either joy or sadness; instead they sprang from a mixture of emotions—emotions she didn't feel capable of processing.

For Justin to saunter back into her life and suggest they start over was too good to be true. There had to be a catch—some kind of conditional promise. *Yes, that's it. He wants something*.

Satisfied with her analysis, Evette opened her eyes. She wouldn't let his hints and insinuations get next to her. "I'm fine," she told him.

At that moment the waitress arrived, bearing their lunches. Feeling rattled from the wave of emotions, Evette took a bite of her salad right away. Then she noticed Justin hadn't started eating.

"Did they get your order wrong?"

"No, I was just wondering if you wanted me to say grace?"

Justin wanted to say grace? That was a first. In the past he had grudgingly paused as Evette said a short blessing over the food. But after awhile she had given up completely.

Now she blushed deeply, having been caught skipping grace. *By him, of all people.*

Evette wanted to groan. She'd so wanted to show Justin how much she had changed, how she'd grown closer to the Lord, how she didn't need a mate to be whole—how she was better off without him. Now he'd gotten her on a technicality.

She wiped her mouth with the napkin and nodded. "I guess I forgot about praying over the meal."

"That's okay." Justin reached across the table for her hand. "Do you mind if I—?"

Evette shook her head. "No, go ahead." She bowed her head as Justin prayed a very short but eloquent prayer.

He began eating, but she couldn't think clearly. She was impressed, to say the least.

He must have felt her watching him because he stopped eating. "Something wrong?"

"No, not really. I admit I'm surprised to hear you praying. You didn't care for things like that before. Do you mind my asking when this changed?"

He hesitated. "It's kind of personal, but I guess I was lonely out there by myself. I think one day I simply felt as if I needed to find out more about God." He shrugged. "It kind of reminded me of you in a way. I felt—I don't know—secure."

Evette listened while he talked. His comments were pretty generic, but she did sense that he was searching for a spiritual change. She thought carefully. In all honesty she couldn't remember if Justin had ever accepted Jesus into his heart. He'd attended church off and on, but other than that he didn't seem too interested in anything having to do with the Lord.

Of course, that didn't prove whether or not a person had a relationship with the Lord. Evette could attest to that. Only recently had she decided to focus on Jesus and live her life for Him.

Now that she had lived both sides of the story, she likened being a half-hearted Christian to being a halfhearted runner or golfer. It wasn't optimal. When she had played sports in school, she had learned quickly that slacking off in her training made for poor performance in the competitive arena. The same went for spending time with the Lord every day, instead of only on Sundays.

In real sports, when Evette's body was strong, she was less susceptible to game-day injuries. In the same way, a well-fed spirit protected her from spiritual injuries. In the short period since she had resumed a daily quiet time, Evette already felt more well rounded. *I feel whole.*

"I felt as if I was missing something," Justin admitted. "I never liked church that much, but the few times I went, I felt that I was getting in on something I needed."

Evette nodded excitedly. Now was her chance to share her own progress. "I know exactly how you feel. The pastor at church talked a bit about this yesterday."

"Really? What did he say?"

Evette was definitely surprised now. The old Justin would never have voluntarily asked for a sermon synopsis. She plunged ahead. "Well, the Scripture he spoke about was in 1 Corinthians chapter 9. It compares a person's walk with the Lord to training for a race. I guess I identified with that since I ran track in school."

Evette stopped to be certain Justin was still listening. "The point is—you have to approach your life as though you're getting ready to run a big race. You have to keep your goal in sight. You can't just 'kind of' do things, but you have to be as dedicated to this life in Christ as a person training for the Boston Marathon is to winning."

Justin nodded. "I've never thought about things in that light before. But I'm impressed with what you know."

"What do you mean?"

"I mean, you've been going to church all these years, and I went only when I was forced to. Now that I'm at this kind of crossroad in my career and everything, I wish I'd paid more attention to sermons and prayer meetings."

She chuckled. "It's not too late. Trust me on this. Why don't you come to church with me sometime? Or even Wednesday night classes? It may feel a little awkward at first—it did for me. But once you get into it, you'll be so surprised at how much you start to understand the Bible."

He shrugged. "I don't know. It sounds kind of interesting. Let me think about it, and I'll let you know."

"Sure."

Justin grinned. "You know, all this talk about the Bible reminds me of back when we first started dating. You used to go to those Bible camps and everything. Do you remember the time when—"

Chapter 9

"Are you sure she remembered my lesson?" Anthony paced back and forth inside the pro shop. It didn't seem like Evette to forget about his class. And her brothers seemed to be deliberately holding back part of their explanation as to where she was. A two-hour lunch break seemed a little far-fetched in his opinion.

"I know she remembered because she mentioned it before she went to lunch," Craig answered. "It's only ten after two so they may have gotten stuck in traffic."

The last sentence caught Anthony's attention. "They?" This was the first he'd heard of Evette having left with another person.

The phone rang, and Craig answered it hurriedly. As he spoke, he motioned for Anthony to take a seat or browse the shop. Anthony decided on the latter.

Moments later the bell on the door announced an entry. Before he saw her, he heard Evette's laughter.

A feeling of dread washed over him as he caught a glimpse of her walking in, her arm looped through Justin's. She seemed a little unsteady on her feet, but if she was hurt she probably wouldn't be laughing. Feeling awkward, Anthony hung back and remained where he stood.

"I will never ride in a car with this man again," she told Craig.

"Still has a lead foot, huh?"

"Lead is putting it mildly. Is there a heavier adjective we could use?"

"Let me remind you that you were the one complaining about being late for your lesson. I did my best to get you here on time," Justin said.

"Next time, let me be late."

"You are late," Craig pointed out. "I'm putting you two on record for the longest lunch break in history."

"Sorry," Evette said. "We started talking about the old days when we were kids and. . ." Her voice trailed off as she stared at Craig. "You said I was late for my lesson. Did Anthony show up?"

"Ahem." Anthony stepped out into clear view. "I was here five minutes early even."

"Oh, no." Evette covered her face with her hands. "I'm so sorry. Of course I'll deduct part of the cost. Let me grab my clubs, and I'll meet you out on the range." Before he could answer, she disappeared into the back room.

Anthony hefted his bag onto his shoulder. "I guess the lesson starts now."

Justin stepped forward and held out his hand. "I know we met briefly, but we weren't properly introduced. I'm Justin Greene."

"Anthony Edwards. Evette tells me you're an old family friend." Anthony felt a degree of satisfaction from using the word *friend*. That sounded so much better than ex-fiancé. He didn't like the idea of Evette's spending time with this guy, no matter how long ago the wedding had been called off.

Anthony couldn't shake the mental image of how natural the two of them had seemed together moments earlier.

"Anthony Edwards—don't you write a sports column for the newspaper?"

Anthony nodded. "Yeah, I sure do. It's been nice meeting you, but if you'll excuse me, I need to get my lesson in. I'd hate to miss out on more time than I already have." He turned and walked toward the exit that led to the driving range.

"I'll see you around," Justin called after him.

I hope not, Anthony thought.

Evette waited for him outside. "I'm so sorry you had to wait. Justin taught his first lesson today, and he wanted to celebrate. Craig and Trevor had already eaten, and Dad and Drew were busy, so he talked me into going." She paused but kept looking directly at him. "I felt as if I should go, you know, because he's been a little depressed about not doing well on the tour, and I wanted to cheer him up—boost his confidence some. I thought we were going to a place nearby, but he wanted to go to the Central West End. It was either there or Clayton or Soulard—so I picked the West End, since that's where he wanted to go in the first place. Then we got to talking and eating, and I totally lost track of time."

He set his bag down and pulled out the pitching wedge. "We start with this one, right?"

"Right. And you're sure you're not upset about my being late?"

This was not a topic he felt comfortable discussing at the moment. Nor was this a good place. He would prefer to take her out to dinner and find out whether or not he had a chance at a deeper relationship than they now shared.

He did his best to remain lighthearted. "Look—you don't have to answer to me. You don't have to give me a full report of where you've been or what you've done—because we don't have that kind of relationship."

She blinked slowly. "Of course I know that," she said in a voice that sounded overly cheerful. "I just wanted you to know that—"

Anthony shook his head. "Evette, nobody's perfect. I can't say I've never missed an appointment or run late. And if you feel as if you need to help your friend get his confidence back, then don't let me stop you."

She bit her lip and looked away. Anthony wished he could rewind the time and take back everything he'd just said. *She's genuinely concerned about Justin, and all I can do is think about my own hurt feelings.*

Anthony considered the distance between the two of them. In two short steps he could have her in his arms.

"For some reason this feels pretty awkward, doesn't it?" Evette asked suddenly.

Anthony nodded. "Yeah. I guess I should admit I'm not too happy about your getting back together with the man you nearly married. I was hoping maybe we were getting to be more than friends."

Anthony heard the door squeak open as Evette was about to answer. He could tell from the look on her face they were no longer alone on the range.

To his great frustration he turned around to find Justin lugging his clubs down the corridor. The man had the nerve to take up residence on the practice mat next to the one where Anthony stood.

"I didn't know you had another lesson today," Evette remarked.

"Nah. I don't have another one. But things are slow inside so I thought I'd come out and work on my long game for a bit."

"Oh." Neither Evette nor Anthony moved as Justin began a warm-up.

Anthony looked to Evette for help. Justin could have chosen at least twenty other practice mats, and in Anthony's opinion his current choice bordered upon rude.

"Do you think you could move down a bit?" Evette suggested. "I'm giving a lesson, and—"

"Oh, I see." Justin gave her a knowing look. "Afraid he might hit a bad shot? I better move for my own safety, huh?"

Evette cleared her throat but didn't answer that question directly. "I'd just like to have a little student-teacher privacy, if you don't mind."

"Not a problem." Justin grabbed his bag and moved all of one space over.

Anthony wanted to groan, and Evette didn't look very pleased. She opened her mouth to say something, but Anthony decided it would be best to leave well enough alone. "Never mind," he said quietly. "Let's get started."

Evette had him review his swing motion then let him start hitting some balls. Not unexpectedly, he did miserably. Anthony did his level best not to shank the ball toward Justin—no way would he give him the satisfaction. But his shots went anywhere but straight.

Whiff, slice, hook, shank, top—you name it; I've mastered every bad shot known to golfers. But even more annoying was the fact that just ten feet in front of him Justin had settled into a rhythm of great shot after shot after shot.

As soon as Anthony messed up, Justin, without fail, hit the most spectacular drive.

After fifteen minutes Anthony sensed that Justin was only out there to have a laugh at his expense. He stopped and watched Justin hit a few.

"He has a great long game, doesn't he?"

Anthony shrugged but grudgingly agreed. "Yeah, I guess so."

When he resumed practicing, Anthony did even worse than at first, if that was possible. Justin's presence had definitely robbed him of any semblance of progress. Evette must have felt so as well.

"Why don't we work on your putting?" she suggested.

Anthony could have hugged her for being so intuitive. "You'll get no argument from me there." He replaced the clubs and followed her to the putting green.

Justin glanced up as they passed him. "Giving up so soon? That's no way to learn the game. It takes time, and you won't learn to drive by quitting."

Anthony inhaled deeply, trying not to say anything he might later regret. If there were academy awards for being annoying, this man would win.

"No one's given anything up," Evette said. "We're going to putt. Why don't you join us?"

Justin hesitated. "I may do that. I'll check inside, though, to make sure I'm not needed."

Anthony frowned. Did she have to invite Justin along? As soon as they were out of hearing range, he voiced the question to Evette.

"Trust me—he's not going to come. He'll find something to do inside."

"I hope so."

Evette sat down on a chair and covered her face with her hands. "Oh, boy, I shouldn't have said that. I ought to go apologize."

Anthony stopped practicing and knelt beside her. "What are you talking about?"

Her shoulders sagged. "What I said to him about putting. I said it on purpose because I was upset. I felt as if he was trying to wreck your lesson—to get you off balance. I knew you were getting frustrated, and I wanted to make him stop."

Anthony swallowed a smile. It felt good to know that Evette wanted to spare his feelings. "I still don't understand, though. Why is that so bad?"

Evette shook her head and lowered her voice a bit. "That's why he came back to St. Louis. He's awesome off the tee and in the fairway, but his short game has totally fallen apart. He can't putt for anything. He's trying to relearn, but he doesn't have much confidence right now.

"Since he did his best to show you up on the range, I couldn't resist tossing out a challenge here on the green. I knew he wouldn't show up because there's no way he'd embarrass himself like that. My brothers have already told him how good you are at this."

Anthony felt a surge of pride to find he was better than Justin at something, but his heart went out to Evette, who was caught in the middle somehow.

"I need to tell him I'm sorry," she repeated. "I know I hurt him."

"Don't you think it might hurt his ego that much more if you go in there and apologize for crushing it?"

"Do you think so?"

Anthony shrugged. "I guess not. If I were Justin, I'd feel embarrassed at first, but after awhile I'd be happy you thought enough of me to do that."

"Are you sure?"

He nodded. "Positive."

Evette stood slowly. "I think we can both agree this session has been a near disaster. Let's pretend it didn't happen and schedule you another lesson. I won't charge you a cent for this."

"I don't mind paying. I mean, I feel guilty about taking up your time."

"No. I can't let you pay. We'll pick an hour when Justin isn't here, or I'll make sure my brothers keep him away next time."

"I like that plan," he agreed. Before Evette could get away or change the subject, Anthony reached out and held her hand.

"Remember what we were discussing before he barged in?"

"Yes." Her voice wasn't much louder than a whisper.

"Let me take you to dinner so we can have some time to talk."

For a moment she nodded her head. Then she backed away from him. "I can't. Don't take this personally, but I'm trying to do things right from now on."

"What?" Anthony felt completely bewildered.

"Do you remember what Gene talked about Saturday?"

"Yeah—but I don't understand why you think we can't have dinner. It's just a date. We'll never get to know each other if all we do is golf lessons."

"I know. But maybe now isn't a good time. It's not that I don't want to spend more time with you, because I am attracted to you. I think very highly of you, and I'm honored you asked me out—"

"But what?" Anthony persisted.

"I'm one of those people Gene talked about. I feel that emptiness, and I've always figured that when Mr. Right came along, it would go away. When I dated Justin, I felt better; but when he left, it got worse. When you started paying attention to me, the same thing happened. I think you're a great guy, but what if we aren't meant to be together?"

Anthony didn't answer. He didn't like the direction this conversation was taking.

Evette continued. "Anthony, we'll have to pray about taking our relationship further. But right now I owe it to myself to learn how to be whole in Jesus instead of waiting for the perfect guy to help me feel complete."

Anthony sighed. "I don't like what this means, but I understand and respect what you're doing. I don't have a right to try to distract you from your relationship with God."

She gave him a wry smile. "Isn't that the reason you started bugging me to come to church more often? You obviously thought I needed to polish my halo a bit."

Anthony grinned sheepishly. "Yeah, I guess that's what I said. I have to admit, though, that I was pretty interested in finding out if you might be that someone I could spend the rest of my life with." He gave her his most hopeful look.

She giggled. "Come on—don't make me answer that right now. Give me some time to get my priorities straight, and then we can see about—anything more."

"Okay. I can't promise I won't ever be impatient, but I will wait." He brushed her cheek lightly with his fingertips. "I'll wait for as long as you need."

Chapter 10

The float trip? I don't think so." Evette lifted her eyebrows. A couple of women from Sunday school class had gotten together for lunch and were discussing an upcoming group event.

Nina laughed. "Why not? It's a chance to be in the great outdoors. For somebody who spends so much time outside, you sure don't seem very enthusiastic."

"A manicured golf course is a good deal different from a wild river," Evette countered.

"Come on—you have to go. We need to have an even amount of people so the canoes won't be lopsided," said Michelle.

Evette shook her head. "Sorry, ladies, but this doesn't sound very fun to me. Besides, you won't know if you'll have an uneven number until the sign-up deadline."

Michelle leaned an elbow on the table and rested her chin in her hand. "And the translation for that would be: You want to make sure a certain Mr. Edwards is going before you say yes. Am I right?"

Evette was speechless for a moment. How should she answer that?

Nina laughed. "Uh-oh, she's tongue-tied. I think you're right, Michelle."

Evette finally shook her head. "No, that's not it. Anyway, what are you trying to say about Anthony?"

"We're not saying anything—except we notice you seem to spend a lot of time talking to him, and he always manages to find a way to sit next to you. People are starting to think of you two as a couple."

"Well, that's not necessarily true."

"So, if someone else is interested in him, you wouldn't be offended?" asked Nina.

Evette sighed. She had suspected Nina liked Anthony, and now she was at a loss. Was it fair to keep other women away from him while she waited on an answer from the Lord? As much as she hoped that one day she and Anthony could have a more serious relationship, Evette felt that being dishonest with Nina would be the equivalent of taking the matter into her own hands, rather than letting the Lord resolve it. "I guess I don't have a clear answer. We've talked about dating, but right now I don't feel ready to move in that direction."

Nina looked puzzled. "So is that a yes or a no?"

"A no, I suppose. We're both attracted to each other, but we mutually agreed not to date."

"I see," said Nina, but the look on her face indicated otherwise. "If I'm not being too presumptuous here—does it have anything to do with that very hand-some man who's been coming to church with you lately?"

Evette blushed. How could she explain this without opening every detail of her life to these women? While they had begun a friendship, she didn't feel close enough to them to tell them everything about herself.

"Not really," she told them. "Justin and I are old friends—in fact, several people at church probably remember him from a few years ago. To make a long story short, we were engaged, we broke up, he moved away, but he moved back last month—and right now he works at my dad's store."

"Does he have a girlfriend?" Michelle wanted to know.

"Honestly, I don't know. We don't get that involved in each other's personal lives these days."

Michelle grinned. "Well, be sure to bring him Sunday, and I'll see if *he* wants to go on the float trip."

Evette chuckled. "Are we still discussing the float trip?"

"Come on, Girl," said Nina. "We're talking about the Niangua River. I've done this before, and it's not terribly intimidating. I mean, you're not going to hit any major rapids or anything like that."

Evette sighed. "Okay. How long do I have to make up my mind? Isn't the trip at the end of August?"

"Yes. But you have to decide by the first of August. It's the first week in June now so you have two months to think about it."

"Okay. I'll think about it, but no promises," Evette said firmly.

❧

Evette was on her stationary bike when the cellular phone rang. Happy for a dis-traction, she reached for the phone. "Hello?"

"Hi, it's Anthony."

"Oh, hi."

He was quiet for a moment. "Are you jogging or something?"

She laughed. "No. I'm sitting on this bike trying to eke out the last half mile."

"Oh. Then I'm sorry to interrupt."

"Don't worry about it. Besides, there's nothing good on TV, so I was in the process of making up excuses for why I shouldn't finish my workout. Your call is a welcome diversion."

"Good, because I have a favor to ask."

"Ask away." Evette slowed the pace of her pedaling so she could hear better.

"You remember my sister Dana and her fiancé, Ethan?"

Evette smiled. "Yes, we've run into each other a few times at church. And Ethan is so charming. What woman doesn't dream of marrying a man who loves to cook?"

"Ahem. Are you taking a shot at my cooking abilities?"

"I don't know. You've never cooked for me."

He laughed. "Trust me—you don't want me to either. Albert says he'd starve if he didn't cook for us."

"That's really sad. Even my brothers can cook in a pinch. My mom made sure of it."

"Yeah, my mom tried to teach me too, but I guess I wasn't paying much attention. But since Albert was a model student in the Mavis Edwards Academy of Culinary Arts, I didn't have to put forth much effort. He cooks, and I eat."

Evette shook her head. "Getting back to this favor—"

"Yes. Remember that Ethan's opening his own restaurant?"

"Mm-hm." Evette leaned forward and pedaled a bit faster. *Just one quarter of a mile to go.*

"Well, they're having a preview party for friends, family, and investors next week. I wondered if you might like to be my guest for the evening."

"This sounds like a serious event," Evette mused aloud. "Is your family expecting you to show up with—anyone?"

"I don't know. I guess they'd be surprised, but I really think it would be good for you to meet them all. Even my brother Max is driving in from Kansas City."

"Aren't he and his wife expecting a baby soon?"

"The end of this month. Of course, my mom thinks they should stay put. She told Max, 'If that baby decides to come early, what will you do?'" Anthony laughed. "Right now she's convinced the baby will be born in the car on the side of I-70. Believe me, she's not too happy about it."

"But they're coming anyway?"

"For now they're holding to the plan. Plus, Stacy's sister Maddy's fiancé has some work in an art show here the same weekend, and they wanted to be here for that too. I think they'll bring Maddy and Jordan to the party with them."

"Wow! This sounds as if it's shaping up to be an exciting event."

"Is that a yes?" Anthony wanted to know.

"I guess so. As long as we don't have to say we're a couple or anything very official. I'd rather be seen as your friend right now."

"Okay, we'll tell them that. But I won't promise that will stop any of them from speculating."

Evette grinned. "I understand. My brothers would do the same. But, to answer your question, I will go."

"Thanks a lot. I'm looking forward to it."

"Me too." Evette glanced at her watch. "I have to run and get ready for work. I have a couple of lessons to teach, and my dad has been hinting that we need to do inventory. Seems he found some inconsistencies in Trevor's method."

"Uh-oh, that sounds like some serious overtime."

"Exactly. Don't panic if you don't hear from me for two or three days."

"The same goes for me. A couple of the guys at work are on vacation so everyone has extra assignments."

"So no golf lessons this week?"

"I doubt it—although Dana's wedding is getting closer, and I want to be able to play with dignity by then."

From the drop in his voice Evette could tell he was getting discouraged.

"Drew told me he's been using a new swing gadget with some of his students, and it seems to work well. Next time you come in, maybe we'll see if it can help you."

"That sounds great. I need to get going, but I'll see you at church. And I'll get back with you next week with more details about this opening."

"Okay." Evette hung up the phone and smiled happily. Although it was sometimes frustrating that she didn't feel a release to be Anthony's girlfriend, it was nice to know he was there for her as a friend. She recognized that other women were interested in him, but he had decided to keep praying and wait for Evette to make her decision.

Now that he wanted her to meet his entire family, she thought all the more highly of him. She also felt more than a bit nervous. *Please, Lord, don't let me make the wrong decision.*

❧

"Okay, how do I look?" Evette twirled in her ankle-length royal blue dress and waited for Anthony's approval.

"You look fantastic. I can't wait to show you off to everyone."

The two of them said good-bye to her parents and walked out to his car. After they drove off, Evette admitted to Anthony that she was extremely nervous. "What if they don't like me?"

He laughed. "Most of them already know you—at least they've seen you at church. I can't think of any reason why they wouldn't like you."

"What about the ones I haven't met?"

He reached over and covered her hand with his, patting it gently. "Relax. It's a party, and everyone will be in a good mood. You don't have to worry about saying the right thing. Just be yourself, and they'll see what I already see in you."

"I'll try my best."

The ride to Ethan's restaurant was far too short for Evette. The butterflies in her stomach were in full force by the time Anthony led her inside.

Dana met them as soon as they walked in. After hugging them both, she turned to Anthony. "You won't believe this, but I think Otis is about to challenge one of our investors to a basketball game."

Anthony shook his head. "Good old Otis. Always trying to get a competition going."

"And you have to stop him," Dana said emphatically.

"Me? Why not Jackson or Albert or somebody?"

"Jackson's not here yet, and Albert is over in the corner with Brienne, looking all googly-eyed. I hate to try to drag him away from her."

Anthony cleared his throat. "I brought someone too, in case you didn't notice."

"I know you did." Dana looped her arm through Evette's. "And I'll take good care of her. I'm going to introduce her to the girls."

Anthony looked at Evette and held up his hands. "I think I'm backed into a corner."

She gave him a brave smile. "I'll be fine."

"All right then." He turned back to his sister. "What do I have to do?"

Dana shrugged. "Get over there and change the subject. Get them talking about something else besides sports. Ethan's in the kitchen cooking his heart out, and he'd be mortified to know that one of my brothers is out here attempting to organize an impromptu tournament. I mean, look at them—they're all wearing suits. And not one of those men is under the age of forty. I seriously doubt any one of them has the game he's bragging about. You have to calm them down before somebody goes out and gets hurt."

Anthony frowned. "I'll do my best. But for future reference tell Mr. Ethan he shouldn't have told Otis about that basketball goal in the back parking lot."

"Come with me," Dana said to Evette. In a matter of moments she ushered her over to a corner table where several women had gathered.

"Ladies, I want to introduce you to someone. This is Anthony's good friend Evette. She goes to our church so most of you have probably seen her. Just for a refresher, let me go over the names. These are my sisters, Sheryl and Latrice. My sisters-in-law Verna, Marva, and Stacy. Then we have Stacy's sister Maddy, my mother Mavis, my aunt Florence, and my aunt Daphne."

Evette smiled and acknowledged each woman. *I only hope I can keep all of these names straight.*

Mavis Edwards was the first to speak. "Honey, why don't you sit down?" There was an empty seat between her and her daughter-in-law Stacy, and the women gestured for Evette to take that chair.

Feeling nervous because they were all watching her, Evette did her best not to trip in her three-inch heels as she made her way to the spot.

As soon as Evette sat down, Dana said, "Ya'll take good care of her, or else Anthony will be fussing at me for years to come." She winked at Evette. "From what I can tell, I think she's a pretty special friend of his." She checked her watch. "Oops! I think I was supposed to pull something out of the oven five minutes ago. I hope Ethan caught it." In a flash she was headed toward the kitchen.

The first few moments after Dana left, Evette felt awkward. The group had been chatting away until she joined them. She felt like a high-school student trying to barge her way into the cheerleaders' inner circle. They all seemed to be sizing her up.

Finally Stacy leaned over and said in a stage whisper, "Mavis might look stern, but she's a real softie. And the rest of us don't bite, so you can relax."

This comment made everyone laugh, and before she knew it Evette started to feel like one of the girls. "Is this your first big Edwards family event?" Stacy asked. With a shrug she added, "You'll have to excuse me if I ask questions everyone already has answers for. I live on the other side of the state so I miss out on things sometimes."

Evette smiled. She liked Stacy already. "Yes, this is my first official family gathering. I guess you can all tell I'm pretty nervous."

"You should have seen me when Max brought me to meet everyone. I was shaking in my boots. To make matters worse, Mavis put me to the test."

Sheryl laughed. "I had forgotten all about that. Mama made Stacy help clean chitlins." She shook her head.

"Honey, in my kitchen, if you don't clean 'em, you don't eat 'em," Mavis said. "And how was I supposed to know she had never cleaned them before?"

Florence spoke up. "I remember that day. After five minutes anyone could see that child had no idea what she was doing. Mavis dear, I think you let her keep going on purpose."

"Maybe I did. It was kind of funny to watch."

"It wasn't funny for me," Stacy cut in. "I was miserable. But I guess I deserved it since I was too scared to admit I had no idea what I was doing."

Latrice laughed. "Evette, the moral of the story is, if Mama asks you to do something and you don't know how, just tell her. It'll save you a lot of stress."

"I know that's right," said Daphne. "Mavis is as sweet as honey most of the time, but every once in awhile she likes to play jokes on people."

Mavis stood up and put her hands on Evette's shoulders. "Ya'll need to stop scaring this girl. I declare, this child is shaking." She kissed Evette on the cheek. "Don't pay attention to them. I do have my practical joke streak, but I only do that to people I know well."

Evette smiled, not sure how to handle all the attention. Mavis sat down and folded her hands in her lap. "Of course, since I hear that my Anthony thinks so highly of you, I expect we'll be seeing a lot of each other." Mavis took a deep breath, creating an atmosphere of expectation. "So you might want to watch out when I get to feeling antsy. I do love a good joke."

Daphne shook her head. "She gets creative about it too. One time she even called me on the phone pretending she was selling something."

Verna laughed. "Not just anything, mind you. She got me with that one too. Claimed she was selling tickets for a ride in a time machine."

"That's a new one to me," said Florence. "Now, Mavis, you are too old to be playing like that."

Mavis giggled, looking very much like a schoolgirl. "See, Florence—that's what keeps me young. You ought to try it sometime. I have to let loose every once in awhile and have some fun. I can't let being old stop me, can I, Evette?"

"Um, I guess not," Evette said, hoping she'd come up with the right answer.

"I like you already," Mavis said.

Evette breathed a sigh of extreme relief.

≈

Anthony watched Evette from the other side of the restaurant. She seemed to be relaxed and having a good time. He wished he could go over and check on her, but the situation with Otis wasn't quite under control. Both Otis and Mr. Davis had competitive personalities, and it had taken a great deal of time and finesse to smooth the rift between them. Apparently one of the two had asked about the other's skill on the court, and within minutes a simple question had escalated into a challenge of who was the best.

Right now they were discussing football, and while Anthony wished he could veer the conversation away from sports, he took comfort in the fact that there was no football field nearby.

"Hey, little bro." Anthony turned and found Max standing behind him. "It's been awhile since we've seen each other. I missed you." He pulled Anthony into a hug.

"Hey, I missed you too. I've been meaning to come up to Kansas City and visit sometime."

"Good idea. Come in a month or two. By then we'll probably be in desperate need of help. We'll take a couple of days off and let you get up when the baby cries in the middle of the night."

"You excited?"

Max nodded emphatically. "We can't wait."

"I'm guessing Mom is a little surprised her prediction didn't come true."

"Yeah, but Stacy and I are thrilled the baby wasn't born on the side of the highway."

"I know I've already told you this, but I'll say it again. Congratulations."

"Thanks. So now that Sheryl and Dana are engaged"—he glanced toward the corner table where Albert and Brienne sat—"and Albert will pop the question to Brienne any day now, that leaves you. By any chance will I get to meet this Evette that Dana mentioned?"

"I brought her with me, but the women have her now." Anthony pointed to the table where the female members of his family had congregated. "I'll be lucky if I get to say more than two sentences to her before the night is over. You know how they get when they're all together."

Max nodded. "We're staying the whole weekend so maybe we can get together before we leave."

"That sounds fun, but it all depends on what Evette's schedule is like. I'm not sure if she has classes to teach."

"That's right. She's a golf teacher."

"She's my golf teacher. I need all the help I can get before Ethan takes the groomsmen out to the course."

Max nodded. "I need to brush up on my game too. We've been running around, getting things ready for the baby, and my game hasn't been a priority."

"Does that mean you guys are coming for Dana's wedding for sure?"

"Oh, yeah. I can't miss my baby sister's wedding. And we'll be back in December when Sheryl and Peter get married—same goes for Albert and Brienne. So what's your date?"

"My date?"

"Yeah. Have you and Evette set a date?"

Anthony blinked. "We're not even engaged. Hey, we're not even officially dating."

"Back up and run that by me again. If she's not your girlfriend, then why the buzz on the family grapevine?"

Anthony shrugged. "Because that's how the family grapevine works. Sometimes stuff that isn't news, is, and stuff that's real news gets overlooked."

"Yeah, you're right. But explain to me why everyone is confused about this?"

"I guess it's partially my fault. Evette doesn't want to commit to a romantic relationship right now. She wants to make sure she is spiritually ready to handle a relationship. Plus, her ex-fiancé called off the wedding, moved out of town for several months, and then resurfaced a couple of months ago. I don't think she's still interested in him, but he seems bent on making it difficult for me to spend any time alone with her. He rides to church with her, he hangs around while I'm having my lessons—and she doesn't really do anything to stop him."

Max tilted his head to the side. "Have you two discussed this?"

"You sound exactly like Albert. And, no, we haven't addressed this situation directly. I don't want her to feel as if I'm trying to push her into a decision."

Max nodded solemnly. "I think it might be in order at least to ask for an update. Do you think she's considering going back to the other guy?"

"I hope not. He's so obnoxious that I can't imagine they would make a good couple. But then again she seems intrigued that he's interested in making some spiritual changes, so—"

"Maybe she sees something you don't, or can't, see."

"That's not a happy thought, Man."

"And that's exactly why you need to have a talk with her. The sooner, the better. Even if she hasn't made a decision about the two of you, I think you deserve to know if this other man has somehow edged into the running."

"You're right. I will."

"And soon. Promise me that," Max persisted. "Just by looking at you, I can tell you've already fallen for her. I don't want to see you get hurt."

"Me either," Anthony agreed.

The meal was scrumptious—roast duck, salad nicois, spinach soufflé, and mushroom risotto, followed by raspberry and lemon sorbet-filled profiteroles, that looked like tiny cream puffs, for dessert. Ethan was an excellent cook, and everyone agreed his restaurant would be a great success.

But Evette had a difficult time enjoying herself because she sensed something different about Anthony. When they arrived, he had been jovial and lighthearted; but now he seemed terribly quiet and contemplative.

Did I do something to upset him? Did I say something wrong? she wondered.

Before she could give the matter any more thought, the party took an unexpected turn. Stacy whispered something to her husband, Max, and in a flash he jumped out of his seat.

For the next few minutes everyone ran around trying to be of assistance, but mostly getting in the way, as Max put his wife into the car and headed to the nearest hospital. The newest member of the Edwards clan had decided to come two weeks ahead of schedule.

Chapter 11

E vette, wake up." Evette could hear Anthony's voice, but it sounded far
   away—almost as if she were in a tunnel somewhere.
   Where am I? She opened her eyes only to squeeze them shut again.
Some place with really harsh lighting, she decided. She opened her eyes again but
blinked rapidly in hopes of giving them a few moments to adjust.

"I have another nephew," Anthony said, beaming. "It's a boy."

The hospital. Now I remember. Stacy had the baby. She stifled a yawn and
smiled. "Congratulations. Have you seen him yet?"

"Just for a couple of minutes. He's so little."

Evette couldn't help but smile. "Most babies are. When was he born?"

"About twenty minutes ago."

Evette checked her watch. "I can't believe it's seven in the morning."

"And I can't believe you slept through the birth."

She shook her head. "I missed all of the excitement."

"It wasn't that exciting. All we did was sit out here and wait."

"Was I the only one who fell asleep?"

"Dad dozed off for awhile, but everyone else stuck it out."

Evette's face grew warm. "I guess I was pretty conspicuous." She buried her
face in her hands. "I didn't realize I was so tired—I remember calling my parents
when we got here to let them know what was happening—but I don't remember
falling asleep. How embarrassing."

Anthony rubbed her shoulders. "Don't worry about it. We all took turns letting you lean on us."

Evette wanted to groan. "Double embarrassment," she muttered. "Please tell
me I did not drool or snore."

Anthony cleared his throat and looked away, but not before she saw him
swallow a big grin.

"Oh, no," she wailed softly. She glanced around the nearly empty waiting
room. "Where is everyone?"

"Standing in front of the observation window oohing and aahing over him."

"Ohh, how sweet."

"Do you want to see him?"

"Yes and no. I'm too embarrassed to face everyone."

Anthony stood and held out his hand. "Not a good excuse. There's no reason to feel like that. You had a long week, and you were worn out. So you fell
asleep. Big deal. Everyone goes to sleep. I won't let you feel ashamed about it."

Evette placed her hand in Anthony's. "All right."

"All right," Anthony echoed. "Let's go see this baby."

The entire family huddled together outside the nursery window.

Amazing how new babies put everyone in a good mood—even people who haven't slept a wink all night, Evette mused.

Anthony maneuvered a corner spot for Evette and him. His mother stood next to them. "There you are, Sleeping Beauty," she said as she gave Evette a hug.

Evette felt her face grow warm.

"Oh, now you know I'm just teasing you. Scoot on over here and take a look at my newest grandbaby."

The little one was pretty well hidden from view—decked out in a massive blanket and a tiny hat—but Evette thought he was adorable.

"He's so precious," she whispered.

"He is." Anthony stepped closer and put his arm around her.

Evette did her best to savor the priceless moment. This family was refreshingly tight-knit—much like her own.

"What did they name him?"

"Jacob Carson Edwards," said Mavis, beaming proudly.

After a few minutes Anthony yawned loudly. "I think it's time for me to get going. Are you ready to go?" he asked Evette.

"I sure am. Do you feel up to getting behind the wheel? Or should I drive?"

He chuckled. "That wouldn't do much good since I'd still have to drive after I dropped you off. I might as well wake up now."

The rest of the crowd began to disperse, and Evette joined in the round of hugs. "Tell Max and Stacy congratulations for me," she told Anthony's mother.

"I will, Honey. And don't be shy and stay away. Has Anthony invited you to one of our Sunday dinners yet?"

"I have, Mom," he answered. "But she hasn't been able to come yet."

"Well, don't be a stranger to us, Evette. We'd be glad to have you."

"I'd like to," she said. Evette had a feeling that even if she and Anthony remained nothing more than friends, his mother would still show her the same warmth.

"Before we leave, I want to find a cup of hot coffee somewhere," said Anthony. "Let's stop by the cafeteria on our way out.

Once they were in the car, Evette did her best to keep the conversation going because Anthony seemed suspiciously drowsy.

"Are you sure you don't want me to drive?"

"I'm sure. So quit asking," he said, laughing. He rolled down the window to let in some of the cool morning air. "Just keep talking to me."

"I'm glad I had the chance to meet your family."

"They were pretty excited to meet you too." He gave her a sideways glance. "They keep asking when we're getting married."

"And what did you tell them?"

"I told them I was waiting for you to make up your mind."

Evette's jaw dropped. "I can't believe you put all the blame on me. I mean— we've never even really discussed—at least, not seriously."

Anthony grinned sheepishly. "I guess I might have forgotten to tell you how I felt." He yawned again and fumbled for his Styrofoam coffee cup.

"You keep your eyes on the road," Evette said, handing him the hot drink. "We'll talk this over later. You're too sleepy to make any monumental decisions right now."

When they reached her house, he looked even more drowsy. "Are you sure you can drive?"

His reply was a gigantic yawn.

"Why don't you come inside and get a refill on that coffee? My mom usually has some going by now."

"Thanks," he said and followed her inside.

Her mother was up and about and, true to Evette's prediction, had brewed a large pot of coffee.

"Your dad went in early this morning," she said as she hugged Evette. "Did everything go well at the hospital?"

"Yes. The baby was born about an hour ago. It's a boy."

"Congratulations," her mother said to Anthony.

"Mom, I fell asleep at the hospital, but Anthony and the rest of his family pulled an all-nighter. I'm going to get ready for work, but could you make sure he looks sufficiently coherent before you let him get into his car?"

Her mother took a look at Anthony and ushered him to a chair at the kitchen table. "I'll do my best, but this boy needs some sleep."

"I know, but he insisted on driving."

Evette took another look at Anthony, who seemed unusually quiet.

"My goodness, he's asleep," said her mother. "You run and get ready, and I'll take care of him."

Evette was relieved to let her mother handle the job. While Anthony might insist to her that he could make the drive to his house, he would be less likely to disagree with one of his elders.

Half an hour later Evette bounded downstairs, refreshed and ready to go to work. She peeked out the front window and saw Anthony's car still parked out front.

She found her mother in the kitchen, but no Anthony. "Where is he?"

"Shh." Her mother gestured toward the living room. "I made him lie down on the couch. He was too out of it to eat or drink anything, so I put my foot down and sent him in there. He should be okay to drive in a couple of hours."

Evette peeked in the room and watched him for several moments. Her mother had thrown a blanket over him, and his stocking feet hung over the armrest. He was out like a light and let out a few snores every once in awhile. *Cute,* Evette thought.

"Thanks for taking care of him, Mom. I hope you don't have anywhere to go."

Her mother shook her head. "Not really. I have to go grocery shopping, but that can wait until this afternoon. After he wakes up I'll do my vacuuming. I'm just glad he got you home all right."

"I am too. You should have seen me, talking nonstop about everything that popped into my head."

"Now are you sure you feel alert enough to make it to work?"

Evette waved her mother's concern away. "I spent the night in a hospital waiting room chair, but I'm okay—at least for the moment. I'll see you this evening."

❦

"Hey, how was the hospital?" Trevor wanted to know as soon as she reached the shop.

"Fine, I guess. I slept through most of it, believe it or not. But the baby's adorable. A little boy."

"Guess what?" said Drew. "Dad has determined that on a scale of one to ten Trevor's inventory skills are a minus two."

"Hey, I made a few innocent mistakes, and now he's in the back having a fit," Trevor defended himself.

"So what does that mean for the rest of us?" Evette asked.

"It means that we have to do inventory twice a month until he feels satisfied that things are being handled correctly. We have to work in teams of three; and you, Drew, and I are signed up for next weekend."

"No way." Evette's heart sank at the prospect. They usually did a full count of all products every other month. The job was extremely tedious—not to mention that being closed up in the storeroom for long periods of time was never fun.

She stared at Trevor. "You must have really messed up."

"Interesting how everyone's so quick to blame, but no one else volunteered to keep track of the day-to-day stock. It gets a little confusing, so cut me some slack."

Evette keyed in her code on the register and officially clocked in. "I can't do it this weekend. Anthony is taking me to the Muny to see a musical on Friday night."

"You have to unless Trevor wants to trade with you. He, Dad, and Justin are scheduled for the next go-around in two weeks," Craig explained.

Evette swallowed her pride and prepared to beg for mercy. "Come on, Trev—please switch with me. He bought these tickets three weeks ago. And they're doing my favorite musical."

Her brother smirked. "Ah, now look at how the tables have turned. Two minutes ago you were criticizing my job skills, and now you want me to show mercy so you can go sit outside and watch some play with your boyfriend."

Evette leaned on the counter. As much as she wanted to keep the date with Anthony, she didn't have much patience for Trevor's annoying foibles this morning. "Are you going to trade with me or not?"

"Yeah, I guess. It's not as if I have anything better to do."

"Thanks," she said.

"So I guess you and Anthony made it official?" asked Justin, stepping over to the counter.

Evette felt strange discussing her personal life with Justin. "Not really," she said. "We're still just friends," she said cautiously.

"Oh, come on—admit it," prodded Drew. "You two are not just friends. I mean, you spent the entire night with his family waiting for his nephew to be born."

"I would have come home, but I couldn't very well ask one of them to leave the hospital and take me home. They might have missed the big event."

"Yeah, likely story," Craig said, laughing.

Trevor singsonged under his breath, "Evette's got a boyfriend. Evette's got a boyfriend."

Craig and Drew chimed in and sang along while Justin stared at her.

Brothers. Evette shook her head, remembering how much fun she'd had with the women in Anthony's family. She loved her family, but on days like today she'd gladly trade one or more of the boys for a sister.

❧

The next week Anthony had to skip Wednesday night Bible study, but Evette went anyway. Since Justin had faithfully attended Sunday morning services with her, she invited him to come along, but he turned down the invitation.

"I like going on Sundays, but I'm not ready to give up another night of the week," he explained.

"I understand, and I'm not trying to force you to go," she told him. "Just thought I'd check and see."

"Thanks for the invite, but I'll stick to once a week for now."

Evette considered his words as she made the short drive to church. For the first few weeks Justin's interest in attending church and learning more about the Bible had been impressive.

But over the past few weeks his interest had waned drastically. He'd even skipped church altogether the previous week. A few of his buddies he'd met on the tour were in town, and he wanted to play a round of golf with them.

While she didn't approve of his choice, she didn't make an issue of it. As she'd had to do, Justin would have to make his own decision about how much he wanted to put into his relationship with the Lord. Evette no longer felt comfortable with the idea of missing church, but she also realized it had taken her years to make that decision.

On the one hand, she was sad that Justin didn't seem as excited about drawing closer to the Lord. She knew her own life felt dramatically different. The empty feeling had all but disappeared, and she woke up each day feeling more refreshed and relaxed than she remembered feeling since she was a little girl. From her discussion with Justin, Evette knew he still felt hurt and confused about his unsuccessful run at the pro tour, and she wished the same change for him.

On the other hand, knowing she and Justin didn't see eye-to-eye on spiritual issues made it easier to ignore the pangs of longing that sometimes resurfaced. While she couldn't deny that her feelings for Anthony grew stronger with each passing day, she still faced a jumble of emotions when it came to Justin. It was harder to walk away from her first love than she could have imagined. His name was embedded in so many of her memories of firsts—first date, first dance, first kiss, first proposal—the list went on and on.

On the other hand, he was also attached to some of her more forgettable firsts—first bout of jealousy (Jacquie Phillips had done everything in her power to get him to ask her to the senior prom); first mistrust (when he'd cheated on her during her sophomore year in college); and, of course, first broken engagement (no explanation needed).

Yet she still found herself wondering if she should give him a second chance. "What should I do, Lord? Which one is the right one for me?"

Chapter 12

What are your plans for next weekend?"

Evette shrugged. "I don't know. But the weekend after that is full. Remember our new inventory system at the store?"

Anthony nodded.

"Well, I was scheduled to work today and tomorrow; but since you'd already bought tickets for the play tonight, Trevor switched with me."

"I see. So how would you feel about going to Kansas City for a couple of days? We'd leave Friday morning and come back Sunday afternoon."

"We? I don't know—"

"Oh, it wouldn't be just you and me. Mom and Dad want me to drive them there to visit Max and Stacy. And Albert thinks he might come too." He cleared his throat. "I hope you didn't think I was suggesting anything—"

"Untoward, unseemly, improper," Evette supplied with a grin.

"Yeah. All of those."

She shook her head. "I know you weren't suggesting anything less than gentlemanly. I just thought I'd tease you a little."

"So will you come?"

"Let me think about it. Give me a few days to see if I can reschedule my lessons and get someone to cover my hours at the store. I have to admit, a short road trip sounds like a great idea."

❧

The drive to Kansas City was perfect. Sunny weather and extremely light traffic made the conditions ideal for a four-hour drive.

They rode in Albert's SUV in order to have more room for their weekend bags. Anthony and Albert sat in front, and Evette sat in back with Mavis and Claude, who were overjoyed at the prospect of seeing their grandbaby again.

As soon as they pulled into Max and Stacy's driveway, Max came out to greet them.

While the men took the bags inside, Evette helped Mavis carry in the baby gifts she'd brought.

Stacy was inside, making sandwiches. Mavis promptly told her to sit down. "Evette and I will do the cooking while we're here."

Stacy shook her head. "I can't let you do that. You are our guests."

Mavis stood her ground. "No, I won't have that. You sit down and enjoy that baby. If we lived closer, I'd let you cook. But since we don't get here that often, I insist on doing my share."

The sound of crying echoed over the house intercom. "I tried to put him down for a nap, but I think he must have realized he's missing out on some excitement," Stacy said. "I'll be right back."

While Stacy was gone, Mavis took inventory of the contents of the kitchen cabinets in order to plan meals for the next two days. If anything was missing, she had Evette take note of it and compile a grocery list. "And I plan to make at least a week's worth of casseroles while I'm here," she informed Evette.

Evette watched as the tiny dynamo of a woman put down stakes and took charge of the household. Within half an hour of their arrival she'd sent Stacy upstairs to nap while baby Jacob slept and had shooed Claude and Max to the living room to assemble a baby swing. Albert was given the task of mowing the lawn, and Anthony was on the sidelines, waiting to be called into duty. "As soon as we finish this shopping list, Honey, you and Anthony can run to the store and get everything."

Evette nodded and continued to do as she was told. She couldn't help but wonder how Stacy felt when it came to Mavis's take-charge attitude.

After spending an hour in the kitchen with her, Evette decided that while Mavis definitely had a strong personality, she wasn't an overbearing mother-in-law type. She truly wanted to help out, but her manner wasn't mean-spirited or condescending.

"Now," Mavis said, wiping her hands on a dishtowel, "please call everybody in here to eat lunch—except for Stacy. I'll fix her a plate and give it to her when the baby wakes up."

Evette called the men to the dining room and helped Mavis serve the sandwiches.

After lunch, Mavis sent everyone back to their jobs. While she started on her assembly line of casseroles, she had Evette accompany Anthony to the store.

"Double-check the list, and please don't forget anything," she cautioned as they headed to the car.

When they were well on their way to their destination, Anthony ventured a question. "So how did you enjoy your first hour under the tutelage of my mom?"

"It was—interesting," said Evette. "Actually I had fun."

"You didn't think she was being too bossy?"

She shrugged. "I don't think so. I think she's just trying to help."

Anthony laughed. "Tell that to Albert. He's still grouchy that he had to cut the grass."

"I thought he didn't look so pleased."

"Yeah, that and the fact that Brienne had to work this weekend and couldn't come. Mom wouldn't let him back out because she said she needed an extra set of hands to help her out. He didn't realize it involved yard work."

"Poor Albert," said Evette.

"Poor Albert? What about Stacy? Mom ran the woman out of her own kitchen."

Evette shrugged. "She seemed pretty grateful for the break."

"You say that now," Anthony laughed.

"What's that supposed to mean?"

"It means, what if you and I were married and Mom came over and did that same thing in our house? Would you think it was nice then?"

The words "our house" filled Evette's imagination with a montage of warm images. She very much liked the idea of "our house" as long as Anthony was in the picture. "No, I don't think so. New babies are lots of work, and my mom always said she wished either set of our grandparents had lived closer when we were little."

Anthony seemed surprised. "So you wouldn't mind?"

Evette grinned. "As long as it didn't happen every day, I would welcome it. I think she's being really sweet."

"Well, I, for one, am glad you feel that way," said Anthony.

Evette sighed happily and looked out the window. There were no words to describe how it felt to fall in love.

❧

"Ah, our traveler returns to the reality of daily life," Craig said as Evette entered the store Monday morning.

Evette closed her umbrella. "Can you believe that wind out there?" She peered out and focused on the dark gray sky. "You know, I really dislike rainy, dreary days. Especially after the weather was so nice all weekend."

"How was the trip?" he asked.

"It was nice."

"Nice? That's all?"

Evette smiled. "I'll give you the condensed version. I spent the first day helping Anthony's mom cook. I think she made twelve casseroles. Saturday we went window shopping on the Plaza. Then we took a boat ride in Brush Creek—it's a waterway that runs along the outer border of the Plaza. Stacy's sister babysat Jacob, and Max took us all to dinner at the Cheesecake Factory. Sunday morning we went to church then returned to the house. I helped Mavis cook dinner, and then we got in the car and drove back."

"What time did you make it back here?"

"Around eight o'clock. I was exhausted and went straight to bed."

Craig sighed. "I think I need a vacation."

"Why don't you take some time off? With Justin around, it always feels like we're overstaffed."

"I think I will. Lisa wants to go to Chicago for the Fourth of July. I'll ask Dad if he can spare me for a few days."

Evette took a look at the daily schedule. "It looks as if you and I are the only ones working until noon."

"Yeah. And nobody's going to come in today with this kind of weather. We might even be able to close early. Justin had a lesson, but the man canceled because of the storm. I tried to call him, but there was no answer. I'm assuming he figured the lesson was off."

"So it's just you, me, and an empty store. What should we do?"

"Go home?" Craig joked. "No, I guess we can always restock shelves. I'll run to the back and drag out some of the heavy boxes, and you stay out front in case someone ventures in."

"Will do," said Evette, as she took a seat behind the register. She found the remote to the television set and turned on the power. Normally her dad insisted it always be tuned to the Golf Channel, but in questionable weather they were allowed to switch to a local station to keep up-to-date.

The phone rang, and Evette answered. "Hello?"

"Evette?" It was Justin, but for some reason he sounded surprisingly unlike himself.

"Justin? Are you okay? You do know your student canceled his lesson, right?"

"I figured he would. I need a favor, though."

She sighed. "I don't know. Craig and I are the only ones here right now so I probably wouldn't be able to leave. Are you having car trouble again?"

"I guess you could say that. I wondered if you or one of your brothers could possibly pick me up and give me a ride home?"

"Where are you?" A flash of lightning tore through the horizon, followed by a gigantic clap of thunder. Evette shuddered. The one thing worse than a thunderstorm was being out in one. She surfed the channels to locate a station giving a weather report.

"At the hospital."

"What?" Evette's stomach turned, and she felt sick. "Did you say you were at the hospital?" Evette turned down the volume on the television and strained to listen to Justin. Why was he speaking so quietly?

"Yeah." He let out a shaky laugh.

"What happened? Are you okay?" Her words tumbled out in a rush. Evette anxiously glanced toward the storeroom door. What was keeping Craig so long?

"I had a car accident, and my car is totally undriveable."

"But what about you? Are you hurt?"

"Not too bad. I have some cuts and sprains—they said I don't have a concussion so there's no reason for me to stay overnight."

Another clap of thunder shook the building. Evette didn't like the idea of going out in the storm, but she hated to let Justin down. "Hold on a minute, and I'll see what we can do about getting you a ride home, okay?"

Evette ran back to the storeroom and hurriedly explained the situation to

Craig. He picked up the extension and got the name of the hospital from Justin, then prepared to head out into the storm.

"Do you think he's okay?" Evette asked.

"I'm not sure. He sounds pretty out of it."

"Yeah, I noticed. Maybe they gave him some pretty strong meds."

Craig gave the interior of the shop a cursory glance. "I hate to leave you here by yourself. Do you want me to call Dad and ask him to come in?"

Evette shook her head. "I doubt anyone will come in now. I'll wait here until you get back."

Craig looked doubtful. "If you feel uncomfortable, lock up and go home, okay?"

Evette nodded dutifully. Craig was the perfect big brother. "I will."

"Be back as soon as I can," he said, tugging on his jacket and heading outside.

True to her prediction, no one ventured to the shop. The weather got worse, and Evette found herself pacing back and forth in front of the window. "Lord, please keep Justin and Craig safe on the road."

Half an hour later Trevor arrived at the store, looking grim.

"Hey, you're not supposed to come in today," she said. "Just couldn't stay away?"

He lifted his eyebrows. "Hardly. I was sound asleep and got a call from Craig demanding I take your shift. He wants you to meet him at Mom and Dad's house."

Dread washed over Evette, and she was reluctant to voice her concerns, fearing what the answer would be. "Is something wrong with Justin?"

"Nothing serious, but he's in a lot of pain. When he talked to you on the phone, he wasn't being totally honest. Craig said the wreck knocked him around pretty good."

"So he took him to our house?"

"Yeah, and he wants you to go and help Mom take care of him."

"I see." Evette got her keys and purse. "I'll see you later."

On the way home she found herself worrying. Poor Justin. She was glad Craig had taken him to the house. He shouldn't have to be alone at a time like this.

At home her parents were busy upstairs, making Justin comfortable in Trevor's old room.

Justin seemed half asleep, but he opened his eyes when Evette came into the room. "How do you feel?" she asked, keeping her voice quiet.

"Not too good," he croaked.

She patted his hand and pulled up a chair next to the bed. "What can I do? Are you hungry?"

He shook his head. "No. . .just. . .sleepy."

Evette looked to her mother. "What did they give him?"

"I'm not sure, but he'll probably need more soon. He was complaining that his shoulder hurt a few minutes ago. Craig went to the pharmacy to get a prescription filled, and he should be back in a few minutes."

Her dad stood in the doorway. "I think we should let him rest for awhile.

There's really nothing we can do."

Evette agreed. "Should I go back to the store then?"

Her dad shook his head. "I don't think that's necessary. I'll go. You stay here and help your mother with Justin."

After her dad left, Evette and her mother retreated to the family room. When Craig came, they gave Justin another dose of medicine, which promptly put him to sleep.

Evette and her mother took turns checking on him to make sure he was okay, but he slept most of the afternoon.

At six o'clock Evette took him a bowl of soup, and he insisted he wasn't hungry but asked for more medicine for his shoulder. Evette sat down next to the bed again. "You have to eat something before we give you anything for your shoulder."

She helped him sit up a little, then fed him several spoonfuls of soup. The medicine still made him groggy. While she fed him, he kept dozing off then awoke to ask her if he could go home.

Evette pressed her hand against his forehead to see if he might have a fever. It felt a bit warm, but she couldn't be certain since she didn't have a thermometer.

"Mom?" she called. "Could you come here for a minute?"

Moments later her mother entered the room. "What's wrong?"

"He feels a little warm. Do you think he could have a fever?"

Her mother felt his forehead and shrugged. "No, his temperature feels pretty normal to me. He just needs some food and rest."

Justin groaned. "Can I go home?"

"He keeps asking that," Evette said.

Her mother shooed Evette out of her seat and picked up the bowl of soup. "Justin, honey, you're going to have to work with me and eat this soup. The doctor told Craig that as long as you got rest and fluids, you would start feeling better soon. You can go home as soon as we think you're up to it."

Justin didn't argue any further but sat up and ate the soup. When he finished, he insisted on walking downstairs to sit in the family room with them.

"I don't think that's a good idea," Evette told him.

He leaned forward and covered his face with his hands. "Please let me go home."

Her mother rubbed his back softly. "Justin, as soon as I know for sure you can get around okay and you can cook for yourself, I'll let you go home. Until then you've got to do what I say so you can get better."

Justin didn't answer, but his shoulders shook as he made sniffling sounds.

Her mother leaned closer. "Now, Honey, why are you crying?"

He shook his head and mumbled something Evette couldn't decipher.

Her mother chuckled. "No, no, you're not being a burden. We want you to be okay, and I don't like the idea of your being home by yourself like this."

"Get me some tissues, Evette," her mother directed.

Evette found a box and handed it to her mother. Her mother passed the box to Justin for him to wipe his face.

Evette could hardly stand to watch this. In all the years she'd known Justin, she had never once seen him cry. Was he really that upset or had the medicine made him overly emotional? To see him in this condition was heartbreaking.

"Let's make a deal," her mother said. "If you want to come downstairs, you have to eat another bowl of soup and drink two glasses of water. Can you do that for me?"

"Yeah," he said.

"All right then. Let's go." She and Evette helped him stand, but he wouldn't lean on either of them. He moved very slowly but finally made it to the bottom. Evette wondered if he would be able to make it back up later on.

Justin sat on the sofa. Her mother wasted no time giving orders. "I've got to check on this roast, and then I'll warm up some soup. You stay here, Evette, and keep him company."

Evette turned on the television and flipped to the sports channel. "Is this what you want to watch?"

Justin shrugged. They watched in silence until the golf highlights came on. At that point Justin started sobbing.

Evette gingerly hugged him, trying not to jostle his bruised muscles.

"Justin, please tell me what's wrong?"

He leaned on her shoulder. "I can't believe you guys are taking care of me after how I treated you. I feel so guilty."

"Don't feel bad," she said, trying to console him. "We forgive you. I forgive you."

"You do?"

"Of course."

"Thank you." He shifted in his seat to find a more comfortable position. Evette watched as he finally drifted off to sleep.

She quietly stood. He must have heard her because he opened his eyes briefly. "Evette?"

"Yes?" she said, bracing for him to ask if he could go home.

"I love you." He closed his eyes and went back to sleep.

Unexpected tears sprang to her eyes. Blinking them away, she placed a light blanket over him and retreated to her room.

Feeling emotionally drained, Evette lay on her bed for several minutes. No matter how much she tried to convince herself that Justin's admission of love was medicine-induced, she couldn't forget his words.

Did he really still love her? Did she still love him?

Did I ever love him?

At that moment the phone rang. "Hello?"

"Hi, it's Anthony. I wanted to see how your day went."

"My day? It was—not too good." Evette tried to hold back the tears, but they wouldn't stop.

"Evette, calm down. Please tell me what's wrong."

She took a deep breath and gave him a detailed account of the day, starting with Justin's call from the hospital and ending with his "Evette, I love you."

"Oh, Evette, I'm sorry your day has been so difficult. Do you want me to come over?"

She shook her head, even though he couldn't see her. "No, that's okay."

"You know I'm not going to let you stay sad like this. What can I do to cheer you up?"

Evette smiled, hearing the concern in his voice. "Okay, tell me something happy. Some good news."

"Let's see—good news. My mom told me Stacy called to tell her that baby Jacob smiles whenever he hears the words 'Grandma' and 'Grandpa.'"

Evette chuckled, thankful for a reason to do so after such a trying day. "Is that so?"

"Yes. That's pretty amazing, considering he's not even three weeks old."

"Got any more good news?"

"Well, I had a call from a sports magazine asking me if I'd like to interview for a position."

Evette sat up straight. "An interview? Really?"

"Yeah." He sounded pretty pleased. "I've wanted to work for them for awhile."

"So if you get the job what does that mean? Will you keep working for the paper?"

"If I get the job I'll have to move to Boston, since that's where the main office is."

"Boston?" Evette tried to remember if Anthony had ever mentioned moving to Boston before today.

"Yeah, it's an in-house position."

"Oh." She tried to sound happy for him. "So when's the interview?"

"I'm flying there tomorrow."

"Wow, this is really fast. You know, I don't think you mentioned wanting to switch jobs before. Is this a new development in your life, or have I not been paying attention?"

"Both, I guess. I mean, I've been thinking about switching jobs, but I sent them my resume around six months ago. I never mentioned it because I assumed they weren't interested. But when I got home from work, out of the blue, they had left a message on my machine."

"Evette?" her mother called from downstairs.

"My mom's calling me. I think dinner's ready," she told Anthony.

"I'll let you go then. Would you pray for me tomorrow?"

Evette swallowed her disappointment. "Sure."

"I'll pray for Justin to feel better soon," he said. "I'm scheduled to arrive back in St. Louis around ten tomorrow evening. I'll probably call you Wednesday to let you know how it went."

After they finished talking, Evette didn't head downstairs immediately. She lay down again, this time deep in thought. How could Anthony have neglected to tell her he wanted to move to Boston? Considering the fact that she felt pressure from him to make a decision about their relationship, this newest revelation didn't add up. How could he not realize a possible move to Boston might affect her decision?

Evette sighed in frustration. This reminded her of the day when Justin called to tell her he was going to stay on the tour full time. In his mind he had already broken up with her but didn't bother to inform her for several more months. *Once again I'm the last one to find out. Am I doomed to repeat the same scenario with different men?*

For once she didn't feel guilty that she hadn't been able to reach a decision about her relationship with Anthony. He might act more holy, but in the end he had turned out to be no different from Justin.

Justin might occasionally come across as annoying and immature, but he was not without redeeming qualities. And at least he apologized, she told herself as she headed downstairs.

Suddenly, the woozy, bruised, soup-eating man on the family room sofa seemed far more attractive and sincere than Anthony Edwards.

Chapter 13

The next day passed a bit more easily. Evette stayed home again to help her mother with Justin, but he improved rapidly. His aches and pains lessened considerably, and he needed only one dose of his medicine.

He still walked with a slight limp, but Evette had no doubt he would be feeling much more like normal by the end of the week.

Evette tried very hard not to think about Anthony's interview, but she was unsuccessful. Besides, she had promised to pray that it went well.

After lunch, while Justin napped, Evette decided to find out what her mother thought of Anthony's news. She recounted her telephone conversation with him and waited for some feedback.

Her mother didn't answer right away but seemed deep in thought as she washed dishes.

"Mom?" Evette asked after a few minutes. "You didn't answer."

"I know." Her mother shrugged. "I'm not sure I have an answer. Have you prayed about this?"

Evette looked at the ceiling. "Yes. I've been praying for weeks about being Anthony's girlfriend, and I thought I had my answer—until this. He knows how I felt when Justin did the same thing, so how could he do the exact same thing?"

"Are you sure it's the exact same thing? You could be jumping to conclusions."

Evette bit her lip. "I don't think so. It's the same thing all over again. First he announces he's leaving, and then he'll want to break up."

Her mother chuckled. "How can you break up if you aren't dating?"

"Mom, you know what I mean. I'm speaking hypothetically here."

"Oh, I see."

Evette didn't miss the smile that spread across her mother's face. She plopped into a chair. "Mom, I know you think this is funny, but it isn't. I was this close to telling Anthony I was ready for the relationship. I even thought I loved him."

"Evette, Anthony and Justin are both good men. Neither one is perfect, but they both have their good qualities. But where Justin purposefully deceived you about his plans to be gone for longer than you had agreed, I don't see Anthony doing the same."

"You believe that whole story about his sending the resume ages ago and not thinking the magazine was interested?"

"I do. Anthony is a man of his word."

"But, Mom, we tell each other almost everything. If this was so important to him, why didn't he ever mention it? I could have prayed with him about it."

"I don't know. It's probably a personality thing. Some people count their chickens before they're hatched, and others don't. I see Anthony as the type to wait and see, especially if it concerns something that's really important to him. In case it didn't work out, he'd be able to cope with the disappointment without having too many people asking how he feels."

Evette shook her head. "I'm the exact opposite. If something big is about to happen to me, I want everybody to know about it so they can be happy for me or help me feel better if it doesn't pan out."

"I know you are," said her mother. "But I'm not like that. I like to keep things under my hat until I know it's going to work out."

"So you think I should assume that's where Anthony's coming from?"

"I think you should talk to him about it. That way you'll know for sure without having to rely on something we came up with ourselves."

"Okay, I guess I can do that. When he calls, I'll ask him about it."

Wednesday after work Anthony decided to call Evette. He still hadn't heard any news regarding the interview, but he wanted to touch base with her.

The phone rang several times, and Anthony was about to hang up when someone picked up the phone.

"Hello?"

He recognized the voice as Justin's. For a man who was supposed to be sick, he certainly sounded robust.

"Hi. Is Evette there?"

"Yeah, just a minute. Eve, telephone."

So now he was calling her Eve. Was that just a nickname or a term of endearment? Anthony tried not to let his imagination get carried away.

"Hello?"

"This is Anthony."

"I know. Justin told me," she explained.

"Oh. I thought I'd call and let you know how my interview went. It took you so long to answer the phone that I thought you might have gone to Bible study."

"No, I decided not to go tonight. Mom and I spent the day helping Justin get things going with the insurance company. It'll cost more than the car is worth to fix it so we're waiting to hear how much they'll pay. Then we had to pick up the rental car, collect the mail at his apartment, and take him to the doctor for a follow-up appointment. After all that, we were too tired to cook, so Dad took Mom out for dinner, and Justin and I stayed home and ordered a pizza. We were in the middle of a Monopoly game when you called."

"I hope he's feeling better."

"Oh, yeah. He's still got bruises and sore muscles, but he doesn't need those strong painkillers anymore. He has a limp from the sprained ankle, but he's feeling well enough to go to work tomorrow."

"That's great news."

"We're all relieved. It was such a shock seeing him in so much pain like that. Thanks for trying to cheer me up the other day. It really helped." She paused then continued talking. "Speaking of our conversation—tell me about your interview." Her voice seemed to have a false cheeriness, and he wondered what could be the matter.

"It was a pretty basic interview, I guess. They seemed to like my work, but I won't know anything until they give me a yes or a no. But thanks for praying— I really appreciate it."

"Anthony—could I ask you something?"

"Sure."

"About the interview—I'm a little curious to know why you didn't mention it before now."

"I told you I thought they weren't going to call. So there was no reason to bring it up."

"Oh." Her voice sounded flat.

"Why? Is there something wrong with that?"

"No—no, not really. I just—I mean, I thought we were pretty close, and we share so much with each other."

Anthony shrugged. "I'm sorry, Evette. Honestly, it never crossed my mind to tell you."

"But what if we'd been dating? Would you have told me then?"

"I don't know. Maybe. But I already said I didn't think they would respond. Does it really make that much of a difference?"

She was silent. Finally she said, "It would to me. I almost feel as if you were being dishonest with me. If I were your girlfriend, don't you think you should give me a heads-up if you're planning to move to Boston?"

Anthony now understood why she didn't seem enthusiastic about the interview. After considering her question for several seconds, he answered. "If we were a couple, then, yes, I would have mentioned the interview."

"Good."

"Good?"

"I mean, I'm glad you feel that way." She sighed. "Oh, Anthony, I'm sorry if I sounded—"

"As if you were interrogating me?"

"Okay, yes. But I'm just so cautious now, and the way you sprang that interview on me I couldn't help but wonder if you had done it on purpose."

"Why would I do something like that on purpose?"

"I don't know. But I couldn't figure out why you wouldn't tell me either, so I feared the worst. I was so scared to think you were planning to leave, as soon as

I realized I was. . ." Her voice trailed off.

"Yes?" Anthony asked.

"Never mind."

"Let me guess," said Anthony. "Justin's in the room, hanging on every word you're saying."

"Yes."

Anthony laughed. "Are you busy Friday night? Maybe we can continue this conversation over dinner?"

"I wish I could, but it's my turn to do inventory, remember?"

"Can't you get one of your brothers to cover for you?"

"Sorry, but I don't think so. Trevor switched shifts with me last time, and I know for a fact he has a date Friday night. Plus I haven't even been to work this week because of everything that happened with Justin. I would feel bad if I tried to get out of inventory."

Anthony did his best to conceal his disappointment. "What about Saturday?"

"I promised Nina and Michelle I'd go to the symphony."

"Sunday?"

"Sunday is good. After church?"

"Yes, I'll take you out to dinner."

"I'm looking forward to it," she said. "Talk to you later."

❦

"That's it," Justin said, closing the ledger they used for inventory records.

Evette placed a hand to her forehead and crumpled dramatically to the floor. Justin laughed and leaned against the wall.

"Boy, am I glad that's done. I can't believe we finished so quickly."

Evette smiled. "Thanks to another thunderstorm, we spent all day cooped up back here. But I guess it's worth it since we finished early." *But if I had known this was going to happen, I'd have accepted Anthony's invitation to dinner tonight. It's not even eight o'clock yet.*

Justin glanced at his watch. "You know, it's still kind of early. Want to see a movie?"

Evette yawned. "I don't know. Do you have one in mind?"

Justin reached down to help her up. "Why don't we ride over to the cinema and see what's playing? If nothing looks good, we can at least get some frozen custard."

Evette blew out a sigh. "I'm a little tired, but, after being in the storeroom for so long, going out might do me more good than heading straight home." She gave him a close look. "But the real question is, how do you feel? I don't want you getting worn out."

He waved away her concern. "I'm fine. Didn't you notice the limp is almost gone?"

"I did. You are a totally different man from four days ago." He was almost a hundred percent again. Yesterday after work he had convinced Evette's mother that he was doing well enough to go back to his own apartment. It was good to see him back on his feet again. At the rate he was recovering, he would probably be able to resume teaching on Monday.

"So are we going?" he asked.

"Yes. I'm ready whenever you are." She followed him out into the shop. Her dad and Craig were preparing to close up.

"You two going somewhere?" her dad wanted to know.

"We're going to get some fresh air," Evette announced. "And we may see a movie or just go for ice cream."

"Who's driving?" asked Craig.

"I will," Evette answered. The issue of Justin's tendency to drive too fast had caused her brothers some concern. Although they were happy he wasn't seriously injured, none of them felt comfortable riding as a passenger if he drove.

"How will I get home?" Justin wanted to know.

"I'll bring you back here so you can pick up your rental car," Evette explained.

"Have fun and be careful," her dad called after them.

The multiplex theater was crowded, typical of a Friday night. After much discussion they decided to watch a new animated movie. At first Justin protested. "It's a kiddie film," he pointed out.

"I know, but I've been wanting to see this one. Please?" Evette asked.

"Fine," Justin gave in grudgingly. Evette offered to buy the tickets, but Justin refused. After he paid at the box office he said, "Why don't you go in and find seats, and I'll get some snacks."

"Okay. Do you still like to sit in the middle of the theater?"

"Yes. And do you still like buttered popcorn and cherry licorice?"

"I sure do." Evette hurried inside to find a good place to sit while Justin headed toward the concessions area.

The theater was full of families, and little kids ran around, laughing and even screaming at random intervals. The ratio of youngsters to adults was probably four to one, and many of the grown-ups wore harried expressions.

Miraculously she found a middle seat with ease. The families seemed clustered close to the aisle seats. Evette figured they wanted to have easy access for the endless rest room trips children were notorious for.

After settling in, Evette surveyed the room once more. The kids were definitely enjoying themselves. She smiled, wondering how it must feel to be free to run around and laugh with abandon, not caring what anybody else thought.

"Evette?" A familiar voice pulled her from her thoughts.

She turned and found Anthony looking down at her.

"This is a coincidence. I didn't know you were into animated films," he said.

"And I thought you were doing inventory this evening."

"Well, we finished early, and a cartoon seemed like a welcome change after spending all day counting and recounting things."

"Uncle Anthony? I need to go to the bathroom!" A little boy tugged at Anthony's sleeve. An even smaller toddler hugged Anthony's leg.

He smiled at Evette. "These are my nephews, Miles and Dennis. They're Latrice and Donald's boys," he said then looked down at his nephew. "Hold on just a minute, okay? Can you do that?"

The boy nodded. Anthony gestured to several seats in the row where Evette sat. "Are those taken?"

"I don't think so."

"Would you mind holding three for us?"

Evette nodded. "Sure, no problem."

As she watched Anthony hurry back down the stairs with the two boys in tow, she realized she'd forgotten to mention she hadn't come alone. *Surely he doesn't think I decided to come by myself—but he probably doesn't expect to see Justin here either.*

While she mulled over these thoughts, Justin returned. "The line out there is so long that I thought I'd miss the first part of the movie," he said.

First things first, she decided. *Might as well tell Justin what's going on.* "Guess who else is here?" she said brightly.

"I have no idea. And here is your candy," he said, handing her the package.

"Anthony Edwards."

Justin didn't say anything but sighed loudly.

Evette pretended not to notice his disappointment. "He's here with two of his nephews."

"Oh." Justin glanced over the crowd. "I don't see him."

She cleared her throat. "He had to leave for a few minutes, but I'm holding their seats." She glanced at the empty seats at Justin's side.

Justin eyed the chairs then gave her an exasperated look. "You're kidding me."

"No. I should have asked, but he was in a hurry—one of the kids needed to run to the rest room, and I couldn't tell him not to sit here, could I?"

"You could have at least told him you were on a date."

"A date?" Evette was flabbergasted. "You never said anything about a date."

Justin didn't seem to hear her question but went on with his complaint. "Why does that guy turn up like a bad penny every time you and I get a few minutes together?"

Evette stifled a laugh. "A bad penny?" she repeated. "I haven't heard that in years."

"I'm serious, Evette. I know we've had our disagreements and misunderstandings in the past, but I thought we were making strides. I thought maybe you might be ready to take me back." He leaned closer. "Don't you remember what I said the other day?" He lowered his voice to a whisper. "I still love you."

Evette spotted Anthony and the boys coming back and quickly shushed Justin. "We can discuss this later."

Anthony eyed Justin and gave Evette a questioning glance. "I guess we had a misunderstanding. I didn't realize you weren't here alone. Should we sit somewhere else?"

Justin merely shrugged, but Evette reassured Anthony the original seating arrangement was fine. Besides, the theater was nearly full.

Justin must have felt apologetic, because he waved Anthony and the boys into the row. "Come on—don't worry about it."

As soon as Anthony had his nephews settled, the lights dimmed and the movie began. Evette didn't know what to do. She could feel both Justin and Anthony staring at her from time to time. The tension didn't ease but grew worse.

At one point Justin leaned over and quite conspicuously put his arm around her shoulders.

Before she could wiggle away, one of Anthony's nephews exclaimed, "Eww—Uncle Anthony, are they gonna kiss?"

Justin quickly removed his arm, Anthony gave her a disapproving glance, and Evette stifled a laugh. The situation wasn't all that funny, but she'd rather laugh than cry. Several people turned around to see what the fuss was about, and Evette wanted to melt into the floor.

The only truly horrible part about this was that she still had to make Anthony understand that she and Justin weren't dating and tonight hadn't been planned. She didn't want him to think she and Justin were sneaking around behind his back.

From the look on his face the resolution was easier said than done.

The film turned out to be rather cute, but by the time it ended Evette wanted nothing more than to go home. Fast. She very much doubted that now would be a good time to try to sort things out with Anthony.

As soon as the house lights flickered on, Evette said good-bye to Anthony and his nephews then ushered Justin outside.

The situation had grown so awkward that staying to chat and going home rated the same on the discomfort scale. She would call Anthony in the morning to explain, and she would set Justin straight on the way back to the store.

"Can you tell me what just happened in there?" Justin asked once they were on the road. "Can you tell me why you invited him and two little kids to be a part of our date?"

"It's not a date. We never agreed to date, Justin. But you know that. You ended the relationship, and I want to keep it that way," she answered.

"Are you sure? Have you even taken time to think it over?"

Evette nodded. "Positive. In fact I've probably spent too much time thinking it over. I like our friendship the way it is, but we are not anywhere near being a couple again."

"Can you at least give me a reason?"

"I can give you a lot of reasons. One, I have a hard time trusting a man who promised to marry me and called it off without any regard for how I felt. Two, I don't think we're on the same spiritual level, and I refuse to get involved with a man who isn't serious about his relationship with the Lord. Three, I'm not attracted to you anymore. Four—"

"You know what—I don't think I want to hear any more." Justin shook his head. "But I think you're just acting out of fear. A lot about me has changed, and you haven't stopped to notice."

Evette sighed. "Yes, you have changed. And I like the new Justin a lot better. But I'm in love with Anthony."

He nodded, looking straight ahead. "I guess I knew that already. I saw it that day I got back and he was at your house eating ice cream."

"I think I knew it then too." She chose her next words carefully. "And I'm sorry if my indecision made you feel—"

"As if I had a chance?"

Evette nodded.

"Don't feel too bad about it. We all make mistakes. I guess I deserve this for what I did to you."

"Don't say that, Justin. It doesn't help either of us to keep dredging up the engagement. It's over, but we still get along. I think that's something of a miracle in itself, wouldn't you say?"

"It is. And I'm happy for you, Eve. You deserve to be happy. I just wish something good would happen for me."

"I'll pray for you to meet the right woman, Justin. I know God will lead you to her."

"Thanks, Evette."

"You're welcome." She remembered Michelle's and Nina's questions about Justin a few weeks ago. "By the way, did I ever mention the float trip my Sunday school class is taking?"

Chapter 14

Anthony awoke to the sounds of loud cartoons and little-kid exclamations. He rolled over and put the pillow over his head. After all the trouble he'd had falling asleep the night before, being awakened at seven o'clock was not appealing.

After several minutes of continued cacophony, he shuffled down the hallway to check on the boys. He held on to the hope that he could convince them to sleep for another hour or so, but that option would only work if they were moderately still and quiet.

To his dismay the boys were not only awake but having an acrobatics competition on the fold-out bed.

Rubbing the sleep out of his eyes, he cleared his throat. "Hey, hey, calm down. Didn't Uncle Albert tell you to stop doing flips on this bed last night?"

The two boys nodded and sat down. They appeared duly chastened, and Anthony felt a bit more compassion. His nephews loved spending weekends with him and Albert. The last thing he wanted was to nit-pick over every little thing they did and take the fun out of it for them. It would take away from the adventure of being away from home for a couple of days.

Anthony remembered well the many scrapes he and Albert had managed to get into when they were young. He also recalled the countless numbers of times their mother had spent chasing them around the house warning them to be careful. He could hear her voice in his head even now: "Watch the lamp! Don't run on the stairs! If you break that vase—! Don't play so rough!"

Anthony located the remote control and adjusted the volume to a more tolerable level. As much as he hated being the bad guy, it was time for a talk.

"Look, fellas—I don't want to keep repeating the same things over and over. I want you guys to have fun. But we have to play safe. No flips or wrestling allowed without me or Albert supervising, okay?"

The pair nodded solemnly.

"Besides, if somebody got hurt, your mommy would be upset with me and Albert. Then she wouldn't let you sleep over anymore, and that wouldn't be any fun, right?"

Again they nodded. "Uncle Anthony, can we play video games?" asked Miles.

Anthony yawned and glanced down the hall toward Albert's room. The door was shut, and he felt a twinge of jealousy that his brother still slept peacefully.

Mornings like this helped him to be grateful he didn't have kids of his own yet. He liked the idea of having a family and often yearned for a wife and kids.

But sometimes these early Saturday mornings and the responsibility of two little boys made fatherhood seem a bit less exciting.

He had strict orders from Latrice to make certain the boys played kid-appropriate games. That meant nothing that involved car crashes or fighting. Instead it meant educational games that helped the boys learn something, like adding or learning new words. And their play had to be supervised. After one hour of video games they had to switch to another activity. "Because I don't want my kids sitting in front of the TV all day," she said.

The list went on and on. Anthony didn't feel up to the task right now.

He scratched his chin and yawned again. Maybe he could change the subject. "Don't you want to watch some of these good cartoons?"

Dennis shook his head. "No, let's play the games now. I saw this cartoon yesterday."

Anthony sighed. It appeared they wouldn't be easily swayed. He cast one more longing look toward his room and sighed again at the thought of his pillow.

He stood up. "Okay. Let me make some coffee, and then we'll play the game."

"Yeah!" The boys, apparently having forgotten his mini-lecture, jumped up and down on the bed. Alarmed at the dangerously creaky noises the sofa sleeper was making under the stress of two jumping boys, Anthony hurriedly got them to sit down and watch television until he returned from the kitchen.

"Remember—no flips, jumps, or wrestling," Anthony called over his shoulder.

Anthony decided to forgo the trouble of the coffeemaker and settle for instant. The sooner he made it back to the family room, the less of a chance there was the boys would get restless and find some new way to break one of Latrice's rules.

Anthony added an extra teaspoon of crystals to the water and put the mug into the microwave.

"Uncle Anthony? I'm hungry." Dennis leaned against the doorway. "Can I have a doughnut?"

"Well, how about some cereal?" Latrice also forbade excessive consumption of doughnuts. Although he and Albert always kept a stash of them in the house, he didn't want to give the boys too much sugar. Especially since they already seemed pretty energetic this morning. They'd had that candy at the show, and then Albert brought out the gummy worms late last night.

"Aww, I don't want cereal!" He stamped his pajama-covered foot on the floor.

Uh-oh. This kind of whining was also on Latrice's list of no-nos. But it also signaled that certain little ones needed a nap. Anthony picked up Dennis and carried him back to the living room. If he could get them both back to bed, maybe he could catch a few extra winks. "No cereal? But I have that colorful kind you like."

"I want some cereal," Miles chimed in.

"I'm sleepy," said Dennis.

That makes two of us, Anthony thought.

He put Dennis on the bed, and the little boy crawled under the covers without any protest.

Miles watched his brother and let out a yawn. "I'm not tired," he announced.

"You aren't?"

Miles shook his head. "You said we could play the game."

"But we can't play without Dennis. We have to wait for him to wake up."

Miles put out a hand to shake his brother. "Wake up. Uncle Anthony said so."

"Leave me alone," Dennis whined. "Uncle Anthony, he hit me."

"Let him rest," Anthony told Miles. He chuckled and patted Dennis's head. "That's okay. You can go back to sleep. We'll wait for you."

Miles yawned again, this time a bit louder.

Anthony turned the TV off and pulled back the covers. "Why don't you lie down while your brother takes his nap?"

The boy protested, even as he snuggled under the blanket. "But I'm not tired."

"I know you're not. You don't have to go to sleep. Just lie here until Dennis wakes up."

"For how long?"

"I don't know. He'll wake up when he's not tired. And no pinching or pushing. Let him sleep, okay?"

"Okay."

Anthony could tell by Miles's constant and prolonged blinking that the boy was quickly headed toward dreamland.

With a sigh of bliss Anthony tiptoed back to his room. As he lay down, he prayed the boys would sleep for at least three hours.

The moment he was comfortable, the phone rang. Sitting up, he groaned and reached for the receiver. He fervently hoped the caller wasn't Latrice or Donald, wanting to say hello to the boys. They seemed to call at the most inopportune times—like now—just as he'd coaxed Miles and Dennis back to sleep.

"Hello?"

"Anthony? It's Evette."

Anthony took a deep breath. The vision of Justin with his arm around Evette had kept him awake last night much longer than he liked to admit. He had tried his best to remain patient while she made her decision about their relationship, but now he wondered if she weren't trying to hold onto him while she decided if she wanted to take Justin back. The last thing he wanted to be was someone's safety date.

Careful to keep his emotions in check, he answered. "Hi, Evette."

"You sound a little groggy. Did I wake you?"

"Not really. My nephews kept me up late and got up early, so I'm a little incoherent at the moment."

"I guess you know I'm calling about last night, but if this is a bad time I can wait a few more hours."

He shook his head. "No, I'm fine." He paused to give her the opportunity to speak first.

"I know this sounds cliché, but what you saw last night wasn't the way it is. Justin and I are officially friends."

"So are you and I, but that hasn't stopped us from developing deeper feelings for each other."

"I know—I know." She sounded tired, and Anthony wondered if her night had been as sleepless as his own. "I admit I was a little—confused. I do have feelings for you, and I was struggling with leftover feelings for Justin."

Hearing her admit it hurt far worse than the suspicion she felt that way. What did she want from him? Love? Plain old friendship?

Anthony didn't think he could deal with this roller coaster she seemed bent on putting him through. One day he felt certain that she loved him, and the next she seemed to lean more in the direction of reconciling with the man who had mercilessly broken her heart.

Anthony rubbed his forehead. Could this get any more confusing?

"Are you still there?" Evette asked.

"I'm still here. I've been thinking, and maybe we both messed up somehow. When I signed up to take those lessons, I asked you to come back to church. I had two reasons for doing so. I wanted to see you more often, but I also wanted to draw you back to the church family. I knew you had drifted away, and I felt it was only a matter of time until you quit coming completely."

"And you were right," she said. "I felt out of touch. I probably would have started finding excuses not to go to church at all. So I'm glad you did what you did."

Was that the sole reason You brought me into her life, Lord? Was it careless of me to let my emotions progress beyond friendship?

"And maybe that was all I was supposed to do," he told her. "Albert warned me from the beginning to examine my priorities. He suspected I had ulterior motives, and I did."

"But I—"

"No, Evette. I have something else to tell you. The magazine called yesterday afternoon. They filled the position I wanted, but they have a temporary opening. They want me to come for a month, and they've indicated they might be able to hire me permanently if things go well."

"Oh." Her voice was flat. This wasn't the way he'd planned to break the news, but perhaps this was better. Not being able to see her face made things slightly less difficult.

"Are—are you going?"

"I think so. I'm not that happy about leaving St. Louis, but if I'm going to go this is an ideal way. I get to test the waters for a month, and if I don't like it, I can come back."

"What about your job?"

"I'm taking two vacation weeks and two unpaid weeks."

"Your apartment?"

He chuckled. "Albert's willing to live alone for a month."

"And—us?"

"I'm not sure there is an 'us.' I know we've both been praying, and I think this job opening is part of the answer. It wouldn't make any sense to start a relationship just before I move to Boston. We'd both be miserable."

"We would."

"I should be back the first week in August—I hope in time for the float trip." Anthony hated to change the subject, but it didn't make sense to get his hopes up and have them repeatedly dashed by the cold, hard facts. Evette was still in love with Justin.

Evette cleared her throat. "Well, I apologize again for waking you so early. When do you leave?"

"Monday morning."

"So you'll be at church."

"Of course. But I think I'll need to cancel our dinner. I'll probably be running around, tying up loose ends, packing, and things like that."

"Oh, of course. I'll pray for you while you're gone. I hope the job turns out to be everything you expected and more."

"Thanks, Evette. I can use the prayer support."

"Anthony?" she asked. "Before we hang up, I want to say thanks."

"You're welcome. But why are you thanking me?"

"Oh, for lots of reasons. But mostly because you reached out to me when I needed that extra push to get things straight with the Lord. I respect you deeply for that."

The thank-you was bittersweet for Anthony. He didn't feel he had done the wrong thing by asking Evette to spend more time with her church family, but she must have agreed to consider a romantic relationship only because she had somehow felt indebted to him.

Anthony shook his head. It wasn't supposed to turn out this way. Even as he tried to think of something to say, another frustration surfaced. He couldn't help feeling that the extra "push" she referred to had helped pave the way for her reconciliation with Justin.

There was no way to deny how he felt about that situation. Jealous. He wanted so much to tell her how much he loved her and beg her to stay away from Justin, but he was too late. Obviously this thank-you from Evette had two meanings. She did feel some amount of gratitude for how he had challenged her to get involved at church again. But she was also thanking him for letting her off the hook about the relationship.

"Evette, you don't have to thank me. I just tried to do what I felt the Lord was leading me to do. I didn't get everything right, but I'm glad my mistakes didn't send you running away."

"I wouldn't run from you," she said.

Anthony was so close to blurting out how he felt that it took every ounce of his self-control to say good-bye and hang up the phone.

This was the way it had to be. Anthony lay down and tried to catch a few more winks. As tired as he felt, though, he couldn't relax enough to fall asleep.

He finally got up and started sorting out piles of clothes to take to Boston. As he worked, he vowed never to engage in a crusade to "help" any other beautiful women grow closer to the Lord.

Chapter 15

Sunday morning Justin arrived at Evette's house just before she left for Sunday school.

"Do you mind if I ride with you?" he wanted to know.

"Of course not."

"And don't worry—I won't mistake this for a date. I did some thinking yesterday, and I'm okay with the friendship."

Evette laughed. "I'm glad we finally see eye-to-eye on this."

"Me too."

That morning, at the end of the service, Justin surprised Evette and her whole family by walking down to the altar and announcing he wanted to rededicate his life to the Lord.

The happiness she felt from this news was shadowed by the fact that she didn't get a chance to say good-bye to Anthony. He was completely surrounded by so many others who wanted to say good-bye that Evette finally gave up. Her family and Justin wanted to go out to dinner, and she didn't want to keep them waiting.

Maybe she could call or e-mail him while he was away. As much as it stung to know he preferred Boston to a relationship with her, she hoped their friendship wouldn't come to an abrupt end.

❧

"Have you heard whether or not Anthony's going to make it back for the float trip?"

Evette wished Nina and Michelle would stop asking her questions about Anthony. In the twenty-eight days since he'd left, she had received only one brief E-mail from him and nothing else. If she'd heard any more news it was because his mother or one of his sisters gave her an update.

Picking at her Caesar salad, Evette shrugged. "I have no idea."

"If he does, we'll have an even number of canoes," said Nina. "I saw the sign-up sheet Sunday."

"So what are you packing?" asked Michelle.

"I suggest you bring clothes you don't care about getting wet and muddy. It's a camping trip, not a fashion show," said Nina.

"I still can't believe you two talked me into this," Evette said. "I don't camp. I don't paddle canoes."

"If you stayed home, you'd be sitting around wondering how much fun you were missing. So try to be at least a little excited about it, okay?"

"Besides," added Nina, "the campout is only for one night. It'll be over before you know it."

"I guess so," Evette admitted. "And the more I think about it now, the more I'm starting to get used to the idea. At least I'll get to take a day off from work. That's always fun."

"That's the spirit," Nina said, smiling. "Hey, does anyone want to share a piece of cake with me? I think the waiter's coming back in a few minutes."

"I'm not that hungry," said Evette.

Michelle gave them a mournful look. "I want the cake, but I'm on a diet. Maybe another day. Oh, girls, guess what?" Michelle said in a conspiratorial tone. "Yesterday Justin stopped by my house and left a bouquet of daisies on my doorstep. Isn't that sweet?"

Evette smiled indulgently. Justin had wasted no time getting better acquainted with Michelle, and as happy as she was for them, it sometimes felt a little strange to hear another woman gushing over the man who would have been her husband.

"You know," Nina said, sounding wistful, "Todd never brings me flowers anymore. He did all the time when we first started dating, but that wore off pretty fast."

"Already?" said Michelle. "You've only been dating for two months."

"No kidding. But he's a sweetie, so I think I'll keep him—despite his lack of floral gifts."

"This has been so much fun, but I need to get back to work," said Evette. "Plus I still need to shop for some of the items from the things-to-pack list we got last week for the trip."

"I need to do that too," said Michelle.

Nina signaled the waiter to bring their checks. "I guess you two have spared me from ordering that cake."

"That's what friends are for," Michelle said, laughing.

Evette paid her portion of the bill and hurried out to the parking lot. She had to teach a lesson in forty-five minutes and wanted to be certain she arrived on time.

As she drove, she analyzed her emotions. For better or for worse, she had changed since Anthony's departure.

Before he'd left, she had been trying to learn what it meant to be whole in Christ, and still she had somehow missed the mark. While she struggled with the desire to have a significant other, she'd also felt secure in the fact that for a time both Anthony and Justin had been waiting in the wings.

She had gone to church, started a daily quiet time again, and begun studying the Bible. But she hadn't been completely honest with herself. That empty feeling still lurked beneath the surface, and after Anthony left and Justin started dating Michelle, it had come back with a vengeance.

Evette had moped around for an entire week, not really bothering to open her Bible. Instead she searched for some kind of balm to soothe her hurts.

She bought chocolate, went shopping, watched funny movies, and cried herself to sleep at night. That hole had grown so large that she sometimes wondered if it would overtake her and transform her into an empty shell of a person.

Finally, one night, as she lay restlessly trying to fall asleep, she remembered Gene's lesson on being whole. Feeling discouraged, she got up and located her Bible. This time she read a bit further in order to gain a better understanding of the passage.

" 'Love the Lord your God with all your heart and with all your soul and with all your mind.' This is the first and greatest commandment. And the second is like it: 'Love your neighbor as yourself.' All the Law and the Prophets hang on these two commandments."

Evette couldn't stop the tears from running down her face. She got down on her knees and asked the Lord to show her how to give every part of her life to Him.

"I want to be whole. And I feel such a void now that Anthony and Justin are gone—I know I'm not supposed to feel this way, but I do. Please show me how to do this correctly."

"Love your neighbor as yourself." The same five words played again and again in her memory.

Do I love my neighbor as myself? After some thought she determined she hadn't been very honest with either Justin or Anthony. She had kept them both within arm's reach until she was certain of her decision.

And now she had neither of them. Yet, if she had been in their shoes, she would have been offended that she hadn't been completely honest about how she felt about them both.

She prayed again. "Lord, I messed up on this part about loving my neighbor as myself. Please forgive me. I want to do better at this. I give it all to You. Everything. The empty feeling, the pain, the confusion—all of it. I'll let You handle it from now on."

Evette stayed on her knees for awhile longer. By the time she finally crawled back into bed, she felt drained but free. So many things that had been bothering her were out of her hands and no longer troublesome.

This new feeling reminded her of how she felt when there was heavy lifting to be done at the store. She didn't pace around the box or fret and frown about how she should handle it. She didn't devise some plan to move it; instead she called her dad or brothers for help. Sometimes they wouldn't get to it right away, but she never took that to mean they wouldn't ever move it. She gave them complete control and knew in her heart it would be done.

She had asked Jesus to make her whole again, and she knew He would.

As her heavenly Father, God loved her even more than her earthly father did.

And, even though she might not understand the process, Evette was determined to let the Lord guide her life completely.

The pastor had preached from Isaiah 55 the previous Sunday. Remembering the Scripture passage, Evette found it appropriate for the change that had taken place in her life: "For my thoughts are not your thoughts, neither are your ways my ways. . .so is my word that goes out from my mouth: it will not return to me empty, but will accomplish what I desire and achieve the purpose for which I sent it."

Since then Evette felt more secure than she ever had. She missed Anthony, but God would take away that void—because His words didn't return to Him empty.

∽

"I can't believe how hot it is this early in the morning," Evette said as she and Justin pulled into the church parking lot the morning of the float trip. "I'm beginning to think that if the boat overturns it wouldn't feel half bad."

"No kidding." He laughed.

Several of the others had already assembled and were loading their bags onto the church bus.

"Do you know how long of a drive it is to the river?" Justin asked.

"I heard it's three or four hours," she said.

Justin lifted his eyebrows. "I hope they fixed the bus's air conditioning."

"Me too," she agreed. A couple of weeks earlier the singles' group had taken the bus downtown to a baseball game and discovered the AC was broken. Although the ride to the stadium was only a little over half an hour, it had still proved quite uncomfortable.

Justin carried both his and Evette's bags as they made their way to the rest of the group.

Nina spotted them and waved. "Evette, I can't believe you actually came. I told Michelle I suspected you would try to skip out on us."

"Ha, ha, very funny," she joked.

"Not too funny, though. She looked pretty hesitant when I picked her up," said Justin. "I kind of figured she was going to find a reason to make me take her back home, but she didn't."

"Well, don't count your chickens before they're hatched." Evette chuckled. "I'm not on the bus yet."

Michelle waved to someone behind Evette. "Well, look who made it back," she said. "You are just in time."

Evette turned around and saw Anthony walking toward them. Two days ago she had seen Dana at the grocery store, and his sister reported that Anthony might not get in until Saturday evening—too late for the float trip.

Immediately he was surrounded by people saying hello and inquiring how his month in Boston had gone.

Evette hung back until the crowd dispersed a bit. As soon as he could, he came

455

over and joined the little group where she, Nina, Michelle, and Justin waited.

The first few minutes were filled with meaningless small talk, mostly about the weather. Since it was so hot, everyone had something to contribute to the conversation, and there were no awkward silences.

Evette felt him watching her from time to time as they talked. She wondered what he was thinking. Had he decided to move to Boston for good?

"I think we should get on the bus," Michelle suggested.

"Right now?" said Nina. "Girl, that bus has been closed for at least a week. I am not stepping into that oven until it's time to leave."

"You know I have to sit in the front, or I'll get carsick," Michelle protested.

"I'll get on the bus with you," said Justin.

The rest of the group seemed to have the same idea, and within minutes everyone started piling inside. Michelle and Justin claimed the seat closest to the front, and Nina and Evette sat behind them.

"Girl, I cannot believe Todd had to work this weekend," Nina said, shaking her head. "He never seemed that excited about coming anyway. I think he signed up for overtime on purpose."

"Maybe," Evette answered, but she didn't pay much attention as Nina continued talking. Anthony sat down in the seat across from them, and, for the moment, he was alone.

He made eye contact with her and smiled. The old butterflies returned. Had he changed his mind about a relationship?

Evette was curious, but the thought didn't consume her, nor did the old void rear its ugly head. She had placed all of this in the Lord's hands, and she wasn't about to try to take it back. Her life was far less complicated without it.

Just before the bus departed, one more car pulled into the parking lot, and a man jumped out, waving his hands.

"Looks as if we have one more," said the driver.

Kaycee, the trip coordinator, checked her roster. "Really? I thought we were all accounted for. Who could we be missing?"

Their questions were answered when Todd boarded the bus.

He flashed a smile at Nina. "I switched shifts at the last minute with someone else."

The bus was almost completely full, and he looked around for a seat.

"I have an empty space here," Anthony said, waving him over.

"Thanks, Man." He sat down as the bus rumbled to a start. Looking across the aisle at Nina, he asked, "Are you surprised?"

"I'm shocked. But I'm happy too," she said.

Evette glanced across the aisle, and Anthony smiled. She returned the smile and watched as Nina and Todd conversed back and forth. Shaking her head, she wondered why those two didn't just sit together since they were talking only to each other.

After an hour on the road Anthony dozed off, and Evette felt a bit drowsy herself. Since she had no one to talk to, she leaned against the window and decided to get some rest.

She woke up as they arrived at the campground. The plan was to set up camp as quickly as possible then drive over to the river and begin the four-hour float trip.

Evette helped Nina and Michelle set up their tent, and they teased her mercilessly when she did a thorough spider check.

"Girl, if a spider wants to get in here, I doubt you can keep him out." Nina laughed.

"Yeah? Well, you can say whatever you want, but I bet you wouldn't be thrilled to wake up in the middle of the night to find some eight-legged creature had taken up residence in your sleeping bag, would you?"

Michelle shook her head. "Come on, Evette. We need to get back on the bus. I brought my strongest flashlight, and we'll do another bug check before we turn in tonight."

❧

"Haven't had much rain this year, you know," the man at the boat rental was telling Kaycee. "River's pretty low in places, but that shouldn't affect the trip. And you don't have to worry about rapids or anything."

Anthony scanned the crowd for Evette. Since Michelle and Justin and Nina and Todd seemed to be paired together, there was a chance Evette didn't have a canoe partner.

He saw her standing near the bus, spraying her arms and legs with insect repellent. He waved to get her attention and jogged over to talk to her.

"Do you have an empty spot in your canoe?"

She chuckled. "I guess I do. Do you need a place to sit?"

"I think so. Do you mind sharing with me?"

She shook her head. "Not at all. I hope you know how to steer it, though, because I've never been in a canoe in my life."

"It's been a few years since I was in Boy Scouts, but I think I can manage," he said. He pointed to where Kaycee stood. "Let's go over there and pick out a boat."

❧

Evette sat at the helm of the metal boat and did as Anthony instructed. Soon they were out on the river, paddling along at a leisurely pace. She had worried about being able to keep up with everyone, but her concerns didn't pan out.

Their group accounted for at least fifteen of the boats on the water, but several other groups had come as well. If nothing else, the first few minutes of the trip resembled a traffic jam on water.

"We can either hang back for a bit," Anthony said, "or we can speed our pace and try to maneuver around everyone else. What do you think?"

Evette's arms already felt tired so she chose the first option. "Let's hang back."

A few minutes later the logjam eased as the faster boaters got ahead of the pack and the novices moved to the rear. Evette and Anthony ended up in the middle.

"How did things go in Boston?" she asked, once they had reached a comfortable rhythm of paddling.

"It was good."

Evette waited for him to elaborate, but he seemed unwilling to say more so she changed the subject to more neutral territory. She went on and on about how things were going in the store, filled him in on local news, and even told him how her mother's garden was growing.

On the positive side, her fears about the river proved unfounded. Not only was it very tame, but in some places it was almost nonexistent. The dry summer had sent the water level to record lows. In a couple of places she and Anthony had to climb out of the boat and push it through the shallow water.

Evette couldn't help but laugh as she recalled how afraid she had been of getting swept away by the current.

After a couple of hours they paddled to the bank and joined the rest of the group for lunch. They had all been instructed to pack their own lunches with them, and Evette had kept their food in a small cooler.

While they ate, Anthony brought up his job again. "They want to hire me, but I don't think I'll go back."

"You don't?"

He shook his head. "I miss the newspaper and my family and—you."

Evette looked him in the eye. *Please let him be serious,* she prayed. "I missed you too."

"Evette, please tell me—were you in love with Justin when I left?"

She blew out a sigh. "No. I wasn't."

"But what about that time I saw you at the movies?"

"It was nothing. We finished inventory early and wanted to get away from work."

"You had turned me down for dinner that night, and I guess I overreacted. When you called the next day, I just—I said everything I could think of to convince myself I wouldn't be hurt if you loved him."

"And I was calling to tell you I love you," she said quietly.

"You do?"

She nodded.

"I love you too, Evette. I've been praying about this since I left. Does this mean you feel ready to have a relationship now?"

"I am now," she said, smiling. "Even though I knew I loved you when you left, I still wasn't ready. But I've been making some changes, and now I know I've reached that point where I can love Jesus and you." She looked down at the ground.

"I've already apologized to Justin, but I never got the chance to do the same with you. I did pray about a relationship with you, but I didn't give the Lord complete control over the situation. I decided to play it safe by keeping you both up in the air, in case it didn't work out with one of you."

She chuckled and continued. "My plan backfired, though. By the time I admitted to Justin that I loved you, you were packing your bags and heading to Boston. Then I didn't have either one of you. I was so disappointed, and I felt so guilty."

Anthony moved and sat next to her. "Let's put all that behind us. While I was gone, I couldn't stop thinking about you. I knew I had been too hasty in making my decision to leave. I felt that I should have let you explain, but I wanted to protect myself from hearing you say you didn't want to choose me. By the time I realized I had made a mistake by leaving, I couldn't back out on my commitment to stay at the magazine for a month. So I had to wait until now. You don't know how nervous I was on the flight home."

"I was pretty nervous too, wondering what you would say when you came back," she admitted.

The others in the group were cleaning up and heading back to their boats. Anthony and Evette followed suit and put their canoe back in the water.

Evette looked around, taking in the scenery. Today was one of the happiest days of her life. She would remember this moment for as long as she lived. Everything seemed to have fallen into place. She loved Jesus, Anthony loved Jesus, and now they loved each other. The circle was complete. Whole.

"I forgot to tell you something pretty exciting that happened," Anthony said, interrupting her thoughts.

She turned around and smiled. "What?"

"I took my golf clubs to Boston with me, and one of the guys in the office was helping me learn."

Evette quirked an eyebrow. "How's that long game coming along?"

"Good. I can drive the ball pretty far now."

"How far?"

"Two hundred yards. Straight."

"Wow! I'm impressed. Or maybe I should be worried. After all, when you took lessons from me, you didn't do very well."

He grinned. "I guess I could say I was a little distracted by my beautiful instructor."

Evette smiled indulgently. "Well, I guess that makes up for it."

"True that. But here's the best part. We played a round yesterday since it was my last day at work. On the seventh hole, a hundred and fifty-five yard par three, I made an ace."

"You're kidding! That's awesome."

"You should have seen me jumping up and down."

"I'm impressed, Anthony. I've never done that yet. Your first hole in one."

"It made me think about you," he said, "and how much I wanted to see you and talk to you again."

"Because I was your golf teacher?"

He shook his head. "No, it was because you were always talking about how you wanted Jesus to help you feel whole. It's kind of a neat concept—whole in one. You wanted to be whole in the One who loved us so much He gave His life to save us."

"Whole in one," Evette repeated. "I like the sound of that."

"Me too," Anthony agreed.

Epilogue

Six months later

A lbert cleared his throat. "Brienne and I want to thank you all for being here to share our special day with us. I especially want to thank my twin brother and best friend, Anthony, for being there for me since day one. Literally."

Evette sat next to Anthony, who blinked back tears. She squeezed his hand, and he gave her a grateful smile.

Albert cleared his throat. "He and I have been fairly inseparable, and we've never really lived apart. So this new phase of our lives will probably take some getting used to."

He turned to face Anthony. "Thanks, Anthony, for giving me first pick when we divided the video games. That is the true test of friendship right there."

The crowd laughed loudly. "And I'm looking forward to taking my place as best man in a couple of months when you and Evette walk down the aisle." He shrugged. "I know I'm looking forward to it because, well, I like wedding cake."

Again chuckles rippled through the hall.

"I love you, and I wish you and Evette all the happiness in the world."

Anthony gently kissed Evette then stood up to embrace his brother.

She wiped away the tears that threatened to make a mess of her makeup. The Lord was indeed good.

Despite their best intentions she and Anthony hadn't found true happiness until they were able to trust the Lord to solve matters in their lives.

And why shouldn't it be that way? A verse she had come across during her quiet time popped into her head: "Though one may be overpowered, two can defend themselves. A cord of three strands is not quickly broken."

Three strands—whole in One.

If you enjoyed
MISSOURI GATEWAYS
then read:

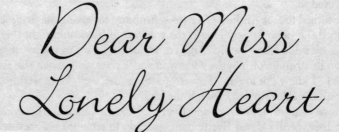

Dear Miss Lonely Heart

Four Stories of Love Within the "Advice Column"

Hope Deferred by Linda Lyle
Wait for Me by Terry Fowler
Mission: Marriage by Aisha Ford
I Do Too by Pamela Kaye Tracy

Available wherever books are sold.
Or order from:
Barbour Publishing, Inc.
P.O. Box 721
Uhrichsville, Ohio 44683
www.barbourbooks.com

You may order by mail for $6.97, and add $2.00 to your order for shipping.
Prices subject to change without notice.

A Letter to Our Readers

Dear Readers:

In order that we might better contribute to your reading enjoyment, we would appreciate you taking a few minutes to respond to the following questions. When completed, please return to the following: Fiction Editor, Barbour Publishing, Inc., P.O. Box 719, Uhrichsville, OH 44683.

1. Did you enjoy reading *Missouri Gateways?*
   - ❏ Very much—I would like to see more books like this.
   - ❏ Moderately—I would have enjoyed it more if _____
   _____
   _____

2. What influenced your decision to purchase this book?
   (Check those that apply.)
   - ❏ Cover   ❏ Back cover copy   ❏ Title   ❏ Price
   - ❏ Friends   ❏ Publicity   ❏ Other

3. Which story was your favorite?
   - ❏ *Stacy's Wedding*   ❏ *Pride and Pumpernickel*
   - ❏ *The Wife Degree*   ❏ *Whole in One*

4. Please check your age range:
   - ❏ Under 18   ❏ 18–24   ❏ 25–34
   - ❏ 35–45   ❏ 46–55   ❏ Over 55

5. How many hours per week do you read? _____

Name _____

Occupation _____

Address _____

City_____ State_____ Zip_____

$\mathcal{H}$EARTSONG ❤ PRESENTS

Love Stories
Are Rated G!

That's for godly, gratifying, and of course, great! If you love a thrilling love story but don't appreciate the sordidness of some popular paperback romances, **Heartsong Presents** is for you. In fact, **Heartsong Presents** is the only inspirational romance book club featuring love stories where Christian faith is the primary ingredient in a marriage relationship.

Sign up today to receive your first set of four, never-before-published Christian romances. Send no money now; you will receive a bill with the first shipment. You may cancel at any time without obligation, and if you aren't completely satisfied with any selection, you may return the books for an immediate refund!

Imagine. . .four new romances every four weeks—two historical, two contemporary—with men and women like you who long to meet the one God has chosen as the love of their lives. . .all for the low price of $10.99 postpaid.

To join, simply complete the coupon below and mail to the address provided. **Heartsong Presents** romances are rated G for another reason: They'll arrive Godspeed!

YES! Sign me up for Hearts❤ng!

NEW MEMBERSHIPS WILL BE SHIPPED IMMEDIATELY!
Send no money now. We'll bill you only $10.99 postpaid with your first shipment of four books. Or for faster action, call toll free 1-800-847-8270.

NAME _____

ADDRESS _____

CITY _____ STATE _____ ZIP _____

MAIL TO: HEARTSONG PRESENTS, P.O. Box 721, Uhrichsville, Ohio 44683
or visit www.heartsongpresents.com